TOGETHER AGAIN

At the dark edge of the forest, the horse slowed. "This will do," said Nicholas, supporting Rose tenderly as she slid to the ground. He leaped out of the saddle, swiftly secured the reins, and stamped down a bed of dry fern. The air smelled of musty bark, crushed leaves, and warm earth. They sank onto the rustling fronds, giving themselves up to each other with stinging ecstasy.

Afterward, glorying in the illicit gift of each other that the gods had handed them one more time, Nicholas said, "This is only half a life, Rose, this life we lead apart."

Rose was married to a man who adored her. Nicholas was married, too, to a woman as beautiful as she was proud. But nothing, not their honor, or their vows, or the strictures of strait-laced New Zealand society, could overcome the love that was born in distant England and refused to die. . . .

ANNE WORBOYS

AURORA ROSE

A SIGNET BOOK

NEW AMERICAN LIBRARY

A DIVISION OF PENGUIN BOOKS USA INC.

PUBLISHER'S NOTE

This book is a work of fiction. Names, characters, places, and incidents either are the product of the author's imagination or are used fictitiously, and any resemblance to actual persons, living or dead, events, or locales is entirely coincidental.

Copyright © 1986, 1988 by Anne Worboys

Aurora Rose appeared previously in a hardcover edition published by E. P. Dutton, a division of Penguin Books USA Inc., 2 Park Avenue, New York, New York 10016.

Originally published in Great Britain in somewhat different form under the title *A Kingdom for the Bold.*

Ø

First Signet Printing, August, 1989

1 2 3 4 5 6 7 8 9

To the memory of my mother

AUTHOR'S NOTE

In the telling of this tale of Edward Gibbon Wakefield's visionary dream my first principle has been to paint a picture, before all the old family tales are lost, of the fears, the sufferings, the excitements, tragedies, and successes of those young people who embarked on the First Five Ships with a curious mixture of naïveté, defiance, and immense courage, to sail to a wild, uncharted land.

The central characters of the novel—those from Rundull and Saxon Mote in England, as well as Oliver—are fictitious, as are Flash Jack, Tilly Bird, and the Rata Hill staff in New Zealand. Otherwise, as I traced the voyage across the world, and the events that marked the first fourteen years of the founding of the colony, I have endeavored to use real people in their historical context, among whom are Major Baker; Sam Phelps; my own great great-grandparents, James and Mary Maxwell; Dicky Barratt; the Stitchburys; Mr. Revans; the missionaries and officials; as well as those Maori chieftains who wrote their names with good and bad will, bewilderment, and blood in the annals of the times.

PROLOGUE

Died. On Sunday last at Quiddenham, the seat of her uncle the earl of Albemarle, to the great affliction of her near relations, and the sincere regret of a numerous acquaintance, Mrs. William Wakefield. This accomplished and beautiful young lady has fallen a victim to a broken heart, in consequence of the distant imprisonment of her youthful husband who, in an inadvertent moment, joined his elder brother (Edward Gibbon Wakefield) in the mad prank of taking away a young lady to Gretna Green. Mrs. Wakefield was the only daughter of Sir John Sidney, Bart., of Penshurst Place in Kent, to which place her remains are to be removed, and great-niece of Mr. Coke of Holkham. She left an infant daughter six months old.

The Times, 15 August 1826

Too many things went wrong that summer. Henry, 17th earl of Rundull, was laid up with a most painful attack of gout. The butler's minx of a granddaughter became pregnant to God knew who. There were poachers all summer on the Rundull estate. The Honorable Nicholas le Grys, younger son and third surviving child of the earl of Rundull, murdered Ned, the village blacksmith.

There was the Bedchamber Plot to darken the already tarnished image of the Queen. At Lady Flora Hastings's funeral people shouted, "Mrs. Melbourne," insinuating disgracefully that the young Victoria was having an affair with the aging prime minister, and threw stones at the royal carriage.

One of the maids of honor, the Lady Felicity le Grys, daughter of the earl of Rundull, was hit in the eye by a rotten tomato. Only the knowledge that her monarch's steely eye was fixed mercilessly upon her prevented her from bursting into tears.

And Edward Gibbon Wakefield came unannounced to Rundull. Edward, who had been out of jail for ten years, and who had never before had the gall to visit the relations of the girl whose fortune he had lost by botching her abduction.

That was the worst of it, in the long run. The fact that Edward came.

1

Ned Taylor, with two weeks of enforced chastity behind him, had been drinking in the Hopper's Maid. His sluttish wife, Gertie, was in Rochester visiting her sister. Ned was on his way home when he saw Rose coming along the riverbank, swinging her skirts. He bounded down the track that led off the road, his hobnailed boots clapping on the stones as he crossed the bridge beneath the willow tree. Hurrying upriver through the twilight, he paused at a hawthorn tree. As Rose came drifting on, he slid into the shadows and waited.

Her beautiful hair, which should have been rolled neatly and respectably into a knot, streamed down across her shoulders in thick unruly waves. Even at this distance, the white mounds of her small breasts showed above her tight bodice. Ned's fingers curled tightly in his sweaty palms.

Rose came level with the tree shadow. She saw the figure emerge stealthily, knew immediately it was not Nicholas, and caught her breath.

" 'Ullo, Rose."

"Ned." Sensing rather than seeing the animal lust in him, Rose faltered, "Fancy . . . seeing you here."

Pulling at the rough material of his smock frock, he shuffled his heavy boots in the grass. Rose made a move to pass, but his hand, black-grained from the anvil, shot out and clamped onto her wrist. When she did not immediately jerk away he slid an arm round her waist. Lonely as she was and loving, Rose automatically returned its

11

pressure. Grandy, who always spoke the truth, had said she might never see Nicholas again. The warmth of Ned's nearness eased her pain.

"Come an' sit 'ere," Ned suggested hoarsely, his senses quickening when the rebuff he had expected did not materialize. He turned her around toward the shadowed tree.

Needing to talk, she would have obeyed him, but in his urgency the smithy made the mistake of grabbing at her, catching her breast with one hand, her shoulder with the other.

"Ned?" Indignant, scared, Rose tried to pull away. "Take your hands off me!"

Somewhere in the back of Ned's immature mind lay the knowledge that speed was the essence of conquest. "What's the matter, Rose?" Looking down at the white skin of her breasts showing above the low neckline, feeling the fleshy softness of the one in his hand, his breath jolted and his eyes bulged. With lust spilling over, he jerked her to him, his knees pushing into her thighs.

"Stop!" she gasped, fighting to keep her feet. "Leave me alone! Let me go!"

He scarcely heard her as he forced her to the ground.

"Ned!" Panic lending her strength, she fought like a fiend, biting, kicking, twisting until, with an angry grunt, he clamped one hefty knee across her legs. "Leave me alone!" she shrieked. With every vestige of strength in her she managed to free one leg. Ned grabbed the flailing limb, slid his left hand along it and found what he wanted. With a grunt of need, he thrust the coarse material of her skirts up around her waist.

"Ned-d-d!" It was only half a scream because his arm now lay across her collarbone, and was moving against her throat. Astride her, Ned snatched wildly at his clothes.

A small bird jumped in the grasses near Nicholas's feet. Then his eye was taken by a movement within the shadow of the big hawthorn.

He strode forward.

Something, someone, was there. An animal? A poacher? Nicholas approached the tree stealthily, his mind sharpened by the knowledge that he might be visible to his lurking prey.

Rose looked beyond the hulking form of the man above her and saw the proud, familiar head, the broad, spare shoulders; saw the line of the gun against the pale mist. In spite of the arm across her throat, she managed a strangled cry.

Nicholas leaped forward. Through the near darkness he saw the large black form of a man in rutting crouch, and the familiar cloud of golden hair framing a face pallid with fear. A volcano of wrath exploded in him. Deafened to Rose's cry by the craving in him, Ned nonetheless sensed something amiss as Nicholas swung high the butt of his gun.

Rose heard her own scream as though it came from someone else. The weapon descended as in slow motion, toward Ned's shoulder. She lifted a hand in protest, also inexplicably slowly. Slowly too, Ned turned his startled face and baleful eyes in Nicholas's direction. He saw, and because, tragically, he ducked, he took the ferocious blow where it would do the most damage. His cranium cracked with a sound that paralyzed both Nicholas and Rose. They stared in mute horror as the body fell sideways and settled bulkily in the shadows.

Out of the silence, eerily, came the thin shriek of a barn owl in flight.

2

Rose's smile had something in it of the intoxication of spring. Child, angel, harlot, she was an awakening seductress. Though unable to either read or write, her innate knowledge of the secrets of living was infinite. Constrained behind the green baize door of Castle Rundull, where she scrubbed stone floors, running at the beck and call of her superiors, she hugged her secrets to herself and dreamed.

At seventeen she was a beauty. She had a pouting pink mouth, green eyes that flashed like emeralds . . . and golden hair that escaped from her demure mobcap in curls as capricious and enchanting as herself.

As she emerged from childhood, Rose listened without understanding to coarse prognostications of what the future held in store for her, and waited with innocent impatience for it to happen. In that spring of 1839 she was joyously ready. Brought up in the tiny village of Rundull, hard by the castle, in a cottage with wattle and daub walls held together by old ships' beams, she knew virtually nothing. The Honorable Nicholas le Grys was teaching her everything.

Snape the butler, spruce in ornately braided coat and knee breeches of the old school, was leaving his pantry carrying the big silver tray. He saw his granddaughter and his heart sank. He knew why she stood there, her eyes burning, one dainty foot tapping in slippers borrowed from an unsuspecting housemaid to replace the heavy pattens that kept her feet dry as she mopped out below stairs. The green baize door marked the boundary between her world and that of the younger son of the Rundulls: a man of strong appetites and arrogant ways. A man not easily crossed. Kitchen maids, Snape knew painfully, were fair game. He heaved a crushing sigh, knowing one could only protect a wench who wished to be protected.

Even in her dark stuff dress, Rose was a picture. Outrageously, she had removed the kerchief from her old-fashioned jacket bodice and slit the front so that her breasts swelled white and firm above the coarse material. Having an eye for style, and imitating the ladies' maids, she had inserted a modern touch by lowering the waist. Her exposed ankles were as delicate as any that peeped from beneath silk gowns above stairs, her fingers as slim and potentially pretty as those toying with samplers in the withdrawing room. Snape knew with frightened pride that, had his granddaughter been born among the Rundulls, she could have made a royal match. He knew too that, as a Snape, she would be used, spoiled, and degraded and likely end up a trollop.

More than once recently, bets had been laid in the village tavern against the orphaned Rosie Snape reaching her marriage bed with virginity intact. The odds, never very good, had narrowed during the summer as the results of Nicholas's attentions began to show in the firm upthrust of her bosom, the maturing of her hips, the soft, pliant sensuality of her mouth. Women bent over washtubs declared she was no better than she should be. The village lotharios eyed each other with jealous suspicion.

"If your Gran finds out what you're up to," Snape warned, "she'll take a whip to you."

Rose's eyes turned wistfully toward the heavy oaken door at the top of the curved stone staircase. Nicholas, who usually waited for her in the hall beneath the clock that always stopped when an earl of Rundull died, was behind it with the guest. Little white petals drifted down her skirt. She was picking a field daisy to pieces petal by petal. Will he, won't he, will he, won't he meet me tonight?

"You've been born a servant and you'll die a servant," Grandy said, solemn in his muttonchops, his rheumy eyes soft with love and a desperate, inner fear that harshened his voice and made his hands tremble, rattling the price-less china on his silver tray. In half a century's service he had risen from boot boy to butler and had seen many a maid used and discarded on the way. "Don't get ideas above your station, young Rose." Only last week he had caught her returning from the meadow, cheeks flushed, wrapped in an aura of illicit loving that had her halfway off the ground. "Your betters don't mind getting you in the family way," he had told her then, "but who's going to marry you after that?"

Rose, young, innocent, and ardent for miracles, knew you could go without all the good things of life and still end up with nothing. Most of the women in the village, including her own sister, were living proof of that. When she was seven years old, she had seen her mother die of fever, too weak from overwork and malnutrition to re-sist. Three years later, her father, protesting his brother's arrest for stealing a much needed loaf of bread, had fallen beneath the wheels of Lord Crosthwaite's crimson barouche with its six high-stepping blacks, and had the life smashed out of him.

But beyond the green baize door, she now knew there was a world full of sparkle and romance. Grandy, with velvet collar and metal buttons, white silk stockings and waistcoat, with a frill on his shirt the size of a handsaw, had a corner in this Arcady. The wondering child knew early in her underprivileged life that he moved around in beautiful rooms warmed by great log fires; that he spoke differently from the lower servants.

"It's the way they like me to talk above stairs," he explained.

Rose could talk like the family now. She used her talent for mimicry to make the servants laugh. "Cor, ain't she a one?" Cook would say, hands on vast hips, rocking back and forth in front of the big wood-burning stove, watching the young girl in her drab clothes glide elegantly up and down the stone-floored kitchen, imitat-ing the countess. "Snape, see that the brandy is ready for his Lordship," Rose would say, her voice high and precise.

But when Rose was with Nicholas she found herself quite naturally speaking like the high-born ladies she overheard outside the village church as they bubbled prettily around the curate or admonished their children. Softly rounded vowels flowed off her tongue without effort. She behaved like a lady, because Nicholas made her feel like one. And he never laughed at her.

There was a heady scent to Nicholas le Grys, a gentleness that was quite outside Rose's knowledge of men. She loved the feel of his fine clothes as they walked together through the woods with arms entwined, carefully avoiding the gamekeeper. She loved the rough brush of his closely trimmed sideburns as he kissed her, and she was transported to another world by the way he talked to her. Throughout the long, bleak nights she hugged such memories to herself, as she lay on her narrow bed in the boxlike room off the stone corridor that led past the kitchens. Life was hard, often unfair, confusing, but there was one thing she knew for certain: when it was good, as it was in the company of Nicholas le Grys, you grasped it with both hands.

In the evening, when he was not otherwise engaged, Nicholas would lounge in the big Jacobean armchair in the hall, his fowling piece resting on his knees, his dark head erect, his eyes deceptively sleepy. When Rose peeped around the green baize door they would exchange a quick, conspiratorial smile. He would rise, and she would dash down the stone-arched corridor, through the servants' quarters, and out into the open, skirts flying, to the hawthorn tree by the river, where the grass lay telltale flat and the night was scented with desire.

The scene for the murder of Ned Taylor was set that evening in the small drawing room that opened off the gallery on the first floor, where the family was gathered to hear Edward Wakefield out.

The earl, sitting severely upright in his favorite winged armchair, was wondering why Edward Wakefield, after all this time, had wanted to visit them. Why he had talked obsessively all through dinner about plans to colonize the new land that Captain Cook had discovered. It was nothing to do with them.

What did the feller want here? Money? He moved impatiently from one bony buttock to the other. Showy young bounder, he thought irritably, looking across at his guest. With one elegantly booted foot on a tapestry stool and one hand at his hip, Edward caressed the curly gold whiskers that were part of his dashing, dandified look. The earl shot a glance from beneath bushy brows at his less than welcome guest, and kicked the King Charles spaniel that lay curled at his feet.

Snape knocked discreetly at the door, went in, and deposited the tray on a Sheraton drum table near the fireplace.

"Brandy, Edward?" the earl growled. His gouty toe was paining him now.

Wakefield inclined his head. "Thank you, your Lordship."

Quietly, impassively, Snape listened as he went about his duties. He remembered Mr. Wakefield's last visit, as if it were yesterday.

On a visit to Rundull when he was thirty years old, already a widower and the father of two children, Edward had heard talk of the countess of Rundull's cousin Ellen Turner, a spirited and well-developed young lady of fifteen, who was heiress not only to the wealth of her own Cheshire family, but also to that of her uncle the high sheriff. His first wife, with whom he had successfully eloped, had died in childbed after the birth of their son Jerningham. Had she survived to the magic age of twenty-one, Edward would have been the lucky inheritor of £30,000, and the second escapade with Ellen Turner would not have been necessary.

Borrowing £40 to buy a carriage, armed with a forged letter purporting to come from the family doctor, Edward had driven up to Ellen's school and announced formally, with just the right amount of concern, that the child's mother had been smitten by a dangerous attack of paralysis. Once safe in the carriage, he had spirited her onto the highway that led to Scotland and Gretna Green.

Over by the fireplace, Nicholas glowered, thinking of Rose waiting in the creeping dusk by the river. He remembered the runaway marriage well. Or thought he remembered. He had been only eleven years old at the time, but family indignation had kept the scandal alive. What baffled him was why Edward, who had planned the abduction in such detail, had in the end lost his bride.

When the family solicitor, a police officer, and two uncles caught up with them in France, the young lady's virginity was still intact. It was all the pursuers needed to know to have the marriage annulled. Yet girls, as Nicholas was well aware, were deuced easy to roll. Momentarily, he forgot that he himself had dealt exclusively with kitchen maids, and some better class whores in the courts off London's Windmill Street. So, what had gone wrong?

Priscilla, the countess of Rundull, remembering that Edward had a daughter of his own, had made a shrewd guess. The earl, who preferred to sleep alone and save his energies for impassioned speeches in the House of Lords, could yet remember the urges and urgencies of youth. In his opinion, when a cove wanted money that badly, had plotted and planned its acquisition that carefully, was as worldly and unscrupulous as Edward, the lifting of a skirt must be at the top of his list of priorities. It had been naïve of the fellow to assume he could get the money without deflowering the spoils. And heaven knew he needed it in the end, for, after the fiasco of the abduction, his trial had cost £6,000. Damned insolent of him now, to turn up here again, in the very place where the plot had been hatched.

And yet, something in the old man had quickened when he realized what Edward wanted with cousin Ellen's money. Rundull had thought, indeed all society had thought his motive had been pure greed. It was only when Edward began harassing Melbourne and the Colonial Office, and when it became known that he was distressed by the fact that three-quarters of the people of England shared less than one-third of the national income, that the penny dropped. Edward had known that the fat, comfortable Whigs in their Westminster clubs were not going to listen to a poor man. His contemporories recalled the words of the eminent Whig ecclesiastic Sydney Smith: "It is always considered a piece of impertinence in England if a man of less than two or three thousand a year has any opinions at all on important subjects."

In the last year of George IV's reign Edward had plucked up the courage to approach his sovereign. "New Zealand?" the profligate king had echoed disinterestedly. "Never heard of it." Later, William IV had snapped, "We have too many colonies already."

"When a man is starving he steals." On his release from prison, Wakefield's accusations thundered across Westminster, reverberating within the House of Lords, where Rundull himself was stung into replying testily that he could not be held responsible for the country's three hundred thousand unemployed.

But there had been recent changes in Parliament and the land. A new, lively young queen was on the throne. There was in the air, like it or not, a feeling for expansion. Whether those in power liked him, or feared and detested him, the earl knew—indeed, all thinking public men of the day knew—that Edward Gibbon Wakefield was now a force to be reckoned with.

The earl eyed him now critically across the breadth of rich Turkish carpet. His blond head and square shoulders were reflected in the gilt-framed pier glass on the red damask wall behind him; almost, Rundull thought irritably, as though he had chosen the position deliberately: the whole man and the strength of him exposed. As though he was a winner, which, by God, he was not. He was as vulnerable as the next man, as his term in Newgate proved.

But he had notoriety now, and he had used it, along with his undoubted charm, to good effect. Men of influence were behind him. The young Queen, unlike her predecessors, was not averse to extending her empire into the South Seas.

"You complain about poachers on your estate," the words emerged softly from their guest's sardonic, well-shaped mouth, "but would they be poaching if they had enough to eat? They do it because they're desperate."

The earl gazed blandly back at him. "It's not that I am unaware of the lot of the poor, dear boy," he said, mesmerized by Edward's dynamism into forgetting the man was already forty-three, "but there are so many of them. If you're criticizing me, then you're wasting your breath. I am, after all, only one landowner. If I were to set about feeding the starving multitudes, how far would I get, in Heaven's name?" He gestured irritably to Snape to fetch his cigars.

"Wouldn't you steal if your children were hungry?"

Replete from a roast pheasant dinner and syllabub, the earl did try to consider what it might be like to be hungry. "It's the way of things," he said uncomfortably at last. "If our Maker had intended us to be equal, He would have made us so."

Henry came quietly into the room and took up his seat on the big sofa. Edward thought, as he looked with tempered disdain at Henry and his colorless wife, that Nicholas should have been the heir. But thank God he was not. Edward would never have bothered to make this journey down to Kent to capture the effete Henry. It was lively, clever, hedonistic Nicholas for whom his trap was baited. A man of spirit, boiling with the passions and prejudices, as well as the arrogance, of those who formed his ancestral line.

A stranger, seeing the hawkish profile inherited from a plundering Border Scot on his mother's side, the strong, sensuous mouth and mocking eyes, could be forgiven for assuming Nicholas to be the inheritor of Castle Rundull and its green rolling acres. But Nicholas was a man without importance to the family line so long as quiet, well-schooled, well-behaved Henry was fit and well. As the younger son of an aristocratic landed English family, Nicholas could sink without a trace. As its scion in a new land, Wakefield could see him not only taking part in history, but shaping its events. The Rundulls had a propensity for lifting the mundane to grandeur. There was a glitter and sparkle to Wakefield's plans. He needed a Nicholas le Grys to carry them out.

"My arrangements for the colonization of New Zealand are as follows," he said aloud. "Listen carefully, my Lord, for I want you to be concerned. Nicholas!"

Nicholas had taken out the gold fob watch given to him for his twenty-fourth birthday in January. He glanced at it, then impatiently out of the window. Twilight was deepening outside. "Get to the point, sir," he snapped.

"I intend to fill five ships with emigrants," Edward continued, watching Nicholas closely. "There are no settlers in the islands as yet. Only sealers and whalers, with a sprinkling of missionaries and naturalists."

"Convicts?" That was Henry, confident in his luck and the laws of primogeniture.

Edward's clear blue eyes flickered across to the elder son. "There are no convicts in New Zealand, and I do not intend that there ever shall be," he said coldly. "I am involved with a convict settlement in southern Australia, but that's twelve hundred miles northwest of New Zealand and quite a different kettle of fish."

Since his release from prison, Edward had been spreading his gospel of a new and better life for the unlucky, underprivileged, and underfed, whom he had met in plenty within the walls of Newgate. They included men who had been incarcerated for stealing a mutton chop to provide for their starving families; men who had dared to protest about their hapless lot.

Snape moved as slowly as was seemly to Henry's chair, deliberately keeping his eyes lowered, to avoid a gesture of dismissal. Gossip about the family was the servants' meat and drink.

"I propose to handpick the first emigrants from the educated classes," Edward said, his head lifting, his eyes fixed avidly on his prey.

The countess uttered a sharp, nervous laugh. "And how are you going to persuade people of good family with everything to lose, and nothing to gain, to sail off with you to the ends of the earth?"

He hit her where it hurt most. He knew how much she loved her younger son. "What has Nicholas to lose?"

Nicholas whirled around, meeting the brilliant blue eyes with fury in his own. It was true he had nothing to lose because he owned nothing, expected nothing but a roof over his head, and—he acknowledged for the first time, resentfully—the charity of his father. Edward's question was one Nicholas had never bothered to face seriously until now.

"Younger sons," commented the earl. "Hmn."

The silence in the room was intense. Nicholas knew only too well what his father thought of his way of life. He and his friends were the talk of the county. "I wish you good evening, sir," he said heading for the door. "I have pressing matters to attend to."

His father lifted an imperative hand. "Wait. Come back and hear our guest out."

Nicholas paused, his dark face flushing with anger. Priscilla looked upset. Only Henry seemed not to be moved. The truth was, he did not particularly care about the fate of his roistering younger brother. It would suit him capitally if Nicholas went away until he tamed down.

"Nicholas!" barked the earl.

He turned reluctantly and went to stand again beside the drawingroom fireplace with its crossed swords above

the mantel, and the molded head of William the Conqueror set into the stone.

"My company is purchasing one hundred and ten thousand acres near a safe harbor in the North Island of New
Zealand," Wakefield was saying, "and portions of this
will be offered to the first settlers at a very reasonable
price."

"Who is to work the land?" inquired the earl, peering
beneath frowning brows at his guest. Surely the man
wasn't expecting a Rundull, even a younger son, to drive
a plow?

"We are offering free passages to carefully chosen
artisans and their families. My Lord, New Zealand will
be a replica of England in every respect but one. There
will be no poverty."

The earl relaxed in his big chair, scowling. The man
was talking nonsense. Poverty was a part of living.

"Snape!" he barked irritably.

"M'Lord." The butler picked up his tray and hurried
to the door. He had been so shaken by the suggestion
that Master Nicholas should go to New Zealand with the
common criminals—or was it Australia, where Gertie
Taylor's father had been banished?—that he had dropped
his discreet servant's mask and stared openmouthed. Now,
as he hurried across the room and closed the heavy oak
door, his old heart was singing. Not only was his little
granddaughter's seducer going to be kept at home tonight, but likely he would disappear altogether. Snape
went down the curved staircase faster than he had done
for thirty years.

Rose was still there, one small foot idly knocking the
door back and forth. "Master Nicholas isn't getting out
tonight," Snape told her, callous in his delight. "And
what's more, he's likely leaving the castle for good soon."

Rose's beautiful eyes widened. "What do you mean,
leaving?" She trotted at his side down the stone stairs.

"Going abroad. Getting married first, I shouldn't be
surprised. You'll likely not meet him again, Rosie." Her
heart-shaped face turned paper white, her lips trembled.
His kind heart contracted in sympathy. "Run along, girl,
and find a nice village lad," he said gruffly. "No good
ever came of getting mixed up with the gentry."

She stood still for a moment, looking lost. Then, with a

bewildered shake of her head, she turned and walked in silence down the vaulted stone passage. At the end, instead of going along to the kitchen, she opened the heavily barred oak door that led into the inner courtyard, pushed it back on its creaking hinges, and disappeared through. Snape put his tray down, but by the time he reached the door the yard was empty. He stood looking around for a moment, then shrugged and went back inside.

Upstairs, restive and quarrelsome, Nicholas scoffed. "The Colonial Office isn't interested in expansion." He knew about the battles with the prime minister. Certainly, it looked as though Edward was winning, but wasn't Melbourne on the way out? It was going to be an empty victory unless he moved fast.

"Your five ships will end by rotting at Gravesend," Nicholas predicted, turning to his father for support. To his surprise, he received a frown in return. The old hypocrite! Why was he not cocking a snook at this clown?

Wakefield's blue eyes snapped, but his voice was velvet. "I think I've enough supporters in and out of Parliament now to make a move. No ships of mine will rot in the Thames. My brother William is sailing in May, and my boy goes with him."

"Not to stay," Nicholas flashed. The man had a genius for twisting facts in order to build up the impression he wished to convey. "I was told by Jerningham the *Tory* is a survey ship." He knew all about the movements of their guest's nineteen-year-old son, a footloose young man with more brains than balance. Jerningham had been boasting for months about his proposed adventure, audaciously leading a native interpreter called Nayti around London like a monkey on a string, telling everyone he was a prince in New Zealand, and cleverly getting society hostesses to lionize him.

"Jerningham would never emigrate permanently," he said now. "You and I know him better than that." Jerningham would embrace any adventure wholeheartedly, but when it was over he would bounce up again in the salons of Mayfair, the fleshpots of St. James's.

"Who knows what the boy will do," the father replied suavely. "Come and talk to him."

"Will you come into my parlor, said the spider to the

fly." Nicholas quoted the words softly so that no one heard. "Good-night to you, sir," he said curtly. "I've already told you I have pressing matters to attend to." He could not announce that he was going to look for poachers, his usual excuse for disappearing at dusk. Not after their guest's comment that poachers were people who had too little to eat.

This time, rather to his surprise, and disconcertingly, no one stopped him. Briefly, with his hand on the door-knob, he considered with alarm that dull Harry and that chicken-breasted, uppish wife of his might encourage Wakefield behind his back. Then Rose's lovely face came into his mind's eye, blotting out anxiety.

He took the stairs two at a time, crossed the hall, and strode along the passage to the gun room. Armed, he had an alibi. Besides, who knew but that he might not come upon poachers? During the past few days, the flock of geese that honked and cackled over the rooftops twice a day as they flew between the ornamental lakes seemed depleted in number. One of the swans had also disappeared. Nicholas had watched with surging anger and that queer, surprising compassion he hid from all but those who knew him best while the swan's mate had died of a broken heart.

He let himself into the east corridor with its arches of coiling stone, then out again on the far side where the passage terminated in a broad flight of stone steps. Hoisting his fowling piece up against his shoulder, he crossed the courtyard. Here he paused, as he always did, under the imposing statue of horse and rider commissioned by the 15th earl of Rundull: he who had patched up the castle one hundred years after Cromwell and his Ironsides sacked it.

The 15th earl, a prominent Whig, helped form the party that became disparagingly known as the King's Friends. Bribery money paid for the entire renovation of the castle, but it was not enough to cover the commission of an armored statue of William the Conqueror on horseback.

Faced with a daunting bill for the finished work of art, the earl told the sculptor he felt it was a matter of some doubt that any knight in armor would keep his seat on a rearing horse while at the same time taking careful aim with a crossbow. It was useless for the poor man to protest that he had fashioned an allegory in stone to burnish the Conqueror's memory. The empty pocket of Henry Lancelot Giles Percival le Grys weighed heavily on the side of disapproval. The sculptor was sent packing with a fraction of his fee.

But Rundull had underestimated his man. In bitter fury, the sculptor invoked the devil to lay a curse upon his work. Anyone unfortunate enough to pass by when the east wind howled around the statue would be doomed, he swore, to a life of tragedy and violence. Should anyone be foolish enough to destroy the work, Castle Rundull would be flooded with evil spirits.

There was a story that Rose's mother, sensing her time had come early, ran from the castle kitchens, crossing the haunted courtyard in her haste. The fact that she had died of fever when Rose was a child, that the father met his death only a few years later, had not gone unnoticed by the superstitious villagers; and occasionally old women remembered that Rose had lain beneath the folds of her mother's cloak that night as she skirted the statue in the teeth of an easterly gale.

It was unfortunate in the extreme that this evening Nicholas should have been carrying a gun. A roisterer, a carouser he was indeed, but he was not a murderer. Striding off with shoulders squared, shirt open, he took the overgrown track that led down to the meandering river Eden, where elderberries, candy-pink foxglove, and rioting dog rose concealed the banks from view. It had been a warm spring with plenty of rain. The meadows were golden with buttercups; somewhere in the distance a cuckoo rendered its double note; and up near the orchard, sorrel coming into flower spread a reddening flag across the slopes.

But Nicholas was in no mood to smooth the jagged edges of this night with the gentle balm of the countryside he so truly loved. At the first bend in the river he hesitated, his nerves jumping, regret for his precipitous exit growing rapidly into alarm. Dull Henry would not take his side, nor would his wife Adeline. Even now, they could be encouraging his father to send him to New Zealand. Twilight had settled over the meadow and a thin mist like a huge thistledown snake lay along the path of the water. Above, the dark outline of the castle rose like a threat.

"Damn the meddling jackanapes!" Nicholas muttered. "Damn him to hell!" But there was no going back now. Somewhere down there in the bushes, if he was not too late, Rose, with her sweet, soft breasts and her plump thighs, waited. The stings and thorns of the night receded. He plunged along the track, thinking only of Rose.

3

"Nicholas," whispered Rose on a breathless, awe-struck gasp, and then again, "Nicholas."

He stood looking down at the body, a crushing sense of doom descending upon him. Rose clambered shakily to her feet, her skirts falling around her calves. Ned Taylor was a twisted hulk in the long grass. In the gathering darkness they could see neither the face, nor the blood. Taking Rose by the arm, Nicholas propelled her along the river path. Twenty yards into the shadowed twilight, where brambles hid the water from view, he paused. "Wait here," he said. "I must go back."

"Don't leave me, Nicholas." She reached out to him.

"Wait!" He was sharply authoritative, and her hands fell away.

He strode back. At the hawthorn tree his spirit nearly failed him. Gritting his teeth, he moved into the shadows. There it was, the body. A bloodstained face, a smashed skull. Nicholas's stomach turned, and the bile rose in his throat. He put a hand to his head. There was a sound behind him, a soft movement as though a small animal crept close. He swung around.

"Don't leave me alone," Rose begged pitifully. He put an arm around her, drawing her against him. "What are we going to do?" she whispered, her voice breaking on every syllable. "Oh, Nicholas. What are we going to do?"

Do? What did one do after killing a man? "I'll take you back. Can you get to your room without being seen?"

"No. No. Please, no. I can't go back to the castle."
She grasped his wrist, her fingers hard, rigid with terror.
"I can't go back." Not there. Alone. To her comfortless
little room near the kitchen, to toss and turn all through
the black night.

"You must," he said, but he spoke gently.

His tenderness was Rose's undoing. She collapsed on
his shoulder, weeping. "Poor Gertie," she sobbed. "Oh,
poor, poor Gertie."

"Who's Gertie?"

"His w-wife."

Silent, tormented, Nicholas smoothed her soft hair. A
little later he said, "Rose, we can't stay here. Where do
you want to go?"

"I don't know. C-could I go to . . . to F-Florrie?" She
wiped her eyes with a ball of a handkerchief.

Briefly, he considered the danger inherent in her suggestion, for he knew her sister's dwelling lay through the
village beyond the alehouse. Someone could see her,
tearstained and disheveled. In the morning, when the
body was found, they would remember. On the other
hand, returning to her own room, she would almost
certainly be seen by one or more of the castle servants.
"All right," Nicholas agreed reluctantly at last. "But you
mustn't tell her."

Rose put a hand to her trembling mouth as though to
hold back the admission of considered guilt. She would
have to tell Florrie.

Holding her close Nicholas led her back to the path.
"I'll take you as far as the bridge. I daren't go any
further in case we're seen."

She looked up into his face with tear-filled eyes. She
wanted to tell him it was all her fault; she wanted to rid
herself of the terrible guilt of not having rebuffed Ned.
The words would not come.

"We'd better hurry."

They found their way along the river path in a silence
punctuated by Rose's soft hiccuping sobs. Nicholas paused
beneath the willow tree. "Try not to let anyone see you."

"What are you going to do?" Rose asked, wiping her
tearstained face once more with her sleeve.

"God knows," he replied heavily. "God knows."

Her face crumpled. "I don't want to leave you."

"You must, darling. And quickly. Anyone could come along here. We must not be seen together. You must get to your sister's place without being seen."

"Oh, Nicholas!" Rose broke down, sobbing.

Taking her by the shoulder he turned her around to face him. "You've got to pull yourself together. All right, tell Florrie, if you must." He added with grim resignation, "Everyone is going to know in the morning, anyway."

She snatched his hand and kissed it, little frantic kisses of gratitude.

He watched as she crossed the stone bridge, a forlorn figure in the gathering darkness. When she had disappeared he turned, striding back along the river, his head held high. Even in the direst trouble, Nicholas le Grys was not one to allow his shoulders to droop, his head to hang. He came once more upon the body and stood looking grimly down. What could one do for a dead man except bury him decently?

He lifted the gun, wiped the butt in the long grasses, then felt his way carefully in the darkness down the riverbank. Cupping a hand in the water, he washed the weapon meticulously, cleaning it of evidence. In the morning someone would almost certainly discover the body. If not, he would have to come down and pretend he had made the discovery himself.

He started to walk toward home, his brain seething. He knew in his heart that the savagery of his blow had scant connection with a normal desire to protect, or even with jealousy. He had killed Ned Taylor, albeit by accident, because the devil was in him. Quietly but potently, he cursed Edward Wakefield for coming out of the past today.

Peering fearfully to right and left, Rose hurried up the narrow cobbled street. Poor, poor Gertie and those innocent little children! They were going to starve now, and it was her fault. As she rounded the corner into the High Street, hoots of coarse laughter and a desultory gabble of voices burst from the open door of the Hopper's Maid. She scuttled into the shadow of a cottage that lay flush with the street and waited, her heart pumping fast, her eyes fixed on the patch of light inside the low doorway. At intervals men took their mugs of ale and drank them in the fresher air outside. But there was no discernible movement, and in a little while she plucked up the courage to move on again.

At the end of the High Street she took to her heels, scurrying across the cobbles and into the alleyway that led behind the ironmongers and the bakery.

And here at last was the mean little cottage where Florrie and Adam lived. "Florrie," she called in a frenzied whisper, her lips against the crack in the rough-hewn oak door that did not close properly because the lintel had sagged, as the frame inched its way over the years into foundations softened by permanent damp. "Let me in, Florrie. Let me in."

Rose's elder sister had been as pretty, pert, and headstrong as Rose, until pregnancy and then marriage, an inadequate diet, and two children in nineteen months had dragged her down. Now, the curl and the warm, honey tones had gone from her hair, the roundness from her figure, leaving a shadowy girl-woman, her body thickened, her thin breasts distended. The familiar listlessness of the poor lay around her like a washed-out rag. Florrie opened the door, saw Rose's ravaged face, and dropped back with a bleat of dismay.

Adam, thin, resentful, uncertain, stood scratching his back as he eyed the girls. In the lamplight he saw the blood on Rose's skirt, the grass in her hair, and turned away, unwillingly recalling that night when Florrie had teased him too far. There had been blood that night, too. Blood on his arm where she had bitten him, and elsewhere too, shaming him because he had not thought she was a virgin. He turned and went sullenly past his wife and sister-in-law, out of the squalid dwelling and down to the Hopper's Maid, though without a penny in his pocket for ale.

Florrie backed onto the wooden bench by the empty fireplace. "What's 'appened, Rose?" And then, with more resignation than interest, " 'Oo was it?"

"He's dead. Ned's dead!" Rose broke down, sobbing.

Florrie sat bolt upright, uncomprehending.

"It wouldn't have happened if he hadn't moved his head," chattered Rose through her sobs. "It wouldn't have happened. He moved his head!"

Florrie, catching the note of panic in her sister's voice,

dragged herself to her feet and hurried over to the corner. There was no indoor tap, but a ragged cloth, still wet from the dish washing, lay on the table. She pressed it to Rose's forehead.

"Calm down, girl, an' tell me what 'appened. Calm down, I tell yer." Rose gulped, but no words came. Florrie waited a moment, then acted the only way she knew. She slapped Rose's face, hard.

Rose recoiled. Nicholas, even in his blackest moments, had been gentle with her. Florrie's native harshness curbed her hysteria, at the same time lifting the lid on a well of despair. "I wish I could die," she wailed. "Oh-h-h, I wish I could die."

Curiosity, impatience, and fear drove out the remainder of Florrie's common sense. She took her sister by the shoulders and shook her roughly. "Wot 'appened? You said Ned's dead. 'Oo killed 'im?"

Rose could not say. The slap had killed her trust.

" 'Oo, Rose?" shouted Florrie.

"I don't kn-now. It was dark."

"Go *on*. Tell me 'oo done it."

"Someone came along and hit him on the head."

"Gertie's comin' back termorrer from Rochester."

The horror within clawed at Rose's stomach. She could not face Gertie Taylor. Nor any of the children. "I wish I could die," she wailed again.

From the sleeping loft came a child's cry, and then another. Florrie rose tiredly. "Now yer've wakened Ossie. I'd better go ter 'im or 'e'll wake the baby."

She seemed to be away for ages. Rose could hear the soothing murmur of her voice as she changed the child. She shivered in the bleak little room. Spring had brought no warmth to the stone floor, and, except in the hottest weather, there was always a smell of damp.

Rose lurched to the single window and peered nervously out, but there was nothing to be seen beyond the cobwebs on the glass and the black wall of night. Then the metal latch on the door rattled and she swung around in fear. Adam burst in, shut the door behind him, and sagged against it as though suspended from a nail, his thin, red mouth damp in a white face.

"Gertie's brothers went after Ned," he said bleakly. "Tom Aiken saw yer together an' told 'em."

A wicked hope reared up in Rose's heart. Perhaps the Almighty would intervene and give Gertie's brothers the blame. "When did they go?"

He listened to the high, queer tone of her voice, and his pale eyes noted her fear. "Jest now." He waited, watching with a foxiness that came of years of looking after his own skin. He was not averse to the thought of Rose's being in trouble, as long as she did not bring it to him. "Yer'd better get back ter the castle," he said. "I don't want 'em comin' 'ere after yer."

Rose licked her dry lips. Her green eyes, huge and tormented, locking on his face, willing him not to send her away, not to learn the truth.

There were footsteps on the bare boards overhead and Florrie emerged, descending the ladder with the sure-footedness of a cat, her puny son on one arm. In her free hand she carried a candle. She looked from her sister to her husband and back. "Yer haven't told 'im," she said accusingly. " 'E 'as ter know. Everyone'll know tonight."

Rose swallowed, tried to speak, backed to a bench, and perched shakily beside the fireplace, where a black cooking pot, suspended from a cast-iron hook in the chimney, hung over dead ashes.

"Tell me wot?" Adam's face sharpened.

"Ned Taylor's dead."

With a scuffle of feet and the speed of a hunted animal, Adam crossed the room. Gripping Rose's shoulders he thrust his pallid face into hers, his mouth slack and ugly with shock. She cringed back in terror. "Dead? Wot d'yer mean, dead?"

In her agitation Florrie dropped the candle. It rolled across the flagstones, spilling the tallow in opaque little pools, extinguishing itself. With small, work-worn fingers she grasped her husband's arm, jerking him away. The baby wailed. "Leave 'er alone, will yer? Leave Rose alone," Florrie screeched.

Lost in the turmoil of his fear, Adam turned on his wife. "Yer tell me 'oo killed 'im, then!" The child in Florrie's arms screamed. "Shut the kid up, or I'll shut 'im up fer yer." Tucking the baby's head close against her heart, Florrie crouched protectively into a corner, soothing him. Adam turned once more on Rose. "That turkeycock done it, din 'e? You been whoring fer months wi' 'im.''

Florrie leaned forward, eyes widening. Adam saw her expression and was cheered by the unexpected opportunity of thrusting a nettle between the girls. "So now yer know it's the Honorable Nicholas's whore pipe she's bin gettin'.''

Rosie and the son of the earl of Rundull! Ned's death, her baby's danger, flew from Florrie's mind and her heartbeats quickened with fearful, unconsidered pride. "Is it true, Rose?"

Her question was overlaid by Adam's brutal thrust. "Was it 'im, the whoremonger? Was it 'im killed Ned?"

'No. No, it wasn't. It was a stranger,'' lied Rose feverishly, screwing the coarse stuff of her skirts into crumpled balls in her hands. "It wasn't him," she shrieked, beside herself with fear. "It wasn't him. And I ain't been whoring with him. I ain't.''

In the ferment of Rose's reaction her sister read the truth. She knew Adam would talk, had perhaps already done so, dangerously, with Ned's brothers-in-law. There were no secrets in the tiny village of Rundull. Never had been. Incest, intermarriage, and lack of money had locked them all together in a bitter kind of harmony. They helped even as they hated; exposed each other's pain, then, inevitably, shared it. They loved, feared, fought, and suffered together as their ancestors had done for hundreds of years. Florrie knew that if the Honorable Nicholas le Grys had killed Ned, only divine intervention could suppress the fact. She said placatingly, "It must've been an accident. I expect 'e thought Ned were a poacher.''

Adam's reply was a thin sneer.

"You won't tell, will you?"

"Yer think they won't know? Unless they think she done it 'erself.'' Adam pointed a grubby finger at Rose. "Would yer like ter go ter the gallows fer yer fancy gen'l'man?'Ow d'yer like ter be 'anged at Newgate, Rose?''

Rose's head drooped and the stains on her skirt came within her line of vision. She slid to the floor, her face on her knees, arms protectively encircling her head, and gave herself up to the agony of total despair. Perhaps Adam would beat her to death, and then it would be over.

* * *

"Every generation, this family throws up a violent man."

The earl spoke ponderously, leaning forward from the depths of his enormous wingbacked chair, his elbows on his knees, his chin resting on the backs of his hands. They were in the library, which was housed in one of the massively rotund medieval towers adjoining the forecourt, originally the outer bailey where the arched main entrance to the castle lay.

The countess, sitting upright on a small gilt chair, opened her mouth to protest, then closed it again. It was true. Violence was inherent in Rundull history. Her husband's own brother had been exiled to France for the murder of his wife's lover. And his uncle had pushed a thieving valet to his death out of the window that looked over the inner bailey where the statue stood. She shivered.

"That's how we came originally to be earls, m'dear. By killing."

His wife drew herself marginally more erect and glared at him. "Do you realize what you're saying, Rundull?" Her voice was high, trembling conspicuously. "That you believe your own son to be guilty?"

"Snape never lied to me. He's been in my service for forty years and he never . . ."

"There's always a first time," snapped his lady, shaken out of her habitual serenity by her fear, and her love for her son. "Or he may be mistaken."

"I believe Snape docs know." His lordship took out a handkerchief and, blowing his nose in short, sharp bursts, gave himself time to consider how much to tell his wife of what he knew. "The granddaughter was involved," he said at last.

"Snape's granddaughter?" The countess's fine brows shot up then, as she digested the disagreeable facts, her lips curled with distaste.

"She's one of the kitchen maids, m'dear."

"The girl must be dismissed immediately," she said with the callous authority bestowed upon her by generations of privilege.

The earl sighed gustily. "What good would that do? Another strumpet will come in to take her place. The only way you'll avoid this sort of . . . er, humph . . . is to castrate the boy, or surround him by pockmarked ser-

vants with harelips." When his wife did not answer he
looked up. Her frozen face was turned toward the rows
of leather-bound books, largely unread, that lined the
walls. "Would you want a son with water in his veins?"
the earl asked aggressively. "Nicholas is only as red-
blooded as his forebears. Men with red blood in their
veins go rutting, Priscilla."

She swallowed the second vulgarity, together with all
its unpleasant implications. Of course she knew young
men behaved unspeakably at times.

"Every now and again a feller runs out of luck, and it
causes trouble. Y'can't keep this sort of thing to your
own class, y'know that." He fiddled irritably with the lid
of his snuff box.

"So you're saying Nicholas was sharing this trollop
with the blacksmith." Priscilla spoke with displeasure and
distaste.

"I said it looks like that."

She rose, picked up a delicate china shepherdess, turned
it over critically, put the ornament down again, and,
lifting her head high, announced with conviction, "Whatever you say, Nicholas is not a killer."

The earl clicked his teeth, took a pinch of snuff, cleared
his throat, then drummed his fingers on the chair arm.

"Why don't you call him in?" suggested his lady at
last. Sooner or later she was going to have to face Nicholas with this insult to her refinement and her gentility
poised between them. "Ask for his side of the story."

"I shall call him in," the earl replied with resolution,
"but the outcome, whatever it is, won't alter what the
dead man's brothers-in-law believe. That's the dangerous
crux of the matter, m'dear. If Nicholas can prove he
wasn't out last night . . ." He paused, shifted uncomfortably in his seat, then ended heavily, "but he was. Snape
saw him leave carrying the gun."

"And Snape has told . . ."

"He didn't have to. Ned Taylor was seen with the girl,
and the girl is known to have been meeting Nicholas by
the river, where the body was found. The village is out to
get Nicholas. That's what I'm talking about, Priscilla.
That's the issue. And if they do, they'll lynch him."

The countess glared at her husband, fear and fury
intermixed. "They wouldn't dare!" She rose, went to the

tapestry bellpull and tugged it. Snape came quickly. "Please inform Mr. Nicholas his Lordship would like to see him."

"Certainly, m'Lady." Snape bowed his head, his face a mask.

"You do understand, don't you, Snape, that what passed between his Lordship and you this morning is strictly confidential." Priscilla gazed at the wall.

"His Lordship made that clear, m'Lady."

"Does Mrs. Snape know?"

"When Rose didn't appear this morning, Mrs. Snape went to her room. The bed 'ad not been slept in. She was obliged to send a messenger to the village. It was 'im come back with the facts I put before 'is Lordship." The butler's distress showed pitifully in the collapse of his normally impeccable English.

"Who was this man, the messenger?" Lady Rundull spoke without emotion.

"A boy, m'Lady, as 'elps out in the kitchen. I did 'ave a word with 'im. And of course Mrs. Snape will see that there's no gossipin' below stairs."

"Thank you, Snape. It was, of course, quite incorrect that Mr. Nicholas was involved." Her words were explicit, her tone carefully careless.

"Of course, m'Lady." Snape's eyes were expressionless. Forty years of service had brought its own harsh lessons.

"Where is the girl, Snape?"

"At her sister's in the village, m'Lady."

"See that she stays there."

"Certainly, m'Lady."

Had there been any doubt about the veracity of the story, one glance at Nicholas's haggard face, his disheveled and wretched appearance, would have convinced anyone of his guilt. It was clear he had not even been to bed, for he was still dressed more or less as he had been last night when he left the withdrawing room. His mother's eyes dilated as she saw the blood on his sleeve.

He came into the room with his normal easy stride and air of alert grace. Before she saw the tortured expression in his dark eyes, Priscilla thought grimly: Small wonder he disturbs people, attracts trouble and love, and hate.

He crossed to one of the high-arched, stone-framed

windows, and stood with his back to it, the light glossing his dark hair. Looking directly at his father, his gaze steady, he said, "Last night I came upon the smithy raping one of the servants. I aimed at his shoulder with the butt of my gun. He moved, and took the blow on his head."

Stunned, they continued to stare at him. Neither parent could have said what they had expected. Certainly not that. They waited for him to go on, and when he did not, the earl said, "Humph!" Then, hopefully, "You thought he was a poacher."

"I don't know. The girl screamed. I went to help her. What would you have done?" Nicholas asked, looking from one to the other.

"Gone on my way," the earl retorted. "You say it was an act of rape. How do you know the girl wasn't enjoying it?"

Nicholas showed no sign that he had heard. "We had better do something about the poor fellow's family."

The earl sat forward in his chair, glaring. "Has it occurred to you to consider your own position? We have it from Snape that this man's relations are after your blood."

Nicholas turned away.

The earl thumped a fist on the chair arm. "D'you hear me, Nicholas? For God's sake, man, are you listening? Feeling is running high in the village."

The dark head rose. The sense of his physical power, his confidence, filled the room. "I can look after myself."

"Nicholas, my dear." Gliding to his side, his mother laid a slender hand on his arm. "In the circumstances, it's possible you may not be able to look after yourself."

His father barked, "I'm talking about a lynch mob. And you're standing there as though you don't give a tinker's cuss."

"You're suggesting I run away." Nicholas's tone was deceptively mild.

"No, son, no. I didn't say that." The fire went out of the earl. He coughed, tapped his fingers on the arm of the chair. "Be a sensible chap and get off up to London for a while."

"No."

The earl jerked forward in his chair, his eyes bulging. "You impudent young pup! How dare you defy me!"

"I will not run."

"And I'll not have a son of mine murdered by the scum of the village on my own estate." Their eyes met and held. Grit and endurance against tempered steel.

Then, Nicholas's mouth twisted. "I can see the awkwardness of that," he agreed sardonically. "All right. I'll ride up to London today. Just for a day or two, until things simmer down."

"Not for a day or two, and not on horseback," retorted his father. "You'll take a closed carriage. And a couple of grooms. Felicity resumes her Waiting today. You will go with her and her maid."

Snape, bulky in the black dress coat and white tie he wore in the morning, stood in the stone doorway frowning at the statue of William the Conqueror that dominated the courtyard. Tanner the Bastard, the Frenchies had called him, that illegitimate issue of a duke of Normandy and a tanner's daughter. A duke and a village girl! Snape's mind turned to Rose and what might become of her; to Nicholas, whom he had loved as a child.

He knew, had always known, the history of the le Grys family. How the first Henry le Grys had come over with the Conqueror in 1066 and how he had, with wisdom and forethought, stayed closely at the leader's side during those years of rebellion and insurrection that followed the proclamation. Rundull Castle and the estates around it had been his reward. Snape raised his eyes to the turrets and battlements that had to be rebuilt after Cromwell's bloody massacre. Nobody, not even the Rundulls, won all the time. He acknowledged the fact with a mixture of relief and uncertainty.

There was a clatter of footsteps behind him in the stone corridor and without looking around the butler moved aside to allow the man to pass.

"Admiring the family benefactor?" The question was unaccustomedly curt.

"It is a terrible pity," Snape said with more bitterness than might be expected from a member of the staff, "that statue was never paid for."

"I'm leaving for London," Nicholas said, annoyed by

the old man's disquiet. "I'm riding Cossack. I could use him in Rotten Row. I may not return for a week or so."

"I would not ride alone, Master Nicholas, if I were you. It would be unwise."

Nicholas's dark brows drew together. He was about to tell the butler to mind his own business, when he read an expression in the pale, tired eyes he had not seen there since he was a small boy and Snape used to pick him up from where he had fallen, soothing him. Without a word, he turned and went on down the long passage, his footsteps echoing on the cold stone.

"Tanner the Bastard," muttered Snape to himself. There were those who were meant to win, however unseemly their beginnings. Perhaps Rose would be one of them.

4

Twenty minutes later, Nicholas, dressed in top hat and frock coat with a jauntily tied cravat, strode into the stone-paved court beside the stables. The butler was there waiting for him. "There's been cadgers and mouchers around the village these past few days, Mr. Nicholas. I've heard tell that the Putnam boys is offering them bribes."

Nicholas grinned. "Tell the Putnams to do their own dirty work. And tell them I don't go unarmed. Look at that whip, Snape." Gingerly, he flicked the springy weapon against the good leather of his riding boots. "A thrashing whip," he said with satisfaction. "Cadgers and mouchers indeed."

Snape wagged his whiskered head in mute and futile reproach. He was certain the boy knew without caring, in his brave and foolhardy way, about the threatening potential of the lower classes. About the gangs of ruffians, who roamed the countryside looking for food, and sometimes even for work: the stinking flotsam and jetsam of life whose bludgeonings, eye-gougings, and thumb-bitings were a feared by-product of the growth of country towns of the 1830s, especially those with fairgrounds to plunder. There was a fairground in the local town of Penbridge.

"What do you want of me, Snape?" Nicholas demanded, laughing, his head back, his dark eyes flashing defiance. "Would you have me a milksop fledgling with a wet nurse in tow, riding in a closed carriage with postilions?"

"It were better so," agreed the old butler, ignoring the mockery inherent in Nicholas's affable banter. "I'd not

41

like to have you tied to a wheel and beaten. That's what
they do, them mouchers. It's been known."

"Tied to a wheel!" repeated Nicholas scornfully. "A
man has to be caught before he can be tied to a wheel."

"It's said they've been known to hold a man underwater until he expires."

Nicholas knew Snape was referring obtusely to the
river Eden that meandered through the estate, crossing
the road down which he was presently to ride. "Let them
try." There was a clatter of hooves on stone and he
glanced up, his face bright and suddenly warm. A groom
was coming toward them across the court leading a high-
stepping bay—newly shod, Nicholas remembered with
disquiet, by the man who had died beneath the butt of
his gun. The gelding's head was raised, his ears pricking
as he sought his young master.

"Cossack." Nicholas strode forward, took the reins
loosely, climbed the mounting block, and flung one leg
over the saddle. "Whoa boy. Whoa there." Even before
he had his feet in the stirrups, Cossack was clattering and
dancing across the stones. Nicholas gripped the reins
firmly in competent hands and settled into a comfortable
seat. The muscled beast swung his hindquarters around,
sending the groom scuttling out of reach of his hooves.

"He'll give me a good ride." Then, in an aside to
Snape, who was standing with head lowered, hunch-
shouldered in his distress, "I'll see you in heaven or hell,
old man, but I won't be there today." Easing the reins,
maintaining control, he waved cheerfully to the outside
servants as he and his magnificent mount rounded the
corner and disappeared from sight.

It was a beautiful spring day. As he went down the
oak-lined drive, Nicholas felt a queer tug at his heart. In
all his scrapes, and he had been involved in a great many
over the years, he had never left the castle under real
pressure. There had been a run or two from trouble to
roister in London or Dover with his friends while the
families simmered down, but they were mere roguish
escapades. Today he had been shaken indeed by the
discovery that he could be so easily dislodged from the
place where he felt himself to be as integral a part as
every stone and beam and arrow-slitted wall. He turned
into the road running between the rolling hills and mead-

ows that he loved more than himself, more than life even. Heigh-ho. The pulse of Rundull would quieten, and he would be back in a week or two.

Above him on the hilltop, the castle brooded, dark as its second son, and as daunting in its moods. Back from the village, beyond the clutter of buildings on a little knoll, the high-roofed Norman church built by Nicholas's ancestors, wrecked by Cromwell, and rebuilt by the 15th earl, lay snugly within its own encircling oaks. Wild pear and apple blossomed at the wayside, and the grasses were tall from the feast of warm spring rains.

The metallic clatter of the horse's shoes echoed between the buildings as they entered the village High Street. With surprise, Nicholas saw it was empty. He glanced, frowning, to right and left, faintly disconcerted. Where were the village women carrying their shopping baskets, or their washing from the well? Where was the local cleric hurrying by in his somber black hat? Burying the smithy, Nicholas wondered uncomfortably? No, it was too soon. He loosened the reins and spurred Cossack to a canter. Out of the village and down the slope he went, faster and faster with his coattails flying in the wind.

Something moved in the sparse bushes by the little stone bridge that spanned the river. He reined in. Fools, he thought contemptuously. Anyone with brains would conceal themselves in the trees on that nearby bank. He rode on with a straight back and undiminished confidence, he fingered the pistol in his holster. A fight! His blood raced in his veins, stirring his guilt at the smithy's death, turning the ignominy of his banishment into a desire for reckless reprisal.

The road narrowed as it led up to the bridge. Nicholas eased the reins and dug in his heels. Cossack gathered up his powerful sinews, thrust out his long neck, and leaped ahead. Nicholas bent low in the saddle, the rushing wind in his face, glorying in the certain knowledge that no man would dare to come within yards of his mount's punishing hooves.

But what the footpads lacked in brains they made up for in immense cunning. Two men leaped from their hiding place, and with the speed of birds in flight, rushed a plank at knee height across the shoulder of the bridge.

The horse was already pounding onto the stone approaches. It was too late to rein in and direct Cossack to jump, too late to turn.

Leaning back in the saddle, his feet thrust forward in the stirrups, his hands sawing the bit ferociously in the horse's mouth, Nicholas knew with a sickening sense of the inevitable there was nothing he could do to avoid disaster. The astonished beast skidded, his forelegs hit the barrier, and they both came down with a juddering crash. Meeting the metal road with stunning force, Nicholas rolled over in a fog of dust and pain. He came to rest dizzily in the grass by the bole of a big-rooted oak. Then they were on him like rats on a cheese, tearing at him with their filthy, bony hands, squealing and shrieking their victory.

"Garrot 'im!"

Through his fading consciousness he heard the dreadful word and felt the touch of cold wire at his throat. Kicking ruthlessly and indiscriminately at his attackers, he flung himself upright. But there were too many of them. He sensed rather than saw their numbers. And his gun was gone. He punched wildly with his fists, whirling on his heels, trying to cover himself from every side, knowing he was hopelessly outnumbered. They scrabbled and snatched at his clothes, dodged and darted. The infernal wire threatened him on every side, as they tried again and again to hook it around his neck.

The bridge was his only chance. He was near enough to the river, if only he could get there. With a powerful lunge he flung himself forward, shedding his coat as he went, leaving it in their hands. He went like a human landslide down the bank toward the water, drivels of dry earth and stones clattering with him. A clump of hemlock partially broke his fall, and then the numbingly cold water closed over him. As he sank, Snape's warning echoed in his ears: "It's said these people have been known to hold a man underwater until he expired."

He bobbed to the surface, swam swiftly into the shadows, searched for a handhold in the rough stonework and, shaking the water impatiently out of his eyes, looked to see if there was a path by which his attackers could come under the bridge after him. He could hear them chattering and rustling through the reeds, closing in on the banks, but to his intense satisfaction he saw they would not be able to get through, for the water lapped the bridge's foundations. The kind of hooligan he was up against, almost certainly born and bred in the slums of London, was unlikely to be able to swim. A stone whizzed past his ear, then another. He crouched lower to avoid the fusillade and the icy water crawled up around his neck. Damn the murdering bastards!

A moment later, a slithering and alarmed snorting, followed by a clatter of metal shoes on the stones over his head, told Nicholas triumphantly what he wanted to know. Sticks and stones would not stop Cossack, if he was unhurt and had made up his mind to go home. Nicholas listened with baleful satisfaction to the mob's cries of rage and frustration as they tried to head the beast off. "Go on, my beauty. Go *on*." There was the sound of a wild scatter of stones, a hammer of metal shoes, and then the rhythmic clatter of galloping hooves fading victoriously into the distance.

So, mute bad tidings would be presented shortly at the stables, and help would come. With great satisfaction, he felt his way along the stone bulwarks of the bridge, found a foothold on a small underwater projection, slid his rear onto it so that only his head was visible, and, shivering uncontrollably with the cold, prepared to deal as best he could with the barrage of stones coming at him from his frustrated attackers on either bank.

A chorus of raucous glee came from the direction of the High Street. Rose rushed to the door of her sister's cottage.

"Come back!" called Florrie. All morning there had been streetcorner whisperings. Adam kept coming in with the news, but he would not allow Rose to go out. When she tried to slip past him, he took her roughly by the shoulders. "Yer go up that 'Igh Street an' yer'll get wot's comin' ter yer." Everyone knew the Honorable Nicholas le Grys was leaving the castle.

"But I must stop him."

"Yer can't. It's too late."

"Don' go, Rose," wailed Florrie. "Don' go. Adam knows." Indeed, he did know that blood ran high, as well as something more. But Florrie did not dare tell Rose what her husband had confided to her, as they lay worrying about the night's events on their lumpy mattress upstairs. Perhaps it was all for the best, she thought nervously. Adam was right when he said a Rundull should not be having his will of her little sister.

Rose stood now by the narrow doorway, listening with growing alarm to the unmistakable cries of triumph that filtered down from the High Street. "I must go and find out what's happened! What they've done to him!" She was already halfway out of the door when Florrie stopped her.

"No, Rose. No."

"I've got to go, Florrie. I've got to."

Florrie's nails dug painfully into the flesh of her arm. "Adam said yer're not to," she screamed. "Yer'll get killed. Yer'll get killed, too."

Too? Rose shook off her sister's clutching hands. Running over the slippery cobbles, she headed mindlessly for the center of the village. At the corner she pulled up with a jerk, her hand to her mouth on a gasp of horror as Nicholas's horse, broken reins hanging loose, head raised, eyes showing white and dilated with fear, pounded by, riderless. The swinging metal stirrups struck him heavily on flank and shoulder as he went.

"Nicholas!"

Adam, who had been standing with the cheering mob outside the alehouse, saw her and came running, a sneer on his thin lips. "They got 'im. They got yer fancy gen'l'man, Rose."

"No! Oh, no! No, no . . ." She crumpled with the agony of her distress.

"I tell yer they 'ave," Adam gloated. "They got 'im. They got 'im. Killed 'im, like as not," her brother-in-law leered. It was not that he especially disliked Florrie's sister, but other people's troubles spread a little balm over his own.

"Go and help him, Adam." Rose's eyes were wild with terror.

" 'Elp 'im! Yer mad trollop! 'E's got wot 'e deserves."

"No. No, it was an accident. Ned died by accident. It wasn't Nicholas's fault." She grasped Adam's hand and tried to drag him with her down the street in the direction from which the horse had come.

"Garn away." He pushed her so that she stumbled. "I told yer not ter come up 'ere."

"Adam, please. Please . . ." She found his hand again and clung to it, begging.

"An' git me own 'ide peeled off of me?" Adam thrust her brutally from him. "Yer must be mad. No one's goin' ter 'elp 'im."

But someone had to. Rose's mind skittered frantically over the possibilities. Who would dare? Grandy! She picked up her skirts and took to her heels, Adam's voice following, on a thin bleat of unexpected concern. " 'Ere, come on back, Rose."

She reached the corner. George Putnam was swaggering toward her, black-browed and threatening. He made a lunge at her, but she dived around him and sped on. The crowd surged forward, their shouts following like a rushing stream.

"Whore!"

"Filthy slut!"

"Come back an' let's all get at yer, doxy."

"Trollop!"

"Wot about my whore pipe? Try my whore pipe, doxy."

"No, mine."

"Mine!"

And then, as excitement rose, there came a great cry: "Let's get 'er! Let's 'ave 'er fer ourselves."

Rose heard the bawdy chorus of obscenities, the stampede of feet behind her, and swung around in alarm. They were coming after her in a mob, lusting and primal. She saw their greedy faces, and a sob of sheer terror burst from her. Knowing she could not outpace them, she turned to the little cottages fronting the High Street. The narrow wooden doors were closed, the windows shut and still. And yet she knew, shockingly, that there were people behind them.

"Whore. Whore!"

They were almost on her. A hand touched her shoulder. "Help!" Rose screamed, and her legs gave way under the weight of her feet.

George Putnam grabbed her around the waist and heaved her up over his shoulder. Rudely, he thrust his way back through the shouting mob. Down the High Street he went, lustful and vengeful and cruel, while she kicked and screamed for help that she knew would not come. The rest of them, men Rose had known all her life, followed like a pack of hounds.

Someone had hold of her skirt. There was the sound of tearing cloth. Her bodice went, the jerk sending her over her captor's shoulder, sliding toward the ground. Featherweight that she was, he tossed her roughly back again. Another hand reached out and the strings of her stays went, the bones falling loose, and she knew with panic and shame—by the lewd shouts no less than by the feel of the coarse fustian of her captor's coat against her bare skin—that her breasts were exposed.

"Leave 'er alone, will yer," snarled Putnam, turning threateningly on the crowd. "Yer can 'ave 'er when I've finished wi' 'er."

"Let me down! Let me go!" Rose screamed, panic-stricken, beating at him with her clenched fists.

Then, suddenly, she was falling, sliding like a wet fish, as George Putnam's legs gave way to the accompaniment of a scream of pain. The hard, gritty surface of the street scraped against her shoulder. She rolled on to her back and knew, unbelievably, that she was free!

Nimble as a rabbit, in her white cotton pantaloons, with stays sagging and hair wild, Rose leaped to her feet. Behind her, a new voice was cursing roundly, less with authority than with towering, roaring rage. Without waiting to see what had happened, Rose dived between the startled men, fled past the once friendly houses, swung left toward the Eden and the castle, ducked over the bridge beneath the willow tree, and pelted along the river path. Running blindly, she passed the hawthorn without pause and reached the water meadow.

Halfway across she stumbled. For the first time, she dared to look behind. There was no one following. A sob of heartfelt, uncomprehending relief escaped her. But she must get help to Nicholas. With a hand to her rib cage she staggered on, climbing shakily over the stile and onto the zigzag path she knew so well. She could no longer summon the strength to run. Her legs were giving way beneath her. She looked around for somewhere to hide. Just ahead, the path narrowed and overhanging broom, blowsy with gold, spread every way. She dragged herself in among long, sheltering grasses, and fell like a stone.

She did not hear the quiet, purposeful footsteps, or the pebbles crunching on the track, but when they paused, she sensed like a young animal that there was someone near at hand. And now she could not run. Could not even stand if her whole life depended on it. With a long, agonized moan of surrender she waited, frozen into acceptance of her fate. Then she was looking into a flattish face beneath a thatch of rough-cut hair.

"Don't run away, Rosie," said Daniel Putnam kindly. "I've brought yer clothes—wot's left of 'em," he added apologetically, averting his eyes from her bare breasts and the coarse white pantaloons tied over her broken stays. "Put 'em 'round yerself."

She looked into his mild, sorrowful face, and the tears of shock overflowed.

"They'd no right to treat you like that," Gertie Taylor's brother said uncomfortably.

She reached out blindly for the familiar drab skirt, torn to ribbons now and filthy. Wordlessly, she tried with shaking hands to pull it over her head. Ripped into a formless jumble of pieces, scarcely a skirt at all, it slid this way and that, evading her trembling fingers.

" 'Ere," he said gruffly, "I'll 'elp yer." Holding it awkwardly with his rough carpenter's hands, he found the waist. He handed her what was left of her bodice. She pulled it clumsily across her breasts, folding it and tucking it in where the buttons had gone.

"Thank you, Daniel," she said weakly. "Was it you saved me?"

"I kicked 'im in the bollocks," Daniel answered, coarsely protective. He shifted uncomfortably from one hobnail-booted foot to the other. "They'd no right ter . . ." He flushed a slow, dark red. His wide mouth turned down with disapproval for which he had no easy rhetoric.

Rose clambered cautiously to her feet. Her legs trembled as though not disposed to take her weight again so soon. "Thank you for saving me, and for bringing my clothes." She glanced along the track, then upward to where the castle lay. "I've got to go, Daniel." She clutched the tattered skirt in both hands.

"Shall I walk with yer? D'yer want me ter 'elp yer?"

"No. No, I don't," she said furiously. "Tell George there'll be dozens of men coming down from the castle to get him. And the police, I should think." The humiliation and pain of her experience welled up in her and burst out in a spitting threat. "Likely he'll go to prison."

" 'E 'asn't done anythin', Rose," Daniel pointed out fairly. "Only tried ter . . ." He broke off as he saw the uneasy trust melt from her eyes.

"There'll be trouble for you all," she threatened, turning on him, punishing him in her misery and frustration for what the others had done.

He shook his big head slowly. "There's trouble now, Rose. Don' come down ter the village again, will yer?"

"I've got to go," she said again, obsessively.

He made no reply, but stood looking at her, his big hands, cracked and roughened by the weather and his work, hanging at his sides. She looked back when she came to the big oak, where the park dipped and she would go out of sight. He was where she had left him, watching her. She lifted a hand in an apologetic little wave. He'd saved her life. Saved her from rape, anyway. Then she forgot him in her anxiety to get help for Nicholas.

Annie Snape, black-clad and bony, with a white morning cap on her head, stood in the doorway rattling the housekeeper's keys she wore at her waist. Decisions, decisions. She had to make up her mind whether to check the contents of the larder or to go after a lazy housemaid who should have finished the upstairs chores an hour earlier.

The door that led in to the little courtyard outside the kitchens crept tentatively open.

"Who's that?" Rose thrust the door back on its hinges and stumbled inside. Mrs. Snape's eyes hardened with anger and condemnation. "Girl! What . . . !"

"Gran, where is . . . ?"

"What have you been . . . ?"

There was no time for questions and answers. Grasping the remnants of her skirt, Rose fled past the old woman, out of the opposite door, along the narrow stone corridor, and up the stairs.

"Grandy!" she shouted as she burst through the green

baize door into the paneled hall, her eyes darting toward the Jacobean oak chair beneath the clock where Nicholas had so often waited for her, gun on knee. She shouted again, "Grandy!" The ancient wood and stone of the hall and gallery absorbed her cry. A great stag gazed glassy-eyed down upon her from above the Rundull family's coat of arms. The clock in its polished mahogany case ticked ponderously into the silence.

She took a step toward the gracious, curving staircase, then paused, swallowing. A kitchen maid did not invade the sacred precincts of the upper household. Unless it was a matter of life and death! Clutching her rags in one hand, Rose sped across the hall and stumbled up the stairs.

A door on the landing was ajar. From beyond it came the tinkle of well-modulated voices. Sick with fright, driven by her inner desperation, Rose entered the room. Henry's wife, Adeline, gave a small shriek. Her needle-point rolled off her lap onto the floor. Lady Rundull came haughtily but precipitously to her feet, her tarlatan-and-lace-covered bosom rising in indignation.

"My Lady." Rose fought the impulse to flee from this terrifying presence. "Nicholas needs help, my Lady. Please send someone down the road. Something terrible's happened."

Anger gave way to pallid shock. Lady Rundull's hand went to her throat. "Nicholas? My son Nicholas? What are you saying, girl?"

"His horse galloped back through the village without him, my Lady. Please send help. He's in terrible trouble."

"His horse!" exclaimed the countess, her voice sharp with disbelief. "You mean the carriage horses?" Yet, even as she said the words, color drained from her face. She knew her younger son.

Behind Rose, a man self-consciously cleared his throat. She turned to meet her grandfather's shocked stare. "Back to the kitchen, girl," he hissed, gesturing in the direction of the landing.

Rose's chin set mutinously. "I came to get help for Nicholas." Then, turning back to the countess, she said, "It's Cossack, my Lady. Nicholas has been unseated. Someone must have attacked him."

"Help has gone, m'Lady," said the butler. He added in

a thunderous whisper to Rose, "Do as I say." Then, apologetically, to Lady Rundull, "Master Nicholas set out on Cossack, m'Lady."

Adeline's pale mouth folded in silent disapproval.

"His father's orders . . . Snape, you know his Lordship ordered the carriage himself." It was as though the countess was trying to convince herself that there was no possibility of disaster. But her face was tight with fear.

"As you say, m'Lady," Snape agreed. "Don't distress yourself, though. Already a dozen men have gone to his aid. One of the stableboys saw Cossack and gave the alarm. Master Nicholas cannot have got far, m'Lady. He'd not been gone an hour."

A dozen men! Rose's face lit up with wild happiness.

The countess saw the glow in her eyes, read it correctly, and turned on her with anger unstrung. "Why are you here, you impudent creature, if help has already gone?"

Confused and defenseless in circumstances that left her inexcusably in the wrong, Rose looked entreatingly to her grandfather for help, but, trained as he was by a lifetime of submission, his eyes were cast down. She had to face the countess alone. "I . . . I came to tell you, my Lady."

"To tell me? You. To tell me!" Her ladyship hesitated, then asked, "Who are you, girl?" Rose, with tears of humiliation behind her beautiful eyes, threw a look of quivering desperation at her grandfather. He said very respectfully, "She's my granddaughter. She's from the kitchens, m'Lady. She means well."

"You are Rose Snape?"

"Yes, m'Lady."

"I see." The ice in the great Lady Rundull's manner gave way to something oddly akin to fear, as she envisaged a cloud of Rose's beautiful hair shining from brush strokes and cleansed of dust; as she recognized beneath the dirt the appeal of her heart-shaped face, the perfection of her young breasts and her slender waist. "You may go," she said distantly.

Clutching her skirt, Rose retreated. As she descended the stairs the countess's high, clear voice floated after her. "I do not wish to have that chit on the premises, Snape."

"She's here on account of my daughter-in-law and my son being dead, as you know, m'Lady. There's no one to look after her."

"You have another granddaughter, Snape, have you not? The girl can live with her."

"There's no room in Florrie's cottage for another body." Grandy's voice was apologetic. Rose hesitated, one hand on the stair rail, listening.

"She's useful, in her way, in the kitchen, m'Lady. She has a small room that would not otherwise be used."

"I want her gone," said the cold voice. "Do you understand, Snape? I want her out of the castle today."

"She's only a girl, m'Lady. Only seventeen."

"If you are unable to accommodate her in the village, tell Mrs. Snape to clean her up and put her on the stagecoach for London this afternoon. A girl with her looks will get on."

Rose did not wait to hear any more. Trailing her fingers along the banister, she continued on down the staircase, then crossed the hall, went through the green baize door, and descended the stone stairs that led to the kitchen.

Alice, sprucely superior in her parlormaid's frilled white cap and apron, was waiting for her. "Slut," she said contemptuously.

Rose walked straight on past, self-absorbed and bewildered. Closing the door of her little room, she flopped down on the narrow metal bed and blankly contemplated the bare wall opposite. London! What would she do in London? What did the countess mean when she said, "A girl with her looks will get on"?

Later, the door opened and her grandmother entered carrying over one arm a stuff dress in a drab shade of brown. Over her other arm lay a cloak. "You're to get into these, baggage." Her mouth was tight.

Over the years of her growing up, Rose had accustomed herself to her grandmother's harshness. Grandy had explained that his wife could not help taking out her resentment at losing her son on the grandchild who had become her unwelcome responsibility. She would not normally risk asking a favor of her, but now, in her special need, Rose looked yearningly up into the old woman's face, searching for signs, if not of love, of at least a little understanding. "Gran, has Nicholas come back?"

"Whether 'is Lordship's son 'as come back or not is no concern of yours, my girl. I'm to give you the fare to London, and you're to get on the stagecoach this afternoon. Those are 'er Ladyship's orders."

Without seeing Nicholas? Without knowing how he had fared? Rose leaped up, her green eyes blazing defiance. "I shan't go . . ." She recoiled in pain as Mrs. Snape, in one efficient movement, threw the clothes onto the bed and boxed her ears.

"Don't be pert with me, miss. 'Er Ladyship 'as given orders that you're to be hoff the estate within an hour, and hoff the estate you shall be. So it was you caused the trouble last night! I thank the dear Lord your mother's not 'ere to see what you've come to."

Rose put both hands to her ears to ease the pain. Tears pricked behind her eyes. Tears of pity for Gertie Taylor and her children. Tears of shame and misery at her own plight.

"The likes of you should be 'orse-whipped," Mrs. Snape went on, encouraged by Rose's abject quiescence. Then, noticing the scuffed and dirty slippers on her feet, the woman's rage boiled up anew. "Where did you get those?"

"I borrowed them."

"Borrowed them? Borrowed them, you hussy! You stole them. Give them to me. Take them off this instant, and give them to me."

The unfairness of her accusation brought some of Rose's spirit back. "I wouldn't steal. You know I wouldn't steal. I borrowed them."

"Don't you sauce me, miss. These belong to Martha. I'll warrant she never loaned them to you. Dirty little thief!"

"I'm not!" Rose shouted hopelessly. This time she saw the blow coming and dived under her grandmother's arm. She tripped on her ragged skirt, regained her balance, and dashed down the narrow stone passage that ran through the kitchen precincts, then out of the door and across the courtyard. Here she hesitated.

If she turned left, following the wall, it would lead her, a hundred yards farther on, to a low wooden door. Rough little stones bit into the soles of her bare feet as she sped along the path. Apprehensively, she tried the iron door handle. It moved. Pushing the door open, she stumbled through into a passageway that led to the kitchen gardens. But there was no shelter there among the low-growing cabbages, potatoes, currants, and beets. She turned right, took to her heels once more, and dived down a narrow alley that led to the main outbuildings.

Beyond the wall in front of her now were the stables. She approached the end of the alley with caution and looked carefully around. There was no one in sight. She crept to the end of the stone wall, and entered the big hollow square around which the stables were built.

Gaining confidence, she went through the door into the anteroom, where Peter the steel boy spent his days polishing bridle bits and metal parts. She looked around cautiously, seeing saddles neatly laid out on their trees, the gleaming, silver-plated harness worn by the shire horses and carriage geldings. There was no sign of the boy. She dashed through. Then stopped again, for Shard, the head coachman, and his wife lived in rooms above. There were domestic sounds of slopping water, a child's cry.

She edged cautiously around the open door that led into the stables proper and made her way down the row of stalls until she came to the big, straw-carpeted manger that was Cossack's domain. Its emptiness sent a chill through her. Folding her torn skirt over one arm, she shinned up the ladder that led to the loft. Here was hay, dry, sweet smelling, and soft. With a whimper of relief she dropped down and lay still.

Moments later there was a clip-clop of hooves. Rose sat up with a jerk. On hands and knees she crept forward. Through the open doorway that led to the courtyard Mr. Oliver the groom was leading Cossack on a short rein. The horse was skittering nervously, his hot breath clouding the cool air. Flecks of foam lay trembling on his shoulders and flanks, and on the groom's loose fustian jacket.

Rose crept back into the nest she had made for herself, biting back her fear, listening for Nicholas's footsteps, knowing he would come if he was able, but hearing only the clink of harness as the groom, whistling through his teeth, rubbed the beast down and filled the drinking trough.

Then he went away, and the air was empty again, except for the soft pad of a hoof on straw, an occasional whinny, and the clank of a shod hoof.

5

Nicholas came, but not until an hour had passed. He had changed out of his traveling clothes and was wearing a loose shirt tucked into white moleskin breeches. Without either stock or cravat, it fell away from his throat, revealing the fine dark hairs on his chest. Rose waited in a fever until she was certain no one was following him, then, snatching at the torn folds of her skirt, she scrambled to the ladder and began awkwardly to descend.

He paused in mid-stride, his dark head thrown back. "Rose! What the devil are you doing here? And what on earth . . . ?" He started forward, his brows drawn sharply together, his eyes clouding as he took in her dishevelment.

Rose jumped down the last few rungs of the ladder and ran to him, the rags of her dress trailing on the stone flagging. "Nicholas! Oh, Nicholas!"

He lifted her chin, looking down into her face, streaked where tears had trickled through the caked dust. "What happened?" But already, angrily, he knew. "Tell me they hurt you and I'll murder every mother's bastard son of them!"

She shook her head, the curls bobbing, her eyes overflowing with tears of joy and relief. "Somebody saved me. Daniel Putnam."

"A Putnam, hey!" Beyond his concern, Nicholas's quick mind took in this new, surprising element. Daniel Putnam, the widow's brother! He held Rose against him while she hugged him to her heart, savoring the piercing sweetness of his presence. "But you're all right, darling.

That's what matters. We'll talk in a moment. I must see Cossack." He ushered her into the stall. Cossack, his first love.

"What happened to you, Nicholas?"

"I had a ducking, that's all." Anxiety for Cossack had already pushed his own grueling misadventure out of his mind. "Hello, boy." He patted the silky nose with his right hand, allowing the bay to nibble affectionately at the fingers of the left. "Let's look at you."

He examined the horse closely. The soft, quivering flesh was unscarred. Cossack pawed nervously with a forefoot and blew through his nostrils. Nicholas smoothed his flank. "A good feed, a good rest, and you'll be fine, old boy," he said consolingly. "It's been a bad day all 'round." Holding a fistful of mane, he led the animal out. The carriage horses came to stand with necks stretched over the gates of their loose boxes, watching curiously as he led Cossack up and down between the stalls. "No limp. Good." He patted the forequarters briskly, shut him in again, pushed the bolt home, and turned his full attention on Rose.

"So, my darling, and what happened to you?"

As they stood there in the manger with the smell of straw and dung and warm horse flesh around them, Rose told him.

"They were going to rape you? By God, I'll have their guts for pigs' swill. I've done this to you," he said. His voice was hard with self-condemnation. "I should have left you alone."

"No. No, you should not have. I love you." Rose remembered with terror what Grandy had said: that the gentry abandoned girls of humble birth like cast-off clothes.

"Do you, dove? Do you really?" He tipped up her chin, slid both arms around her. "Yes, I believe you do."

"I'm to go to London, Nicholas," she said when his arms loosened and she could speak again.

"London? What do you mean?" He spoke sharply, pushing her away so that he could look into her face.

"Her Ladyship ordered it."

Nicholas's brows drew in. "My mother! What the devil . . . ?"

"I'm not to be allowed to stay here. My grandmother brought me traveling clothes." Rose's voice trembled less at the memory of the slap than at the brutality of her own kin in so willingly obeying the countess's orders.

Nicholas's eyes stayed on her, questioningly.

"I was to get the stagecoach. But I knew you'd come to Cossack, so I ran here to hide. I had to see you. I had to be sure you were all right."

"My love, I am all right. What the devil were you going to do in London? Were you going to Cavendish Square?" Nicholas added in a puzzled voice, "There's nobody there." The family maintained a mansion with stabling for use in the London season, but the season was not on them, and the house would be empty.

Rose looked uncertainly up into his face, her green eyes enormous. "Your mother said I would 'get on.' "

Choking rage mercifully stilled his tongue.

"You're going to London. Could I go with you?" Rose asked wistfully.

"What would I do with you there?" he asked gruffly, holding her small hand in his, smoothing her golden hair back from her forehead.

"I could look after you." Her face was alight and eager. "I've helped Cook, and watched the ladies' maids pressing with flat irons. I could get your meals and care for your clothes."

"So you could," Nicholas said softly, his mind darting ahead, burning resentment driving him to do what he knew would hurt and anger his mother, who had hurt and angered him. "So, I believe, you could. Now, what shall we do about it? You can't go in those rags. And barefoot."

"I haven't anything else." She said the word innocently, and wondered at the mute anger that sparked in his dark eyes. But the anger was directed against himself, for he had never noticed that she met him always in the same dress. Her loveliness and her warmth transcended whatever drab garments she wore.

"I'll think of something," he said. "Later." His glance darted around the bare interior of the stables. There were several coats hanging on pegs on the wall outside the stalls. He took down one of them, and draped it around her shoulders. It was long enough to hide her right down to the toes. "Take your skirt off. There's not enough of it left to cover you decently, but you could use it to hide that hair. We may not be able to avoid being seen, but we can at least make sure you're not recognized."

Obediently, Rose dropped what was left of the garment to the floor, picked it up, and stood mutely in her coarse pantaloons, while he tore off a square of material and folded it into a triangle. "That should do." He planted a kiss on the end of her nose.

She went with him to the stable entrance, then stood quietly at his side while he looked cautiously around the stone-paved yard. Only the tinkling fountain broke the silence, and a pigeon cooing softly as it preened its white feathers.

"All seems to be clear." He took her hand in his and squeezed it, then let it go. "Don't talk. Just follow me."

They fled together over the soft, green turf, around a stone bastion at the base of a crenellated gray tower, and came to a low oak door. Nicholas led Rose inside, bolting the door behind him.

As her eyes grew accustomed to the windowless gloom, Rose saw the narrow stone stairs ahead and knew where she was. The family's quarters were served by a series of back staircases, used by the skivvies when they came with their mops and pails to clean. She had never been up the stairs, but she had helped carry water as far as the bottom landing. "I can see well enough," she whispered.

They climbed in silence. On a landing so tiny that it barely held them both, he halted, a finger to his lips. Then he opened the door carefully and peered out.

"Come on." He led her into a wide, carpeted corridor and shut the door behind them. "This way." She had to run to keep up. "Here's my room." He opened a door on the right, nudged her inside, then closed it swiftly behind them.

Rose was stunned by her surroundings. "Is this where you sleep? All alone?" The room was so vast it dwarfed the four-poster that stood in solitary splendor against one wall. She stared in amazement at the big stone fireplace with its polished steel basket already set with logs. A fire in one's bedroom! And those armchairs! Such a carpet!

She moved silently across the room, drawn to touch the satiny wood of a chest of drawers, then to a wardrobe with shining brass handles. She caught a glimpse of herself in the cheval looking glass and turned quickly away.

Nicholas watched her. She examined the little set of steps standing beside his bed, then moved toward the marble-topped washstand. She ran her fingers wonderingly along its cool, smooth surface, unable to come to terms with such splendor.

"Try the bed for size." Emotionally unstrung, he took refuge in gentle lechery. She climbed the steps and sat down on the brocade cover, head back, marveling at the ornate ceiling.

"It's soft," she said dreamily, innocently spreading the whole picture of her life out before him, driving nails of guilt into him, because he had known about her circumstances without, inexplicably, he realized now with another shaft of self-directed anger, really being properly aware. Clearing his throat, he strode over to the wardrobe and opened the door. "You had better get in here. I'm going to ring for hot water so you can clean yourself up."

She glanced automatically at the washstand.

"No, I'll have a tub brought up. You're filthy, my darling."

"In here?" she asked, bypassing his robust criticism. "A tub in your bedroom?"

"Why not?" He spun some clothes along a rail to make a space for her to hide in. "Sorry about this. It's going to be a bit close but you won't suffocate." Obediently, she stepped inside and sat on the floor. Curled in a ball, with her knees under her chin, in her grubby white underwear, she looked heart-rendingly vulnerable. She smiled trustingly at him.

He fastened the door, crossed the room swiftly, and jerked the bellpull. A housemaid came hurriedly adjusting her little white cap and long apron. Damn! She was the one who had brought the hot water when he returned from his ducking.

"Tell Snape I want to see him right away, then wait in his pantry until you're sent for, Watling."

"Certainly, Mr. Nicholas."

The butler came panting, his side-whiskers aquiver. "Master Nicholas?"

"Come in Snape, and shut the door." The butler obeyed. "What has happened to Rose, Snape?" Nicholas asked, looking the old man square in the eye.

"Her Ladyship has ordered her to London, Master Nicholas."

"And she has gone?" With an elegant gesture, Nicholas flicked an imaginary piece of fluff from his shirt front.

"There was some trouble, Master Nicholas, and she's disappeared."

"I see." Nicholas pulled at his left ear lobe. Snape took the opportunity to glance around the room. Nothing. But she could be under the bed. He hoped most earnestly she was not. "I'm somewhat chilled, Snape," Nicholas went on. "Ask Watling to bring my tub back. And some more hot water. Clean towels, too. I am not, by the way, ill. My mother need not be told. And I'll be relying upon you to see to the housemaid's discretion. I've asked her to wait in your pantry. She's aware that I've already bathed." His eyes took on a steely look as he gazed into those of the old man. "Do you understand?"

The butler's heart sank, but he met Nicholas's eyes unblinkingly. "Yes, Master Nicholas."

"There is the matter of clothes, Snape. Female clothes."

"Mrs. Snape has some ready, Master Nicholas. But I'm afraid the stagecoach will have gone."

"There's no call for the stagecoach, Snape. Bring the clothes, but in the most discreet manner possible. See to the tub now."

"Certainly, Master Nicholas."

"Master Nicholas took a bath only a short time ago," the housemaid grumbled. "What's 'e want another one fer?"

"He is cold, Watling."

"Then why 'asn't 'e gone ter bed? I could bring 'ot bricks."

"Nobody asked for your advice, girl," returned Snape, crushing in his misery and despair. "If Master Nicholas prefers to rid himself of his chill in another hot tub, that's his business. And it's not something to discuss below stairs." She tossed her head, and he snapped, "I'm issuing you with an order, Amy Watling. Understand? You are not to discuss Master Nicholas's habits with the other servants. He can have six baths a day if he wishes."

She met his warning look sulkily. "Course I understand orders. It's why they're given I don't understand."

Mrs. Snape was not in the kitchen precincts. The butler went into Rose's tiny room. The cloak and dress his wife had offered her for the coach ride to London lay on the bed, and beside them some cotton stockings. There was a pair of black button boots on the floor. Snape rolled everything into a ball, put it under his arm, and went ponderously back the way he had come. As he was passing the kitchen door his wife emerged.

"Mr. Snape!" Her sharp eyes noted the bundle. "And where, may I ask, are you taking that?"

"You may ask, Mrs. Snape, but I think you already know. They're for Rose."

"Where is she?"

"I was not told. I have merely been asked to bring her clothes."

The housekeeper's eyes narrowed. "Who asked you?"

"Mrs. Snape," said the butler impassively, "Rose is leaving. Put her out of your mind. As m'Lady has said, she will do very well in London." Deeply hurt and offended by his mistress's treatment of his granddaughter, Snape resorted to unaccustomed sarcasm. He lumbered past his wife, ascended the servants' staircase, opened the door into the hall, and went up to Nicholas's room. At the door he paused, knocked discreetly, and waited. Nicholas turned the key, opened the door, and took the bundle.

"Thank you, Snape." He closed the door and locked it again, then went to let Rose out of the wardrobe. She unrolled herself like a kitten, greeting him with a faintly nervous smile.

"Are you all right?"

"Yes." She stood on one leg rubbing the toes of the other foot against her ankle. "Do all the family have a room like this to themselves?" she asked, her eyes wistful.

Nicholas cleared his throat. "Oh, er, well . . ." There was a moment of inarticulate emotion. He took her hands, looking tenderly down into her face. "Would you like to see my sister Felicity's room? She went back to London early this morning, so we'll not be disturbed."

The Lady Felicity le Grys, who waited on the Queen! "Oh-h-h," said Rose, overawed. Then, with two skips she was over at the bed, excitedly picking up the drab stuff dress Snape had brought, stepping into it, and dragging it across her front.

Nicholas took the stable jacket, sniffed at it with disdain, and tossed it carelessly out of the window. "I'll see if the coast's clear." He strode toward the door.

"It doesn't fit! And my stays are torn!"

Her frustrated wail brought him back. "Take them off."

Her eyes flew open wide, then she saw his teasing expression, and her lips curled up at the corners in a mischievous smile. "Why not?" She jerked giddily at the strings. The whalebone fell around her hips, then onto the floor. She stepped out of the garment, gave it a lighthearted kick, and watched it disappear beneath the bed.

Laughing, he went back to the door, opened it, and stepped outside. "There's no one around," he said. "Come on."

Rose never forgot Lady Felicity's room. Early afternoon sunshine streamed through the tall windows and over the beautiful Aubusson carpet, touching its floral design with gold. The ancient wood of the Jacobean four-poster glowed darkly, a foil for its pale silk hangings. There was a tapestry stool with gilt feet, and an exquisite little armchair with curved arms and pink velvet upholstery. Rose stood quite still, her hand on her heart.

"Oh, Nicholas, it's so beautiful. I never knew there was anything as beautiful as this." On tiptoe, she crossed the room, hesitating before an elaborate looking glass. She ran her fingers lovingly over the exotic birds, the little Chinamen, the goats, seashells, and flowers with which its frame was carved, murmuring soft, unintelligible little sounds of admiration and delight.

It was no impulse that took Nicholas across to the wardrobe. He had known defiantly, when he brought her here, what he was going to do. Only three dresses hung on the rail, for his sister took most of her wardrobe to Buckingham Palace for her waiting. He beckoned. "What do you think of that?" he asked carelessly, turning one of the gowns on its hanger.

Rose automatically wiped her hands on her skirt, then touched the fine tarlatan with small, reverential fingers. "Oh." The sound came softly, like the purr of a cat.

"Here's a cloak. Green is your color. To match your eyes. Try it on."

"Could I? Really?"

Lifting the velvet garment from its hanger, he dropped it over her shoulders. She went to the looking glass and stared at herself in amazement. She pirouetted across the carpet, the rich folds swinging this way and that, glowing as they caught the light. Then reluctantly, with reverence, she took the cloak off. There was no envy in her only a deep, unquenchable longing.

Nicholas said abruptly, "Don't put it back."

"What?" She was startled at the harsh tone of his voice, but then she saw that his eyes were soft.

"Don't take it off, I said. Keep it."

"Keep it?"

"Keep it!" Now he was angry. But not with her. He was already moving rapidly toward a big mahogany chest across the room. He pulled open one drawer after another. "Come here, Rose."

She joined him slowly, dreamily, looking down at the green cloak. Together they gazed at piles of carefully folded underwear, white cambric with frilled edges bunching delicately one upon the other. "How lovely!"

"Take what you need," he said. "Take something to wear."

She fingered the luxurious lace. "I . . . couldn't."

"Why not?" he asked impatiently, his head on one side, his eyes brilliant with a new kind of exhilaration. She looked uncertainly up into his face.

"It . . . It's not mine." This was stealing. Taking Martha's slippers had been a different matter, for she had meant to put them back. But she was going to London now, and there would be no returning these garments. Yet, as Rose's fingers hovered over them, her conscience began to recede. She lifted a camisole and shook out the folds. There was threaded ribbon at the neck; it was whiter than snow, and as soft. Nothing she had ever touched had prepared her for the softness and delicacy of Lady Felicity's underwear. As the ribbons drooped silkily over her hands, she grew venal. She chose swiftly, before Nicholas could change his mind, thrusting the frothy garments possessively under one arm.

The mischief done, he dropped a kiss lightly on her lips. "You'd better have a dress too," he said, going back to the wardrobe and jerking the tarlatan gown from its hanger. He reached for a pair of slippers with bows that lay on the shelf above.

"My sister ain't much bigger than you, if at all."

Reverentially, she took the dress he held and stood gazing at it, her lips parted, her eyes enormous.

"Wait here," Nicholas said gruffly. "I'll see if there's anyone in the passage."

He went out of the door, leaving her dizzy with excitement, clutching the lacy underthings in her arms with the dress laid on top, and the slippers in her fingers.

"It's deserted."

She hurried after him along the passage to his bedroom, the cloak swinging heavily around her. The tub had arrived. It lay by the newly lit fire. Nicholas locked the door carefully. Rose put the underwear down on the bed, undid the cloak and laid it down, then spread out the dress.

"Come on, leave your booty or the water will grow cold."

"Oh, Nicholas! Nicholas, Nicholas!" She shook her head, and, leaning down, trailed her fingers in the silky, warm water. Odd images, foreign and unwelcome, stabbed at her memory. Cold water in a tin basin. The coarse soap they made below stairs for use in the kitchen, scraping her skin. She needed to absorb the delight of this munificence before she became a part of it.

Misunderstanding her silence, Nicholas said teasingly, "I don't at all mind seeing you naked. Beats me how a woman can give everything, then balk at exposing a bit of bare skin." But his laughter was soft and indulgent as he pushed down the sagging neckline of her gown baring her breasts, cupping them in his hands. Her body was suddenly quiescent, her mouth trembling. He put a finger beneath her chin and lifted her face.

"Why, you're just a natural courtesan," he murmured softly, brushing his lips against hers.

"What's a courtesan?"

"Mistress to Nicholas le Grys."

He turned away abruptly and, going to the bureau in the corner, took a cheroot. With hands that shook, he lit a lucifer match. "I won't look until you're clean." It was a promise to himself. An order. He opened a window and leaned out, his elbows on the sill. Already somebody had found the stable jacket and removed it. He felt the familiar pulsing of his blood that came when he courted danger.

Rose's dress fell to the floor. She slipped out of her mean undergarments, then stepped with a squeal of delight into the water. With a little moue of pleasure, she put her nose down on the soap that smelled luxuriously of lavender and was soft as honey, then spread it joyfully all over her body. Her eyes dreamily traced plaster cherubs in the ceiling as she slid down in the tub, her hair floating on the surface of the water in a golden cloud.

Outside, the air was still. Away in the distance, Nicholas could see the road to the village and, beyond, the village itself, its tiled roofs and a tower buttressed by trees. He was afraid, now, to turn and look. Loving her as he had always done, in tree shadows and long grasses shaded by night, he had never seen her in all her naked beauty and, in spite of his rash remark that he did not at all mind seeing her stripped, he knew his yearning for her was already teetering dangerously beyond control. He smoked his cheroot in short, uneven puffs, craving the relief and excitement of flinging her dripping wet onto the carpet.

There was a tap at the door. With a little gasp of alarm Rose sat up, splashing water over the side of the tub.

Nicholas swung around and rapidly crossed the room. "Who's there?"

"Snape, Master Nicholas."

Nicholas turned the key, but he opened the door only a short distance. Rose watched in alarm. The butler, poker-faced, held out a tray. "Some refreshment, Master Nicholas."

"Thank you, Snape."

"Would you care to have a room prepared?"

"No, thank you, Snape."

"It would be no trouble, Master Nicholas." He added pointedly, "I would prepare it myself."

"I said, no. Perhaps you could spirit a dinner up this evening, though. One dinner, Snape. I shall of course be dining with the family."

"I understand."

Kicking the door shut, Nicholas carried the tray to a table by the window.

"Oh, Nicholas, Grandy knows I'm here now!"

"Someone had to know, otherwise you'd starve." He lifted the covers. "There's cold venison and turkey, tomatoes, mashed potato, and a bowl of fruit. It smells good and you must be hungry. When did you last eat?" She was sitting up in the bath like a young Venus, pink-cheeked, her soft, back-turning lips smiling seductively. Her naked shoulders were white and marble smooth, the tips of her breasts dark buds. Nicholas swallowed.

"Will you pour the water over my hair now?" she asked innocently. "Then I'll get out. I am famished. I can't remember when I last ate." So much had happened.

Nicholas reached for the jug. "Close your eyes and hold your breath." He splashed water over her hair, tossed her a towel, then went with fierce determination back to the window. After a while his craving came under control.

He was going to have to take a carriage now to London. The brougham perhaps, with its shaded interior. His groom could ride Cossack to the other side of Penbridge, where they could safely change places. Then it occurred to him that, if Rose's identity was to be kept secret, he would have to stay with her. Grooms, as well as housemaids, had prying eyes and wagging tongues. Thirty miles in a closed carriage! He swung around scowling.

Rose stood straight and slender in Felicity's lacy bodice and frilly petticoats. Her hair, rubbed partially dry, reminded him of many things: of autumn beech, of chestnut fillies, of the golden light on the wild, sweet meadow grasses as the sun went down. Something seemed to change direction in him. Something that weakened his immediate hunger and strengthened his long-term discomfort. He watched her pick up the dress and slip it with deft movements over her head. There were tiny buttons all the way down the back. Nicholas did them up. When he had finished, he turned her to look at him. What a lady she made!

"Why are you looking at me like that?" Rose asked.

"I'm sorry," he replied, brushing his hair back roughly from his forehead. "I didn't realize. I was making decisions. I will take you to London. But we will have to go in the night. Or at dawn."

"And you will let me look after you?" she asked sweetly.

He nodded. She put her soft arms around his neck and kissed him, her lips delicate and sweet. He undid her fingers gently, turning her around. "Eat your food," he said. He watched her move elegantly across the room, her petticoats rustling around her, her back as straight, her head as high as any well-bred miss of his acquaintance, and a pain began somewhere, gut-deep, as his mind grappled with the enormity of what he had done.

6

————•————

The Lady Priscilla Rundull, impeccable in a frilled Babet cap and a bombazine morning dress, met Snape on the landing. "You have got rid of the girl, Snape?" The words were framed less as a question than as a warning.

"To London," he replied obscurely, but without lying, bowing his head deferentially, so that the expression in his eyes was hidden from her.

"Master Nicholas seems to be an uncommonly long time about his ablutions, Snape." Her fine, pale brows lifted. She was not unaware of a certain bond between her butler and her younger son. While Snape's loyalty to his Lordship was undisputed, she suspected he covered up for Nicholas when the son's interests clashed with those of his father. "Kindly inform him that the earl wishes to speak to him in the library as soon as is convenient."

"Very well, m'Lady. Master Nicholas was concerned with his mount. He's been to the stables."

"You did not, I trust, mention the matter of the girl to him?"

"No, m'Lady."

Priscilla rustled into the library, adjusting her bishop's sleeves as she went. Inevitably, Henry was there. She felt faintly irritated that he, who had heretofore shown little feeling other than jealousy for his younger brother, should be taking such an uncommonly close interest in the affair.

"Whoring around Haymarket is a damned sight safer than whoring around here," Henry was saying as his

70

mother entered and closed the door behind her. The frosty look she turned on him conveyed not only her dislike of his vulgarity, but also her irritation at the predatory air he presented. He rose thinly to his feet, offering his mother a seat on the Knole sofa, a copy of the one Lady Dorset brought with her when she married their neighbor, Sackville, at Knole House.

"Nicholas will be here directly," she said as she sat down, her spine erect, her eyes chilly. "Is it really necessary for you to be present, Henry dear?"

"Very necessary indeed, Mama. I, too, wish to see the family's future safeguarded." Sharp-eyed and seedy in claret-colored waistcoat and gaiter pantaloons, Henry looked like a caricature of the country gentleman he affected to portray. No matter how precise he was with his attire—and he was precise rather than clever, the countess thought critically, looking him up and down—it was the clothes that strutted, diminishing him. Though she disliked comparisons, and tried to love both sons equally, she was reminded with a little rush of warmth of the fact that Nicholas's apparel, however dandified, served merely as an expression of his lusty personality.

"Do you not consider your father and I capable?"

"Indeed, Mama." Henry fingered his pale whiskers. "But if I may speak plainly, where Nicholas is concerned you're inclined to be a little too lenient."

"Your tone indicates," she reproved him sharply, "that, as the younger son, Nicholas scarcely merits consideration."

The earl said, "H-rr-ump!" and Henry looked away, not with disdain, for he would never be rude to his mother, but committing himself nonetheless to her assumption.

Nicholas entered abruptly, looking grim. He kicked the door shut then, with head high and feet planted wide apart, stood fingering the edge of his swiftly tied cravat.

"I'm glad to see you're none the worse for your adventure," said his father, looking him over reprovingly, but not without a certain warmth. "I've sent a message to the high sheriff. The matter will be investigated, but we've already established the fact that the ruffians who attacked you had no connection with the village."

Nicholas's brows knitted darkly together. "So it was sheer chance," his voice was weighted with sarcasm, "that

I happened to be passing when a particularly vicious mob of itinerant wanderers was in the neighborhood?"

The earl tapped a gnarled finger on his chair arm. There was a soft, hissing sound of air expelled between his teeth. A sign that his temper was on a short rein. "We all know better than that, but it can't be proved. What we've got to face now is the fact that the village has outwitted us. The authority and safety of the family is in jeopardy. Once such a situation gains hold, it may be difficult to eradicate. Edward Wakefield and his friends are changing the thinking of the people. There's a feeling of unrest. The rights of our kind are being questioned, even by our own kin."

"It's clear," put in Henry, meticulously adjusting the skirts of his long-waisted frock coat, "that the Putnams are determined on revenge. That's what we're talking about, Nicholas."

"Of course," Nicholas agreed, his voice cold to hide his guilt. "The breadwinner's dead and the widow, I understand, has five children. Did you expect them to bring us a bouquet of field flowers? Let's offer her work in the castle."

"In the castle?" exclaimed his brother incredulously.

"Why not?"

"The brats won't starve," Henry pointed out vapidly. "There are three brothers to help feed them."

"It occurs to me," said Nicholas, looking hard at Henry, "that you need to be reminded that old Joseph, the father, was transported to Australia for stealing a sheep from the estate. As Edward Wakefield said last night, when a man is hungry, he steals." The sharp astonishment on the faces of his three listeners turned swiftly to outrage. Knowing he sat on a powder keg of bigotry, Nicholas went on, "And the brother is in Brixton jail for bag snatching. An honest man may snatch a bag when he needs money for food. It occurs to me also that in a world where the le Grys are in the habit of winning, Putnams lose."

In the stunned silence that followed, he looked with interest from one member of his family to another and, perversely encouraged, added, "Perhaps it's as it should be that the rights of our kind are in dispute." A new, passionately felt emotion was driving him to admit, for the first time, to an unacceptable disparity in people's lives. It was something of which he had been only vaguely aware, until he saw the expression on Rose's lovely face as she handled his sister's lacy camisole.

"Rights!" barked his father. "What are you talking about, Nicholas?"

Nicholas remained standing with feet apart, his dark head still high but now a little to the side. "Putting some 'rights' into the hands of the workingman," he said provocatively.

The earl reached for his snuffbox. "Rights!" he scoffed dismissively. "They wouldn't know what to do with 'em."

"Perhaps they should be taught."

The earl shot him a sharp glance from beneath lowered brows. "And who's to pay for educating riffraff?" Then, without waiting for a reply, he added with resignation and a certain relief, "Anyway, you're off to London. You'll have to take rooms. I can't open up Cavendish Square for one person."

Henry said coldly, "What Papa is trying to say is that you're going to have to stay away for a long time. Not a week or a month, as you may have thought. Years," he said in a thin voice. "What do you think about Edward's plan? You weren't enthusiastic when he put it to you last night, but circumstances have changed. You've changed, too, it seems. Perhaps, since you talk like a socialist, this new life he plans is right for you."

Nicholas took a threatening step forward. "How dare you sit there, you smug jackass, and calmly order me to leave my country?"

"Now, now," remonstrated the earl tetchily.

The countess rose and glided between them, placing a hand on Henry's arm. "I think it would be better if your father and I talked to Nicholas alone."

"I'll thank you to remember that you're not the squire yet," Nicholas said with some acrimony, "and may never be. Heirs have been known to die of a fever or the smallpox."

"Henry, please leave the room." His mother nervously increased the pressure of her fingers on his wrist, tugging a little to turn him toward the door.

"Very well, Mama. But . . ."

"No buts," snapped Nicholas. "I'm leaving for London

tonight, but I warn you, Henry, I shall not stay away. And neither shall I go to the Antipodes. My place is here." He pointed a forefinger toward the floor, indicating in the gesture not only the Rundull estate, but nearly eight hundred years of ownership of which he was an unequivocal part. "Given time, this matter will blow over. And besides," soft laughter flickered in his dark eyes as he added, "I may be needed to provide an heir."

"I shall provide the heir," retaliated Henry, in the same wintry voice. "Adeline is in no hurry. She's only twenty-four."

Walking with long, confident strides, Nicholas went to the door and flung it open, standing by insultingly to shut it after his brother's departure.

Color rose dully in Henry's face. "Papa, I must protest. This matter concerns me."

The earl gazed vaguely at the opposite wall, whistling through his teeth. "Not entirely. Your mother is right. It's better that we talk to Nicholas alone." Henry reluctantly crossed the room. Nicholas bowed with a mocking smile.

"If you had done as your father and I wished," said Priscilla unhappily, when her younger son had, unforgivably, slammed the door on her elder, "this would never have happened. It wouldn't have hurt you to travel to London with Felicity and her maid. No one need have known you were in the carriage."

Nicholas smiled disarmingly. "What does it matter, Mama? Cossack and I emerged unscathed. Quite an adventure, you must agree."

"No, dear boy. It was not a mere adventure. It was the beginning of an uncommonly awkward business," replied his father testily. "Henry is right. You will have to stay away."

"So you, too, wish me to go to the ends of the earth?" Nicholas demanded incredulously. "A pox on Wakefields and their harebrained schemes! You would never have thought of it if Edward hadn't put in an appearance." He prowled to the stone-girt window and frowned down on the hillside below, uncomfortably aware of his parents' waiting silence. At last, he turned. Moving slowly but lightly for so powerful a man, he came to stand before them again. "We've had our troubles before and they've blown over."

Priscilla glanced away, embarrassed by her son's overt sexuality, seeing it at the core of everything that was happening.

"Henry is wrong when he says the authority and safety of the family are in jeopardy. For the moment, the Putnams are disturbed, and they've managed to upset some of the villagers, but it won't last."

His mother turned deliberately to look at the gilt-framed portrait of the 12th earl, who had endured years of exile for murdering his wife's lover. "I think you underestimate the Putnams." She smoothed her skirts, which already lay in elegant folds. "It may well be that they'll soon lose their hold over the rest of the village, but I've talked at length to Snape, and he's of the opinion that the Putnams themselves will neither forget nor forgive. They now have the responsibility of their brother-in-law's children. And their sister back on their hands." She drew in a long breath and let it out on a sigh, as though the coming admission cost her something in dignity or pride. "The Putnam family, as you said, have suffered greatly already, with the father having been transported. And a brother in jail."

"Now a member of the Rundull family has killed one of them!"

His father, puzzled by the brooding quality of his son's comment, shot him a keen look.

His mother's fine features crumpled. "They've taken an oath of vengeance, dear."

"Hobgoblin stuff!" Nicholas laughed derisively.

"If one man is determined to kill another," pronounced the earl, weighing each word with the power of his conviction, "and he is not in a hurry, there will eventually be an opportunity."

During the silence that followed, Priscilla took a lace-edged handkerchief from her reticule. "I have only two sons," she said emotionally. A moment later, taking herself in hand, she added, "Besides, there's that other matter. Adeline shows no sign of producing an heir."

Nicholas's quick mind darted over the dreary possibility of interminable dull canters in Rotten Row. Of shooting on other people's estates. Of filling in time while his mealymouthed sister-in-law submitted dutifully to his brother's attentions in their four-poster bed. "I'll go," he said, his voice harsh, the very real horror of his situation rendering him more than usually incautious. "London will suffice to amuse me for a while, but I'll be back the moment I'm bored."

His hand was already on the doorknob when his father rose, deliberately clearing his throat. Nicholas hesitated, then glanced at his mother, who quickly looked away. The silence in the room was palpable. His Lordship adopted the stance he used for addressing the House of Lords when he did not expect, nor intend, to be contradicted. His thumbs were in his waistcoat, his stomach forward, chin in, his pale eyes glowering beneath graying brows.

It was a familiar moment, bringing with it, uncomfortably, a memory of a small boy's apprehension. The earl was showing the inherited strength that had kept the le Grys family close to the throne and to the land, to the administration of the country and all it stood for, down through the centuries. "When you go to London," he said, "you will consider carefully what you need to take, because it is my intention not to allow you to return until either you or Henry have sired an heir."

Jerningham Wakefield was nineteen, tolerably handsome yet lacking the glossy charm that had ensured his father's riding high in public life. His face, unmarked as yet by living, held an expression of empty content; in animation there was a look of high excitement, rather than of lively intelligence. His strength, if indeed there was strength in him, was forged by a genuine loyalty to and admiration of his family, men of the moment with their hands lightly on the reins that steadied him.

"Melbourne is hot for the plan," he said.

"And therefore the Queen," observed Nicholas dryly, knowing what everyone knew: that the young Queen, if not putty in the prime minister's hands, was at least his very willing pupil. They were in the library of the Wakefield house in Chelsea. The big table in the corner was strewn with maps and charts, plans and papers. Jerningham was beside himself. The survey brig *Tory*, armed with eight guns and small arms for the ship's company, was already waiting at Gravesend, filled with stores, provisions, and goods for barter with the New Zealanders.

"Sixty million acres!" Jerningham exclaimed, flinging out his arms as though encompassing them. "An area nearly as large as Great Britain. Untouched."

Nicholas yawned. "Untouched. Uninhabited? Gad, it sounds awful."

Jerningham was too excited to be put out by his friend's disinterest. "It's the challenge of the century. How I wish I could make you see." Beyond his own wishes, also, he had explicit orders from his father to make Nicholas see.

"After the challenge has been met, what does one do? Perish from boredom?" In the forefront of Nicholas's mind was the fact that, unlike himself, this son of Edward's had nothing to lose.

Jerningham's eyes lit up with something of the Wakefield zealotry. "For the colonists, the challenge will never end. Imagine having thousands of acres of your very own! Virgin, fertile soil, forested and fed by rivers. Wonderful country that you can ride over for days at a time. Doesn't that entice you?"

Nicholas grimaced. "Frankly, no." His mind had flown inevitably to the thousands of acres that could come to his heirs one day if Adeline proved barren; that could be his own if Henry did not outlive him.

"Come with me down the Kings Road and I'll show you the kind of exotic plants that grow wild in the New Zealand bush. They're being naturalized in Knight and Perry's nursery gardens."

"Not interested, dear boy."

Somehow, Nicholas had to be coaxed, tempted, seduced.

"Father's arranging for thoroughbred horses, and shire horses for the plows, the very best cattle and sheep— Romneys and shorthorns, every kind of animal—to go out. You could take Cossack. In fact, any number of thoroughbreds. Ships will be chartered especially to carry livestock."

Nicholas lifted a cigar cutter from a small table, turned it over, turned it back again, opened it idly.

"Do you realize you could have an estate ten times the size of Rundull, and put your brother's inheritance to shame? I wish you could come with us in the *Tory*." His uncle William had refused to overload the survey ship, even for a Rundull. He eyed the back of Nicholas's head speculatively. "I could get you invited to the breakfast party at the West India Dock Tavern. There's to be roast meats and game. And guns going off. Come along. Be my guest. The Earl of Durham will be there as governor of the company, and Joseph Soames, who, as you may know, is England's largest shipowner, as deputy."

"Joseph Soames, eh?" Nicholas put the cigar cutter down and turned, but his mouth was cynical. "You have my reluctant admiration. Your father certainly has a genius for attracting influential people."

"And Dr. Dorset is to be ship's surgeon. You'll remember he was with my uncle in Spain."

Dorset, who had led a great cavalry charge, and who was the only officer to come through unscathed. Momentarily, there was a leaping light in Nicholas's somber eyes, then it died and, with a violent movement, he shook his shoulders back. "The thin end of the wedge?" he suggested, referring to the invitation to breakfast. "Hah!"

"I just want you to see how right this whole operation is for you," Jerningham said, ignoring Nicholas's exclamation of contempt. "You could get yourself a passage on one of the first emigrant ships and join us there. They'll be off in September. Oh, come, Nicholas. Can't you see what a devil of a time we could have?"

"Frankly, I'm aghast at the thought." How clearly he could see through the son's guileless persuasion to Edward's sorcery. "Why don't we talk about something else?" Propelled by the trapped, irritable energy in him, Nicholas prowled off to the end of the room. He'd suspected the motive behind this invitation to luncheon, and he had been right.

"Did Father tell you about the opportunities for absentee speculators? You must bring this fact to your father's attention. The country's a gold mine."

Nicholas paused in his pacing, his eyes resting sardonically on Jerningham's unabashed face. "May I ask what you've invested? Has any of your good money gone into the venture?"

"Yes, you may ask," Jerningham replied with easy goodwill. "The Wakefield stake in Port Nicholson—that's where we're starting—is a thousand pounds. What could that be worth in the future?"

Nicholas thought it might be worth nothing at all, but, in spite of himself, he was impressed that the family was prepared to back the scheme with their own money. "New Zealand," he rolled the name over his tongue. It had a foreign sound. He altered the accent. "Niew Zeland. Dutch, ain't it?"

Jerningham flinched. Privately, he thought Nicholas, for all his grass roots in Kentish soil, had a foreign look himself. Frenchified, from his Norman ancestors. "It was discovered by a Dutchman, but the name has been anglicized. The Maoris call it Aotearoa. The Land of the Long White Cloud. What could be more English than that?" He flung himself into a chair, swinging his legs boisterously over the arm. "They say the place is so healthy men die only from drowning or drunkenness. The former as a result of the latter, no doubt."

"And what are the Dutch doing about it? They're no less adventurous and venal than we are. Perhaps they've discovered pitfalls in paradise. The pitfalls, with respect, that may have eluded you."

"There are no pitfalls." Jerningham spoke unequivocally. "It is simply that there was nobody in Holland of the caliber and foresight of my father. You don't find his type among foreigners. Come, Nicholas, parcel up your gold and join us." Jerningham kicked his legs in the air and bounced back onto his feet.

Nicholas leaned against the map table, his arms folded across his chest, part of him amused against his will by Jerningham's unbridled excitement, part of him wishing that the boy would grow up. "What, may I ask, do cannibals do with gold? Dangle it in lumps from their ears?"

"They'll use money the same way as everyone else. They'll be buying the goods the traders bring."

"And do you call yourself a trader?"

"No. But I could be. It just happens I'm not at the moment. My uncle William and I are arranging to buy land on behalf of the company."

"And paying for it with gold?" Nicholas's eyes flickered to Jerningham's face.

"We're taking all sorts of things. The natives aren't actually ready to use money yet."

Nicholas caught the suggestion of evasion. "You were advising me to bring money. Gold, you said."

"Of course. We'll be starting a bank. Money will be used almost immediately."

"But not to pay the natives for the land?"

"Well—later." Under Nicholas's quick questions, Jerningham evinced a shade of discomfiture. "We're bartering, to begin with. We're taking guns and—"

"Guns? What would the natives want guns for?"

"Oh, come, Nicholas, I've already said it's a hunter's paradise. I'm told the game is so friendly it looks down your gun barrel."

"If the natives have been living on game all their lives, they must already have satisfactory methods of catching it. Have you considered that they might turn your guns on each other? Or on you?"

"Nonsense. They're peace-loving people. Educated, too, in a way. The missionaries are doing their best to turn them into brown-skinned, Bible-banging Englishmen. Two chiefs called Shungi and Waikato visited England twenty years ago. Mr. Kendal, one of the missionaries, took them to Cambridge to be near Professor Lee, and between them they compiled a grammar for studying the Maori language."

"I am *not interested*. Can you not get that into your thick head?" Tucking his hands beneath his coattails, Nicholas walked slowly across the room to stand at the window. Staring out into Hans Place, listening to the clip-clop of hooves as carriages rolled by in the soft spring rain, seeing Rose's sweet face upturned, her hunger flickering from the depths of her lovely smile, he considered, with a feeling of deep disquiet, the fact that black cannibals in a far-flung corner of the earth were being educated as she, white-skinned and sharing his bed, walking on his arm through the streets of civilized London, was not.

"If I were to take you seriously, which I don't," he said at last, "I'd have this to say: Why should this experiment fare any better than the American colonial one?"

Jerningham leveled his bright look on Nicholas's face

and replied with the utmost confidence, "My father's planning has been meticulous."

"His planning of my cousin Ellen's elopement was meticulous, too, and it landed him in jail. If he can't manage the abduction of a fifteen-year-old girl, how's he going to colonize a country?"

Jerningham rose hotly to the bait. "As you very well know, Papa was clubbed with a jail sentence for no better reason than that he was a gentleman. If he hadn't been a gentleman, if he'd seduced the girl—a mere consummation of the marriage, you'll agree, hardly a seduction—he'd have been rich, and become a voice in the land without the long, punishing fight." Guilelessly, Jerningham ignored the fact that the fortune was to have come from a branch of Nicholas's family.

"Your father has a diabolical genius for dropping other people in Queer Street," said Nicholas bitterly. "The carrot you dangle in front of my nose does not tempt me, and for no one simple reason. Edward, having made a mess of your uncle William's life, as well as . . ."

"Uncle William obviously don't bear a grudge for that. If he did, he wouldn't be involved in this project now."

"Then he's either a saint or a fool," Nicholas replied contemptuously. "I have no hesitation in saying I hold your father entirely to blame for my present situation. If he hadn't delayed my departure from the castle, Rose would have been with me when the smith came by."

"I'd expect a le Grys to stand by his own misdeeds, but"—Jerningham's eyes lifted slyly to wait for his guest's reaction—"if Father did set a train of events in motion that culminated in your exile from Rundull, then it's right that he should offer you a new home."

"What smooth-tongued rogues you both are." Nicholas took a turn about the room, feinting little kicks at the carpet, working off his unbridled irritation at being caught while Jerningham played the fox. Then, realizing this conversation might well be reported, he added cruelly, "Your father's record of failure is deuced high, and it goes back a long way. He walked out of Westminster School, was expelled from Edinburgh High School, then was thrown into prison. Whitewash him as you will, in the eyes of the world, the man you're asking me to follow is a failure." He paused, giving the words time to sink in, then added scathingly, "A leader of men ought to be able to avoid detention at her majesty's pleasure."

All the pent-up hope in Jerningham and the strain of endeavor burst out in an explosion of injured wrath. "How dare you! A swell who's never had to fight for anything! A Rundull! One of the kings of privilege! Educated by a tutor! What a nerve you have to criticize a man who couldn't tolerate the barbarism of a public school! Do you know what the Bishop of Adelaide said to his clergy when they complained of hardships in the tough convict colony my father set up in South Australia? He said, 'You should have been a fag at Westminster in my time.' "

There was a long silence. The air pulsed with the hostility between the two men. Nicholas pushed his hands deep into his pockets, fuming, pondering on the fact that his privileges lay poised on a razor's edge. When a Rundull fell, he fell heavily.

Jerningham, remembering with apprehension his father's command—"I'm relying on you to get the boy" —and already regretting his loss of control, came to stand beside his guest, resting a conciliatory hand on his shoulder. In the back of his mind, a germ of revenge already grew.

"Why not do what my father did with his prison sentence?" he suggested, in as mild a voice as he could manage. "Why not turn adversity into opportunity?" The words cost him a good deal, for he was deeply angered by Nicholas's criticism of his father.

"Your project sounds more like an opportunity for the kind of underprivileged people your father met in jail."

"There will be no convicts in New Zealand." Jerningham kept his voice calm.

But *convict* was an emotive word for Nicholas now. "Why not? I've no doubt many of them are very decent fellows. If I were without food, I'd steal," he said.

"And I'll wager you'd get away with it," Jerningham replied warmly. "That's why my father's after you, Nicholas. Because it's guts and brains he wants in his colonists, as well as good blood. How you would fall on your feet! You'd be one of the leaders. You'd be able to say what you liked."

"I say what I like now." Nicholas went back to the

bookcase, gazed without interest at the shelves, took up a book, then put it back again.

"My father's friend Leigh Hunt went to prison for calling the prince regent a fat Adonis of fifty."

Nicholas's chuckle was sardonic in the extreme. Privately, he thought Leigh Hunt was a fool. History had shown that the men at the top were those wily enough never to fall foul of the establishment. A Rundull might murder his valet, but he would cut off his right hand before insulting his sovereign. He smiled. "I never knew you to show any sign of a crusading spirit before."

Jerningham flushed. "Would you not be the first to agree that what's in the blood will come out in its own time?" Mutely, he indicated his cousin, Elizabeth Fry, gazing piously at them out of a dark frame on the far wall. "And cousin Hannah is married to Thomas Fowell Buxton, the emancipator of slaves."

Nicholas prowled restlessly back across the room. "You are indeed well connected with busybodies."

Jerningham watched him balefully from beneath lowered lids. His father had warned him to use his last card only in extremis. Rashly, he took the plunge. "Now what about that little strumpet you've got in your rooms, decked out like a lady?"

Nicholas swung around savagely.

"You can't make a lady of her," Jerningham went on, artfully pretending not to have noticed his guest's reaction. "She don't sew or draw or read. She ain't a doll. When you walk her 'round Mayfair showing her off, you can't introduce her to your friends. You've made a prisoner of the poor little trollop. Now, if you went out to New Zealand, you could do a great job of setting up equal opportunities for her and her kind. Under Father's plan, in another generation or two, men like you will be marrying girls like her, and thinking nothing of it. You could even take her with you. There's plenty of room in steerage."

The silence in the room was deadly. In a way, frightening. "She'd find a husband easily enough," Jerningham continued, unabashed. "There'll be men by the score, and very few women for a while. She would be able to take her pick. With a good class of artisan for a husband, her descendants could be prime ministers. What's she got here? She's too pretty for service. No lady in her right senses would employ her. And it'd be a pity for her to end in a whorehouse, which is the only alternative."

He felt rather than saw the violence in Nicholas's face and hesitated, then, recklessly playing the last card his father had given him, added, "You've got Rose's future in the palm of your hand." He steeled himself to look Nicholas full in the face, opening his eyes wide with spurious innocence. "Why not marry her and take her with you?" He saw something flare in Nicholas's eyes, then fade. "She looks like a princess, God knows," Jerningham murmured slyly.

The sheer outrageousness of his host's attack knocked Nicholas sideways. He brushed a hand across his brow, the anger in his eyes giving way to cloudy shock. "Because I have to think of the succession. Adeline may not bear a son."

"Of course she will. Think about it, old chap."

Think about marrying Rose? About the son of a kitchen maid one day inheriting Rundull Castle? Or, and here was the rub, think of never returning to Rundull until he had married and impregnated some high-born nitwit with his seed. Recovering, he said in a stinging voice, "You're onto a good thing, Jerningham. You've had a voyage 'round the world dropped into your lap. You're about to start a magnificent adventure. And you know Mayfair's here to come back to. It's what you like. What you're good at. Playing games."

Jerningham's face darkened, his future boxed up like a toy.

Nicholas strode out of the room, picking up his tall hat as he went, jamming it down on his head. "Thank you for lunch." His gratitude came like a curse.

7

It was three weeks since Rose had come to London. The city's lively, noisy, colorful streets were glades of heaven for her, with Nicholas at her side, handsome and rakish in his daring, plum-colored frock coat, flowered and hand-embroidered waistcoat, and pale breeches. Together they would sweep past friends and acquaintances as though their business was too immediate and too confidential to be shared. Sometimes, to Rose's delight, an irreverent swank would wink at her, but always when Nicholas was looking away.

In the set of rooms he had taken in St. James's, Rose slept in a comfortable four-poster bed with hangings: a bed that bounced when she jumped on it, and curved voluptuously around her when she settled to sleep. There was a mahogany washstand in the bedroom, and a wardrobe in which to hang the beautiful dresses Nicholas had bought for her. Sometimes, when he was at one of his ceremonial breakfasts or musical soirées, Rose would spread the dresses out on the bed and spend hours buttoning and unbuttoning them with her small, adept fingers, rejoicing in the touch of soft lawn, percale, or tarlatan.

Nicholas took her to the fair at Greenwich, and to Astley's circus with its exotic French equestrian troupe. They walked together in Vauxhall Gardens listening to the music and watching the fireworks. They saw Monsieur Phillippe's miraculous juggling, and in June, Nicholas promised, he would take her to the gayest, brightest, rowdiest, most colorful event, called Derby Day, where she could have her fortune told by gypsies, and see the racehorses actually racing.

Sometimes, lying back on the bed in his fashionable chintz dressing gown and yellow morocco slippers, smoking a cheroot, Nicholas would say lazily, "Dance for me, Rose."

Pretending to be shy, she would start slowly to pirouette, her skirts swinging, and he would watch in silence, not looking lazy at all. He would take the cheroot from between his lips, lift himself on one elbow, and with his dark eyes smoldering say softly, "Faster, Rose, faster," meaning he wanted her gown to whirl outrageously up around her calves to expose her lacy underdrawers. And when that happened, he would leap up and clasp her to him, pulling off her nether garments with expert fingers, while she shrieked with excitement. The cheroot would smoulder in the ashtray, forgotten. Rose asked nothing more of life than that this should never end.

Inevitably, though, there were problems. Once, Nicholas said, "Mend this, will you, Rose," holding out his bright yellow waistcoat showing a tear in the embroidery. Unable to bring herself to admit she knew nothing of fine mending, Rose had gone with him to the Burlington Arcade to find a linen-drapery and haberdashery shop.

As they waited for the parcel to be wrapped Nicholas asked, "Is there anything else you want."

"Perhaps the lady would like a sampler to embroider," suggested the elegant young man in white collar and neckcloth, who was serving behind the counter.

Nicholas saw Rose's embarrassment and misread it. Tossing some more coins on to the counter he said, "Yes, why not."

Rose was silent as they walked back to the rooms. Admissions of the kind she was being forced into now could set Nicholas pondering on the fact that their relationship lay outside the realms of real life.

"Then why did you agree to mend my waistcoat?" he asked impatiently, when at last she plucked up the courage to tell him she had no knowledge of embroidery.

"Because you wanted me to. I thought I could try," she said. And then, in a warm rush, "I'd do anything for you, Nicholas."

"Ah, sweet Rose, sweet Rose."

That evening he watched enigmatically as she brought out the sewing material. The thimble slipped off her finger and rolled away. Nicholas went down on his knees to find it but, not accustomed to being waited upon, she was there first. They met on the floor, laughing. Spontaneously, he kissed her, and they were delightfully diverted by one of their hedonistic games of love.

If only the ladies' maids at Rundull had been less snobbish and disagreeable, Rose thought regretfully when the game was over, and she set about threading the needle again, she might have learned how to manage this ridiculous thimble that made her finger feel as though it had been chopped off and stuck on again. She picked up the yellow waistcoat and under Nicholas's absorbed and sympathetic gaze she put all her untutored sense and inventiveness to work. The tear came miraculously together.

"Clever as well as beautiful," he said, leaning back on the sofa, long legs apart, his cheroot between his teeth, as he held up the garment for examination.

Her smile was warm with relief and gratitude.

"Why don't you have a look at the sampler now?" he suggested, tossing it into her lap.

How beautiful it was! There was a tree to embroider, and a kitten, and a small child, some lettering, and a complicated border. Rose fingered it lovingly, sliding the glowing silks through her fingers, ingeniously pushing the paper with the mysterious lettering on it out of sight beneath the linen.

Nicholas found it. "Here are the instructions." She sat with eyes cast down in waiting despair.

Chastising himself for a tactless fool, he put a finger beneath her chin, forcing her to look up. "There are more important talents than reading, my darling, and you have them all."

The next morning, Rose opened the door to an unprepossessing woman wearing linsey-woolsey and an old-fashioned pelisse.

"Mrs. Finglass at your service," she said. "I've come about the embroidery lesson."

"Oh!" exclaimed Rose delightedly. Nicholas was full of surprises. She backed into the hall, gesturing to the woman to follow her. "Do sit down. There. Over there on the sofa." She hurried to Nicholas's desk, and picked up the sampler. The woman took off her bonnet, patting the frilled cap she wore. Her eyes darted swiftly around the room.

"As I understand, you're to start from the beginning," she said.

"Y-yes." Was starting at the beginning in some way a fault? Mrs. Finglass was frowning, taking needles, cottons, and cloth out of her reticule. Rose drew up the sofa table.

"I want to know how to sew this," she said, showing the sampler. "If you could just show me . . ." She broke off because the woman was clearly not listening.

"This is gentlemen's rooms," said Mrs. Finglass at last in a damning voice, her sharp eyes flickering from the sporting prints on the walls to the uncovered tables, the heavy, masculine chairs.

"Er, yes," stammered Rose. Nicholas lived here, and he was a gentleman.

Mrs. Finglass treated her to a long, unnerving look.

"What is the matter?"

Mrs. Finglass folded her mouth thinly. "You may not start with that. You 'ave to learn the stitches first, miss. I 'ave 'ere a piece of calico. We will do the stitches across it one by one."

"Why can't I work the sampler?" asked Rose, baffled by the sudden show of animosity.

"You can when you've practiced the stitches. We will do feather stitch now."

"On this piece of plain cotton? Why?"

"On the cotton, if you please."

Rose followed the woman's instructions with resignation. The same stitch, repeated again and again, in a long line that used up a great deal of thread, and meant nothing. "Two stitches would have been enough," she protested. She would see feather stitches in her dreams! "Now, do please show me another stitch. One I'll use on the sampler."

Mrs. Finglass looked annoyed. "I only teach one stitch in a morning."

"One stitch! But why? Do you mean you have to go now?"

"No. I am to stay for two hours. But I only teach one stitch. You must practice it for the two hours. That's the way to become proficient."

"But I am proficient," protested Rose, sliding her tongue with alacrity around the unfamiliar word. She held up the piece of calico. "I could never do those stitches better if I practiced for a hundred years. Please," she begged, "I do want to be able to work the sampler. Please, Mrs. Finglass. That's all I want to do." To make something beautiful, she meant, to show to Nicholas. How could he be expected to waste his money on long rows of stitches that were all the same?

Mrs. Finglass heaved an irritated sigh. "You've put me right out of my stride, you have. All right, here's your herringbone, but it's not likely as you'll take it in."

Swiftly, Rose threaded the needle again. Her fingers moved more deftly all the time. She held the thread just so, neither tight nor loose, and this time she went right to the end of the row without protest. When she had finished, she held the plain piece of calico at arm's length, eyeing it critically. "Look!" There was no response. "Mrs. Finglass! May I now be shown the next stitch?"

"It's not the way I teach."

"Please," Rose insisted, "I wish to learn every stitch. Now." She thrust the dreary piece of calico at her reluctant tutor.

"It's not the way . . ."

"It's the way I wish you to teach me."

Ungraciously, the woman took the materials from Rose's hands. Rose watched her, intent as a dog with a bone. She was stitching swiftly, quite deliberately swiftly. Chain stitch. Satin stitch. Stem stitch. When she put her needle down, her eyes were dark with malice. "If you can follow that . . ."

"I'm sure I can. Thank you." Rose added politely, "You need not come again."

The woman lifted her thin nose and drew a long, slow breath. She looked up, her gaze directed pointedly at Rose's polished golden head, innocent of the Babet cap that Nicholas refused to buy.

"One does not deliberately hide one's crowning glory," he had said lightly. "You don't really want one of those things, do you?" Rose had thought only that ladies wore caps, and that she was not a lady. It had not mattered at the time.

"I was hov the impression," Mrs. Finglass abandoned her refined mode of speech, "that I 'ad come to give lessons to a gen'l'man's wife. I'm not haccustomed to dealin' wi' kept women. It's ladies I learn, not jumped-up servants an' whores."

"How dare you! How dare you call me a whore!" Rose leaped off her seat, sending the precious sampler flying.

As though the release of her venom had restored her to a sneering kind of good humor, the woman smiled faintly. "I am habout to go. And much good may the lesson I give do fer you." She picked up her bonnet, tied it on her head, and flounced out.

"Your sampler's lovely," Nicholas told Rose when he arrived back. "My own sister couldn't do better." And he looked at her with such pride that all the misery of the incident disappeared.

Next morning, Rose wakened to a feeling of acute discomfort. There was an inexplicable hardness and soreness to her breasts that she had never known before. Later, she was dreadfully ill.

She did not tell Nicholas because Florrie's experience had taught her that men reacted badly to illness. Although she was sick again the next morning, and the next, she was well enough again within the hour, and eventually, because there was no one to talk to about it, she pushed the problem to the back of her mind.

That night, Nicholas arrived home from his gambling the worse for drink. Apprehensively, Rose waited for the shouting to start. She knew men beat their wives when they were drunk. But he only looked at her ruefully and staggered into her arms, murmuring, "My beautiful scented Rose. My flower." She held him close, while wild and ridiculous promises hurtled off his tongue.

"I'll buy you bonnets covered with roses. Roses for a rose. And pearls for your throat. We'll drive in the park on Sunday, and I'll introduce you to the Queen." Then he tried unsuccessfully to make love to her, and laughed, saying the brandy had got him. "Never leave me, Rose," he said, holding her tightly, and sounding so vulnerable that her heart filled with a new, compassionate love.

The next day he did buy her a bonnet, trimmed not

with roses, but with tiny pearls, and another with *mentonnières* of yellow lace under the brim and a little spray of violets on either side. He took her for an airing in the open landau that was kept in the mews of the Rundulls' town house in Cavendish Square. It had been exciting, driving through the park with Nicholas, preening herself under the admiring glances of the arrogant young bloods on their prancing steeds. They went out often after that. Then one day they came upon Lady Felicity, driving with another of the Queen's attendants in an elegant curricle and pair. Rose lost her breath with shock.

"Lift your head and stare right back," said Nicholas mischievously.

She could not. She averted her face, wishing miserably she could drop through the floor. The horrified expression on Lady Felicity's face froze her to the bone.

Later that day, accompanied by one of the Queen's ladies in waiting, because, Nicholas explained later, maids of honor were not allowed out unescorted, his sister came to the rooms. Rose, curled up on the four-poster, heard raised voices behind the closed door, a sharp rebuke from Lady Felicity, and Nicholas's uproarious laughter. When they had gone, he said, "Felicity don't want your cloak, so consider it your own."

Nor, to Rose's puzzled surprise, did Nicholas's sister want the long underdrawers and prettily decorated muslin petticoat she had borrowed. Having acquired some delicate linens of her own, she had washed them beautifully in scented soap, working painstakingly and meticulously on the frills and lace edgings. Now they were parceled up neatly, waiting to be sent back. Out of the past, she remembered Grandy saying philosophically, as though, being accustomed to the fact, he did not really mind, "They don't care what we do, Rose, so long as we keep out of their way." Lady Felicity did not even require her honesty. Rose felt a strange sensation that she no longer existed.

Nicholas went alone to grand functions. They both knew and accepted that Rose could not accompany him. "Dress up to see me off," he would say, and she would go downstairs on his arm in her emerald green cloak with one of the lovely new gowns underneath. After he had gone she would return upstairs and work happily on her sampler until his return. The tree was finished already, and the child's face. She had been right about her ability to puzzle out the stitches. She was an adept needle-woman now.

And then the invitation came to the ball at Bucking-ham Palace. It was beautiful, carrying a crown and the sovereign's initials prettily scrolled at the top. "You must wear your very best dress," Nicholas said, just as though she had been included.

"I'll wear my oyster silk," she replied solemnly.

"And your tiara."

"Of course. My best one?"

"The one with the hundred and ten diamonds will do." She giggled delightedly.

The le Grys family, who had moved into their Caven-dish Square mansion for the occasion, sent their dress chariot, the one that was elaborately decorated with ar-morial bearings and crests, summoning the errant son to dine with them. How magnificent Nicholas looked in court finery, his black dress coat falling away from a white satin waistcoat and his long legs encased in pale cassimere breeches! With the addition of a cocked hat, he seemed to tower—not like a giant, rather more like a god—Rose thought, her heart ready to burst with pride. One passerby after another stopped to stare.

Nicholas seemed not to notice when Mr. Shard, the head coachman, bewigged and splendid in his livery, ignored Rose. The postilions, who were, after all, only ragamuffins from the village, nonetheless turned away when she tried to ask them about her family. Never having seen them at Castle Rundull dressed like that, in leather breeches and snowy linen shirts puffed above the waistbands, narrow-brimmed hats with gold cording and smart lube jackets, she was at a loss as to how to deal with them.

" 'Ave a good time, Guv," an old man called good-naturedly, as he rattled by in his jingling costermonger's cart. A flower seller offered Rose a posy, then she no-ticed Nicholas getting into the coach without her. "Aren't you goin'?"

Rose was moved by the woman's concerned interest.

"He's off to the palace," she confided. "The Queen is giving a ball for a Russian prince."

The flower woman snatched her posy back. "I thought you was a lady," she sneered. Rose shrank into herself, but Nicholas, who had overheard the exchange, leaned out of the window and bowed to the crone in a way that was as prime an insult as a box on the ears. Then he smiled at Rose as the woman flounced off, her face evil with dislike, and Rose smiled back, her heart swelling with gratitude.

As the carriage rolled away, Rose's spirits sank. Though Mr. Shard was a very superior servant in the castle heirarchy, he had always been kind to her before. She trailed back upstairs and stood leaning against the window. It seemed suddenly as though a wall had risen between herself and her past. There had always been a wall ahead.

She looked unhappily down to the street. People moved briskly to and fro; there was the sound of voices, a shout of excitement. Never in her life had Rose felt more in need of warmth and human contact. Yet Nicholas had told her she must not leave the rooms unaccompanied.

Her pulses quickened. He would not be back until the early hours, and need never know. If she looked like a lady, as she now had plenty of discomfiting proof that she did, who would dare accost her? Running to the wardrobe, she took out her beautiful cloak and the tarlatan dress.

Nicholas had not been specific with his advice. He had omitted to tell her that ladies did not wander unaccompanied around the streets, especially in the evening, and, more especially, dressed in emerald green velvet.

8

"**H**ey, miss!" A new fearful excitement had Rose on her toes. She passed the cigar shop where Nicholas bought his Havanas, and hurried into the glare and bustle of Piccadilly. There were the lively clatter of horses' hooves, the pungent smell of dung and dirt and unwashed bodies, a man with a performing monkey on a stick. The streets were alive with hurrying hansoms, hackney carriages, idling wayfarers leaning on their canes or gossiping at street corners. People looked at Rose, and looked again.

"Hey, there! Hey!" At the sound of a friendly voice, she swung around and came face-to-face with a smart gentleman in uniform, driving a cabriolet with the tiniest "tiger" in dashing livery on the step. The man winked and jerked at his reins. Thrilled, terrified, Rose tossed her curls and fled breathlessly up a side street.

The streets grew narrow, the buildings closed in on either side. She paused, looked around apprehensively. Piccadilly seemed a long way behind. The smells were different here. And the people. The odor of savory food mingled unpleasantly now with that of animal dung. The warm, busy sounds of the affluent West End were replaced by the sharp clicking of pattens, so familiar to Rose from the castle kitchens. Head-scarfed women hurried in and out of courts and side streets carrying pots or bundles of firewood. One of them paused, looked at Rose with the same expression the policeman had worn. Then, to her utter disbelief, she spat on the pavement at

Rose's feet. Rose grasped her skirts protectively and jumped aside. Deeply offended, she hurried away.

Across the way, a woman with a shawl around her thin shoulders, a wailing baby in her arms, and a man's cloth cap at her feet was singing in a thin, reedy voice. Passersby were tossing coppers into the hat. Rose remembered with a surge of excitement that she had a shilling. For the first time in her life, she had something to give away. She swung around, meaning to hurry back to St. James's, but was stopped by a solidly built gentleman in surtout and striped peg-top trousers. " 'Ullo, deary. An' what's a pretty young lidy like you doin' all alone so far from 'ome?" The man twirled his cane, touching it against his saucer-shaped hat, fiddling with his yellow neckerchief.

"Walking," Rose replied politely, stepping aside, not liking the cold, calculating look in his eyes nor his oily, wheedling voice.

"Walkin', is it then?" Quick as a knife, the fellow slipped an arm through hers. "An' 'ow would yer like ter come walkin' with me, my pretty?" Indignantly, Rose tried to jerk her arm away. "A young thing like you ought not ter be wanderin' 'round alone."

"I'm perfectly all right. Let me go. You're hurting me."

"Perfickly all right, is it? Now my doxy, it's all kinds o' trouble yer could get into, bein' as yer're 'ere alone." He brought his face down close to hers, so close she could smell the stale tobacco and cheap drink on his breath. "Come wi'me now, an' we'll 'ave a little talk," he said confidentially.

"I don't want to talk to you. Let me go. Let me go!" She pulled and tugged in desperation, but all the time his strong blunt fingers were digging hurtfully into her flesh, and he was pushing her backward toward a door. The door opened. She screamed, but before the scream was halfway out, his hand, calloused and smelling of the streets, came down hard against her mouth. She dug her teeth fiercely into his flesh and kicked like one half crazed. "Let me go!" Then she was through the door, and it was clattering shut behind her.

"None o' that, m'dear. None o' that. I warns yer." The man spun her around. "Now, look down 'ere," he said in a suddenly kindly voice. "There's friends o' mine as want t' meet yer."

They were standing at the top of a short flight of steps. An untidy crowd of people was gathered at the foot. There were men in cloth caps and the broad-brimmed beaver hats of draymen; women with flamboyantly high, old-fashioned hair styles, painted faces, and excessively low-cut gowns. Rose searched frenziedly for a kind face and, finding none, shrank back. One of the onlookers moved forward, his sharp eyes running over her from top to toe.

"Move, I said." Her captor gave her a rough shove that sent her teetering down the steps.

A man approached and began to smooth Rose's cloak with venal fingers. " 'Ullo Ben," he said softly, "wot yer got 'ere?"

In a panic, she searched the faces again for help, knowing despairingly there was none.

"Sit down, my pretty. A brandy fer the lidy, Mr. Potter, if you please." The talk around the bar faded, but still they continued to look at her. The man called Ben came strutting behind her and grasped the collar of her cloak. "You won't want ter be sittin' in this 'ot thing," he said.

Rose clutched feverishly at the garment. A dozen men and women closed in on her, curious, watchful.

"Please, it's mine." It was that dreadful day in the village High Street all over again. She was alone against the mob. The cloak was jerked from her shoulders.

A harpy with black stockings and coarse masses of red hair stretched out a thin claw. "I'll look arter it, Ben."

"Put it away careful fer the little lidy. Careful, I said, mind. We wouldn't want anythin' ter 'appen ter a nice, stylish cloak like that now, would we?" Looking cunning, the girl crept away.

"Give it to me," shrieked Rose, but the cloak was whisked out of sight, and someone thrust her backward so roughly that she fell against the bar.

"Ah! 'Ere's yer little tipple," said Ben heartily. "Thank you, Mr. Potter. Jus' what the lidy needs. 'Ere yer are, my dear."

"I don't want it. I want my cloak, and I want to go home."

"You can't come inter a wine bar an' refuse ter drink yer 'ost's good liquor," the bully warned her, his voice mildly threatening. He looked across at the barman for agreement. "Can she, Mr. Potter?"

The barman shook his head.

"C'mon, my doxy. Real little flower, ain't she, lads?" Looking for approval, Ben surveyed the faces of the grinning gap-toothed old men, the evil-eyed crones and tarts. "Drink it up, my beauty, an' another one or two like it an' we'll be orf ter my place."

His place!

Rose's terrified eyes swiveled again over the assembled mob.

"Yer want as I should 'old yer nose an' pour it down? Open yer mouth, doxy. Come on. Open yer mouth. Come on, luv. Yer niver goin' ter enjoy yerself until yer drink it, so yer might as well." Some of the sharp, strong liquid went down Rose's throat. She coughed helplessly.

" 'Er bonnet's in the way, poor gurl." Rose clutched uselessly at the air, as a woman in a stuff dress trimmed with tatty artificial flowers jerked her bonnet ribbons, and whisked it away.

"Oh, please . . ."

A woman in scarlet sateen put the bonnet on, tied the bow with a flourish, and danced up and down the room, flinging her shiny skirts high to cries of approval and a round of applause. The man Ben released his hold on Rose in order to put the glass down and clap his hands.

Enraged by her loss, maddened with terror, suddenly free, Rose lunged at the woman in red. "Give me my bonnet! How dare you!" The onlookers set up a cheer. Suddenly the place was in a turmoil. Women shrieked, men shouted. There was the sharp crack of glasses breaking. A man carrying her cloak over his arm was making off up the stairs. Rose flung herself after him. Hard hands grabbed her, and the next moment she lay spread-eagled on the filthy floor.

Then, without warning, the uproar ceased. A voice was raised in inquiry. "What's all this, then?"

She opened her eyes. The crowd had parted. A large man in a high black hat and blue cloth coat, trimmed with brass buttons and gold braid, was looking down at her.

"Causing a mischief, was you?" He took her roughly by the arm and hauled her to her feet. She staggered a little, her head spinning. Her dress was torn, the frothy pleating of her chemisette hung in ribbons. She clutched at the edges of her bodice and looked around groggily at the silent crowd. Their faces now were blandly innocent. Rose wept inwardly.

"Nice little girl like you, well dressed an' all," said the policeman, shaking his head. "Got on in the world, hadn't you," he added, looking with suspicious eyes at the torn tarlatan. He took a notebook and pencil from his pocket. Rose staggered against the bar. Any moment now, she knew, shamefully, she was going to be sick.

"Drinking," said the officer, licking his pencil, sounding personally affronted. "Well, well."

An uncouth voice said, "She were drinking brandy."

"Brandy?" repeated the representative of the law, scandalized. "You'd better come along o' me. Brandy, you said?" he looked around the silent assembly. They nodded their heads, disapproving to a man. "And making a public nuisance," he added. "What's your name?"

Tears of humiliation and despair, misery and bewilderment, caught in Rose's throat. She put a hand to her head where it hurt and felt a wet, sticky lump. She blinked groggily at the blood on her palm. Nicholas! Oh, Nicholas! Her head had begun to spin again. She was going a long way away, riding on air. In the far distance a voice was asking, "What's your name? What's your name?" But then there was only the spinning. Faster and faster . . .

In the state ballroom at Buckingham Palace, sitting down for a well-earned rest between a lively quadrille and schottische, the Queen cast an approving eye over Nicholas le Grys, the brother of Lady Felicity. "He really is a devilishly handsome fellow, Marm," agreed Lord Melbourne, rubbing at the skin hanging loosely from his bony chin. "But tonight is for the young Tsarevitch, not for the problems of your subjects, however attractive and sympathetic they may be."

"If I am to be a good queen, my Lord, then the problems of my subjects must take precedence over my pleasures," retorted the Queen, in an early display of exceptional spirit and piety. Normally she would have added, "and certainly over foreigners," but she was already half in love with the Russian Grand Duke, and sorely regretting her offer to put him in the way of her maid. "You know how greatly devoted I am to my ladies and maids of honor."

"I do indeed," replied the prime minister sincerely, though his mind inevitably reverted to the Lady Flora Hastings debacle. Maybe the fact that that particular maid had come in for such a rough time was the poor creature's own fault.

"Lady Felicity le Grys is quite my favorite," Victoria continued warmly, "and I am very much concerned about this problem that is exercising her. Her father wishes Nicholas to be absent from the estate for some considerable time."

Turning his shrewd old eyes on his sovereign, Melbourne noted a rise in her color. "Would it be indiscreet of me to ask what the young man has done to be sent from home?"

"It is a private matter. In fact, I do not know, and if I did, I would not be disposed to repeat it, for I have had enough of scandal," retorted Victoria, flinching inwardly. She, also, was inevitably reminded of the mystery of Lady Flora's expanding waistline. "The family has it in mind to send him to New Zealand. Do you think he would make a good colonist?"

"Not if he's to be forcibly transported like a convict," replied Melbourne mildly.

Diverted, she remarked, "It is unfortunate, is it not, that the prime mover in this splendid venture should have himself been to prison?" Her rosebud mouth tightened in the way the prime minister knew so well. "I would like to meet Mr. Wakefield, but I really cannot entertain a man who has served a term of imprisonment."

"I am sure he will bear you no grudge for that. But let me say this. Had Mr. Wakefield not been to prison, then I doubt he would be pursuing the project at all. Fiery he is, and often mistaken, but he may well go down in history as a hero. I'm sorry you feel unable to meet him. He's a royalist, and a man of immense charm. You would be captivated by him. It's to be remembered, Marm, his crime was abducting a young lady of considerable means in order not so much to pursue his own ambitions in

Parliament as to use the power money brings to alleviate the misery of the poor. He hasn't been contaminated by rubbing shoulders with jailbirds, only strengthened in his resolves."

"Mmm." The Queen's eyelids drooped. When she had spread a balm of virtue over the profligate past, when the good name of the court was totally restored, maybe she would be able to meet such men.

"As to young le Grys, Marm," the old man gave his sovereign a dry look, "it's my impression he would be as attracted by lofty aims as a fly to a spider."

"You may be right, but he has a fancy for excitement. And is adventurous."

"There's one method—a very common and invariably successful method—of quieting a young man down." The prime minister turned a tolerant eye on Nicholas as he whirled by, leading one of the prettiest guests through a lively waltz. "Marriage is adventure of a kind."

"We will come to that. I'm sorry you are not enthusiastic about his virtues as a colonist."

"On the contrary, as a willing colonist I think he could be a remarkable success. But I did not get the impression he was willing." Melbourne turned amused eyes on his hostess.

"I did not aim to give you the impression he was unwilling, my Lord. Mr. Wakefield has especially invited him. As you said yourself about the American colonies that we have lost, the colonists were not closely tied to our great families."

"It's true," conceded the prime minister. "Give Mr. Wakefield his due, Marm—he is leaving no stone unturned to ensure that you will reign over this one."

"Oh, I do. I do," replied the Queen happily. "Now, with regard to Nicholas. We, Felicity and I, feel it would be wise to ensure he takes with him a nice sensible girl from a good family. He would then be prevented from any wild excesses to which he may be disposed." She lowered her eyes, fanning herself vigorously. "I think I must after all tell you what Lady Felicity has told me, but you must understand this is entirely confidential, my Lord. He is involved in a most unsuitable liaison."

"Ah." The Prime Minister rubbed his chin again, hiding a smile.

"These matters usually run their course, then blow over," he said comfortingly.

The Queen smoothed the fine silk of her ball dress. "This is not, as you seem to think, a petty matter. There's a girl here tonight of whom you have a slight acquaintance. The daughter of the Earl of Woolege. She is of strong character and mild temperament. Felicity and I have come to a decision.

"Lady Cressida has those virtues of blood and character that Mr. Wakefield requires in his colonists. I know her well, I believe her to be dutiful, modest, and brave. I'm certain she would follow her husband. . . . Oh! The grand duke is coming this way." There was no mistaking the towering prince's movements in a crowd. "The long and the short of it is," said the Queen, flicking her fan this way and that, more than a little excited by the approach of her handsome guest, "we wish you to put pressure on the matter. Here, tonight, is an atmosphere full of romance . . ." She looked up, her eyes starry. "Ah, Alexander, come and sit beside me. You must tell me about this *grossvater* that you wish the band to play tonight."

"It's a German country dance . . ."

The prime minister, grumbling inwardly, dragged himself to his feet and left. Dutiful and modest—these were characteristics the Queen admired, but were they attributes to attract a young blood of Nicholas le Grys's temperament? He shook his head doubtfully. Odd that the Queen, who was so reluctant to consider marriage for herself, should prove so enthusiastic a matchmaker for others. He glanced back, saw her glowing face raised to the young Tsarevitch, and his heart sank. A pretty kettle of fish that could be

The Lady Cressida Amhurst was sitting on a Queen Anne sofa between her somewhat elderly parents. Lord Melbourne knew her history well enough. As the youngest of five sisters, she had had to wait her turn in the marriage stakes. It had not been easy to produce even four, much less five, husbands of the rank and standing that the old earl desired. At the critical moment, when the fourth daughter had been married off to one of the Queen's German relatives—there was always a "bank" of likely suitors on the Continent, when offers of high-born Englishmen ran low—the girl contracted the small-pox, and no one saw her for a year. The earl let his Berkeley Square house that season, and the family stayed at their country seat, Saxon Mote in Suffolk.

Rumors were not easy to scotch in the hotbed of gossip that flourished at court, and all kinds of nonsense was talked about the girl when she did not reappear. It was even said, perhaps out of envy of her luxuriant golden tresses, that she had lost her hair and now wore a wig. Likely suitors scurried in the opposite direction. Melbourne, compassionate in his own way, felt it was possible that the elderly countess, relieved at having the girl restored to them, had kept her shackled by sheer love. But she was of marriageable age. Well past it, in fact, at twenty-one. It was high time an offer was made.

Nicholas was standing alone, leaning nonchalantly against a doorjamb, scowling down a line of twittering ladies waiting on little gilt chairs to be asked to dance. The scowl came from his heart. He had been shocked to discover, over dinner at Cavendish Square, how determined were his family's plans to send him off to the colonies. When Melbourne spied him, he was anxiously going over the dinner-table conversation in his mind.

"We're told the country's ideal for the growing of corn," his father had remarked, as casually as he might have said, "Pass the butter will you please, m'dear." "If the Corn Laws are repealed—the League is determined they will be—any amount of it can come here."

"And olives and almonds," Henry had added, gulping down his chicken giblet soup. "Think of the profit in olive oil. I'm trying to help you, Nicholas," he said soothingly, seeing the murderous expression in his brother's eyes.

"Do we have to discuss this matter over dinner?" Priscilla asked nervously. But her husband felt they did. Nicholas knew why. They had him in a trap tonight.

"I've read the reports Charles Darwin wrote," the earl said. "He was out there in *Beagle*. He declares grapes will grow twice as quickly in New Zealand as in France or Italy. I can arrange for you to take vine roots. Any number of them. In no time, it seems, you could be bottling your own wine."

Nicholas glanced up and saw the prime minister approaching. Melbourne hesitated, considering tactics. Wily old bird that he was, he knew this swashbuckling young man with the rake's air and the arrogant eyes was not one to be either pushed or led. He greeted Nicholas casually, then added, "I want a private word with the earl and countess of Woolege. I wonder if you would do me a favor, young man, and remove that beautiful daughter of theirs. Keep her out of the way for a good half hour, if you will."

"Of course, m'Lord." Negligently, Nicholas approached the Woolege daughter. Cressida was as comely and as light on her feet as any other wench in the ballroom. Gad, but how Rose would turn the heads in such a grand gathering, he thought, as he whirled his partner into the throng. With the ribbons and baubles of high fashion, would she not dazzle and amaze!

Cressida, too, had gold hair—yellowish hair, he corrected himself—but as faded as an old skirt compared to Rose's crowning glory. He half closed his eyes, watching her through his thick, dark lashes, seeing Rose in the Woolege diamond necklace, the glittering drop earrings. The longing and disquiet in him unleashed a raging energy, and all at once he was rushing his partner in and out of the dancers, moving at double time to the music in the way a mazurka was never intended to be danced.

Much later he bade his family good-night, declined a ride in the carriage, declined also a bed, tentatively offered, in Cavendish Square, then went out alone to find a cab. The sky was full of stars as he swung merrily along the Mall. The grand Rundull equipage with its six matching bays rolled smoothly by, and he waved, thinking gleefully of Rose in the big bed, waiting for him. The earl looked annoyed. But then he had been annoyed since ten o'clock, his normal bedtime.

Over the jangling of harness and the beating horses' hooves, Nicholas's baritone lifted on the air:

> "O my Luve's like a red, red *Rose*
> That's newly sprung in June;
> O my Luve's like the melodie
> That's sweetly played in tune."

He was going to his dear love, his refuge, and his

delight. Already, in his mind's eye, he could see her: her gold hair spread on the pillow, her dark lashes lying curled against her cheek. She would wake like a kitten, as she always did, stretching luxuriously, smiling even before she opened her eyes.

"Hurry up, hurry up," he urged the driver, his heart-beats quickening, his need for her burning unbearably.

Outside his rooms, Nicholas paid off the driver with a flourish. Dashing exuberantly past the doorman, he took the stairs two at a time. Without pausing to light the candle that stood on a table inside the door, he felt his way across the dark hall, and opened the bedroom door.

The faintest glow of early morning combined with the flare of the gaslight to show him the empty bed. He stumbled forward, touching the covers in bewilderment. "Rose!" The name was more than a name. It was an agonized cry of distress. "Rose!" He felt his way back to the hall fumbled for the lucifer matches, struck one, and lit a candle. He did not search the rooms. He knew she was not there. The scent of her had gone. Shocked, he sat down on the big sofa, his hands on his knees, and stared blankly into space.

9

"O my Luve's like a red, red rose
That's newly sprung in June:
O my Luve's like the melodie
That's sweetly played in tune."

Jerningham Wakefield was a heavy sleeper. Three hand-fuls of stones rattling against the window served only to drive him, with a muffled groan, onto his opposite side. The fourth brought him fully awake. He sat up in bed with a jerk, nightcap askew, his heart beating fast with excitement. Time to start for Gravesend?

Outside there was darkness. He fell back on the bed, disappointed, wondering what had wakened him. The sound came again. He swung his legs out of bed, pulling his nightshirt down over his knees. Someone was throw-ing pieces of metal, or stones, against the window! Nayti, his young Maori guest, he thought with a sleepy grin. Nayti, playing the fool on his last night in civilization.

He padded barefoot to the window and, lifting the sash, thrust his head outside. Down below, in the glow of the street lamp, he could just discern a form spread-eagled on the seat of a hackney cab, his cocked hat awry.

"Who's that?"

The cabby was standing in the street, looking up at him, right hand poised ready to take aim. "Sir, there's a gentleman to see you." He climbed stiffly back onto his box.

What a picture of inebriated disarray! "Who is it?" he called.

"Nicholas le Grys," came the slurred reply.

"Devil take it, Nicholas, is this the way her gracious majesty sends her guests home?" Jerningham burst into a hearty peal of laughter. "I'll come down and let you in." Pulling his gown around him, he slid his feet into the Chinese slippers that had not found a place in the overfull trunk standing ready in the lobby downstairs.

As he crossed the landing a light appeared beneath his father's door. "What's that infernal row?"

"It's Nicholas, Papa, come to say good-bye." Jerningham added good-humoredly, "Rather the worse for his evening, by the look of him."

"Grasp the nettle," said Edward Gibbon, manipulator of men.

"I'll do my best."

"Good lad."

It had been an immense disappointment to the Wakefield family that Nicholas had steadily refused to be cajoled into throwing in his lot with the colonizers. Refused even to discuss the idea of marrying Rose, which would have put him directly into their hands. The earl of Rundull, faced with a daughter-in-law from his own kitchens, was, the Wakefield family knew, more than capable of delivering a kick that would send his erring son to the colonies for life.

Jerningham opened the front door and hurried out into the misty street. Nicholas, holding onto the wheel of the cab for support, was paying the driver. "Come in, old friend. Tell me all about the high jinks of the upper crust." He offered a steadying arm and they went together into the house.

In the front parlor, Jerningham lit the gas. The flaring light showed a room stuffily overfurnished, in accordance with the style of the times. Pictures and photographs, shaded lamps, antimacassars on velvet chairs, artificial flowers beneath glass domes, a heavily leafed aspidistra in a shining copper pot. The fire was black and inhospitably cold. "Sit down while I fetch the port."

Nicholas fell loosely into the chair. Looking up, he saw a stern pair of eyes gazing at him from the opposite wall. Elizabeth Fry, teetotaler! Staggering to his feet, he turned her picture to the wall. His host came back with a decanter and two glasses. "It probably don't mix with champagne."

"I was drinking brandy," said Nicholas, having forgotten about the champagne.

"Brandy and port?" Jerningham hesitated, his better nature coming briefly to the fore; then he shrugged and poured a measure. "D'you realize that today is the most exciting day of my life? I shall be aboard *Tory* by noon, and tomorrow we head out for Plymouth Sound.

Nicholas, thinking of Rose, tried to pull his scattered thoughts together. Jerningham was going away, but for the life of him he could not remember where.

"So what happened at the palace?" Jerningham's eyes sparkled. "How I would have liked to be there! It's ironic that the origin of my father's best deeds render him socially untouchable."

Nicholas stared down into his glass.

"Gad, you're drunk! Where've you been? You didn't really get like that at the palace, did you?"

"How do you know what happens at the palace?" Nicholas had not intended to be surly, but neither was he ready to confide his reasons for drinking half a bottle of brandy at his rooms.

Jerningham bridled, mistaking Nicholas's rudeness for arrogance. Underneath, and it was underneath that showed when a man was the worse for drink, Nicholas thought of the Wakefields as middle class. Jerningham made a mental note to pay him out. "Now tell me, who was there, dancing a noble quadrille?"

"The Queen was there," replied Nicholas, manifestly and unnecessarily precise. "And the grand duke, and a lot of stiff-necked notables, all behaving with considerable decorum." Heaven alone knew what had happened to his tongue. "The prime minister toadying Whiggishly. Lord knows where he'll turn when the Tories throw him out. And rows of giggling wenches decked out like . . . like . . . May blossom."

Jerningham snorted appreciatively. "May blossom!" he repeated. "Does this mean you've met a twig of May blossom that's to your taste?"

Nicholas gulped his drink and his head spun.

"Whom did you partner, Nicholas?"

"Lady Cressida Amhurst. Remember her? The wench with the pox and the wooden leg and bald pate?"

Jerningham looked startled. "She was there? How does a wench execute the waltz on a wooden leg?"

"She hasn't got a wooden leg. Nor a bald pate," Nicholas said categorically, adding, "She's remarkably pretty."

"Really? Last year, when I went with my father to Canada on the Durham Mission, our letters from home were full of gossip of Woolege's girls. Lord Durham mentioned there might be a good chance for me, if no one of the right standing offered. Leftovers," said Jerningham, good-humored because life was presently offering him something far, far more to his immediate taste than a successful marriage, "were ever the happy lot of young men without prospects. If she's still available when I get back from the Antipodes," he grinned mischievously, "should I consider her?"

Nicholas was staring at the wall, seeing a collage of two golden-haired girls, one glowing and radiant, the other demure. "She looks like Rose," he said.

Jerningham's brows shot up.

"She looks rather like Rose," Nicholas amended. Jerningham waited, watching his friend closely. "Rose," offered Nicholas, his voice breaking as he remembered why he was here, "has gone."

There was silence in the room. Jerningham's heart began to beat a little faster. How he wished his father would bestir himself and come downstairs, he who would manage this situation so much more smoothly. Suddenly, the solution leaped into Jerningham's mind.

"Then you're free to marry this girl who's so like Rose, and join Uncle William and me in New Zealand," he said innocently.

"Rose has gone," repeated Nicholas.

Jerningham, his mind alert and keen, said sympathetically, "I appreciate her disappearance must be a shock. But you knew it had to come. You can't keep a girl like that shut up in rooms in London. She was bound to get bored and run off to her own kind." Placing a hand on Nicholas's shoulder, he said warmly, "Papa could arrange for you and your entourage to have quarters in the first emigrant ship. You could bring your own staff in steerage. If the Lady Cressida looks like Rose, then grab her and bring her to New Zealand."

Nicholas rubbed two fingers across his forehead. "I was talking about Rose," he muttered.

"Your father wants an heir," Jerningham pointed out craftily. "Cressida could provide an heir. Rose could not."

"Rose could. Of course she could."

"No, old fellow. That's just what Rose could not do. You can't have the next earl of Rundull great-grandson to the butler."

"The Conqueror. Bastard to a tanner's daughter."

Jerningham chuckled indulgently. "Remember 1066 was a long time ago, Nicholas. You know Papa's plans. The seeds of our new country must be of good stock. Lady Cressida's children would be wellborn."

"Rose could have a dozen shons. Shon," he repeated irritably. "God damn it, Jerningham. Port on brandy!"

Jerningham grinned. "It won't do you any harm. Drink it up." The plan formulating cunningly in his mind took firm shape. "You mean Cressida," he amended. He paused a moment, then repeated the name. "Cressida, Nicholas, who looks like Rose. In view of Adeline's being barren, you have the responsibility of producing this well-born son. Cressida's son." Surreptitiously, he topped up Nicholas's drink.

Nicholas began to sing softly, "O my luve's like a red, red rose." The despair had gone. In his mind, the two girls began to merge. He was glad he'd come. Jerningham's company, for once, was proving a comfort.

Afterward, Nicholas remembered Jerningham helping him into the gig. But that was all.

"O my Luve's like a red, red rose . . ."

They pelted down the road, past the nursery gardens at Chelsea, past the new town houses the city merchants had built on the drained swamps of Belgravia, their voices soaring on the night air. At Hyde Park Corner, where the cows were still asleep at the roadside, Jerningham tightened his reins. As they entered Piccadilly he brought his horse to a stop. Nicholas looked up. "Where are we?"

"Outside Roddy Cameron's house, and here he is, creeping home. Hello, Roddy!" A young man in top hat and the newly fashionable long-waisted frock coat leaned against a lamppost in the misty gaslight smoking a cheroot. He smiled complacently at the occupants of the gig. "Time you were indoors," boomed Jerningham good-humoredly.

"Time you were there, too," their friend retorted, leaving the safely of the post, and staggering toward them. "What are you rackety fellows up to?" His tall hat fell into the gutter, and he stooped to retrieve it.

"To propose to the Lady Cressida Amhurst, who looks like a rose," announced Jerningham, his heart beating faster with excitement. "Hop aboard, Roddy, and come with us." The young man slammed his hat back on his head at a rakish angle, and weaved closer, throwing away the stump of his cheroot as he came. Wobbling dangerously, he raised one foot to the step.

> "O my Luve's like a red, red rose
> That's newly sprung in June . . ."

Nicholas, head back, his dark hair falling in a windblown tangle, filled the night with his beautiful voice. A window went up with a crash and a nightcapped head appeared.

"What in the name of all that's human is going on down there?"

"Nicholas le Grys at your service." Jerningham stood up precariously in the gig to effect a bow. "On the way to propose to the Lady Cressida Amhurst."

"Then get on with it, young fellow, and allow me to finish my sleep. Roddy! Is that you, Roddy? Come in this minute, my boy."

Their passenger swung obediently but dangerously off the step, overbalanced into the street, and staggered toward his front door.

Jerningham whipped up the horses. That a fellow should be so lucky! Roddy Cameron was one of the greatest gossips in town, and as for his mother . . . By mid-morning the news would be halfway around London. They sped noisily over the deserted granite setts of Piccadilly, Jerningham's voice rising to a victorious shout.

*   *   *

"As fair art thou, my bonnie lass,
So deep in luve am I
And I will luve thee still, my dear,
Till a' the seas gang dry."

They swept into Berkeley Square, and Jerningham allowed the sweating horse to slow to a walk. Its breath billowed mistily in the cool air. "Here we are!"

Nicholas blinked up at a tall gray stone house. He knew this house, or thought he did, but he could not remember to whom it belonged.

"Where are we?"

"Your rose is here. Your love who's like a red, red rose," said Jerningham glibly. "Stand up. We're going to sing together at the top of our voices, and get her out of bed."

Nicholas blinked up at the house.

"Come on," urged his friend. "Come on. Stand up and sing up."

"O my luve's like a red, red rose . . ."

"Louder. Louder," urged the mischief-maker.

A window went up with a clatter, and then another, and another. "There she is!" cried Jerningham triumphantly.

Nicholas blinked and there she was at a window, her golden hair framing her sweet, pale face.

"Rose!"

"Marry me!" shouted Jerningham in the best imitation he could manage of Nicholas's voice. "This is a proposal." There were faces at every window now, and laughter too. Here and there a ribald comment. Lights went on in houses on either side. Then there were more faces, more cries of encouragement. More derision.

Jerningham was beside himself. "Strike up again. At the top of your voice, Nicholas. At the top of your voice!"

Nicholas held out his arms to the dear face smiling down at him. They sang over the laughter, over the insults from angry citizens wakened from their sleep. Jerningham's riotous good humor was infectious. The louder the protests, the louder they raised their voices.

"I want to get out," said Nicholas urgently. But

Jerningham was wielding the whip, urging the horse to move on.

"It's too early, old fellow. She's not even dressed. Blow her a kiss, and we'll come back later."

"Let me out, you clown. Let me out." But the gig was already sweeping victoriously around the square. "Rose," Nicholas shouted helplessly, losing his balance and collapsing into the seat. "Rose!"

His mischief done, Jerningham made off toward St. James's.

Nicholas wakened to a thunderous knocking on his door. He staggered from the sofa where he had fallen only a few hours before, his black dress coat crumpled, the embroidered satin waistcoat awry, his frilled shirt crushed, the stock limp, and his head feeling as though it had been hit with a sledgehammer. Lurching across the room and into the hall, he pushed open the door and stood looking at the doorman with loathing.

"What the devil is all this rumpus about?"

"Sir, there's a messenger downstairs from the court as wants a word with you."

Nicholas put a hand to his head. A messenger from the court? God in heaven! The Queen! "Send the man off," he ordered, his voice rough with shock. He retreated into his rooms and opened the windows wide, took a long, dizzying draft of air that smelled of horses, dung, and dust, then sat down heavily on the sofa. But he had forgotten to shut the door, and when he looked up, the man was standing nearby, an apologetic expression on his half-whiskered face.

"What is it?"

The man shifted from one foot to the other. "I'm very sorry to trouble you, sir, but a messenger's come from the court, sir. He's been sent by the girl . . ."

"What girl?"

"She was brought in last night for brawlin' in Covent Garden or thereabouts."

"Brawling?" Nicholas's eyes were fixed starkly on the man's face.

"She spent the night at the Old Bailey in a cell."

Rose! "Get me a cab," he said tersely. "Have him

wait. Ask the boy to tell them I'll be at the court presently."

Rose's cell had a stone floor that had not been cleaned for a very long time. The one tiny window, barred and set high in the wall, let in very little air. She had spent the night huddled in a corner, crying. The stench was appalling. Fourteen unwashed bodies, and herself in a worse state than the others, for this morning she had been sick again. Her vomit lay where it had fallen, for there was no basin. Some of it was smeared disgustingly on her dress and in her hair.

A thin old man came along ringing his handbell. "Court's open." Rose was too deep in hopeless despair even to look up. It was hours since she had persuaded that boy, with fervent promises of money from Nicholas, to go to St. James's. Yet, Nicholas had not come. Several of the women who had been quarreling noisily moved over to the bars and addressed a chorus of insults to an approaching officer. There was the sound of a key in the lock.

"Snape," said the turnkey, "there's a gen'l'man what's come to bail you out."

Grasping the rags of the tarlatan dress around her, Rose stumbled to her feet. Nicholas had come! Someone spat viciously on her bare arm, but she scarcely noticed. In a hail of expletives from the other prisoners, she blundered stiffly toward the barred door.

Nicholas, waiting uncomfortably in the outer court-yard, slapping his cane against his boots, caught his lower lip between his teeth as Rose, in the guise of a filthy street urchin, came into view. Her uncombed hair drooped on her shoulders, her beautiful eyes were red and swollen from crying. Even at this distance, she smelled vile. His bewilderment changed to disbelief, and then reluctantly to disgust. She came trustingly toward him, whimpering like a puppy. Hating himself, he took an involuntary step backward, Felicity's damning voice ringing through his mind. *"What do you think you can do with a kitchen maid? She came from the gutter and she'll go back there, because that's where she belongs."*

He wanted to upbraid Rose, yell at her, tell her she had let him down, shattered his dream, proved everyone right, and himself wrong. He wanted to turn and march away, leaving her in the squalor that, after all, as Felicity had so ungraciously pointed out, was her heritage.

An official came importantly forward. "Brawlin'," he said. "Common brawlin', sir. The court's waiting. Do you wish to speak for her, sir?"

Nicholas passed a hand across his eyes. It was a bad dream. He would wake up in a moment.

"She is your servant, sir?" asked the man.

"Nicholas." The green eyes gazed up at him, dark now with fear.

"Tell the court I'll pay whatever fine there is." Nicholas swung on his heel so that he did not have to look into those drowning eyes.

"Nicholas." It was the cry of a small animal, the runt of the pack, somehow knowing with utter despair that it was going to be abandoned. Propelled by something beyond his control, Nicholas turned as the ragged figure was led away. She looked so vulnerable that his face twisted with a pity that grew and grew until he had to crush it.

Running from the cutting knives of his conscience, he hurried out into the street, but the clatter of carriages, horses' shoes, gigs and cabriolets, the shouts of drivers, and the rattling of carts went so painfully through his head that he was forced to return to the relative quiet of the court. He stood staring at the wall, mindlessly whipping his calves with his cane.

When the case was over, a court official called him to pay the twelve-shilling fine. He produced the coins in angry silence, throwing them down in front of the man, who took his emotional fury for lordly disdain and said fawningly, "Thank you, sir. Thank you, sir."

He strode off through the court with Rose pattering at his side. Even without turning to her, he could have described with accuracy the expression of humility, fear, and shame on her face. He kept his face averted as he led her to the coach stand. There was a tattered hansom waiting, a dingy gray transport, whose elegant past showed here and there in the yellow outlines on the wheels, and the nearly obliterated coat of arms on the panels. A thin horse stood patiently between the shafts, its head droop-

ing. The driver, hands in pockets, leaned hunch-shoul-
dered against a lamppost.

Nicholas spoke to him sharply, giving the address. The
man jumped to attention and opened the door. Nicholas
pressed a shilling into Rose's hand. She looked up at him
pitifully, her lips quivering. "Aren't you coming with
me?"

"I'll walk." He slammed the door violently, shutting
out the unacceptable. The hansom rumbled off, and he
strode behind it, slapping his calves once more with his
cane, harder and harder until, even through the thick
Hessian boots, the pain went beyond pain and brought
numbness. On the next corner there was a public house.
He slammed the door open with his fist, and shouldered
through.

10

Nicholas brushed a hand across his brow, drew in his breath with a sharp hiss, and emptied the glass of the last mouthful of brandy. Better go back to his rooms now, and get on with what had to be done. He'd been out of his mind to bring Rose to London. What mistakes a man made when the lust was in him.

It was true, as he had told his sister, that many well set-up young swells of his acquaintance had a mistress. It was also true, as she had retorted and as he had refused to admit at the time, that they chose women either from their own class or from a rung or so down the ladder. Cavorting in the long grass of the Rundull estate with kitchen maids was one thing, Felicity had delicately inferred, but bringing them to London was quite another.

Felicity was right. You shouldn't run against the tide. The lower classes were primitive. His father was right. They were where they were because they had not learned how to behave. Nicholas rose to his feet, threw a handful of coins on the counter, then went out into the street to look for a ragamuffin who would get him a cab.

Stepping down in St. James's, reaching for his purse to pay the driver, Nicholas froze. The Rundull town chariot with the family's coat of arms on the door was drawn up not more than a dozen paces away. The coachman in top boots and cockade sat dreaming on the box. Flinging some silver to the cabby, Nicholas strode forward, his face dark with apprehension.

"Shard?"

The man wakened with a jerk, and respectfully touched his hat with the whip handle. "Mr. Nicholas, sir."

"What are you doing here?"

"I've been sent by his Lordship to bring you to Cavendish Square, Mr. Nicholas."

Nicholas considered the summons grimly.

"There's a letter for you, Mr. Nicholas. I delivered it up to them rooms."

The shock brought some of the events of the night before tumbling back. He remembered going to the Wakefields, but not why. He rubbed his forehead. After drinking the brandy, which was supposed to make him forget Rose, he had had a muddled idea of going to New Zealand with Jerningham and of taking her with them. But the brandy and champagne had caught up with him, and he had passed out on the way to Hans Place. He could recall no more. Raw from the events of the morning, Nicholas's temper flared. "Be off with you, Shard."

The coachman's brows came down in a worried frown. "I've been sent to get you, Master Nicholas, an' bring you back." Nicholas noted the change from "Mister" to "Master" and his wrath grew. That was the trouble with servants who grew up with the family. They still saw one as a small, naughty boy. It was Shard who had taught him to manage horses. Shard's grandfather had taught his own father four-in-hand driving on the coachman's box.

"You heard me," Nicholas barked, swinging on his heel, leaving the coachman in no doubt as to his intentions. He turned at the door, snarling an afterthought, just in case Edward had been in touch. "Tell my father I was in my cups last night." He took a fob watch out of his waistcoat pocket. The stagecoach might already have gone. He'd have to hire a post chaise for Rose. He set off up the stairs at a run.

She heard his footsteps on the landing and went quietly to the door. Seeds of a plan, stylish in its execution, unswerving in its resolution, new to her, but old as time, had begun tentatively to sprout in Rose's brain. She had bathed her eyes with cold water. The swelling had eased. Her hair had been swiftly washed and lay smoothly, demurely, over her ears. Golden ringlets danced on her forehead. Her lawn dress, showered with rosebuds and totally unsuited to morning wear, exposed the rounded, creamy curve of her breasts. The skirt bunched out over her hips, accentuating her shape. Her big emerald eyes were limpid wells of desire. Her mouth opened tremblingly like the flower of her name.

Nicholas looked at her and, as Rose had tremulously planned, his mind filled with her vivid, tantalizing beauty, her enchantment, her sorcery, and her signature over a million promises. Swiftly, he closed the door and strode forward, a fiery, urgent thirst raging through him with joyous familiarity.

"Sweet," he murmured, his lips against her scented hair, his whole being on fire at the touch of her soft, pliant body. "Sweet, my darling love."

They stood with their hearts beating together, then he moved her tenderly to arm's length and looked at her. This was no kitchen maid, no street bawd, no giver of cheap sensations. This was a woman of eroticism, sympathy, and tenderness. A woman who—how could he have forgotten?—had transported him time and again to undreamed heights of rapture.

He bent her head back against the curve of his arm and kissed her, parting her lips softly at first, as though they had only just met and this was a trial kiss; then hardening, until the wild singing in his heart merged with the male need in him, and he swept her up, striding with her into the bedroom, flinging her onto the bed, groping for the fastenings of her dress, her stays, her ribbons and bows. Send her back to the village? May God forgive him for the thought. She was his. He would never let her go.

A long time later, lying side by side in the disheveled bed, Rose whispered, "I have to tell you what happened."

"No." He put a finger to her lips. "It's all over. I have a plan."

She moved his fingers gently with her small ones. "But I want to tell you, Nicholas. I want to explain."

"No. It doesn't matter. It can never happen again. Listen, my darling. Last night I saw my friend Jerningham Wakefield, who is sailing for New Zealand today."

Protectively, hungrily, he held her close, telling her what was in his mind. Passenger ships were to go in

September. He and she would join one of them. It would be a magnificent adventure, but, above and beyond that, they would leave the kitchen maid behind.

Rose's heart sang as she listened and visualized the dream. To go over the seas in a sailing ship! To a land of milk and honey, where she would become Nicholas's wife. The new Rose answered, tremulously at first, and then with conviction. "Yes, yes. Oh, my darling." Anything could happen. If you really wanted it to.

"I'll buy land. Jerningham's father will arrange that we get on the first passenger boat, so that I shall have first choice of land." He put his lips to her hair. "As my wife, as the wife of the biggest landowner, for I shall see to it that I am, you will be a person of importance. A complete cross-section of English society is going. Gentlemen of independent means, to be squires and own the land; tradesmen to supply their needs; mechanics and craftsmen to build their houses; laborers to make their roads, and man their farms." Edward's rhetoric rolled easily out of his memory, and over his tongue.

No one would dare cut the wife of the Honorable Nicholas le Grys of Castle Rundull in Kent, sister-in-law to one of the Queen's maids of honor, daughter-in-law to Lady Rundull, who had waited for Queen Charlotte.

He lifted her hand to his lips, possessively, and kissed her arm right up to the elbow. He traced her delicate profile with his fingers. How soft her skin was. "We'll take Cossack," he said, "and a mare for you. I'll teach you to ride." Rose, who was so clever, who learned about clothes so quickly, who could embroider like an angel after only one lesson, would soon learn to ride. Edward Wakefield's words scattered through his brain. *"You could be a king in this new land."*

You could do anything if you were king.

He looked down confidently into Rose's beautiful face, seeing her vividly as the lady of the manor. His lovely consort. His queen.

Bright-eyed, aglow with excitement, Rose drew herself into a sitting position. "I think we ought to answer that door."

Nicholas started, then burst out laughing. "Poor Shard." He kissed her again and leaped out of bed, pulled on his strapped pantaloons, flinging a shirt loosely round his shoulders, running a hand through his disordered hair.

It was his brother Henry who stood on the step. Henry, impeccably dressed in high boots and riding smalls, an expression of enormous irritation on his thin face. "Papa asked me to call and see you into the coach," he said coldly. "What's keeping you, for heaven's sake? Shard's downstairs with orders to bring you." He saw the satiety, the arrogant amusement in Nicholas's face, and turned away, embarrassment showing in his eyes. "You'd better hurry," he mumbled. "I'll wait, but I'm not prepared to wait more than a few moments. I've an appointment."

"The deuce you'll see me into the coach!" flashed Nicholas. "I'll go when I'm ready."

"Nicholas." Henry turned back, his face serious. "I promised Papa I'd see you into the coach. I *must* see you into the coach."

Nicholas grinned. "What's he so worked up about?"

"God in heaven! Haven't you read the note?"

"No."

"You're a casual bastard."

Nicholas slammed the door in his brother's face and went back inside. Something of Henry's concern had crept into his consciousness. An envelope emblazoned with the family crest lay on the table. He stood looking at it thoughtfully for a moment, before taking up a paper knife and slitting it open. The single sheet of parchment crackled as he unfolded it. The message in his father's huge scrawl was brief.

The Earl of Woolege is to wait upon us at noon. Have the goodness to be here a half hour earlier.

Nicholas blinked. Disjointed memories from the night filtered through his brain. He remembered Woolege from the ball, but not that he had spoken to him. He'd danced with the daughter. He wondered whether Woolege had something to do with Wakefield's plan. Edward was a past master at gathering the great and important behind him.

He felt the touch of a hand on his arm. Rose, voluptuously folded into his dressing gown, looked up into his face. "I have to go to Cavendish Square," he said regretfully. "I won't be long."

"No."

He stood looking down at her in surprise. "Don't go," she said urgently, putting her arms around his neck, lifting her face. "Don't go. Not now. Go tomorrow."

Gently, he put her away from him. "I'm not going to tell them about us. Not yet." A letter sent back by the captain of the ship would suffice when the marriage was a fait accompli.

"Please, Nicholas, don't go."

"What's the matter, darling?" Rose's eyes were enormous. One hand lay against her heart in the semi-theatrical gesture that came so naturally to her.

"I don't know. I only know that you shouldn't go. I know it, Nicholas." She grasped one of his hands, holding it close between her palms.

He looked down at her with all the consuming love he felt for her in his eyes, but with no conception of the wringing of her heart, the bleak, ominiscient dread that enveloped her.

"Nicholas . . ."

He did not hear the lost, despairing cry as he left. The outer door opened silently and a cold wind spun up the stairs, streaked across the hall, and set Rose shivering. Then it banged shut, and he was gone.

In normal circumstances, Nicholas would have ordered Shard to drive him around to the mews to say hello to Cossack. He decided it was better not to keep his Lordship waiting today. He stepped down from the carriage outside the imposing, pillared façade. Shard and his equipage rolled away.

The door was opened by a footman in livery. "Good morning, Quick." Nicholas offered his top hat.

"Good morning, Mr. Nicholas." The servant was about the same age as himself. Tall, blond-haired, with a good English face and honest eyes. Nicholas had known him since he came into service at fourteen, and had always liked him.

"Are you happy in your work, Quick?" Nicholas asked as they crossed the hall.

"Perfectly, Mr. Nicholas. Why do you ask?"

"I'm emigrating to New Zealand and shall need house-hold staff. I wondered if you'd care to come with me."

The man's eyes blazed. "Oh, Mr. Nicholas!"

"That's settled, then. What kind of mood is my father in?"

"Very good, Mr. Nicholas."

That was a surprise, in the circumstances. Nicholas's spirits rose.

"And thank you very much. I'm grateful," the foot-man said, then added, his eyes consideringly on Nicholas's face, "I would not have thought of leaving his Lordship's service, sir."

"Don't worry. It's all in the family." There was no spite in Nicholas's nature, but his eyes tilted now with sardonic amusement. The family might consider the loss of a servant or two a small price to pay to get him away from Rundull. He paused at the entrance to the high-ceilinged, stately drawing room, pale and elegant with its Adam fireplace and smooth plaster walls; modern by comparison with the stark, aged grandeur of Rundull Castle, where a stone buttress stood at loggerheads with paneling, and vast Flemish tapestries kept out the cold.

"Thank you, Mr. Nicholas. Thank you very much," Quick said again.

The good-humored smile faded from Nicholas's face, as it struck him forcefully that he might have made a mistake. It would be nigh on impossible for Rose to command a houseful of servants, who had, in another incarnation, been her superiors. "I'll talk to you later, Quick. Don't mention it to anyone for the moment." He would have to withdraw his offer and look elsewhere.

Rose heard the insistent knocking and dragged herself awake. Had Nicholas forgotten to take his key? She slid off the bed, and hurried through the rooms, her face soft with sleep. She opened the door, then recoiled sharply Snape, familiar in his dusty black coat and muttonchop whiskers, stood on the step.

"Grandy!" Rose's hand flew to her mouth. "Grandy, what are you doing here?" She backed away.

He followed her into the room, and closed the door quietly behind him. "Come, my darling," he urged her gently, "gather up your things. I'm taking you back to Rundull."

"No." Rose's face was sheet-white. "No, Grandy. No. I'm to stay with Nicholas."

His eyes swept over her with reluctant, compassionate distaste, noting the bright hair loose on her shoulders, Nicholas's dressing gown that dragged on the floor.

With a heavy sigh, he sat down on the straight-backed sofa, prepared to argue a little, to give the shock time to subside. "As I've always told you, him and the likes of us don't mix. I've been sent to take you away."

"Not by him," Rose denied fiercely. "He'll be back soon. You may as well go now, Grandy, because he'd be very angry to find you here."

The butler looked at her with compassion. "Dearie, he's not coming back."

She would not allow the words to sink in. She would not have them meet the fear that had lodged at the back of her mind when Nicholas had read the message and had said he had to go. "Go away," she screeched in terror.

Snape rose and took her cold, trembling hands, holding them firmly in his. "Listen, Rosie. This young scoundrel is to be married."

She became icy cold and still. Inside her head a voice shrieked, "He's going to marry me!" but she made no sound. The ghosts of generations from the past—the raped, the degraded, the defeated, the always-losers—came with their sighs to scoop the warm, solid present from her and to replace it with agonizing pain.

"He's marrying the daughter of another earl, as is right," said Grandy, trying to sound matter-of-fact, and not succeeding because the child's agony had communicated itself to him, alarming him with its intensity.

"No." Rose's lips formed the denial but the words were a mere breath.

"Yes, dearie. Ive been told to tell you, though goodness knows, I'd rather not. It's a lady by the name of Lady Cressida Amhurst he's proposed to, and they're sailing for New Zealand because, as you know, he can't stay at Rundull . . ." The old man's voice trailed off, and he let her hands go, fishing in his pocket for a handkerchief.

"Get your things, dearie. Young Barney Herd, who is to go as Master Nicholas's valet, will be coming over shortly to collect his clothes. 'Twere better for you to be gone then."

Mindlessly, moving as a puppet moves, she went into the bedroom and sat down on the big four-poster bed, the scene of their giving and taking. She reached out, and her fingers closed convulsively on the muslin gown Nicholas had torn from her in his passion such a short time ago. She held it against her face, and a terrible keening came from the depths of her, rising to the ceiling and filling the room, an agony outside her control. She heard it as from afar, yet knew it was herself, dying. After a while she was aware of Grandy on the bed beside her, holding her against his heart, clumsily, not knowing what to do, how to stifle the shocking sound.

"Hush, Rose, you'll wake the dead. Hush, my darling." She could not.

"I'm going to have to get your Gran, Rose," he said at last, desperately. "She's waiting in the coach. I'll have to get her if you won't stop. But I don't want to, you know that."

The wailing stayed, shredding her, and after a while the soothing hand, the hard shirt front were not there. The animal in her sensed danger. Like a cat leaping, Rose came back to life. She raced to the outer door, banging it shut. But she was too late. Mrs. Snape, high-bosomed, black-bonneted, avenging, pushed the door wide. Behind her came Barney Herd, brisk and lively in his low-crowned hat and button boots.

"Hello, young Rose. My! You do look a treat!" His leering eyes took in Nicholas's dressing gown. "How's tricks? I come to get Mr. Nicholas's things. Orl right if I go in?"

Rose felt her grandmother's hard hand on her shoulder, then she was spun round and pushed into a chair. She heard Barney's "Tut, tut!" as he made for the bedroom with his cheeky, bouncing walk. Then he paused, pointing at Rose. "I'll need that gown. Part of Mr. Nicholas's wardrobe, huh."

"Get on with your work," snapped Mrs. Snape, sitting stiffly beside Rose. Grandy stood uncomfortably by the table, looking blankly out of the window. From the bedroom came sounds of drawers opening and closing, of locks clicking. After a long while, Herd came out dragging a trunk. "Every good thing comes to an end, eh, Rose?" he taunted her, not wholly unkindly.

"Give over," said Snape sharply.

"That gown don't belong to 'er, Mr. Snape."

"Leave it. Leave it, I said." With unaccustomed belligerence, Snape escorted the manservant to the door and returned, his face crumpled with pity.

Rose said, "He asked me to marry him. Nicholas and I were to go to New Zealand together."

"Oh Rose. Do I have to say it again? The gentry don't marry the likes of us."

Rose's face hardened, but the vulnerability grew in her staring eyes. "If he wasn't going to marry me, why did he ask me?"

"The gentry are a law unto themselves, dearie. Only they know what they mean. Come, little girl, put your things together. His Lordship's given me the use of a carriage, and I'm to take you to Rundull."

She flinched. "Lady Priscilla . . ."

"M'Lady is here, in London, where she'll stay for the season. Or at least until the wedding."

"I don't believe it," said Rose. "I don't . . ." and then, remembering the ghastly moment of rejection in the court that morning, her voice broke. She remembered, too, with driving shame, Nicholas's expression of disgust as he turned away from her. But he had come back after that, and asked her to marry him. She sat up with a new sense of urgency. Something could be done. Something must be done. Then she recoiled, as her grandmother dealt her a stinging slap on the shoulder.

"I said get up, you little varmint." The tough, sinewy arms pushed her gentle grandfather away when he tried to intervene. "Get dressed and out of this disgusting den of sin. What would your poor dead mother say! She must be turning in her grave."

"If my mother was here, she wouldn't let you treat me like this," Rose sobbed. As she stumbled into the bedroom she heard her grandfather murmur his sad agreement and felt gentle warmth suffuse her. A strength beyond anything she had ever felt before stiffened her spine and lifted her head.

"Rose!"

She looked up at the dark, hard figure of her grandmother standing in the doorway.

Anne Worboys

"I swear," her voice rang out clear and determined, "on the soul of my mother I shall not be parted from Nicholas."

She scarcely saw the woman move forward, she came so fast, but the blow felled her like a ninepin. She lay against the bed leg thinking dizzily, It will be all right. It will be all right. "I swear it," she whispered, but under her breath, so no one heard.

11

———————————

"And about time, too," growled the earl, looking up from his high-backed chair. "What kept you?"

"I had important matters to attend to. What is it you want of me?"

The earl reached out toward a carved gilt console table, from which he lifted a sheet of writing paper between finger and thumb. "I have received a note from Edward Wakefield."

Nicholas loosened his waistcoat, flung out his coattails, and relaxed thankfully against the brocade cushions of the Queen Anne sofa, one long leg stretched to full length, the other bent elegantly at the knee. "Edward is nothing if not an opportunist," he observed, glancing up casually at the fat plaster cherubs on the ceiling.

The earl frowned sharply. "Read this."

Nicholas thrust the paper away. "I can imagine what's in it," he said sardonically. "Edward will have one of my feet already on the gangplank. However, this morning I have given the matter some thought, and I've come to a definite decision that ought to please you. If he can arrange accommodation on the first passenger boat, I'll go."

"Splendid. Splendid!" The earl folded the letter down the center and slapped it triumphantly against the back of his hand. "Now let's get on to Woolege." He took a gold watch out of his fob pocket, glanced at it, then back to Nicholas. "He'll be here soon. First of all, there's to be no mention of your rooms in St. James's. That's a closed chapter. So far as the Wooleges are concerned, you're living in this house, and have been here all along. We have arranged for you to move in today."

Nicholas jerked erect in his seat. "What do you mean, you've arranged? And what the devil has the earl of Woolege to do with my domestic arrangements?"

The earl slapped his open hand down on the chair arm. "Damn and blast you, son, I'm talking about the scullery maid you've had in your rooms. Everyone expects a young man to sow his wild oats, but he don't expect to mix 'em up with his marriage. What I'm saying is, Cressida don't know anything about the matter, and with that baggage packed off home, she need never know."

"Cressida?" Nicholas asked faintly.

"It's by the by now, of course, but I'll say in passing I never knew even the wildest buck propose to a lady, then bed his whore within an hour. I'll give you this," the earl growled, his eyes gleaming beneath lowered, bushy brows with a hint of reluctant admiration, "you've got the blood of the old Rundulls, and their mettle."

Nicholas came slowly to his feet. "This is preposterous. I didn't propose marriage to the girl." Even as he said it, he felt a growing sense of dread.

"That you did," retorted his father, banging one fist down on the table with such force that a small porcelain ornament rocked dangerously. "There's no point in denying it. Half London have the story on their tongues."

Nicholas put a hand to his forehead. There had to be an explanation. He remembered returning to his rooms and finding Rose gone. He recalled taking a half bottle of brandy from the cupboard. He remembered the pain, the desperate need for oblivion.

"I must have been blind drunk. A man can't be held responsible for what he does when he's so drunk he can't even remember." Yet already memory had begun to return.

"O my Luve's like a red, red rose . . ."

But he had sung to Rose, not the Wooleges' daughter! To Rose! He and Jerningham. In the gig. They had gone to his rooms. Surely. Rose had been at the window. Yes, she had been there. At the window. He could see her now. Clear as day. Golden hair falling on either side of her face . . .

The picture shattered. Rose had been in jail! Nicholas looked at his father. His father looked back at him without compassion. "That you were so inebriated," he said scathingly, "that you cannot remember, has very little bearing on the matter. The facts are not in dispute."

Nicholas jerked to his feet. He strode to the end of the long room and back. His face was ashen. A nerve twitched in his cheek. He came to stand before his father. "I can't be held to an offer I made when drunk." His voice was fierce.

"You can be held to an offer you made, drunk or sober. How dare you stand there bold as brass and tell me, *tell me* . . ." In his fury, the earl of Rundull spluttered into silence. A half moment later he said more calmly, but still with total resolution, "Woolege is on his way. You're obliged to ask properly for the gel's hand now, and, should she accept you, you will marry her. D'ye hear me, sir? *You will marry her.*"

Nicholas's pacing came to an abrupt stop. He said ferociously, "Drop it, Papa. I do not intend to marry her. I will *not* marry her."

His father's quiet voice broke through his bitter thoughts. "Then I wish you luck in getting out of it, with, as I said, half London already talking. You woke up everyone between Hans Place and Berkeley Square, not to mention all the Wooleges' neighbors . . ."

Nicholas went to the window and stood looking out into the garden. He would have to tell his father about Rose. He swung around, white to the lips. "This morning, I proposed to another girl. I've asked her to come to New Zealand with me."

The earl's facial muscles jerked. He glared at Nicholas, the color rising purple to bloat his face and neck. With both hands on the chair arms, he rose to his feet, chin thrust out. "How dare you propose to two of 'em! How dare you, sir!"

"I told you, I was not aware of having proposed to the Woolege girl. I have no recollection of it."

"Who is this other gel?"

"It doesn't really matter. What's done is done. I'm not as unchivalrous as you think. I can't marry both of them.

To avoid trouble, no doubt I could quickly marry . . ."
With his father's pale, bloodshot eyes murderously on
him, he paused.

"Who? Who? You haven't told me who!" thundered
the earl, bringing a fist down on the console table. A
porcelain figurine shot off and bounced across the carpet.

Nicholas considered his situation with horrifying clarity. He could not, would not, marry Cressida Amhurst.
Marrying Rose now would undoubtedly mean being cut
off with the proverbial shilling, but he could take an
assisted passage and travel steerage. Comfort was something Rose had done without all her life. He would not
be penalizing her. As for himself, it might be rather
amusing to turn the tables on those damnable Wakefields
by traveling steerage. And the future was now a challenge indeed. Here was an opportunity to find out if
Nicholas le Grys was made of the stuff of his ancestors.

The earl saw the lifted head, the devilment in the dark
eyes, and rose sharply erect, apoplectic with shock. "It's
that strumpet you've got in your rooms! You've proposed
to Snape's granddaughter! How dare you! You, the likely
inheritor of a title that goes back eight hundred years,
have the audacity to tell me you proposed marriage to a
kitchen maid and a whore!"

"The *unlikely* inheritor," Nicholas corrected him, holding back his own anger at the insult to his future
wife. "And, as for Rose," he added coldly, "when she's
my wife, she will not be a kitchen maid."

His father sat down slowly. There was a silence in the
room. The grandfather clock in the corner struck the
quarter hour. "Whatever happens to this girl," he said
deliberately, "wherever she lives, she will always be the
scum of the village. The scum of the village," the earl
repeated, "because that is what she is now, and that is
what she will stay. People don't change, Nicholas. People
are who they are, and they remain that way. Anyway,"
said his father, with awful finality, "the girl has been
collected by Snape, and is already on her way to Rundull,
where you may not go."

Florrie wriggled out of Rose's convulsive, welcoming grip.
"I don't see as, 'ow you can stay," she protested. "People

are goin' ter know yer're 'ere. They must know already. They'd 'ave seen you arrive."

"There was nobody." Rose's eyes pleaded with her. "I opened the door of the coach at the alley and ran."

"I wonder Gran didn't come after yer. She must've known where you was goin'."

Rose's lips trembled. "She tried to, but Grandy held her back." Fear swamped her as she saw that Florrie, in a defensive reaction, was withdrawing her small resources of caring, tucking them away out of reach. Panic put urgency into her voice. "Nobody saw me, Florrie. There was nobody in the alehouse. Nobody anywhere."

"Just because they didn't open their doors an' shout at yer don't mean they weren't standin' back from their windows spyin'," wailed Florrie. "What's Adam goin' ter say when 'e finds you 'ere? The Putnams could make things nasty fer 'im. An' even if 'e let yer stay, yer wouldn't be able ter walk out into the 'Igh Street or the fields. Yer couldn't imagine what they've done ter Daniel fer 'elpin' yer git away."

Rose's mouth went dry with fear. "What've they done to him?"

"They've put 'im out of their 'ouse, an' 'e's had ter go an' live up at the castle with one of them grooms. Someone put somethin' inter 'is ale—deadly nightshade they do say, an' 'e was sick almost ter death. What they'll do ter yer if they catch yer, I 'ate ter think." Florrie backed away. There were too many cruelties crowding in on her in that dark, little stone-floored room, with no legacy of hope.

"Florrie, I have to go somewhere. I can't go back to the castle. I can't."

"I don't see why not," Florrie whined self-protectively. "Why couldn't yer stay in London?"

"You don't know what London's like." Rose shuddered. "And I haven't any money." She wiped her eyes with the back of her hand. Somewhere along the road her lace-edged handkerchief had been lost.

"No." That was something Rose's sister understood. There never was any money. Never had been. But she had also done without food, which Rose had not, without rest, without comfort. She was unwilling to suffer anymore. "Yer've got ter go."

"Florrie, you're my sister!" Rose looked into her sister's indifferent eyes, willing her to respond.

But Florrie was too poor, too tired, for loyalty. Besides, one learned by example, and the Putnams had thrown Daniel out. "Yer'd better go," she repeated mindlessly.

Rose went to the door, drowning in hurt and a bitter incomprehension of human fallibility. She did not love Florrie, had never loved anyone except Nicholas. And Grandy. And, perhaps, more as a haven than a person dimly remembered, her mother, who had been the first one to let her down, by dying. But Florrie was her sister, her very nearest flesh and blood. Deeply, instinctively, Rose knew that families were supposed to give protection. That, even without love, one did not turn a relation away.

At the door, she turned, abject in her humiliation. She had been going to say, childishly, "They'll probably kill me, then you'll be sorry," but Florrie, with her stringy hair, her dull eyes, her thin, hunched shoulders, looked so pathetic that the reproach died on her lips. She lifted the latch and went out into the stinking little back street, more poignantly than ever aware of the pitiless conditions of her sister's life—a world away from the patchily rich, stricken insecurity of her own. She picked up her pretty lawn skirts and, lost, directionless, tiptoed through the debris of potato peelings and refuse in her dainty satin shoes.

It was Mr. Dugdale the curate, in his black shovel hat and button boots, who found Rose, sitting on the riverbank, crying. He led her with sympathetic deference to the neat brick house that had been built for him, with 1837 marked into the cement over the door, and the garden full of the sweetness of fallen blossoms.

"Don't ask her questions," he directed his wife. Mercy Dugdale looked with astonishment at the black eye Rose had somehow acquired during her rough exit from Nicholas's rooms, at the expensive gown, but she kept an obedient silence as she showed Rose to a small room at the top of the back stairs.

Beyond tears, beyond talking, Rose ate cold pork and potatoes, then fell with relief into a small, hard bed that bore no resemblance to the one she had been sharing in voluptuous comfort with Nicholas.

She wakened to a bright morning, and was promptly sick in the flower-patterned ewer. Mercy Dugdale, coming up the stairs with a cup of tea, put it down and held Rose's head, then helped her back into bed.

"Is there something you'd like to tell me?" she asked, sitting by the bed and smoothing Rose's brow, her eyes full of apprehension, as well as genuine concern.

Rose, shaking like a leaf, read the expression in her hostess's eyes. "It's just that I've nowhere to go. It scares me," she said.

"I didn't mean that, dear."

"That's all. I don't want to go to the castle, and my sister can't have me. That's all." Rose looked at the wallpaper, counting the berries on a trellis, then the squares of the trellis itself. Her heart was thumping in a highly irregular manner, so loudly she felt certain the curate's wife would hear it. She did not like having to lie in this house. It was a bit like lying in church.

"I meant, you're not well." Mercy Dugdale's contemplative brown eyes were gravely questioning, but there was no solace, Rose was quick to note, behind them. No eventual safety. She recognized the thinness of the woman's concern.

"I'm sorry I was sick," she said meekly. "I was upset yesterday. I'm always sick after I've been upset. I'm all right now. I'll get up. Mr. Dugdale said I might help in the house."

"Of course, dear. I expect he told you we won't be able to pay you anything, but you may have a bed and food in return."

Rose, while grateful, wished fervently that her warm wickedness had not to be confined in so upright a household, their god being quite different from the one she occasionally called upon. She knew instinctively that theirs did not allow for human error. She had a feeling He preferred not to concern himself with errant kitchen maids. At least until their spirits were humbled. Rose's spirit, now that she had a roof over her head, was rising on stout wings.

She was not ill again. The sickness failed to withstand her fast-developing sense of survival. Word went up to the castle of her employment at the Dugdales and Grandy arrived, puffing and concerned, carrying a carpetbag full of the clothes she had brought from London.

"Don't wear them, dearie," he advised, forbearing to tell Rose of the tussle he had had with Mrs. Snape in order to prevent her putting them—wages of sin that they were—into the kitchen stove.

"No, I won't. I don't have to. Mrs. Dugdale gave me this dress." Rose smoothed the brown stuff skirt over her hips. It was a period of acceptance.

"We're going back to London," Grandy said unhappily. He told her the number of the house in Cavendish Square. "If you should be in trouble, go there." He put some coins into Rose's hand. "This will more than pay for the stagecoach."

Rose's heart began thumping again. She knew, even as her fingers closed over the money, that it would be used. But not how. Her plan had yet to fall into place.

Grandy did not kiss her. He never had. Not because he was lacking in affection, but because outward signs of loving sat awkwardly on the Snapes and their like. As he turned away, he said diffidently, "It's the London Season. That's why they've gone. But they'll come back here after the wedding."

The sudden reality of the nightmare froze Rose to the bone. "When?" she asked, through lips so stiff she could scarcely form the word.

"He's to be married on the fifteenth of July." Then Grandy added swiftly, not looking at her, "And they'll be going to the cannibal country early in September. There'll be comings and goings up on the hill, I daresay, because I've heard tell he'll be taking some of the servants with him."

The following days and weeks passed in a kind of trance. Rose was no longer aware of watching eyes. Her own eyes looked straight ahead, blinkered. In her there was a sense of waiting. During the day she helped the maid with light housework. The girl, incensed by Rose's detached indifference, gave up trying to draw her out. In the kitchen, in silence, Rose stitched at her sampler.

"Fair give me the creeps, she does," Cook told her employer. "I told her I'd learn her, but she just smiled."

She did not know that Rose had become a sponge. To take lessons might have brought into the open plans that she herself was not yet ready to face. She learned the culinary arts by watching Cook's every movement.

The curate found her in his study with a duster in one hand, looking with childlike, puzzled eyes at an open copy of the Bible. Not having suspected Rose of piety, he was deeply moved by the change wrought in the atmosphere of his God-fearing home. "Would you like me to teach you to read God's word?" he asked kindly.

Rose nodded.

"The Father's ways of bringing the wayward to His flock are many and diverse," he told his wife that evening, as they sat over dinner. "I propose you should take her to church on Sunday. I think you might find it an edifying experience. Especially if you could find time to go over the morning service in the prayer book with her first. She has a mind as quick and receptive as a child's."

It was true what he said, but Rose had also a relentless determination to succeed. Demurely, obediently, the new lamb went to the high-towered Norman church, with its vast, vaulted roof, its cold stone pillars, and its sarcophagi that held the remains of the past earls of Rundull. She sat in the hard wooden pew with Mercy Dugdale, following the psalms, singing sweetly, filing the words indelibly in her mind, learning to read.

Then one day, Daniel Putnam arrived at the back door of the curate's house.

"I don't know as you ought to see him," Cook told Rose with concern. " 'Twas the Putnams caused all the trouble, weren't it? Anyways, he won't go until I tell you he's here, so I'm telling you, but I'm also sayin' I think you should sit there and keep on with your embroidery while I send him away."

Rose folded her sampler neatly on her lap, and stood up. The strain of the weeks in limbo had taken color and curve from her cheeks. Her dark-fringed eyes were enormous. "I'll talk to him," she said. "Daniel's not like the others."

"Want me to come with you?" asked Cook anxiously.

"No."

He was standing by the wisteria several paces from the door, a thick-chested, solid man, his mouse-colored hair brushed forward over small sideburns, his cord breeches and smock very clean. He looked shy, dependable, and kind. Rose felt a surging wave of optimism and a sense of a drawbridge rising, of chains around her wrists falling away.

"Hello, Daniel." She smiled as she stepped out onto the brick path.

"I 'eard you was 'ere." Surprised at his serene reception, he shuffled his feet with pleased embarrassment. "Saw you goin' to church, too. 'Ow are you gettin' on?"

"I'm all right. The Dugdales have been kind. I hear you've left your family."

"Yes. The Dowsetts 'ave given me a bed."

Rose knew the extent of the undergroom's accommodations over the stables. They had two bedrooms, and three children to house. She said, "That was good of them," and wondered with self-absorbed concern how long they would allow him to inconvenience them. She walked farther into the garden, testing the feeling of having Daniel at her side.

"It was kind of you to save me that day," she said demurely, her long lashes fluttering up. "I'm sorry it turned out so badly for you."

"Don't matter." He looked down at his country highlows, and scraped a lump of dirt off one square toe.

Rose reached up and plucked a leaf from a silver birch, then tossed it from one palm to the other. She felt the tightness around her mouth relax. The strain, which had been manifesting itself in two sharp little lines between her brows, fell away. She bent down to pick up a chestnut the winter squirrels had missed, and tossed it to Daniel. He threw it clumsily but delightedly back.

It was the fifteenth of June.

12

On the twelfth of July Rose put her few possessions into her grandfather's carpetbag, and left.

Because she cared little for the opinion of those few people who knew her, a sense of guiltless freedom swept through her as she took to the road. She did not flatter herself that anyone was particularly marked by the seventeen years during which she had paused in the village of Rundull.

She had no plans to take Nicholas from the girl he was to marry. Lady Cressida might wear his ring, but Rose knew fiercely that she would never experience the magic that had been between herself and Nicholas. You could beget children without that. She would bear Nicholas no grudge for producing heirs, she told herself. If it had to be. If it was God's plan.

God's black and wicked, cold, uncaring plan.

Well, she had a plan of her own.

It was not far to the London Road, not above three miles, and the morning was a fair one. Rose caught the stagecoach at Penbridge and left it at Hatchett's Hotel and Coach Terminus in Piccadilly. From there she went to the tavern in Cork Street where Nicholas dined frequently with his bachelor friends, and, feeling safe in the drab brown dress and shawl Mercy Dugdale had given her, waited patiently outside. When men spoke to her, she turned her black-bonneted head away, closed as a box. An hour later, when Nicholas had not come, she plodded indomitably to Regent Street to stand outside

Verey's restaurant, watching and praying as the Reverend Dugdale had taught her to pray. "Our Father which art in heaven . . . Send Nicholas, please."

When twilight closed around her, when the doors were ostentatiously and noisily locked, when God, ignoring her prayers because of her earlier blasphemy, had turned his back, when the Peeler who had passed several times was beginning to show aggressive interest, Rose trotted purposefully off to the nearest cab stand and hired a hansom. Alighting at Cavendish Square, she looked around cautiously. She noticed a cobblestoned entrance that looked likely to lead to the mews. She turned the corner, and tiptoed the length of the dirty alley. There were candles burning in the small windows of the servants' quarters above the stalls. She waited, listening, but heard only the stamp of horses' feet, an occasional snort.

She made her way along the row of stalls, peering over the stable doors until she located Cossack. Timidly, she held out a hand to him. He came forward, muffle-footed on the thick straw, his long ears flicking. Quietly, she slipped the bolt and entered. No one had told her a highly strung thoroughbred might resent the intrusion of an interloper, and in a moment kick her to death. Cossack was her catalyst. He had brought Nicholas to her before. The great beast watched with curiosity and vague surprise as she made a nest in his straw and curled up. She had long since eaten the cold cabbage and leg of chicken stolen from the curate's kitchen that morning, but in spite of the hunger she eventually dropped off to sleep.

She wakened to vague stirrings of danger and found herself looking into the startled eyes of a stable boy.

"Cor, Mr. Shard won't 'arf cut up rough when 'e finds you 'ere," the child said, his pale eyes popping. Rose scrambled stiffly to her feet, assessing the unprepossessing little instrument fate had sent her.

"What's your name, boy?" She summoned up the dimpling smile she had been using to drive Daniel Putnam half out of his wits with bewildered happiness.

"Oliver."

"What do you do here?"

"I 'elps out." He indicated the wooden washing bucket at his feet.

"Do you get paid?" She fingered the coins in her pocket.

"No. I gets scraps and sometimes ale."

"Now look here, Oliver. If I were to give you sixpence, would you do something for me?"

His colorless little eyes sharpened, and the starved face narrowed with suspicion. "You got sixpence, miss?"

"Yes, I have. And what's more, I've got important friends. If you keep my secret and help me, I'll help you. I might be able to get you work. Not helping out. Real, paid work."

"Proper work! Oh, miss!"

Rose pressed a coin into his hand. "This is to show I trust you. Now I want you to trust me." She drenched him with the full flood and warmth of her enticing smile.

The boy put the sixpence in the side of his mouth and bit on it. "It's silver, miss!" The puny muscles of his thin body tightened, like a kitten at its first scent of a bird.

"Of course it's silver. Now listen carefully. I want you to go to Mr. Snape . . ."

The boy backed away. "Oh no, miss. I couldn't do that. 'Im what's the butler, you mean? I couldn't."

"If you don't, I'll have to take the sixpence back. And there'll be no job. Now, do as I say. Go to the back door and tell whoever opens it you've something very important to say to Mr. Snape. Say there's no one else you can tell."

The boy's face paled beneath the ingrained dirt. "I never talked to a butler, miss. 'E wouldn't listen to the likes o' me."

Pretending diffidence, though her heart hammered with apprehension, Rose turned away. "If you're not clever enough for that, you wouldn't be able to do the job I have in mind that my friend could find for you," she said.

At last he ventured, "What was you thinkin' of, miss, in the kind of work?"

"There's no point in thinking about it if you won't see Mr. Snape." She held out her hand for the sixpence. "Give it back to me, Oliver. I'll talk to Mr. Shard, after all. He'll take my message for nothing."

The lashless eyes screwed up tightly with fearful determination. "I'll go," the boy said. "Wot's the message?"

"Tell him he's to ask Mr. Nicholas to come and see Cossack."

The boy's expression of disbelief tangled with Rose's shaky confidence. Fear of disaster roughened her voice. "Go," she said gratingly. "Go now." He went, looking terrified. The gelding, sensitive to the change in her, pawed the straw, snorted, and shook his great head. Rose allowed a great sob to escape. "Make him come," she whispered, addressing the empty air, too guilty to approach the Deity directly. God, the one with whom she had been living for the past few weeks, was Mr. Dugdale's instrument, and she had let the Dugdales down.

Nicholas dragged himself out of sleep, shedding the familiar nightmare. He had been alone in a clearing surrounded by trees. Somewhere near, hidden, women were waiting. He could not see them, and because of that, he could not order them to leave him alone. He was tired, so agonizingly tired that his shoulders drooped and his arms hung limply at his sides. There was supposed to be an army of men helping him, but they too had disappeared. It was the fourth or fifth time he had dreamed the same dream and he was fed up with it.

"Who's that?" he called.

"It's Snape, Mr. Nicholas. May I come in?"

Nicholas grunted. "It's a devil of an hour to waken a man," he grumbled. "What's amiss, Snape?"

"There's a message, Mr. Nicholas, from the mews. You're asked to go to Cossack."

"Cossack?" Nicholas rocketed into a sitting position.

"It's urgent, Mr. Nicholas. There's a stable boy come to the door."

Nicholas was out of bed, jerking himself into his pantaloons, thrusting his feet into boots. He crossed the room with swift strides. He was already descending the stairs three at a time when the old man reached the door.

Rose heard the clatter of hurrying feet on the cobblestones. Stumbling to the stable door, she came up against Cossack. He nudged at her with his velvet nose. She was obliged to raise an arm to push him back, and it was thus, with her hand on his forelock, that Nicholas saw them. Her arm dropped to her side, and the horse stilled.

Nicholas came slowly forward, blinking. "Rose!"

She held her breath.

"In two days I am to be married." His voice was calm, but his fingers gripped her arm hard.

Rose's huge eyes gazed at him with mute hunger.

His mind flew back to the Buckingham Palace ball, when he had seen her in his mind's eye, bedecked in Woolege jewels. Dear God! That he should have to be tormented so. "I am going to New Zealand." Her nerve-tearing silence brought out the guilt and the despair in him. He added, "How dare you come here! How dare you!" He hit her hard across the face.

She staggered, crumpled, seemed about to fall. Then the shock she felt exploded in a violence that more than matched his own. There was a coil of rope suspended from a nail. She snatched it up, dashed after him, and as he turned, lashed it across his face. She had forgotten she was a nobody from his father's kitchens. That she had accepted she could not marry him. Out the fireball of pain inside her she screamed, "You were going to take *me* to New Zealand. You asked *me* to marry you. You said you loved *me!*" Nicholas fell back, and she hit him again, and again. Momentarily, he stood stunned, a hand to his eyes.

"You . . ." She broke off, choking, as she saw the blood on his dear face. My love.

His hand came down. He stepped forward. Grasping her by the shoulders, he shook her savagely. Then suddenly she was back in the manger, projected violently onto the nasty softness of warm horse droppings. There was a sharp crack as the stable door slammed shut. The sound of his footsteps echoed into the distance. The empty silence filled up with Rose's agonized sobbing.

Later, spent, she became aware of a gentle touch, and gazed into Cossack's big, soft eyes. He lifted his head, then stretched it down to her again, his trembling velvety lips brushing her hair.

"Oh, Cossack." Her defeat lay on her spirit, heavy as lead. She had gambled on Nicholas's enduring love, and lost.

Her grandfather found her—puffing from the exertion of running down to the mews, concerned, angry, outraged, yet knowing guiltily in the back of his mind that, had it not been for his pieces of silver, Rose could not be here. He looked at her, at her beautiful, pitiful face, her old brown dress covered in bits of straw, then beyond, to the limitless pain of despair. His jowly face twisted. "Come with me, dearie," he said, his concern evident in the ragged edges of his voice. "Lord only knows what Mrs. Snape's going to say." He saw Rose's carpetbag, and bent down to pick it up. "We'll get you clean, anyway," he added uncertainly.

They came through the area door together, the raindrops shining on their hair and shoulders. Mrs. Snape, passing through the passage leading to the kitchen, jumped as though she had been shot.

"Lord'a' mercy!" she cried, too staggered to be immediately angry. "How did you get here?"

Snape, never one to be thrusting, replied with entrenched calm, "She's to stay."

The housekeeper recovered. Her knuckles found her bony hips through her black skirt, and her long feet squared up for battle. "I beg your pardon, Mr. Snape," she challenged him threateningly, chest outthrust. "Her Ladyship . . ."

"There's nothing more to be said, Mrs. Snape."

Rose's scared glance met the housekeeper's outraged glare, then she followed her grandfather up the back stairs. He turned toward the front of the house, into a narrow passage, then along it to the far end. He opened a door, and Rose looked in astonishment into a bright little room. There were pansies and forget-me-nots on the wallpaper. A smallish bed stood against one wall, its polished mahogany headboard fashioned with ornate curlicues. There were a dressing table in the same prettily curved style, a wardrobe with a scrolled front, and a patterned rug on the floor. By the window stood a small chair with a shell-shaped back.

An unearthly stillness came over her. She went to the window and looked out on the leafy square, at the houses rising like palaces opposite.

Nicholas, she thought giddily, must have given orders that she was to be cared for. After all."Grandy!" she turned, clasping her small hands over her breast. "Am I to sleep here?" It was a prayer with a question enclosed. Here, in this lady's room, she meant.

The old man's face sagged. "I've been told to bring you here, that's all, Rose. I don't approve of your coming any more than Mrs. Snape does, and that's a fact." He wiped a hand wearily across his brow. "It's trouble. And it's wrong. If I could stop it, I would. I've said this before, and I'll say it again—Mr. Nicholas is a gentleman, and you're a headstrong, willful little girl, who's too pretty for her own good. You've been a headache to me, and you're going to be more than that to Mr. Nicholas before he's through with you." Snape turned, signing to her abruptly to follow him. He moved heavily back down the passage and paused at a door. As he opened it, Rose, coming tentatively up behind him, looked in a tiny room containing a tin bath, a looking glass, and a small stool. "There'll be some hot water brought up," he said.

"Grandy!"

He raised a hand to silence her. "Clean yourself up."

"Grandy!" Her bewilderment warred with excitement. "Did . . ."

"Ask no questions and you'll be told no lies," said the butler unhappily. "I'll come and tell you when the water's here. And while I'm away, Rosie, lock the door."

Rose did as she was bid, then went like a homing pigeon back to the window. In a daze, she looked out through the mist of sweet summer rain, over the leafy green trees, and between them to the grass and summer flowers. A hooded phaeton rolled into view, the horse stepping high. From the opposite direction appeared a lady driving her own carriage, with a liveried groom behind, and a pair of elegant dalmatians escorting. Rose slipped swiftly out of her filthy dress, turned it carefully inside out, rolled it into a ball, and put it by the door with the heavy shoes and stockings Mrs. Dugdale had given her. Then she went back to the window and waited in her chemise and long pantaloons.

The day wore on interminably. The rain ceased, and the sun came to shine through the window, its rays warm and soothing. With wolfish hunger Rose demolished the food Grandy brought after she'd bathed, and several hours later was looking for more. Rifling through the carpetbag, she found the Bible Mr. Dugdale had given her, but she was too hungry to read; too excited and curious, bored and frustrated to concentrate. She took her sampler from the carpetbag, began to sew, and immediately pricked her finger. She licked the blood away and began again, but her hands became damp, and the thread stuck to her palms. The stitches grew more uneven. She was ruining the picture. With a sharp sigh she put the work down and opened the Bible once again.

It was evening when Nicholas came. He arrived exquisitely attired in knee breeches, a white satin cravat so large it covered his shirtfront, his broad shoulders encased in a coat of magnificent blue with a velvet collar. He closed the door and stood against it.

"Nicholas." She rushed impulsively toward him, her eyes bright with sweet urgency.

He put up a hand to stop her. "No," he said, vehemently.

Obediently, she paused on tiptoe.

"Devil take it, Rose," Nicholas blurted out suddenly, "don't look at me like that. I can't help what's happened. Tonight there's to be a ball at my fiancée's father's house in Berkeley Square." He looked down, smoothing the frills on his shirtfront, touching the diamond pin in his cravat. She noted with interest that his fingers trembled.

"Yes?" She tucked the word *fiancée* away with the rest of her newfound knowledge. That woman was his fiancée. That lady, Rose corrected herself, that he was to wed.

"Rose, would you like to work here until we sail? The family will return to Rundull immediately after the wedding."

Rose put a hand to her mouth to stifle a gasp.

"You could do a parlormaid's work. Snape would advise you."

"Oh yes," she whispered, agonizing over the wickedness of his suggestion. This was what her grandfather knew and had been afraid to tell her.

"Most of the servants will return to Rundull with the family."

She had been going to ask him why she was in this pretty room at the front of the house, but there was no need now. She had to be hidden from those who would return to Rundull.

"Lady Cressida is borrowing some staff from Saxon

Mote, her family home in Suffolk. They won't know you."

Rose came toward him. This time he made no move to stop her. She put gentle arms up around his neck, savoring the dear enchantment of him. "I love you, Nicholas," she whispered, pressing her cheek against his shoulder. "Say what you said when you left me in St. James's."

He drew in a quick breath. "I can't, Rose, my darling. You know I can't." But he put his arms around her.

"You can," she told him fiercely, every nerve willing him to obey. And then, when he remained silent, "At least you can say you love me. Say that, Nicholas. That you love me."

Suddenly his face was soft and vulnerable. "Oh, Rose. Rose, you are my cross," he said in a tortured voice. He thrust her from him, flung the door open, and left.

She was at the window when Shard drove up to the pillared front door, resplendent in his wig, with bright buttons on his waistcoat, and an embroidered overcoat reaching right down to his heels. She watched with burning eyes as the family emerged, the ladies bejeweled in tiaras and glittering diamond earrings. Lady Adeline appeared, skinny as a rabbit in a wonderful silk gown with a brilliant ruby necklace circling her neck.

And then came Nicholas.

The other men stood on the outer perimeter of her consciousness. Nicholas, taller than the rest, broader, finer, more splendid. As he stepped into the coach, he turned, and for a brief, heart-stopping second, looked right at her window. Then the door closed, and the carriage rolled away.

As dusk fell, Grandy came with a pile of clothes over one arm, and a box of sewing materials. He laid them on the bed saying, "Here's your parlormaid's dress, dearie. If it don't fit you'll be able to fix it, I daresay. Master Nicholas has given me some money, and I'm to take you for a drive."

"A drive?" Her eyes softened and grew moist as she realized the trouble Nicholas was taking on her behalf.

"I've sent the boy, Oliver, to find a hansom. Put on the cloak and your black bonnet. And mind you tuck your hair out of sight under this."

Ignoring the frilled day cap he held out to her, she

looked up yearningly into his face. "Grandy, is the Queen going to the ball?"

"I believe so. It's said she encouraged the match and is well pleased." Snape broke off, his caring showing in his sad eyes.

Obediently, she tucked her golden curls beneath the muslin cap, and spread the cape around her shoulders. Then, with a grimace, she put the ugly bonnet on her head and glanced in the looking glass. Even in this horrible disguise, she knew that she was prettier than the Lady Adeline in her silks and jewels. And, no doubt, a hundred times bonnier than this fiancée Nicholas was to marry.

They went together through passages miraculously emptied of servants, and out via the mews. Oliver was waiting by a hansom. As Snape slipped him a coin he turned his sharp little face, and the pale eyes flooded with recognition.

"Oh miss, it's you. You promised . . ."

Rose's reaction was swift, mindless and confident. "Wait," she replied, instinctively feeling Oliver could be a part of *the plan*. The plan that was coming, in the secret recesses of her mind, to maturity.

On the day of the wedding, after the bustling morning exodus, the house was quiet as a tomb. That evening, when bride and groom returned to the house, Snape called the remnants of his Rundull staff together to meet their new mistress. Rose, hoping no one would notice her, turned toward the door, but Fred Quick, hugely enjoying himself, shot out an arm to bar her exit.

"We don't want 'er Ladyship to jump through the roof when a new face appears of a sudden, do we?" he asked of no one in particular. "Everybody's got to meet the new mistress."

Rose cast an agonized glance around the room and caught Mrs. Snape's steely stare. Then Snape shuffled them into place and opened the door. Sick with fright, Rose moved forward with the little procession.

She knew Nicholas was standing with his wife in the hall because she could hear their voices, but, with her eyes cast down, she saw nothing except the long black skirt of the maid who preceded her. Her face was hot as a furnace. Sweat gathered in her armpits and ran down her neck. She could hear Nicholas's voice, but not his words. Then the skirt in front of her disappeared and her own name came through loud and clear ". . . Rose Snape, parlormaid." Her head came up and, for a brief, astonished moment, two pairs of eyes met; one green as the sea on a wild day, the other pale as aquamarine. Rose had a startling impression of herself with the life spark submerged in gentility.

"Rose is Snape's granddaughter," Nicholas was saying, and she knew she should make a bobbing curtsy. She knew also that, if she did, her knees would give way, and she would fall headlong to the floor. She saw Lady Cressida's fine brows draw together in a quick frown, more of bewilderment than displeasure. Her own soft lips parted in a smile of dizzy delight. Nicholas had married a girl who might be her own sister. Nicholas, who would not say he loved her, had given her proof beyond doubt that he did.

Then Lady Cressida was saying something about the two small households merging, and hoping those who would travel with them to New Zealand would be friends. Her voice was calm and cool. Measured.

Back in the kitchen uproar broke out. ". . . cheeky strumpet!" That was Mrs. Snape, and Fred Quick was saying, "You'll be dismissed, my girl mark my words."

Barney Herd said more kindly, "I should've thought you'd learned your lesson, young Rose." Across the big scrubbed table, the Woolege servants whom the new mistress was taking to New Zealand regarded her with curious eyes.

Rose felt Grandy's fingers on her arm, heard his anger. Forgetting that her belongings had been moved to a servant's room in the attic, she stumbled to the door and fled up the narrow stairs to her refuge at the front of the house. Locking the door, she dropped into the shell chair, put her head back against the velvet and felt sweet contentment spread through her like a benison.

Suddenly *the plan* was no longer a wickedness. It was a

giving of herself with total confidence, knowing Nicholas truly wanted her.

But she must find a way to carry the plan out alone. Nicholas had a sense of duty strong enough to annihilate them both.

13

The lie was as transparent as a piece of gauze.

"She doesn't look the slightest bit like you," Nicholas said. "And as for the obligatory curtsy, to tell you the truth, she has recently been raised to her present position of parlormaid because Mama couldn't spare one of hers for you. She's not accustomed to meeting the lady of the house. It was fright, that's all."

Cressida sat down on a brocade chair by the window, her back rigid, her face expressionless. "I should like to get rid of her." Her fingers tapped on the chair arm.

Nicholas went over to the fireplace and standing directly in her line of vision turned, head high, to pose in the way that was so typical of him, one foot lifted to rest on the fender. "On what grounds, my dear? We've agreed that our circumstances call for a skeleton staff. None of them is expendable."

"Would you understand if I said that I object less to her insolence than to the fact that we bear a most unfortunate resemblance to each other?"

"You would compare yourself to a parlormaid?" he asked, looking amused. He took his foot down from the fender and moved away, wandering idly, his hands beneath his coattails, right up to the end of the room. He stood frowning at the portrait of his mother in her low-cut, tubular-shaped gown of the twenties. At the housemaid peeping around the door behind her, remembering inconsequentially but with feeling how his father disapproved of the fashionable ploy, and thought the girl ought to be painted out.

"I would like the girl to go."

Nicholas counted five before turning around. Then, equally slowly, he walked back down the length of the long room. "Madam," he asked, with the utmost politeness, standing feet apart before his wife, "have I unsuspectingly married an autocrat?"

Her pale, pretty eyes searched his face feature by feature, as though she had never seen him before. "No," she replied at last. "You are to be master of your own household. I have already promised to love, honor, and obey you, and I cannot imagine any circumstance in which I would break that promise. But I would like to make this one request on our wedding day." She paused, cleared her throat. "I want that girl to go."

"Very well. You shall have your wish. She shall go tomorrow."

"Thank you." Cressida swallowed. "I don't mean that she should be thrown out on the streets." She spoke quickly now, wearing an expression of uncertain gratitude. "Perhaps we could find her a situation. No doubt I could persuade a friend . . ."

"There is no need. She can go back to Rundull."

He turned and abruptly left her.

When Snape came to inquire of Lady Cressida what time the young couple wished to dine, Nicholas was not with her. When dinner was announced he emerged from the library, marginally drunk. They ate their meal in silence, then repaired to the drawing room. Snape came with coffee, cheroots, and port.

Cressida sat stiffly on the sofa, pleating the silk of her skirt between finger and thumb. Nicholas waited for the butler to leave the room.

"Perhaps you'd care to join me in a glass of port, my dear," he suggested. "Let's drink to our union. I would have done that at dinner, had you not refused the wine."

"I felt if I refused the wine you might not have it yourself," Cressida replied distantly. She closed her hand over the little pleats, crushing them. "It was clear to me that you had had enough."

"How little you know me," Nicholas retorted lightly. He lifted his eyes to her face. "But of course you don't know me at all, do you? In the event that you didn't drink, I had your share."

She rose from her chair, her pale face very still. "I would like to retire." She glided forward, head high, and cracked her shins against the curved leg of a Queen Anne stool. She caught her breath, but her face remained expressionless.

He looked at her tauntingly. "It is not seemly in a lady of your breeding to show such ardor. I scarcely expected my bride to trip over the furniture in her desire to hurry on the act of consummation. Surely such impatience is a male prerogative?" She stood with eyes cast down, still and white. Goaded by her very acceptance, he added cruelly, "Might I not beg ten minutes, even, while we drink to our future?"

There was a small silence, then, lifting her eyes to his face, showing no sign of what effort the words may have cost her, Cressida replied, "Yes, I would like to drink to our marriage."

He handed her a glass. She took it with an unsteady hand. His eyes moved downward to the curve of her bosom showing provocatively above the stiffly boned front of her gown. Deliberately, he put a finger inside her décolletage and lifted one breast. It burst easily out of the tight corsettop, the darkened tip bulging grotesquely. There was an automatic stiffening of her features, then she summoned a smile. With a furious kind of shame at his own cruelty, he rubbed a finger across her nipple. "I see," he said at last, when she neither moved nor changed her expression, "you have been well instructed in your wifely duties. Give my congratulations to your mother, my dear."

Only in the gulping down of the port and in the set of her suddenly peaked face did Cressida show any sign of emotion. She put the glass down on a Chippendale sofa table, adjusted her bodice, and left the room, closing the door quietly behind her. Her shinbone stung as she went up the stairs, but she did not limp. She held her back as straight as a lance, but there was a choking sensation in her throat.

She opened the door of the room she and Nicholas were to share and crossed to the window, her feet silent on the thick carpet. Candles guttered in their sconces, patterning the elaborate ceiling with flickering shadows. She looked at the big canopied bed with distaste and a certain controlled fear. Today in the eyes of God and beneath the warm, approving gaze of her Brittanic majesty she had given up all protection and security in exchange for . . . for this man with the burning eyes and angry, cruel mouth. She had given her hand to a stranger who loved a servant girl. Her breasts heaved with the weeping inside. But she had been raised from stock that down through the ages had borne crushing misfortunes and risen again with spirit undaunted. In the soft glow of night the long dead ancestors crept close, wrapping their courage around her like a blanket, whispering that they had been tested and come through. There was no going back. On the other side of the world, in a new country, might not her husband forget the sordid little adventures of the past? There, she told herself, she would find love.

She went to the little escritoire in the corner and penned a note, then crossed to the tapestry bellpull. Her maid came running.

"See that this is delivered to Nurse immediately, Yorke."

"Now, m'Lady? Tonight?" The girl quickly drew a veil over her expression of dismay, for there was to be a celebration below stairs.

"Tonight," said Cressida firmly. She turned to the dressing table and began to take the pins out of her hair.

Down in the library Nicholas contemplated the black day. The Hastings family had refused to attend the wedding because the Queen was going. The tragic death of Lady Flora only ten days earlier had blighted the festivities. Since the results of the postmortem had been made public, and the poor lady-in-waiting was revealed to have been suffering from a tumor on the liver, instead of the illegitimate baby the court anticipated, London had buzzed night and day with reviling gossip.

The queen's coach had been stoned on its way down the Mall, and a crowd in Hanover Square outside St. George's church hissed her as she alighted. As if that was not bad enough, Melbourne had announced with revolting assumed modesty that he could claim some credit for this glittering match that joined two of England's most illustrious families. The government was indeed gratified, he said in a long speech, that the flower of this glorious land should choose to go out and colonize New Zealand; to make it England's own.

The only good thing about the God-damned, ill-omened day was the fact that no one seemed aware this particular bloom was a victim of the God-damned hereditary system of this God-damned glorious land. And then the prime minister, emerging into the street, had been hit with an egg that splattered across his elegant shirtfront, narrowly missing the bride's finery. "Why don't you go back to the palace with your young missus?" somebody jeered insultingly, and another crone yelled, "Poor little Lady Flora. I 'opes you an' the Queen 'ave 'er death on yer conscience through heternity." It only needed Rose to step out of a pew and say she knew of some just cause why this couple should not be . . . to complete the nightmare.

Nicholas's shoulders slumped. Guilt sealed the hate he bore for the poor young creature he had taken—only God and Jerningham Wakefield knew by what means—to be his lady. Given a fair chance, she would no doubt make not only a very good partner, but also an excellent wife for a colonist, which was, he knew, something more. By the time they sailed, he had told himself, he would have come to terms with his fate. He had not counted on Rose's turning up again.

He went to the bellpull, waiting in silence until the butler arrived. "Bring me brandy, Snape."

"Certainly, Mr. Nicholas."

"And Snape, where is Rose?"

The butler's startled eyes flashed indignation. "I've had her things moved to a room in the attic with the other servants. If I may say so, Master Nicholas . . ."

"No, you may not," snapped Nicholas. "You are not employed to give opinions. And kindly resist the temptation to call me Master Nicholas whenever you decide you know better than I. I am the head of this household, Snape, and I do not need advice from my staff." He paused briefly. "I intend to get quietly drunk. No doubt, given time, I will sink into blessed oblivion."

"Perhaps that would be a good idea." The butler stared unemotionally at the wall.

"Can you imagine, Snape, what it is like to be in my position?"

"I'm very sorry, sir, I'm sure."

"I'm asking you, Snape," Nicholas fixed the old man with eyes that were dark with pain, "if it ever occurred to you to consider the responsibilities of a man in my position. Perhaps you have inquired of yourself if you could make a good job of it."

"I would try, Mr. Nicholas. I've always felt there are great advantages in being born the son of an earl, sir."

"And great disadvantages?"

"If you'll excuse my saying so, sir, there are great disadvantages in being born a Snape." He lifted his balding head and added deliberately, "And particularly in being born a very pretty girl of the name."

"That, Snape, is a criticism," said Nicholas coldly.

"Yes, Mr. Nicholas. In a manner of speaking, it is. I would not be making it, as I am sure you realize, were it not for the particular circumstances." He turned, his shoulders hunched, his old face suddenly tired. "If you will excuse me, sir, I will bring the brandy."

"Before you go, Snape, Rose is to return to Rundull tomorrow."

"I'm sure that's wise. I'll tell her."

"I'd prefer to tell her myself. In her new situation as parlormaid I'm sure she would not feel she was stepping too far out of line in bringing the tray with the bottle of brandy. And two glasses, Snape."

In silence, Nicholas coolly contemplated the butler standing indecisively before him. At last the old man repeated, as though hoping to be corrected, "Two glasses?"

"Two glasses, Snape."

When he had gone, Nicholas prowled restlessly the length of the room and back. His mind, in spite of the wine and port he had drunk, was clear, and there was a new warmth in him as though something of the essential goodness of the old man had seeped into his pores. Rose must be protected, that was the message and he accepted it. He had made his bed—not true, of course, others had made it for him—but he must anyway lie on it.

He would say good-bye to Rose now, she would go back to Rundull, and that would be the end. One day, when he was an old man, he would no doubt look back on the year 1839 and remember it only as the year he married and went to a new country, got himself a brace of sons on a good and dutiful wife, and returned to a world that had forgotten his youthful escapades.

He looked up as the door opened and Rose came in. Their eyes met, and he caught his breath.

"Grandy has given me ten minutes to talk to you. Ten minutes, Nicholas." Rose's words ran swiftly one upon the other. "He says you have something to say. What is it? That I may not stay here? I know that."

He took the tray and put it down, then tilted her face up to look at him. "There are certain things one cannot do to a human being," he said, because he had made up his mind to say it, though he had not anticipated his voice would come out jolting and creaky as a dray on a country road.

"You can do anything to human beings," replied Rose. It might have been her sister Florrie talking, so stark and painful was her acceptance. "But there are some situations that don't work. My being in your house is one that doesn't work." Her wonderful green eyes flickered to the brandy bottle. "Grandy said I'd better not drink that. He called it gut rot."

Nicholas felt a new stillness creep into him. "What are you going to do, Rose?"

"Go back to Rundull. To the Dugdales, I expect."

"The Dugdales?"

"When Grandy took me back before, I ran out of the coach in the village because I was afraid to go to the castle. The curate took me home with him because Florrie couldn't have me. I expect they'll have me back," said Rose. "You're married," she added, folding her hands together and looking down at them with frail dignity. "But do you ever get the feeling we belong together? That nothing can really part us?"

He lifted her hands and kissed them. "If I were to agree with you, darling . . ."

"You can agree with me," she replied. "I'm not talking about wedding rings and households. I got the curate to read the marriage service to me and I learnt it. I've thought about it since. 'Those whom God hath joined together let no man put asunder.' God's not in church. He wasn't there to join you and Lady Cressida together.

It's the vicar who joins people. Or the bishop. Or the curate."

"He does it in God's name, Rose." Nicholas's eyes were somber.

"And does God say he should?" Suddenly she was passionate, the pink deepening in her rounded cheeks. "God doesn't say anything. How can he? He isn't here, and people make up things for him to say."

"What the clergy says is in the Bible, Rose."

"Is it? Have you read the Bible?" She looked at him with eyes overflowing, sparkling like underwater jewels.

"Well, no. I must admit I don't seem to have had time . . . yet. Rose, where is this conversation getting us?" He took a handkerchief from his pocket and tenderly wiped her eyes.

"I just wanted to say, there's a feeling I have that God has joined us together, you and me. Before we were born, perhaps. And that's the joining that may not be put asunder."

There was a tap at the door. It opened, and Snape stood looking at them.

"Just a moment, Grandy," said Rose, without turning her head. "Please. Just one moment."

Reluctantly, the old man backed away. "There's one thing I'd like to ask of you," Rose said. "You have to take carpenters to build your house in New Zealand. Well, there's Daniel Putnam. He's a carpenter. He's without a home. He's living in the stables at Rundull because he daren't go into the village."

"A Putnam?" Nicholas's brows drew together sharply.

"He saved me that day you were attacked. I told you, the mob was after me, and he saved me. Could you possibly take him to New Zealand with you? I'd be so grateful if you would."

"A Putnam, Rose!" Nicholas repeated incredulously. "You're asking me to take a member of the family who are the cause of my going?"

"No, Nicholas. *I* am the cause of your going. Daniel's honest and straight and hardworking. He's not at all like the others. He'd be loyal. I swear he'd be loyal, Nicholas. I swear it."

Nicholas's eyes narrowed. "Why should he be loyal to me when he's not loyal to his family?"

"Why should he be loyal to a family who have driven him out?" she countered.

"If he's a carpenter he can go by himself. All he has to do is apply to the New Zealand Company for a passage. He can go free. He doesn't even need a sponsor."

"What can I tell him to do?"

"Do? Take himself off to the company's offices in Broad Street to make his own application. Frankly, Rose, I wouldn't want to sponsor a Putnam."

Rose dropped her eyes so that Nicholas might not see the excitement and relief in them. "What's the name of your ship, Nicholas?"

"*Aurora*. Why?" His eyes twinkled. "Have you in mind to come and see us off? That would put the cat among the pigeons."

She dimpled up at him. "You'd like that?"

"I'd like it fine, but I don't think you should."

"As you wish," she said demurely. "Oh, and there's another matter, Nicholas. There's a little boy named Oliver who helps out in the stables. Could you take him with you?"

Nicholas's dark face took on a whimsical look. "Why, Rose, I didn't know about this side of you."

"You did say there was plenty of work to be had. He's willing, and he'd be very grateful. He's only a little boy, and he seems to be starving." It did not occur to either of them that the boy's starving was a blot on the Rundull escutcheon.

He kissed her very, very gently. "You're making it impossible for me to let you go. Come, sit down. Let's talk."

"No." She moved away a little, releasing her hands from his, afraid of his questions.

"Why are you asking these favors of me?"

"They're the only two people, apart from Grandy, who have ever done anything for me. Promise me, Nicholas. Promise me you'll take Oliver."

"I promise." The door opened. Without really seeing her grandfather, Rose crossed the room and passed him in the hall.

After she had gone, Nicholas sat for a long time staring into space, then he stood up. A marriage, no matter what kind of a marriage, he told himself grimly, had to be consummated. It was one of the rules of the game. He could always close his eyes and pretend his wife was Rose.

He took the stairs step by step, then went slowly along the Turkey-carpeted passage that led to the big room he and his wife were to share. In answer to his tap on the door, a quiet voice said, "Come in."

She was sitting at the Sheraton dressing table, her fair hair with its gold lights streaming over her shoulders, a negligée draped around her. She stood up to face him as he came through the door. "I thought you would be in bed." He glanced at the big four-poster with its high white pillows, and the monogrammed sheet turned down by the maids.

She had not known how she was going to react when the moment arrived, only that she would do the best she could. Now, those reserves of goodwill she had tried so hard to foster were snatched away by the wretched insult of his churlish indifference. The cutting edge of hurt rose in her, defensively. "Like mutton waiting to be carved?" she asked, her voice brittle as eggshells. "I didn't care to, since I had no way of knowing how long you intended to dally with your slut. Don't bother to look surprised. Of course your staff have been indiscreet, and mine were concerned enough to tell me."

"Get into bed." Without waiting to see if she would obey him, he went into the dressing room, and with angry, jerking movements disrobed, wrapping himself in the fashionable Greek-style dressing gown he had purchased along with all the other new clothes for his wedding. He came back into the bedroom tying the sash. She was still standing. He looked at her from beneath black brows, his mouth hard as a stick, hating her for the same reason that he had been attracted to her in the first place. For her intolerable effrontery in resembling Rose.

"If you're thinking it's your duty to divest me of my virginity," she said, her anger manifest, her hurt lurking pitiably beneath, "it has gone long since, so you can save yourself the trouble. I have to inform you that you're not alone in being banished to the colonies."

He lifted his dark head, his eyes malignant now, and waiting. "What do you mean?"

Fear was uppermost, but the pain in her drove her on.

"Did it not occur to you that my father was uncommonly enthusiastic about accepting your offer, sir?"

There was the faintest heightening of color in Nicholas's cheeks.

"I'm gratified to see you didn't know," she spat at him, taking courage from that faint sign of vulnerability. "The matter was put down as smallpox at the time, though I do believe there was a deal of intelligent gossip when I was tucked out of sight. Until the child was born and adopted, I mean. Like you and Rose Snape, we couldn't marry." She paused, then the vicious words fell one over the other. "The father was one of our coachmen. Incidentally, a very attractive man. I'm sure you must know my parents were originally more ambitious for me. But for this misadventure they would not have allowed me to go to a younger son. They'd have stuck out for a prince of the blood, or at the very least a belted earl."

Nicholas drew a sharp breath, but the words kept running on, out of control.

"I wouldn't have told you, if you hadn't brought that baggage into the house."

Nicholas's hand went to his hip, then paused, the fingers curling as though he held the butt of a gun. But he did not move. Nor did he speak. His eyes had taken on a faintly quizzical look.

Cressida clutched at the lacy garment she wore and moved defiantly toward him, her head high. "Not that I mind a roll around the bed with you," she added, devil-driven. "I've enjoyed these romps very much in the past. My parents were good when they discovered I was pregnant and allowed the father of my baby to spend nights with me. A woman needs a man when she's with child. Of course, I'm no more in love with you than you are with me, but I'm quite prepared . . ."

She broke off as Nicholas moved across the room, his face expressionless. At the door he turned, bowing coldly from the waist. "I hope you enjoyed your little confession. I like to think you will take pleasure from spending the first night of our marriage alone, my lady wife. And all the other nights. If ever I wish to sire a son upon you I'll give you notice."

He walked back down the passage as slowly as he had

come. In his mind was something Shard had told him as a
boy, when their pedigree spaniel bitch was raped by a
mongrel from the village and produced a litter of half-
breed pups. "They're no good for proper pedigree breeding after that," Shard had said. "Spoils them, somehow."

At the top of the graceful, sweeping staircase he paused.
The chandelier in the hall had been extinguished, but a
shaft of moonlight from a high window showed him the
way. He went slowly down and stood at the bottom,
mindlessly fondling the head of the heraldic beast that
held a shield sporting different quarterings of the le Grys
family.

As he stood there he realized that, now the first shock
to his pride was receding, he really did not give a damn.
The story probably wasn't true anyway. He'd married a
venomous bitch. Perhaps that was what he deserved. He
wondered bleakly how long his span of life was to run,
and if it was going to be like this all the way.

It was then he felt a slow, growing sensation of warmth.
A feeling that, by some miracle, he was no longer alone.
He looked up. Rose stood in the doorway that led to that
other, smaller staircase and, though he could see her only
faintly, he seemed to sense that she was smiling and
beckoning to him. He went swiftly across the marble
floor, seeing her clearly now, holding out her arms.

14

The Company offers a free passage to its Settlements (including provisions and medical attendance during the voyage) to persons of the following description, viz: agricultural laborers, shepherds, miners, bakers, blacksmiths, braziers, and tinmen, smiths, shipwrights, boat-builders, wheelwrights, sawyers, cabinet-makers, carpenters, coopers, curriers, farriers, millwrights, harness-makers, boot- and shoemakers, tailors, tanners, brick-makers, lime burners, and all persons engaged in the erection of buildings.

Adult Cabin Passengers will be allowed a space of two tons each, and adult Steerage Passengers, half a ton, or twenty cubic feet each, for luggage.

By Order of the Directors

JOHN WARD, Secretary

New Zealand Company's Office
5 June 1839

Rose's eviction from Cavendish Square the morning after the wedding was a miracle of silent efficiency. Nicholas had been gone only minutes from her bed when a woman entered her room with the air of one who not only had a divine right to be there, but who was accustomed and able to annihilate opposition.

"Get dressed."

Rose knew a brick wall when she saw one. Obediently, she put the bedcovers aside and pattered across to the little shell chair where her clothes lay. With unexpected courtesy the woman turned her back. Struggling with her corsets, Rose ventured timidly, "May I ask . . ."

"No, you may not. Put your hair up, if you please, and put on your bonnet and cape."

Rose obeyed meekly. Untroubled by the upper-class sin of pride, the realization that she was being escorted off the premises brought only relief that the remainder of her grandfather's money should remain intact. Her plan was certain to incur expenses. Besides, if perchance she was being taken to some distant place, she would need money for running away.

Surprisingly, they left by the front door, and surprisingly again there was no one to see them go. The house had been swept clear of life. The ancestors in their gilt frames gazed down calmly as though accustomed to enforced exits of small kitchen maids in ugly black bonnets and ill-matching capes. In the square stood a closed carriage. The old horse nosed lethargically at some early-morning itch.

The woman bustled her aboard. In silence, she settled herself opposite, Rose's carpetbag, like a crumpled hostage, on her knee.

They crossed the river, driving, Rose noticed, at an angle to the rising sun. The village of Rundull lay to the southeast. Very soon she knew they were on the Dover Road, the main route to the south. She settled down with a sigh of relief. There were little shops to look at, busy street markets, and, quite soon, green fields with full-leafed trees. Later, they passed pretty Kentish cottages with red hanging tiles and Kentish taverns. Riders dressed for a long journey passed them by.

The sun was sinking as they clattered down Penbridge High Street, past the familiar gibbet that dangled threateningly outside the old Elizabethan Inn. As they stepped down the woman remarked, not unkindly, that Rose was a strong girl, capable of the short walk to Rundull. She added pointedly, "I shall be at Cavendish Square until the ship sails, seeing to m'Lady's peace of mind."

Rose said good-bye politely, picked up her carpetbag, and set off along the road to the village. She was back where she had to be.

*   *   *

The first tentative steps toward execution of *the plan* were taken in the curate's garden as Rose and Daniel walked together beneath apple trees heavy with fruit. The sun was below the horizon and a red glow lay above the green hills on which the castle stood. Rose looked up into Daniel's face. "You can't go into the village, and nor can I. We're prisoners, Daniel."

He wanted to put his arms around her, to tell her that while he was here she would be safe, but he was not accustomed to showing his feelings. He shuffled his big feet and smiled, his arms hanging uselessly at his sides. "It won't last forever, Rose. They'll forget."

She lifted her shoulders on a quivering sigh. "They'll never forget, Daniel. Never. I wish there was somewhere we could go. How long can you stay with the Dowsetts?"

"They'll let me stay."

"But you mustn't take advantage of their goodness."

"Take advantage?" Daniel, who had never taken advantage of anyone in his life, looked at her uncomprehendingly.

She bent to pick a dandelion, frowned, carefully plucked the golden petals one by one. "You'll wear your welcome out. People who ask you to stay don't mean you to be there forever, you know."

His brow creased. "There's nowhere I could go. I can't go 'ome. An' no one in the village would take me in. Where could I go, Rose?"

The magic question. The door opening on a sweet madness that had to be. "Why don't you emigrate?" She took a dancing step to avoid the daisies, reached up to break off an apple twig and set it, to his acute embarrassment, behind Daniel's ear. "Why don't you do what the Honorable Nicholas has done? He says there's a wonderful future for ordinary folk in New Zealand. Wonderful." She lingered on the word, lifting it intriguingly on her tongue, her green eyes on his, mesmerizing him.

"I'm not on 'is staff, Rose, nor ever would be, the way things are." Daniel shuffled his feet again, looking away, uncomfortably remembering matters that were better forgotten.

"No. Lucky you."

Confused by the relief and concern in her voice, he

turned his weather-lined face, frowning. "What d'you mean?"

She picked a half-grown apple off the tree and tossed it from hand to hand, her eyes bright, her bud mouth turned back into a smile. "I mean, if you had to leave here as his servant, you'd stay a servant all your born days."

" 'Ow could I go otherwise, but as 'is servant?" Daniel turned innocent eyes on the dangling bait.

She threw the apple high and watched it fall among the daisies. "You can have a free passage simply for being a carpenter. The government wants all kinds of artisans, but especially carpenters, because every family that goes out will need a house. There's lots of timber in New Zealand, but no houses yet." She repeated what Nicholas had told her. "Why Daniel," she fluttered her eyelashes, "you could be famous for building the very first house in New Zealand. You'd be a man of substance in no time at all. Employing men yourself, I shouldn't be surprised."

His confusion grew. His face flushed, his mouth opened like a beached fish. "Me?"

"Oh really, Daniel! If you were my brother or father or . . ." his humility exasperated her into saying boldly, ". . . husband, I'd make you go. It's the only way out for you." Her brilliant eyes rested on his face. The dark blood rose until his plain features were the color of a turkey cock. "Why Daniel," she slid an arm coquettishly, warmly, encouragingly, through his, "what on earth has made you blush? Is it because you've a mind to marry? Because if you do, you certainly can't stay here. It's one thing for the Dowsetts to give you a bed, but they wouldn't want a married couple foisted on them. Who is this girl you're sweet on then?"

The unearthly stillness of the country twilight crept stealthily around them. Rose moved into the deepening shadow of the apple tree, knowing that darkness would make it easier for this shy, inarticulate man. "Tell me, Daniel. Tell me, who is your secret love," she teased him, laying a hand on his arm, lifting her face sweetly so that it was close to his.

"Rose," he muttered, his voice so hoarse with emotion she scarcely recognized her name.

Slowly, with a look of dewy wonder, acting as she had

never acted before, Rose put her soft arms around his neck. Daniel's face crashed headlong into hers, all the passionate longing in his timid soul expending itself in a bashful lunge. His whiskers scratched like wire as the big, dry mouth awkwardly sought hers. "Why, Daniel, how was I to know?" she gasped when she could extricate herself.

It was easy, after that. His sheepish incredulity and his gratitude were fertile fields for her sowing.

"We'll emigrate, like you said," he mumbled, his face crimson, his eyes shining in wild ecstasy.

"If this is really what you'd like to do, of course I'll go with you," she told him demurely, her lashes fluttering down.

"Would you, Rose? Oh, Rose." Daniel found her mouth this time, a direct hit that bruised her lips and flattened her nose.

"Let's talk about it." She brought out the information piecemeal and diffidently, allowing him to think she had overheard folk talking below stairs. "There's a ship called *Aurora*. It's the name of a star, I think. I looked it up, I mean, I read about it in one of the curate's books. No, not a star. More a light in the sky." Rose clasped her hands together, her face upturned to his. Daniel thought he would never be closer to paradise than at that moment. "A light in the sky, Daniel. Doesn't that sound like a new beginning for us? We must get a passage on that ship!"

The next day, his humble spirit winging on a cloud of glorious disbelief, the last few coins of Mr. Snape's money in his pocket, Daniel traveled obediently on the stagecoach to London. Where a man of greater intelligence would have been suspicious, he saw only a miracle, and thanked God.

As soon as arrangements for D. Putnam, carpenter, and spouse, steerage passengers on the good ship *Aurora*, were complete, they were quietly made man and wife in the old church at Rundull. The curate was not surprised to hear that Rose needed to be married. His wife had hinted as much when the girl was with them before, but he was indeed amazed to hear the culprit was quiet, stolid Daniel Putnam. The village talk had been all of the Honorable Nicholas le Grys. He had wished to lecture

Daniel on the wages of sin, and particularly that of fornication, but Rose begged him not to because, she said,
Daniel did not know about her condition, and she would
prefer to be safely married before breaking the news.

On September 13, her plain black bonnet firmly anchored over her bright hair, her face demure, Rose prepared to descend from the hackney on the quayside at
Gravesend. Suddenly a trumpet blared across the water,
there was a crash of cymbals and a brass band struck up a
lively tune. With one foot already on the step, she slewed
round, rigid with shock.

"Daniel!" Oblivious of her anxiety, entranced by the
sight that met his eyes, Daniel scarcely heard her. He
was looking with delight at the gaily decorated tents, at
the three little ships, festooned with flags that tugged
gently at their mooring ropes. More flags flew high over
a great marquee. Rose grasped his arm, shaking it in a
frenzy. "What is it? What is it? Is it a fair?"

"It's a send-off, I think." Daniel was pleased and flattered. "They're givin' us a grand sort of send-off."

Rose's heart failed a beat. She was going to be exposed. Before she could even get onto the ship! She
snatched up the box containing her precious bonnet with
the violets on it, and leaped to the ground.

Daniel looked after her in consternation. "What's the
matter?"

"What's the matter! Everything's the matter!" Rose
quite forgot she had promised herself to be always polite
to him. To remember with gratitude that he had married
her when she needed him. Half mad with fright, she cast
around her, looking for camouflage of any kind, seeing
nothing but faces with eyes to recognize her. Any of the
grandly dressed ladies promenading up and down might
be the Lady Cressida! Any of the gentlemen in tall hats
could be Nicholas! Standing in groups, glancing dangerously this way and that, were artisans in cloth caps who
might be from Rundull. "I'm going on board," she told
Daniel in a high, sharp whisper. "I'm going ahead."

"Wait a minute. 'Ang on, love. There's our luggage
to . . ."

She did not wait to hear Daniel out. With her head
down, her skirts swishing around her, Rose sped across

the quay to where the crowd was thickest. She came up against a tall, beefy man in a red neckerchief, a man big enough to serve as a screen. With a sigh of relief, she slid in beside him. Lifting a tight, strained face to his, she asked, "What's the rumpus about?"

"There's directors of the company coming from London," the fellow replied, jogging heavily in time to the band's playing, looking delighted, as Daniel had been. "There's going to be important folk making speeches, and there's to be a banquet with roast beef and plum pudding and John Barleycorn. We're to go in style." She stared at him, her lips parted, her eyes glazed, as he described what he knew of the appalling arrangements.

No effort had been spared to expose everyone to one another. Rose's heart palpitated with fright. Daniel, carrying their meager possessions, caught sight of her. "There you are!" he exclaimed, his plain face rumpled with bewilderment. "Why did you run away from me?"

"I don't feel very well." She turned her head lest Daniel should read the fear in her eyes. "I really don't feel very well."

"You're not going to be sick, are you?" he asked in dismay. "P'raps you oughtn't to go aboard."

She pressed forward, tripping blindly over the cobblestones, the thrusting, heaving, good-natured crowd making it easy for her to hide among them. Looking neither right nor left, she scrambled up the gangplank. Along the deck she went, following a shawled figure laden with parcels, keeping her head down.

"I don't feel well," she repeated mindlessly, her voice high and shaking, as she hurried down the stairway into the bowels of the ship. "I don't feel a bit well." She was chattering like a monkey in an effort to keep from thinking.

An official asked for their names.

"Over there. Stall number forty-eight."

Daniel, beside himself with worry, hurriedly pulled aside the curtain that served as a door to their quarters. Rose rushed in headlong. If the accommodation was inadequate in both size and privacy it was at least a refuge from immediate danger. Her heartbeats slowed.

"We'll not have to go ashore to listen to those speeches, will we?"

"I'd like to join in," Daniel admitted diffidently.

"I don't feel well," she muttered again. Daniel put their belongings down, and then there was scarcely room to stand. Rose fell onto the narrow bunk.

"Can I get you somethin' Rose? A drink of water?"

"No," she muttered. Would they be able to send her packing as they had done from Cavendish Square? "No, thank you, I mean."

"What then? What can I do? Are you going to be sick?"

"No. No." She clutched at his hand. "Don't leave me, Daniel."

"No, I won't. I won't." Daniel's face was as long as a horse's nose. She had been so happy on the drive down, teasing him, singing little snatches of song, her eyes bright, her cheeks rosy. "Where d'you hurt, Rose? 'Ave you got the bellyache?"

"No."

"Shall I go, then? Go out on the quay, I mean?"

"No. No. Don't leave me." She had to think of something. Anything. She sank back on the bed, her nails digging into her palms, her eyes screwed up so tightly in concentration that the long lashes all but disappeared. She did not know what to do. Banquets, the man had said. More than one banquet meant more than one day's wait. They couldn't stay here, the two of them, locked in this tiny cubicle day after day!

She heard the banging of boxes and rustling of skirts as the other passengers shuffled past, and envied from the bottom of her heart their uncomplicated lot. She listened to the bossy officials allocating space and tried to think how they might help.

"What'm I goin' to do about you, Rose?" Daniel sounded unnerved. "I'll look for a doctor. They said there's to be a doctor on board."

A doctor! The sweat of another kind of fear dampened her forehead, and trickled down her back. "I'm going to be all right. Just, just let me stay here for a while." And then, with relief, she knew what to do.

She sat upright, her eyes smiling, lashes fluttering, a faint color returning to her cheeks. Lovingly, she put both arms around her husband's neck. "You go out, and enjoy yourself," she said. "Likely there'll be a lot of fun to be had. I'll be perfectly all right. If you see anyone from Rundull," she added with the utmost carelessness, as though it really did not matter at all, "don't tell them I'm here."

"But . . ."

She held her cheek against his so that his whiskers scraped her skin. "Remember, we wanted to make a new start. Just you and me together. You and me, Daniel," she cajoled him, smiling at him with her eyes.

"Yes, but . . ."

"Don't tell anyone you're married. That's what I mean."

"Yes, but if they're on this ship they'll . . ."

She lost her poise. "They won't be on this ship. Why should they be? I told you, there are five ships going." Impatience and fear whipped the smile from her eyes. "Don't talk to them, then. You know what they tried to do to me in the village. Your own family!" Unfairly, she implied he had been guilty too. "If you don't care about a new start, then think of me. I'm your wife and you've to, you've to . . . you've to forsake all others for me! Haven't you to forsake all others?"

"Y-yes."

"Then start by forsaking those horrible people from Rundull!"

"It weren't them, Rose," Daniel protested, his long arms hanging at his sides, his short legs enveloped in the packages that contained their pathetically few worldly goods. "Not Mr. Nicholas's staff. . . ."

"Daniel!" she shouted at him, her terror filling the tiny stall. The shuffling and chatter in the other stalls ceased. Daniel backed away, tripping over a box, righting himself.

"You stay and rest," he muttered.

He went out with a feeling of having bitten off more than he could comfortably chew. The women in his family never got into a state when they felt ill. Rose was practically hysterical, and she didn't even look like throwing up. He lumbered along the narrow, ill-lit passage, fighting against the unruly tide of emigrants looking for their accommodations. If he stayed away for half an hour or so, she'd calm down, he persuaded himself.

In the event, it was five interminable days before *Aurora* was ready to go. *Oriental,* inexplicably, left on the fifteenth. Rose, a prisoner in the confines of her stall, listened with irritation to the cheering, as the first brig to be ready was towed out into the Thames. "Why can't we go?" she asked fretfully, but Daniel could only repeat at sixth-hand what people were saying. The formalities were not complete.

Then, at last, on the eighteenth the cheering rose anew as they too were towed into the middle of the river, followed closely by *Adelaide*. The *Duke of Roxburgh* was to leave from Plymouth, and *Bengal Merchant* from Glasgow.

Daniel had no problem remaining unobserved. There were nearly five hundred emigrants divided among the ships, their ranks swelled by friends and family who had come to see them off. Anxious to please Rose, he wore his cap well down over his eyes. Several times he saw Barney Herd, and turned his back. Barney belonged to a part of Rose's life Daniel had effectively blotted from his mind.

As *Aurora* moved down the Thames on an ebb tide, Rose slid her feet to the floor. Now, at least, she could get up. Daniel had told her that single men were confined in the bow, women in the stern. It had not occurred to her that the divisions were merely for night time. That steerage passengers would have a free run of their section of the ship during the day. That, anyway, they were all bound to meet at meals.

Throwing a shawl around her shoulders, skirting the narrow-fronted stalls of her steerage companions, she went on up the stairway and out on deck. Intoxicated with freedom, she held out her arms so that the cool breeze ran up her sleeves, and down the neck of her dress. The sky with its scurrying, feather-white clouds that she had not seen for days, was beautifully blue and high. Seabirds wheeled elegantly, squawking their curious, raucous farewells.

The wind hissed in the rigging and a seabird, white as snow, gray as silk, with a golden bill, floated in to settle on the rail. Soon England would disappear. What had it given her but Nicholas, and were they not turning their backs on it together? she thought happily. Then she remembered Grandy and a lump came into her throat. There was suddenly a strange sensation of loss: A feathering in her brain, a trembling of her hands, as though she had gone one move too far, stepping as it were, right off the edge of the map.

"Be a good girl," Grandy had said. Her head had come up, her eyes sparkling, her wickedness lying on her like a crown. Grandy was old, she had thought then, and her life was her own. Now she remembered the warmth of his arms about her unexpectedly, the sudden bewilderment of it; she remembered too her sister, who had been her friend until Adam and poverty and the kind of hopelessness that put survival before love, came to separate them; she thought of her mother, lying eternally in Rundull soil.

She was still standing there, her beautiful eyes hazed, her lower lip caught between her teeth, her fingers tight on the rail, when Barney Herd found her. He knew about the unmarried girls who were to spend their nights in charge of a matron behind a forbidding-looking iron grating aft, as far away from the single men as a 550-ton ship would allow. He was on his way now to renew acquaintance with a pretty young seamstress he had met during the jollifications.

"You!" he gasped, his eyes protruding with shock.

Rose gulped. "You," she echoed defiantly, clutching her shawl around her, automatically backing away, her heart pounding. "What're you doing here?" What are you doing in our part of the ship, she meant.

"I'm with Mr. Nicholas, o' course. You knew I was goin' with him. My Gawd!" said Barney, his Adam's apple jumping. "My Gawd, Rose."

In the stillness that followed his words Rose felt a very real terror.

As Nicholas's valet, Barney would have access to the poop deck. He could go straight and tell Lady Cressida she was aboard. Galvanized by the fearful possibility of exposure, she acted with every ounce of strength and all the talent she possessed. Opening her eyes wide, imploring him prettily to believe in her innocence, she murmured, "Mr. Nicholas? On *this* ship?"

"I smells a rat," said Barney bluntly, unconvinced by Rose's winsome guile. "May I be so bold as to inquire whether 'is Lordship arranged this?"

"How could he?" She tossed her head. "You know I left London the day after the wedding."

"Well, I got to hand it to you, Rose. . . . But, my Gawd! What's 'er Ladyship going to say?"

"It's nothing to do with her if my husband's granted a passage," she flared. "He's an independent man. If he wants to emigrate . . ."

"Your husband!" Herd's eyes popped.

"Now really, Barney. You're not very flattering. Don't you think a girl with my looks might get herself a husband?"

Slowly and deliberately, Barney Herd set his feet apart, put both hands on his hips, and looked down at her. "Orl right, give it ter me."

Rose's lashes fluttered.

"Who'd you marry, Rose?"

"Daniel Putnam. I'm Mrs. Daniel Putnam now."

Barney swallowed and his Adam's apple jumped again. "My Gawd!" He wiped his brow.

For the first time, in the wake of the valet's astonishment, Rose recognized with awe the enormity of what she had done.

15

The captain of the *Aurora,* fastidious, white-gloved Theophilius Heale, had groaned inwardly when Gibbon Wakefield, whom he knew to be the strut and stay of penal reform, offered him his present commission. The money was good, but he knew from his midshipman days what the transporting of a load of convicts across the world implied, having endured many a disagreeable night watch, while the screaming of the wind in the rigging merged eerily with hideous laments from the pitiful souls below in their stocks and chains. The West Indies, the Napoleonic Wars of his youth, and trading in the islands of the Pacific had proved vastly more to his taste. He was therefore pleasantly surprised on being told he was to take to New Zealand twenty-one cabin passengers of eminence and distinction, along with a steerage comple-ment of respectable artisans.

"No convicts will ever go to New Zealand," the great man had assured him with a smile.

On the poop deck now, as the brave little vessel slid silkily on a straight keel into the Channel, he engaged Lady Cressida le Grys in conversation. "Of course your maid may come to you at any time to perform her duties. And your husband's valet as well."

"We may go below to visit other members of our household?"

Heale rubbed his chin. He had no intention of crossing swords with the daughter-in-law of the earl of Rundull. "In my view, it's the mixing of the classes that lowers the dignity of a ship. As Mr. Wakefield said in his excellent speech, we all commend the enterprise of the working classes in going to a new land, and, we hope, to a better life, but . . ."

Clutching at the skirts she had reefed and double-reefed against the wind Cressida eyed him silently. What a snob the man was, she thought irritably, yet knowing she was a little mad with the volatile emotions triggered in her by the sight of the tiny cabin that Nicholas and she were to share. Palatial though it might be by steerage standards, she had known at first glance it would never contain their mutual resentment for the duration of the voyage.

"Anyway, tell your husband not to worry about his men," Heale's heartiness overlaid the uncertainty of her silence. "I've made provision for Major Baker to assemble all the male adults for daily drilling just as soon as we say good-bye to Land's End. Apart from the obvious necessity of training, it will counteract boredom."

"Obvious necessity? What do you mean?" Cressida snatched at her pretty bonnet as the bow breeze caught it, trying desperately to take a calm and intelligent interest in what the man was saying.

"In a cannibal country there may well be times when they'll need to defend themselves." Heale leaned toward her, adding confidentially, "Between you and me, I'm of the opinion that many of our passengers are sailing in total ignorance of what they may encounter on the other side of the world."

Cannibal country? Cressida repeated the words to herself as if puzzling over their meaning.

Holding her apprehension at bay, she asked, "Why should they have to defend themselves, Captain? Should there be any trouble, surely we are all bound to act under the command and direction of the New Zealand Company's officers, some of whom I know served with great distinction in Spain and Portugal, as well as with the Foreign Legion."

"Don't worry your pretty head, m'Lady."

Constraint of human emotion was something Cressida had learned in the nursery, but anyone who knew her well would have seen signs of something more than disquiet in the puckering of her features, the fluttering of her hands. "How can I help but be alarmed when you say such things? I really must ask you to explain, for I've read all the company's literature, and they're at pains to portray the natives as a friendly race, even partially educated already by the missionaries, and most anxious for white men to come among them," she said.

"Indeed, that is so."

"Then the reason for the 'obvious necessity' of training eludes me."

Heale frowned up at the tall masts. Lord defend him from intelligent women! He had not expected a catechism. "It's exercise the working people need," he said, dissembling. "You must realize, m'Lady, on a ship of this size steerage is bound to be cramped."

"That surely depends, not upon the size of the ship, but upon how many people you've taken in relation to its size."

"I took the number allocated to me by Mr. Wakefield."

"And how many was that, may I ask?"

"Er, eighty-five adults, I believe."

"And children?" Cressida persisted.

He shifted awkwardly. There was a look in his eyes that said these facts were none of her business. "In the region of, er . . ."

"You must know, Captain."

"Forty-two."

Cressida, calculating swiftly, failed to suppress a gasp of dismay. "A hundred and twenty-seven!"

"The ship's not overburdened, I assure you."

"How cramped the poor things must be!" Her consternation flung her own dilemma out of her mind.

"No more cramped than is usual." Like the earl of Rundull, the captain was impatient of sentiments about the poor. If God hadn't intended them to be poor he would not have inflicted poverty upon them.

She turned away from him. She wanted to say, "If one treats people badly, they will behave badly." She knew. How she knew. In the past two months she had become a stranger to herself, bottling up her misery and disappointment until it festered like a sore. Nurse would not listen. Nor her mother. When a girl married, they inferred, she took what came her way.

She glanced behind, saw the dear, familiar green land of England receding at a frightening speed, smelled the salt drifting in to replace the sweet, dry scents of summer, and stifled a convulsive little gasp. She had to bite her lips to stop herself crying out loud to this heartless man that he must stop the vessel and let her off—let them all off—all these innocent people who were "sailing in ignorance of what they may encounter on the other side of the world." The seagulls swooped and cried, the wind whistled in the rigging. She wondered why Nicholas had not told her New Zealand was peopled by cannibals.

The captain saw her apprehension. "Don't you worry . . ."

Her control broke. "Please, Captain. I am not accustomed to being treated as a toy. If I have, if we have all been misled as . . ."

"Indeed, I'm sure you were not misled," he countered hurriedly. "Is not your husband a friend of Mr. Jerningham Wakefield?"

"Yes. Yes, he is."

"Well then," the captain blundered on heartily, "I'm sure he must know as much as there is to know about New Zealand, and would not have brought you if he considered the expedition hazardous. Talk to your husband. . . ."

She swung away, leaving his words to scatter on the wind. Talk to Nicholas! After two months of marriage the gap between them was as wide as on their wedding day. "Life is what you make it," her father had said. Life was what men made it, Cressida thought bitterly, and tears stung behind her eyes. Cannibals! Was it not enough that she should be going to the other side of the world with a man who did not love her?

She went to the rail and stood looking out over the gray waters of the Channel, a hard little pain inside growing and rising toward her throat, threatening to break out in a cry of despair. Then she remembered Nurse's earthy advice. "There's no trouble that can't be cured, my Lady, by doing something for someone else."

She swung around. "Are there any arrangements for schooling the children?" she asked. That was something she could do. Teach the children.

"There is only one. His parents . . ."

"I mean the steerage children. You said there are forty-two of them cooped up below."

"Mr. Langford has already been appointed education officer, and Mr. Wallace has volunteered to help him. They'll take classes for the males."

"But what about the females?"

"Females?" he echoed quizzically.

"Some of them must surely be female."

"Possibly," he conceded. "Very possibly."

"But you don't feel they are entitled to an education?" He remained silent, bull-eyed, his kindliness assassinated by her violation of the social niceties. She saw by his reaction that she was unforgivably interfering, but she did not care. "I am accustomed to ride and entertain myself vigorously," she said. "The voyage is to be a long one. Six months? I anticipate I could become exceedingly bored unless I find some way of employing my time. I could teach these children." She clasped her fingers tightly together, praying that he would agree, thinking she would go mad if she had nothing with which to divert herself.

"I'd hazard five months." The captain whittled her figure down with a bland smile. "*Oriental*, the crack ship, may even do it in four." Cressida did not smile in return. In sudden impatience, the captain said pointedly, "Forgive me for asking, but are ladies no longer content with their sewing and the conversation of their husbands?"

"No," said Cressida, remembering with a scalding sense of defeat and shame the endless nights at Cavendish Square, when she had sat alone with her needlework, suffering retribution for the trouncing of Rose Snape; taking her punishment for Nurse's protective intervention, which had seemed such a triumph at the time; learning the hard way that old servants, whose reliability was as solid as the very land the earls of Woolege owned, were unable to carry their protection across the barrier of marriage.

Without a lessening of his rigid naval bearing, the captain shifted awkwardly from one foot to the other. "It is indeed to your credit, m'Lady, that you should think of educating the working-class daughters, but, as I said before, it's important to me to maintain the dignity of my ship."

"I was not talking of cultivating the society of the assisted emigrants, Captain, merely of taking a class of girls in reading and writing. Perhaps not only girls. I'll be bound there are both men and women without education, and without the means to pass the time."

"I imagine education would be wasted on such people."

Ignoring the inference that she close the discussion, she retorted, "I have taught my maid to read and write. If, as our sponsor has promised, New Zealand is to be a better land for the underprivileged, then should we not all cooperate to that end?"

Captain Heale drew in a sharp breath and expelled it with energy. Perhaps he should simply stand aside and let these young people have their heads. Time alone would tell what they made of Wakefield's Great Britain of the Southern Hemisphere. Certainly, nobody but themselves would suffer if they built up a country without a working class.

Then, to his relief, Nicholas appeared from the hatch, formidably handsome, with his crisp dark hair tossed by the wind, his tall hat in his hand, the full skirt of his double-breasted coat flapping in the breeze. They stood in silence as his lazy stride brought him nearer.

"So, Captain, we're on our way. The great adventure has begun." He paused, his long legs in the light doeskin pantaloons set wide apart, the straps tight beneath boots polished by Herd to a mirror gloss.

"It has, indeed."

Nicholas took Cressida's arm. "May I remove my lady wife? Her maid has unpacked and returned below. We must sort ourselves out, now."

"Of course." The captain bowed stiffly, his face relaxing. "I've enjoyed our conversation, m'Lady, and look forward to many more."

"Thank you, Captain." She smiled at him, a small, apologetic little smile. "I would be pleased if you would give consideration to my suggestion."

Noting the change in her manner, Heale inclined his head courteously. Ah, well, some of these fillies needed a bit of taming. That young colt looked just the man for the job. Clasping his hands behind his back, he began pacing with studied precision up and down the deck. He reached the rail, swung around and paced back, enjoying the tug of the wind, glad to be at sea again. The next time he turned, he was looking into the lively blue eyes of his first officer.

"What is it?"

"I think you ought to know there's a runaway aboard."

The captain slapped a hand to his side in immediate vexation. "Stowaway?"

"No. She's in cabin number two, fully paid for, and a delightful lady into the bargain. Miss Annie Frederick by name. I saw two Runners searching the crowd on the quayside, and I saw the minx fling a shawl over her head and grab a baby from one of the assisted emigrants, which she proceeded to, er . . ." The officer hesitated.

"All right man, what did she do with it?" demanded the captain impatiently.

"She pretended to feed it."

"Put it to her dry breast?" Heale was scandalized.

"Yes. The Runners passed on, and she scuttled into the crowd, going aboard. She's a very respectable lady, sir. I talked to her."

"Respectable! Bah!" snorted the captain impatiently. "What is respectable about that kind of behavior? And why was I not told before?"

"Because she begged me not to. She's very persuasive, sir. And you were busy. I decided not to bother you. You can still put in at Dover or Plymouth, if you must. She is going out to join a member of the survey party—a Mr. Stitchbury, who is a friend of Mr. Wakefield's son. She's not without either influence or money and . . ." The two men eyed each other, the one with uncertain disapproval, the other hopefully.

"I'd leave her alone if I were you, Captain. I've done my duty in reporting the situation, but I think you'll find she will be a great asset. There are only twenty-one cabin passengers, sir, and it's a long voyage. She's a comely lass and could enliven things considerably." He turned his eyes to the captain's face, and his voice slowed interrogatively.

"It's monstrous, of course. Monstrous!" The captain quickened his stride, his face marked with the lines of his displeasure. They paced together the length of the poop and back. "Send her to me, Mr. Vine. I'll judge the situation on its merits."

Nicholas and Cressida strolled across the deck together, the salt wind whipping at their clothes. "What scintillating suggestion did you have for our worthy captain, my dear?"

"If it's part of the marriage contract that I should repeat all private conversations to you, then surely I should have been informed of it," she replied tartly.

Nicholas's head was aching damnably from an overindulgence in brandy at a select little dinner on *Mercury* the previous night. The New Zealand Company's bigwigs had chartered their own boat, and had come down to Gravesend to see the first ships off. "Is it possible that a sea voyage will have the effect of blunting that sharp tongue of yours, my dear?" He smiled as he spoke, for the benefit of passengers who might be looking their way. "Good afternoon. Yes, it's good to be afloat at last." They nodded, their smiles serene, but Cressida's eyes, if the passerby had but noticed, were lit by something deeper and brighter than mere goodwill.

They came to their own door. A pretty girl with bobbing curls and a lively face was emerging from the cabin next to theirs. She extended a friendly hand. Cressida took it. "We must introduce ourselves," the stranger said, "for we are obliged to live cheek by jowl for a long time. I know who you are. I've made it my business to put the passenger list to the faces, and I am so pleased," she declared warmly, "that we are to be friends."

She had removed her outdoor wrap and bonnet. She was wearing an elegant yellow gown piped with green. Her manner was so charming, the picture of her so pleasing, that they momentarily forgot their ill humor. "I am Annie Frederick," she went on. "And Mr. le Grys, I know you are a friend of Mr. Jerningham Wakefield, who is also a friend of the man I am going out to New Zealand to marry. He has sailed in *Tory*. Is this not the most wonderfully exciting adventure?"

Her excitement was infectious. It lifted their spirits.

Nicholas said good-humoredly, "We shall take a leaf out of your book and quickly get to know everyone."

"Oh, yes. We must make it a friendly voyage."

A voice from the end of the passage called, "Miss

Frederick!" They turned their heads. The first officer was there, apologetically smiling.

"If you could spare a moment . . ."

Nicholas reached out casually toward the door but Cressida, with a swift, independent movement, opened it and they went inside. Nicholas closed the door after them. In the appalling closeness of the tiny room, they faced each other. "Not quite the master bedroom of Cavendish Square." He surveyed the narrow bed and meager floor space. The silence lengthened. Nicholas leaned back against the wall, his dark eyes still, his face inscrutable. "In the new circumstances, might it not be advantageous to strike the truce that anyway has to come, if we're going to live out our allotted span? Assuming, of course, that we're lucky enough to arrive."

Quivering, Cressida turned her head away and began untying her bonnet. She put it down on the bed, a confection of flowers on grosgrain that matched her eyes. Those pale eyes, Nicholas was thinking, like a wash in the wake of Rose's vivid coloring. She slid unsteady fingers through the curls that lay loose on her forehead, straightened her dress, glanced down at her dainty boots. Her voice was as emotionless as his as she asked, "What are you suggesting?"

"I'm suggesting this is rather a narrow bed. I'm a normal man with all a normal man's instincts." Her suddenly stiff back, her continuing silence, provoked him into adding tauntingly, "And you, my fair lady, by your own admission, are well endowed in the same direction."

A sharp uprush of anger combined with fear wiped the stillness from Cressida's face. She bent down again, adjusting the flowers that had blown flat on the rim of her bonnet. "You're suggesting you may wish to use my body?"

But her apparent coolness, her question that was meant to shame him, only brought out the devil in Nicholas. "I wouldn't want to embarrass you by looking for comfort among the single women in steerage. Anyway, why should I go there, when you have confessed to liking a roughing up?"

Maintaining an outward show of impassivity, by a miracle keeping the humiliation hidden, she turned, keeping her eyes lowered. "I've been talking to Captain Heale.

We might not arrive in New Zealand for six months or more. We may even, as you have inferred, be wrecked and have to make do with a desert island." Her emotions broke through and she stumbled, "W-would you wish me, in these circumstances, to be p-pregnant?"

He watched her contemplatively, his teasing and his animosity suspended.

"I mean, would you wish to endanger my life?" When he still did not answer, she said bitterly, "Fornication— and it is fornication we're discussing—may lead as easily as an act of love to pregnancy."

"You're suggesting that all married men on board should abstain from claiming their conjugal rights for the duration of the voyage?"

"I think that would be wise. If you feel unable to control your animal instincts, I'm prepared to sleep on the floor, since, as you infer, proximity is the problem."

He burst into a gust of incredulous laughter.

But the hurt had gone too deep, and she lashed out, "I am to forget you spent our wedding night with your slut!" She saw his face darken, hesitated, then rushed on, "And every night since, presumably with some London trollop. I am to forget that because suddenly you have nowhere to put your, your . . ."

In the depths of his eyes, a light flickered briefly, like a small, crude flame. When she choked on her own lewdness, he emitted a hearty yell of laughter that hit the walls of their tiny cabin and buffeted back at them. Two scarlet spots patched her cheeks. In that moment of illuminating passion, she had never looked more like Rose. "Why," he said softly, "we may yet make something of this travesty of a marriage."

On the small aft deck Rose raised terrified eyes and met Barney's uncompromising stare. Why, oh, why had she ventured out? What a fool she had been. A dozen untenable possibilities flashed through her mind. Would Lady Cressida tell the captain? Would the captain put her ashore at Dover? What would Daniel's reaction be if he had to suffer the public disgrace of being off-loaded along with her? Exposed in the limelight of the public gaze, would everyone see what, miraculously, no one had noticed so far? Daniel had amiably agreed not to tell anyone their marriage was only a matter of days old, but faced with a rumpus, who knew what would spill out? She had to fight.

"May I be struck down," she declared tossing her golden head, risking hellfire and damnation, "if I knew Mr. Nicholas was on this ship. Daniel couldn't stay in the village, and he . . ." The words were tumbling over each other. "He didn't know where to go. And I did know, from Nicholas, that carpenters was wanted in New Zealand." In her panic, Rose's English lapsed. "So I told 'im, but 'e wouldn't go by 'imself. 'E wouldn't, 'e simply wouldn't, so I, I . . . 'e'd saved me life. You know 'e saved me life. I owed 'im . . ." Her voice quivered, the tears starting to her beautiful eyes. "I owed . . ." Her heart-shaped face, marble white now, crumpled.

Something of her genuine distress, her helplessness, pierced the shell of Barney Herd's disapproval, and weakened the loyalty so newly growing in him for his master's lady. He was not a cruel man, and he had known Rose all her life. Besides, without being disloyal to his friends in the cabin class, Edward Gibbon Wakefield had, perhaps inadvertently, put germs of independence into some of their servants' heads. Glimpses of a new and heretofore unguessed-at freedom had flashed across the valet's facile mind. There was a sense of optimism among the young men in the bow, tactfully not yet put into words, that for the assisted emigrants fate might have something better in store than they with their humble pretensions had heretofore reckoned on.

His thin mouth twisted into a wry but not unsympathetic grin. "You may be struck down," he agreed, "but you could postpone it, like, if you stayed in your bunk 'til we 'aven't no more ports we could stop at. Land's End, like, would be safe to come out. Fred Quick's on board, and 'e ain't exactly trustworthy. I mean, 'e's all over Mr. Nicholas and 'is lady. There's the boy Oliver, and Will Trent who's to look after Mr. Nicholas's 'orses." He saw the gratitude in her face, and added slyly, "If I ever need a favor, I'll know where to look, eh Rose?"

"Oh yes. Oh yes, Barney."

"Orl right," Barney told her kindly. "You go off an' get seasick, what's sensible kind of behavior."

*   *   *

Up in the first-class saloon the passengers eyed one another with intense interest. Twenty adults and a child were to be closely confined for five or more months. Dr. Stokes, the ship's surgeon, older than the others, began asking the young people where they came from.

Miss Frederick swiftly left the saloon. She had no intention of allowing herself to be quizzed until the ship was safely past Land's End.

She knew from the entertainingly indiscreet Jerningham Wakefield, with whom her lover had sailed, that the Scottish couple were both twenty years old. The same age as herself. That he was the younger son of Sir John Maxwell of Ayrshire. That his wife, though one would never have guessed it from her pretty voice and her stylish clothes, was the local shoemaker's daughter with whom he had eloped. She knew, too, that Mr. Maxwell had a thousand pounds in gold with which to pay for his land.

As she hurried out on deck, thinking warmly of the most wonderful man in the world to whom she was running away, she wondered, with a gurgle of suppressed amusement, who else among her new companions was a victim of the conventions, or of fate.

In her bunk in the bowels of the ship, life was far from perfect for Rose. Good-natured passengers, worried that this pretty little matron should be ill on such a calm sea, came to keep her company.

"Perhaps you're expecting a happy event," one woman suggested shrewdly, settling her bulk as best she could on the foot of Rose's inadequate bunk. "When was you married, love?"

Rose implied demurely that such a happening was not outside the bounds of possibility. "I'd be glad if you didn't tell anyone." She gave the woman her most disarming smile.

"Of course, dear. I understand. It's your little secret, isn't it?"

It was indeed. Confined all day in the cramped quarters below decks, Rose sweated in misery. Ventilation was poor. The air grew more and more stale. The creaking of the ship's timbers frightened her out of her wits. A sudden lurching as a squall hit them would send boxes flying around the floor and small objects sliding beyond the curtain, to be lost forever. She gritted her teeth and saw it through.

At last they passed Land's End, the magic, long-awaited point of no return. As the ship began to pitch and toss in the Bay of Biscay, as the steerage passengers fell misera- bly into their bunks, as the fetid smell and stomach- turning sound of vomiting grew disgustingly in the confined, airless space around her, Rose swung her legs over the side of the bunk, jerked at the strings of her stays until they were tight enough to allow her to fasten her skirt, and happily ascended the cabin scuttle. As they stood on the narrow deck side by side, Daniel, too pleased and relieved to delve into the mystery of his wife's illness, took Rose affectionately by the arm. "I've got to tell you somethin'. Barney 'Erd an' Fred Quick is on board this ship."

And Nicholas! A leaping warmth went right through her, turning her eyes to green emeralds, swelling her heart. She saw a puzzled look cloud Daniel's face, and made her eyes fly wide with pretended shock. "That means . . ."

"Yes," he agreed, looking at her uncertainly.

"Oh dear." But the happiness in her drowned the dismay she had fully intended to show.

"You don' sound very worried, Rose," said Daniel. "You said you didn't want 'em, on no account, to know."

The laugh she had meant to sound careless emerged like a peal of bells. "What can we do, Daniel? We can't jump overboard and swim back to England." With danc- ing fingers, she pulled the ribbons of her violet-trimmed bonnet up under her chin, tied a beautiful bow, and, brimming with sensuous serenity, smoothed the ends.

Daniel watched her closely. "Where'd you get that, Rose?"

Surprised, she turned her lovely, glowing face. "I bought it. It's pretty, but it was quite cheap," she lied brazenly. Daniel's mouth tightened, and a little warning note sounded in her head. "I-I'm good with clothes." Daniel continued to look at her in silence, and for the first time, Rose wondered apprehensively if she had underestimated him.

That night she put the bonnet away and begged some trimmings from a resourceful milliner, who was even now happily employed stitching up confections for disconsolate women whose headgear had blown overboard. She embellished the bonnet she had worn to the ship, garlanding it so lavishly with flowers, feathers, and bows, that in the end it was almost prettier than the one Nicholas had given her. Though there was no looking glass in her stall, she knew she looked enchanting from the smiling expressions turned her way.

But as the men ogled her, their less comely wives frowned. A month ago, Rose would have tossed her head and gone on her way, but here in the narrow confines of a tiny ship, there was nowhere to go. Besides, she knew apprehensively that she was soon going to need the goodwill of her own kind. With bored resignation she stripped the old bonnet, leaving only a nodding bunch of feathers at the side.

The waif Oliver followed Rose like a dog. Whenever she appeared on deck or at the long trestle tables for meals, he was there, his thin, apprehensive, pallid little face lighting up with hope at sight of her. Partly irritated by his devotion, partly flattered, she accepted his attentions, and gradually acquired a sense of responsibility for him. She knew now the dreadful story of his parents' death.

"They was 'anged," said Oliver.

"Why?" Rose felt her eyes popping.

Oliver shrugged. Any one of two hundred crimes, from blacking one's face or writing on Westminster bridge to murder, brought poor folk to the Triple Tree.

"Do you remember it?"

"Yes. We all went to Newgate in an open cart an' the folks follered be'ind, jeerin'. The 'angman put a noose round me ma's neck, an' I screamed an' screamed, an' someone dragged me out of 'er arms. There wuz a man wot sold pies at the foot of the scaffold. 'E 'anded me over the 'eads o' the mob an' dumped me on the cobbles."

"And then?" she asked, fascinated in spite of the horror the story evoked.

"Don't remember."

She learned piecemeal about the life he led, fending for himself as best he could, sleeping in doorways, finding a space big enough to curl up in in the verminous warrens of the rookery north of Leicester Square. With nothing better to do, the child would go to Newgate to watch the hangings. He soon discovered that folk in the fever of blood lust could forget about their picnic baskets. Those chickens and loaves were to keep him alive. The hangings did not bother him. They became a part of the background to his life.

Once past the Bay of Biscay, the sea was pleasantly calm. *Aurora* scudded along swiftly with a following wind. Those who had been ill rose from their bunks in the bowels of the ship, leaving behind them stale, malodorous air that was to linger for the remainder of the voyage. Up on deck Rose and Daniel watched with delight the leaping and bounding of phosphorescent flying fish and the moon, so huge and bright in its waxing, so mysterious in its waning. Sometimes Rose had a feeling of merging to become a part of the hissing of the waters as they broke on the curved oak of the ship's hull, of the dreamy sighing of the wind in the rigging, of the miracle of the mysterious night.

"You haven't been a proper wife since we got on the ship, Rosie," Daniel grumbled, dragging her out of her private heaven.

"It's bad enough listening to other people groaning and grunting through the curtains, without knowing they're listening to us," she returned. "You'll have to wait till we're on dry land." She pushed his exploring hand impatiently away and straightened her skirts.

"But it's only been once, Rose," he pleaded.

"It's not my fault we got married with nowhere to go," she pointed out. "Count your lucky stars the curate was good enough to let you come into my bed the night we were wed, or it wouldn't even have been once." Yet, she knew one loving had been necessary. Daniel might be thickheaded, but he was not as thickheaded as that.

"Sometimes I think you're hard, Rose."

"I'm sorry. I don't mean to be." In her quicksilver way, suddenly penitent, she rested her head endearingly on his shoulder. "We'll have a house of our own soon, and then it'll be different," she murmured dreamily, floating away on a rosy cloud of self-deception. She would face the inevitable when she had to. As they crossed the deck she twined her arm through his and gave him a guilty little peck on the cheek.

16

Mr. Langford was delighted with Rose's suggestion that classes should be started for the steerage adults.

"One of the ladies has kindly offered her services for just such a project," he said, omitting to add that only the captain's opposition to so grand a personage associating with the lower orders had kept him from taking up the offer so far.

Rose was jubilant. Thirsting for knowledge, cheating audaciously, she had managed to ingratiate herself into the children's classes, sidling in at the last moment, her pretty face winsomely apologetic, holding Oliver by the hand, and sitting so self-effacingly on the floor that neither Mr. Wallace nor Mr. Langford had the heart to evict her.

In the steamy heat below decks she now canvassed inert, disinterested passengers.

"Learnin' don't do nothin' for a woman," grumbled Daniel. "Likely you'll look down on me."

"If you get some learning yourself," Rose retorted good-humoredly, "you could look down on me."

"I could never look down on you," he replied with heavy-footed sincerity. Yet he was discomfited by the widening chasm between Rose and the other passengers. Workingmen's wives did not embroider. They mended and patched, and that was the end of it. Rose was thought to have ideas above her station. Daniel could not but agree. Miraculously, he had missed one sneer addressed directly to his wife, "You'll 'ave more to think about and

proper useful work to do when that baby o' yourn comes."
They had been married for twenty-six days. It was still
too soon for Daniel to know.

Rose spent hours poring over the Church Missionary
Society's *Grammar and Vocabulary of the Language of
New Zealand,* learning to read in both languages, intriguing her tutors, fostering doubt and suspicion in her
kind.

"Kiwi. A wingless bird."

"Wingless bird? I thought you said you could read,"
scoffed one of the steerage women.

Rose lifted her eyes from the page. "I can read quite
well. It does say here 'A wingless bird.' "

The woman sneered. "You've a long way to go before
you're heducated, my girl."

Unbashed, Rose returned eagerly to her studies.

Kumara, sweet potato. *Poi,* a toy for a child, attached
to a string and twirled rhythmically to the accompaniment of a song or dance. She closed her eyes, visualizing
herself dancing with the little boy, twirling the ball on its
piece of string. Dancing . . . dancing . . .

"I thought you was learnin'," scoffed Daniel. "You got
yer eyes shut."

"I am learning," she replied, patiently accepting the
breaking of the spell. "The Maori name for a house is
whare, Daniel. It's *whares* you'll be building."

" 'Ouses'll do fer me. We don't 'ave to learn to talk
heathen, Rose. We're not goin' to change into natives."

"Mr. Langford thinks it would be courteous to make
an effort to speak the language. He says the Maoris are
making the effort to speak ours."

"Of course they are. I don't suppose they want to
be 'eathens all their lives."

Rose looked worriedly across the long gap that separated them, then went back to her precious dictionary
and forgot.

They scudded south on a stern breeze. Major Baker
ordered the male passengers out on deck. As one drilling
followed another, speculation mounted, and the words
savages, cannibals, and *heathens* were bandied about.
The educated élite grew tight-lipped. Some steerage women
wept and wished to go home.

A company official, employing *sangfroid* that would have done credit to Edward Gibbon himself, explained that the drilling was only for fresh air and exercise. "There are very few Maoris," he told them. It was what Jerningham had said, and Nicholas still did not believe a word of it. The saber rattling excited him, but he was worried for the women and children. He made a decision to divert them.

"I'll get up a concert, Herd," he said to his valet one evening while dressing for dinner. "We've a deal of talent up here. I'm trying, without much success so far, to persuade the captain to allow steerage passengers to join in." Heale was unbending in his determination to keep the classes apart, only reluctantly giving permission to Nicholas and Cressida to assemble their household once a week in a broad gangway in the middle of the ship, so that Cressida could satisfy herself as to their well-being.

"What do you think about having the steerage up, Herd?" Nicholas asked now, as he reached for his cravat.

Barney Herd's reaction was sharp and immediate, for he knew Rose would not absent herself from a concert where Nicholas was to perform. "Honest ter God, Mr. Nicholas, I don't think as most of them would know a concert from a 'ole in the ground."

Nicholas chuckled. "Oh, I don't know. Hand me my studs, there's a good fellow. And be careful with them. Can't replace anything now, and Captain Heale is a great one for keeping up standards. He's got the ladies wearing their jewels to dinner."

"That's what I meant, in a manner of speaking," Herd replied, snatching with relief at ballast for his argument. "It's a big jump, like, to the steerage folk."

"According to Mr. Wakefield, they're all going to be translated in a flash into independent landowners. Everyone his own master."

"That's as may be, Mr. Nicholas."

"Have you a taste for being your own man? Deuced awkward for me if you do."

"I'll believe it when I see it, as they say." But Herd did not meet his master's eyes.

More than one of the cabin passengers had expressed concern at the trend of Edward's speechifying at Gravesend. In the evenings, over brandy and cigars, while the germs of disquiet multiplied, Nicholas found himself considering the daunting prospect of running a servantless estate. Jerningham had said a balance was to be kept between land, labor, and capital. "Otherwise, before you can say knife we'll have the laborers buying up the land, and gentlemen left out in the cold without servants." Nicholas remembered saying scornfully, "So New Zealand is to be a land of opportunity! For all your fine talk I'll wager this new country will grow up as class-structured as England."

Now he looked thoughtfully at Herd, wondering if, anyway, he would have use for a valet in the new life. "Mr. Langford and Mr. Wallace go down to the bowels of the ship every morning to teach children the three Rs," Nicholas remarked idly as he buttoned his waistcoat. "My lady wife, being short on occupation, offered to assist them with a class for adults."

"Oh, no, sir. Oh, no," exclaimed the valet, appalled.

"Why not?"

"They're pretty rough, sir," said Herd, hot with apprehension.

"She's county-bred, Herd, and seems to get on well with country folk."

"I'd suggest m'Lady sticks to 'er own kind, all the same, if I was you. They're rough, them steerage," the valet repeated.

Nicholas put Herd's advice to Cressida that evening. He had settled on the edge of the bed, tormenting her with his interest, as she drew her nightgown over her clothes, and proceeded to wrestle with her stays.

"I see it as my duty to bring education to the underprivileged," she snapped, provoked out of her studied calm by his lewd stare, dreading the moment when he would drop his clothes to the deck and stand before her naked. "In the eyes of the church we are one," he had said when she protested, taunting her with the eternal theme of their suffering. "Why should you not enjoy looking at what is yours?" The corsets fell with a small plop to the deck and she bent to pick them up, her cheeks fiery with embarrassment. She stepped over to the bed already made up on the floor.

Suddenly tired of it all, Nicholas heaved a huge sigh. "Does the unreality of our circumstances never occur to you?" His eyes dwelled on her face as he waited for her reply.

She stiffened. She knew only too well, had always known, that tied as she was to such a virile man, she could not remain untouched indefinitely. With a scarcely perceptible movement she turned, but only a part of her face came into view. He did not see that she was frightened.

"We need to have a quiet and very serious talk," he said.

She moved with quick, nervous little steps toward the far corner of the cabin and sat down on the brass-bound sea chest. She looked so like Rose with her hair falling around her shoulders, gold silk on white cambric, that his heart wept. "I wish you would come and sit beside me," he said. She did not move. "Whatever we feel about each other now, we must sooner or later face the fact that our future lies together. We're going to share children, and a home. We may even die together. I think it's time to take stock."

Cressida looked down at her hands. Even knowing that to live with indifference was to die slowly from the core outward, she could not take the first step. Not if she was to show maidenly decorum. Not, anyway, after the insults.

"If it helps," he said gently, "I did not arrange for Rose to come to Cavendish Square, and I would not have gone to her if you hadn't . . ."

His ill-chosen words rekindled her bitterness. "Oh, how facile men are! Can't you see it takes more than words to undo . . ."

Nicholas leaped to his feet. There was violence in his manner. He began purposefully to undo his clothing.

"Nicholas!"

It was a cry of sheer terror, but it served only to stimulate him. Besides, that was not real fear, he told himself. By her own admission, she was accustomed to fornication. Heedless of her state of undress, Cressida dived past him toward the door. He put a foot on the skirt of her nightgown, and she fell with a shriek to the deck.

He was adept at picking up a girl of her size and flinging her on the bed. Rose loved him to take her like this. His arms went lustfully around her, then with shock he saw her eyes were wide as saucers, starting with fear.

She did not move. Two enormous tears rolled onto the bedcover. A vast and unexpected compassion overwhelmed him. "Why did you marry me?" he asked. Her mouth worked in a desperate effort at control. "Cry," he found himself saying gently. Her body heaved with sobs. He was amazed at the pent-up passion in her. He smoothed her brow, kissed her gently on the hands. At last she was calm. She said in a small, distant, but very dignified voice, "I lied to you."

Nicholas frowned. "Is that supposed to answer my question?"

She wiped her face with the sheet, sniffed, and pushed her damp hair back from her forehead.

"Here, blow your nose on my handkerchief. It's not ladylike to sniff."

Obediently, like a child, she blew her nose then, clutching the handkerchief to her breast, she said in a rush, "It wasn't true. About the baby I mean. I wanted to hurt you . . . You had hurt me so much."

"You mean, you are a virgin?"

"Of course."

He laughed. "Of course," he repeated. It scarcely seemed to matter, now.

Her eyelids fluttered up, apprehensively.

"Can I have my answer? Why did you marry me?"

"I was in love with you." The words emerged like an admission of guilt. "Since I was eight years old."

"Eight!"

"Do you remember coming to S-Saxon Mote one summer? Our f-fathers were very friendly at the time. There was a three-day shoot."

"Yes," he replied uncertainly. "I believe I do remember."

Her voice grew stronger. "I told my parents I was going to marry you."

"What did they say?" he asked, incredulous, in a way amused.

"They laughed. But I never forgot."

"I don't recall that you gave any sign of this, er, passion."

She said with a little hiccup of distress, "You seemed always to be chasing some other girl. You treated me rather like a sister. Then I got smallpox, and I thought that was the end. I knew you would never marry anyone who was . . . imperfect."

"But you're not imperfect. You're lovely." Nearly as lovely as Rose. Like a pale print of her when the light had faded.

"I wasn't marked at all. I wanted to do the season last year, but my parents wouldn't have it. They insisted I wasn't well enough."

"Were you?"

She lifted her fingers, and with the utmost tenderness stroked his cheek. "I found out later my sister Fanny had told my parents what I had confided to her—that I was going to set my cap at you."

"Oh?"

"That year you had been in a deal of trouble."

"Yes."

"Everyone said you were wild. My parents thought you'd never quiet down."

"They were so afraid of your carrying out your threat that they kept you away for a season?"

She nodded.

"Then how did you get back into society?"

"You must have heard the rumors—that I had been badly scarred. All sorts of nonsense was being bandied 'round. My parents rushed me to London at the beginning of last season to let people see for themselves. After my illness, anyway, I had lost some of my liveliness. They hoped you wouldn't be interested. Then you danced with me at Buckingham Palace and you said things that made me think . . . Why did you say," and she quoted his words, " 'Don't press me. I might say more than I ought'?"

That she reminded him of Rose? Nicholas groaned inwardly. "I don't remember," he lied.

"I thought you meant to speak to my father first, but instead you got drunk and came to Berkeley Square, shouting at the top of your voice that you wanted to marry me. You serenaded me. It was so romantic . . ." Her eyes were puzzled, questioning.

Dear God!

"Papa and Mama were horrified, of course. Your behavior only proved to them that you deserved your bad reputation." She twisted her wedding ring around her finger. "I was wrong to insist, was I not? And I got my punishment." The silence was painful to them both. Cressida broke it in a rush of words. "Why did you come at five o'clock in the morning and propose to me in that exciting way, if you didn't want me? I told my parents, people say what they really mean when they've had too much to drink. I said you must have been afraid my father would turn you down. And he would have if I hadn't insisted. Why did you do it, Nicholas?"

He leaned down, pressing his face into her shoulder so that she would not see his and be hurt further by the lie he had to tell. "I'd have asked for you, sober," he said. "It's just that, it was a bit soon. I hadn't finished sowing my wild oats. You should have been four years younger. I needed a little more time."

"And I looked like that girl?" She could not resist stabbing herself with a sword that had lain at her side for months.

A shadow crossed his face. "It's time to forget and start again." He undid the little buttons at her neck and bared her breasts. "Let me love you the way you deserve to be loved." She turned her head obediently and offered her face, the lips sensuously parted, her eyes glowing.

He felt the pain deep in his heart. Ah, God, how she could look like Rose!

17

————◆————

Cressida lay against Nicholas's encircling arm gazing at the ceiling, sensuously hoarding this new and surprising love within her, feeling forgiveness flowing and spreading its balm over the ugly spikes that months of bitterness had caused to form within her soul. The early-morning tropical sun burst in a benediction against the porthole. The wind sighed in the rigging as *Aurora* sped on her way south.

Stealthily, so as not to wake her husband, she crept out of bed. In the mirror she saw the new softness, and with it her old sweetness returned. The long unhappiness had tensed her muscles, hardened her mouth, aged her. Now she was a young girl again, her eyes liquid with satiety, her mouth tremulous. Even her skin seemed finer. It was the face of love she looked at, and joy. She picked up her brush and shook her thick hair down her back, stretching the lively curls into shining waves. Then she polished her hair with the piece of silk that had lain unused in the brass-bound chest. She put her head back, closed her eyes, and thought that being loved was like little bells ringing in one's heart.

When she looked again Nicholas had opened one eye. She came over and stood beside the bed, smiling shyly down at him. He saw the change, and reached out a hand to take hers. "Happy?"

"Oh, yes." Intoxicated by it. "May I ask you something, my darling?"

He smiled lazily in return. "Of course. What do you want to know?"

Her lids fluttered down. "Something maybe I've no right to ask."

"Then why ask?"

"Because . . . because I . . . I need to know you better," she faltered. Having given her heart into his keeping, she needed to know it was safe.

He kissed the back of her hand, seeing it as thinner than Rose's. "You've got a lifetime to get to know me. I thought we agreed last night the past is to be forgotten." He looked up at her gravely.

"Just this one question?"

"All right." Privately he reserved the right to lie.

"Where did you go in the evenings when we were at Cavendish Square?" She sat down on the bed.

He patted her hand again, but this time it was half in irritation. "I played cards with my friends." He hesitated, then, knowing it was not a reply she wanted, but a committal to the right answer, he added, "Did you think I was whoring?" Only in the catching of her breath did she show any sign of reaction. She stood in silence until he put a finger under her chin and lifted her face so that she had to look at him. His voice was kinder now. "Had you considered how unbearably humiliated you would have felt had I given the wrong reply?"

Her face had flushed a dark red, her trembling fingers playing with the little crocheted buttons at the neck of her nightdress. "I feel humiliated when you . . . Do you have to use such indelicate words?"

"You've married an indelicate man, my dear."

He took her other hand, pulled her down beside him, and looked into her face. "Last night you wanted this marriage to work," he said. "Do you still want that?"

She nodded.

He smoothed the soft flesh of her arm, kneaded the smooth little rump beneath the thin nightdress. How soft she was from that one loving! His voice was gruff with emotion. "Then do as we agreed. Kill the past."

She fought a swift battle with herself, her nails digging into her palms. "I will," she promised.

"Although there is something you might remember," Nicholas added, looking at her keenly, "you were in love with a rake. Everyone warned you of it. You didn't care then. Now that you've married the man, you must not expect him to turn into a muling, puking child. A marriage ceremony don't change anyone, Cressida."

"I didn't know what was meant by wild," she faltered, her cheeks reddening again, her lashes dropping over her pretty eyes.

"Oh? Then what, may I ask, was your idea of wild?"

She cast around for something he would accept. "Hunting. B-being brave in the hunting field . . ." She saw his incredulous grin and faltered.

"Do go on."

"It was said you were always first in at the kill, and no hedge was too high for you to jump." She kept looking at him uncertainly for signs of that merciless amusement she knew so well, but a veil had come down over his features. "And I knew you and your friends drank." The nervousness went suddenly. "You organized a one-horse cabriolet race 'round the park at midnight, did you not? And they all ended by turning over. Except you." Now there was real pride in her voice.

"And you swam the Thames one night." Gaining confidence, Cressida grew bright-eyed and eager.

Yes. Jonnie Hurstmoncieux was drowned, but he had walked naked back across Hungerford Bridge and caused an uproar. She was so pretty in animation. "You liked that?" he asked softly, his fingers digging pleasurably into her thigh. She was less pliable than Rose. Less relaxed. Altogether less. But she was here and Rose was not.

"I mean, it was very brave," she said, her color deepening as she felt the sensuous pressure of his hands.

"I see." Drawing her toward him, he asked, "Did you enjoy what I did to you last night?"

Her eyes swerved away in deep embarrassment. "Oh, Nicholas, a lady doesn't . . ."

He captured both of her hands, drawing her implacably closer. "Once you marry the wild buck the vicarious living stops."

"W-what do you mean?"

"Don't look so startled. If a lady wants love from a man, she must be prepared to give him love in return."

"Oh, but I do love you. I said I've always loved you."

There was a long, deliberate silence. His eyes did not leave her face. Cressida's lids fluttered and her color heightened.

"Ah, yes," said Nicholas softly, smiling, teasing. "You know you have to answer my question before we can go on."

She tried to pull her hands away. There were tears of agonized embarrassment in her eyes. He held her, laughing softly.

"I know it's a wife's duty to submit."

He said gently, "Passion is not, as young ladies are taught to believe, a man's prerogative. If it were, then every act of love would be an act of rape. Now, did I rape you?"

"No. Oh, no!" She was shocked.

"Well, then . . . put your arms 'round my neck."

He was going to do it again. In daylight! "Nicholas!" Cressida's voice rose on a soft little shriek. "We're having a serious talk!"

"I agree." But he spoke detachedly because, with expert hands, he was already swinging her nightdress up around her neck. "Why do women have to wear . . ."

"Nicholas!" she cried again, frantic with shame. "We're talking . . ."

He jerked her to him, stiff as a ramrod in her nakedness. "So we were. Let me repeat my question. Did you enjoy . . ."

It was too late for answers, then. Too late for Nicholas to finish his question. Afterward, as they lay back on the bed, he lifted her fingers dreamily to his lips. Her body was soft as warm wax beside him, and as yielding. One leg was thrown over his. There was sweat on her face.

"There's really nothing to talk about, is there?"

She smiled back, tremulously. All the shock and the shame had flown away. She was suffused through and through with a wonderful sense of giving and receiving. Nicholas's arm tightened around her, and she snuggled closer. If only life could stay like this.

"Lesson number one," he said softly.

She gave a little gasp of dismay and leaped up, automatically clasping the sheet to her naked breasts. "Lessons!" she repeated in horror. "I promised Mr. Langford

I'd take that class of adult steerage passengers this morning. Oh, my goodness, what's the time?"

Nicholas collapsed against the pillow, roaring with laughter. "If you must do good, then you had better hurry up and dress, and while you're at it, think of a more acceptable excuse than the truth for being late."

"Are you still certain you want to take on this task?" asked the captain. "When you didn't appear at breakfast we thought you might have changed your mind, m'Lady."

Langford good-humoredly bypassed their captain's disapproval. "She is clearly delighted to be taken up on her offer. Look at her, Captain."

Cressida's lashes drooped demurely over her sparkling eyes. She knew how different she looked. She had been conscious of the spring in her step as she approached, the lilt in her voice as she spoke. Wanting to be pretty for Nicholas, she had put on a delphinium blue bodice, the long, pointed waist accentuating her slender figure, the bell-shaped skirt elegant in its simplicity. Her bright hair, hastily drawn into puffs over her ears, fell in soft curls around her face.

"But you must have breakfast first," the captain said, giving way reluctantly.

"No, really. I said I would be ready at nine o'clock. It's after that now. It was my own fault that I slept in." Cressida flushed prettily.

The class was already seated. Mr. Langford stood aside at the door to allow the new teacher to precede him. She entered with her head high, and a smile on her lips.

"That's m'Lady from London," whispered Oliver, who had insisted on coming with Rose to the adult class. "Mr. le Grys's lady."

Inexplicably, in her confusion and distress, Rose found herself looking into Daniel's face for help. Daniel, who had never seen Lady Cressida, smiled back. The sweat stood out on Rose's face. She closed her eyes. All at once, with a feeling of wonder and terror, she felt the baby rolling over. She opened her eyes. Her gown was moving precipitously, as though there was a puppy hidden beneath the folds. The class must be staring at her! Everyone! Especially Lady Cressida! And more especially, even Daniel.

"She's nice. In London she allers smiled at me," whispered Oliver happily.

I'm going to be sick, thought Rose in a panic.

"Wake up." Daniel's elbow brought her back to the insupportable present. In mortal fear, she peeped through her lashes. She could see Lady Cressida's lips moving, but because of a roaring in her ears, she could not hear the words. She screwed her eyes tightly closed, consciously receding from a present too shocking to face.

"Rose?"

She managed to open her eyes, this time to look at Daniel, silently begging for mercy. The baby was rolling again. Stop. Stop!

"I thought you'd gone to sleep." Daniel, carrying the identity of their teacher with puzzled discomfort in his mind, looked sullen. Mr. Langford, having effected his introduction, had gone. Lady Cressida le Grys, standing with her back turned, was writing on a small blackboard borrowed from the children's classroom. The adults attended in obedient silence, mainly uncomprehending. Rose sat still as a mouse, pretending she was a million miles away.

Cressida, in a cold calm as of Calvary and death, somehow held the shock at bay, while an inner voice taunted her with her naïveté. There was no anger at first, only an unfathomable sense of injustice, and a return of the so-familiar humiliation. Mercifully, her mind froze beneath a cloak of saving shock. The lesson had to continue. She kept her head high, her eyes on a level with the tops of their heads.

She had meant to go among her pupils, speaking to them individually to find out how much, if anything, they knew. Now, she could not risk looking into the eyes of that girl and seeing the triumph that would be shining there. She spoke as she had not intended to speak, formally, treating them not as individuals but as a body. The lesson seemed less like an hour than an eternity. Her throat grew parched and her eyes stared with the effort of maintaining control.

Mr. Langford, returning to free his voluntary assistant, stopped dead in the doorway, his face falling. Cressida saw him, snapped the lesson to a swift conclusion, put the chalk down, thanked the class for their attention, and glided out through the door.

"How did it go?" Langford asked with concern. "You didn't have any trouble, I trust?" Her face was white as the writing on the board.

"No. Indeed, they were very attentive." She turned glazed eyes and a humorless smile on him, then walked ahead, the insult of Rose's presence in every line of her stiffened back, her rigidly held head.

"Don't feel you must continue," Langford said uncomfortably, as she grasped the iron banister and fled aloft toward the shelter of the cabin class.

She did not answer, only marching straight across the deck as though she had not heard. She managed to hold herself in control until she had locked the cabin door behind her, then, standing by the bed—their bed—shame and despair broke over her in suffocating waves.

It was her wedding night all over again, but this time with hope extinguished. She had a despairing sensation of being rudderless on a malevolent ocean. Of seeing Rose Snape, with her angel's face and the Giaconda smile, laughing while she died.

There was a knock on the door. The handle rattled.

"Cressida?"

"Go away," she said. If she had to let him in, she would kill him. Or herself.

"Cressida? What the devil's up?"

"Go away."

There was a long silence. Then, "Are you ill?"

After a while she heard his footsteps on the deck, leaving. She fell on the bed, dry, racking sobs bursting from her.

Purposefully, Rose led Daniel up to that part of the foredeck they had made their own. They settled down side by side on the neatly coiled ropes, shaded from the sun by the scimitar curve of the jib sails. It was another cloudless day. The little ship, propelled by the weight of its wind-filled canvas, slid through a lively sea. The air was warm and salt in their nostrils. A sailor hurrying by gave them a friendly salute.

"I want to tell you something, Daniel." Rose took a deep breath.

"I'm going to have a baby." She felt like a pricked balloon, sagging with the release of her guilt.

"You would if you'd just let me get at you," muttered Daniel, misunderstanding.

"I'm having it now. Now Daniel. *Now.*"

Daniel's eyes were down-bent and concerned. He knew women imagined things when they hadn't enough to think about. "We only did it once."

"It only takes once." She reached for his big, calloused hand, smoothing the rough skin, the gnarled knuckles.

"I mean, I'm pregnant, Daniel. That's what I mean."

The only sound was the slap of canvas against the booms. Daniel considered the matter in silence. Then he turned startled eyes on her waistline, and for the first time consciously recognized the bulge. "But we've only been married two months." He frowned, looking back at her middle. "We only did it once," he repeated.

"Some people blow up fast," she said breathlessly. "Maybe it's twins. Or a very big boy. I should have thought you'd be glad. You want a family, don't you?"

Daniel shifted uncomfortably. Rose's strange way of looking at things left him tongue-tied. When folk married a baby came every year. He'd never heard of a woman asking her husband if he *wanted* a family. He remembered how slim she used to be, and wondered why he had not noticed the change. "But if you've got that big in two months . . ."

"Don't worry, Daniel," Rose chattered, excited now, relieved that he had not guessed the truth and hit her, as Adam hit Florrie when he was upset.

"You're goin' ter need a sack to wear," said Daniel crudely, "if you get ter be four times the size o' that." In the back of his mind something formless, no more than a small discomfort as yet, had begun to grow and stir. His shoulders slumped as he leaned on the rail, staring out over the mighty ocean.

"Look, Daniel, there's a porpoise!" exclaimed Rose, nervously.

Daniel's eyes passed over the curved creature as it leaped exuberantly beside the ship, then settled in bewilderment on his beautiful wife. If he had not kicked his brother George in the balls . . . But he had.

In the late afternoon, when Cressida had still not appeared, Nicholas went again to the cabin door. "Madam," he said in a low, angry voice, "let me in, or I shall get the captain and have the lock forced."

A moment of silence. A patter of footsteps. The key turned. The cold malevolence of his wife's face was a shock. She did not speak. Baffled, he could only stare at her. "What's the matter? Have I hurt you?"

Ignoring his question, she went to the porthole and turned her back. The creak and rasp of the ship's timbers was the only sound. Nicholas sat down on the bed, hands clasped between his knees. When he felt he could wait no longer he said with heavy, impatient patience, "You'd better pull yourself together. Herd will be coming up to set out my clothes for dinner."

"Get your own clothes. Herd may not come in."

He stared at her back. After a while, he rose and laid a conciliatory hand on her shoulder. "Cress—"

She swung around, her face contorted with loathing, and flung his hand away as though it burned. "How dare you touch me! Don't you ever touch me again."

He strode out through the door, slamming it behind him. He flung himself down on a box beneath the towering mainmast in the waist of the ship. Up on the poop the captain paced to and fro. The setting sun cast a golden pathway across the darkening water, and the sky was brilliant with tropical reds, purples, blues, and golds. The wind in the rigging made a distant, hissing sound. Footsteps approached and paused, but Nicholas did not look up.

"What's the matter, lad?"

Nicholas lifted his head, sucked in his breath, then expelled it in a heavy sigh, leveling his tortured eyes on the doctor's kindly countenance. "D'you know anything about women, Stokes?"

"I know when I hear them scream behind the cabin door there's something very wrong." His unprofessional bluntness belied the look of concern in his eyes.

Nicholas dropped forward again, face in hands, elbows on knees.

"Some wives need taming, but I should have thought you had a way with women. A very potent way, if I may say so. I would guess you're a young man of experience.

I'd have thought even such a lady of character as your wife would not be impervious to well-laid charm."

Privately, the doctor was curious to know why this oddly assorted pair had married. Le Grys's background would give him an open field. He would have expected either a gay and flamboyantly pretty girl, or one of those doelike, adoring creatures who hung on a man's every word.

Eventually he suggested, "If you'd like me to talk to your wife, perhaps an older man might be able to speak without offence. Would you care to have me approach her tactfully at a convenient time? As a medical man, I mean."

And hear that their three-month marriage had been consummated only last night?

The doctor rested a sympathetic hand on Nicholas's shoulder. "Women can be the very devil at times."

Nicholas lifted his head, laughing harshly. "God damn it, you're right," he acknowledged, slapping both hands on his knees. "Would you care to join me in a game of cards tonight?"

"A splendid idea, my dear fellow."

"I'll meet you in the saloon immediately after dinner. I must go now and send a mesage to my man. I'm not changing, in spite of the captain's wishes."

When he reeled down the passage at midnight, and tried the cabin door, it opened to his touch. Cressida, to his befuddled surprise, had not made up her bed on the floor. She lay on the extreme edge of their mattress swathed tightly in a sheet. She appeared to be asleep, but when he leaned over her eyes opened, and she gave him a stare cold enough, he thought, to freeze the blood in his veins, had it not been so heavily laced with brandy. He dropped his clothes in an untidy heap on the floor, and fell down beside her. "You needn't have bothered to wrap yourself up," he muttered. "If I want you, I'll have you." But in his heart he knew it was an idle threat.

Sleep came swiftly, and with it the worrying dream of the trees and the two women, and the strange state of helplessness. He wakened with a vile head and a filthy taste in his mouth. The other side of the bed was empty.

18

To the utmost distress of all, death came to them before Christmas. "The child would have died anyway," Dr. Stokes prophesied, "had the family stayed at home." The new country with its expected sunshine might cure lung disease, but the sea never had. The poor little mite was sewn up in canvas and the captain read the funeral service. It was a sad day, and a frightening one.

Having finally left the warm tropical seas behind, the Roaring Forties began as a release and a relief to them all. Fair-weather sails came down, and the little ship bent under heavy canvas. Shoals of whales dipped and blew as they lumbered up against the hull. There was new excitement in singing sails and high-flung spray. The ship went as far south as the captain dared take her. Cressida, feeling one day a sudden chill, looked anxiously at the barometer and saw it had plummeted. They were hurtling along at a terrifying speed. Major Baker said apprehensively that they were carrying too much sail. One of the officers corrected him with asperity, "We carry only three, and are about to reduce to two."

"Two hundred and forty-five miles a day," said Captain Heale, looking pleased. The fastidious snob had been replaced by a doughty sailor, fully stretched.

Soon snow blanketed the ship. The crew battened down the hatches, and the helmsman was lashed to the helm. As the weather worsened and the sturdy vessel tossed like driftwood, four sailors added their strength to the wheel. Men not noted for their piety, finding themselves staring into the grim, gray face of eternity, went off to pray. The virtuous had been on their knees for days. There was no hot food, for they dared not light fires in the galley. Inevitably, the boiling sea smashed through the deckhouse. Crewmen were swept horrifyingly around the deck. Down in the lower decks the noise was appalling. The din of the waves and the wind, the creaking of the timbers, joined to form a perpetual shriek.

Rose clung to her cot, certain that Nicholas's child was about to add to the chaos by launching itself into the mêlée, long past caring about Daniel's reception of a premature birth. He sat on their little box beside her, stolid, white-faced, and withdrawn, offering no comfort, less from lack of sympathy than because he did not know how.

Water poured down companionways and through closed hatches. It sloshed around the passageways. When the worst of the storm was over, soon after Christmas, those who recovered first went to work with mops and cloths. Charcoal stoves were produced to dry the bedding.

It seemed to Nicholas that he was alone in enjoying the storm. Had he the remotest knowledge of sailing, he could have battled his way to the wheel to help their gallant captain and his men.

"Have a brandy with me, Doctor," he offered, as Stokes entered the saloon and collapsed tiredly into the seat opposite. "It will do you good."

"All right. A small one. Wasn't it Dr. Johnson who said being at sea is like being in prison with the added chance of being drowned?" The good man managed a weary, sardonic smile. "By the way, there's a boy in steerage I've been treating for boils. A touch of scurvy, too. There's a history of malnutrition. He's an unprepossessing little wretch, but all he really needs is good food. He tells me you're his sponsor, though he doesn't seem to know you."

"Oliver," said Nicholas heavily, thinking of Rose. "A friend asked me to bring him. Being under age and without a trade, he would not have been given a passage. Heaven knows what I'm going to do with him when we get there."

The doctor brightened. "I'm staying to take up land.

Give him to me. I would see to his education and give him a start. He's going to need doctoring until he's well."

"You can have the boy." Nicholas thought with a feeling of aching loneliness as he poured the brandy that one could scarcely keep an "unprepossessing little wretch" as a memento.

"There's one other matter young man, if you can spare me a further moment," Stokes said.

Nicholas settled himself with head high, legs apart, hands on his knees in that essentially masculine way he had of sitting, confidence and sexuality in every line of his body. Lady Cressida, the doctor thought, eyeing him wryly, was never going to have this young ram by the horns.

"I was going to ask your wife if she'd give me a bit of help," he began, "but it might come better through you. There's a girl in steerage swears she's only three and a half months pregnant, but my guess is she's too near her time for comfort. She weathered the storm, but I'm not certain she is going to make landfall before delivery."

Guessing hard-heartedly at the reason for the doctor's concern, Nicholas grinned. The company had given him a free cabin and two shillings a head for each adult emigrant landed alive and in good health, with a bonus of fifty pounds if all went well.

"Young Oliver says the couple are from your estate."

Nicholas blinked.

"A man called Daniel Putnam."

"Putnam?" The name was a shock. "Yes, he's from Rundull. He's not one of my staff, though."

"You didn't sponsor him, then?" The doctor's face conveyed his surprise.

"I had no need. Unlike the boy, he is in possession of the qualifications laid down by the company, and I've no doubt the local curate gave him a good character. We had trouble with the Putnams."

"Is that why he left?"

Nicholas laughed harshly. "No. And, to be fair, this one is a cut above the rest of his family. As I understand it, he emigrated to get away from them. He'd had to leave home because of ill feeling and was living with one of our grooms. But no," Nicholas repeated heavily, "he's not one of my men. I was asked to help. That's all."

The doctor leaned forward, brows raised, eyes intent. "Can you remember exactly when you were asked to help?"

"In July." On his wedding day. The worst day of his life.

"Is anything the matter?"

"No."

"Putnam was living with your groom because he had nowhere to go," the doctor repeated thoughtfully. "That presupposes he had nowhere to take his bride. It may be the answer I'm looking for. The couple could have been married just in time to catch the sailing, by which time the girl could have been well on with her pregnancy." He gave an exasperated little snort. "The wife seems such a smart little thing, I'd have thought she would realize you can't fool a doctor. Thanks, le Grys."

"I'll go down and see him," said Nicholas, thinking aloud. "He did this friend of mine a good turn. I'll make it my business to find work for him and see his wife's cared for. Let me know if you need m'Lady. I've no doubt she would talk to your patient."

"Capital."

"Herd," said Nicholas that evening when he came to the cabin, "there's one of the Putnams aboard."

His valet stiffened.

"I'd like to have a word with him. Ask him to meet me this evening, there's a good fellow. Tell him to bring his wife. I'd better see her, too."

Herd gaped.

"What's the matter, man? Why are you staring at me like that?"

"You don't know as 'oo Daniel Putnam married, Mr. Nicholas?"

"How should I know? I wasn't even aware he was married until today."

"You didn't know as 'e married Rose Snape?"

The silence in the cabin was palpable. Herd, gazing glassy-eyed at his master, saw Nicholas's color fade, saw the stunned shock in his eyes give way briefly to a leaping light, then saw the shutters come down.

"Rose Snape!" he repeated, his voice cool, his face blank. "So, a Putnam and a Snape! Well, well. There's quite a crowd aboard from Rundull, then." He picked up the cravat Herd had put out for him, examined it closely. Was this the explanation for his wife's behavior? He gazed out of the porthole at the dancing waters, his mind racing. Turning, he said casually, "I trust you're all taking advantage of the schooling that's being provided in steerage, Herd. Are you going along to Mr. Langford's classes?"

"Yes, Mr. Nicholas. We all go."

"And the Putnams? Do they attend?"

"Yes," Herd said diffidently, "Mrs., er, Rose got the class together. It's only young Oliver an' Rose was real interested at the start. They made the others go. Daniel don't go now."

"Oh? Does he not care to take advantage of this splendid opportunity to acquire some education?"

"I dunno as to that, sir. 'E went to the first one. 'E's turned sour. 'E don't do nothin' now."

"Sour, eh?" Nicholas picked up a cuff link and tossed it idly from one palm to the other. "Don't bother about asking him to meet me, then. Even a sweet Putnam is not to my taste. Convey my felicitations to them both, and say I'll see them on terra firma."

"What's that sir?"

"What's what Herd?"

"Terra firma. What time, like?"

Nicholas grinned. "Tell the fellow to apply to me for work when he's ready."

Later that evening, when Nicholas came to the cabin, Cressida looked up from her Maori grammar without either welcome or interest. "You are early."

"I have something to say to you." He closed the door and leaned against it. "Why did you not tell me Rose was aboard?"

There was a look in her eyes more pitiful than hate, but just as deadly.

Crossing the short space between them, he leaned down, took the book from her, and placed his hands on her shoulders. With compassion he looked into her eyes. "I didn't know." He did not apologize. He could not say he was sorry for the lifting of the misery, the boredom and despair that had dragged at his coattails from Gravesend to the southern seas. She jerked her chin up, tried to turn away.

"She came without my knowledge. I want you to know that," Nicholas asserted, his eyes steadily on hers.

Something in the way he spoke seemed to affect her. Her lips trembled, hope flared in her eyes. "You did not know?"

"I have not lied to you, and I will not, except perhaps in a manner that would save you intolerable pain."

"Do you not see this girl's being aboard as intolerable pain to the wife who promised to love you, and who would wish to honor that promise?"

"It would have been an outrageous thing to do," Nicholas said, "to ship my mistress out deliberately on the same vessel as my wife. If you had come to me with the story . . ."

"How could you expect that of me?" she said, her face white, the skin tightly drawn across her cheekbones, her mouth downturned and trembling.

She missed the look of frustration on his face, as he turned sharply and went to stand at the porthole. "Anyway, she is married."

"Oh." Cressida wrung her hands. "Then why, oh why, if she has a husband, has she come?" Forgetting she had promised herself never to break down again, she began to cry silently.

"Come," he said, lifting her to her feet. He held her close against him, looking down at her golden head, feeling warm and gentle, thinking of Rose and how her golden hair shone in the lamplight. "We have to learn to live with what fate sends," he said, shelving the problem of his two women because there was nothing he could do about it.

Her head came up. "You expect me . . ."

"I want to make up to you for what you have suffered. I am truly sorry. But we are man and wife, and that's an end to it." He began to undo the buttons at the back of her dress.

She stood numbly, acquiescent, remembering what her mother had said, that it was a wife's duty to submit . . .

The fog came down more densely still, filling the passengers with dread. Petty bickering quarrels broke out in steerage. The storm, they agreed, had been nothing like as bad as this eerie, sinister silence. Men stopped shaving. Women who had refused to go to bed in the storm reiterated that if they were to die they would die fully dressed. Then on December 31 the glass suddenly rose, and a gale blew up.

On January 16 the southern island was sighted and Rose's son decided to enter the world.

By four o'clock the following morning, all hands were out on deck to see the land: a long range of mountains, on the one hand towering majestically to the clouds, on the other, green with forest and vegetation to the water's edge. By breakfast time many of the passengers were lining the rails. The lively Miss Frederick came running, her curls bobbing outside her yellow bonnet, her eyes bright with excitement.

"Mr. le Grys, I have a message for you. I met Dr. Stokes, and he told me to tell you a child has been born to the young wife of one of your men."

"A boy." Nicholas made the comment with complete conviction. He had known Rose would have a boy.

Misunderstanding him, she replied lightly, "Ah! So you heard." She turned to look out upon the mountains ahead. "How beautiful is our new country! A new life for a new land," she said musingly, shielding her eyes against the sun's glare on the water. She turned back, looking up into his face. "That's what the doctor said." She quoted again. " 'A new life for a new land.' "

Nicholas swung away and crossed the deck. Latecomers, hurrying to the first view of their destination, met him with happy faces, jostling each other as they came.

"Have you heard about the baby? I declare, if this is not an omen."

"It is, indeed."

"And the father is one of your men, I understand. Why, Mr. le Grys, you have begun already to make history."

"I? It is the mother who makes history." At the door to his own cabin he did not even pause to knock, flinging it open, bursting in, the pulsating life in him filling the room. Cressida, dressing for the elements in a jade bonnet and matching pelisse, smiled up at him. He stared at her, feeling the cold settle around his heart, and with it a totally unacceptable sense of guilt. "The child was delivered last night."

The smile on her face froze. They stood in silence. Then he came forward and, looking uncertain, held out his hands. Standing stiffly, she said in a small, uneven, but very dignified voice, "I will arrange for you to see . . ." She swallowed, then went on. "It would be expected that we should have a degree of interest in the family."

"The child is not your affair," he said gently. "I'll speak to Stokes."

"No. I will arrange it. That will look better. Tomorrow, when we come in to land would be a good time, for naturally you will be concerned about arrangements for your staff to go ashore."

"I told you, I did not sponsor him." Nicholas was suddenly angry, realizing she had not after all believed him.

"Then he shall come onto your staff," Cressida replied, "so you can see to the family's comfort without provoking gossip. It is convenient that he is a carpenter, for we shall need someone to build our home. I am sure he's a good man and has been grievously taken in. He, at least, deserves our help."

Nicholas came and stood in front of her, his fingers tightly curled, his knuckles resting on his hips. "Did you not know that it was the husband's brother who, being after my blood, caused me to be sent to this wretched colony?"

"I am sure it is a very uncomfortable situation for both of you, but that does not alter the fact that we must do what we can with the cards that have been dealt us."

He went on staring at her, this newly strange stranger. Then he swung around and strode away.

In the tiny hospital room below, Rose lay with the child in her arms, whispering promises over his downy head, touching her lips to his toysized fingers with kisses light as thistledown. "One, two, three, four, five," she counted, marveling at their diminutive perfection, at the strength of their grip as they curled around hers. How like Nicholas he was! The same black hair, the same dark eyes, already a hint of the same enigmatic look as he gazed up into her face. Nicholas and she, as one. What a precious sharing this was. Her green eyes were soft as rainwashed moss.

Daniel had been brought in by the doctor, half led, half pushed, shuffling his feet, hanging his head so that he might not see the child. The doctor had made hearty noises. "A fine son, Putnam."

"Look at him, Daniel," Rose suggested uncertainly. He lifted his downcast eyes, wherein lay all his inarticulate humiliation. Ignoring the child, he looked at her, and she saw with shock how she had in her folly and obsession diminished him. "Daniel," she said, still uncertainly.

I oughter 'ave knowed," he muttered. "You wouldn't be marryin' the likes of me. Not you." There was no bitterness there, only an all-enveloping, crushing despair.

She extended a hand, guilt and compassion intermixed, and took his rough fingers. "He's a lovely baby, Daniel. Do look at him."

Daniel glanced down, then quickly away. She went on fondling his fingers. "I don't know what to say," he said miserably.

She saw with relief that he was not going to be able to say anything and smiled winningly at him, thinking of Nicholas, impatient for him to come. "Just look pleased," she said encouragingly. "Everyone will be so happy for you."

A grating sound came from his throat. He did look down at the child then, but only briefly. "I got to get used to it," he said, as though getting used to the boy was something he was perhaps willing, but inadequate, to do.

19

Where was *Tory*?

The fourteen male cabin passengers were gathered in the saloon to consider their situation. Too late, they asked each other why they had not waited in London for word of the survey brig's safe arrival, not knowing that leaks from Parliament to the effect that Melbourne had been hustled into outlawing the company's arrangements had panicked the company's directors into pushing their five ships out to sea. Now they approached Captain Heale about the possibility of returning home. "We cannot land if no preparation has been made for us. If *Tory* has gone down."

Mr. Maxwell remarked comfortingly, "Captain Chaffers is a very experienced sailor. He has already taken *Beagle* around the world. He brought Charles Darwin to the South Seas."

Nicholas said with a cheerfulness he did not feel, "A pox on you for doubters. *Tory* carries on her prow a bust of the Duke of Wellington. How could she fail to win through?"

They chuckled and went to bed quietly.

As the saloon emptied, the doctor detained Nicholas. "Would it be impertinent of me," he asked closing the door quietly, "to broach a matter concerned with your private life?"

Nicholas stiffened.

The doctor tugged at his whiskers, eyeing Nicholas thoughtfully. "Without mothers and grandmothers and aunts, our ladies are going to find themselves facing a very great void that busy husbands are not going to be able to fill." He paused. "I hope you will encourage your wife to confide in me, should she feel like so doing."

"Of course." Nicholas looked at him boldly.

There was a flash of irritation in the doctor's eyes. "You're hotblooded and foolhardy, young man, but with the love of a good woman behind you, I've no doubt you will come through. There's a rightness about you that could mature into greatness. But I would not put all my money on it, Nicholas le Grys." Thrusting his hands beneath his coat-tails, Stokes walked purposefully across the saloon, then back.

Nicholas went coolly to a cupboard affixed to the wall. Taking out a bottle of brandy and two glasses, he poured a measure into each. "Let us drink to the love of a good woman, then," he suggested, raising his glass.

The doctor sipped his drink in startled silence. A moment later, he lifted his head and added, "The child's mother has immense strength of character and purpose. I do not believe she needs help to get on. I think she can safely be left, now, in the hands of fate."

Almost imperceptibly, Nicholas's shoulders squared. "In the hands of fate?" he asked, a faint smile disguising his very real disquiet. "I had thought you a responsible man." He put his glass down. "Good-night, Doctor. It is time we were in bed."

He strode out onto the deck. An armed guard was there, pale sentinels against the sky. Nicholas leaned on the rail, contemplating the land he did not want, that was to give him the life he did not want. The darkening hills crept close. So, if *Tory* had gone down, within a few days they would be on their way home. And then what? He lit a cheroot and smoked it through to the end. He threw the stub into the water as night, their first New Zealand night, crept close and swallowed them.

As the sun rose over the misty mountains, a dawn chorus like a ringing of small bells reawakened hope in the hearts of those who came up on deck. At mid-morning, a little flotilla of canoes rounded a point and moved toward them, sending snatches of song on the eddying breeze. The brave, uncertain faces of the watchers relaxed. The red ocher sides of the vessels, quite fifty feet in length, were ornamented with tufts of white feathers. They carried grotesque figureheads with protruding tongues and quantities of black feathers to represent hair. One of the canoes pulled out in front and swung alongside. A native stood up in the prow, grasped the ship's ladder, and began to clamber aboard.

The guard stood ready. Surrounded by his senior officers, the captain waited impassively. Those onlookers who had dared to stay clustered together in silence. The burly Maori jumped over the rail, his bare feet landing with a slap on the deck, his thick-lipped face cracking into an enormous grin.

He was an imposing man, the feathers in his headdress adding immeasurably to his height. A richly fringed and ornamented cloak was thrown over one shoulder. There was a bunch of white seabirds' feathers at the side of his head. His face was decorated with blue painted whorls and innocent of hair, with the exception of a small tuft of beard on the point of his chin. He carried, like a badge of office, a highly polished weapon made of a soft green translucent stone.

"Haere mai," he said. *"Tene koutou."* It was a greeting they had mostly learned. Welcome. Hail to ye all. He handed a piece of paper to the captain, saying in English, in a soft voice quite devoid of menace, "This no fast ship *Oriental.*" He pronounced the name "Orry-entle." "Colonel Wide-Awake say *Oriental* come first."

"But *Aurora* has come in first." Captain Heale swelled visibly.

"All many chiefs and princess," the Maori said quaintly, approvingly, eyeing the onlookers in their tall hats and pretty bonnets.

The watchful faces smiled hesitantly.

Captain Heale raised his eyes from the paper. *"Tory* went off a fortnight ago to explore the coast," he said, addressing his first officer directly. "This is not from Colonel Wakefield, if that is whom the man means by Wide-Awake. It is in an illiterate hand, and not easy to decipher." He leaned over the rail, his gaze sweeping across the upturned faces in their canoes below. "They seem friendly enough," he said. Thoughtfully, he weighed up his Maori visitor. "I wish to send five men ashore. As there will not be room in your canoe for five extra men, you may leave five here with us."

"Plenty room . . ."

"I must ask you to leave five of your men."

The Maori grinned slyly, then, leaning over the rail, called down to his men in the canoes. There was a scramble, and five young natives clambered aboard. They were younger than their leader, and wore straw mats slung carelessly across their bodies. Their faces, though more lightly marked, were decorated with the same blue paint.

The captain turned to his second officer. "Take three or four men with you, Mr. Sedgwick, and go with them."

Nicholas stepped forward. "With your permission, Captain, I should like to go ashore."

"And I," echoed Mr. Wallace and Mr. Maxwell.

Cressida gave the faintest of gasps, quickly stifled. Miss Frederick heard, and put a hand on her arm. "You have married an adventurous man," she whispered, smiling, but at the same time chiding her. To Nicholas, who was arguing with the captain, Miss Frederick called, "Look out for Mr. Stitchbury and bring him to me. He does not know that I have managed to come." There was a ripple of laughter. Miss Frederick had captured the interest and affection of all.

Followed by the other two men, Nicholas hurried across the deck and disappeared below. They returned armed. Mr. Maxwell received a quick kiss and words of reassurance. Nicholas merely waved as he went over the side. "Wish us luck. We will perhaps return with some fat pigeons for dinner." Cressida turned swiftly away.

"How proud you must be of him," said Miss Frederick with warm compassion.

Cressida bit her lips.

They watched the canoes growing smaller in the distance, the white men working enthusiastically at the paddles, their hosts laughing at their clumsiness with the strange implements. The captain indicated that his brown-skinned guests should accompany him up to the poop. The onlookers turned away. "I wish I felt competent to speak with them," Cressida said, feeling lonely and all at once inexplicably unwell.

"But surely you are competent," protested Miss Frederick. "You have spent so much time studying. With only fifteen letters in the alphabet, I am sure we can all master the language." She made a laughing little grimace. "As you know, I have spent too much time in dancing and gossip."

"It was wise of you to enjoy yourself," Cressida said generously, thinking with sadness of the nights she might have danced away beneath the moon, if only things had been different.

"We shall have to guard our complexions, if today is a true sample of what the climate has to offer." One of their fellow passengers, coming up beside them, tilted her bonnet over her eyes.

"If I believed the sun to be our greatest enemy," asserted another pessimistically, "I would be more sanguine about the future than I admit to being now."

Cressida turned on her sharply. "Then pray don't spread your apprehensions. We are here to stay, and it is right that we should make the best of it."

There was a breathless silence. No one could ever remember hearing the elegant and withdrawn Lady Cressida le Grys show so human a failing as the losing of her temper. They were stunned, then slyly intrigued. One of them, recovering, said kindly, "You do not need to worry about your husband, my Lady. The hostages are well guarded up on the poop. No harm can possibly come to your dear man."

"Of course no harm will come to them," agreed Miss Frederick, slipping an arm through Cressida's and leading her away.

They loitered on deck. At midday, a member of the crew of *Tory* came aboard with an English whaler, explaining that he had been left on D'Urville Island to watch for the five ships. *Aurora* was to proceed to Port Nicholson as soon as the quintet returned with their Maori escorts. His amazement that *Oriental* had not come in first further increased the captain's good humor.

"I am in danger of becoming a hero."

"I declare, the buttons on his waistcoat will pop off," whispered Mrs. Maxwell, "he is so puffed up with conceit."

The two men looked with amazement at the natives under guard on the poop. "I would advise you to let them go."

But the Maoris were thoroughly enjoying the hospitality. Grinning cheerfully, they came down onto the deck and mingled with the passengers. Fishing lines were produced, and enough rock cod were caught to feed the entire ship. Canoes, large and small, came out from the shore. A fish hook was bartered for a basket of potatoes. More men went ashore in a canoe, returning with native flax, and a variety of shells. Down in the galley, the cooks were busy. Basketloads of shellfish came up on deck, steaming. The passengers gathered around eagerly, helping themselves to the new luxuries.

Before the adventurers could return, a squall came sweeping across the water. They had stayed ashore too long. Now the wind and tide was against them. There was renewed excitement and consternation among the ladies as the captain's boat put out to rescue them from the lively, perilous waves.

Mrs. Maxwell stood at the rail, fighting back her tears, Cressida beside her, erect, still-faced. Everyone knew that the devoted Mary Maxwell, though she spoke, dressed, and behaved like a lady, had been born the daughter of a village shoemaker. Now, they whispered cattily, that breeding showed. Cressida, rubbed raw by the inescapable problem of Nicholas's child below, of her patched-up marriage that had slipped again into disarray, envied the woman her very real emotion.

At last the boat tied up alongside. The Maori hostages left with many expressions of goodwill. The natives of Port Nicholson, they said, awaited the settlers with eagerness and warmth. "Good-bye. Good-bye," they shouted. The immigrants returned the compliment. *"Haere ra."*

Nicholas, coming aboard wind-blown, wet, and exhilarated, tossed a brace of wood pigeon, twice the size of its English counterpart, to a member of the crew. "The birds sit on the branches and look at you. It seems indecent to kill them," he said. Without even looking in Cressida's direction, he strode purposefully across the deck. Aware of probing, curious eyes, she moved swiftly to the rail, turning her rigid back, holding her humiliated face up to the balm of the hurrying breeze.

The passengers crowded around Mr. Maxwell, eager to hear the news. "But my husband is chilled," his wife protested. "Would you have him catch cold?" She hurried him away. Mr. Wallace, happy in his bachelorhood, chuckled as he leaned against the rail, holding court.

Outside the tiny hospital cabin, Nicholas, his dark hair rumpled, his wet smalls clinging to his legs, was saying impatiently to the stalwart matron who barred his way, "Great heavens, woman, do you think I am likely to rape your patient?"

Her face expressed shock, outrage, and curiosity. "Dr. Stokes said . . ."

Placing both hands on her broad shoulders, Nicholas turned the woman none too gently to face the empty corridor, then opened the door and stepped in.

Rose was sitting up, the child in her arms. Her beautiful green eyes were mysterious, translucent. Nicholas stood looking down at them both. Momentarily, an expression deeper than love and richer than pride showed on his dark face.

"But what sort of triumph is it, Rose?" he asked softly.

"Look, Nicholas." She lifted the small bundle. "Take him. He's yours." Her mouth curved up at the corners, her cheeks dimpled.

"And what am I to do with this splendid gift?" he asked, not moving.

"Love him." She added sweetly, with all the warmth and richness of giving that were her, "He ties us together."

"Prettily spoken, my love, but we have no right to be tied together. You have no right to be here."

She hesitated a moment. A tear came onto her lashes and trembled there.

"The child is your responsibility," said Nicholas, as though reciting something he had learned by heart. "I came to tell you that. I will see Putnam gets work, and that you and the boy are safe. But I cannot claim him as mine."

She regarded him calmly. "He is your child. It is not a matter of claiming him."

Nicholas moved impatiently, emotion warring with the decisions he had made that day, as he forged through the bush, raised his gun, smelled animal scent and the musty dampness of the leaves, felt his nerves singing with the rattle and clatter of streams. He had brought this man's world back with him, and it pressed at the walls of the tiny room that was already suffocating him with its narrowness, its cleanliness, its unreality. "He belongs to Putnam."

"Daniel does not want him."

There was a shivering silence. The baby gave a quick sigh, almost a gasp, then closed his eyes. Nicholas crossed to the bed. Rose drew the child nearer, holding him protectively against her swollen breast, looking down at him with heartbreaking tenderness.

"That will be my vengeance, Rose," Nicholas said. "To give a Putnam my child to bring up." He lifted the bundle, and swing around so that the boy faced the porthole, and through it the rolling, bush-clad hills. "Look well on that, young man," he said, "for it is to be your heritage. Your home."

"And yours, Nicholas." Rose looked up at him, the flaw in her confidence showing in the gravity, the insecurity, behind her eyes.

"No." Nicholas's expression changed, the line of his jaw grew hard. "Before God, Rose, I swear I shall go back. Rundull is a part of me, and I can no more live without it than I can die off its soil. I shall have it, mark my words. I shall go back there, and I shall stay." He turned, giving the hills a cursory glance, lightly condemning them. "The child may have this wild, unholy land."

"You're saying you wish your brother dead," she cried in distress. She was afraid of him when he looked like this.

Nicholas's mouth twisted. "He wished me as good as dead in sending me here."

"Forget him, my darling. You have an heir now, and will get your own lands."

"Heirs do not come from the wrong side of the blanket, even a colonial blanket."

"Don't mock him," said Rose sharply. "He is your son." The words came less as a reminder than a warning and as a warning they were a reminder, too: of Rundull misdeeds, Rundull tricks and Rundull violence, Rundull loves and Rundull hates.

"He will always be your child," said Rose, and, startled, he heard the tone he had himself used when he said Rundull would be his.

"I have decided to call him Giles. It is one of your names."

"Giles Putnam!" Nicholas gave an incredulous shout of laughter. "There's audacity for you!"

"Giles," said Rose resolutely.

"What makes you think he will grow into the sort of fellow who can cope with such a name?" Nicholas held the child before him, scrutinizing the small face. The boy stared back at him with eyes that were penetrating, aware, and somehow old. Unnerved, Nicholas turned to the cot and dropped the babe unceremoniously in.

"Before you say anything," said Rose in a rush, "I want to tell you . . . you may not love soil or grass or buildings better than human beings. You may not!"

"Soil!" Nicholas exclaimed in astonishment. "You call Rundull . . ."

"Yes, I do," she replied passionately. "That's what Rundull is. Stones and dirt and furniture and . . ."

"Rose," said Nicholas, smiling in spite of himself, "if you had been born there . . ."

"But I wasn't, was I?" she snapped. "I was born on a doorstep. I thought—when you took me up to your room at the castle, and your sister's room, and I saw all those lovely carpets and beds and pictures and drapes and the bath before the fire—I too thought this was more important than people. For a while. But *you* are what counts, Nicholas. And me. And the baby." She paused, her eyes enormous, a sea of quivering tears.

Nicholas gazed enigmatically back at her.

"I'll *make* you understand," she added, and the tears ran down her face.

"What about Master Putnam, the poor wronged husband who is to give the child his name?"

"Somebody had to marry me," replied Rose illogically, brushing the tears away, resuming an equally illogical self-confidence. "I will always be grateful to him. And I will be good to him if he will let me." She lifted her eyes again, the dark, damp lashes turned back against lids and rounded cheek. "But I don't expect he'll let me, do you?"

"Possibly not," Nicholas replied solemnly. "To him you are, after all, only a scheming hussy."

"Am I that to you?"

"I think you're a survivor, Rose," he said. He glanced down at his sea-soaked smalls, at the cuffs of his sleeves, dried now and caked with salt. "I've been ashore, as you can see."

"Was it exciting?" Her voice was eager, her eyes bright.

"Yes."

"And beautiful? Is the country beautiful?"

"Yes."

He sat down on the bed, widely set knees supporting his elbows, and, head down, ran his hands through his hair. She watched him, smiling sweetly, her warmth extended. "I am so glad, so very glad you enjoyed your day. Oh, Nicholas, how wonderful it's going to be!"

He frowned and glanced down at the child. A nervous tic jumped in his cheek. The babe stared back, unblinkingly. His head began to ache. He closed his eyes.

"Nicholas," Rose whispered. Nicholas bent and kissed her.

She smoothed his damp, tangled hair, and drew him down so that his cheek lay against her breast.

20

The security of the colony would entirely depend upon the settlers themselves: for, by conducting themselves towards these people in a kind and conciliatory manner, they might easily secure their attachment and prevent their suspicions; but, if by adopting a contrary demeanor, they should have the imprudence to provoke their resentment, the very worst consequences might be expected to ensue.

Information Relative to New Zealand
June 1839

The next day they moved on, but a nor'easter kept them off the Heads. On the second afternoon another Maori canoe came out, carrying amidships a vaguely familiar, fair-haired man of compact build.

"That's Colonel Wakefield!" exclaimed Nicholas. "By God, it's about time."

But there were those who did not share his impatience. The colonel's arrival was living proof that *Tory* had survived. As Edward Gibbon's brother clambered aboard, the immigrants greeted him with cries of very real pleasure, yet it was Nicholas, scowling, conspicuous by his height, who drew his attention.

"How pleased my nephew will be to find you here. He so much desired that you should come."

"Where is Jerningham?" Nicholas inquired crisply as they shook hands.

"He has gone off in a cutter to investigate the possibility of buying land in the Wanganui district."

Angry at Jerningham's nonappearance, scarcely knowing what he would say to him when they met, Nicholas curtly presented Cressida.

"Did you have to show your dislike so openly?" she asked when they were alone. "Colonel Wakefield was delighted to find you with a bride."

"I do not dislike the colonel. I scarcely know him." The name Wakefield had become a canker nonetheless.

On Wednesday, January 22, the gallant little bark tacked into Port Nicholson with *Helena*, a vessel owned by Sydney merchants, which had come on a trading and land-sharking expedition. The passengers lined the rails, braving the boisterous wind that tore at the ladies' flowered bonnets and tugged their skirts, pouncing on the gentlemen's hats, flinging their coattails into a wild dance. The impatient and the anxious paced up and down, missing nothing of the headlands and sandy bays as they fled by, wild and magnificent in their virgin state.

Captain Geordie Bolts, who piloted *Helena*, was a mine of disquieting information. His gossip went through the ship like a forest fire. The chief at the local *pa*, though he had expressed himself delighted to receive the settlers, knew nothing of land allocation. The mountains and plains, the rivers and beaches, he said unequivocally, belonged to the tribes. The missionaries had advised the tribes against selling.

There were alarming rumors that Governor Gipps of New South Wales was preparing a proclamation to the effect that all property should be deemed to belong to the crown. No one, and that included the company, would legally be able to buy directly from the Maoris, even should they wish to sell. The men in their tall hats and frock coats marched up and down *Aurora's* middle deck, seething with indignation. They knew the company had already bought a hundred thousand acres. The settlers had bought this land from them. Paid for it in London! Besides, they could not believe that they were to be under the jurisdiction of the goveror of a convict colony. Where was Mr. James Busby, the British Resident?

He was four hundred trackless miles to the north. It was his job merely to conciliate the goodwill of the native chiefs. He had no power and no authority. With sinking hearts the immigrants realized it was as well Busby had no influence, for those Bible-toting, declared enemies of the company had been his sole companions for six years, and were therefore his friends.

They dropped anchor between a green and tranquil island and Petone Beach. "They have already commemorated one of the men who landed us in this pretty pickle," commented one of the gentlemen sardonically. "That is Somes Island."

"What are we going to do?" they asked each other, looking apprehensively across the bay at a two-mile sweep of sunlit sand. With growing bitterness, they heard that the Maoris had built Colonel Wakefield an office, storerooms for the company's goods, and sleeping accommodation for himself and his nephew, but that they were to make do with tents.

Women wept and wished to return home. Men declaimed. There was a feeling afoot among the wilder elements that they might as well take over a tract of land of their choice, squat on it, and to hell with the consequences.

The lively ones—Mr. Wallace, Nicholas, and a few others—leaped into the longboat and went ashore. The longboat returned swiftly, and the crew began the laborious job of conveying to the beach such necessities as tents, provisions, and cooking stoves.

Maori canoes came alongside—light, graceful vessels without topsides, but with tapering heads and sterns well peaked up at either end—smaller than the one that had met them farther out, quick and handy to paddle. The half-naked savages lashed their cafts to the chains and scrambled aboard, bringing fish and potatoes, bartering shells for tobacco. They offered transport to all and sundry in return for trinkets, a razor, a ribbon sash. Their childlike friendliness won the hearts of the immigrants.

The next morning, in spite of their declaration, some of the steerage women left the ship. The children, many of whom were suffering from boils due to the restricted diet, were anxious to be out in the fresh air. Their mothers wished to look for fresh greens and fruit. Soon there were whole families on the beach, reveling in the kind of freedom many of them had never known. The young ones ran up and down, shrieking with delight, throwing handfuls of golden sand at each other, tumbling in it. Dusky-skinned children came from the local *pa* to gape at them, astounded by their blond hair, exclaiming in astonishment over their pale skins.

Nicholas went ashore every day, vibrating with energy, returning after dark to fall exhausted into bed. He and his companions investigated the various possible sites for the town. The Wakefields favored Petone; the thinking immigrants, who had studied maps and listened to their pilot thought Port Nicholson, with its deep, sheltered harbor, a far more favorable site. Colonel Wakefield had said eleven hundred acres exclusive of quays, streets, squares, and public gardens had been bought from the Maoris for the town. But where was it? The colonel, vacillating, said he would prefer to wait until all five ships arrived before making decisions.

"May I not go ashore?" Cressida asked on the third day of waiting.

"While the ship remains," Nicholas replied, "I wish you to take advantage of the protection it affords."

With tremendous strength of will Cressida suppressed a very improper hope that they might stay aboard and return home again. "What shall we do if we cannot have the land?"

"We will have to take up arms and conquer." Nicholas's hands went deep into his pockets, his shoulders straightened.

"Oh, you men with your wretched conquering zeal!" exclaimed Miss Frederick, who had come up behind them. "Let us make friends with the natives. Surely good nature must achieve more than guns."

"As an educated woman, I am surprised you know so little of historical fact," Nicholas replied crisply. "Good nature has never, to my knowledge, carried more weight than arrows, guns, or cannon."

"Oh fiddle," she retorted. "Let the Rundulls be satisfied with conquering England. Your wife and I are intent upon friendship, as I am sure is Mr. Stitchbury." When Nicholas had gone, she said, brightfaced, "Lady Cressida, these men have taken the adventure wholly upon themselves. I propose to go ashore today and I suggest you come with me. I too have been studying the Maori language, and should like to try out something of what I have learned." She saw the expression of doubt on Cressida's face and added, "We are going to have to stand on our own feet as never before. Obeying one's husband and doing that is a poor mix. Pray send for your maid that she may escort us."

It was Barney Herd who came instead. "I'm very sorry to 'ave to tell m'Lady that Yorke 'as fell in love wiv' a man as is a sawyer, and 'as left your employ."

"Left my employ?" echoed Cressida in disbelief.

"Without a by-your-leave, m'Lady, and that's a fact."

"But . . ." Cressida, recovering her composure, said sharply, "Please send her to me."

"She's not 'ere, m'Lady. She's gorn ashore. This man, name of Edwards, ma'am, 'as took her."

Cressida was outraged. "You must bring her back, Herd, if only for the sake of decency."

"They're to be married as quick as may be, m'Lady. The sawyers is ter go out inter the bush, an' wants a woman ter cook for 'em. Edwards is ter work some sawmilling machinery for a gen'l'man 'oo's arrivin' on *Oriental*. She's done very well for 'erself, Yorke 'as, if you'll pardon my sayin' so, m'Lady."

"But this is outrageous! I have paid her passage. She is my servant."

"I don't know as she 'as ter be," replied Herd, shifting uncomfortably from one foot to the other. "Mr. Wakefield talked about opportunities for the likes of . . . Yorke's 'ad a opportunity, beggin' your pardon m'Lady, and she's took it."

"The Captain will not marry them!" declared Cressida indignantly.

" 'E's given young Yorke a lecture, m'Lady, about 'er responsibilities like, but she's not ter be talked out of it. An' if he don't marry them, there's clergymen comin' on other ships that will. Missionaries, too."

"You're a mine of information, Herd," said Cressida, trying with tight face and stiffening lips to smile at him.

"I been ashore, m'Lady, finding out things."

"I see. Now, tell me, Herd, who is to look after my clothes and attend me?"

Herd did not answer.

"If all the servants do this . . ." Cressida caught her breath.

"I'll be stayin' with Mr. Nicholas, m'Lady," he said reassuringly.

Her voice softened. "Thank you."

As he walked away, Miss Frederick looked down at her slim white hands, the smooth palms turned upward, and remarked, "It would seem we must prepare ourselves for washing dishes and lighting fires."

"You are teasing me," said Cressida, with a nervous little laugh.

Miss Frederick, provokingly, did not reply. Suddenly weak with shock and despair, Cressida had to bite her lips to keep from saying, 'Would you be so gay and adventurous if you were to find your man had his mistress with him, and their child?'

Cressida stood alone and lonely as Miss Frederick was rowed to the jetty that had been run out by *Tory's* surveying team. Willful disobedience would do nothing to help her marriage, she told herself. Endeavoring to stifle her feelings of disappointment, she trailed back to her cabin and settled herself down with her *Maori Grammar.*

When Nicholas returned that evening wearing the now familiar mix of arrogance and guilt, Cressida's heart sank.

He closed the cabin door and leaned against it. "I have arranged for a *whare* to be built for the Putnams. They cannot take the child to a tent."

Cressida laid aside her embroidery. "Of course," she managed her reply without emotion.

Momentarily, he looked taken aback, then said in a clipped voice, "There were problems. The common Maori is as yet unwilling to work for us. As a favor to me the chief—Te Puni is the fellow's name—had some of his *Rangitira*—aristocrats—build it. He is under the impression—" Nicholas brushed his dark hair back from his forehead, seeming momentarily to waver, then said in a voice that was cold to hide his guilt—"he did it for me. He would not have granted me the favor, had I told him the dwelling was for an artisan. It will be necessary for Rose to go ashore in clothes of style and good material . . ."

She put a hand to her throat, her eyes widening.

"No, m'Lady, I do not intend to ask you to loan your

own garments. She is in possession of plenty of her own. She can easily go ashore as a lady."

Cressida's words were full of indignation, but she kept her voice calm. "And her husband? Have you provided him with pantaloons of cassimere and a tall hat? If so, you are wasting your time. I have seen the man. And have you considered what you are doing to this girl? The gentry will never accept her, and her own kind . . . What of her own kind, if you make her a peacock in a pen of domestic fowls? Can you not see how you would place her in a very invidious position?"

Through the ensuing silence came the chatter of passengers in the corridor. Cressida's eyes flickered. "Why are you telling me this?" she asked as the footsteps died away.

"Because people may comment. I shall expect you to have an answer."

Swallowing her humiliation, determined that he might not see the effect of his arrogance and cruelty, Cressida nodded. What was left to them but the dignity of the family, she thought bitterly.

Nicholas extended both hands with genuine gratitude. Pretending she had not seen, Cressida moved over to the sea chest, saying, "It is time we dressed for dinner. Had you heard that my maid has been corrupted by opportunity, this commodity the Wakefields have been presenting to the lower classes as highly desirable?" Her voice rose, cracked a little. "How unfortunate for us that the Maoris should be so class-conscious, for it seems we are to lose our servants and therefore our dignity. What say you to this red gown for dinner? It goes so well with my rubies, and who knows but that this may be my last opportunity to wear them."

He moved toward her, his manner gentle, his gratitude showing in the softened lines of his features. "Cress . . ." She was noisily rustling the gown, shaking it as though it smelled of mothballs or harbored fleas.

"Cressida," he began again. "It is a situation we . . ." He looked at her imploringly.

"I know," she said. There was a flash of fear in her eyes. Then she lifted her head. He placed his hands on her shoulders, leaned forward, and kissed her very gently on the cheek. Blinded by tears, she turned away, and began to lay her clothes very carefully, with little precise movements, on the bed.

The next morning the ladies left the ship along with the final installment of goods and chattels. Miss Frederick, seeing Rose in the accompanying longboat, demure in pale muslin with the violet trim back on her bonnet, the baby held closely in her arms, turned with amazement to Cressida. "Why, how very clever of you, Lady Cressida, to loan the girl some of your clothes! You do have the greatest good nature!"

Cressida looked away, silent in her anguish. "I did not loan them, dear Miss Frederick. She has somehow acquired them herself."

"But how could she?"

"The maids at Rundull sometimes received hand-me-downs from the family."

"Oh, but that outfit is surely no hand-me-down," expostulated Miss Frederick. "Or if it is, I am greatly surprised."

"In my sister-in-law's situation as maid of honour to her majesty," replied Cressida stiffly, "she needs a large wardrobe. Though Lady Felicity's clothes are certainly quite unsuitable for Mrs. Putnam, one of the upper servants may have contrived to . . . Stranger gifts than an unsuitable gown have been given, I am sure, on the occasion of a marriage."

The Putnams' erstwhile steerage companions watched with expressions of amazement as the ill-assorted Putnams disembarked and crossed the beach. Hiding in the precarious comfort of her dream world, nervous of Daniel, Rose had not made enough friends on the voyage. Now, it mattered. Those who had championed her in the later stages of her pregnancy looked at her grand clothes and felt taken in. Those who had not forgotten the saucy miss who came aboard at Gravesend sharpened their knives. Rose sensed their dislike. She knew that most of them had never owned a new gown in their lives, and she was sorry to upset them. But Nicholas had said the chief was a snob, and that she must impress him by speaking and looking like a lady.

Two women, whose husbands had been tiresomely attentive before her pregnancy became obvious, moved directly into her path and delivered a public insult in the

form of a low curtsy. "You haven't seen my baby," she
said, looking down at the little face in the crook of her
arm, then smiling up at her tormentors. As they hesitated, trapped by their ill will, she added ingenuously,
"He's really quite famous. He's the first white baby to be
born here."

"There's lots of babies been born here. Lots of missionaries' children and whalers' children," came the unfriendly reply.

"The first settler," Rose corrected herself, determined
to please.

"Settler?" repeated a carpenter's wife in waspish outrage. "Your husband's a common workingman like ours."

There was mocking laughter. Rose flushed. The word
"settler" had fallen automatically from her lips because
Giles, as Nicholas's son, would one day have land and be
a settler.

"Why, she's only a baby herself," murmured one of
the older women kindly, "and probably don't know the
difference."

Rose smiled winningly. Her face, warm with gratitude,
and bright with the tension of the moment, was so stun-
ningly beautiful that it split the onlookers into factions of
envy and reluctant admiration.

"Rose!" shouted Daniel from the edge of the grass.

One of the younger brides peered at the baby and said
artlessly,"He don't look at all like you, Mrs. Putnam.
Nor your husband."

Deftly, Rose tucked the shawl about the baby's head,
hiding the telltale hair. "They're all born with black
hair," she said. "All babies are. Sometimes it falls out
and they turn fair."

"That they don't," snapped a forthright woman with a
north country accent. "I've got five bairns, all born fair."

A whiff of tobacco came downwind, and a shadow
larger than the rest fell beside her. "So here is the new
arrival, having his first taste of his own country," said
Dr. Stokes benignly. "What a handsome little fellow he
is, to be sure. What's his name to be, Mrs. Putnam?"

Rose lifted her head and said proudly, "Giles, Dr.
Stokes."

The murmuring ceased spontaneously. An astonished
silence fell.

"Well, that's as good a name as any," said the doctor kindly.

A mean-eyed woman said, "Giles! Is that a name for a decent workingman's boy? Ask her as to who the father is, Doctor, and see what she says."

"The father is Mr. Putnam," the doctor replied firmly. He added, the heat in his voice carefully controlled, "For shame! We are a small community and will not survive without according each other honor and respect."

They listened, but their hearts were not with him. They had been a long time with very little to think of except their own precarious safety, and a victim was an acceptable diversion in the desert of their minds.

"Rose!" shouted Daniel again.

Rose smiled at the women, tentatively soliciting their goodwill. "I have to go," she said apologetically.

There was a stir on the outer perimeter of the crowd, and a voice called, "Do stop. Just for a moment." A bright-faced woman in yellow gingham with ribbons around her slim waist hurried through, laughingly using a frilly parasol to clear her path. "Mrs. Putnam, do allow me to see the baby before you take him away."

There was a delicate earthiness about the newcomer, and an air of genuine interest. Rose warmed to her. "Of course you may look at him. He is enjoying the attention."

The silence was electric. The crowd had heard the lightening of Rose's voice, the softening of her vowels. They met each other's eyes with disbelief, then one by one they melted away, whispering. Rose was unaware of employing that facility she had absorbed through Grandy, of using one voice for her fellows and another for her superiors.

"How beautiful he is! How lucky you are to have begun your family already," the newcomer was saying. She touched the baby's downy cheeks, his dimpled chin, smoothing the fine black hair.

Rose glowed.

"I declare, Doctor, you are going to be kept busy when we start building our nests."

He bowed graciously, his eyes twinkling. "I shall be very pleased, Mrs. Maxwell, to be kept busy on such a happy matter."

She smiled again at Rose and pressed her hand. "Run,

dear. Your husband is approaching with great impatience. I must apologize for detaining you."

Absurdly warmed by the small kindness, Rose glided away across the sand. Daniel was coming to meet her. Without a word, he held out his arms and took the baby, then turned, and they went together toward the bank.

Dr. Stokes looked after them, rubbing his whiskers. "Mrs. Putnam seems to be a woman of rare spirit, and a loving heart. There's a kind of exaltation in her face. For a village girl . . ."

Tugging at her bonnet ribbons, laughing, Mrs. Maxwell said, "I was a village girl myself, Doctor, as I am sure you are aware."

He coughed discreetly. "You have married exceeding well, Mrs. Maxwell, into a family of considerable stature."

"Oh, indeed," she replied with a wry sort of pride. "My husband was brought up to treat his elders with respect and to address his superiors only as your majesty."

"Well, there you are. You behave like a lady, and speak, look, and dress like one, otherwise I am sure Mr. Maxwell would not have married you. You do not need to compare yourself with Mrs. Putnam."

"Compare myself?" She laughed merrily. "I will not hesitate to say I should like Mrs. Pitnam's face and figure, though perhaps you might say she is too pretty to be a real lady." She gave the doctor a sideways, mischievous glance, then heaved a sigh. "As for me, as my mother-in-law has been gracious enough to acknowledge, I am one of God's creatures. No more nor less. I have a husband whom I love, and who loves me. I hope to lead a useful and interesting life with him. What else is there, Doctor?"

"How I wish there were more of your kind," he replied.

Oliver was waiting, his thin face already pink from the sun. He helped Rose up the bank on to the grass. "My!" he cried with gusty admiration, as he took in the muslin gown and violet-trimmed bonnet. "You do look pretty! I never seen yer dressed up like that. Don't she look pretty, Daniel?"

"*Have* never seen." Rose corrected him automatically. She did not want Oliver teaching Giles to speak in the vulgar manner. Giles was to be a gentleman.

Daniel stepped up onto the bank and handed the baby to Rose. "C'mon then," he said.

They went into the bush together, Oliver and Rose quivering with excitement, Daniel plodding along. They filled their lungs full of the delicious land smells, the musky fragrance that lurked among the tree boles, savoring them with near ecstasy. "Oh, Oliver!" cried Rose. "Isn't this just . . . Isn't it—" She broke off, defeated by her own exhilaration.

He leaped into the air, his bony little body throbbing with life and a hiatus of delirious joy. Impetuously, recklessly, he jumped at low branches, fell on all fours, rubbed his hands through the brown carpet of leaves, flung them in handfuls into the air.

"Why, Oliver," exclaimed Rose, amazed at his antics, "have you never before been in the country?"

"No." He raced ahead, swung around precipitously, dashed back again. Rose put a hand on his arm. They all three paused to look at the little birds darting through the branches, peeping at them with their heads cocked to one side. Bigger birds scurried to and fro on the ground. There was a babble of soft voices and they turned. Maori children were coming along a sidetrack carrying fishing lines.

"*Tenakoe*," said Rose, smiling at them as they approached. They hung their heads as they passed, looking shy, but farther on they paused and stared. On being discovered, they burst into suppressed giggles, then scattered down the path and out of sight.

"Come on," urged Oliver.

"No. We must not hurry." Rose was dizzily aware of her new surroundings. "Look!" she whispered. A dingy little creature the size of a small thrush, with the plumage of a chaffinch, alighted on a branch nearby, then opened its beak and sounded a peal of silver bells. Even Daniel smiled. A parrot with reddish brown and scarlet feathers alighted at their feet. Searching for grubs, it began to tear up the loose soil at the root of a tall tree. They stayed to watch, delighting in the creature's antics, its beady stare, its incredible trust.

They emerged into the sunlight of a clearing overhung around its small perimeter with luxuriant foliage, the sun dappling the leaves on drooping branches. And there was the house Nicholas had had built for them. Rose stared, blinked, and stared again. The walls were made of the velvety brown trunks of the punga tree fern, the roof neatly woven with palms.

"What d'yer think of it?" asked Oliver with an air of proprietary importance. "I seen them making it."

A monstrous antithesis flashed across Rose's inner eyes; a picture of the cottage where Florrie and Adam lived, with its always damp, cold stones, its odor of rotted peelings and babies' urine. She looked down at her own child and thought in distress of Florrie's sickly, white-faced urchins. One day, she vowed passionately, as she listened to the soughing of the wind in the trees, the distant surging of the sea, she would share this miraculous escape with Florrie and Adam. And Grandy, if he would come.

She went forward across the sunlit grass and, thrilled, bewitched, stood in the doorway of the Maori *whare* looking in. The room was quite twenty feet long and oblong in shape, the walls strengthened by planks of prettily grained wood. It was lined with neatly packed bundles of bullrushes, held in place by glazed canes the thickness of a finger. The roof, which was supported by one post upholding a ridgepole in the center, was made of reeds tied firmly together with strips of flax, and there was a partition at one end, forming a small, doorless room.

Daniel muttered, "This is a heathen's house, Rose. Let's go back to the tents."

"No, Daniel." She grasped his hand and drew him inside. "No."

Oliver, bright-eyed as a hopeful winter starling, cried, "I wish I could live 'ere with you, Rose. Couldn't I make a mattress of grass in that corner over there?"

Rose let go of Daniel's hand. "But what would Dr. Stokes say? You belong with him."

"Just fer a little while," entreated Oliver. " 'E woildn't mind. I could run messages and 'elp with the cooking. Please let me. Please, Rose."

She turned back to Daniel, but he had disappeared. She heaved a quick sigh. "Yes," she said. "Yes, you may. So long as you tell the doctor."

"*Tenakoe.*"

They turned in sharp alarm. It was their first experience of the creeping quiet of the natives. In the doorway stood a burly Maori, his feathered mat slung negligently, like a Roman toga, over one shoulder. Rose's startled eyes jumped from his fearsomely tattooed face to the snowy white albatross down puffing from his ears, to his bare feet, then back with apprehension to meet his fierce stare. He carried in one hand a greenstone club decorated with parrot feathers, in the other a menacing spear. A thrill of fear went through her. Like a peace offering, she extended her arms, just fractionally, for the native to admire the baby.

With a rough gesture, he indicated that he was not interested. "Me no like bab-ee until it have milk teeth. Very sweet then to eat."

Rose's eyes glazed. "Sweet?" she queried starkly.

"Sweet meat," he replied, adding with disdain, as he gestured toward the child, "No good now. No taste. I give you thousand acre for him when he cut teeth."

Her head spun with shock. "Did not the missionaries tell you it is wicked to eat people?" She spat the words at him like a mother cat.

He nodded casually, then changed the subject. "Very good house." He indicated the building with pride.

"Yes. Yes, it's lovely."

Te Puni's appraising eyes moved from the top of Rose's pretty bonnet to the hem of her muslin skirt, then back to her eyes. "You are lady," he said approvingly, then added with thunderous condemnation, gesturing toward the door, "but your man *kuki*."

Rose's eyes flickered nervously.

"English slave."

Bewilderment set tight little tucks between her brows, and at the corners of her puckered mouth.

"If your man chief he kill father of bab-ee."

So he knew Nicholas was Giles's father. Or had guessed. "English people do not kill one another," she said fiercely. Then she remembered that she had been directed by Nicholas to make a friend of this man. It was more than even her loving heart could manage. "I think it is better that my husband builds a house for us," she said. "He is a carpenter and can put his hand to it very easily."

"He *kuki.*"The native assumed once again his over-bearing and provocative manner.

"No," she replied stamping her foot.

"He common man," the chief stated with disdain.

"If you like, yes.".

His incredible face, blue with those grotesque designs, was only inches from hers. In her nostrils was the forest smell of him, the dankness of fungus, the scent of tree bark, the strange perfume of the birds whose feathers decorated the woven mat he wore. She pushed past him, stepped through the dark-skinned children, and out into the sunlight. Oliver followed. They exchanged uneasy glances.

There was the sound of voices. "Look!" exclaimed Oliver with relief.

A group of barefoot Maori women was approaching along the path, their black hair dancing on their shoulders, their long bone earrings swinging. They, too, were smiling, their white teeth flashing above the tattoos on their lower lips and chins. They all wore a plaited band across their foreheads, ocher colored, black, and that strange red of the canoes. Their plain tunics were fastened with a girdle around the waist. A scatter of naked brown children came running behind.

"*Tenakoe,*" they called cheerily. One of them added in English, "we come see bab-ee."

A beautiful plump woman, apparently the acknowledged leader, came up to Rose, and leaned forward until their noses touched. The gesture appealed to Rose's sense of the ridiculous, but she kept a carefully grave face as she allowed them, one by one, to rub their noses against hers. They admired the baby. "Nice black hair. All the same the Maori!" Rose joined in their good-humored banter, laughing nervously, agreeing with them. The children gathered around, their big black eyes, with their amazingly white irises, full of wonder.

"You have bed for bab-ee?" asked one of the women. Rose shook her head.

"We make. Today. Here." She was carrying a basket skillfully woven of pale flax. "For bab-ee."

"How kind you are." Rose once more looked around for Daniel, wanting him to share the gift."Daniel!" He appeared from behind the *whare* dragging his feet in his heavy boots, looking humble and frightened out of his wits.

Her eyes flicked nervously toward the chieftain. He lifted his head arrogantly, and his lips curled in an expression of contempt. He went to the end of the building and began to walk up and down, working himself deliberately into a rage. His antics must have been a signal for the women to leave. Murmuring excitedly, they headed back the way they had come, the children trailing behind them, waving.

The chieftain stopped pacing. With a baleful look at Daniel, he jumped in the air, bringing his feet down hard on the ground. Mesmerized, Rose stood rooted to the spot clutching the baby, as the Maori waved his arms, rolled his eyes, put out his tongue.

Daniel looked stunned.

Suddenly a sinewy, sunburned young man emerged from the trees. He was attired in brown moleskin trousers tied with flax over strong boots, and he wore a blue serge shirt confined at the waist by a leather strap into which were tucked a sheath knife and a tomahawk. In one hand he carried a flax stalk which he used as a walking stick.

"Chief Te Puni!" he roared.

The rolling eyes steadied, then brightened with pleasure and real warmth. " Pastor!"

"What was he doing?" Rose asked the newcomer, still rigid with a mixture of terror and excitement.

"Proving what a temper he is in, that's all."

Daniel looked at Rose in an agony of misery and despair.

The Englishman went to stand in front of the native chief, his lank, frail-looking frame bent over the flax stick, his stance somehow conveying the utmost authority. He spoke in Maori in a firm tone, and at great length. Te Puni replied with courtesy, though not without some baleful glances in Daniel's direction. After a moment or two of silent indecision, the native stepped aside and went off down the track.

Their visitor turned. Looking at him full face, Rose saw and understood the chief's submission. His plain features, dominated by wide-set clear eyes, were lit by an almost unearthly radiance. "Maoris are quite childlike in some ways, but very tractable if you're careful with them. May I introduce myself? I am Octavius Hadfield. I'm a missionary." His emaciated face split into an angelic smile. "And you are Mr. and Mrs. Putnam. I've talked to Mr. le Grys, who, as I understand it, had this house built for you. It was an error of judgment, but everything is all right now."

"Rose," Daniel said hoarsely,"we can't stay 'ere." He addressed himself to Hadfield, "The Maori don't want us to . . ."

"Te Puni's changed his mind," broke in the pastor good-humoredly.

"He says—" broke in Daniel desperately.

"The house is an accomplished fact, and if we are to avoid further trouble, here you must stay. Te Puni's all right. A bit of a show-off."

"He said he would eat the baby," said Rose.

"A chieftain would never eat a newborn baby. I've told him to behave himself and he will obey me." He turned again to Daniel. "Putnam, if you and the boy will come back to the beach with me . . ."

"I'll stay with Rose," replied Oliver with thrusting vehemence.

"Oh, very well," Hadfield replied cheerfully."You come with me, Putnam, and I'll show you where to find your issue of gear."

21

The wind rose, blowing black clouds into the bright sky, swirling around the tents, pushing the canvas, tugging at the ropes. Cressida stood at the entrance to the tent that Herd and Fred Quick had erected, feeling the new, secret life stirring within her, feeling defiled by its existence, shamed.

We are as animals, she thought bitterly, and I have behaved like an animal in conceiving the child. Help me to find the grace to survive. The wind caught at her bonnet, sending the ribbons high in the air, teasing out tendrils of hair, lashing them back across her face. Out on the restless ocean, *Aurora* was making ready to sail.

"Do what you can to sort things out," Nicholas had said, squeezing her arm in a gesture of sympathy as he left. "There is nowhere else to go, so you may as well make the best of it."

She went inside and looked bleakly at the piled boxes, the small camp beds, thinking with overwhelming humiliation of the little thatched dwelling to which the kitchen maid had gone.

"Lady Cressida."

At the sound of the familiar voice outside her tent, she brightened and lifted the flap. "Oh, Mrs. Maxwell!"

She looked no more than sixteen with her bonnet gone, her hair blown free of its pins, her cheeks flushed, eyes sparkling. "May I come in? I declare, this wind . . ."

Cressida drew her into the shelter of the tent. "How glad I am to see you. My husband, in an endeavor to find out exactly what the situation is, has gone to see Colonel Wakefield."

"I will stay only a moment. My husband has already received some intelligence which has caused him to make a decision. I came to tell you we are leaving."

"Leaving!" Cressida cried, hope soaring giddily. "You are going home?"

"Oh, no." The shoemaker's daughter laughed merrily. "Our return would be far from acceptable to my husband's family." She sat herself down on the trunk, spreading her skirts happily around her. "We are to move off to the north. Mr. Maxwell has convinced himself, after listening to a selection of whalers, natives, and missionaries, that the capital will be built where men of influence have established themselves. Perhaps in the Bay of Islands where the British Resident lives, or a little to the south, near a bay called Manukau, where there are already missionaries. It does seem, Lady Cressida, that the company has taken the law into its own hands with regard to appropriating land."

"But we must surely stick together," cried Cressida, shocked and distressed. "There are so few of us. We cannot afford to lose each other." Even as she spoke, she saw with a sense of intolerable loneliness and bitter envy that her friend, with a loving husband at her side, did not need her. Her hurt showed in the tartness of her reply. "Do you not feel under an obligation to the company?"

"We do not feel any responsibility for the folly of the company, my dear Lady Cressida. We were not told that the British government was antagonistic to the company's plans. It seems that those who stay here may never get the freehold of their land. There are to be accredited land sales shortly in the north. My husband wishes to be there in order to take advantage of them."

Cressida forced a smile. "I am sorry if I spoke sharply. Sometimes I worry about the loneliness, but that is selfish of me."

"Like me, you have a wonderful husband. And we will meet again," Mrs. Maxwell told her warmly.

"Of course," she said without hope, thinking that this was a country where it would be of no avail to closely guard friendships for, by the very nature of pioneering, they would be broken up like driftwood. "How will you go? With Captain Heale?"

"No. He is to take our chattels." The visitor's voice rose, liltingly "We are to walk."

"Walk?"

"It is an opportunity to see the country. We have already commissioned a Maori guide, and another to carry a few belongings. It will be such an adventure! I shall be forever in possession of tales to relate by the fireside to my children and grandchildren."

Another voice calling from outside brought her out of her brown study. Cressida turned and parted the canvas flaps. Miss Frederick stood silhouetted against the glare of the sea, her skirts dancing, one hand steadying a small hat.

"Oh, my dear, do come in," Cressida cried, her voice all but breaking. "I am reeling from the most stupendous news Mrs. Maxwell has brought."

The visitor sat down also on the trunk, her face long, her eyes misty with disappointment. "I have heard it. How I envy them. If only that wretched, hateful Mr. Jerningham Wakefield who has captured my Stitchbury, would appear. And what of you, m'Lady? I cannot imagine that Mr. le Grys will want to tolerate the situation as it is here. We wait and wait, and nothing happens. Colonel Wakefield is distressingly indifferent. Even his surveyors are in the wrong place—at the Hutt—while everyone is saying the town must be built on the harbor."

Cressida could only say, "Do you realize, Mrs. Maxwell, how far you will walk?"

The young woman nodded, her eyes sparkling. "Four hundred miles, or thereabouts."

"I declare," cried Miss Frederick, jumping up from her seat and clapping her hands together, "I shall persuade Mr. Stitchbury to follow your excellent example. And you must consider it, also, Lady Cressida. I beg of you, consider it."

Cressida felt cold, and not only at the thought of losing her friends. Now she must make the ignominious admission to Nicholas, immediately upon the birth of his mistress's baby, that she could not travel, for she too was expecting. "I shall endeavor to persuade Mr. le Grys to make something of what is here," she said. "It may appear at the moment to be a sorry lot, but I am sure he will. . . ."

"Of course," said Mrs. Maxwell kindly. "Of course. And now I must be on my way, for there are arrangements to be made."

In solitary anguish Cressida watched her friends go off across the sand.

Nicholas made his way to the end of the beach and strode into the storehouse built on a slope with trees behind. Maori children playing on felled logs gazed up at him. "*Tenakoe.*"He strode right past them. The culprit, wearing the tall white hat that was his badge of office, stood by his desk, urbane, genial, pleased to see him.

Nicholas rasped, "Colonel! You have been here for two months, yet not a single residence has been built."

"How were we to know our crack ship would be beaten by *Aurora*?" the colonel asked quizzically. "There are wooden houses in frame aboard *Oriental.*"

"Not everyone has ordered a wooden frame house. We were told we would be accommodated temporarily in homes that the natives would construct. If it is possible for you to be provided with accommodation, why have not the settlers been accommodated?"

Without apology, Wakefield replied,"This is little more than a storeroom." He gestured toward a bed set up in the farthest corner. "I sleep over there."

"I sleep in a tent. And what is more to the point," Nicholas added cuttingly, "so does my lady wife."

"You must understand, we had to have shelter for the company's perishable goods."

"How dare you, sir, consider your goods before your people! Could not you envisage the ill feeling your misapplied diligence would create?" The question was rhetorical; it was evident the colonel did not feel compelled to reply. Nicholas continued, "Where are the laborers? You presumably employed native workmen on this building."

"Let me explain, dear boy. Before we went off in *Tory* on our land-buying expedition, we asked for houses to be erected. It seems the natives did not fully understand. Chief Wharepouri, who is supreme head of the local tribes, was under the impression that a mere half dozen immigrants were coming. The Maori, it appears, cannot visualize numbers over one hundred. We are having difficulty making them realize the immensity of our project."

"Are you telling me, sir, that we must fend for ourselves?"

Wakefield's pale eyes settled calmly on Nicholas's angry face. "My brother was diligent in seeking out immigrants of exceptional potential. You have brought your own staff. Let them also aid you in persuading the natives of our methods. Teach them the advantage of wage-earning. They are accustomed to work only for the next meal."

"And what are they to do with these wages, sir?" Nicholas asked.

"When the rest of the ships arrive, stores will be built."

They both looked up sharply as Octavius Hadfield, his clothes hanging on his emaciated figure as though tossed there by some mischievous wind, burst through the door. With a brief nod to Nicholas he walked right up to the desk and stood looking down at its occupant.

"Colonel! I have something very serious to say to you."

"There is nothing for us to say to each other," retorted Wakefield coldly. "I have now heard that a deputation headed by my brother Arthur waited upon Mr. Dandeson Coates of the Church Missionary Society in London, who said that, though he had no doubt of the respectability and purity of our motives, he is opposed to the colonization of New Zealand. He intends to thwart us by all means in his power. . . ."

"Colonel—"

"We do not therefore expect any regard or consideration from you," the colonel continued obdurately, coldly looking up at the missionary, "and we are very well aware of the mischievous nature of your interference. The Reverend Henry Williams has been following us just one step behind on our land-buying expeditions, in a vain attempt to stop the Maoris from selling."

"Your payments for land have already resulted in a battle of horrific proportions," retorted Hadfield. "Seventy men lie dead, slaughtered in the most appalling circumstances. Your company has blood on its hands, Colonel. It was indefensible to take a hundred and ten

thousand acres in return for the kind of trash that was
bound to cause trouble. Jew's harps," he said scathingly,
"sealing wax, pencils, umbrellas." He paused, drew a
long breath through his teeth, then added, distastefully,
"Muskets, gunpowder, and tomahawks. What did you
expect but that you would start a war?"

"We have come to colonize," retorted Wakefield, "and
to arrange for a better life for underprivileged people of
our own country. Our own people, Mr. Hadfield. And
yours. Charity begins at home."

Hadfield straightened. "Captain Hobson of the Royal
Navy, who is our governor-elect, is bringing a treaty to
be signed by every chief in the land. It cedes to our
queen absolutely all rights and power of sovereignty,
guaranteeing the tribes undisturbed possession of their
lands, and the exclusive right of the British government
of preemption of such lands as the Maoris are prepared
to sell. I warn you, Colonel, the government will not
recognize the validity of any land titles given without her
majesty's authority."

There was a pregnant silence, then Wakefield said with
civil incivility, "Our queen has not given authority for the
adoption of the vast tracts taken by the missionaries. Has
not Mr. Williams himself annexed a farm of four thousand acres in the north? Mr. Fairburn, I believe, has
helped himself to a whole county, and Mr. James Shepherd owns all the land from Kirikiri to the Hokianga
forest, a distance of approximately fifteen miles." He
added with deliberate censure, "My company pays for its
land."

Grim-faced, impotent with anger, Nicholas turned and
went out the door. On the edge of the beach he stood
looking out across the water, white-crested now from the
darting wind, and contemplated with acute disquiet the
precariousness of his situation.

There was no going back. That was the only certainty.

He stepped down onto the sand and walked briskly
beside the water, his hat gripped in his hand, the wind
dragging at his hair, blowing the sand into whirls that
stung his face and gritted on his lips. He went to the end
of the beach before turning. There was a woman coming
toward him, her skirts flat against her thighs, a shawl

wrapped closely around her head. For a moment he thought it was Rose and, heart leaping, he started forward.

"I saw you from the tent," called Cressida. "I guessed by the angry way you hurried along the interview had not gone well." They came face to face, and she gave him a tentative smile. "I came to tell you, in case you are concerned on my account, that I find this new mode of living quite diverting. You will not run away as some are thinking of doing?" Her eyes were pleading, but her voice was strong.

"No, by God, I'll not run, and neither will I wait upon decisions that may be made by incompetent fools." They walked the length of the beach in silence, but together. The seagulls swooped and rose, uttering their melancholy cries.

The picnic on the beach continued week after week. *Oriental* arrived to swell the numbers, and with it the workmen acquainted with foundry and milling trades. A Wesleyan missionary, who had walked four hundred miles to greet the immigrants, held divine service on board *Aurora.* Captain Heale unceremoniously dumped the remaining cargo that owners had not had time to claim and gave a farewell dinner, inviting his favorites, along with the leading settlers from other ships.

The lively young sons of founders Lord Petre and Sir William Molesworth, having eventually found their boiler washing about in the sand at high tide, grimly refused Heale's invitation and, working side by side with their men, put their machinery back into operating order.

Some wanderers in small schooners and cutters arrived from Van Dieman's Land, and a grog shop was established on the beach. Here, to the distress of the respectable immigrants, a disorderly assemblage of sailors and stray whalers gathered nightly.

A sow, the first tame pig to land since Captain Cook, gave birth to a litter of piglets. Goats were unloaded. A few Lincoln and shorthorn sheep arrived from Sydney. Colonel Wakefield went out to the Heads in *Cuba* to bring in the *Duke of Roxburgh,* whose captain had been lost overboard in a gale. One by one, the first five ships arrived.

Word came that the dreaded treaty had arrived at the

Bay of Islands in the north, that forty-six chiefs had appended their signatures in return for the bribe of a blanket. The missionaries were now bringing the paper south. No chief was deemed to be too unimportant to append his signature or mark.

The young and independent, the rash and rich, announced they intended to choose their land and set up their machinery. Possession, they announced with optimism and vigor, was nine tenths of the law. Leaving the clamor behind, they tramped off with their men. On the banks of the Hutt River, a mile from the sea, where the company's surveyor had pitched one of his tents, they cleared a space for the foundry. Within a few weeks, they promised, they would be offering nails and other iron articles, stoves even, for the new homes.

The Honorable Francis Molesworth took his men upriver, and not only marked out a farm, but, ignoring threats of forfeiture, began felling timber for farm buildings. Seizure and occupancy, it was discovered, was something the Maoris understood. The first axemen in a primeval forest could lay claim to the surrounding trees.

Individual settlers, moving slowly and carefully, at last persuaded individual Maoris to build native houses for them. Payment was agreed at four blankets, the brown-skinned laborers adamantly refusing money.

And one English cow, accepting her new country with equanimity, wandered among the dwellings, browsing contentedly on native shrubs.

22

One or two weddings were held every Sunday, as men came to recognize their need, after a hard day's work, for a cook and home comforts. One woman was heard to say she was sorry she had married in Scotland, for she could have had an independent gentleman here.

The town, people decided, should grow up at the port and, acting on a new feeling of autonomy, they began one by one to settle there. Te Puni, concerned about the blankets and beads promised to him for Petone, demonstrated his displeasure by lighting a bonfire in view of the beach, where he and his relatives danced, brandishing spears and chanting far into the night.

But he had reckoned without the stoical quality of the British. As they watched the warlike figures silhouetted in processional movements against the flames, they smiled their tight, brave smiles, and drew on hitherto unguessed-at resources of inner strength.

At last it was agreed, pending the outcome of negotiations with Westminster, to grant a temporary allotment of twenty acres of land to each of the settlers who had paid in London. Nicholas sought out Chief Wharepouri, grand seigneur of all the natives in the southern part of the North Island, who understood some of the white man's laws.

There was a method of buying land that was precise in the Maori mind and totally acceptable to Nicholas. Having astutely chosen a block that encompassed a high hill, he led the willing chieftain to the summit, where they both climbed the tallest tree. With his naked arm raised, as Wharepouri explained carefully, to a height where Nicholas could see the dark hairs beneath, he turned slowly around, marking a circumference that Nicholas deemed roughly to encompass a thousand acres. That was to be le Grys land. Nicholas gave him £1,000 in gold and Wharepouri was satisfied.

"But how can you be certain you will be allowed to keep your property when the whole matter is investigated?" Cressida protested, wanting to wait until the courts were set up.

"At least twenty acres is legally mine," Nicholas retorted. "The company holds my payment for eighty more. I am prepared to fight in court for the other nine hundred odd. Anyway," he added with an illogicality that startled his wife, "I am confident we will be able to keep it as long as it is needed."

"Are our lives to be governed by the fact that Adeline may not bear a son? What a sorry plight we may find ourselves in if she does." But Nicholas was already walking away.

When Herd, who had promised to remain loyal, sent a message that he had found employment to his liking in a sawmill, Nicholas merely asked, "What do I want with a valet?" His day wear consisted of moleskin trousers, a blue serge shirt, and a much-prized cabbage tree hat with a black ribbon. "Tell the cowardly villain to put his best foot forward and see that I get timber for my house."

Cressida took the news that a whaler had annexed her cook with less equanimity. "He's been in this country ten years, m'Lady, and has a very comfortable house," the woman said, looking embarrassed but firm.

"Which is more than I can provide for you at the moment," Cressida replied bitterly, but she graciously attended the wedding in the small mission chapel and offered the couple her good wishes. With apprehension, she watched her maids talking to two young men who intended to seek their fortunes in the north.

That night she wrote to her mother: *Please send me a very ugly cook and some trained, ugly, housemaids.*

Plows were arriving, hundreds of bricks and millstones. Nicholas met every ship in order to importune skilled workmen. Sawyers were busy in the new mills. He let it be known he was prepared to pay well for his timber, and good wages for men to pit up the kind of house that would keep a clutch of carpenters and masons busy for some time. They must have a residence quickly. It was to be the first, the biggest, and the best.

Daniel found work in a sawmill at the Hutt River, trudging there every day, returning tired in the evenings.

Oliver kept Rose supplied with news. "We're all learnin' to swim. Even tiny natives can swim as good as fish. Their parents throw them in the water when they're babies. You must throw Giles in, Rose. He'll swim."

Rose reached out longing arms for her child. "Hand him back to me, you monkey. How cruel!"

"Is it?" the boy who had seen his parents hang asked in surprise. "They say everyone swims if they 'ave ter." He was a growing encyclopedia on Maori ways. Oliver's thin little face seemed to broaden day by day, his strength to grow. Rose listened to the stories of his exploits, serene in the knowledge that this was the life her little boy was to inherit, growing up plump, merry, and strong like the native children, swimming like a fish, as Oliver said.

The natives had become her friends. They came every day and taught her their lullabies. They led her to a stream and helped her wash her baby's clothes. They brought yams and peaches, *kumara*, the sweet potato, and cabbage from their cultivations. They taught her their language, and she taught them hers. They talked to her of their *Arikis*, their priest-chieftains, eldest sons of eldest sons, who traced their descent back to the Maori gods, and they enchanted her with legends of noble warriors fighting wars over beautiful Maori maidens.

They showed Oliver how to build a native oven. Oliver, having lived by his wits in London, had no difficulty in finding a spade to do the job.

The food they cooked in Oliver's oven, a round hole lined with small stones containing a fire, was delicious. Wild pig, fish, and pigeon brought by the Maoris, who were generous to a fault, would be packed in leaves, placed over the hot stones and covered with soil. Then Oliver, delighting in his new prowess, would pour water into the center to create steam.

"When are you coming to live with me?" Dr. Stokes

would ask Oliver quizzically. Meanwhile Daniel protested, "You're turning native, both of you. Why have you no white friends, Rose?" It was the inevitable consequence of being a peacock in a pen of domestic fowls.

She illuminated the *whare* by means of an extempore chandelier made with sticks lashed to the main pole like cross ties. Brilliant blossoms from the pohutukawa trees that fringed the sands clustered around the candles.

Those were magic weeks. Early every morning, after Daniel had trudged off down the path that led to the Hutt Valley and his work, Rose would feed the baby, then she and Oliver would set off to the beach carrying the basket between them, often accompanied by Maori children. When ships came in, they mingled with new arrivals, enjoying the chatter and fuss. In the middle of the day, when the sun was hot as an oven, they went into the bush, following the Maori tracks, learning from natives the names of the trees and the friendly birds. During the long, languorous afternoons they studied. Rose was reading now with ease, and her writing improved daily.

"What're you goin' ter do with all that learnin'?" Daniel grumbled.

Sensing that her new accomplishments made him feel inadequate, Rose replied kindly, "I shall be able to help you, Daniel."

" 'Elp me? 'Elp me bang in nails? With readen' an' writin'?"

"You're not always going to be a carpenter," Rose told him encouragingly.

Daniel grunted. "What's wrong with bein' a carpenter, I should like ter know? What was Jesus Christ, then?"

Rose was shocked. Daniel had been good to her. She did not want him to go to hell.

Barney Herd told Rose about his secret plans to start his own sawmill. As soon as there was enough money saved from his wages, he intended to write to England for the necessary machinery. Fred Quick, though this too was a secret as yet, had plans to join the whalers as soon as the season started in May. Though life was hard and rough, there was big money to be made. Old loyalties grew threadbare as the new life took shape. A man's world was the taproot, and roots grew out of doors.

Inevitably, Daniel was offered accommodation at the Hutt. "Mr. Molesworth says 'e'll take me on permanent an' I can 'ave a proper board 'ouse when 'is is finished, but there's a cottage the Maoris 'ave put up close by the river where we can live comfortable fer now."

Rose looked wistfully around their cozy habitation. "is it as nice as this?"

"You're married to me."

She heaved a small sigh. "Yes, Daniel."

"And Rose?"

"Yes?"

He shuffled his feet. "About them fancy falderals . . ."

"I won't wear them. I told you, I had to look like a lady that day, or the chief would not have allowed us to live in his house."

"You're not a lady, Rose."

"Of course I'm not." She ruffled his hair. "I'm the wife of a humble workingman." She laughed merrily and made a face at him.

They left early the next morning, Rose carrying the baby in his flax basket, his clothes folded neatly around his feet. Herd and one of his workmates transported their belongings on a stretcher fashioned from flax matting strung between two poles. Daniel carried the rest. It would have been easier and quicker by canoe, but that meant advertising their departure. The natives knew, anyway, as they knew everything. Oliver was sent to tell Nicholas the *whare* was free.

Cressida, swallowing her pride, moved in. The Maoris who came to welcome her were met by a frosty glance and left in silence. Only Te Puni, puffed up with pride now that, after all, he had his great white chief and his lady installed, was accorded an interview. Fred Quick took over the little earth oven and, gradually, as the gifts of pigeons, suckling pig, and vegetables came from the *pa* by Te Puni's orders, Cressida relaxed.

While Nicholas worked at bringing in plows and other farm machinery he had purchased from the company, supervising the staff he had acquired, the laying out of the timber, Cressida, her porcelain complexion carefully shielded from the sun behind a wide-brimmed bonnet and veil, would wander over the estate in the company of the ebullient Miss Frederick.

"It is going to be so magnificently . . . *immediate,* collecting one's own produce, even cooking it oneself! You will be glad your cook ran away with the whaler, Lady Cressida, when you have once known the novelty of producing meals yourself, I am sure. To be useful to your husband and truly share his life, that is going to be our greatest joy. Why, my dear friend, what a tame existence we lived at home! And how separated we were from real life.

"Mark my words, in a year you will declare you never could go home to sit like a stuffed ninny waiting for time to pass, and people to call, and tea to be brought. Perhaps Mr. Stitchbury will take it into his head to do as Mr. le Grys has done, and buy from the natives."

Cressida said with a nervous smile, "My husband is headstrong and impetuous. I would not like to think of him as leading Mr. Stitchbury astray."

"But would you have married him if he was a cautious mouse?" Miss Frederick answered the question herself. "I doubt it. Those who dare are bound to win. It is love that makes everything possible. Love of your wonderful man—for he is wonderful, Lady Cressida, is he not?" Without waiting for a reply she prattled exuberantly on, "So handsome, strong, and purposeful, so dominant, and yet with such a heart!"

Cressida smiled affectionately at her friend. "I pray you will settle here." Mrs. Maxwell's departure had left such an emptiness. If Miss Frederick were to go now, there would be no one. Only Nicholas, so handsome, so strong, so deeply, unjustly, embarrassingly, and hurtfully in love with someone else.

Mr. Stitchbury arrived and Cressida saw immediately why Miss Frederick had been attracted to him. He was indeed a man to cross the world for: lively, adventurous, enterprising; the same type of man as Nicholas. He planned, also, to take up land the same way Nicholas had done.

"And be damned to Sir George Gipps, that stuffed shirt who thinks he can hold life and death jurisdiction over the whole of the South Seas!" Mr. Stitchbury laughed. "A governor in charge of a penal colony? A *penal* colony, by God.

"As to that Irishman in the Bay of Islands. I knew

Hobson at home. A hero no doubt," he allowed, "when it comes to hustling pirates out of the Caribbean—y'know he was the bold and dashing model for Marryat's book—but what can he do here, all alone in the north, blustering out his secondhand orders? A man-o'-war without guns is no ship at all. Let them come after me and take my land from me if they can and dare. Besides, the powers that be will be kept far too busy around the towns to bother about those with the wit to set themselves up hundreds of miles from the main centers."

"May we walk, as the Maxwells have done?" asked his radiant bride.

"We will find a schooner going north and see some more of the coast. I hugely enjoyed my trip in the *Guide* to Taranaki and the Middle Island. You will enjoy this also, my dear."

"And so I shall," declared Miss Frederick, forgetting her own plans in a moment, looking up with delight into the face of the doughty young man who had enticed her across the world.

They were to be married at the mission church by a minister of the Kirk of Scotland who had come in the *Bengal Merchant*. Cressida, starting out on what should have been the happiest of days, heard a shout of hearty welcome. She looked up, then recoiled with shock. In ghastly slow motion, she saw again a sweating horse with clouds of steam billowing from its nostrils into the cool mist of early morning Berkeley Square, two young men standing eager-faced in a gig, looking up at the window where she stood in her night clothes, her hair streaming over her shoulders.

"Marry me!"

She had never heard Nicholas shout before. Nor since. His anger, when it came, was cold, snapping, and low-toned. Poised now in her delicate finery, the ostrich feather nodding on her hat, the buttons at the waist of her breathlessly tight gown undone, she felt all at once discredited, stripped of dignity, deflated, and cheapened out of countenance. She stared at the newcomer as at a ghost.

"Cressida! I wish to present to you Mr. Jerningham Wakefield." The scheming maverick wore a grin of huge delight.

"M'Lady, how glad I am to see you here."

She did not answer, for she could not. And then she was saved by the slow procession into the church.

Afterward, in the privacy of the leaf-scented *whare*, in the soft glow of candles on their stark bracket, so rudely makeshift now without Rose's floral decorations, she faced Nicholas, but before she could speak, he said, "You took me to task for being curt with the colonel on board ship. May I ask you a similar question? Did you have to show such dislike for his nephew? Luckily he is quite an insensitive chap and devilish conceited, so it will not worry him. But I thought we agreed we must make the best of things."

Her hands twisted together, and her heart beat quickly as she relived the shock. "That night we met at the palace ball. What happened after you left?"

"Devil take it, that was a long time ago," he said shortly. "I was with Jerningham. Why do you ask?" Something beyond his reach, a vague stirring, made him uneasy.

"Do you remember coming to Berkeley Square?"

He had never remembered that. Only seeing Rose at a high window. And the next day his father said he had proposed to Cressida.

"Of course," he said, lying and guiltily aware of having told his wife he never lied. "One does not forget proposing to one's wife."

She lifted her head, saw the duplicity and the kindness, and turned away. "I had better tell you this, for women are beginning to notice, and I shall shortly have to speak to Dr. Stokes. I was unable to do up two buttons at the waist of my gown today. You did not notice they were undone, or you would have remarked upon the fact. We are to have a child. You and I. It would seem I became pregnant that night," her voice broke, "immediately before discovering your mistress was aboard the ship."

Nicholas heard her out, his face betraying nothing of the possible effect of her words. "It is perhaps a good thing, anyway," Cressida added, "that you should have a real s-son." She corrected her inept interpretation. "I mean, a son of your own . . ."

"I know exactly what you mean," Nicholas replied

gently. There was a long pause; then he asked, "Why did you not tell me before?"

"You will understand, perhaps, when I say that as soon as I was reasonably sure, there was the matter of . . . that child's being born. The circumstances . . . It is true we agreed to forget, but things have not been the same between us since then."

He moved toward her, then hesitated, rebuffed by her impenetrable calm and inhibited by his own guilt. It was a moment when either one of them might have found words that would bring them spontaneously together with warmth and pity, with forgiveness even.

"It is not so late," she said at last, turning away, "but I am increasingly tired these days. I am sure you won't mind if I retire."

The emotion he had felt a moment ago collapsed in the face of her apparent indifference. He watched her straight figure glide into the bedroom. Cursing himself for his inadequacy, he threw open the door and went outside.

In the faceless darkness he leaned against a tree trunk, listening to the rustlings of the small night creatures around him. It was eerie here, and curiously unfriendly, as though lurking strangers watched with passive ill will. Did it matter, he wondered, who stood behind him, sweetening his leisure, providing him with the son that would hold Rundull to the le Grys breast, after this ridiculous colonial interlude was over? With a girl who looked like Rose he ought to be able to make a life that worked on all levels, as it could not with Rose herself. A gold ring without the brilliance of a diamond was still a gold ring.

He turned toward the sea. It was light, for the moon was nearly full, the silver water fluffy with wavelets where the stalking wind had kicked it. "The breeze will drop soon," they said, but it seldom did.

So he was to have a son. An heir, as he had told Rose, from the right side of the blanket. Why, then, should he be filled with resentment?

He went across the grass, then turned, and following the shore line, walked fast toward a row of trees on the horizon, crow-black against the golden moon. He had asked his wife for love, asked her unfairly, knowing he could not reciprocate because she was not Rose. He came to the rocks and the low cliffs, scrambled up, and continued on.

"I will walk until I am too tired to go on." It was what he was accustomed to now, being too tired to go on.

More than an hour later he returned. The *whare* was in darkness but he could tell by Cressida's breathing that she was not asleep. He lay down beside her, and slid an arm beneath her slender body. Her breasts felt large and hard. Why had he not noticed? She turned her head, and he kissed her, tasting the tears on her cheeks.

"Time to start again." But he was aware as he said it of the uncertainty of its promise. He kissed her once more, and she moved a little closer. Without desire, he held her close, gathering what comfort he could.

23

The Hutt River Valley was so beautiful it brought tears to Rose's eyes. Great kauri pines hovered over the lesser hinaus, the birches, the totara trees. The Putnams' new home lay on the clay bank of the river. On the opposite side there were flax bushes, their tall spikes of red blossom filling the air with the scent of honey, the scarlet rata vine drooping over the water. In the green gloom of the bush the *ka-ka* hoarsely croaked as it searched for grubs among the tree roots. Robins hopped to the doors of houses and peeped in. All day, bell birds chimed their songs around the perimeter of the riverbank village. The parson bird, trim and dapper with his white feathers curled coquettishly on his throat like clerical bands, sang morning hymns of praise.

The bush rang now with the sound of saws singing their way into the hearts of trees. Maori flax workers came by singing, their canoes packed with cats, dogs, pet suckling pigs squealing among the baskets of flax and potatoes, the women paddling, poling, or tracking, as the different parts of the river required. Rose and Oliver watched the natives cutting and scraping flax with mussel shells, seeking the silky threads that would become much-needed twine. The fantails flitting daintily from twig to twig watched them with their beady eyes.

The bigger children learned how to build rafts for themselves by binding bundles of bullrushes with flax. They guided their giddy craft with great dexterity. They made the most of the heady freedom that could not last, for already there were threats of a school's being built at Petone or Port Nicholson.

The flour mill was a going concern. Men with white clothes and white faces hurried like ghosts to their mid-day meals, then hurried back again. All was bustle and urgency. You could have what you wanted if you wanted it badly enough. That meant work. Overnight, timorous forelock-touchers changed into lusty, muscled men. Their wives roasted and baked and boiled in a battle to meet their appetites.

Oliver, while good-naturedly acknowledging that Dr. Stokes was his guardian, quixotically stayed with the Putnams, asking nothing more than that he should help guard the baby and share their lives. Perhaps sensing that he wove an invisible thread holding them together, Daniel allowed him to stay. Every morning he rose early to lift the raupo shutters and tie them to the eaves. He was anxiously proud of his ability to light the fire. He learned from the Maoris how to catch pigeons. He set traps on a quiet stream near the *miro* trees. Miro berries made the pigeons thirsty. His cunningly placed snares caught them when they drank.

They lived virtually free on the birds Oliver caught, the sow thistles he found growing wild, the shellfish, trout, and crayfish he brought from the river.

He found out how to make lamps from pieces of rag wound around sticks and set upright in a pannikin of fat. The flaring light that served better than the tiny candle flame for reading was magical, full of colors that stunned the senses.

Gradually, other men's wives responded to the warmth that Rose exuded, and tentatively offered their friend-ship. Though she now wore what they wore—a coarse stuff skirt with a blouse of plain linen, and a half sack as apron—the story of her coming ashore in her muslin gown and violet-trimmed bonnet was legend, and their doubts and suspicions found shallow graves. Besides, some hus-bands could not take their eyes off her; some had diffi-culty keeping their hands to themselves. Rose was a tactile person. She used her hands for warmth, for greet-ing, for persuasion. Men did not always understand.

Daniel came to her with his wages. Ten shillings that first week. Rose stood in the doorway of their little home, the bright coins catching the sunlight in the palm of her hand. "We must save for our house."

"Mr. Molesworth promised us a house." Having been dependent all his life, Daniel could see no other way.

"We want one of our own."

"We don't *need* to pay if he lets us use—"

Briskly but kindly, she interrupted him. "Now Daniel you must remember those talks the company men gave us on board ship." Rose never forgot anything. Daniel had taken very little in. Putting the money carefully in a tin, she dug a hole in a corner of the living room floor, and pressed the tin in.

Already a farm for Giles had become an attainable goal in her mind.

As more immigrant boats came, the Maoris grew apprehensive.

"You said only a thousand white men come," Te Puni told the colonel.

"There are about a thousand here now, Chief."

"All these are thousand? My heart is dark. You will be too strong for us."

In vain the colonel endeavored to explain the English wished to be friends.

"My nephew, Te Wharepouri, who is young and strong, speaks of making war."

"War? What reason can he give for this?"

"He said there are soldiers coming."

"A detachment from the Eightieth Regiment. Yes."

"Listen to me, Wide-Awake. When the great warrior Hongi Ika was dying, his relations and friends were gathered to him for farewell, and he said to them, 'Be kind to the Europeans. Welcome them to our shores, trade with them, protect them, live with them as one people.

" 'But if ever there should land on this shore a people who wear red garments,' " Te Puni went on, his black eyes glittering, " 'who do not work, who neither buy nor sell, and who always have arms in their hands, then be aware that these are a people called soldiers, a dangerous people whose only occupation is war. When you see them, make war against them,' said Hongi Ika, 'that you may not be enslaved, and that your country may not become the possession of strangers.' "

"Wherever Englishmen go there will be soldiers to protect them," Wakefield retorted mildly.

Te Puni ruminated darkly. "Chief Te Tao Nui went up to this governor of yours and licked his hand. We do not like this. Perhaps your king-governor bewitched him with the sacred piece of paper when he put his name on it at Waitangi."

Wakefield smiled. "It is an English habit to kiss the hand of the Queen's representative. Your chief was merely adopting our English ways."

Another long silence, then, "The treaty paper we must sign for a blanket says the Maori people will be protected by your queen. Why should she speak of protecting us if there is no war expedition coming?"

"It may be that our queen intends to defend you against those Europeans who are venal, or merely thoughtless."

"A woman!" he said in disgust. "And she is not even here."

Some young Maoris, exhibiting their disquiet in their own way, vandalized a garden. It was the first sign of real resentment.

The full complement of the five ships spread itself gradually across the three settlements. A disenchanted few waited on the beach for a vessel to take them home. The manager and clerks of the Union Bank of Australia came ashore with their well-lined safe and settled down to business in a prefabricated hut. Dr. Evans, lawyer and erstwhile headmaster of Mill Hill School, who had steered the company's plans from his house in Hampstead, became chief justice and busied himself with a small committee, setting up a system of law and order.

Over on the harbor a council was set up, the machinery of a provisional government established. Plans were drawn for the appointment of officers, the regulation of finances, the selection of sites for a powder magazine, an infirmary, a library. Two taverns appeared on the waterfront at Port Nicholson, Thorndon, or Brittania, whatever the town was to be named. Some of the more grateful pioneers favored Wellington, in honor of the Iron Duke who had loaned so much enthusiastic support to the project.

Seven hundred Lincoln sheep, sixty Aberdeen Angus

cattle, a few shorthorns, and two horses arrived from Port Phillip in New South Wales. The land-hungry who had established themselves bid fiercely for the stock, and Nicholas, with a small area of land already cleared, bought his share. He had plans to cross his Lincolns with Romneys. Later, his flocks would be Romneys, pure bred. He bought one of the horses, too, a lively little cob. Maoris who met him riding fell about laughing. Such strange creatures, horses. They encircled him, commenting excitedly on the long legs of his mount that were so unlike those of a bullock.

Nicholas rode the boundaries of his land and was surprised that its beauty and wildness excited him in a way Rundull never had. Every single acre would belong to him when he got security of tenure. Arrogantly, conspicuously, he sited the house outside the twenty acres that were his legal allotment.

Wind came in vengefully from the southeast, throwing a heavy surf onto the beaches, and with it, rain. Cressida invited the ladies to abandon their battle with tents and join her in privileged comfort among the trees. In the cozy *whare* they sewed and knitted little garments for Maori babies, answering the call of the missionaries who had pledged themselves to fight infanticide. If pretty clothes could be provided, the mother often became reconciled to a female birth and allowed the child to live.

The ladies from England, sewing industriously, came to know those with whom they were destined to spend the rest of their lives. The homesick among them were cheered. Brides desperately missing their mothers were heartened by loving attention from older women who had left sons and daughters at home. It was a good period. A time of building and growing united.

Then word came that the Hutt River had overflowed its banks, flooding the habitations nearby. That a group of hostile Maoris were laughing fit to split their sides at the predicament of the unfortunate immigrants. Several boats, with Jerningham Wakefield at their head, set out upriver to give assistance, but the force of the current drove them back.

The Putnam residence, situated a little below the others, was screened from the river by a small raised bank, which acted in the circumstances as a dike. As the rising waters seeped slowly into the other dwellings, their occupants gathered up their possessions in an orderly fashion and left.

Rose, happily absorbed with the baby, singing the sweet Maori lullabies Daniel would not allow her to sing in his presence, heard nothing of the move. When rain began to drip through the roof she opened the umbrella, thoughtfully provided by the company, and placed it over the baby's basket. When the drips increased she piled their meager collection of clothes onto a barrel and covered them with a rug.

There was no warning. The wave came rushing through the front door, the only door, with a menacing whoosh, funneling downward in a chute the breadth of the doorway. With a shriek of alarm Rose lunged toward the basket and lifted it high, making a wild grab at the umbrella that was already floating away. With the basket in one hand and the umbrella in the other, she swung this way and that, searching for a way of escape, knowing there was none. The windows were too high, and too small. The rising tide swirled up around her knees. With her skirts clamped to her legs, she splashed clumsily to the barrel, maneuvered the clothes into the basket, and settled it in their place. Then she snatched a floating wooden box and, using it as a precarious step, managed to climb onto the barrel, edging the basket adroitly onto her lap.

Heart thudding, breath held, she gazed in mute terror at the muddy water, dancing with debris, swirling around her. It had already drowned her camp oven. Now it was rising against the sides of the barrel, touching her feet. Giles, wakened by the jolting, chuckled and gurgled with unsuspecting pleasure.

"Darling, you're safe," Rose said, her voice cracking. She smiled down at him, her eyes glassy, her lips stiff.

Where was Oliver, who was always at hand when she needed him? And then she remembered with a sinking heart that he had tramped off earlier to bring his precious pigeon snares home.

"Help!" she screamed. The sounds rose a few feet to the soaked roof thatch, losing themselves. "Help!" she screamed again. "Help! Help!"

She strained her ears. The silence was eerie. Then

came the gurgling of water working its way through the wall slabs, pushing out the clay, and the drip, drip, dripping from the roof.

The baby, sensing Rose's distress, began to whimper. "Hush, little one, hush. I'd sing to you if I could." She could not remember any of the lullabies taught to her by the Maoris. She searched her mind frantically and came up with songs she had learned on board ship. Songs that brought memories of Nicholas.

" 'The harp that once through Tara's halls . . .'" She sang right through her entire repertoire. Only "Home, Sweet Home" defeated her because this was her home and it was drowning.

" 'Twas the last rose of summer . . .' "

24

"**W**ho's there? Who's inside there?"

A man's voice came in through the half-submerged doorway.

"Help!" screamed Rose. "Help! There's a baby here. Quickly, please save my baby . . ."

"I'm coming. At least I think I'm coming," came the tentative reply, "but this is deuced difficult." The prow of a small canoe nosed through the door. Strong arms reached out to grasp the wall on either side and spin the craft into the room. "Great heavens!" A solidly built man of thirty-four or -five with wide-set blue eyes, his wet hair straggling around his face, looked up at Rose in amazement. "How did you come to be left?"

"I got caught. . . . I didn't know. . . ." She saw his quizzical eyes on the barrel and dazzled him with her smile. "I had to keep the baby dry."

"By God, you'd drown the poor little trout rather than get him wet!" exclaimed the man. "Here, hand him to me, then I'll hang on to the barrel while you slide aboard." He took the basket, peeped curiously inside, then placed it on the floor of the canoe. "Nice little codger. Pity to send him back when he's only just come. Right, young lady, give me your hand."

Rose slid obediently into the narrow vessel, but when she reached back for the rest of their clothes, he grasped her arm. "There's little enough room for us."

"I've got to take them." Rose panicked at the thought of losing the few clothes they owned.

"I've no doubt the company will fix you up with some more. Act of God and all that. If you overload this little . . . Watch the basket, girl, I'm turning around now." He maneuvered across the room, nosed through the door. The waters outside swirled and eddied around half-submerged bushes, bounced over tree roots, tugged at frail plants. Rose's hand tightened on the handle of the basket. There were tree branches and pieces of timber flying past. The man's alarm showed in his face.

"Take me back!" Rose shrieked.

"Sit still," snarled her rescuer, "and shut up." Working frantically with the single paddle, he edged the little craft toward the shore. Nearby, a soaked *manuka* bush pushed its way up out of the water. He grasped its rough foliage, holding on grimly while the swirling waters fought him for possession of the canoe.

Rose looked back into the raging torrent behind her and all control went. Behind the *manuka* was the bank. Leaping to her feet, holding the basket in a vicelike grip, she lunged forward, her left arm swinging the basket ahead, her right reaching out to snatch at the tough little bush. The sharp, coarse wood of the hidden branches struck her palm. Her fingers closed around it and hung on.

Behind her there was a shout, but it lay outside her immediate concern—the baby's safety. She fell, half in the shallows, half sprawling on the bush, but with the hard ground beneath her. The basket was out in front. The baby was safe.

Hands came from everywhere, pulling her upright. "The baby. Keep the baby dry!"

"Ssh, Mrs. Putnam." They tried to quieten her. "Are you all right?"

She was vaguely conscious of shouting. "I'm all right. Cover the baby." She looked around wildly for the basket. Someone had taken it. She pushed violently at one of the men standing in her way. "Give him to me. Give him to me!"

"Of course." They humored her, holding the basket under her nose to prove the child was still in it. In an agony of apprehension she looked down at the startled little face.

"Oh, my darling!" Rose lifted the basket, holding it tightly against her breast.

Behind her the shouting rose, then broke into anxious exclamations.

"Run, run. We might catch him at the next bend."

"The canoe's half full of water!"

She turned quickly, for the first time remembering her rescuer. He was floundering helplessly amidships, his paddle swirling far out of reach on the wild brown waters as his little craft flew on its way. Her arms tightened around her precious bundle. At least Giles was safe. Nicholas's baby was safe.

The women took her to higher ground, to the shelter of a hastily erected tent, while the men scattered off downriver in a fruitless endeavor to catch the canoe. Nobody leveled any blame, for they were not blameless themselves. They had been working to save their own possessions. It had not occurred to any of them that Rose did not know what was happening.

Oliver came flying back through the bush, crooned over the baby, and clung to Rose's side. "They say Mr. Wilshire's safe."

"Who's he?" Rose, holding the child close, asked vaguely.

"It's Mr. Wilshire that saved you both. Lucky fer 'im there's bends in the river an' the canoe struck a flax plant."

There were others who said that even a heartless, self-centered woman like Mrs. Putnam could not kill Alain Wilshire, who had survived the French Foreign Legion, the Napoleonic Wars, the pirates of the Caribbean. And, anyway, the Maori princess he lived with had had him *tapu'd* so that evil spirits could not touch him.

Jerningham Wakefield, having abandoned his attempts to navigate the swollen river, hurrying along the bush track, arrived at the settlement in time to witness the commotion Rose had caused. Gad, what a beauty! he thought. Even with her soaking clothes clinging to her—especially with her soaking clothes clinging—those superbly full, upthrust breasts, tiny waist, rounded hips, golden hair loose and tumbling made a picture Titian would have given his eyeteeth to paint. No wonder that cool dog had brought her with him! He was still smarting from the glare that tight-lipped bitch Lady Cressida had given him when they met at Stitchbury's wedding.

Someone gave Rose a blanket. She was so dreadfully wet, poor thing. Yet, watching her fold it, then drape it artfully around her figure, inexplicably infusing the gray woolen square with style, the women turned away. The men never stopped talking about her. They said Putnam couldn't hold a girl like that. There were wives who lay awake at night asking themselves whose husband she would take.

Jerningham gathered the homeless together and they set off toward Petone where they would have to go under canvas again. Kind people offered to carry the baby and keep him dry but Rose refused them. Taking only small and intimate possessions, they trailed off back to the beach, leaving a pile of their salvaged goods covered with a tarpaulin until a free bullock dray could be found to transport them.

Nicholas saddled his bay and rode in to Petone to see if the survivors needed help. Concern and goodwill had become endemic in the colony. They knew a high morale depended on the wellbeing of all. On the track he met a Maori who told him the river was in flood. Nicholas had seen the riverbank cottages that were provided for sawyers' families, and knew Francis Molesworth had secured one for the temporary use of the Putnams.

Grim-faced with anxiety, he dug his heels into his horse's flanks, taking the shortcut across country to the edge of the bush, splashing through puddles, leaping over tussocks that lay in his path, ducking under branches to keep on a straight course. The rain beat in his face, swept under his flying oilskins, ran in rivulets down his saddle and into his boots. Inevitably, as he entered the bush his mount slowed, for the track was narrow. They made what pace they could, and eventually came to the bullock track.

He saw the bedraggled party in the distance, Rose and Oliver swinging the baby basket with an umbrella fixed above, Rose in her blanket, as lithe and sinuous as one of the Maori maidens, her face lifted to the rain. He sat forward on the saddle, watching as they came, the reins loosely clasped, his earlier distress at her presence, his vows to his wife, dying within him.

"Nicholas!" Jerningham strode out in front, a great bundle supported on his back, his trousers tied at his knees with flax bands, a waterproof hat low over his face. "Nicholas, to the rescue! Make a dash back to the beach, there's a good chap, and find my uncle. He must be warned. Accommodation is needed for these people."

Nicholas looked down at Rose. "Are you all right?"

She nodded, her face glowing.

"Shall I take the baby?"

Jerningham grinned. "Try and get it from her!" Yet, even as he spoke, to everyone's astonishment, Rose lifted the umbrella. "The basket is soft," she said, looking up at Nicholas. "Very pliable. If you bend the sides in he will stay dry."

Stunned disbelief settled over the crowd. Bending down in his saddle, Nicholas took the basket from her, balancing it in front of him. Momentarily, he was tempted to offer Rose a pillion seat and thought better of it. Then Oliver said, "Rose is soaked, Mr. le Grys. Could you take her, too?"

He grinned. "Why not?"

Jenningham, his face a study, dropped his pack and clamped both hands around Rose's waist. She was featherlight to lift. Unselfconsciously, she slid both arms around Nicholas, clasping him tightly, while the crowd stared. Everyone knew who Nicholas was, as they knew all the leading colonists, but especially Nicholas, son of the earl of Rundull, whose sister was maid of honor to her majesty.

"I'll run," said Oliver, leaping away, splashing through the puddles with flailing arms and whoops of excitement. Some of his street sharpness was going, but the years of having to win stood him in good stead. The other children set out after him, but half-heartedly, impeded by the rough, slippery surface of the track, the rain that was driving against them. Oliver was already a long way ahead, out on his own as always. Rose pressed her face against Nicholas's back, her senses on fire. They cantered easily down the track on the windward side of the trees where there was shelter from the worst of the driving rain.

"He has grown." Head half-turned, Nicholas shouted into the wind. He had not seen the baby since that first day on board ship, had not particularly wished to. He thought himself detached. Now he recognized, in his lively anxiety, his publicly taking Rose on his horse's rump, the shallowness of his attempts at reconciliation with his wife.

"He is the handsomest baby in the world." Rose clung to Nicholas's hard body, feeling his warmth through the oilskins. "He looks like you."

"Such flattery!" But his derision was warm. They passed Oliver who was losing the impetus of his first wild burst of speed. The boy made another conscious spurt, taking the flying mud pellets from the horse's heels full in the front, laughing.

They trotted up to the company's headquarters. The colonel saw them and met them at the door. "Very good of you, young man." He took the basket. Nicholas leaped from the saddle and lifted Rose down.

"I want shelter for Mrs. Putnam," he said, slicing boldly through the colonel's typically diffident concern.

"We're getting tents set up now."

"No. Find her accommodation in one of the prefabricated buildings." He turned to Rose. "Where are your clothes?"

"I lost them."

"Not those," he replied impatiently.

"Dr. Stokes has them."

He addressed a bemused Wakefield, "Look after her, Colonel. Get her a dry blanket." As he galloped off, Nicholas thought in a disturbed way that he was probably not doing Rose a favor by bringing out her finery. He shrugged. She probably had no friends to lose.

A trading vessel brought a copy of Hobson's appointment to the position of lieutenant-governor, under Sir George Gipps of the convict colony. Feathers were newly ruffled.

"He should have demanded governorship," the citizens declared indignantly. "Six years in the doldrums following the Napoleonic Wars must have softened his brain!"

A mill had been established now, also a still, and an iron foundry. Young Betts Hopper, formerly the leisured son of a lord, discovered he could get more out of his foundry than any of his men. Gentlemen were learning with some satisfaction the art of doing things for themselves.

A printing press was brought by *Adelaide* and Samuel Revans was appointed managing editor of *The New Zealand Gazette*.

Gardens sprang up. Boats and barges were built using native honeysuckle from the Hutt Valley. Nails were fashioned from iron hoops. The Maoris brought wild pigs, wild honey, ducks, and pigeons to sell. They were learning about money, at last. Mr. Charles Grace, claiming to have been a professor at a Scottish university, opened a school in a wooden building behind the hotel. Grateful parents enrolled children who were running wild. Through the windows the pupils could see the comings and goings of the Maoris, the constant traffic of small boats from vessels anchored out in the harbor. After so many months of freedom, they did not take kindly to discipline. A permanent school was to be built from sun-dried clay bricks at a little distance from the fascinating harbor. Meantime, Mr. Grace's Academy flourished in gentle chaos.

Oliver was sharp and willing. He had a mind that soaked up learning faster than his teacher could deal it out. He borrowed books from the school library and shared them with Rose. Every evening, he walked to the Hutt to check that the Putnams were all right. Daniel grew irritated. "This house only needs one master, young Oliver," he growled. Oliver said he worried about the river, though Cornish Row, the newly built street with its neat little cottages, had been set on an elevated shingle ridge, well out of reach of the treacherous waters. Privately, Rose knew Oliver considered himself more capable than Daniel of looking after her and the baby.

As houses sprouted along the harbor edge Mr. Heaphy, draftsman to the Company, whose father had been official artist on the Duke of Wellington's staff as well as portrait painter to the Princess of Wales, recorded the changing view. From the schooner *Jewess*, while the captain and owner Frederick Moore traded, he painted the wild coastline, the deep-cut bays, the Maori habitations.

Ingeniously, Moore and Heaphy built themselves a house on the slopes above Lambton Quay and called it Clay Castle. Laboring up into the hills with tomahawks, they brought back saplings, bundles of flax, reeds, and supplejacks, wove them industriously into place, then plastered the walls liberally with clay. The raising of the flag was a sign that one of their uproarious gatherings was scheduled and an open invitation to the young blades of the town.

Ships came from India and China with chests of tea, bags of rice, preserves. Carpenters worked feverishly putting up shops. Public buildings rose. Daniel was offered two shillings sixpence a day to work in the town, and refused. "Two shillings and sixpence is the going rate," he said suspiciously.

"Tenpence a day more!" Rose cried. "Don't you realize that's five shillings a week? Half as much again as you're earning now!"

"What do we want with all that money?"

"We want a farm, Daniel," Rose explained patiently.

Daniel's face turned wooden. "I'm a carpenter."

"A carpenter can be a farmer. All he needs is the money."

Daniel stared at her, his eyes blank with incomprehension. Then he looked down at his hands, large, useful hands that knew what to do with timber and nails, struts and stays. Only that.

Rose saw the defeat in his face and felt it too. Giles, with Nicholas's blood in his veins, needed land, and horses to ride. Flinging her arms across the slab table, collapsing face-down on the wood, she burst into a flood of tears.

Daniel put a tentative hand on the shining golden head. "Rose? Rose, don't yer see, it's gen'l'men as owns farms."

She saw a way through. "Couldn't we save up for a little bit of land so that I could keep chickens and ducks— for eggs? We could have a vegetable garden." She appealed to him prettily, taking him by the hand. "Daniel, a carpenter should have his own house here. . . . It's different from how it was at home. We could save on two shillings and sixpence a day. There's lots of land, and lots of timber. You could build it yourself."

He shifted uncomfortably from one foot to the other. He knew things were different here, but not in a way he yet understood.

"Daniel, you will, won't you? Because you're really very kind."

Overwhelmed by her sweet insistence, he blurted out, "When are you going to be kind to me, Rose? When are you going to let me . . ." He flushed a dull red.

She struck a bargain with him. "If you will take this job at half a crown a day, I will let you, Daniel. I promise. I told you Dr. Stokes said we had to wait a while."

It was Alain Wilshire who had offered Daniel the money. Rose decided to see him herself. One of the women generously offered to look after Giles, and Rose accepted.

It was a wonderful day, balmy with breezes from the south and a sky of heavenly blue. She swung along the bullock track that was badly rutted from the wheels of the loaded drays and the cloven hooves of the ox teams. She undid her blouse, leaving it wickedly open, and tossed her skirts high, dancing on the sweet wayside grass that sprang out of the rich loam of leaf mold as soon as the trees were felled and the sun came in. Now and then she paused to listen to the twitter and whistle of the birds.

Eventually, she came to a familiar track that led to Te Puni's *pa*. She hesitated, gripped by nostalgia and a certain curiosity to know whether Lady Cressida had left the *whare*, then on impulse turned down the path and ran the short distance to the clearing. There were Maori women lazing on the grass before the *whare*.

She stepped forward, calling a happy greeting. *"Tenakoe."*

"Haeremai." Come to us.

They rubbed noses in that artful, tickly way that made Rose want to laugh. She answered their questions about the baby, and asked after Mr. le Grys.

The great man had gone. Lady preferred a wooden room or two to a Maori *whare*. They did not like Lady Cressida, nor did they understand her. Rose bid them a warm farewell and hurried on. She could not believe her eyes when she saw the harbor. Sailing barks and schooners danced on the wind-brushed water, jetties poked their long brown noses out to sea. A Maori woman with a heavily tattooed face wandered past carrying a flax string of plump, silvery fish crumbed with sand. Rose sat on a stone and looked around her. How the place had changed! Sailors wandered by. A man in a tall hat stopped to speak to her. She stood up and went on her way with her head averted. She had heard of the land sharks from New South Wales, the speculators, the young gentlemen who hung around the beach as though it were an English watering place, hoping to make a quick killing and return to England.

The town was surprisingly neat and tidy. There were gardens everywhere. And the white cottages! Springing up as though house seed had been indiscriminately scattered. Here, a potato patch, there seedbeds neatly marked. In the center of the flat, behind one of the jetties, she came upon a large unfinished building with oiled calico windows and an imposing sign over the door announcing it as Barratt's Hotel.

She knew about Dicky Barratt, the most famous European in the Cook Strait area. An English sailor, he had settled in New Plymouth in 1828, married a chief's daughter, and, with Te Wharepouri and Te Puni, held out in the Waikato invasions of Taranaki. In 1834, with the survivors, he migrated to the Cook Strait area and established a whaling station at Te Awaiti, a bay at the northern end of Middle Island. Tentatively, Rose pushed open the door and walked in.

"Mrs. Putnam! What brings you down from the Hutt?"

Rose glowed with pleasure, her weariness falling away. "I have come to see Mr. Alain Wilshire," she said. "I thought you might know where I could find him."

Barratt reached into his pocket and brought out a golden sovereign. "I'll tell you where you can find Flash Jack. And give him this, if you please. He will know why." He led her to the door. "Go along the front to the end where there's four buildings under way. They're his. And go carefully, little lady."

Rose thanked him. "I've walked all the way from the Hutt without mishap, and the road was rough."

"That's not what I meant," Barratt replied obscurely.

She did not turn around, or she would have seen him standing watching her, hands on his hips, shaking his head. "So that was Aurora Rose!"

25

Wilshire was balancing on a sawhorse directing his workmen. Rose recognized him immediately. He was a tall, tough-looking man—barrel-chested, with iron sinews. He saw Rose, as did his workmen. Eyebrows shot up. The banging of hammers ceased. The men leered and glanced at each other.

"Get on with your work." Wilshire delivered orders the way his workmen hit a nail, hard and clean. He jumped down and walking tall, with a lusty seaman's stride, went to meet Rose, his eyes roving across her upthrust breasts, her trim waist, and rounded hips.

Having no access to a looking glass, Rose was unaware of her enhanced beauty; of the new softness that had come with Giles's birth. Now her cheeks were pink with the embarrassed glow engendered by Dicky Barratt's laughter. Her plain bonnet lay back on her shoulders, her bright hair fell softly around her face, its tendrils lifting on the breeze.

Wilshire thought he had never seen anyone lovelier. Rose felt the piercing intrusion of his lightly lashed blue stare. With her eyes on his, she found the buttons at the neck of her blouse and hooked the collar together. His look, compounded as it was of shrewd laughter and suspicion, reminded her that she had accidentally kicked his canoe away from the Hutt riverbank. He had the air of a man who might be intolerant of human error.

She said breathlessly, though she had not planned an apology, "I wanted to thank you, Mr. Wilshire. I was so

glad you came to no harm that day. I didn't get a chance
to apologize. I had to save my baby, you understand."
He went on gazing at her, his lips faintly twitching.
Discomfited by his continuing silence, she tried a dazzling smile. "Well, you're safe, aren't you—" She broke
off, confused. "I'm to give you this from Mr. Barrett."
She held out the sovereign. "He said you'd know . . ."
She stumbled to a halt, unbearably embarrassed by his
stare.

He was listening to her voice, marveling. How in the
name of heaven had that dreary clodhopper Putnam got
her?

She burst out in a rush, "I came to tell you my husband will accept your offer."

His hand hovered over hers, a large hand, a rough
sailor's hand etched with cutlass cuts, the raw thrash of a
wire rope splitting—a calloused hand that had known the
ungentle wash of frozen seas. He seemed about to take
the coin, but instead, with practiced dexterity, closed her
fingers over it. "Keep that," he said.

"Keep it? Why?" Even as she queried the gift, Rose's
hand clenched. A week's wages already. To go toward
Giles's farm.

"Because I say so," Wilshire replied. "If I'm to be
your husband's boss, I have the say, have I not?"

At his gritty tone, her brows flew up in surprise. Then
unexpectedly, he laughed, a great hearty rambunctious
laugh, and she joined in. He took her arm, turning her,
taking her down the dirt road toward the sea, but with
such long strides that she had to run in little bursts to
keep up with him. "Let's make the arrangements now.
Your husband will have to give Molesworth a week's
notice, so I'll expect him to start on the fifteenth. I'll
send some men to transport your belongings."

Rose gazed up at him, hypnotized by her stupendous
luck.

"There's a cottage along here not far off completion,"
he was saying. "I'll put my men onto it and have it done
by the time you move in. You won't want saws and
hammers making a racket and upsetting the baby."

In her excitement Rose tripped on a jutting stone, and
he caught her, jerking her upright with deft gentleness.

"There's plenty of room for a garden. There'll be no

fence around the building until the land sales are agreed, so you'll take your chance with roving animals, but if your husband likes to build a pen you could have chickens."

"Oh."

Wilshire let her arm go and stopped on the rough track. His eyes flickered across her plain blouse, her stuff skirt. "Is that company issue you're wearing?"

"We lost everything in the flood. Except the bonnet. Someone found this." She lifted it from her shoulders, pressing it down on her head, screwing up her nose. "I'd rather they hadn't. It's not very . . ."

He stuck his hands in his pockets. A grin spread across his features, exposing strong, exceptionally white, and rather large teeth. "You're right. It's not very. I shall have to find you another."

"Find me another!" echoed Rose, blinking in surprise.

"Why not? I'm a trader. I've a stock of fine materials waiting for my store to open. Sometimes I let the wives of my employees have them cheap. In fact," he added casually, fingering his whiskers, "there's a particularly fine bolt of cotton that got . . . damaged. A, er, leak in the ship's hold. You can have it as a gift. It would match your eyes very nicely." He paused, saturating himself in their glow. "And there's some linsey there for everyday wear."

His kindness overwhelmed her. She had a burdensome feeling of sin for having treated him so badly. "You might have been drowned. Oh, I am so sorry," she babbled, "that I jumped out of the canoe."

There was again that twinkling of the eyes that was not really forgiveness. More a shrewd assessment of her hustling, tumbling guilt. "As you said, you had the baby to look after. Let's move on. The house I'm thinking of moving you into is just down the hill from Dr. Stokes's place, so you could be seeing quite a lot of young Oliver."

"You know Oliver?" Rose indulged in a delighted little skip, then ran to catch him up. The offending bonnet bounced back on to her shoulders.

Alain's eyes rested on her hair. "Oh, yes. I know him well."

"He's my best friend," she said happily.

"Come on," said Wilshire with lively impatience.

She sucked in a great mouthful of the salt air and pressed her red lips together to hold it there, her lungs stretched, her eyes sparkling. He watched her, enjoying her delight. They turned left up a grassy slope. There were white-painted cottages here, with quaint verandas like jutting jaws.

He pointed. "That's it."

Rose stood on the rough path, gazing in amazement at the unfinished building. There was gingerbread along the eaves, like lace, as yet unpainted; a wide veranda shaded by a curved roof; big window frames so that the rooms seemed open to the sky. It was magnificent. The realization of a dream.

The front door was not yet on its hinges. They went in through the gap. Rose walked on tiptoe. "This is the kitchen?" Her voice came out in a kind of squeak. Alain watched her face, but he did not answer. It had to be a kitchen, for there was an iron stove standing against the wall. A kitchen with a big window and the sun streaming in! With a back door opening onto grass, and the hillside sloping away to the town and the harbor. She darted into the square room next door, and another similar. Two bedrooms! She swung around, looking to the right. This had to be the parlor. There was a bay window! Rose's imagination ran riot. She could already see herself sitting in the window with her sampler, looking out across the town to the dancing, white-capped wavelets of the harbor. She ran back to the kitchen, obsessed with its size, the wide, open look. The sun had splashed through the window and was spilling across the floor.

"Come outside," said Wilshire gruffly. He seemed to have a frog in his throat. "There's a lean-to washhouse."

And a copper pot gleaming above a little kiln with its own chimney! "Oh!" She hurried back, touching the plank walls with her fingertips as she passed, feeling the life in the wood.

"Oh, Mr. Wilshire!" She grasped a support, swinging one booted foot, carelessly exposing an ankle. "How can I ever thank you!"

He surveyed her upturned face. A bloody Botticelli angel, he marveled. Aloud he said, carelessly, "Call me Alain. Everybody does."

Unselfconsciously, she picked up her skirts and danced

around the room, kicking at loose wood shavings. She bent down and picked them up in her hands, holding them to her face, sniffing their new-wood scent, tossing them, watching them fall like confetti.

"What made you pick Daniel? Of course he's a good carpenter . . ." She looked up and their eyes met. There was a rush of recognition, a quiver of shock. She saw the face of Ned Taylor, the village blacksmith, reflected in the man's eyes. Then it went.

"Yes," said Flash Jack Wilshire, smiling. He really had the nicest smile.

She flushed, laughing at her momentary foolishness.

"He is the best carpenter I know. That's why I want him. I'm letting you have the house to ensure he stays." Wilshire touched her arm in a gesture of reassurance and warmth, the fingers trailing, lingering. "That's settled. Now I'll take you home. We'll go upriver in my ketch."

"I have asked him to clear off," Nicholas said when Cressida protested fearfully about the Maori who squatted at the bottom of their garden polishing his spear. "I will try again." Crushing his plush hat onto his head, he strode outside.

The man was old, his mat in rags. Beside him lay a stick. He looked up, his jaws working over the tough, stringy kauri gum the natives chewed.

"Tenakoe."

"Haeremai."

Speaking in Maori so far as he was able, Nicholas said, "This is my land. Te Wharepouri has been paid well for it, and I have his assurance that the arrangement is legal in the Maori way."

"My ancestor still live here," retorted the old native stubbornly.

"Lives here? Where? There is no Maori *whare* on my land."

"In cave."

"Take me to him," retorted Nicholas boldly, thinking to call the native's bluff.

"I take you, but maybe he not come out. He big lizard."

"He what?"

"Big lizard. My ancestor big lizard."

Nicholas squatted down on the ground beside the old man, eyeing him with friendly curiosity. "Your ancestor will be safe," he said at last, picking a grass stalk, sliding it between his teeth so that the delicate sap ran lightly onto his tongue. "And of course you may walk over the land as much as you wish."

It was a milestone. He felt he was beginning to understand the natives. He looked up at the window. Cressida had disappeared. Better not to tell her, perhaps. He chuckled to himself as he strode off across the hillside to his work. The sheep, his sheep, regarded him with their bright, impertinent stares. The watchful mothers stamped their feet willfully, guarding their lambs as he approached. There had been sheep in plenty at Rundull but he had never been aware that they had personalities. He never came close to them.

Cressida had gone back to the letter she was writing to Felicity.

Perhaps you have heard from Saxon Mote that our servants have all left us now. It is not that there has been trouble between us, but they have gone in order that they may better themselves. It has been somewhat inconvenient for us, I must confess, but it does not really signify, for of what use is a disloyal manservant or a maid? We shall easily replace them. There are ships arriving all the time, and I have great hopes of training some of the pretty Maori maidens.

Would she dare to bring one of those loose-hipped beauties into the house? Nicholas was not seeing the kitchen maid now. "I will not pretend anymore to be asleep when he comes to bed," she vowed, knowing she had made this vow before and broken it. The nights were intolerable anyway, lying stiffly on her side of the bed, listening to the melancholy call of the bittern down in the swamp, the shrill cry of the weka. She returned to her letter.

I must tell you of my new accomplishment. Sometimes I wonder at my frivolous and useless life in the Old Country, as the new colonials have lately chris-

tened England. Each morning I am up betimes to
turn my hand to bread baking. And I have actually
made several cakes.

Her arms ached from the never-ending labor of baking
bread. The yeast bottles burst, always in the middle of
the night, waking them with a sound like gunshot so that
she was certain marauding Maoris had come. The bread
either raged up over the tin or sulked down into a nasty
little gray oblong that had to be soaked before even the
hens would eat it. One day, busy with her baking, she
became aware of a shadow falling across the kitchen.
Looking up, she saw a native standing in the doorway.

"What do you want?" she asked in Maori, but the
intruder merely grinned. She tried ignoring him, creepily
aware that though he made no move to enter he followed
her every movement with his eyes. Suddenly, as she took
the loaf from the oven he stepped forward, gesturing,
demanding the bread. Panic-stricken, she flung the hot
loaf outside onto the grass. When Nicholas came home
she was still leaning against the door with fast-beating
heart, still trembling.

"Could you not try to make friends with them?" he
asked, looking tired, and she knew, upsettingly, that he
was thinking of the kitchen maid who had such a warm
relationship with the natives.

Leaving her letter now, Cressida lowered herself stiffly
into the balloon-back chair and sat staring in front of her,
hands clasped across her protruding belly. She smelled
unpleasantly of wood smoke and ashes. Her skin was still
sticky from the heat of the kitchen. Her nerves were
always on edge, and she was increasingly tired. Her whole
body quivered with tiredness. At Home (now she thought
of it with a capital H, as though she had no other), she
had been so strong, riding to the hunt, staying out all day
in all weathers, walking, dancing the night away.

God give me that peculiar strength needed for housework and cooking, she prayed silently. On the bare plank
wall opposite, which would later be lined with papered
canvas, hung Goya's portrait of her mother. Sometimes
Cressida thought she saw outrage in the eyes looking out
of the priceless gold-leafed frame. Nicholas had been
incredulous when she insisted upon distributing personal

treasures around the half-finished dwelling. Even she had several times grown alarmed for the portrait's safety, when the wind in angry mood whistled through cracks in the wood.

Across the bare room, the horsehair ottoman was gathering crumbs of sawdust. The tasteful Berlin work on the cushions was turning faintly wood-red but, willfully, she did not care. She had to have something from home, something familiar, to look at and to touch. Her eyes lingered guiltily on the beadwork. I will clean the cushions, or put them away. Soon. But she never did.

Her precious pianoforte was still safely in its zinc case. Every day she resisted afresh the temptation to unpack it. Last week in an unhappy, irresponsible moment, she had persuaded the carpenters to help her unroll and hang an Aubusson carpet, like a tapestry, on a wall. It hung there heavily, warmly, exotically, sagging beneath the weight of its rich beauty.

"You would put a nail through that?" Nicholas had shouted when he came home, his face blank with disbelief. Part of the change in Nicholas was his shouting. It was as though he brought the wind and the hills and forests with him at the end of the day. He spoke to her sometimes as though she stood on the opposite side of the valley.

"I must have something to look at," she had shouted back.

He had not understood. "There is so much to look at." He gestured beyond the window. "That carpet will fade in the sun," he said at last, flatly, when she did not reply.

I, too, will fade, she thought now, plucking at her apron, that humiliating gift handed to her with a sort of kindness by her departing cook.

Soon the builders would be calling her in their cheeky way. "Hey, missus, we're parched. Get us some tea, will yer?" Nicholas had admonished them, asking that they address Cressida as m'Lady, but in the wake of their newfound freedom they had changed into cocky, confident men. They knew Nicholas was well aware that they only worked up here, away from the town, because he paid high wages. That they could get another job tomorrow, and nearer to their homes.

"Of course they can boil their own billy," Nicholas had

acceded, "but if you want your home finished in a hurry, you would be advised to make it possible for the men to keep working."

Swallowing the ever-present sense of outraged disbelief, Cressida slipped into the role of a working colonial wife. She drew water from a well the Maoris found for them, while the workmen from their ladders, sawhorses, and half-built chimneys watched her enigmatically.

A bullock dray had labored up the track carrying a tank sent by the trader Wilshire, but it had not filled, for rain came too lightly on the blustering, dancing wind, merely brightening the lawn, mischievously dampening the timber and corroding the wet concrete.

"I will carry the water in," Nicholas promised, and then forgot. Every day he was out at daybreak, working harder and longer than his men, chopping down the smaller trees with an axe, firing the fern, gathering the dry *manuka* that was so excellent for touchwood to light the kitchen fire. When he came in ready to eat half a shoulder of mutton with half a loaf of bread and fall exhausted into a chair, Cressida knew with grudging sympathy she could ask no more of him.

Cressida resumed her seat, picked up her pen. As she did so, a fearful churning began inside her. The brave lies had risen up to attack her. They hammered at her throat, tugged at her breath. She heard as from a long way off an inhuman cry of terrible distress. Then another, and another.

There were hands on her shoulders, hard but gentle hands.

"Now, missus," said a gruff man's voice, "don't you take on like that. It'd fair break a man's 'eart ter 'ear you, it would."

Her eyes were closed, uselessly, against the tide of tears. They coursed down her face to spill onto her swollen bosom; they seeped wetly through the cotton of her stretched gown.

"Poor young missus," the voice went on. "We're terrible sorry, we are, and that's a fact. Me mate is makin' yer a cup o' tea. 'Urry up there, young Alf," he shouted.

Cressida fumbled with the small, soaked square of linen and lace that was her handkerchief, trying without success to cover her eyes. "I'm sorry," she whispered, meaning in some complex and confused way that she was sorry she could not hold up her head and set an example as she was brought up to do.

"Now, don't you be sorry, young missus," the voice went on kindly. "You're orl right. You jest sit there awhile an' calm yerself while I 'urries up the tea."

In an agony of embarrassment Cressida lifted her head, straightened her back. "You're very kind," she said stiffly, when he returned with the tray.

"That's orl right, m'Lady." He spoke quietly, and to her infinite surprise, with some measure of respect. "That's perfeckly orl right. Me mate and me—that's 'Ector out there—we don't like to see you un'appy, m'Lady. Anytime you want anythin', you jest ask." Like a glow from a warm fire, his kindness spread through her, melting the tension, disposing miraculously of the shame.

Tears of gratitude rolled gently down her cheeks. "You're very kind, U-Upton."

"That's orl right, m'Lady. Glad ter 'elp. I'd like it if you'd call me Jemmie, though. I'll be 'ere workin' for a while. Call me Jemmie, and we'll get on fine." He was watching her, his eyes steady. "Orl right, m'Lady?"

"A-All right, Jemmie," she said. She watched his back as he went off across the room with his cocky, lively gait. At the door he turned, winked, then swiftly disappeared.

26

———◆———

Now that she no longer had to carry water from the well, Cressida found life considerably more bearable. Every evening, when the workmen went home, they left a row of cans at the back door, full to the brim; every morning, they replenished the empty ones. They made her a butter cooler in a bank beneath a red beech at the back of the house. Hector, the bricklayer, dug out a burrow and fitted a drainpipe, carefully preserving the exquisite tracery of maidenhair fern so that it acted as a curtain over the entrance.

Jemmie, the red-haired carpenter with a cheeky grin, the one who had come to Cressida's rescue, always noticed first when the wood box was empty. He would put down his tools for an hour and chop up some of the small *tawa* trees Nicholas had carted home and left haphazardly on the woodpile.

"How very kind you are to me, Jemmie," Cressida said one day as he brought the wood in, feeling vexedly tearful again, though she could not have said why.

"Nuffin' ter cry about," said Jemmie gruffly, as he dropped his armful beside the stove.

"No. Of course not. Perhaps I have taken cold."

Did carrying a baby make one cry? There were so many questions to ask, and no one to whom she might address them. If only her mother were here, or Mrs. Stitchbury, or Mrs. Maxwell. Mrs. Maxwell had written that she was happier than anyone should ever expect or deserve to be. Her dear husband had taken up land near

Auckland, and they were prospering. Cressida swallowed hard over the lump in her throat. She must not be envious, for envy was a sin. But the isolation was dreadful.

Sometimes, thinking about the baby's arrival, a kind of panic took hold. The home paddocks were mainly cleared, and Nicholas spent his days far out on the estate. The house, too, would soon be finished; the workmen no longer at hand. She broached her worry to Dr. Stokes. He had merely patted her hand. First babies took their time. So long as Nicholas called in around midday every day. But Nicholas was too busy to come back every midday.

She jerked the apron firmly over her distended belly and thrust her arms into the sudsy water in the tub, bashing the clothes against the corrugated washboard. If I stop thinking, perhaps I will stop crying, she thought distractedly, the tears dropping into the foaming suds.

Those were pleasant interludes in the day now, when she made refreshments for the men. "Coo-ee, Jemmie, Hector, Bert, Paddy!"

"Tea-o," they would say to each other, looking pleased, clambering down ladders from the roof. They would sit on wood blocks in a half circle facing the back door, while she perched inelegantly on her upturned box in the kitchen, for there was as yet no stool. Cressida grew as fond of them as she had been of the servants at Saxon Mote. She worked at forgetting their surnames. She would never forget the hostility in the face of the sawyer who had married her maid when she met them in the town and forgot Yorke should now be addressed as Mrs. Edwards.

"Her name is Alice, m'Lady," said the fellow. "If yer don't want ter call her Mrs. h'Edwards, that is."

Cressida had plenty of time to dwell on the past as well as on the future. Would the servants of Saxon Mote have preferred to have been addressed by their Christian names? In this new world where people dared to complain she was acquiring a new view of things.

One day Jemmie's wife, Lily, arrived, carrying a small child on her hip. "Us come to give you a lesson in bread making," she offered, stepping uninvited through the door into the kitchen. "Jemmie told us as 'ow yer cook run away."

"How very kind!" Cressida exclaimed, blinking hard, searching in agitation for a handkerchief in her apron pocket. "I think I've got a cold." She blew her nose hard. "May I take the baby? Do sit down on that, er, box, I'm afraid. Would you like a cup of tea?" Tea was their lifeline, their class bridge, their comfort. They sat together at the kitchen table, stimulated and warmed by the novelty of each other's nearness.

"Yer can't learn to bake off the top of yer 'ead like that," Lily said scornfully when Cressida told her of Cook's airy departing instructions.

Later, when the lesson was over, the bread in the oven, she stood back, looking up at Cressida, knuckles on her square hips, her honest face puckered. "Things is goin' all topsy-turvy fer yer, ain't they? But you'll soon git a new cook," she added kindly. "Anyway, it's better you should know. You might get a girl what's not proper trained."

"I have asked my mother to send me another cook."

"Let's hope she's got an 'arelip an' a beard, then," remarked Lily pessimistically. "It's cooks them single men want, an' no mistake."

"M'Lady looked tired ter death," she confided to her husband. "It ain't right fer delicate ladies the likes of 'er ter 'ave ter do the work of all her parlormaids, an' kitchen maids, an' laundry maids an' cooks." She added bossily, "You 'urry up an' finish this 'ouse, Jem, so she can 'ave a servant afore she does a proper mischief to 'erself. All puffed up an' pale she is, an' y' can see what a beauty she used to be."

The next time Lily came she brought a book of cake recipes all laboriously penned in a childish hand. Cressida made a fruitcake, which she proudly offered to the men for their tea.

"It's a pleasure fer us ter work fer a real lady," said Hector, settling his bony frame on the chopping block. "Jus' like 'ome."

Nurtured by their daily kindnesses, Cressida softened. When Nicholas came home one evening, she seemed almost gay. "Tomorrow the men are going to line the little parlor for me."

He glanced up from his six-month-old copy of *The*

Times, his eyes widening in surprise. "I thought you wanted the drawing room finished first."

"The men feel I should as soon as possible have a room of my own. It was their decision. Mr. Wilshire has received a consignment of the very latest wallpaper designs. Jemmie is to pick up samples and bring them to me tomorrow."

He noted bemusedly the touch of pride in her tone. Once he had commented she was good with the lower classes. Confound it, she sounded as though they were managing her now. He put his paper aside, smiling. Had Rose looked like that when she was carrying their child? Had she, too, blossomed in this voluptuous manner? He rose from his chair, the weariness from the long day's toil falling away.

She recognized in his movement something more than sensuality, a kind of loneliness, a need, and her newly warmed spirit went out to meet it. She smiled at him in return. "Paddy said his younger boy could build a henhouse. It would be nice to have our own eggs."

He crossed the room and took her hands, looking down at her, noting the flush in her cheeks. "Do you realize you will have to feed them? Until we get the quarters built for shepherds, and a full-time handyman."

"I will manage," Cressida replied, knowing she could turn to her new friends. "It would be better, I think, if we had our own produce."

He bent and slowly kissed her. She did not stiffen, nor did she pull away. He put both arms around her and rested his chin on the top of her head. Neither spoke. The clock in the corner ticked quietly. He kissed her again, very gently, then led her out to the veranda. They sat together on the rough sofa the men had put together for her out of planks, and which she had covered with a giant cushion stuffed with *raupo* flock. In front of them, the verdant valley crept in dusky silence toward the town, tree-spotted, forest-edged, black from its recent burning, yet already showing green. The sky in the west was faintly stained with the last red rays of the departing sun.

"There's a vine called passion fruit that grows apace here," Cressida said. "I intend to use it as a curtain to make a shady room of part of the veranda."

"Have you come to terms with all this now?"

She recognized that he had not asked lightly. "I have tried all the time to come to terms with it," she replied. "If I have not wholly succeeded . . ."

"I know," he said. "I have not had the time nor the energy at the end of the day. It has been hard for you. But soon, when the staff quarters are built, and I have acquired permanent help . . ."

She sensed his unwillingness to commit himself. "Are you still thinking of Rundull?"

"How can I not?"

"You must accept the fact that Adeline will have a son," she replied, the new spirit and hope in her infusing her with courage. "That when your father dies there may not even be a welcome, much less a place for you at Rundull."

He said quietly, "I pray every night that Adeline may not have a son. Sometimes I even find myself praying that my brother will not survive. You'll be mistress of Rundull one day. There'll be no skivvying for you there." His voice was full of guilt.

She put a hand on his arm. "Please. I beg of you not to think like that."

He stood up precipitously, gave her a bleak smile, then strode into the house. A moment later he was back, jerking himself into a fustian jacket, balancing a gun dangerously between his flailing arms. Bouncing heavily down the veranda steps, he strode across the delicate new grass and was swallowed up by the gloom.

Word came that *Aurora* had been wrecked on Kaipara Bar when the wind failed. No one knew what had happened to Captain Heale. Word came also that the governor's wife had arrived at the Bay of Islands. They discussed with considerable unease the possibility that Hobson might be successful in making Kororareka the capital of New Zealand. Captain Arthur Wakefield, who would have sailed in *Tory* as the company's principal agent, had he not been unexpectedly promoted to a command in the Mediterranean, had elected to retire from the navy next year and to begin the colonizing of the Middle Island. When that was accomplished, the town of Britannia would indeed be well-placed in this long, narrow land. Nightly, in their houses and in the taverns, settlers chewed over ways and means of persuading Westminster that Britannia should be made the seat of government. With a prefabricated government house already on the high seas, there was an urgency to decision-making.

May rushed in on a cold breeze from the south, and the whaling season began. Fred Quick disappeared to join the five hundred white men hungry for whale oil. In her cottage overlooking the bay, Rose experienced the first pangs of homesickness.

There must be some way, she felt, that she could get Florrie and Adam out to share her good fortune. Rose took up her pen and wrote to the curate at Rundull.

She described her little house and told him the family could stay with her until they were settled. She told him, also, how healthy even the sickly emigrants had become. She enclosed the £3 Oliver had dug out of the silt in their cottage after the Hutt River flood so that Adam could take the stagecoach to London and make enquiries at the company's offices, and picking up the baby, she set out for the post office.

It was a fine life, and she wanted her family to share it.

After church on Sundays, the outlying settlers having come into town, there were lunch and tea parties in the houses ringing the bay. Since Rose did not fit easily into any social category, and as no one would have thought of inviting Daniel anywhere, the Putnams loitered on the church steps and drifted around the town, chatting to people they had known at the Hutt, and to those who had traveled steerage with them on the ship. Rose enjoyed these occasions. The clergy and their wives were unequivocally friendly, the gentry unfailingly polite.

The Wakefield plan for a classless utopia had not materialized. If during the week they tentatively extended feelers beyond their class-consciousness, on Sundays, when the tall hats and elegant stocks came out, when delicate buttoned boots peeped beneath fine gowns, they automatically remembered their places. It was a day that brought homesickness more often than not and a tired acceptance of the old order of things that had been good enough for their fathers, but was now, sometimes confusedly, not quite good enough for them.

Nicholas and Cressida came into town. Rose, aching to

catch Nicholas's eye, knowing she must not, watched them discreetly from a distance.

How brown Nicholas had become. How beautiful! Though he walked decorously enough twirling his cane, with his wife's hand lying elegantly on his forearm, Nicholas always looked vaguely uncomfortable as though he no longer felt at home in the Sunday clothes of a dandy. Having a facility for ignoring the unacceptable, Rose turned a blind eye to the bulge beneath Lady Cressida's cloak.

With Alain's gift of pretty cottons she had discovered a talent for dressmaking. She made herself gowns that were suited to her new life. But she toiled alone. Even though her behavior in public was demure in the extreme, and she was patently the most devoted mother in town; even though no woman could say with any honesty that she ogled other people's husbands, she did not manage to make friends.

Working-class wives whispered jealously in corners that she had more clothes than was good for her, and weren't her necklines too low? Men of every class ogled her in vain. She knew she was pretty, but it was only important for Nicholas to notice.

The Maori friends Rose had made when she lived near the *pa* continued to visit her. They came when Daniel was at work, squatting on the grass beside the veranda. Matrons toiling up the hill to their cottages looked the other way, pretending they had not seen this breaking of the rules. Rose assiduously practiced her Maori. One of Te Puni's wives brought her a woven mat for the parlor floor.

"They'll be comin' fer tea next," Daniel said truculently.

"They don't like tea. And what's more, they don't like going into English people's houses."

" 'Ow d'yer know?" inquired Daniel, looking at her suspiciously from beneath his heavy brows.

"Because I invited Wi Tako in when he brought me the sweet potatoes."

Daniel was outraged. "I'm not goin' ter 'ave a dirty nigger in my 'ouse!"

Rose, not easily moved to anger, stamped her foot. "How many times do I have to say, they are not niggers!" She would have liked to tell Daniel that some of her brown-skinned friends spoke better English than he did. Daniel's sloppy speech offended her. Chief Matangi, a venerable old sage with silver hair and long beard, had pronounced Daniel a *pakeha tutua*. A poor creature. Rose could not tell Daniel this, even in anger, because Giles's presence reminded her unremittingly why Daniel was here to be criticized.

She tried to soothe her conscience by giving him a pretty and comfortable home. She knew there was wallpaper in the newly opened stores, but, aware that the house they lived in did not belong to them, she had covered her walls with pictures cut from old copies of the *Illustrated London News*. Alain brought an opossum rug for the bed. She had never before known the touch of real fur.

Rose christened the cottage Aurora. Flash Jack Wilshire had one of his men stencil the name over the front door. She sat as often as she could on the veranda. It was all very well for the gentry to remain hidden in their homes, but who was going to call on her? Gentle folk smiled as they passed by, but they did not come in. Working-class wives continued to keep their distance. Rose, amused and stimulated by occasional visits from Flash Jack, busy with her baby, her reading, and her home decoration, came to accept with a certain equanimity her situation in no-man's-land.

All around them the town grew. Blanket and coal charities having been left behind in the old country, erstwhile ladies bountiful turned their minds to planning for public utilities. There was a library to organize. The school. Later, when they were settled, when Government House was erected on the hillock Colonel Wakefield had benevolently offered free to Westminster, when Mrs. Hobson—popularly thought to be young, cultured, and beautiful—was in residence, there would be balls and parties. Already the ladies were looking out their ball gowns in anticipation of genteel excitements.

Then Mr. Eaton's boy was murdered by Maoris. The town shuddered and went to ground. At the inquest, it was said he had been stealing potatoes from native gardens. Such rough justice was fair by Maori law. The coroner had difficulty making the natives understand that as subjects of Her Majesty Queen Victoria they must abide now by English law.

"A woman!" The culprits roared with laughter. Women had no standing in Maori law.

The settlers grew seriously alarmed. With no police there were no laws, and therefore no reprisals. The colonists told each other stoutheartedly that only a few unimportant natives had turned against them; the chiefs were friendly. Nonetheless, they looked forward to the arrival from the Bay of Islands of a detachment of soldiers from the 80th Regiment.

Word came that Hobson had left Kororareka to live in Auckland. The gentlemen nodded their heads sagely. The pig-headed fool was learning. He would turn up here soon and settle in, putting Britannia and its deserving pioneers on the map.

The colony had its first fire. The rush roofs of Cornish Row burst into flames, and overnight a host of laborers were made homeless. With the aid of householders, Colonel Wakefield managed to get them under cover. A fund was set up to replace their belongings. Rose gave a shilling out of the beginnings of her new savings.

"Where d'yer get that?" Daniel asked suspiciously.

"I saved it. Everyone is expected to help if they can." Rose floated along easily on the tide of change, but, "Gawd Almighty," muttered Daniel, looking lost, "who d'yer think yer are?"

The excitement of the blaze had hardly subsided when the first earthquake arrived. Fearless in her fascination, Rose leaned against a wall as the house rocked on its foundations. Daniel stood stock still, paralyzed, his eyes bulging. Neighbors, thinking their houses were being pulled down by the natives, rushed outside firing muskets and pistols. The Maoris were vastly amused.

A Wakefield club was established, the subscription high, and membership limited to twenty members. Jerningham invited Nicholas to join. "I am too busy at this time to be involved in the affairs of the town," Nicholas replied curtly.

"But you joined the Pickwick Club," Cressida reminded him.

"Indeed. I do have some public spirit, my dear, but I

have no wish to canonize the man who has so radically changed the course of my life."

She turned away to hide the hurt. Things had been better between them lately. Sensing her discomfiture, he slid an arm around her shoulders and held her briefly close.

"Folks are talkin'," Daniel complained to Rose one evening. "It ain't seemly fer yer ter entertain Mr. Wilshire while I'm at work."

"Entertain? Oh, really, Daniel!" She laughed merrily to cover her apprehension. Alain carried the gossip to her; entertained her with seafaring tales; flattered her outrageously; brought her pretty things. He was the only member of the colony who made her feel she belonged.

"Don't bother to pay me," he would say carelessly, as he handed her a reel of silk or a ribbon for her bonnet. "I've taken it off feller m'lud's wages." It was a black art they shared, this ability to create small wickednesses. He had a look about him of cunning, yet his eyes were clear as bush pools and honest as mutton. He said he was the illegitimate son of a French countess; that his father was an English duke at whose stately home he had been raised in Gloucestershire; that he had left England after fighting a duel with his half-brother. His stories brought a sparkle to Rose's eyes and zest to her day.

Though he behaved monstrously, selling old flintlocks to the Maoris and overcharging when goods were short, he spoke like a gentleman and commanded immense respect.

She was at her best with Alain because he stimulated her, brought laughter, as Daniel never had. Daniel's life was not for enjoying: It was for plodding through, while keeping a wary eye open for disasters. The fresh winds of the new country had not blown optimism his way.

Aware that her delight in her new life, her growing enlightenment, the enrichment of her self-teaching was driving them farther apart, Rose tried hard to take Daniel with her, but he would not rise. Once she made an effort to open his mind to what he was doing to her at night, jabbing her hurtfully, scrambling roughly and heavily over her, grunting like a porker. And never, never kissing her.

"Yer don't talk about those things," he replied, looking embarrassed.

"But you're hurting me. Can't I talk to you about that? Please, Daniel, let's talk. Do let us talk about that."

"Yer're my wife. A man's got 'is rights."

Sometimes she closed her eyes, gritted her teeth, and willed herself to think of Nicholas, but it didn't work. Once she cried and Daniel said violently, the only time he had ever brought himself to refer to the way she had deceived him, " 'Ow d'yer git that brat if yer don't like it?"

She knew then she had rubbed him raw by her wickedness. That she had tried a mild and naturally kindly man too far. She kissed him and smoothed his hair. "Daniel . . ."

"Shut up," he said, though not unkindly. "I've 'ad a busy day an' I want ter go ter sleep now."

27

———◆———

Rose was beginning to understand Britannia's troubles. The missionaries, who were determined to protect the Maoris far beyond the desires of the Maoris themselves, had the ear of the governor; and the governor had decided to stay in Auckland like an ostrich, pretending that the New Zealand Company and its settlers, who had more than one hundred thousand acres in the south, did not exist. Somehow, they must acquire recognition.

The Wade/Pearson affair forced their hand.

All Britannia knew John Wade, who had settled in the area, and everyone was on his side when a dispute arose with Captain Pearson of *Integrity* over the carrying out of a charter. Wade applied to the town's magistrate, and the captain was ordered to appear for questioning in the little courthouse behind Barratt's Hotel.

Pearson refused. Arrested, he steadfastly declined to answer questions on the grounds that the magistrate, not having been appointed by an elected government, had no right to ask them. The magistrate was in a quandary. There was as yet no jail where Pearson could be committed for contempt. The only other alternative, the stocks, where wayward wife beaters and Sam Phelps the drunken bullock driver occasionally languished, was unthinkable.

Tory was idling at anchor on the windblown waters of the harbor. The laws of England did not allow one captain to detain another on his ship, but, and to Captain Chaffers's embarrassment, Pearson was put aboard.

Yet Pearson's ship sailed at dawn!

Down on the waterfront gaggles of idlers took bets on who had won the battle. Had Pearson left in command of *Integrity,* and if so, who had helped him escape? Flash Jack's name was on everyone's lips, for no one had seen him last night and he had a reputation for taking matters into his own hands. But beyond and above that, if Pearson was right and their magistrate was not a magistrate at all, they wondered whether Britannia was to be overrun by libertines, while the governor dillydallied up north trying to make up his mind where to live.

Poor John Wade's cause was quite forgotten. The young blades in the taverns guffawed over the possibility of Sam Phelps suing the company for his weekly incarceration in the stocks, on the grounds that no one in the vicinity had the right to arrest a drunk.

Rose was rocking her baby on the veranda when she saw a figure turn up the grassy track that led between the houses. Recognizing Alain's seaman's stride, she jumped to her feet, smoothing her linsey gown to rights, wondering if he would notice she had already made up the warm material he brought her last week. The nights were cold now, though the sun would melt honey, and the breeze was mild enough. But winter was coming, their first winter. How cold it would be, no one could as yet tell.

"Hello, sweet Rose," said Flash Jack, stepping onto the veranda, chuckling as he noticed her new gown, nodding approvingly. "But why have you changed your hair?"

Rose flushed. "I thought you had come to tell me what happened to *Integrity.* Oliver will be 'round later and you know how dearly Mrs. Stokes likes to be first with the news. Tell me—"

"I'll tell you nothing until we've got to the bottom of this very serious matter," retorted Flash Jack. "Ah, how pretty you are, my poppet, when you're disconcerted." He moved around her emitting soft little whistles of surprise. "Now tell me, my lovely, why you think you should look like a governess."

"The Queen does her hair this way," replied Rose defensively, fingering the tight little ringlets over her ears, the neat bun at the nape of her neck.

"Then leave it to her. She's a prim miss anyway," Alain said carelessly.

Rose caught her breath. Never before had she heard anyone criticize the Queen. It was like laughing in church.

Resting both hands on her shoulders, Flash Jack looked gravely into her face. "Glory in your beauty, Rose, and wear it like a halo." He read something behind a shadow in her eyes and added softly, "God has given you your own particular cross, and your own particular power. Go down your own path and you'll find out how to use it. You'll find nothing if you trail after the mediocre ones. You're for the mountains and the valleys, Rose. It's not going to be easy for you, but that's what you've been given. Don't underestimate the value of your loveliness. It will carry you through."

She did not know what to say to him. Riddles like this, which she had come to expect from him, infused her with excitement, and at the same time a touch of fear. Later, in the night, remembering, she wished she had asked him to explain.

"Make me a cup of tea, sweet Rose," he said now. He bent to retrieve the packet he had dropped, rustling the paper in his noisy way. "I have here a pound of the finest blend out of China, just arrived."

Rose dimpled. "You bring me too many things. Let me pay for this."

"You'll not pay for it because I'm not giving it to you. Put it in a separate tin and mark it Flash Jack. Don't you dare give any of it to Feller m'Lud."

"Alain!" But hurrying into the house, picking up the kettle, she forgot in an instant about Daniel. The power of Flash Jack's personality drove Daniel out. He wandered in after her and stood, hands in pockets, in the center of the small kitchen that she had made as pretty as her parlor. He sniffed the aromatic air appreciatively, looking around at jars filled with ti tree covered in tiny white and pink flowers, at the new, bright curtains drifting in the breeze.

Rose often wondered if it was true what they said, that Flash Jack lived with a Maori woman, and if so, what kind of home they shared. There was a shine about him as of polished brass. She could not imagine him living with a native.

There was a shout from Giles. Swift and silent as a cat, Alain disappeared. She found him on the veranda standing by the child's basket, his eyes intent. A shock went through her. She waited with fast-beating heart. He met her look and his silence was still as the bush. "Captain Pearson has sailed for Auckland to tell his tale to the governor," he said innocently.

"How do you know?" she asked, flustered, then hurried on, accusing him to cover her embarrassment. "They say you rowed him to his ship and were well paid. Is it true?"

Alain's eyes gleamed. "Ah, sweet Rose, there are some matters better kept secret. But I'll tell you this. He intends to inform Captain Hobson that the citizens of Britannia are setting up a republic. That is his vengeance."

"What's a republic?"

"It's high treason, that's what it is. It's living without a queen. God works in mysterious ways," said Alain, in an unlikely show of piety. "I'll wager a new pair of slippers to a tankard of ale our precious governor will come running. And that's what we want, isn't it?" He rubbed his hands together. "Hobson can pull the New Zealand Company's flag down with everybody's blessing, and what a day it will be when the Union Jack rises in its place. Our first state occasion.

"There'll be flags flying and bells ringing," Flash Jack galloped on. "All the ladies will turn out in their finery, and the gents will be in full rig. What of you, Rose? They tell me you have silks and satins from London, and a bonnet trimmed with violets. Or is this mere idle gossip?" He saw her shock and grinned. "And there is another tale afoot . . ." He looked down at his feet, crooked one knee, stared at it, then grinned again. "Let's leave it at that, shall we? What's a woman without mystery?"

That evening, while Daniel was sitting hunched in a chair blankly contemplating the wall before him, Rose broached the subject of Flash Jack's visit. "State occasion!" he echoed. "What d'yer mean?"

"He thinks the governor will come and read a thing called a proclamation to say our queen is also to be Queen of Britannia."

Daniel stared.

"What I'm telling you, Daniel," said Rose, wheedling

nervously, "is that everyone has to get dressed up in their best and join in."

Daniel grinned foolishly. "Yer want me ter strut 'round like a turkey cock, pretendin' I'm sumpin' I'm not? I 'aven't got no ideas above me station. Not like some I could mention."

She picked up his rough hand and pressed the back of it to her cheek. "Couldn't you try to change, just a little bit? Just for me?"

"I'm like I was when yer married me, Rose. You was pleased enough ter get me then."

Ignoring the barb, Rose smiled at him prettily. "Folk change all the time, Daniel dear."

"They got no right. I wish yer wus what yer wus." He looked up at her with an odd mix of pride of possession and nervousness. "Yer're a common workin'man's wife, Rose," he said. There was a kind of pleading in his voice.

She ruffled his thick hair, which was growing heavily, determinedly, forward and down, like a thatched roof.

"Git away. Don't mess me about."

She stood looking down at him without rancor because she knew he did not dislike her. Brought up in a loveless climate, he simply did not understand. "You're an old man," she said sadly.

Squashing his hair back into place he replied indignantly, "I'm twenty-five."

"You're sixty-five," she said, suddenly resentful. "And next year you will be seventy-five. Daniel, if you don't escort me to the proclamation . . ."

"You can go by yerself. You go fer walks by yerself an' down ter the stores," Daniel pointed out reasonably.

"But I would like you to come with me. You are not in the village of Rundull now. It's different here." She added, quoting Flash Jack, "We can make our own rules. Anyone can be stylish if they want to."

"I'm a plain man," retorted Daniel heavily. "I was born a plain man and I'll die the same."

"Then I," flared Rose, "will go to the proclamation with Flash Jack Wilshire, because I am not a plain woman, and I'm only eighteen, and I want to have some pleasure before I die. Since you don't care what people think of you, you shouldn't mind me appearing with another man." She waited for Daniel to protest, hoping against hope he would assert his rights, so that she might not have to do this wicked thing.

Daniel rose. "It's time fer bed," he said.

In her exasperation she shouted after him, "I am only eighteen," the words pursuing him down the passage. "Only eighteen," she repeated unhappily.

Daniel did not turn. "Come ter bed."

When he had finished with her, she thought about what Flash Jack had said. If there was really to be a fête day, with the outlying settlers coming into town, it would not be like Sundays when the gentry walked decorously out in front. They would mill together in a crowd. She and Nicholas.

Why should she not be escorted by Flash Jack Wilshire? He did not give a fig about what people said. Under his patronage she would be able to talk to Nicholas. It had been such a long while since they talked, really talked, together. Time and again as she strolled on the waterfront with Giles, she had strained her eyes toward the hills, looking for a lone horseman, but Nicholas had not come.

She made wild, audacious plans. She would wear one of the dresses he had given her. The most beautiful. The oyster silk. But her heart sank. What was the point of wearing a wonderful dress if it was to be covered with her drab brown cloak? Then she had the solution. A truly wicked, outrageous solution. But I will do it, she vowed.

She awoke to a sky feathered with clouds. Little wavelets danced along the shore as she hurried down to town. The Maoris squatting outside taverns and stores were huddled into their mats. One or two swaggered proudly, draped in a red blanket, boasting their connection with land sales, or the signing of the contentious treaty.

Flash Jack was standing in the fitful sun outside his store, legs apart, hands on hips. He wore a vulgar orange waistcoat with brightly shining buttons over his frilled cambric shirt. His narrow-brimmed hat with its trim of gold cording sat jauntily on the back of his head. His jackboots shone like glass, and as though he were a buccaneer there was a brace of pistols in his belt.

Rose remembered that his generosity had until now been voluntary, and she hesitated. Then it was too late for he had seen her and was approaching.

"Mrs. Putnam." He clicked his heels and bowed. "Is there something I can do for you?"

Hugging her drab cloak close against the wind, she looked up at him with big eyes. How fortunate, she thought nervously, that today's weather should remind him of its possible inclemency on the great day. She said breathlessly, "Daniel doesn't want to go to the proclamation. . . . He won't escort me." She smiled winningly up at him.

Flash Jack's eyes twinkled. "Ah! Then may I have the pleasure?"

"How kind," she replied, trying to appear gracious, thinking that at any moment her thumping heart would burst right through her stays. "But you did say everyone should wear their best . . ."

"Come on, Mrs. Putnam. Out with it," Flash Jack said breezily.

Her eyes flickered down. "I had a beautiful green velvet cloak once, but I lost it."

"Lost a beautiful green velvet cloak!" he echoed, his bright eyes widening with affected amazement. "As I remarked yesterday, you are indeed a lady of mystery. So," he said, teasing her, "if you are to set the colony by its ears on Proclamation Day—or any other day for that matter—you must be provided with green velvet, and some silk for lining?"

Rose's cheeks flamed. Laughing gently, Alain lifted her hand and kissed it. She stood frozen. Nicholas was the only man who had kissed her hand before.

On the day of the celebrations Rose shut herself away in the spare bedroom, where her finery was hidden. Carefully and with intense love she lifted the oyster silk gown, dropped it over her head, and rustled it down on her hips. Her fingers trembled as she did up the little buttons over her bosom and at her wrists. She picked up the violet-trimmed bonnet and set it on her head, then took the new green cloak and swung it around her shoulders.

There was a sound behind her. She swung around to see Daniel standing in the doorway, his face as red as his flannel shirt, his head down like a bull.

"Rose!" His cry was animal, too. "Yer niver goin' out like that."

"Aren't you proud of me, Daniel?" She stood with her head on one side, hiding her terror, swinging the velvet folds.

"No. Git out o' them. . . ."

A loud voice overrode his protest. "Are you ready, Mrs. Putnam?"

They both jerked around. Flash Jack, in his outrageously striped satin coat, frilled cravat, and buckskin breeches, filled the front doorway like a giant. Daniel fell back.

"Well, Putnam," said the visitor genially, "don't your wife look a treat?" Without waiting for the reply of which Daniel was patently incapable, he flapped his gloves against the back of one hand and added, "Aren't you coming, man?"

Daniel turned his back.

Overwhelmed with pity, touched even with a little shame, Rose put a hand on his hunched shoulder. "Daniel, everyone will be there."

"Who's goin' ter look after the brat?"

"We can take Giles with us." With a little rush of excitement she remembered Nicholas had not seen his son since the day of the flood.

Daniel lumbered out of the back door, slamming it behind him.

"Come on," said Rose in a small voice, and picked up her gloves.

As they made their way toward Flagstaff Hill, townsfolk and country folk came hurrying in from all sides. Sailors were swinging ashore in rowboats. Out in the bay where ships' bows lifted elegantly on the ruffled water, their pennants streamed aloft. The wind sweeping up the hill caught bonnet strings, threatened tall hats.

Chiefs sported their best Kiwi-feather cloaks. Te Wharepouri, accompanied by two of his wives wearing sharks' teeth necklaces and greenstone earrings, strutted like a Roman emperor in his highly prized dogskin mat. Groups of ordinary Maoris squatting on the ground rubbing noses exchanged news in their traditional wailing chant. Some dusky children, looking uncomfortable in missionary issue shirts and trousers, led a pet piglet on a string. Rose, high-stepping with excitement, searched the crowd for the tallest head, the darkest hair, the most handsome face.

Jerningham bounced along beside Nicholas, recounting the tale that was sweeping through the delighted colony. "The shouting came just after dawn. Nightcapped heads were popping out of windows all over the place. There was *Integrity* riding at anchor, and Jack the Giant Killer, in the person of self-important little Constable Cole, marching up to the flagstaff with thirty soldiers in tow. Not Willoughby Shortland, mark you! He skulked aboard, preserving his dignity. Thirty soldiers to pull down our company's ragged old flag!" Jerningham all but collapsed with laughter.

Cressida gazed straight ahead, frozen faced, wishing their uninvited escort would go away.

Nicholas, too, was scarcely listening. He had a feeling of having left Jerningham behind. More brains than balance, people said of the young Wakefield. Even the Maoris called him *tiraweke,* a chattering bird. In a disinterested way, Nicholas thought he would get his comeuppance one day.

"Mr. Shortland," said Cressida stiffly, "by the very nature of things, is going to be unpopular. So would be the Pope in his position, or Mary Magdalene. He is too close to the intolerable Mr. Hobson. That is his real crime." The Hobsons and Shortlands were neighboring Devonshire families. Shortland had served under their governor in South America, the Mediterranean, and Jamaica.

"Come, my dear," said Nicholas as they reached the crest of the hill, "let us draw closer while Mr. Shortland reads the proclamation, and express to him our pleasure in this event." He was glad—weren't they all?—that the colony had official recognition at last. It remained only for Britannia to be made the capital. For Cressida's sake he would welcome the coming of society. Now that their house was finished, the pianoforte and all their treasures unpacked, and more furniture ordered from England, she was talking of holding glees, and of, shortly, when she found a cook, inviting some of the leading colonists to dinner. They had to fill the empty years somehow before they could return home.

They crossed the rough grass to the flagstaff where the Union Jack was to be hoisted. It was then that Nicholas saw Rose. He stopped dead, staring at her as she leaned sunnily, unacceptably, on the arm of Flash Jack Wilshire.

He had never felt jealousy like that before, tearing into him sharp as a dagger, jagged as the teeth of a saw. Cressida, looking up in concern, saw the fury in his eyes as they fell on the man at Rose's side; saw Rose elegant as a queen in a silk dress far, far more beautiful than her own, her face alight, the red lips parted in a silent cry as Nicholas's eyes met hers; saw the naked emotion in both faces. She saw the head lift, the neck arch like an elegant plumed bird enticing her mate.

Oh, no. No! *No!* Cressida rocked on her feet. She felt her knees give way, then, in appalling slow motion, the ground seemed to rise and rise and rise, hideously threatening. Closer and closer it came, darker and darker, until, with black finality, it exploded in her face.

Only when he heard the cries of distress from onlookers and the rushing of feet did Nicholas realize, with numb surprise, that his wife was lying crumpled at his feet.

"Whore!" said a malicious voice in Rose's ear.

She swung around to face the woman who had suggested, on the day they left *Aurora*, that Giles was not Daniel's son.

"Jezebel!" Another of the steerage passengers planted her insult with venom.

"Take no notice," said Alain, jerking her around so that she had her back to the troublemakers. And then there was Dr. Stokes, looking grim as he rushed to Lady Cressida's aid, nice Mrs. Stokes looking right through her. Some of the gentry cast her amazed, withering glances, then swiftly turned away.

" 'Oo do you think you are?" That was one of the Hutt Valley wives.

"She is Mrs. Putnam, you silly woman," said Flash Jack in a loud, angry voice, but he released Rose's arm. She had a shocked feeling of being abandoned. "Glory in your beauty," he had said, dismissing the demure hairstyle that might have set folks' minds at ease and brought her friendship.

Lieutenant Shortland had begun to speak. Flash Jack was listening intently. Rose hung her head, wishing she could fall into a hole in the ground.

At last the formal proceedings were over, the flag hoisted on the mast, the cheering dying away. Flash Jack took a cheroot from his pocket, put it between his strong teeth, and stood looking down at her, his eyes enigmatic. Without moving, he seemed to have receded. She could hold out no longer. A more sophisticated woman might have pleaded a headache. Rose said, "I want to go home."

He replied in a voice that sounded sincere, "Nobody wins all the time."

Win. She had been snuffed out like a candle. She did not, because she could not, say good-bye. She walked off with her head lifted but inside the loneliness was deep as a well. Because she did not turn she failed to see that he stood watching her. She made her way past the groups of squatting Maoris, the children playing with their cats' cradles and their *pois*. At last she was in a kind of safety behind the buildings at the bottom of the hill.

Now that there was no one to see, she allowed the tears to fall. Was it so very wrong to appear in public with Alain? Even as she asked herself the question, she knew in her heart that it was the dress and the emerald green velvet cloak that had caused the trouble. And now Alain had turned against her because he had seen that expression on Nicholas's face. Nicholas, looking as though he would draw a sword and cut Alain to pieces.

28

Daniel returned from work smoldering. "You should 'ear wot folk are sayin' about yer."

Rose was working at her sampler, her ever present comfort. She lifted her head high. "I've done nothing wrong," she said, thrusting into the back of her mind the fact that she had caused Nicholas's wife to faint, that she had upset Flash Jack who was so kind to her. She was unrepentant about breaking the social code. Her only regret was having made Nicholas angry.

"There's a place called Kororareka in the north." Daniel stood before her, his head thrust forward, his big boots somehow making his short legs look shorter. "It's 'ad whites fer twenty years—sailors an' missionaries an' traders. They say I could get work there easy enough."

"Leave Britannia!" A part of Rose, the heart of her, pulsed to life. "I will not go," she said. She knew by the way Daniel's shoulders slumped that he understood something of her determination.

After a while, he said cruelly, "You got no friends. You didn't really 'ave any before. . . ."

"People forget," she replied, sounding calm and confident.

And it seemed they did. The next time Mrs. Stokes passed by she smiled and waved. Oliver was in and out of the house as usual, sharing his schoolwork, bringing Rose books from the doctor's library. Alain did not come again. She missed his cheery visits.

* * *

Platina arrived off Petone beach. Immediately news flew through the colony that Government House lay below decks in all its rumored glory. There were sixteen bedrooms, servants' rooms, a schoolroom; clerks' and secretaries' offices; detached kitchens; a terrace veranda a hundred yards long supported by iron columns. A hundred and fifteen yards of Brussels carpet; ornamented ceilings; a marble mantelpiece for every room!

Britannia was to be the capital after all!

Twittering with excitement, ladies brought out ball gowns and inspected them carefully. The muddled beginnings of the colony were forgotten as a vision of their old way of life floated before their eyes.

Colonel Wakefield, jostled by the eagerness of the colonists into forgetting that the only reason *Platina* had come here was because his brother directed her to the same destination as *Tory,* went aboard in high spirits to sign for the prefabricated mansion. He returned dismayed. Captain Wycherley had explicit orders to hand the prize directly to the governor.

Peppery Dr. Evans, in his official capacity as chief justice, threatened to hold the ship until Hobson promised to make Britannia the capital. But Wycherley was not to be coerced by barefaced blackmail. Only half the freight had been paid for in advance, and he knew any discrepancy might lose him the rest of the money. Colonel Wakefield hurried aboard a schooner that was making ready to cast off, resolute in his determination to bring Governor Hobson to see for himself the central position of the settlement and its highly favored harbor.

The colonial secretary settled into a half-built house and prepared officiously to set the colony to rights. "You are here as squatters," he told the settlers. "I am awaiting instructions to warn you off what are now crown lands."

They held a hurried meeting at Barratt's Hotel and invited Shortland to attend. It began quietly.

"I have paid the company in London for my hundred acres, and I have paid the Maoris a pound an acre in gold for the rest of my land," said Nicholas. "I have now built my home, and I will not be dislodged."

"The combined forces of our most noble majesty, the governor, and yourself will not unseat me," declared Mr. Betts Hopper.

"I am prepared to go to court to battle for my rights," said Mr. Molesworth.

"Put your energy into dealing with those land sharks that arrive daily from Sydney, for we do not want them," shouted Mr. Langford.

"Nor do we want your wretched police," added Dr. Stokes. "Look to them, Mr. Shortland, if you will, for feeling is running high. Bring us some respectable Peelers from the Old Country." The New South Wales police Shortland had brought, accustomed as they were to convicts and bush rangers, to rewards for conviction of drunkenness with violence, were parading aggressively up and down Petone Beach with fetters and manacles dangling from their pockets. Robberies were ignored. There was no profit to be had from arresting a sober thief. And they were not sober themselves. They were so bored in face of the good behavior of the citizens that they searched houses and confiscated liquor, which they drank themselves.

"Bring us respectable Peelers." Heckling spread through the room.

At last, his self-importance stripped to the bone, Shortland outlined his powers. They were not great. He had been commissioned only to establish a post office and a postal service to the north.

"Nobody will take on a mail run in that direction," they had told him. The local Maoris were still at loggerheads with those they had conquered and displaced from their home here years before. Smarting with mortification, burning with blood lust, they lurked in dark forests ready to waylay any of their conquerors who might try to pass through.

"But the missionaries Henry Williams and Hadfield have traveled through this land with their Waitangi Treaty," he retorted.

With exclamations of contempt, they told him the good men of the church with their blanket bribes were always safe.

Shortland listened, vexed and worried. He had come to deal with insurgents, and found only intelligent good citizens who wanted a fair deal from Westminster. A sea mail service was established between Thorndon and Petone. In unfavorable weather the postman was obliged to walk. The post office was a raupo-thatched hut. Pigs strayed in and out, for tame animals had free run of the town. The wild wind blew through cracks, scattering letters indiscriminately. Nonetheless, it was a start.

Colonel Wakefield returned disconsolate from the north. The governor had refused to budge. *Integrity* with the house aboard, put to sea again, and for a little while the colony was depressed.

It was nearly midwinter now and there was snow on the Rimutakas to the north as well as all the way down the alps that lay like a spine along the Middle Island. The townspeople shivered in the wind that swept across the narrow channel of wild water outside their sheltered harbor. They shut themselves in their houses, blocking drafts with rugs, rags, and tent flies, anything that came to hand, complaining that their cottages had been put up in too much of a hurry; that the green timber had shrunk. It was much colder at home, but their blood had grown thin in the hot summer, their memories short.

Rose never complained. When the wind blew strong and cold she would stand on the veranda with the sweep of it through her hair and gratitude in her heart, for having escaped the dark kitchens of Rundull and the black sleeping cupboard where she had left her childhood. Every day she thanked God that Giles would be brought up where the future was sweet and warm with hope. The tin in its hiding place behind the stove was filling up with coins.

But her happiness was to take another tumble. Suddenly, one morning, when Rose was testing a ham with a fork, her stomach began to churn. Rushing outside, she was violently sick. Afterward, hunched whey-faced on the kitchen stool, she remembered how she had recently cried out in pain when Daniel leaned on her breasts in the night. And there was that other thing that she had twice determinedly ignored. Daniel's baby was on its way.

In mindless panic she climbed up onto the kitchen table and jumped off. Staggering in anguish to the parlor, with her ankle throbbing painfully, she dropped into a chair and gave herself up to mute and miserable contemplation. What kind of child would Putnam seed produce? A boy as dull as his father? As violent as those uncles who had pursued her down the High Street of Rundull?

How desperately unfair life was! How absurd her prayers! Clearly God did not listen.

She put on her bonnet and shawl, tucked Giles into his flax basket, and wandered disconsolately down to the waterfront. Sam Phelps, the colorful town drunk, resplendent in a wide-skirted green coat ornamented with brass buttons and a crimson traveling shawl, came rattling along in his wagon. Looking down at her from his high seat, he winked. Vastly cheered by her own daring, Rose winked back.

He jerked at the reins. "Whoa there, Shortland. Whoa there, Cole." Sam rechristened his buffalo bullocks following each court appearance for drunkenness, exacting retribution by naming them after those magistrates who had offended him. Public abuse of his beasts was his revenge.

"Mornin' Mrs. Putnam. And how be you this fine day?" he bawled out.

An enchanting idea leaped into Rose's mind. A ride along a country track in this rough equipage might get her out of her predicament, as jumping off the kitchen table had not.

She looked up. "Where are you going, Sam?"

"I'm takin' this 'ere load o' provisions up to Mr. le Grys's estate."

A thousand incoherent desires flew through Rose's mind. She must see Nicholas again. Touch his hand. Look into his eyes. She had not spoken to him on Proclamation Day. The disappointment of that was still an aching void. Her imagination created a picture of Nicholas lifting Giles in his arms. Then Lady Cressida crept in. Rose allowed herself to face, for the first time, the outrage of that woman's pregnancy. In her condition, she thought defiantly, Lady Cressida was unlikely to emerge from the house.

She put a hand to her heart to quiet its thudding and gave the bullock driver her prettiest smile. "Would you take the baby and me for a ride? I've never been out that way."

"I'd be pleased, so long as yer 'usband don't mind."

"Of course he wouldn't mind."

"C'mon, then." Affably, Sam moved over. "Can you

climb up if I takes the basket?" He extended his big, scarred hands.

Thrilled, Rose settled on the hard seat and placed the basket between them. Sam leaned over to peer in. "Nice little feller. 'Oo's he like?" His gaze settled on Giles's black hair.

"He's like my family. They're all dark," Rose lied brazenly.

Phelps's eyes rested on the golden curls that peeped from beneath her bonnet. "Ho-hum. Gid-up you Cole an' Shortland. It'll be bumpy, Mrs. Putnam." With a jangle of harness and rumble of wheels they moved on.

Soon they swung around a sharp bend into the darkness of the forest. A crimson-flanked *kaka* raced heavily across the path with a loud, grating screech. "Miserable bastard, beggin' yer pardon, Mrs. Putnam," commented Sam, looking after the creature malevolently. "That boid's got a real nice whistle when it likes."

Rose fluttered her eyelashes at him. "I can do it." Pursing her lips, she imitated the *kaka* the way her Maori friends had taught her.

Sam chuckled. "Pretty clever, that."

Rose beamed. "Oh, what a wonderful day!" she exclaimed, too excited to keep her high spirits in check. Lifting her head, she took a great gulp of scented air. She wanted to sing with the birds, laugh, and scatter her happiness all around. As they emerged from the forest the leaf-patterned sunlight danced across the bullocks' backs and flickered along the basket, so that Giles started, blinked, and smiled. Rose lovingly drew the sheet forward to shade his face.

"You jist struck it lucky, Mrs. Putnam, you did," Sam remarked conversationally. "I run into Mr. le Grys down fer the meetin' in Barratt's 'Otel. They're ballotin' fer town sections. All the monied folk is in town. Survey's bin done at last an' they're pullin' straws fer the favored blocks, like. Town blocks is thought ter be val'able investments."

Rose's shoulder slumped. But her disappointment was rapidly overlaid by another shock. In Nicholas's absence, his wife, in spite of her condition, must come out to sign for the load. The ride took on a defiance, an impertinence, that was never intended.

"You had better put me down," she said, laying a trembling hand on the driver's arm. "I suddenly don't feel very well."

"Giddap there Cole, you lazy ole 'ump." Sam swung his rawhide whip high, bringing it down on the meek creature with a blistering crack.

"Put you down 'ere?" he repeated, his rough eyebrows shooting up.

"Can't put yer down now, Mrs. Putnam, dear. Them's wild pigs roamin' round 'ere. Why, they'd eat you alive, a nice little lidy like you. And the bebby too. You'll 'ave ter come with me all the ways now. Puke over the side if yer need to," he added with disarming vulgarity, "but I can't put yer down."

Oh no! She must go back. She must. They were lumbering along a stony edge beside a bright, rushing, tumbling creek. She sat forward in her seat, one hand gripping the handles of the basket. She would wait until they reached a reasonably clear patch, then jump.

"Giddup there, Shortland, you fool." They turned and began to move up a lightly wooded hill. The bullocks bent their great horned heads, thrusting their shoulders forward. There had been recent fires. Tree stumps still smoldered, the smoke rising in the still air. How Nicholas had been working! Some white-faced cattle paused in their contented chewing; a little flock of sheep set up a baaing, then whisked away, tails swinging.

"Look out there in front, Mrs. Putnam. There's the 'ouse."

Lost in her thoughts, Rose started, then gazed. Nicholas's house!

Built on a spur to command a view of the valley, its wide roofs sloped gently to shade verandas that bordered the house on both upper and lower floors. Big windows gleamed in the wintry sun. "It's a mansion!" she whispered. Then she remembered Rundull with its acres of lichened stone and the house shrank and grew flimsy before her eyes.

There was someone on the lower front veranda. A woman. Lady Cressida. Panicking, Rose let go of the basket to grasp the driver's arm, her fingers digging into his flesh. "Please let me off, Mr. Phelps. Sam. Please let me down."

"Orf 'ere, Mrs. Putnam! I'll never let you orf 'ere. Gee up there, Cole, you ole misery. Damn me, but these bullocks . . ."

"No, Sam, really," Rose burst out in dreadful agitation, her eyes riveted on the distant figure, her fingers once again gripping the handle of Giles's basket, loosening, gripping again. She flung a dismayed glance behind, assessing the height of the dray. She could not jump with the baby. It was too high. "Sam, let me down. I want to walk. You can pick me up on the way back. Please, Sam," she begged desperately, her pretty, wheedling ways forgotten, her face frightened. *"Please,* Sam."

"You jest set there an' we'll drop our load an' be turnin' 'round in next ter no time." He took a hand off his reins in order to pat her wrist. "Folks in Port Nicholson think little enough of me now w'out I drop a young leddy an' her bebee ter be eaten by wild pigs. Or cannibals," he added, with a knowing, wide-eyed nod.

The figure on the veranda moved, disappeared around the corner, reappeared a moment later on the other side, paused, and moved on again.

"There are no cannibals here," Rose protested, close to tears "And the Maoris say wild pigs don't attack unless they're cornered."

But he was not to be moved. "Git up there Cole, yer rotten ole hag. Gid-*dup!*"

In her distress, Rose began to pound the seat with her fist. The figure had come into view again, larger now as they approached. It was Lady Cressida. They were nearing the bottom of the fenced garden. Sam said, "There's somethin' wrong. Sure, an' there's somethin' wrong 'ere."

Lady Cressida seemed to jerk, as though losing her balance. She reached out to the wall. Using it for support, she went around the corner of the building. This time she did not reappear.

The bullocks came to a halt. Sam dropped the reins. They both stared at the empty veranda.

"P'rhaps you should go in, Mrs. Putnam, an' see if all's well."

"I don't think . . . I'm sure you . . ." Rose floundered.

"She won't bite yer, y'know. She's a 'uman bein' fer all she's a h'earl's daughter."

"Sam, *please* . . ."

Her reluctance and distress at last made the required impression. "Orl right. Wait 'ere. The team's too bone idle ter move without I drive 'em." Sam thumped to the ground with a grunt and disappeared around the back of the dray. There was a clanking of chains as he undid the flap. Loading a bag onto his back he lumbered off across the grass.

From somewhere behind the homestead came a series of excited barks. Rose sat very still, her eyes fixed on the windows. The silent house stared glassily back at her.

Phelps came around the corner of the house at a run, his great boots pounding the turf, his arms flailing. "Git down orf that there seat, young missus," he shouted, "an' git inside. 'Er Ladyship's in trouble. There's a bebby due any moment an' she's all by 'erself. 'Urry up now. I'll get orf back to town an' call the doctor. 'Urry up, I tell yer. 'Ere, gimme that basket."

Rose sat frozen.

" 'Ere. Git down." He grasped her arm roughly, jerking her so that she half fell. He caught her in his arms, released her, and handed her the basket. "Put the boy on the veranda an' git to 'er, quick." With that he leaped up onto the dray, dumped his load unceremoniously on the ground, and clambered into his seat. "Git inside, Mrs. Putnam, will yer," he shouted as Rose stood bewildered, straightening her clothes, then, turning all his coarse attention on the bullocks, he yelled, "Git on there, yer buggers, an' back ter town!" With a rattle and jangle of harness, a creaking of shafts, the dray groaned around in a tight circle and set off noisily down the hill.

Rose wanted to dash into the trees screaming, but she could not move. She stood as though rooted to the ground trying to come to terms with this ordeal. Then she was crossing the grass and going up the steps onto the veranda. Her mind was numb. The door facing her was shut. She reached out tentatively, turned the handle, and went through.

Cressida stood at the bottom of the stairs, her face crumpled, her bloated body sagging against the newel post. Perspiration stood out in blobs on her forehead and chin. She heard Rose's entrance and looked up. Fear and hatred crept through the big hall as the two women faced each other; then, as in a paroxysm of grief, Cressida sank clumsily to her knees, pressing her forehead against the varnished wood of the stair rail.

Rose's heart fluttered with fear. "Tell me where I can find a blanket. You had better stay where you are."

"I . . . must . . . get . . . into . . . bed."

"You can't." Galvanized to life by a picture of mother and baby washing like flotsam down the stairs to the hall below, Rose put Giles's basket down against the wall, instinctively placing it at the farthest point from Nicholas's wife, swiftly discarded her bonnet and cloak, then, grasping her skirts in both hands, sped up to the landing.

She faced a barrier of closed doors. One by one she flung them open. They were all empty except the last, which held an enormous four-poster. She had a vague impression of shaded silk drapes, a confused memory of Lady Felicity's room at Rundull, then she was grasping the silk bedcover in her hands, flinging it to the floor, and filling her arms with blankets. Turning, she ran breathlessly to the top of the stairs and pattered down, the blankets trailing behind her.

Cressida was lying on the floor with her eyes closed. Folding one of the blankets in half, Rose spread it alongside her, thinking with a queer dispassion that Lady Cressida looked as though she was going to die. Then she half rose on one elbow, opened her mouth, and uttered a bloodcurdling scream. Unnerved, Rose too lost control. Her hand leaped like a viper's tongue, and she slapped Nicholas's wife soundly across the cheek. Cressida fell back, her eyes whitely on her enemy. Rose's panic subsided into shaky relief.

As though the slap had settled something between them, Rose said, almost kindly, "If you can roll over a little you will be on the blanket. It will be better for you."

Cressida moved awkwardly. Then her face twisted with pain, her mouth opened but before the scream came her eyes swiveled around, meeting Rose's eyes. In the breathless silence that followed she gritted her teeth and obediently fell to one side. Rose gently moved her legs and wrapped the blanket around her.

What did one do if the doctor did not arrive in time? Giles's birth had happened so quickly Rose could scarcely remember it. "Like an animal in the fields," the rough

midwife had remarked. She wondered if she should remove the patient's drawers. Lady Cressida's drawers! She
repressed a faintly hysterical laugh. Cressida lay still with
her eyes closed. Rose went out to the veranda and,
shading her eyes, looked down across the green valley,
knowing that there was no possibility of help arriving for
a long time. Reluctantly, she retraced her steps.

Cressida opened her eyes, saw her, and, gritting her
teeth, reduced the coming scream to an agonized gasp.
Rose fell on her knees, grasping Cressida's hands with
compassion. "The doctor will be here soon," she said,
lying. "Sam Phelps is a very fast driver. He'll go like the
wind."

"Do you know what to do if he d-doesn't . . .
doesn't . . . ?"

Rose wanted to yell that she did not know. She wanted
to run away and pretend all this was not happening. "Of
course. Haven't I had one of my own?"

Giles. The air between them was again a shiver of
mistrust. Automatically, Cressida withdrew her hands.
"There's some water boiling on the stove," she said,
turning her head away.

Boiling water! When Florrie was confined the old women
in the village had talked of boiling water but Rose had
not been allowed in to see how they used it. She stood
up, looked around, saw that a passage led off the hall,
and followed it to a sizable kitchen. An enormous table
stood in the center of the room. Flames crackled noisily
in an impressive-looking stove, and a black kettle steamed
merrily on the hob. It was warm in here, considerably
warmer than in the hall. There were neat cupboards on
the walls, all varnished to a pale gold color with the
marks of the wood showing through. But it was not
pretty like her kitchen. There were no curtains. No flowers. This was a kitchen for a servant. Yet there were no
servants.

She went back into the hall. "Would you like me to
make you a cup of tea?" she asked diffidently. Perhaps
that was what boiling water was used for.

Mutely, Cressida shook her head. Her hands went to
her face, wiping away the sweat. Again, in spite of her
animosity, Rose felt a rush of sympathy. She went back
to the kitchen and found a cloth, dipped it in water,

wrung it out, and returned to the hall. Kneeling down, she gently washed the patient's face. Then she picked up one of her hands, frail as the claw of a young bird, yet surprisingly ingrained with black. Rose stared at it for a moment before wiping the sweat away, past rancor merging with a bitter kind of satisfaction.

Back in the kitchen, memory leaped out of the haze of the past. She seemed to remember seeing some sort of cord tied to the bottom of Florrie's bed. She hurried back to the hall. "Is there a rope anywhere?"

Cressida's face closed, but not before Rose had seen a flash of fear. "Oh, really," she exclaimed impatiently. "It's a way of helping with the pain, I think. You pull on something. I could tie a rope to the banister for you."

A faint flush crept across Cressida's face and something like gratitude or relief. "You'll find plenty of rope at the back of the house. In the stable block."

Rose picked up her cloak, swung it around her shoulders, hurried back to the kitchen, then went on into the yard. Shivering, she drew the cloak close. She passed a fowl run, and there in front of her was the stable block. She went toward it, thinking of Rundull, of the pale lichened walls of ancient stone curving around the castle, enclosing the stables snugly. How strange it seemed for Nicholas to be here in the midst of all this newness. Beyond, on the brow of the hill, great kauri pines stood like giants with totaras in front, their bark peeling in papery strips below the brownish yellow leaves.

It was then she saw the old Maori woman coming through the trees toward her. In one hand she held a flax kit. Her luxuriant hair, part gray, part ebony, hung free around her shoulders, and she wore the plain, shapeless mat of the common Maori. Rose halted. The woman padded nearer, silent in her bare feet.

"*Tenakoe.*" She was old, her face deeply lined and unusually dark. She was also extremely dirty and smelled vilely of damp wood and stagnant swamps.

"*Tenakoe,*" Rose replied politely. Then, speaking in Maori, "What do you want?"

The old woman gestured toward the house. "I come for picca-ninny."

Piccaninny. Baby. Child! "What do you mean?" Rose chattered in a frenzy of shock, all knowledge of the

Maori language evaporating. "What do you mean?" Everyone knew Maoris ate newborn baby girls. Te Puni had said he liked the flesh of children who had their milk teeth. Giles! Giles was here. Giles, who was cutting a tooth. Her knees wobbled with fright.

The woman moved on, scuffing her callused feet through the dust of the yard. Rose ran after her. "You can't go in," she shouted, grasping the woman's arm, trying without success to jerk her around to face the way she had come. The crone shook her off. "You can't go in," shrieked Rose, striding out in front, swinging around and waving her arms as though chasing a flock of sheep. "Go away. Go away."

But the Maori had an insidious way of sliding by.

Picking up her skirts, Rose dashed across the yard and through the kitchen door, slamming it behind her, leaning her full weight against it. No attempt was made to open the door. No sound at all came from outside. Rose waited with creeping alarm. Then her nerves split as a scream of sheer terror erupted from the hall. Picking up a poker, she flew out of the kitchen and down the passage. The old woman had come in through the front door. She was squatting on the floor beside Cressida. Rose's eyes flew to Giles's basket.

"Send her away! Send her away!" Cressida's eyes were staring from a blanched face. Rose move automatically forward, then paused. The Maori had taken a bundle of green leaves from her flax kit. With a calm and competent air she began carefully to unwrap them.

Slowly, Rose eased the poker down. Cressida, too, calmed. When the leaves had all been removed the native held a black sticky-looking mess in her hands. Cressida looked at Rose imploringly.

"I think you should taste it," said Rose uncertainly. "It might help." Cressida turned her face away. Then another pain came. She opened her mouth to cry out and the brown fingers slipped the mixture into her mouth. She collapsed in an all consuming sob. The Maori began undoing the buttons on Cressida's loose gown. Cressida's eyes, huge with fear, fastened on Rose's face.

The Maori reached into her kit and, bringing out something that looked like a stone, began to rub gently at the patient's lower back. A moment later, Cressida closed her eyes. The lines of agony in her face smoothed away. The Maori began muttering in a singsong voice, as though intoning a prayer or chant.

Giles was gurgling and kicking. That black memory of Chief Te Puni crawled up once more into Rose's mind. Her eyes slid over to the woman, intent on her self-imposed task. But what was her self-imposed task? To get the newborn baby and eat it? Well, it was not born yet. There was still time. And Giles was the important one. Giles with his sweet flesh and his milk teeth. Swiftly, she picked up the basket, and crept with it to the door on the opposite side of the hall.

29

Rose paused by the front door, brushing the leaves from her skirt, straightening her hair. She heard the mewling cry as she reached for the doorknob. She flung the door open. Cressida was still on the floor, her eyes closed, one arm flung wide. She looked as though she was dead. The Maori was on her feet, the infant in her arms. Rose came in like a tornado. The woman turned, her eyes coal-black circles in wrinkled sockets.

"Wahine" she said.

A girl. Afterward, Rose never knew exactly what happened, only that the naked slippery form of the child was clutched in her own arms and she was shouting, beside herself with terror, ordering the woman to go.

The Maori crouched, suddenly barbarous, wizened, tough, and sinewy. But she was old, and Rose was young and strong. Without taking her eyes off the woman, she managed to put the child down on the blanket, placing her roughly within the confines of Cressida's arms. Leaping up again, she flew at the murderer, thrusting the heels of her hands against those bony shoulders with a violence she had not known she possessed. "Get out!" she shrieked. "Get out!"

But the old savage was fast, and slippery as an eel. She took a step backward, then sideways, shouting Maori words Rose had not the time to translate, pointing to Cressida. Or to the baby. She lunged again. The Maori evaded her once more. Rose turned on her heels, her eyes scanning the walls. On the mantel was Nicholas's

gun. Rose dived. Her hands fastened on the cold metal
of the weapon she had no idea how to fire, and she
swung around, holding it high.

"Get out or I'll shoot you dead." The hag hurled
obscenities, but she did not move. Quivering, Rose advanced step by step and, reaching her, pushed the barrel
of the gun into the narrow, hollow chest. The face turned
ghoulish with evil and dislike. She began to back away.

Rose kept walking, forcing her down the passage toward
the kitchen. She backed slowly, still retaining her predatory crouch, an unintelligible babble of insults streaming
from her lips. They came to the kitchen. With one final
baleful glare the old woman lurched out of the back
door.

Rose trained the gun on her as she skulked across the
yard. A dozen times the crone stopped, swung around
screeching barbarously, then moved on. Rose did not
take her eyes off the shambling figure as she passed the
stables, the wood heap, the little group of native shrubs
that had been left when the house site was cleared. Then,
with a last threatening gesture, she slipped in among the
sparse trees on the outer edge of the forest, and disappeared into the gloom.

Five minutes passed. Ten. Rose lowered the gun, closed
the door, and went back inside. She was trembling and
sweat trickled wetly down her back.

Cressida was leaning on one elbow, the baby held in
her free arm. Rose gaped. "I thought you were dead."

The paper-white face twisted. "Oh, what a brutal creature you are."

"I didn't mean . . ." Rose was mortified that her exclamation of relief should have been so wantonly misunder-
stood.

Regaining a bitter kind of poise, Cressida said distantly, "I think I would have died without her."

"Of course you would not have died," Rose snapped.
"Why should you? There is something you ought to
know. Maoris eat girl babies." She placed the gun carefully on the floor and burst into tears.

"Only their own girls," retorted Cressida coldly. "Only
because girls are no use to them as warriors, and conse-
quently they don't want to feed them. Why should they
eat an English child?"

Rose swallowed, wiped her eyes with her sleeve.

"I tried to attract your attention to tell you the poor woman came to help, but you wouldn't look or listen. You were hysterical," said Cressida, enunciating her words with spiky clarity. The chill of them struck Rose to the very bone. "If you had learned the language you would have known what she was saying, that there was more to do. The gun was not loaded," Cressida added, stripping Rose of every vestige of dignity, "so I supposed you couldn't do too much harm, except of course to make an enemy of the Maoris, which I have no doubt you did. They do not forget insults, you know."

Her eyes filled with tears. "I've got a terrible pain. There is something called the afterbirth . . ." Her face crumpled and she fell back on the floor looking vulnerable again, and terribly frightened. When the spasm was over, she began again, "The woman did know what she was doing. She is, I am sure, an accredited midwife in the native sense. She was saying, I think, that she must get rid of the afterbirth." Cressida emitted a little wail of despair. "Now what am I going to do?"

Even in her pain and distress she excluded me, thought Rose bleakly afterward, knowing that together they would have managed somehow.

Leaving the gun where she had placed it on the floor, she turned and went numbly out of the room, impotent hatred stirring. She stood with one arm curled around a veranda post, her forehead pressed against the cold wrought iron. Stung to fierce resentment, she told herself she was glad the baby was a girl, that Nicholas would not be pleased. Then faintly through the silence came a familiar sound.

She leaned eagerly over the veranda rail, straining her eyes into the distance. They burst into view around a spur, two riders bent low over their horses' necks. She swung around the post, giddy with relief. They disappeared into a belt of trees, then reappeared flying up the slope toward the house.

With a little whoop of delight Rose ran down the steps and dashed eagerly across the new grass of the lawn, skirts flying. They raced right up to her, then leaped out of their saddles. The withers of their mounts were foam-flecked, the great bodies steaming. "She's had the baby,"

Rose cried. "She has had the baby. Oh, how glad I am you've come!"

"Had it, has she, by God!" exclaimed the doctor, wrestling with the straps on the pommel of his saddle as he tried swiftly to extricate his leather bag.

Looking at Nicholas, who was looking at her, Rose said, "Your wife's all right." She did not want to be the one to tell him the baby was a girl. Let Lady Cressida see the disappointment on his face, she thought, pain flaring from the wounds she had inflicted.

Nicholas thrust the reins into her hands. "Take them to the stables and rub them down. Can you do that? They're very hot and could take a chill. Give them a drink when they're cooler."

She stood there a moment with the reins in her hands, vengefully triumphant because Nicholas had put the welfare of the horses before his wife who had been so cruel to her.

When she had finished her task with care and pride, feeling, after the blundering ineptness of the morning, competent and useful, Rose sped back through the yard and into the house. One of the blankets still lay at the foot of the stairs, but Cressida and the baby had gone. She picked up her cloak. There was a sound upstairs and Nicholas came across the landing. She could tell by his closed expression he was thinking about the baby being a girl. Nicholas already had a son, she told herself fiercely. Nicholas had Giles.

At the bottom of the staircase he looked up, and their eyes met. He gave her a helpless, wry look and shrugged. "How do you come to be here?"

Misunderstanding, she replied, "I came for my cloak, and to get some water for the horses."

He nodded absently. They went together through the kitchen. In the wash house she waited while he found a bucket and filled it with water. They walked in silence to the stables. His face still wore the closed look.

The horses crowded him thirstily, jolting the bucket so that some of the water spilled. They tried to get their noses in together, slurping noisily, splashing. Suddenly the cob flung up his head, and with a great snort of satisfaction, showered her with the droplets that clung to his lips.

Nicholas laughed, and the dark look went. He put the bucket down. Still chuckling, he took a handkerchief from his pocket and wiped her face. She stood still as a mouse, her heart leaping as his arms went around her shoulders and waist, as she felt the pressure of his thighs against her flesh, the hardness of his ribs on her breasts.

"Oh, Nicholas," she whispered, her voice breaking with the loneliness of the long months of waiting, clinging to him in an agony of explosive tenderness. He began to love her, his lips hard and at the same time petal soft, his kisses slow and vibrant. His mouth traveled down her throat, his fingers digging urgently into the front of her gown. He lifted one breast, kissing it with a rage of tiny kisses that drove her out of her mind. Heaven alone knew what might have happened, then, she thought afterward, had not the mare emptied the bucket, and in a gesture of satiated relief, lifted it on her nose and tossed it into the air. It came down grazing the sleeve of Nicholas's jacket. He jerked away.

"Pas devant les chevaux," he said, switching the passion to pulsing laughter, and before she could ask him what he meant, added, "Oh God, Rose, how I miss you!" He buried his face briefly in her neck, squeezing her shoulders so hard they hurt.

"Your little boy is here, Nicholas," she said sweetly, all the love she felt for him there in the softness of her voice and the green of her translucent eyes.

"Here?" His dark brows shot up.

She slid an arm through his, warmly, covetously, drawing him with her to the door. "Come."

"Where are you going?" he asked, looking perplexed as she led him away from the house.

"I hid him. There was an old Maori woman here."

"Yes." Nicholas looked quizzically down at her. "Why did you drive the old girl away?"

"Because Maoris eat baby girls."

"Oh, I see. I must explain that to my lady wife." But already he had remembered the sewing afternoons in the thatched *whare* at Petone. The dainty clothes Cressida had made to encourage Maori women not to eat their daughters.

Rose told him as they crossed the clearing about meeting Sam Phelps. But not the other thing. Her pregnancy, which was, in a way, a betrayal. They picked their way deeper into the forest.

"What are you going to call your farm, Nicholas? It cannot be known forever as Mr. le Grys's estate."

In his gentlest mood, he asked indulgently, "What would you have me call it, Rose?"

"I would call it Rata Hill."

"Then Rata Hill it shall be."

"Look up," said Rose. He raised his eyes to a great *kauri* pine towering above them. "Once upon a time," said Rose softly, "a seed fell or was dropped by a bird into the fork of that branch, and a thin creeper grew out of it, downward, until it reached the earth where it made roots. Then, when the roots were established, it started upward again, wrapping its coils 'round the trunk, feeding on the mother tree, and sending out branches of its own, until, as you see is happening here, the host tree decayed and died and the rata became the tree, supporting itself."

They stood in silence for a moment. Nicholas frowned.

"Your son is lying in that hollow tree."

"They say the vine kills the tree in the end," he said.

Struck by the tone of his voice, she looked up sharply. His face wore a dark, withdrawn expression. Then he shrugged, smiling, and said, "Someone walked over my grave."

She laughed, liltingly. "Don't let them. Nobody has the right." They came up to the green curtain and she drew it aside. "It kills the host in the end," she agreed, "but not for years." She reached into the dark hollow heart of the tree and withdrew the basket. Giles blinked sleepily up at them. "Look at him," said Rose, running a finger gently through his curls. "Is he not a tiny copy of his father?"

Nicholas's hard features softened. He touched the rounded baby cheek. Giles looked back at him. "He is summing me up. Does he look at everyone like that?" Nicholas asked.

"He treats everyone differently. He adores Oliver, and cries when Daniel comes near."

"And how does he treat you, my love?"

"I think he feels superior to me," said Rose, accepting the fact with humility. "I think he knew, when he was born, that he was an aristocrat. I told you, didn't I, at the

time, that you should not have said what you said. I think
he is going to find it hard to forget."

Nicholas sat down in the curve of a fallen branch that
lay across the bole of the tree, and drew her down beside
him. She relaxed close against his side. "You are a funny
little thing."

Giles screwed up his eyes, opened his mouth, and
cried. Rose undid the front of her gown, bent down,
picked him up, and rained a shower of soft kisses on the
back of his neck. Then most tenderly she put him to her
breast. The leaves rustled softly and that curious flight-
less bird, the *weka*, came stealthily out of the undergrowth, head down, tail flitting, beady eyes alert. He
progressed right to their feet, hesitated, then pecked with
his strong beak at the toe of Nicholas's riding boot.

"Cheeky fellow."

"Don't you love their friendliness?"

A flicker of irritation crossed his face. "Birds belong in
trees."

"It's different here," said Rose softly. "Everything is
different."

"And you like it that way?"

"I had nothing to lose."

"What have you gained, Rose?"

She looked down at the baby. His dark eyes were
steadily on hers, his jaws working, the milk white around
his mouth. She struggled to find the words. "You are
nearer to me," she said at last. "Nearer in my heart," she
corrected herself.

They fell into a long, companionable silence. Giles
finished his meal and lay back in Rose's arms, his eyes
closing, the dark lashes making little fans on his creamy
cheeks.

"We had better go back." Nicholas heaved a sigh and
stood up, brushing the damp moss from his moleskin
smalls. He waited while Rose settled the baby, then
picked up the basket. They walked together out of the
deep shade into filtered sunlight, across the clearing, and
into the yard.

Dr. Stokes was in the kitchen. He turned to them a
face as black as thunder, and as threatening. "I would be
very much obliged if you would make my patient a cup of
tea, Mrs. Putnam," he said.

Rose glanced across at the stove. The kettle was already near to boiling. Her mouth buttoned up mutinously, the wounding affronts still stinging in her mind.

"And you, le Grys, I would like a word with you." He turned and marched out of the room. Nicholas put the basket down and followed him unhurriedly.

There was a plain brown teapot on a shelf, and beside it a tin of tea. A silver pot and a hot water jug stood on a tray together with a silver sugar bowl. Rose vacillated. She chose the brown pot. In a cupboard she found delicate china. Large, white kitchen cups hung on hooks. With a regretful sigh, she picked up a shell of a cup painted with flowers.

Through the drawing-room door she could hear the voices of the two men raised in anger. She went on up the stairs. As she reached the landing a door below was flung open. Looking over the banister, she saw the doctor hurrying out, bag in hand. She heard Nicholas say in a cold but very polite voice, "Your mount has been take care of. If you wait here I'll resaddle him."

"Don't bother. I'll do it myself. Good day to you. I will return this evening with a nurse, and if Mrs. Putnam is still here I will transport her home."

"I would be grateful. But where will you find a nurse?"

"I will bring someone," Dr. Stokes said, cold and convincing.

Rose paused to tap at the bedroom door, then opened it. Nicholas's wife was lying back on the pillows, the baby in a cot at the bedside. Rose crossed the room and put the tray down on the bedside table. Cressida's eyes noted that some of the tea had slopped from the spout.

"I'm sorry."

"Were you not instructed to set silver . . ."

"Your maid when she returns will no doubt bring you a tray properly prepared. The doctor asked me to fetch you a cup of tea. I have done that. I would have done it for anyone in the circumstances whose maid was not on hand," Rose said, burning with the insult of Cressida's manner. "Where is your maid, and the rest of the staff?"

"There is no staff," replied Cressida bleakly. "Only a boy who does odd jobs, but he went into the town today. They are all so independent . . ." She broke off, biting her lips, humiliatingly aware that she had been seduced by the girl's pretty voice and outrageous manner into speaking to her as an equal.

"I will stay until someone comes."

"There is no need."

Rose opened her mouth to say she was isolated here until the doctor returned, then with a certain regretful compassion closed it again. There was a little silver bell on the table. She placed it within the patient's reach, and went quietly out of the room.

I will not have her thinking of me as her servant, she said to herself indignantly, holding her head high as she went off down the stairs. Barney Herd is a whaler. Fred Quick is a sawyer. We are people, now. She may not like it, but she will have to put up with it. She went with quick, pattering footsteps and erect carriage into the kitchen, drew up a stool, and sat down to await Nicholas.

There were hoofbeats outside, as the doctor rode away, then Nicholas came through the door. He pushed it shut behind him and leaned against it, looking down at her. Several moments passed during which neither spoke. Rose became aware of the kettle steaming merrily on the hob. Of Giles making snuffling baby noises in his basket. Her heart swelled with such happiness she could scarcely breathe. It was as though they were together in their own home. She looked up, her eyes liquid with love.

"That's more like you," he said, smiling, "I have never seen you in a brown study before."

"I have taken your wife a cup of tea," she said. "Would you like one?"

"I would rather drink the baby's health. If you will come with me to the drawing room I will open a bottle of champagne. Have you ever tasted champagne, Rose?"

She lifted the basket, jumped up from the stool, and, dimpling delightedly, went with him.

"M'Lady says the child is to be called Beatrix," he said as they crossed the hall. "Is that a good name, Rose?"

"I daresay."

Upstairs, faintly through the open door, there came a clink of glasses and the sound of soft laughter.

Cressida's face twisted. She closed her eyes tightly, but the tears pushed through, trickling slowly down her cheeks. After a while she reached over the side of the bed and found the baby's tiny hand, then fell back on the pillows, still clasping it within her own. "Beatrix. To make happy," she whispered.

It was at once a hope and a prayer.

People were surprised and sympathetic when Rose did not immediately recover from her miscarriage. It was her first experience of invalidism and she contemplated with amazed pleasure the effect it had on her neighbors. They gave her seed packets sent from home, balsam and pansies and sweet william for her spring garden. Mrs. Stokes sent Oliver to the cottage bearing delicacies cooked with her own hands. Mrs. Revans, the wife of the managing editor of the *New Zealand Gazette,* which had been set up by subscription among the principal colonists, brought her copies of the paper.

Rose found herself acquiring a passionate interest in local affairs. She read about the Union Jack being hoisted in a northern town named for a gentleman called Lord Auckland, Governor General of India, about their own governor drinking the Queen's health at the foot of the flagstaff, about the Maori canoe races that followed, and the whaleboat races with gentlemen competing against sailors. She joined in the partisan indignation that Britannia, colonized first, had not these official excitements. She agreed they must somehow persuade the governor to come to see Britannia.

Milly Picton, a pretty Cornish girl who lived with her husband and baby in one of the cottages close by, came often to visit. She became Rose's first friend. While Rose rested, Milly would take their children out in a four-wheeled cart her husband had built for their boy.

It was a placid time. A time of growth. Rose accepted with amused grace the gifts brought to her by the neighbors in whom patronage had been born, and was slow to die.

30

───────◆───────

Spring came, and with it a gentling of the boisterous wind. The flower and vegetable seeds Rose had sown in her garden burst through the soil like green frills on a brown skirt. She had planted a bed of pansies on either side of the path that led to the front door. Pansies with smiling, welcoming faces to meet her as she approached. Daniel never smiled when she came in. Often he did not even look up.

Hollyhocks were to grow at either end of the veranda and verbena at the steps. Behind the cottage, by the henhouse, pumpkin seeds erupted into leaf, like tiny hearts, and the spinach was a thick fuzz of green.

"You must thin the plants out," Mrs. Stokes told Rose. But want had been bred into Rose's bones. Using the handle of a teaspoon, she lovingly edged the frail embryos free of their soil, then transplanted them with words of apology and encouragement into a new bed. The apple and pear pips she had brought from Rundull came sturdily through.

There was talk of a vast crate of books brought by the *Glenbervie,* donated to the New Zealand Company's immigrants by well-wishers in London. They were held in the company's store awaiting the erection of a library. Rose chafed at the delay. She asked Mrs. Stokes if the books could not be released.

"They will be released when they can be properly housed," the doctor's wife replied.

"I could house them," Rose offered eagerly. "I've got

room. Daniel could make shelves in our parlor. And in the passage. It is wide enough to take books on either side. I could start the library now." It came to her that by having a library in the cottage, she might even make some friends.

"Oh, my dear." Mrs. Stokes looked nonplussed. "There will be a committee of ladies set up to administer . . ."

"Why should the gentry administer it? Ladies have their own books."

Recovering, Mrs. Stokes said kindly, "Oliver can bring you any book you wish from my library, providing you look after it."

Rose turned away. "Providing I look after it," she repeated mutinously.

It was in Mrs. Stokes's library that she discovered Jane Austen, and a new world was opened up for her. She identified cursorily with the shy Fanny, suffering with her in her cold sitting room, praying that she might win Edmund. She named her pets after the characters. Beady-eyed Mrs. Norris sat on a clutch of eggs that, with luck, could produce a dozen chickens. Fanny, Maria, and Julia laid every day. Eli, whose name she had culled from the Bible, strutted cocksure among his plump wives and wakened everyone at dawn with his joyous crowing.

Each day, as she swept out the henhouse, chattering happily with the clucking inhabitants, Rose felt a renewal of pride of ownership. "You're all mine," she would say gloatingly, as she surveyed her brood, marveling at the miracle of her new life.

On the beach one day she came upon some boys teasing a small marmalade-colored kitten.

"It's our cat. We can do what we like wiv it," the biggest bully told her defensively.

"Folks who are unkind to animals may not have pets." Rose picked up the cowering creature, and fondled it protectively against her bosom. Gradually, its fast heart-beats quietened. The boys turned and walked away, their heads bowed, kicking sulkily at the sand with their toes. Rose tucked the kitten at the foot of Giles's basket and carried them home together.

She christened her diminutive pet with two drops of water from a cup. "I name you Edmund." Edmund, who might marry Fanny by the end of Jane Austen's book.

Within days, the furry skeleton showed signs of filling out. He gamboled happily around the cottage, patting little balls of wool, chasing his tail, drawing shouts of delighted mirth from the baby lying propped up by cushions on the veranda. Later, grown stronger, Edmund climbed up on the henhouse roof to clean himself in the sun and tease the fowls. But their shelter had been well constructed by Daniel's competent hands, and besides, Oliver brought the cat so much fish that he soon forgot his hunting instincts and grew sleek, fat, and lazy.

Then one day Flash Jack returned. Rose was sitting on her veranda putting the final touches to the sampler Nicholas had bought her in London. She saw the large-limbed, somehow majestic figure striding up the grassy slope, his luxuriantly wavy hair fluffing out beneath the bell-crowned hat set back on his head, and felt a little burst of excitement at seeing him again. He came right up the path without speaking, placed one hand on the rail, and bowed. "Good afternoon, Mrs. Putnam, I trust you are well."

Rose dimpled. "I thought you had gone away," she said innocently, knowing perfectly well he had not.

He ascended the steps slowly, deliberately, taking time to look around, anticipating change. Flash Jack noticed everything. Rose presumed that was why he gleaned the news before other people. Behind that relaxed air he was the most vigilant man she had ever known.

"Do sit down."

He lowered his big frame into the chair that stood nearby for Daniel's use, though Daniel never sat outside. "I have come to tell you the town is to change its name. There, you are first with the news."

Rose dropped her embroidery into her lap and looked at him, smiling, wondering if he really thought she cared to be the first to know, hoping he merely wanted an excuse to visit the cottage again.

"The directors of the company in London have decided we should honor the Iron Duke," Flash Jack went on, lighting a cheroot, blowing the smoke high, watching it drift away on the breeze. "Britannia, anyway, is a prodigiously stupid name, do you not think?"

"Britannia? For Great Britain? Why is that a stupid choice?"

"Because it makes plain the fact that we are forever an offshoot of the Old Country. May not our children's children consider we lacked enterprise?"

"I don't know what you mean."

He chuckled. "Your children may not, in a whole lifetime, even visit England. They will be true New Zealanders. Why should they feel they owe allegiance to England?"

"Are you saying we will become foreigners?" asked Rose doubtfully.

He considered her answer. "You have an original mind. I had not thought to become a foreigner myself."

"Original? Is that an insult or a compliment?"

"A compliment, I assure you. But, in saying that, I must add a warning. The possession of an original mind will not necessarily smooth your path through life, my dear Rose."

She waited for him to explain, but his silence obliged her to speak. "Who is the Iron Duke? I am sorry to appear ignorant, but I don't know."

He shifted in his seat, smiled a little. "Have you not heard of Waterloo?"

"Of course." But she had not.

"Then you know the Duke of Wellington was the hero of that battle?"

She stabbed her needle into the linen. "Women do not like war. Don't you know that?" And, without waiting for a reply, "I would prefer the town should continue to be called Britannia rather than be named after a man who makes wars. However," she shrugged, "nobody is likely to take any notice of me."

"I am willing to wager that before long you will be making people take notice." Flash Jack spoke with such considered gravity that she looked up sharply but he did not elaborate.

"Alain. I want to ask your advice."

"Please do. I am flattered."

"You know, don't you, that a library is about to be built?"

He nodded.

"The committee is to be composed of the gentry. But the gentry have books of their own. Should it not be administered by those who need the books? It is not that

I have no books," she explained hurriedly. "Mrs. Stokes is very kind in loaning them to me, but if the library is for the use of the people . . ." She stopped, nonplussed by the tiny smile playing about Flash Jack's mouth. But he was watching the kitten.

"Since I have been here, I have come to dislike patronage," Rose rushed on. "I wish to be independent. I think those books, which were never intended for the use of the gentry, should be unpacked and used by those who need them. Do you think it would be . . . impertinent, I think Mrs. Stokes would . . ." She stopped as their eyes met.

"Yes," he said. "Yes, like Mrs. Stokes, I think the ladies of the Library Committee would consider your intrusion impertinent. But, unlike Mrs. Stokes, I do not myself think it impertinent. Is that the answer you want, Rose?"

"Oh." She had been unaware of the fact that she was holding her breath. Now she let it out slowly. "What should I do, then? Can you tell me what to do, Alain?"

"Get the common people on your side."

"The common people do not like me much," said Rose with raw honesty.

"Only because you are different. People are afraid of what they do not understand."

As summer approached, a small parcel of wool went to London and the *Gazette*, now renamed the *New Zealand Gazette and Wellington Spectator*, trumpeted delightedly that the colony's first wool had realized two shillings a pound. The sheep farmers, admittedly on appropriated land, were nonetheless on their feet. More sheep and cattle arrived from England and New South Wales. A new vessel came every three days. They brought sugar, spices, exotic groceries, coal from the Middle Island, flour from Sydney.

The brick kiln flourished. Solid-looking public buildings rose on strong foundations. Roads began to appear where muddy tracks had wound before. There was great happiness among the assisted immigrants. Children who had never known waste carelessly tossed away pork bones they had not bothered to gnaw clean. They ran barefoot on the beaches, grew brown and wild and confident.

They stuffed themselves on apples and peaches and pears carefully wrapped during the summer glut, and hoarded in boxes to be enjoyed during the short, sunny winter months. The whalers and traders across Cook Strait, who had been settled there for twenty years, had orchards galore. Even the Maoris of Petone planted fruit trees now.

"It is going to be so different for our youngsters," parents sighed happily. They saw their boys as sheep farmers all, striding their own acres, traveling in horse-drawn carriages from their homes into town.

But the rich and ambitious did not want for discontent. The ballot for land had proved unsatisfactory. Some families found themselves in possession of estates forty miles away, while absentee landlords, Englishmen persuaded by Edward Gibbon to invest in his venture, obtained remote possession of valuable blocks that lay fallow in the center of the town. "Eyesores," people called them. An insult to those intrepid spirits who had the courage of their convictions and crossed the ocean for their claims.

There were more stormy meetings in Barratt's Hotel, and a group of dissidents embarked in the wake of the town planners and surveyors for Wanganui, said to be a hundred and twenty miles to the north, where the land was considered fertile and the natives more cooperative. There had been trouble lately with the Wellington Maoris. The novelty of the blankets and baubles and gold having worn off, some of them wanted their land back. Settlers talked themselves hoarse trying to make the troublemakers understand the meaning of a bargain signed and sealed. Native extremists burned down several houses in the Hutt Valley. Others contented themselves with trying to stop the surveys, ransacking gardens, frightening women alone in their houses.

Then there was the problem of the native reserves in the town area. The Maoris' habitations were slovenly and dirty. Could not Colonel Wakefield remove the town natives with their horrible *whares* to an outlying district?

"No," he replied uncompromisingly. "The arrangement was that they should retain one tenth of the town for their own use. One tenth of all lands." It was sheer bad luck if one drew a section adjacent to a native reserve. The unlucky families waxed indignant to no avail.

A series of advertisements appeared in the press, announcing that five hundred mechanics and laborers were wanted in Auckland. Top wages would be paid. The whole town erupted. Vociferous blame settled on Mr. Shortland's head, for rumor said he had put word around that there was no work to be had in Wellington. Irritation changed to fury when it was discovered that ships paid for out of public revenue were to be sent to pick up the skilled tradesmen wanted for the building of the new capital. Employers were angrily reduced to raising wages in order to keep their skilled men.

Colonel Wakefield, incensed, tore up Governor Gipps's announcement that his land purchases were invalid. Hobson was arranging for land commissioners to sort out the claims. That was the last straw. Another mass meeting was held and an appeal drafted to Queen Victoria, demanding the recall of Governor Hobson on the grounds that he was inept, weak, and kowtowing to the natives at the expense of the whites; that he was under the influence of the greedy missionaries who had grabbed huge holdings of land for themselves. The list of his sins and omissions went on and on. The fact that he had declared Auckland the most central position for the seat of government, without traveling further south to see the thriving town of Wellington, proved him to be wrongheaded, incompetent, and a cad. Fearing the letter would not arrive if conveyed through the proper channels, they sent it via Valparaíso, defiantly, and with conscious disrespect, passing a copy to Hobson in Auckland.

"We could go to Auckland on a free passage," suggested Daniel, not looking at Rose, already wearing an expression of partial defeat.

She knew he wanted a fresh start where they were unknown. Where Flash Jack could not call on her, and without the ever present ghost of Nicholas. "The government is offering no more than Alain already pays you," she replied, picking up Nicholas's baby, who must never be separated from his father, holding him close against her heart.

Nicholas had acquired two more horses. His stables were now completed, and he had bought a solidly built buggy for transporting Cressida and the baby into town. The

Woolege family was sending all manner of things: a pony cart; Charmy, Cressida's mare; her favorite dog; and two young cats bred at Saxon Mote.

Paddy's son Ben moved into the newly completed accommodation over the stables. Anxiously meeting ships in his search for a married couple who would work as cook and handyman, Nicholas arrived home with three young farm laborers.

"Please, cannot you manage without all these men?" Cressida asked him, desperation in her eyes at the thought of cooking for six. Nicholas had always had help on the land, but still she had none for the house. Several of the ladies had tried to train Maori maidens, but the scrubbing and delousing was more than Cressida could face, particularly when she heard they were anyway slovenly in their work and incomparably lazy.

Nicholas said apologetically, "I must take what offers when it offers, my dear." With a thousand acres to clear and lay down in grass, there was no time to be lost. In this climate of warm rain and sunshine, burnt-off forests could erupt into fern at a frightening pace.

"Do you not understand that I am still weak from the birth of the child?"

Of course he did. To understand and yet be unable to produce a miraculous remedy was a frustration in itself. Hands in his pockets, coattails tossed over his forearms, Nicholas paced up and down the drawing room, eyeing the unpolished floorboards surrounding his wife's exquisite Persian carpet. Sometimes, looking on the comic mix of the old and the new, his sense of the ridiculous set him laughing out loud. But today he was grim. "I am having to understand a good deal about life that was not required of me before," he replied, avoiding those big, pathetic eyes. "We are breaking new ground, m'Lady. We must learn to think as pioneers, forgetting entirely the concept of life at home. I, too, wish that moving into a large house automatically meant there was a flood of servants from which to choose, but unfortunately they cannot be produced at the wave of a magic wand."

"With the best will in the world I cannot see myself as a mix of lady of the manor and cook, housemaid, and nurse. Can you not see that you ask too much of me?"

"By the same token," Nicholas pointed out without

self-pity, "I must pose as steward, handyman, shepherd, groom, and laborer."

Cressida turned her face away. "Oh, how hard you are! How cruel!"

He crossed the room and stood before her, hands on her shoulders. "Would you like to go home?" he asked compassionately. "I will send you back to England with the child if that is what you want."

She shrugged his hands away. "Such empty promises you make! You know I cannot leave you. That I would not be welcome at home. My people—and yours too—consider that a wife is bound to her husband by duty."

"Duty!" There was a queer twist to Nicholas's mouth. He went to the window and stood looking out over the rolling hills and forests, over the land that in spite of everything was beginning to clutch at his heartstrings.

"I should have thought that woman . . ."

He turned sharply. "I did not invite 'that woman,' as you call her, to assist at your confinement, madam. But the fact remains that you would have been in a pretty pickle had she not arrived. It is over now, and with luck," Nicholas's mouth twisted again, "the situation will not arise again."

"I am bound to meet her in public places," Cressida burst out distressfully. "If your heart was in the right place you would persuade her husband to take up the offer of employment in Auckland."

"I would deem it disloyal in the extreme, m'Lady, while feeling is running so high over the government's dastardly crimping, to encourage any skilled workman to go to Auckland," said Nicholas, still smarting from her reaction to his ill-considered offer.

She blew her nose on a small handkerchief. The crumpled lace edging, which had not seen a flatiron in months, was hard and rough.

"You seemed to have immense spirit when we met," he said.

"Do you not know that courage comes from a sense of being wanted and loved?" Suddenly, she cried out in a way that wrung his heart, "I am so lonely. I have nothing and nobody. No family. I have a child to care for, and no more than my natural instincts to guide me. It is not enough, Nicholas. Can you not see how lost I am?"

Nicholas sat down beside her and put a gentle arm around her shoulders. "I will do my utmost to find a man whose wife we can employ as cook," he said. "I do not know what we can do about a nursemaid. Why do you not send for the dragon who brought you up? She will no doubt set the whole colony to rights, including the government."

He jumped to his feet, lifted the lid of Cressida's little writing cabinet, and laid a sheet of paper down with a quill pen beside it. "Write today, and I will ride into town with the letter. Let us have the ogre. At least she will be loyal, and as I recall, far too hatchet faced and grim to attract the snatch of even the most desperate bachelor."

He went out to saddle his horse, wishing things could somehow right themselves by magic, while he put his attention to his farm.

31

As if by magic, Cressida's problem was solved that day. Dispatching the request for her old nurse to travel out and join them, Nicholas came face to face in the post office with a demurely dressed young woman who looked at him boldly from hazel-colored eyes.

The postmaster said, "Mr. le Grys, this young lady is looking for a situation. I have heard you are in need of staff."

It was as easy as that. Too easy, as Nicholas later realized. The girl said her name was Tilly Bird. No one believed that was her own name, and neither did anyone believe her story. She said she had emigrated to New South Wales as a servant, then worked her way across to New Zealand as a cook, in order to escape from the rough elements of Australian society.

It was soon patently clear that the girl had no cooking experience. Cressida set out to teach her all she knew. It was the blind leading the blind, but such was the girl's wit and intelligence that she soon mastered all Cressida could convey and, left to her own devices, dealt with the mysteries of the temperamental stove. After several evenings studying the receipt book, she turned out a tolerable pudding.

Cressida, quick-wittedly noticing the mark of a ring on the third finger of her otherwise sun-browned left hand, deemed it politic to keep her discovery to herself.

Black-haired, with delicate cheekbones, a small pointed chin, and an elegant way of walking, Tilly Bird reminded

Nicholas of a young, sleek cat. And she was watchful and wary as a cat, too. Because of lack of communications, riders often came unheralded to outlying districts, confident they would be accorded an enthusiastic welcome. Life could be lonely for the wives. Tables would be cleared after tea to make room for dancing, and when everyone was happily exhausted there would be singing around the pianoforte, followed by cake and wine. But Tilly Bird, on such occasions, was never there to help. She was always the first to spy a conveyance or a rider approaching up the long hill. Then, as though she was the soul of tact, she would disappear. She never reappeared until after the visitors had gone.

"What shall we call her?" Cressida wondered, reminded of that shaming confrontation with the husband of her erstwhile maid. "It seems we may not now address the lower classes by their surnames, and I cannot with dignity call the girl Tilly."

"Lower class?" queried Nicholas dryly. Tilly Bird did indeed drop her aitches, but only when she remembered to do so.

Cressida ignored his show of skepticism. "I shall call her by her full name," she decided.

Tilly Bird was indefatigable. With her curls bobbing outside her housemaid's cap, she sped lightly around the house, cleaning, washing and polishing, singing prettily to herself when she thought no one was listening. Once, when Cressida and Nicholas returned from visiting a neighbor, they found music sheets in disarray in the pianoforte stool. Curious beyond bearing, Cressida ventured, "It must be lonely for you here, Tilly Bird. Would you like me to give you some pianoforte lessons so that you might amuse yourself when we are out?"

"No thank you, m'Lady. I am far too busy," Tilly Bird replied pleasantly. There was never another sign that she had touched the instrument.

When told guests had been invited, Tilly Bird would ask for the visitors' names. "As though she has a right to know," Cressida remarked to Nicholas. She was amused by the girl's confident manner of speaking, her level-eyed look when she asked. The two women became good friends. Cressida found herself unburdening her problems, knowing instinctively that nothing would be repeated. But it was like talking to a sponge. She grew accustomed to the fact that her servant offered nothing in return.

Paddy's son Ben proved an energetic and amiable handy-man, grooming the horses, keeping the stables clean and the harness bright, ready with a never-ending supply of kindling and firewood for the greedy stove. When Cressida returned with a plant or a packet of seeds given to her by a generous neighbor, she had only to show her prize to Ben and he would go cheerfully for his spade. The kitchen garden was magnificent with its long rows of pearl-green turnips side by side, with beans running skyward at tremendous speed, with corn already splitting to show gleaming golden cobs, with little sugar beets.

Nicholas's team of tree-fellers worked like beavers. The cleared land daily encroached on the bush. All around, all the time there were little drivels of smoke as the fire ate into tree stumps, leveling them to a black patch that would turn green with amazing speed. Plans were already in hand for building a woolshed, so that next year Rata Hill could do its own shearing.

Cressida grew more cheerful. There was time in the evenings now for her to change her clothes and arrange her hair before Nicholas returned. Time also to rest a little after feeding the baby. The rest brought her strength; the company, good humor. Nicholas would come in to find his bath already run. At first he was amazed, then pleased. "With a little more practice you will make an excellent valet," he said.

Cressida flushed prettily.

Word came that the long awaited pony cart from Saxon Mote, Cossack, Charmy, the dogs, and the cats had arrived, along with a consignment of furniture for the house. Leaving Beatrix in the capable hands of Tilly Bird, Cressida and Nicholas hurried into town. Brought up, as they both were, with the charm of old stones, old wood, and the ghosts of bygone generations, it was the brash newness of their surroundings that somehow offended them. Old and familiar possessions would add a patina to Rata Hill. Standing together on the pier while the ever present wind tugged at Cressida's riding habit, threatened her black beaver hat, and tugged at her veil, watching with intense shared excitement as their animals were conveyed to the shore in a punt, they forgot their differences. Nicholas felt for Cressida's hand, caught her fingers, and squeezed them.

The horses came down a ramp with their heads tossing, their manes flying, the incoming tide swirling around their fetlocks. As soon as they cleared the water, Nicholas and Cressida ran forward, grasping the halter ropes, greeting them with affectionate cries of welcome.

Nicholas's eyes were soft as he gentled his favorite. "Remember me, old boy?" Cossack lifted his head and looked at the new land, trying out his strong feet in the sand. He flicked his long tail, tangled now for want of grooming, nuzzled his velvet lips at Nicholas's fingers. Charmy seemed nervous. She had not enjoyed the voyage, the sailors said, but there was no doubt she was pleased to find her mistress. She, too, lifted her hooves, stamping them daintily, tossing her mane, looking at the gathering crowd with nervous astonishment.

Nicholas noticed the brightness of his wife's eyes, how her cheeks glowed as she fondled the mare, scratching behind her ears, blowing gently into the mole-soft nostrils. He knew he was grinning from ear to ear like a schoolboy, but he could not help it. The cob had been adequate, but he was not Cossack.

Then the dogs were brought in. There was an uprush of excitement as Herod and Bertie, catching sight of Cressida, strained at their leashes. Slavering with excitement as the punt came nearer, they lost their wits and tried to jump into the sea. Then Bertie broke away from his handler, and in an ecstasy of welcome hurled his big, fluffy body at his mistress. Nicholas let go of Cossack's reins and caught Cressida as she lost her balance. For a moment they were clasped tightly in each other's arms, the dog battering them both with his big front paws. Nicholas, laughing, held her a moment longer than was necessary. She felt warm, soft, and yielding.

They trotted home together, Charmy between the shafts of the pony cart with Cressida at the reins, the hack she had ridden into the town and Nicholas's cob trotting behind on leading reins. The cat basket lay on the floor at her feet, two furry faces gazing big-eyed through the bars. Nicholas rode his gelding. The two dogs bounced around them, leaping up on their hind legs, barking, racing ahead.

"Do you know, I rode in this cart on my nurse's knee," Cressida said contentedly, running her free hand across the familiar buttoned leather of the seat.

Nicholas refused Cossack full rein. "You've been cooped up too long, old boy. You're unfit. Take it easy awhile."

Herod proved unequal to the long run to Rata Hill, but Bertie the Irish setter refused to give in. He arrived exhausted and fell asleep, looking blissfully at home, on the drawing room carpet. Ivor, the spaniel, having finished the journey on the floor of the cart, went on to explore the house with enormous interest, sniffing at the unfamiliar scents, dashing upstairs and down, pushing doors open with his nose.

That evening, as they finished reading their copious mail and began happily unwrapping copies of *The Times, John Bull, Blackwoods Magazine,* and all the other reading matter that was no less welcome for being six months old, Nicholas looked across at his wife. "Let's hold a Christmas ball," he said impulsively. "It is time we had a housewarming."

Radiantly, Cressida returned Nicholas's smile. "A ball! What a good idea!"

"Tilly Bird!" he shouted, driving his voice across the hall and down the passage toward the kitchen. He added, frowning, looking at his wife, "I thought we were going to have some bells installed."

"It seemed to be tempting fate at the time," Cressida smiled. "But perhaps we should now. Tilly Bird, I am sure, would prefer not to be shouted at."

The girl, looking considerably less like a maid than a happy young member of the household, came at a run, with one of the cats in her arms.

"We were thinking of holding a ball," said Nicholas. "Could you manage supper for . . ."

The glowing face went still, its color receding.

Cressida broke in nervously, "I will, of course, give you all the help I can."

The young face remained closed.

Some sixth sense, some seed of self-preservation born of the long months of weariness and despair, awakened in Cressida's mind. "You would not, of course, be expected to serve the guests. I was thinking of cold meats, salads, and fruitcakes." Nicholas watched her with amused cynicism.

Tilly Bird smiled. "Ask as many people as you wish, m'Lady. I am sure we can manage."

When she had left the room, still with the cat in her arms, and Bertie huffing importantly at her heels, Nicholas's eyes met Cressida's thoughtfully. She looked away, saying in a rush, "How lovely it will be for us to have such an entertainment. It is high time we returned some of the hospitality we have received."

Nicholas arose and closed the door. "I think we should talk," he said quietly. "That girl is not, never was, a servant. I have for some time suspected that we have a fugitive on our hands."

Cressida looked up sharply, traces of panic in her face. "It's none of my business. Nor yours."

"As responsible citizens, we must consider it our business."

"Then in this matter you must consider me irresponsible," retorted Cressida defiantly. "I do not care if she has robbed Windsor Castle and murdered the guards. I will defend her to the death. She is my cook and my friend, Nicholas. She is a person I cannot do without. You have said yourself we must cut our coats according to our cloth. I have done that."

Guiltily, he considered the hardships she had endured, the loneliness. "But if she has done wrong . . ."

"If Tilly Bird turns out to be the runaway lady of our own governor, he shall be sent from here with a flea in his ear, but he shall not have her back," Cressida declared extravagantly. "You have said I lack spirit. Look to the spirit I am showing now!"

"Defiance suits you." He smiled tightly, turning away with an ache in his heart, remembering that other face, the one that was always full of life. "Very well. We will leave the matter for a while," he said. He did not like the idea of employing a fugitive gentlewoman in his house. The colony threw up some deuced awkward situations, there was no doubt.

Down in the town there was an echo of his sentiments. One evening a young artisan and his wife called on the

Putnams. Unaccustomed as she was to visitors, Rose met them at the door, eager and bright eyed. The man introduced himself as Sam Woodward. "Mr. Wilshire told me you're interested in the library. He said you might have some ideas about gettin' it goin'. Me wife here and me are keen readers but we've got nothin' to . . ." He stopped talking with a grin because Rose was clapping her hands in delight.

"Please come in. Do please come inside." Thrilled, sparkling, aquiver, she ran ahead of them. Daniel was sitting in his straight-backed chair staring, as usual, at the wall. She cried exuberantly, "Daniel, jump up, jump up, we have visitors. They've come to talk about getting the library started."

As though they had mentioned treason, he picked up his outdoor boots, which lay where he had dropped them on the floor beside his chair, and slunk off to bed.

Rose's advertisement in the *Gazette* caused a furor. The gentry's response varied from chilly amazement to downright hostility.

"The working classes think they can run a library without help!"

"A meeting of artisans and their wives in the coffee room at Barratt's Hotel? A meeting of *artisans!*"

Daniel was at work when the deputation of ladies called upon Rose. They stood at her front door, a solid bank of well-corseted flesh and muslin, their virtuous expressions beneath the nodding plumes of their bonnets obliquely softened by the warp of their patronizing smiles.

In a flurry of confusion, Rose invited them into the parlor. The one who had introduced herself as Mrs. Sheraton had evidently been chosen as spokeswoman. She pointed to a low stool positioned before a chair. "Sit here, my dear," she said. Then, with great dignity, she seated herself in the chair.

It flashed through Rose's mind, with volatile resentment, that this was her house.

"Come, my dear," said the visitor sharply.

Never in her life, except for her brief little outburst to Lady Cressida over the tea tray, had Rose defied a member of the gentry. To her horror, she found herself moving toward the stool, but before she could sit down there was the sound of a man's step on the path outside, followed by the stamp of heavy feet on the veranda boards. She turned quickly. With polite, irritated expressions, the ladies also glanced toward the door.

Flash Jack's voice rang through the cottage. "Mrs. Putnam." He was already in the open doorway to the parlor, one hand raised to the lintel, the other at his hip. "Well, ladies," he said, speaking genially, though there was a kind of violence in his manner, "I am sorry to break up this little meeting, but I must take Mrs. Putnam away." He turned to Rose. "Your husband is in a bit of bother."

Rose's eyes flew wide.

"Just a small accident," he explained kindly. He turned his attention to the visitors. "My humble apologies, ladies. Perhaps Mrs. Putnam will invite you another day when it is more convenient." His eyes glinted like steel. "It might be better to come one at a time, though. That would be a fairer deal."

Rose stood in the little hall as the ladies left, her head spinning, her hands trembling with the aftermath of shock. Flash Jack had taken over so suddenly and so forcefully she scarcely felt it was her place to say good-bye.

"Mrs. Beck," he said as that lady bustled disconcertedly out. "Mrs. Norman." He inclined his head. "Mrs. Charge. Mrs. Wright." Another bow and this time, with no attempt to hide an ironical smile, "Mrs. Sheraton. Good day to you all."

He stood watching them until the last one reached the end of the path, bowed again deeply, then turned to Rose.

She looked up at him mistrustfully, her eyes dancing, her lips twitching. "Daniel . . . ?"

"No, of course not." He grinned. "I heard the cannibals were on their way up the lane. Luckily, news travels fast to my store. Having tipped you into this, I felt duty-bound to haul you out."

She collapsed into a chair laughing uncontrollably. "It was terrible. I didn't dream . . . But I thought I would be able to . . ."

"Ah, Rose, you overestimate yourself," said Flash Jack compassionately, planting a cheroot between his lips and lighting a lucifer match. "You lack cunning. That is your problem. It takes years of experience to defeat the velvet-gloved bullies from the shires, and you aren't ready for the fray—may never be ready, for it is an art form to which they are born. They have jostled for position and bossed each other all their lives. One woman like that can crush a small rose such as you with her little finger." He added whimsically, "I wonder why they bothered to come as an army."

"You said people are afraid of me," she supplied, feeling confused.

"I said people are always afraid of what they do not understand. That is another matter."

"I have no desire to run the affairs of the town," Rose said, still trying to unravel his words. "I only want some books to which I believe I have a right. Don't you see, I don't wish to be beholden to the likes of them."

"Nor should you be." Flash Jack's weather-lined face was suddenly grave. He paused, looking down at her with a curious sadness in his eyes. "You have a certain strength and tenacity for what you want, have you not, Rose?"

"Perhaps." Again, she scarcely knew what he meant.

Then he surprised her by saying, as he gave her arm a squeeze, "Be sure you do not want too much. And be doubly sure you want what is right for you."

She knew he was not talking about the library now. There was a look in his eyes as though he wished to see into her heart. Her mind flew to Nicholas, and she wondered if Flash Jack knew. It is none of his business, she thought passionately. It is nobody's business but ours.

The Rata Hill ball was a great success. Leo brought in wild suckling pig ready for the oven, and legs of lamb. Tilly Bird, Ben, and Cressida worked for days beforehand getting the food ready. The reception rooms were bowers of scented greenery, scarlet with the splash of rata blossoms, and delicately white where starry clematis had been twined.

The officers of the 80th Regiment, which had after all not been needed as protection and was preparing to rejoin its unit, rode out resplendent in red jackets and gold braid. It was like a small cavalry charge, Cressida thought with excitement as she watched them cantering up the slope toward the house in early twilight, leaving the buggies and gigs to labor along behind. Sam Phelps, persuaded into upholstering his dray with an enormous *manuka* mattress, conveyed a jolly party of mothers and daughters, as well as a young man who brought his accordion.

Jerningham Wakefield and the young bloods from Clay Castle arrived together on sweating steeds. Flinging one leg over the saddle and leaping to the ground, Jerningham cried in his exuberant way, "I thought you would not mind an old friend's gatecrashing. My uncle is on his way, but too circumspectly for my taste. We left him a long way back."

"Of course we would have invited you," Cressida said, surprising him with her show of warmth. "We had thought you were in Wanganui."

"Even to such outposts of the empire as Wanganui news of great import will filter through," replied Jerningham, bowing deeply. "I have brought you a ham, cured with my own hands. It is the first of many. The natives supply me well with pigs. I look forward to a brisk trade on the coast."

"How very kind." The hams imported from England were arriving now in such bad shape that no one would buy them.

Those who already knew the house led the others upstairs to shed their cloaks and readjust windblown coiffures. "My one servant has worked so hard for your benefit I have had to send her to rest this evening," Cressida told them, "so you must make your own way." She smiled charmingly. "But you have all become so independent. I am sure you would prefer not to have to submit to such tiresome attentions as you have left behind at home."

"Some of those dames were laughing through their tears," Nicholas remarked as they turned away, eyeing his wife with a whimsical look. She was dressed in a low-cut gown of pale gold silk, and she wore the Woolege ruby necklace, with more rubies dangling from her ears. The late setting sun had caught the gold of her hair and fired the gems. The flowers behind her, yellow banksia roses and honeysuckle climbing sturdily up the veranda posts, might have been deliberately arranged by an artist's hand. She was aglow like a fire on a winter's night.

She was another Rose. He felt the warmth stirring in his loins, and his arm slid around her. She looked up at him, her lips parted, her eyes, by a curious trick of light, verging on sea-green in the shadowy light.

Then someone called in a merry, teasing voice, "Nicholas, old chap, you have the rest of your life in which to admire your lady. The musicians wish to know if they may tune up."

He turned aside, ruefully, and the moment was gone.

The amateur band was pronounced magnificent. One of the guests had brought his violin, another a flute. The dancers swept through the hall and onto the veranda. The stars came out, bigger and brighter than anyone remembered, and the full moon rose, a pale gold ball. The scent of the dewy grass, roses, and trees filled the air. Mr. Lyon, who had had an official sowing of the first Scotch thistle at his Petone farm on St. Andrew's Day, caused a happy stir by arriving in his kilt. He marched up and down the lawn at midnight playing a lament on the bagpipes.

The lavish supper was the object of many congratulations. They exclaimed at Cressida's amazing efficiency. "And you have a cook! You must be the last household in the colony with such a luxury."

"I have been lucky," she agreed serenely.

"I do not believe the woman is exhausted," one of the guests chided her playfully. "I believe you have hidden her in case one of us should steal her away."

Cressida, her face flushed from a Scottish reel, her eyes bright, nodded lightheartedly. "I would trust none of you to meet her. You are right."

They danced until they were exhausted. As the sun lightened the eastern sky, the guests saddled their horses, climbed into their gigs and buggies, and trundled off down the slope calling their weary good-byes. Nicholas, finding Sam Phelps in a drunken sleep beneath the *totara* tree, threw away his empty bottle and went to get help.

Ben was in the kitchen tentatively sampling leftover champagne. He looked up shamefacedly as Nicholas entered. Nicholas jovially clapped him on the back. "Come, drink a toast with me." He filled another glass and raised it high. "To you, old fellow, and Tilly Bird. What would we have done without you both?" He tossed down his own drink, though knowing he had had enough, and waited, chuckling good-humoredly, while Ben choked the bubbles from his throat and nose. "Now help me to get old Sam up into his seat. He's a scallywag, but I'm told he drives equally well, drunk or sober." He put his glass down on the table, already regretting his courtesy to the boy, for the extra glass had gone swiftly to his head.

Host and hostess stood at the veranda rail, arms entwined, watching the last guests go. "I love you," said Cressida, leaning her head against his shoulder, gazing up into his face. Her golden hair merged fuzzily with the roses that climbed the post behind her. Nicholas pressed one of them gently against her cheek. "Rose," he said.

There was a flash of uncertainty in her eyes, then she felt, or smelled the rose, and she smiled faintly, with hope.

He slid both arms around her waist, dragging her against him. "Tonight," he said with rising excitement, "we will beget another son."

"We have a daughter," she said, showing faint distress in the trembling of her lips, her eyes beseeching.

He looked down at her blankly, the dream shattered, his mind again crystal clear. "Ah, yes. To bed." He was suddenly unbearably tired.

Some of the more affluent immigrants were now putting their money into goods, importing and selling merchandise of every description. Good black satin stocks, London-made boots and shoes, ladies' kid gloves could all be had at any one of three stores. The ladies were thrilled because John Telford, banker turned store owner, was giving a big dinner for the opening of his new building, inviting all the leading colonists. Wellington was becoming positively gay.

There were picnics in the little bays as more and more families acquired their own boats. People with houses close to the shore managed to make a lawn flat enough for croquet.

How strange and novel was that first sunny Christmas! The weather was too hot for traditional food, but they cooked and ate it nonetheless. Children, freckled and tanned, splashing happily in the warm sea, were dragged home protesting, to be stuffed with hot baked ham and black plum pudding. There was more food on the tables now than the working classes had ever dreamed of.

They did not allow Rose to take charge of the library books but she and the lively young Woodwards, bringing themselves onto the committee, nonetheless forced the hands of the ladies to the extent that the reading matter was unpacked and distributed usefully. In the eyes of the working classes, Rose gained stature. The gentry, hiding their resentment, began to treat her with a soupçon of unwilling respect.

New Year was celebrated in English style. Fat bullocks were slaughtered, bells rung, cannons fired, flags hoisted. Plans were made to celebrate the arrival of the first settlers with an anniversary fête. In an attempt to restore good feeling, they persuaded the Maoris to hold a canoe race. Prize money was offered. Rice with sugar, considered by the natives to be exotic and delectable, would be provided for a feast. Then there would be an artisans', or, as they preferred to call it, a "popular" ball, staged in a large warehouse on Te Aro beach.

When she heard of the ball, Rose plotted and dreamed. Daniel would never go. But she would see Nicholas on the day, for Mrs. Stokes had said the gentry would certainly attend the popular outdoor events. Rose's spirits were sky-high that afternoon, as she cooked a batch of scones for Molly Picton, who was ill, made her some tea, and walked down to the edge of town with Giles and Billy Picton in the baby cart.

At the end of the beach, a track ran away through the bush to a clearing. It was a warm day, golden with butterflies, and bright with sunlight. She laid her rug on the grass, lifted the babies out of the cart, then settled herself in a comfortable niche between two exposed tree roots, with her back to the boles and her skirts spread around her. She was half asleep, dreaming of Nicholas, when a rustle of footsteps broke into her consciousness. She opened her eyes slowly, smiling as Oliver came toward her. He was a good-looking boy now that his face had filled out, his legs grown sturdy. Even his hair, which had been mouse-colored, had bleached to a attractive pale blond. The pasty whiteness of his complexion had darkened to a handsome tan.

"How did you know I was here?" Rose asked, sun-saturated, too lazy to move.

"I was going fishing and I saw you disappear into the trees." He settled down beside her, chewing a grass stalk, watching the two little boys playing happily together.

"I wanted to tell you I wrote a poem," he said.

"How clever you are!" She had given Oliver a volume of Mr. Wordsworth's sonnets, found among the library books.

"Giles will be having a birthday soon," he remarked.

One year old, thought Rose, marveling. Nicholas and I have a son one year old. How she wished they could celebrate the birthday together. "I shall make him a cake." At Rundull Castle there was always a cake when one of the family had a birthday. Giles was a Rundull.

Oliver looked surprised. "Can he eat cake?" He fell on his knees, crawled across the rug toward the babies, and examined first Giles's then Billy's gums. "They've both got teeth!"

"Milk teeth," said Rose.

"Well," said Oliver, "they can't eat milk with their teeth, so I don't see why they shouldn't try a bit of cake. You could have a two-baby party."

Rose smiled affectionately at him. "Will you recite your poem to me?" She spoke sleepily, her eyes half closed.

"If you promise not to laugh."

"Of course I won't laugh."

Oliver took a deep breath and began.

> "I climbed on high in the kauri tree,
>   And took the starry clematis . . ."

Never again could Rose hear poetry without wanting to scream. It happened so silently, with such horrifying suddenness, that neither of them could have said from which direction the Maori came. They saw him with disbelief, in the center of the rug, both hands extended toward Giles. Then Giles was under a dirty brown arm, his head down, already sliding beneath the mat the man wore, his little legs sprawling.

32

Rose's scream was primal. In a flash she was on her feet and running, running blindly after the Maori as he fled into the forest. Within seconds, he had disappeared without sound or trace. Panic-stricken, crazed, she floundered, falling headlong, clambering to her feet, lurching dementedly as she searched for a trail, helpless in her despair. The forest surrounded her with impenetrable gloom. The man and her child had gone.

"Nicholas!" she screamed. "Nicholas! Oh, God, send Nicholas. Help me. Help me!"

Where was Oliver? She was alone in a confusion of agonized disbelief. "Oliver!" There was no reply. Even the birds were silent.

With her mind driven by something so black and terrible she could not face it, she floundered, searching and screaming. Panic gripped and shook her. She no longer knew where she was or what she was doing. Something touched her arm. A hand.

"Rose. Rose." She felt a bundle of softness against her breasts. Uncomprehending, her arms closed automatically around it, and she looked down in bewilderment. The small, startled face looked back at her.

"Oh, my baby!" Nicholas's baby.

"He's all right," said Oliver, his voice quivering, full of fear. "Quick. Hurry, Rose. Quick, run."

He would not allow her time for relief. They floundered back through the rough undergrowth, the prickly bush lawyers catching at their clothes, ripping Rose's

358

skirts and her stockings, which were already in rags, tearing at her hair until it hung down her back, leaf-filled, all the pins gone. Oliver, at her side, kept her from falling.

They staggered into the sunlit clearing. As Rose paused, Oliver plucked at her arm. "We've got to go."

"Billy." She was staring at the empty rug, the abandoned cart. "Where's Billy? Where's Billy?" she screamed, the nightmare returning.

Oliver did not answer.

"Where's Billy?" She began to run this way and that. The horror caught again at her throat. She told herself to stay calm. She began to frantically search.

Oliver laid a hand on her arm. He was looking up into her face with a strange and desperate intensity.

"Where is Billy? The Maori didn't take him. Only Giles." She remembered very distinctly that Billy had been left on the rug.

"Oliver! Where is Billy?"

He was wearing the expression he had worn that day she came upon him in the mews behind Cavendish Square. Even his features seemed to have changed. They were scrawny and small and sharp, with an air of defeat behind.

"It was 'im or Giles," said Oliver defensively.

Rose's face twisted with illogical outrage.

" 'Im or Giles," said Oliver in the raw Cockney voice he had lately left behind.

In silence Rose fought to come to terms with what Oliver had done on her behalf. There was a look on his peaked, uncomprehending face that he must have worn as his parents swung by their necks from the Triple Tree. He reached for Rose's hand, but he did not speak.

"You, you . . . you . . . ?" Rose could not ask the question.

"I caught 'im," said Oliver. " 'E didn't mind which one 'e ate."

Rose's legs gave way. She sat heavily on the ground. Giles rolled onto the grass and began to cry. Rose wanted to cry, too. Or die. She could not speak to Oliver again. She thought she never would.

They abandoned the cart and the rug with its ghoulish associations. With tacit agreement they took to the hills and came in behind the town like fugitives. As they approached the houses Rose spoke for the first time. "Give me your shirt, Oliver." Silently, obediently, he took off the torn, dirty garment and handed it to her. "You were fishing," she said, speaking with desperate calm, "and your shirt got washed out to sea. That's what you must tell Mrs. Stokes, because if she found it torn and dirty like this, she would ask you what happened. Do you understand?"

He nodded.

Holding the heavy baby precariously on one trembling arm, Rose put the other one around the boy's shoulders and kissed him. It occurred to her then that she had never kissed Oliver before. Perhaps nobody had. She said, choking, "Promise me not to tell anyone."

"It was 'im or Giles, Rose," quavered Oliver, begging acceptance of his terrible deed.

"You know what a promise is, don't you?" she asked, looking closely into his eyes.

"Yes."

"Now promise!" It was a threat.

"I promise."

"No matter what anyone says to you, or to me, you will say you were fishing this afternoon. Fishing. Do you understand?"

"Yes." She brushed the few remaining pieces of leaf from his hair.

"And smile when you go home. There's nothing to feel glum about. Billy's mother is having another baby. It wasn't your fault the Maori came." With a flash of terrifying guilt she remembered Lady Cressida's words on the day her baby was born. *You have made an enemy of the Maoris. They do not forget insults.*

Rose waited until Oliver was out of sight, then on trembling legs she hurried down the hill, steeling herself to do what she must do. To tell Mrs. Picton her baby had been kidnapped, which was true, in a way; and that there had been nothing she could do to save him.

The following weeks passed in a blur of distress. In a mindless panic over what would happen to Oliver if the truth was discovered, Rose muddled her story and brought suspicion on herself. There were interviews with the police, with magistrates, with a horrified Mrs. Stokes (who was thought to have influence with Rose). Even with Lieutenant Shortland himself.

Lady Cressida had already told how Rose had upset the old crone who appeared out of the bush the day Beatrix was born. The Maoris, everyone now knew, were cunning and terrible in revenge; patience itself in waiting for an opportunity for *utu*. She had put every child in the colony in jeopardy.

Had Mrs. Putnam, as the Pictons suggested, given the baby to the cannibal to save her own skin? Flash Jack was right when he said Rose lacked cunning. Driven to her wits' end by their questioning, she mindlessly told them that Chief Te Puni had offered her a thousand acres of land for Giles when he was sweet-fleshed, with milk teeth.

So Mrs. Putnam had deliberately taken another woman's child into the forest and sold him for land! A thousand acres! Let her be tarred and feathered! Te Puni, fearing the vengeful god of the missionaries, denied both the earlier threat and the fact that he or any of his tribe had a part in the kidnapping. Cannibalism, he reminded the authorities innocently, had been outlawed by the whites.

Jim Picton, on his way out of the courthouse, had to be restrained from attacking Rose. His wife vowed she would never again speak to her. The bulk of the colony followed suit. They threw her off the Library Committee, proving how frail had been her perch. Daniel, angered by the insults so unfairly heaped up on his own head, tried to persuade her to run away. They must go north to Auckland where he would easily find work; or even farther, to Kororareka. Rose would not go. More than ever, now such dangers were known to be at hand, she was determined Giles should be near his father.

The town became a seething hive of enemies. She holed up in Aurora Cottage, reliving her mistakes in intolerable nightmares. Sometimes she was running down Rundull High Street with the louts of the village after her; sometimes she was fighting her way out of the crowd on Flagstaff Hill, with the cannibals tearing at her silk dress, while the draymen and tarts of Covent Garden ran away with her green velvet cloak. Sometimes she was standing in a clearing watching Giles, a hand's reach away, being put into a Maori oven. And every night she woke up screaming.

A reluctant Daniel collected reading matter for her and she read voraciously. With her head in a book, she could forget for a while about Billy Picton, about what Oliver had done, about what was to happen to them as a family. When she was not immersed in a story, when she was not having her nightmares, she cried. If only Nicholas would come. If only Florrie and Adam would send word that they had decided to join her. The limitless space around her was empty. Her future was a frightening blank.

And then she knew, though she could not face the fact, because it was the final straw, that she was again pregnant.

One Sunday morning, just before a church service which Rose dared not attend, the Reverend Hadfield came. "I am told," he said when the good mornings were done with, "that neither you nor your husband have been attending church."

Rose's eyes filled with tears.

"I have not come to ask you why," he said briskly. "I have come to escort you there. You are two of God's people and shall not be refused His blessing." Without waiting to be invited, he walked into the parlor. "Ah! How I wish I had more time to read." Picking up one of Rose's library books, he lowered his long, bony form into a chair. "Ten minutes?" he inquired casually, making his question sound rather like an order. "Could you be ready in ten minutes? There is a young Maori woman coming to look after your little boy. She is a friend of yours and therefore as responsible as they come."

The Maoris were not responsible, as everyone knew, but they were accustomed to babies. Children with the novelty of a white skin could hold their attention for hours.

"Who is she?" The natives whom Rose had thought were her friends had let her down.

"Epecka Matenga. I know she visits you. That is why I asked her," the Reverend Hadfield replied gently.

She never forgot that first reappearance in public: she, holding her chin so high her neck ached; Daniel shuffling along like a prisoner in chains; the faint hiss from the back row that caused their sponsor to swing around and give the culprits a look that should have laid them dead; the intolerable length of the walk up the aisle, to the front seats that had been held vacant for them; the sermon preached, she afterward discovered, at Mr. Hadfield's insistence, on Christian acceptance, charity, and love.

There were prayers said for the Pictons, who had gone, with everyone's blessing, to find work in Auckland. Rose prayed fervently that they would have lots of children, and forget. Afterward, the frail young missionary stood with Daniel and Rose on the steps of the courthouse that served as a church, drawing people around them. There were some who marched deliberately away, but others, tentatively and perhaps with shame, offered a tardy hand of friendship.

The scandal, town-bred and town-fed, had not reached Rata Hill. Nicholas and Cressida sat through the little drama in puzzled silence. They were to lunch that day with the newspaper proprietor. Helping his wife into the pony trap, Nicholas said, without meeting her eyes, "Go on ahead, my dear. Cossack is frisky. I will catch you up easily enough."

She flicked the reins across Charmy's back and moved off, the skin drawn tight over her cheekbones, her eyelids sliding down to hide the scalding shame and humiliation of this new recklessness, this further disloyalty. She knew where Nicholas was going, and that he would not catch her up before she reached Mr. Revans's house. She would have to steel herself to enter alone and make excuses for him.

It was too bad that this trouble had blown up, bringing the girl back into their lives just when their marriage had been working so much better.

She closed her eyes and willed herself the strength to stand up under this new blow.

Leaving Cossack in the yard behind the courthouse where the churchgoers tied their mounts, Nicholas strode off through the town. Flash Jack Wilshire was locking up his store. The two men greeted each other civilly. "How do you escape the zealotry of God's henchmen?" Nicholas asked with brisk envy.

"I imagine they believe me to be beyond redemption." Pocketing his keys, turning to leave, Flash Jack dropped his thunderbolt like a man tossing a piece of wastepaper into a basket. "By the way, le Grys, I believe you harbor my cousin's fugitive wife at Rata Hill."

Caught off guard, Nicholas's astonishment was evident in the parting of his lips, the widening of his eyes. "The deuce I do!"

"Lady Teresa Bolingbird. Wife of Lord Cheney Bolingbird of Hurstpoint Hall. He took her to Australia, where he has acquired a deal of land, but she flit one night and crossed the Tasman Sea, not guessing she was aboard a brig I had chartered."

Nicholas played for time. "I know of no Lady Teresa Bolingbird."

"She goes under the foolish name of Tilly Bird, a pseudonym unlikely to fool anyone of intelligence, unless they're desirous"—Flash Jack's light eyes glittered—"for personal reasons, of remaining in ignorance."

The jab struck home, as it was intended to. "You must know my wife would not wish to employ a lady in menial work," Nicholas snapped, scowling.

Flash Jack's lips moved halfway between a sneer and a smile. "I would not put any trick past m'ladies if they could see a way to avoid soiling their pretty hands. However, that aspect aside, I must warn you that my cousin is coming from Australia, in a barque that is sent to convey government bigwigs for the anniversary celebrations. I have heard from him that he believes his wife to be in Wellington. You know as well as I do that he will have no difficulty in locating her. With a following breeze, his ship could be here today."

"You wish me to return her to her husband?" asked Nicholas curtly.

"Nothing of the sort. If Cheney had conducted himself in a gentlemanly manner, she would not have run away. I merely desire you to know that you employ as cook the daughter of the earl of Dexter. The rest is up to you." Flash Jack turned and strode away.

Stung, Nicholas glowered after him. Damn him for a galling blackguard. And damn Cressida for putting him in so ignominious a position. Why had he not followed his own hunch and questioned the girl? He strode off irritably, up the hill toward Aurora Cottage. People standing in their gardens watched him come. Others peeped curiously from behind their curtains. He turned toward them boldly with a frozen smile. It would not hurt Rose for the neighbors to know the Honorable Nicholas le Grys was calling on her today.

He came to the gate. The land surveys having been completed and Flash Jack now being in possession of titles to his property, Daniel had been allowed to erect a little white fence with a picket gate. Nicholas opened it and strode up the path. A Maori girl sat cross-legged on the veranda, playing with a ball on a string. Nodding to her briefly, he rapped at the door.

Rose appeared with the child in her arms. A sweet Rose, somehow smaller, paler, infinitely vulnerable. There were dark circles under her eyes, and the eyes themselves, without their luminosity, seemed shrunken. At sight of her the ferment of ill humor in him went. A sweet wave of tenderness swept through him, driving out the bile, cooling the hot Rundull blood.

"Oh, Nicholas!" The flood of warmth and relief that he brought took her strength away.

The Maori girl rolled her body forward in that graceful way the natives had, and rose to her feet. "I go now."

"Thank you for your help, Epecka." Rose led her guest into the parlor and put Giles down on the floor. All the misery in her rose in a tide, and as she tried to speak her voice broke. Nicholas took her in his arms. She was as frail as thistledown.

"What happened, Rose? What have they been doing to you, my darling?"

She took his hands and held them against her cheeks, kissing them frantically while tears spilled through his fingers.

"Tell me. You must tell me, my darling."

It was a long time before she could. It was as though she had to have this little respite first, savoring the fact that their love had not perished, before she told him the little she could tell. "I was in the forest with Giles and the Picton baby."

"Yes. Go on. What happened?"

"A Maori came and took Billy Picton." Her lips trembled. "That's all, Nicholas."

But that, he was certain, was not all. He said gently,

holding her against his heart, "You must tell me every-thing, Rose. I might be able to help."

The tears that now came so easily ran down her cheeks. "You c-couldn't bring Billy b-back to life. He's d-dead, Nicholas. They a-ate him. The m-missionaries found the bones."

For a while he was too appalled to speak. Eventually he moved her gently away so that he could see her face. "Did you have to choose? Is that it?"

She nodded, gulped, her glance sliding away. She knew if she told Nicholas the truth he would thrash Oliver. With pride and fear, she knew he would never allow her to take the blame.

"Oh, God!" He held her very tightly for a long time, comforting her, treasuring her, refilling his own deep well of need. The ever present horror Rose had lived with crept away in the silence. He took a linen handker-chief from his pocket and wiped away her shimmering tears. "It is what any mother would do," he said compas-sionately. "It was natural. You must face up to them and tell them that. You must make them see."

Her face crumpled with distress. The tears gushed up again. "I, I can't. They have been so cruel. So dreadfully cruel . . ."

"Does Daniel not help?"

"I can't ask him to stand by me. Not after what I have done." It was an uncomfortable moment. They both looked down at Giles. Sweeping the child into his arms, Nicholas perched on the edge of a chair, holding him out on his knee so that they faced each other. "He sits there like a young king," marveled Nicholas. "As though he has the right."

Rose smiled, the tears sparkling on her lashes. "He has the right," she said with total conviction. She came to stand beside him, one arm lovingly around his shoulders. "He has the assurance, as you say, of a king."

"Then you must have the assurance of a queen, my Rose. This is your country now, and you must somehow learn to cope with it. You know you cannot call upon me. Or rely upon me."

Yet he had come as soon as he heard of her trouble. Her heart lifted sweetly. She would be able to face peo-ple again now.

"There are the anniversary celebrations in a day or two. Make Daniel take you to all the entertainments. Go out and enjoy yourself. It will help you to forget."

Rose was not listening. Here they were together, a little family. She glowed with love and happiness.

"I must go." He handed the baby over. "We are lunching with Samuel Revans," he said. "As the editor of our only newspaper he should do something. I will try to influence him. It ought not to be left to the goodwill of a missionary."

He strode off down the hill feeling greatly disturbed. Leaving Cossack tied up behind the courthouse, he walked to his hosts' house. The exercise dissipated some of his emotion, but not enough. Rose's sweetness, bringing with it the inevitable sense of loss, clung around his heart.

As he came into his hostess's drawing room, Mrs. Revans was saying, "Young Mr. Hadfield already has something of the reputation of a saint. The Maoris seem to revere him."

Her gently patronizing voice reminded Nicholas that all his life he had heard people taking for granted kindnesses done by those whom they did not consider to be their equals. For some time now, he had been aware of a new feeling building up in him. Flash Jack's criticism this morning had pinpointed it.

With scant deference, he bid his hostess good-day. His eyes were already sweeping the room, looking for an audience. "Would you prefer, gentlemen," he asked bleakly, "should your wife find herself in Mrs. Putnam's position, that she give your child to the cannibal in order to save the infant of a neighbor?"

There was a flutter of indignation and surprise. Faces turned toward Cressida, who was sitting ashen faced. The light from the window falling on her features gave them an oddly gaunt look.

Standing in the middle of the room, long legs apart, head high, wearing his Rundull arrogance like a flag, Nicholas added, "I think, Revans, you should write a leader along the lines I have suggested. Mrs. Putnam has been punished enough for anything she may have done. But has she in fact done anything at all? Not one of you has answered my question. May I put it to you again, a little differently perhaps. You are all family people. If a

Maori came with a tomahawk when your wife was in charge of your child and mine, which child would you prefer her to hand over?"

"Oh come, sir," spluttered one of the men.

Nicholas glanced his way with contempt. "Unless our host protests, I should like an answer."

"The Putnams come from Mr. le Grys's estate," apologized Mrs. Revans with a peacemaking gesture. "He feels obliged."

"They are not my protégés," he retorted curtly. "I speak for them only as human beings. Edward Wakefield's plan for this country was that everyone should have a square deal. The town has not given a square deal to Mrs. Putnam, and that has been underlined by the fact that no one has answered my question."

"Nor will they," replied Revans good-humoredly. "You shall have your editorial, le Grys. Now let us go in to lunch before it grows cold."

"How you humiliate me," whispered Cressida savagely as Nicholas took her arm.

He scowled. "At least your humiliation is private," he retorted, "as Mrs. Putnam's was not."

They drove out of the town in bitter silence, broken only by the clatter of Charmy's dainty hooves and the call of the bush birds, as though Rose with her sweetness and her treachery, her vulnerability and her corrosive tenacity sat between them. At last, when Cressida could keep her bile in check no longer she burst out, "That woman would cause trouble wherever—"

Nicholas snapped, "You are by way of causing a deal of trouble yourself, m'Lady. It seems you employ as cook, housemaid, children's nurse, dairymaid, and skivvy the Lady Teresa Bolingbird of Hurstpoint Hall, daughter of the earl of Dexter."

She turned and stared at him, her hands tightening on the reins, her face freezing over her distress. It was as though in her heart she had always known. "I will talk to her," she said, and then volunteered uncertainly, "perhaps we could share the work. We are, after all, friends."

"You may not even do that. Her husband is on his way to claim her." Nicholas repeated what Flash Jack had said. "Lord Cheney Bolingbird is his cousin. The scamp is indeed well-connected." He added unkindly, "You may have to answer to his Lordship not only for misusing his lady, but also for failing to accept his cousin. Perhaps Flash Jack should have been invited to our ball."

"Connections on the wrong side of the blanket are not socially acceptable, as you well know. Besides," Cressida added frostily, touching the chestnut's rump with a dexterous flick of the whip, "it is said he lives with a native woman and has innumerable half-caste children. I have not yet become so colonial that I will invite such a man to my home. I intend to live here as I lived in Suffolk."

Nicholas nodded. "Without charity. I understand."

"You are intolerable!"

"I do not mean to be unkind, Cressida. I truly believe there is a new feeling growing up in the colony. I think you should tread carefully. There is to be an Anniversary Day ball—"

"Which I propose to attend," she interrupted defensively. "I have said I will."

"I am speaking of a second ball, to follow the so-called popular jollifications. It is to be held in a wooden storehouse on Te Aro beach. I believe all the young aristocrats intend to patronize it. I think it would be politic for some ladies to appear. Charles Heaphy and Frederick Moore have invited their friends to foregather at Clay Castle and ride over together. You ladies would be a stabilizing influence and add tone to the proceedings."

Cressida turned on him an incredulous look. "I do not believe that respectable gentlemen will attend. And certainly I shall not."

"Very well, then. You will not mind if I uphold the family honor?"

I shall mind very much, she said bitterly to herself. She felt wan and shaken by the events of the day. If only the wretched Putnams could be persuaded to go north. And yet, she thought with despair, the going of the poor bereaved family had precluded that.

They did not speak until they were in the house. Cressida removed her large hat and veil. Nicholas called in Tilly Bird. She came at a run in her usual way, but when she saw their expressions her face fell. Then she shrugged and grinned shamefacedly.

"So you know. I can tell by the way you look. What do you intend to do with me?" she asked, unfastening her apron and tossing it over the back of the buttoned couch, translating herself in the flick of an eyelid from servant to guest.

They were startled into amused silence.

"Let me ask you this," she said, drifting to the wood settle with its painted panels, "if you knew me to have been married, for money, to a man whom I did not know at all well, who lied to my parents, and who did the most dreadful, unimaginable things to me in our bedroom—"

Cressida, her face flaming, broke in, "My dear, perhaps we could talk between ourselves—"

"Oh, fie!" She discarded Cressida's protest with the wave of a hand. "Mr. le Grys knows what men can do. If they are pigs, that is, which I am sure he is not."

Keeping a straight face, Nicholas replied, "I hope it will please you, Lady Teresa, to remain here as our guest. But I must warn you that your husband is on his way. He will undoubtedly be directed here by the townspeople, for our friends are aware that we have a servant whom they have not seen. Besides, the postmaster who introduced you to me will undoubtedly be approached as the person most likely to be *au fait* with local affairs."

She rose and went restlessly to the window.

"I already have a hiding place. If m'Lord comes for me, I shall be in the hollow tree where I spent the night of the ball." She looked from Cressida to Nicholas, then back to Cressida, and her face took on a peaky look. "You did not ask where I was. I believe you did not particularly care. I was at the time a work horse, yet of less concern to you than Charmy and Cossack. More like your hacks and the shire horses who pull the plow and fend for themselves in the fields. Yet," her mouth twisted, "I had made it possible for you to have your ball."

Cressida flushed.

"I am not criticizing you," Tilly Bird continued, "but it is a very lonely feeling one has when one is hiding in a tree, knowing nobody cares what has happened, only that one should return when it is necessary for some more work to be done." She heaved a quick sigh, then added, "Someone had already used the tree, for I found a toy there. A baby's rattle."

Cressida looked bewildered. Nicholas's face was still, wiped clean of all expression.

"I confess I also neither knew nor cared about the lower servants at home," Tilly Bird went on. "Those who made my life comfortable. But I am glad I have had the opportunity of this reshuffle of the cards. I have already learned a great deal, and one thing in particular—it is not necessary to be a man's chattel."

"If you are talking of working to support yourself," said Nicholas, "you will always be at the mercy—"

She cut in sharply, "I do not intend to be at the mercy of anybody. I believe, if I behave as I have been taught to behave, people will respect me."

"If you tell them who you are, they will respect you," retorted Nicholas cynically.

Tilly Bird looked at him with her head to one side. Cressida flushed and glanced away, knowing that he was thinking of the kitchen maid.

"Your husband will be here very soon," said Nicholas. He repeated what Flash Jack had told him.

"Mr. Wilshire, you know, is my husband's cousin. I have not met him but I understand him to be something of a rogue." She looked brightly from one face to the other. "I begin to wonder if I was wasted in my sheltered existence at home. I very much enjoyed my trip across from Australia." She grinned mischievously. "Perhaps I have the makings of a lady adventurer."

33

Samuel Revans's editorial "whitewashing," as some of the meaner spirits suggested, Rose's behavior went a long way to restoring tranquillity, but it was Flash Jack Wilshire who gave her back her inner strength, inevitably blackening her reputation in the process. Braving the public, obeying Nicholas, she had taken Giles into town to buy some wool. Flash Jack saw her as she entered the store.

"Good morning, Mrs. Putnam," he called cheerfully and reached up to a high shelf. "I have a replacement for you," he said, lifting down a parcel.

Rose came up to the counter, smiling uncertainly. "A replacement for what?"

"For your green gingham skirt and blouse."

The gingham she had been wearing when . . . She turned to run. Flash Jack snatched at her wrist. Holding on to her with one hand, he lifted the countertop on its hinge with the other.

"Come through," he said. "I want to talk to you."

Rose felt she would faint with fear and shock. She had begun to believe the torment was over, yet here it was again. Flash Jack ushered her into a small room at the back of the store. He took Giles from her and placed him on the floor. She was vaguely aware of bales of cotton piled one upon another, cardboard boxes, reels of twine, fishing tackle; by the window, a small desk. Pulling out one of the chairs, he signaled her to sit down. She sat awkwardly, her eyes huge with apprehension, the knuckles of her hands showing white where they clasped the edge of the chair, her heart jumping.

He seated himself facing her.

"I saw you come out of the forest." He spoke casually, crossing one leg over the other, reaching for his cigar box. "That's how I knew your clothes were ruined."

She waited, weak with dread. Giles's eyes roved around the room, then lifted to hers with Nicholas's quizzical look.

"What happened, Rose?"

Her mouth closed like a trap.

"If you can't, or won't tell me, I'll tell you."

"No!" The remorseless hysteria that lay beneath the surface of Rose's serenity rose like a tidal wave. She clapped a hand to her mouth to hold back the scream that never would quite go away.

Flash Jack was shocked. It showed in the startled brilliance of his pale eyes, the parting of his lips. "Great heavens! What a state you're in!" He stood up, hesitated, then, pulling out a drawer, lifted a bottle of brandy onto the desk. "Someone has to lance this wound," he said. He took two glasses from a cupboard and poured a measure into each. "Take up your drink, Mrs. Putnam." Nervelessly, obediently, Rose raised the glass. The liquor had a familiar smell, bringing recollections of another place, another world. A London basement. A sneering, venal mob. Her hand trembled.

Flash Jack's voice spun through the threatening memory, pulling her back to the present. "Drink it down at one gulp. One gulp, I said, and mind you do that."

She was not in London. She was thousands of miles away and Flash Jack Wilshire was being kind. The ghosts receded. Rose did as she was told. She felt the top come off her head. Her eyes started like organ stops. Her breath went. She gagged, coughed, spluttered. In the distance she could hear Flash Jack, laughing softly.

"Now you'll find you are strong as a lion."

She blinked, wiped tears from her eyes, and coughed fiercely over the flame in her throat.

"Firewater," he said cheerily. "Just the thing for the job."

Rose smiled tremulously, blinking away the tears.

"Now let me tell you my theory about what happened in the bush that day."

"No, please. It isn't necessary." But her protest was halfhearted. The edges of her pain and fear were somehow blunted.

"Oh, but it is. It is very necessary. Listen to me, Rose Putnam." Flash Jack leaned forward, his arms on the desk, looking into the depths of her eyes. "I have seen Revans's editorial. It was well meant, but written by a man who does not know you. It's my view that if some native, or natives, came for children in your care you would let none of them go. Am I right, Rose? Unlike the gossips, I believe there never was a choice. I believe you would fight to the death for any child."

"You do not know," Rose muttered.

"Ah, but I do know, because I know you. I know about the animal and the peasant in you. A peasant cares for her child as none of the virtuous ladies of the parish can. An animal fights for its young. That is why I know young Oliver gave the other baby away."

Rose's eyes flew wide. "No! No! He didn't. I swear he didn't, Alain! I swear!"

Ignoring her protest, Flash Jack went on. "Now, what are we to do about Oliver? That is the question that's bothering you, is it not?"

It was no use fighting him. He knew. Besides, the brandy had taken her strength. "I brought him here," she said. "He did me a good deed."

"Then you have repaid him well. Now, I want you to tell me what happened that day."

"I don't know what he . . ." And yet, she did. At that moment she saw brilliantly in her mind's eye what had been smothered in the secret recesses of her mind. Oliver, crafty and quiet and swift as the cannibal himself, slipping in and out of the trees, sliding through the bushes, as he was accustomed to slide around butchers' carts with food snatched from ghouls too fascinated by the hangman's maneuvers to notice.

She said urgently, leaning forward across the desk, hammering the wood with her fists, "He did it for me. He knew I couldn't live without the baby." She added fiercely, "If you tell, Oliver's whole life will be ruined, and he will not understand. He will not understand," she repeated. "Do you not see? You will do no good for either of us. He is such a little boy." Her voice broke.

"No," replied Flash Jack very deliberately, "he is not a little boy. How old is he, Rose?"

"I don't know. Maybe ten." She misread the look in his eyes, adding swiftly, protectively, "Maybe eight."

"I think he is nearer fourteen. And I think we would be doing him a great disservice if we did not make him understand. Don't worry, Rose. I shall not tell. But even a plant needs pruning, and I doubt Dr. Stokes knows where to apply the knife. I will take young Oliver away on my next trading trip. He will be useful, and I don't doubt he will be pleased to earn some holiday pay while the school is closed for the summer."

Rose's head had been drooping, her lids falling over her eyes. Oh, the relief! The blessed relief of telling someone. Of having the responsibility of Oliver taken from her. She felt herself drifting.

"Poor little trout," said Flash Jack, smoothing her hair, arranging one arm more comfortably. Perhaps he had been a little heavyhanded with the brandy, but it would not do her any harm in the long run. Taking a length of silk from a shelf, he crumpled it into a pad and placed it beneath her head. He looked at her for a moment, his weather-marked, life-marked face gentle, then turned away with regret. When he kissed her for the first time he did not intend that she should be asleep. He went back into the store, closing the door quietly behind him.

It was unfortunate that there should have been a window in the side of the storeroom. Next day the news was all over town that Mrs. Putnam had been lying across a desk in Flash Jack Wilshire's store with a brandy bottle beside her.

It was late on the evening of the select subscription ball. Rose, lost in her dreams, sat in the parlor with her embroidery on her lap. She and Nicholas were dancing the night away at Barratt's Hotel. His eyes sparkled at her from the darkened windows where moths battered their silken wings, his "Faster, Rose, faster," came with the wind through the chimney, setting her feet tapping and calling up nostalgic memories of their days together in St. James.

Oliver, who had escorted Dr. and Mrs. Stokes down the hill, came in on his way home to report on the glittering scene. "Why didn't you go down to watch, Rose?"

Stifling a sigh of longing, Rose replied, "I daresay it's all right for boys to stare at folks, Oliver, but it wouldn't be right for Daniel and me."

"There's lots of grown-ups there, gawping."

Rose wished Daniel was absent, so that she could ask how Nicholas looked, what he wore. Was he more handsomely dressed than everyone else? The most distinguished man there? Did he ever think of her, Rose wondered yearningly, when he danced with his wife, looking over her head and pretending, as she did when Daniel did those terrible things to hurt her? A huge moth fluttered in and crashed against the lamp. She started, heaved an enormous sigh, looked across at her husband.

"Daniel," she said after Oliver had gone. "Would you take me to the Popular Ball?"

He raised that heavily thatched brown head, the eyes incredulous. "Take you ter the ball?" he echoed. "Why? Where's the point? You don't know 'ow ter dance an' nor do I."

"Could we not go and watch, and learn how to dance?"

"I don't want to make a fool of meself an' I don't want ter see you—

She contradicted him hotly, "I am sure I would pick up the steps with ease. And I would not make a fool of myself. I'd like to learn to dance."

He shrugged his thick shoulders, grunted negatively.

"I'd go by myself," Rose said resentfully, "if I could, but as you well know, I cannot."

"And that's as well," Daniel said, assuming the expression he wore when he thought of the way men followed Rose with their eyes.

"I believe you would like to chain me up until all my looks are gone."

Daniel did not reply.

"Wouldn't you?"

"There's no call to shout at me," he said, getting up from his chair and shambling off toward their bedroom.

There was a sharp rapping at the front door. They both looked around in surprise.

"Don't open it," said Daniel. "It's too late ter be answerin' doors."

Throwing him a defiant look, Rose went down the passage. As she flung the door open a cloud moved across the moon, but not before she made out the familiar, bulky figure of Flash Jack Wilshire.

"May we come in?" He stepped over the doorstep, leading a dark-skirted, bonneted figure by the hand. "I have brought you a guest, Rose." He glanced across at Daniel hovering in the darkened passageway, the yellow lamplight from the parlor behind him. "Is that all right, Putnam?"

"It's your house," muttered Daniel.

Breezily ignoring his grudging reception, Flash Jack turned to Rose. "May I present Tilly Bird, who has run away from the marriage bed of my caddish cousin."

The girl had stepped forward and was holding out a friendly hand, meeting Rose's pleased and astonished scrutiny with level eyes and a smile. "I do hope my unexpected arrival will not inconvenience you, Mrs. Putnam."

"This is not a mansion," said Flash Jack looking around, hands in pockets, "yet it should be possible to keep her out of sight if you are willing to take a little trouble. As soon as possible I shall find her a berth on a schooner so that she may go north."

Rose was both enchanted and intrigued. Flash Jack with a cousin! She had never imagined him belonging to anybody. "Of course you may stay, Mrs. Bird, and welcome," she said warmly.

There was a moment of startled silence. Flash Jack looked back at the girl. His large white teeth shone in the lamplight. Tilly Bird flushed defensively. Rose, too, was on the defensive. "Perhaps you are not Mrs. Bird at all," she suggested, her eyes suddenly bright with suspicion. She turned to Flash Jack with controlled indignation. "You must know I would not give a friend of yours away, Alain."

He swung around to address Daniel, "And you? Are you of a mind to give this lady away?"

Daniel fidgeted, scratching his shoulder, looking baffled. "Why should I?" he muttered.

Flash Jack swung back to Rose, eyes glinting. "The lady is hoist with her own petar. I think it was you calling her Mrs. that took her aback."

"You are not married, then?"

Tilly Bird's discomfiture melted away and she laughed merrily. "I am indeed hoist with my own petar, and by pure conceit. It was truly the Mrs. that confounded me, for I have never been addressed so. Being a lady, I did not change my title on marriage. And you are right, Rose, my name is not Bird." She sensed Rose's quickly veiled shock and grasped her hostess's hands warmly. "I am Teresa Bolingbird. You must call me Teresa. Let us be friends for the brief time I am to be here. I hope you will not mind if I call you Rose."

Mind? Before she could gather her whirling wits, Teresa said, "Alain says you have a little boy, so I brought this for him. I found it in a hollow tree." She took a package from her pocket.

Rose removed the paper. Her face flamed as she stood looking down at Giles's rattle. "You have come from Rata Hill!" she said, startled into indiscretion.

"So it was you who hid in the hollow tree?" countered the other girl, her eyes going from Rose's embarrassed face to Daniel's suddenly closed one.

Rose managed lamely, her eyes cast down, "It is somewhat difficult to explain."

"Mrs. Putnam is herself something of a mystery," said Flash Jack. "Ho! Well!" He flapped his cape noisily against the broadcloth of his pantaloons, stretching like a long-necked bird.

"But there is no mystery at all about me," cried the visitor, breaking up the difficult moment. "Cressida le Grys, who is my friend, has diverted my husband to the ball at Barratt's Hotel. Nicholas kindly called Alain to fetch me. I rode here on Cressida's pony."

Rose's eyes were like saucers.

Flash Jack said, "I must be off now, or every dance will be taken. No doubt they have already been taken, for there are ten gentlemen to one lady in this wretched town." He turned as though to go, then slowly revolved on one heel, his eyes settling on Rose. "Since I am unable to escort my cousin to the ball, perhaps you would care to accompany me, Mrs. Putnam?"

"I, I . . ." stammered Rose. She glanced automatically in Daniel's direction, but he had disappeared.

"Come, come. You are surely not going to tell me you have nothing to wear. No silk gown? No velvet cloak?" Reaching across, he took the rattle from her. "Pray don't tear the thing to pieces. It was not meant to be so ill-treated."

Upset beyond bearing by Daniel's poignant retreat and Flash Jack's teasing, Rose blurted out, "I have never learned to dance."

Teresa said, "I shall remedy that. I shall teach you. In our new and different circumstances we must all help each other."

Rose was on tiptoe with excitement. "Yes, yes!" she cried. "You shall teach me to dance. And then, Alain, will you take us to the Popular Ball?" She gazed up at him with wide, beseeching eyes, thinking Nicholas would surely attend, and she would be able to dance—oh! to dance all night—with Nicholas!

Flash Jack looked down at her quizzically.

"Now that's settled," said Teresa, curtailing the silence. "You, Alain, must persuade Cressida to arrange entertainment of his horrible Lordship that evening. Then you shall escort me to the ball."

"And you," said Flash Jack, addressing Teresa, "shall dance every dance with le Grys, for he proposes to attend along with a number of unattached gentlemen." He fingered his whiskers. "You will be off to the north betimes, and the local busybodies cannot link a man's name scandalously with a woman who is not to be found."

"And with whom shall you dance?"

"With Mrs. Putnam because, as she will tell you, her husband is unlikely to attend."

Rose said demurely, "Of course," knowing that Nicholas would not allow her to dance with anyone else but him.

"It is such a long time since I have had any fun." Teresa clapped her hands and gave a little skip. "Oh, what a daring and delightful escapade!"

When Rose crept in beside Daniel later that night, she was far, far too excited to sleep. When she did drop off,

she dreamed she was dancing with Nicholas in her beautiful silk gown, and shouting giddily and quite disrespect-
fully, "Teresa, Teresa come and join us," while Lady
Cressida, who was not actually a Lady anymore, lurked
in the shadows, and dear Grandy stood in the doorway
looking amazed.

Rose awakened to a feeling of strangeness. There was a
warm hump breathing heavily in the bed next to her, but
someone was in the kitchen. Lady Teresa? In the kitchen?
Heavens! She threw a wrap around her shoulders and
pattered disconcertedly down the passage to investigate.
Giles's cot, which had been moved out of his room into
the parlor, was empty.

Her guest was indeed in the kitchen, fully dressed in a
pretty blue skirt and a lacy cream blouse. "Ah, Rose,"
she said, looking up brightly, "I have collected three eggs
from the fowl run, lit the fire, and changed your little
boy." Behind her the kettle steamed merrily on the hob.

"Oh, you should not have!" gasped Rose, horrified.

"But pray, why not? I am a dab hand at changing
babies, for I have had a deal of practice with Cressida's
child."

"You shouldn't be working in those clothes," Rose
managed, gulping down her embarrassment at Teresa's
assumption that she was friendly with Lady Cressida.

"But whyever not? Now that my secret is out, I may as
well wear my own clothes. When I worked for Cressida I
had to wear such a drab outfit, which I bought in Sydney
for the purpose, and it was dreadfully bad for my morale." At Rose's expression of surprise, she added, "Clearly
you do not know of that. I will tell you later. Meantime,
there is work to be done. I shall get breakfast for you and
Mr. Putnam, and then I shall do some cooking for you."

"Oh, no, you must not cook."

"Then how shall I employ my time? And I must keep
my hand in, for how am I to earn my keep except as a
housekeeper or a cook?"

"Can you not go home?" Rose ventured, feeling totally out of her depth with this strange creature.

"Oh, my dear, how naïve you sound." Teresa put both
hands to her forehead and brushed back the dark curls.
"You speak as though I am mistress of my destiny, but

what woman is? Come, let us breakfast. You shall employ your time telling me the story of your life, as I shall tell you mine. There is little enough to tell, goodness knows, but perhaps yours will be more interesting." She glided right up to Rose, scrutinizing her features, looking deeply into her eyes. "You are the wife of a carpenter, and yet in a cupboard in the room where I slept last night there are clothes fit for a queen."

Rose reacted with a soft little gasp of dismay.

Gripping her wrist, still looking into her face, Teresa whispered, "Are you also a lady, Rose? Are you, too, the runaway daughter of a nobleman?"

Rose's head came up sharply. It was a strange moment. Then her guest tossed the question aside. "There is time enough to tell me. So, I am to teach you to dance before the ball!"

It was odd, but the earl's daughter brought them all together in a quite inexplicable way. Oliver came. Oliver with his new vowels, his natural friendliness, his careless regard for Daniel, his love for Giles. Oliver was the doctor's son, now. Teresa assumed he always had been. She even brought an unaccustomed smile to Daniel's lips, as she took Rose through the paces of the polka and the schottische. Oliver acted as her partner. She taught them the rudiments of a Scottish reel, the lancers, Sir Roger de Coverley, humming the tunes, dancing all the other parts herself until she fell into a chair from sheer exhaustion.

It was the happiest time Rose had spent since the far off halcyon days in Nicholas's rooms in London. She remembered Nicholas's saying, "We aristocrats are nothing if not resilient. It is the secret of our survival." In Teresa's resilience Rose recognized a different kind of courage from her own. The girl was a fortified island. It is being unafraid of people that makes all the difference, she thought. It has been my lot to be afraid of people all my life. She wondered with a breathless little rush of optimism if it was a yoke she might one day throw off.

Teresa poked her inquiring nose and her nimble fingers into everything. By midday she had the answer to most of her own questions. "You are, of course, Nicholas's mistress," she stated matter-of-factly, standing in the doorway to the kitchen watching Rose stir the soup. "And that darling boy is Nicholas's son. The resemblance is amazing. Tell me, Rose, is Mr. Putnam a cuckold, or is he your protector?"

"He is my lawful, wedded husband," replied Rose defensively, her cheeks vivid. "I am not Nicholas's mistress now, for he has a wife."

Teresa laughed merrily. "Oh, fie! When did marriage preclude a man having a mistress?"

In her consternation Rose dropped the soup ladle. Edmund leaped for the window, a streak of offended fur and claws. Giles crowed. She picked him up and held him against her heart, showering the top of his curly head with little warm kisses, hiding her face.

"Nobody knows about Giles," she muttered resentfully. "I would thank you to keep the truth to yourself. If you tell—"

Teresa held up her hands in mock horror. "A girl who tells the secrets of others risks having her own exposed. Of course I will tell nobody. Rose, will you allow me to wear that beautiful oyster silk gown to the ball?"

Her best, her very loveliest gown that Nicholas had given her! She said timidly, beseechingly, "You will look after it?"

"Of course. What fun it will be! What an escapade! You shall dance ever dance with your lover, and I shall dance with Cheney's wicked cousin. What a flash fellow is Alain! He has been good to me, there is no doubt. Perhaps"—Teresa went on thoughtfully, one finger to her lips—"if Cheney divorces me I shall marry Alain. Is it in the rules for one to marry one's ex-husband's cousin, Rose?"

"I don't know what you mean," said Rose, momentarily feeling the ground sliding out from under her feet.

"I mean, does the church allow it?" And then, acknowledging that Rose did not know the answer, Teresa smiled.

The next day, fate favoring the "populars" the sun rose in a cloudless sky. Windy Wellington was at her best. Flags were run up on the housetops. Every vessel in the harbor was bedecked. The colony was presenting proof that it had weathered a full year and was on its feet. Soldiers paraded up and down in their glamorous red coats, eyeing the young single girls. Gentlemen swung their canes and doffed their tall hats to acquaintances.

That day was, on a certain level, a turning point. Nobody put the change into words, but everyone sensed a difference in the atmosphere. The line that divided the gentry from the working classes was blurred. The ladies discovered it was not so easy to be haughty with women who were dressed arguably as well as themselves. Some of them, indeed, wore their new raiment with distinction. Schoolmasters were driving out the flat cockney vowels, and insisting upon pronounciation of *h*s and *g*s Parents experimented and tentatively followed suit. Men, who for the first time in their lives had money jingling in their pockets, walked with confidence and pride. It had not become a classless country overnight, and perhaps it never would, but the citizens were more comfortable with each other.

Daniel, never at ease with Rose in her vivid moods, wandered off by himself. She and Oliver plunged happily through the crowds, stopping while people admired the baby, chattering, laughing.

It was easy to find Nicholas. He was standing alone, hands in his pockets, coattails flung over his forearms, his tall hat on the back of his head as he rocked from heel to toe, gazing over the heads of the moving crowd. Oliver swerved around in a half circle. "Let's go and talk to him."

"Hello, you two," Nicholas called casually, strolling forward, smiling at them both, but particularly at Rose. "And how is the young man?" Children rushed past, grown-ups paused, doffed their caps or their tall hats, moved on. Miraculously, nobody seemed to think there was anything odd about the Honorable Nicholas le Grys talking to Mrs. Putnam. They chatted happily, like old friends. Friends without secrets to hide. Nicholas had heard about Oliver's sailing with Flash Jack Wilshire to Auckland, Kororareka, and the Middle Island. "You're a mightily traveled young man. What are you going to do with your life?"

"I'm going to be a farmer." Dr. Stokes had a farm conveniently close to the town. "I'm learning to ride," Oliver added.

Nicholas's eyes flickered. "Why don't you teach Rose

to ride? I think she would take to it like a duck to water."

Oliver's eyes swept across to Rose. He was nearly as tall as she was. "Would you?"

She nodded, her face radiant, her eyes sparkling. "How I would love it!"

"Well, then, I will," promised Oliver, "as soon as I can ride properly myself." They saw Nicholas often after that, as they saw everyone coming and going. During one meeting Rose managed to say casually, "I believe you are going to the Te Aro ball tonight. I am so looking forward to it."

He grinned, doffed his tall hat, and wandered on looking lifted, Rose thought warmly. As though someone had given him a thousand pounds.

That evening Flash Jack called for Rose and Teresa in a buggy. Daniel, looking lost, hovered in the kitchen. Rose, a blush of scarlet on her cheeks, saw his discomfiture and felt a pang of genuine concern. "How I wish you would come with us, Daniel," she said kindly, not wishing it at all, but needing to console him.

" 'Ow can I?" he retorted, his eyes down-sloping, his voice truculent. " 'Oo's goin' ter look after the brat?" But he eyed her hungrily, slender and curved in her pale-blue flowered brocade, with a jeweled comb Teresa had loaned her in her hair.

Tonight Daniel was not shocked by his wife's clothes as he had been when Rose emerged from her room on Proclamation Day. They seemed only to depress him. The goings-on of the past several days had knocked him quite off balance. He could not say he disliked having the strange girl in the house, but he felt certain her coming there was wrong. And then Flash Jack came striding up the path, filling the little cottage with his flashing gold watch chain, his striped buckskin, his fluted ruffles, side whiskers. Daniel slunk out of the back door and went over to the henhouse, where he stood with his back to the cottage, jerking belligerently at the netting door, testing it for strength as though he expected foxes or snakes to come in the night.

34

They left the house in silence because there was, inevitably, a certain guilt to their going. As she climbed up into the buggy, Rose burst out defensively, "Why should I stay in just because he won't—"

But Flash Jack cut her off, echoing impatiently, "Why indeed?" And then they were on their way, rattling and bumping over the uneven road.

"You shall introduce me as Miss Flora England," said Teresa, looking up at Flash Jack from beneath her dark lashes, "for my middle name is Flora, and of course I come from England." She laughed merrily, mischievously. "I shall say I am visiting the Putnams, which is true, but beyond that I must ask you to say nothing, for I do not know what my future is to be, and if I am to be able to return here with dignity sometime after the hue and cry is over, then it is better there should have been no untruths told on my behalf."

Rose glanced across at her with respect and awe. "How I wish I had a big house and garden where you could hide."

Teresa shrugged. "It is kind of you," she said, "but if you had a big garden you would doubtless also have staff as has Nicholas, and they would talk. I must go away." Suddenly Rose saw an expression of fear on her face, but it disappeared so swiftly she wondered if she had imagined it.

Nicholas was waiting for them. Rose recognized his tall, broad-shouldered figure in the distance, and her heart began to race. How beautiful he was, dressed in fine black broadcloth and ruffled shirt with his thick black hair shining and his air of lazy grace. The rush of love that swept through her seemed to lift her off the seat. She thought her stays would burst with the swelling of emotion, tightly laced as they were over the unacceptable bulge that sharp-eyed Teresa had not noticed. She wanted to rush up and touch him to make sure he was not a shadow or a dream.

A railed enclosure made of saplings and the slender brown trunks of the *punga* trees had been erected beside the hall. Flash Jack reined in behind a jam of horses and bullock drays, buggies and pony carts, all waiting their turn to enter. He jumped down, but before he could offer his hand to Rose, Nicholas was there, his eyes slanting and dangerous, his arms extended to take her waist. At that moment they both felt a strengthening of the ties that had stretched and jerked them apart, pulled them together, tossed them and hurt them but never quite broken.

Rose was unaware of the murderous glare in the pale eyes of the man who had brought her.

"Come, Alain," said Teresa serenely, putting a gloved hand through his arm, "let us move on."

The two girls were as conspicuous in their fine gowns as they had known, outrageously and without a care, they would be. Teresa had pinned a little circlet of pearls in her hair where it was knotted at the back of her head, and at the last moment laid a pretty little *ferronière* across her forehead. "Nobody will guess it is gold, or that the jewels are real," she remarked carelessly, but Rose knew that they would, and it was part of Teresa's daring, now that she was safely protected, to want to set the colony agog, to create a little dangerous excitement with which to counteract her fear.

The low-built warehouse was so thickly lined with the enormous curved leaves of the *punga* fern that it was like a cave in the bush. Here and there lanterns had been hung from the rafters, but their wicks were low so that the whole interior was shadowy and mysterious. Narrow wooden forms were set along walls. There were a few chairs for the band. The floor had been sprinkled with a chalky substance, but the surface was still rough. Nobody cared. There was an overwhelming air of uninhibited excitement. They were still cock-a-hoop from the successes of the day. The Clay Castle mob, as they were popularly named, having raced all the way on horseback, carried their winner in shoulder high, waving jubilantly, singing a rollicking glee at the top of their merry voices.

Rose was delirious. Part of her wanted to hold on to Nicholas and never let him go. Part of her wanted to dance with every one of the young men who rushed toward her each time the band struck up, their bold eyes flashing, arms outstretched, pretending they had not seen Nicholas. He stood with one hand nonchalantly on his hip, tyrannical and disdainful, ignoring their impertinence, ready to sweep her into his arms.

Familiar faces flew excitingly by. There was Barney Herd with his eyes popping out of his head; Will Trent, Nicholas's groom, who had disappeared the day *Aurora* made landfall; Fred Quick, now a prosperous sawyer with his own gang of men. For all Nicholas appeared to notice, they might not have been there. He swung Rose in and out of the lancers and quadrilles as though only he and she were on the floor, the others merely puppets, conveniently playing their part. They danced the polka with fast, crazy, physical abandon. No one would ever have guessed Rose had learned it only the day before.

"You must dance with Alain," Teresa whispered in Rose's ear as they came off the floor, after an hour or more of Nicholas's desperate possession. "He grows progressively more annoyed, and I fear there will be trouble."

Thrilling at the possibility of trouble, nonetheless Rose looked up into the bold, tender face of her love. "Might I dance just once with Flash Jack?" She saw a quick look of impatience in the dark eyes, felt his fingers tighten on her arm, and added apologetically, "He did bring me here."

"You want to dance with that swashbuckling cockalorum?" Holding her at arm's length, looking ready to eat her up, Nicholas pretended incredulity.

Glorying in his possession, Rose flushed like a field poppy. "Not really," she whispered. "But he brought me—"

"Somebody had to bring you," retorted Nicholas hard-heartedly. "My love, you are mine for the night, and I will not give you up."

But there came a time when both of the girls were whirled away on an excuse-me waltz. Suddenly neither Flash Jack nor Nicholas was to be seen. The young bachelors dived like hawks. Somebody persuaded the band to keep playing and playing, the tunes leaping on each other's backs—the polka, the galop, the valse—until all the women cried out for a respite. Rose looked for Nicholas, but he was nowhere in sight.

Then Teresa came out of the shadows and grasped her hand. "Rose! Look over there. At the doorway."

Rose turned. Looking tumbled and angry, Flash Jack and Nicholas were pitching their way through the crowd. Flash Jack's satin waistcoat was torn, his right eye was closing. One of Nicholas's eyes also looked strange, and his beautiful white shirt was filthy, the frill dropping across his broad chest, exposing the fine dark hairs.

"Oh dear, they have been fighting!" exclaimed Teresa. "How willful and foolish of you not to dance with him!"

"Nicholas wouldn't allow me," whispered Rose, ill-considered pride showing through her consternation.

There was a clap of delighted laughter and some whoops of derision. The Clay Castle mob gathered around the girls again, fencing them in. Rose scarcely heard the rush of eager questions, the flotilla of dance requests, for she was watching Nicholas striding across the floor. He shouldered through the young gentlemen, contemptuously ignoring their cheeky taunts, and then she was snatched in a hubistic demonstration of ownership, and was whirling across the floor, out of the door, and along the rough path toward the horse enclosure. Nicholas paused momentarily to sweep her up in his arms. Finding Cossack, he flung her up on the pommel, and vaulted into the saddle. Almost before his feet were in the stirrups, they had cleared the low rail and were galloping through the moonlight toward the bush hills. Rose's head was up, her lips were parted, her hair, broken loose, streamed against Nicholas's face. She was afire with the touch of his lips on the nape of her neck, the sensuous pressure of his hand on her breast.

At the dark edge of the forest the horse slowed. "This will do," said Nicholas, supporting her tenderly as she slid to the ground. He leaped out of the saddle, swiftly secured the reins, and stamped down a bed of dry fern.

The air smelled of musty bark, crushed leaves, and warm earth. They sank onto the rustling fronds, giving themselves up to each other with stinging ecstasy. Their passion raged—mystical, feverish, delirious, ecstatic, and all-consuming.

Afterward, as they lay together in sweet serenity, glorying in the illicit gift of each other that the gods, relenting, had handed them one more time, Nicholas said, "This is only half a life, Rose, this life we lead apart." His arms tightened around her. "I have tried to make a success of my marriage. I have truly tried." He buried his face in her shoulder.

Rose said in a small voice, "Marriage to me would have worked. Here."

"Yes," he said at last, "but I could never take you back to Kent with me."

"Why should you return to Rundull?" she asked fiercely. "It will go to your brother."

He leaned up on one elbow, looking down into her face, smoothing her hair. "There is a madness in me, Rose. It is possible for me to inherit Rundull. I cannot release myself from the notion. Besides, I know, I seem always to have known I will go back to Rundull."

"Then I will have to go, too."

His face twisted when he thought how far she had come from squalor and poverty. He kissed her very tenderly. The moonlight filtered down upon them through a spangle of dew, at once a benison and a warning.

Next day the town was abuzz with gossip. Who was the young person calling herself Miss Flora England, who had attended the Popular Ball in a beautiful silk gown such as no artisan could afford to buy for his daughter or his wife? Everyone agreed she was a gentlewoman. The young bloods riding from Te Aro beach at sunup were agog with the mystery. Matrons bustled off, bright-eyed, to gossip with their neighbors. Everyone tried to contact Flash Jack Wilshire in the hope of gleaning further information. But Flash Jack had disappeared. On a trading expedition, it was thought.

A frenzy of surmise flew between the overstuffed chairs.

Somebody came up with the suggestion—and they wondered why nobody had thought of this before—that Mrs. Putnam was a high-born lady, thrown out by her family and finding shelter beneath the roof of the carpenter Putnam. Certainly, she and Miss England were intimate friends, if one could judge by the way they were said to have whispered behind their fans. They remembered the muslin gown and the bonnet trimmed with violets Mrs. Putnam had worn when she came ashore. And they recalled that the gown she wore on Proclamation Day had been of silk.

Now what, they wanted to know, could be made of Mrs. Putnam's dancing so much with Mr. le Grys? Was she actually a friend of the family? The gentry remembered Nicholas's demand that Mr. Revans write an editorial after she gave poor Mrs. Picton's baby to the cannibal.

And who gave Mr. le Grys the black eye? The artisans who knew had banded together in guffawing secrecy. That kind of gossip was considered to be the sole prerogative of men. They would never tell their wives. And as to the gentlemen, when asked they seemed surprised. "What black eye?" they said carelessly, winking at each other behind the ladies' backs.

Several of the young bloods, concocting flimsy excuses, called at Aurora Cottage. But to no avail. Miss England had disappeared as mysteriously as she had come. They looked over the ships in the harbor. The *Sainte Marie,* in which the fine-looking Roman Catholic Bishop Pompallier had arrived, had pulled up anchor and left. Flash Jack's schooner had also weighed anchor. That, they conceded, was a more likely transport.

Rose did not know where Teresa had gone. When she crept, sated with love, into the cottage as the sun was lightening the eastern sky, and dew lay over the morning hills, she saw the door leading to Giles's room lay open. The cot stood once again by the window. The bed was neatly made up.

In February of that year, some of the *Duke of Roxburgh*'s passengers sailed for Taranaki, the ship's decks heaped with furniture, animals, plants, and children like a Noah's Ark bearing the germ of a new colony. They planned to call their town New Plymouth. The spherical Dicky Barratt and his train went along, but Barratt's Hotel kept its name and with it the memories. The new owner gave a bumper dinner, inviting the leading male colonists, and put Colonel Wakefield in the chair. They were celebrating Governor Gipp's approval of the company's purchase of 110,000 acres.

The ladies, who were beginning to demand rights in exchange for doing their own housework and cooking, were furious. "If you ignore us now, you relegate us to the role of servants," they said.

The gentlemen, alert to the modifications that were being made on the old ways, considered. It was not thought ladylike to make demands, but they had to admit that they themselves were less gentlemanly now. Somebody had said he would wager an eel to a sackful of onions that, when the top hats wore out, they would not be replaced.

"Are you saying this matter of getting titles to your land is not our concern?" the wives asked indignantly. "It is very much our affair." They did not win that round, but they made a point. If they were not to be languid and important in their own homes then they must have public stature and sharing.

In May, Cressida's nurse arrived, along with the ugly cook and two housemaids.

"If your mother had looked the length and breadth of England," expostulated Nicholas, "I am certain she could not have found so ugly a creature as your new cook."

Cressida laughed gaily. "I believe Mama did, as you say, look the length and breadth of the country."

"Was it really necessary to send one who is pockmarked *and* with teeth missing?"

"Yes," replied Cressida soberly. "Yes. I do believe so. It is the only kind we will keep."

More logs were sent off the property. Nicholas was anxious that his woolshed should be built, like the house, from his own pines. Inevitably, the carpenters who came to build the woolshed at Rata Hill took back into town tales of the housemaids who brought them their billy tea. Soon, on the flimsiest of excuses, young artisans began to appear at the back door. Plain girls that they were, the maids delighted in their unexpected popularity. Cressida grew nervous and was short with them, importuning Nicholas to take them to task, to point out with some severity that he had paid their fares.

It was to no avail. Ill feeling grew on both sides.

Within a week, the naughty creatures were scampering off to town every evening, on the rumps of hacks borrowed from the farmhands' employers. Before the month had gone, it became obvious that they too would go, just as soon as accommodation could be provided for them. Nicholas wryly berated his own single hands for not falling in love with the girls. "I would have built you houses on the estate," he said. But he spoke too late. They were all learning their lessons the hard way.

The Dragon, as Nicholas dubbed Cressida's nurse, ignoring advice that Maori maidens were dirty and lazy, took it upon herself to visit Te Puni's *pa* and return with two giggling native missionary-educated girls called Esau and Manata. Having deloused them and scrubbed them down with carbolic soap, she braided their hair and proceeded to instruct them in the arts of English domesticity. At first they sulked. Then they ran away. Te Puni sent them back.

If they were slow to learn and lazy, they were at least amiable. And they were silent about the house in their bare feet, the Dragon having failed utterly in her efforts to get them shod. Ben came upon Manata straining the milk through a grubby duster. "They're dirty brutes an' no mistake. I dunno as 'ow 'er Ladyship can do with them."

"Beggars can't be choosers," returned the Dragon tartly, omitting to add that she had recently caught Esau washing dishes with a flannel used for cleaning the floor. But the Maoris did introduce novelty and variety. They scraped potatoes with *pipi* shells brought up from the beach, and the house was filled with their soft, melodious voices in sweet harmony. The Dragon never cured them of the habit of taking themselves off for a swim in one of the river pools, considering the break well worth the scolding they received.

There was now a household at Rata Hill. Cressida walked once more with swishing skirts and head held high. Another kind of milestone had been passed in the strange climb toward their uncertain future.

That year of 1841 was fraught with troubles. News came in May that a Taupo war party was moving south. The warriors were said to have ravaged Waitotara, killing and eating those too old and infirm to flee. The Wellington natives under chiefs Wharepouri, Te Puni, and Taringauri, head of the Ngati-Tama tribe, mustered several hundred men and held them ready. There was talk of recalling the 80th Regiment, of setting up fortifications. The town worried about its outlying settlers. Men working far out on their estates worried about their wives. Nicholas taught Cressida to handle a gun.

The Dragon would have nothing to do with firearms. She thought they were far more dangerous than the Maoris. "I'd like to see one of those heathens come into m'Lady's house," she would mutter. "Over my dead body."

Nicholas thought privately that Maoris would not dare.

Meetings to discuss the safety of the settlement were held in the coffee room of Barratt's Hotel. Someone pointed out that the Maori uprising could surely, with tact, be contained as a purely native affair. They called on the young missionary Octavius Hadfield. With all the complexity of trouble between the natives, the government, and the missionaries, he alone remained aloof from criticism. Employing his particular brand of calm and courageous reasoning, he turned the warriors back.

Lulled into a false sense of security, Englishmen bought Hutt Valley land from the Company and built houses. Taringakuri laid claim to the land in the Maori way by demolishing them. Homes did not count. The man who cleared and cultivated land automatically became the owner. The chief built a village on the riverbank and fortified it with palisades. The settlers appealed to the governor, who drove the wedge deeper between officialdom and the settlers by declining to interfere.

After the miracle of Teresa's visit, life for Rose fell flat as a pancake. As a new pregnancy advanced people grew kind, but there was no fun. The general feeling was one of smugness that little Mrs. Putnam had at last met her Waterloo. With two children to care for, there would be little time for mischief.

In August, Joseph Putnam was born, making his unwelcome arrival on a cold day when the wind shrieked through the town, driving dust into spirals, and sending the harbor into a ferment. Rose glanced without interest at the screwed-up red face, then looked away, confounding Dr. Stokes.

She tended the child dutifully, and fed him, but she did

not love him. He was a blood tie with the mob who had
chased her down Rundull High Street with rape in their
hearts, and a symbol that perhaps the worst of life might
still be there, clinging to her heels long after she had
thought it had been left behind. When shown the new
arrival, Giles also looked at him without interest. Daniel
chose the name, adhering to the old world with its old
hates, calling the child after his own father, who had
been transported to Australia for stealing a sheep from
the Rundull estates.

Toward the end of that month, without bothering to
notify the settlers in advance, Governor Hobson came.
The Maoris, to whom dignity was paramount, gazed in
scornful amazement at the government brig *Victoria,* which
was smaller than any of the immigrant ships. The Maori
language was not rich. There was only one word for
woman. Its meaning was dependent upon the manner of
utterance *wahine.*

Colonel Wakefield hurriedly ran up a flag, and a few
sympathetic citizens went down to the beach to watch
Captain Hobson disembark, but the majority expressed
their bitterness by continuing with their affairs. Rumors
were rife of waste at Government House, of the numerous sinecures at the gulf of Hauraki. The governor had
levied customs duties and taxes to the tune of a thousand
pounds a year on Wellington, yet allowed them not a
penny of the public revenue accrued.

Wellington's public institutions were in a bad way. The
jail was a disgrace. Sixty prisoners, chiefly mutinous or
runaway sailors, were huddled together in a wretched
native building large enough to house fifteen or twenty at
the most. The postmaster in his dilapidated reed hut was
forced to stuff the letters into potato sacks. They blew
away if he attempted to sort them on the table. And, to
add insult to injury, on pure hearsay Hobson pronounced
the Middle Island uninhabitable. Yet they were awaiting
only the arrival of the colonel's sailor brother before
founding a town there—already provisionally named for
Admiral Lord Nelson.

A levée was held for the governor, but few attended.
Their wounds were too sore. They would never forgive
him now for failing for so long to recognize them, for

short-sightedly making Auckland the capital without seeing Wellington's splended harbor.

Captain Arthur Wakefield arrived on *Whitby* while Hobson was taking a disinterested look at the land on the other side of Cook Strait. At the dinner held aboard, the great body of independent settlers remained seated, upending their empty glasses when the chairman proposed a toast to the governor. Hobson had to make amends before he could be honored. He admitted his errors but declined to rectify them. Since an unfortunate attack of paralysis, his health was deteriorating, but the anger he generated in the settlers' hearts left no room for compassion.

Rose listened without particular interest to the town's indignation. She did not equate public order with private happiness. Daniel had been kinder since she had given him a son of his own, and he seemed more at home in Flash Jack's house, but the arrival of Joseph, the fruit of Daniel's pitiless insistence and her duty, had lowered her spirits. She had a feeling of having let Nicholas down. Never seeing nor hearing of Beatrix le Grys, she found it difficult to convince herself the child still existed.

The months passed, and still Nicholas did not come into town. People said he worked harder than his men. "Like there's a devil driving him." The colonel wanted him on the Legislative Council, but he was not to be persuaded. "Let those whose futures are irrevocably here indulge in petty power," he said. "Mine, God willing, is not."

Some of Rose's loneliness was assuaged by visits from missionary-educated Maoris. They would come unheralded and squat cross-legged on the grass, proud in their shell necklaces and ear ornaments, their white teeth flashing in brown faces as they laughed, their glossy hair prettily adorned with carved combs of white bone. They told her folk tales that had been passed down from generation to generation and Rose was charmed, English folk history having in the main passed her by.

Inevitably, though, the Maori obsession with war and killing drove a wedge between them. "I will not listen to atrocities," she told them firmly one day in November.

"We eat only those slain in battle, and slaves," they protested ingenuously. "People who are dead are only bodies. Besides, their eyes will give our warriors strength for battle. You ask us to explain about *uto*, but when we do, you say you will not listen."

Rose sighed sharply. She knew they were thinking on another level; killing was not atrocious to them. They just wanted her to know how brave they were, and how important was *uto*, their word for revenge. But everyone said the immigrants should try to understand the Maoris. "I will listen."

Epecka continued, "Our war party overtook and slew the chief. We roasted him, then his tongue was cut out and packed in a calabash with the dripping. Our people covered the tongue with the tattooed skin from his buttocks, and we sent it to his tribe. That was *uto*. The tongue that ate Tiwaewae, our kinsman, was eaten by his kinsmen, and his death suitably avenged. It is necessary you accept *uto*, Rose, or you do not understand the Maori."

But Rose was feeling sick. "You must go," she said, abruptly.

"It's not the color of their skins," Rose told Daniel later, desperately needing to talk to someone of her own color and creed. Desperate, also, for comfort. "I tried to tell them about Florrie and Grandy, but they said disdainfully, 'Florrie live all the same the Maori, eh?' They want to look up to us. They think Grandy is a slave." They would eat him, she thought, shuddering.

Daniel grunted. "Ignorant savages."

His unthinking, unsympathetic reply drove out her wits. "Daniel, I'm pregnant again," she burst out. Better to tell him than tell no one. In her loneliness and despair she even imagined for a moment that Daniel would understand.

"That'll keep yer out of mischief," he replied, grinning.

Rose picked up Edmund and cried furious tears into his fur. "I will not have a baby every year," she said defiantly, lifting her head. "I will not."

"You'll 'ave what's given yer," retorted Daniel unfeelingly.

Rose sat down at the kitchen table opposite him and held out her hands, taking his rough ones, lifting her face appealingly. "Daniel, be nice to me."

He lifted his downcast eyes, and she was surprised to see them dark with hurt. "What about the Te Aro ball, then?" he asked.

Shock stemmed Rose's tears and stiffened her spine.

"Yer thought no one would tell me? There's allers someone wants ter cause trouble." Daniel pulled his hands resentfully out of her warm grip. "I'll tell you wot 'e said. 'There's only one way ter keep 'er kind at 'ome. Keep 'er in the family way.' "

Rose crept off to her little parlor to lick her wounds. Foremost in her mind was the fact that she was now, suddenly and unexpectedly, in Daniel's power. If he kept her pregnant all the time she would lose Nicholas! She thought, with rising hysteria, that she must write to the curate again. Florrie and Adam must come. She *must* have someone to talk to.

Rose was far from unique in her suffering. While the men could be diverted by hard work or the arrival of the first steam saw or the formation of an Agricultural Society, all the women were lonely. In times of excitement and happiness they forgot, but when they met the random disasters of life, as they all did from time to time, they missed the sympathy of warm arms and wise counseling. Erstwhile innocent brides grew hard little cores of defense and self-reliance. As time passed their inner resources grew.

Mrs. Stitchbury wrote to Cressida from a sensuous heaven that smelled of the sweet grasses and stocks and heliotrope; of balmy sea breezes and sunshine. Her joy and her happiness came flying off the page at every line. She lived in a wonderful little cottage her husband had built, in a virgin bay full of the cries of sea birds and the sweet soughing of the sea.

She had two children now, and hoped God would give them another the following year. She was indeed blessed, she wrote. Even her family had forgiven her. They could not be restrained from sending her little luxuries—cloth to be made up for the children, so many seed packets that she scarcely could find the time to plant them all. The garden was already driving her wild with its beauty. She lived in a drift of flowers that filled the air with perfume all the year round.

Schooners and cutters on their way to Auckland occasionally called with mail and provisions. When there was time, which was not often, their captains might come ashore and stay a day or two. She had not seen a white woman since leaving Wellington, but it did not signify. She was as happy as a sandfly. Stitchbury himself was trading in timber as well as farming. One day, when Mr. le Grys was less busy, perhaps they would come and visit?

"She does not say if the fellow is making a success," remarked Nicholas, frowning. They were all obsessed with success, for themselves and for each other. It was their justification for having done what they did.

Cressida looked mistily out of the window over the rich, rolling green acres of Rata Hill; at the white sheep, incessantly baaing and answering, the small ones leaping and chasing, their tails flicking. So many of them to be dipped and shorn and mustered. To be saved from predators. To be fenced in, driven, guarded. What is success? she wondered. Surely it is happiness.

She had learned to live with what fate dealt her, as she had learned to live with the tearing wind, the jerking and flapping of the curtains, the noisy slamming of doors, the regular, monotonous sound of the lowing cows waiting to be milked, the clanking of buckets and urns, the closeness of life in the raw. God willing, the memory of the lot of a squire's lady of Saxon Mote or Rundull would fade altogether in time.

Mysteriously, because it had been Nicholas who suggested Nurse's coming, her arrival seemed to have driven him further away. She had seen real malevolence in his eyes when he looked at her. He did not dislike Cook, now that he had learned to live with her ugliness.

She could never have guessed the reason for Nicholas's antagonism. Every time that starched figure came into the room, chest outthrust like a prow of a ship, he had an instant vision of a small chamber with flowered wallpaper, a chair with a shell-shaped back, an empty bed.

Nicholas understood himself now far better than he ever had before. The screaming scarlet of the sunrises, the shriek of the wind, the live weight of an axe in his hands, the aching of his muscles, the peace of the silent nights—the weka's cry did not disturb his sleep—had brought him face to face with a man he had sensed within him, but never seen.

He knew now that when he climbed the stairs the morning after his wedding, to the room where he had left

Rose, one part of his mind had made a decision which he had not consciously recognized. With Rose at his side, laughing, loving, sharing, learning, he felt there would have been none of this accursed hankering after Henry's demise, the persistent hunger for what was not rightly his. They would have built another Rundull in the Southern Seas.

A kingdom for their inheritors, the wealth of handsome, strapping sons Rose would have given him. What did it signify that they should be born out of wedlock? With Felicity at Court, something could doubtless be done about that. And if not, well, in another generation the matter would be forgotten. Was not Robert FitzRoy, their governor-elect, great-grandson of the Duchess of Cleveland and Charles II? That gentleman's ascent from the wrong side of the blanket had done him no harm.

But it was far, far too late.

35

The new baby came in July 1842, only eleven months after Joseph. He was an appealing little mite, so much smaller and less stalwart than the robust Joseph that, in spite of her resentment at bearing him, Rose could not dislike him. "But I will not have another," she vowed. "Daniel has two sons now, and that will do."

Daniel stood looking down at his child more with satisfaction than with pride, and watching his heavy features for a show of warmth, Rose realized with a creeping chill that he was thinking of the boy less as a son than as a trap for her. A trap whose jaws it was in his power to strengthen every year. She said resentfully, "I thought you would be pleased to have another boy."

"We'll call him Ned," returned Daniel, as though he had not heard.

"Ned?" she whispered. "You cannot call him Ned."

"Ned," repeated Daniel, "after Ned Taylor wot yer fancy gen'l'man murdered."

Rose fell back weakly on the pillows. "Daniel," she cried piteously, "don't hate me. I know I've done wrong, but please don't punish me like this."

"Ned," repeated Daniel triumphantly and stumped out of the room. She knew then that she had gone too far in attending the Te Aro ball, for it had been the final straw that broke the back of Daniel's resentful tolerance.

The next day, when Rose's milk refused to come, Dr. Stokes asked with concern, "What is the matter, Mrs.

Putnam? Tears? You've got a beautiful little boy. You should be as happy as a lark."

Rose's mouth buttoned up against her misery. "Daniel wants to call the baby Ned."

"And what would you like to call him, my dear?" the doctor asked genially. "It doesn't seem to me an insurmountable problem. I am sure you can choose one name each. What would you like to call him?"

"I'd like to call him Charlie." Rose snatched at the first name that came into her head.

"Why not? It's a nice name. Edward Charles, or Charles Edward. Humph!" said the doctor, looking fierce. "I'll speak to that husband of yours. Anyone who upsets my patients has to answer to me."

"What an odd little creature Mrs. Putnam is," he remarked to his wife that night, shaking his head thoughtfully. "Strong as a lion one moment, falling into pieces over the most inconsequential matter the next."

When Mrs. Stokes walked over the following afternoon with some hot soup, she found Rose quite recovered. "The baby's name is Charlie," Rose announced. She was sitting up in bed with the bundle in the crook of her arm. "Charlie Putnam. I don't know what name Daniel may have registered, but I shall call him Charlie, and that is that."

"She is strong as a lion again," Mrs. Stokes reported to her husband that evening. "I believe she accepts this baby. Perhaps it will be a turning point for them."

There was a turning point approaching, but it was not one either of them could have envisaged at the time.

In October of that year the road linking Port Nicholson and the Hutt was to be ceremoniously opened at last. It had been an altogether uncomfortable project, and everyone was glad when it was finished. There had been discontent over wages; threats to burn down Colonel Wakefield's house; trouble with the Maoris, who despised roadworkers, who in turn despised the natives' dark skins and refused to pander to their precious dignity.

By tacit agreement, Sam Phelps, as the town's most colorful character, was to be first on the road with his dray and team of bullocks. Crowds had turned out less for the official ceremony than to see whether the drunken, foulmouthed driver would treat this honor with decorum.

Daniel, who usually stayed a few paces behind Rose as she pushed the baby carriage Flash Jack had given her, indicated new confidence by walking at her side. She never heard him call the new baby Ned, for she had closed her mind against the name. "His name is Charlie," she told people with spirit whether Daniel was listening or not. Even Giles, who was now two and a half years old, called him Char.

From their vantage point in the crowd, Rose looked up longingly at the well-dressed citizens in their gigs and buggies and pony carts; at the young bloods on their mounts lining up for a race. Oliver was going to teach her one day to ride, but it was impossible if she was always pregnant. She thought longingly of Teresa, who had shown her how much fun there was in life if one was brave and strong—and lucky. But Joseph had brought her luck plummeting down. And Charlie kept it there. She could almost wish Teresa had never come and taught her to dare and dance and be gay. Her brief stay seemed to have marked Rose forever. Her going had left a hole as deep and empty as a well.

She was startled out of her wan reverie by the sound of her name being called. "Hey, Mrs. Putnam, dear. It'd be a honor if yer was ter sit up beside me on this hauspicious occasion." Sam Phelps was standing erect in his wagon, waving his whip, yelling over the heads of the onlookers. Rose's head came up, her hands slid off the pram handle, and she started automatically forward, the dreary months of her pregnancies falling away.

"Rose!" bellowed Daniel, but she was already running. Sam, his flushed face wreathed in a proud smile, reached down. Someone in the crowd took her waist in his hands and tossed her aboard, skirts flying.

She looked out breathlessly, radiantly, over the upturned faces, some laughing, some frowning, some whispering, and some giggling, but all looking her way. She felt like a queen in her little sailor hat with the ribbons. The skirt of her India muslin dress and her petticoats caught in the breeze and flew up like a cloud of thistledown over the coarse tweed of Sam Phelps's coat, wickedly exposing her calves. The young gentlemen on their horses pranced closer, their eyes devouring her audaciously, their red mouths laughing. It was the artisans' ball all over again.

"Garn! Git on yer blinkin' Shortland! Stir yer blinkin' stumps, or I'll cut yer blinkin' tail off," shouted her driver exuberantly. "Git on or I'll whip the skin off yer."

Rose gasped and came down to earth with a thump. Lieutenant Willoughby Shortland, colonial secretary and chief magistrate, was promenading with his little retinue along the beginnings of the new road. He turned his cold red face and glared.

"Are you applying those expressions to me, Mr. Phelps?"

Sam grinned innocently. "I weren't a-speakin' ter you; I'm a-driving me bullocks. Them's their names."

The crowd roared with delighted laughter. Jerningham Wakefield and his cronies were splitting their sides. "Bravo," cried the young blades on horseback, letting go of their reins and clapping. Colonel Wakefield, dignified in his tall white hat, swinging his cane, stared stonily ahead.

The wagon creaked swiftly onto the open road, followed by a train of buggies and pony carts. "Oh, Sam!" cried Rose, her face flaming. "Sam!"

But he was unabashed. "Keep yer hies open fer anymore henemies," he guffawed. "I'll change the critters' names ter fit 'em."

Oh, what did it matter! The crowd's amusement filled Rose with excitement and fired her blood. She bounced forward on the seat, clutched the iron bar for support, and threw back her head. The wind caught her little sailor hat, flinging it onto her shoulders, tossing it by its ribbons. Oh, but this was such fun! "Git on yer blinkin' Shortland," she cried giddily, and they laughed together until their sides ached.

There was, inevitably, a certain shame attached to the colorful day. On arrival at the Hutt, Flash Jack appeared mysteriously on a great prancing steed, and without a word lifted Rose down. In stern silence he brought her home on his pillion.

"Did you think I made a fool of myself?" she asked demurely, not at all sorry for what she had done, feeling that she had canceled out all the long, weary months of boredom. He only turned and looked at her with a grim smile.

Oliver reported having seen Nicholas start forward with a furious expression on his face, but that Lady Cressida had caught him by the coattails. Muttering angrily under his breath, he had turned away.

"I am a person now, Oliver," Rose said, consciously proud.

Oliver grinned. He was getting to be a young man and understood a great deal. His holiday trips away on Flash Jack's schooner, which were not holidays at all, but long days of work—hauling in sails, scrubbing down decks, cooking, learning the facts of life—had broadened and stretched and strengthened him. He knew Rose would not have done what she did if she had been a real lady. But there was a special charm to Rose's indiscretions. As with Sam Phelps, the town was grudgingly working toward an acceptance of the fact that Wellington was a more colorful place for her presence.

The gentry, too, made mistakes. Samuel Revans, writing about his life to indiscreet friends in England, boasting as the gentlemen did of their newly discovered prowess, remarked that he had done numerous odd jobs of carpentering, including the erection of two water closets. The letter was published. Nicholas roared with laughter when a shocked note came from Countess Rundull, saying she hoped very much that they were not growing into a coarse nation.

It was inevitable that a certain coarseness should have drifted in. The gentlemen had more opportunities here for manliness, for rage, for happiness, for going over the top in every way. Life grew regrettably less and less genteel. There were those vexed working bullocks whose ears were so attuned to swearing that they would not respond to refinements. The ladies would have to be deaf not to hear, and children were always naughty enough to imitate.

Colonel Wakefield imported a thoroughbred from Sydney for his motherless daughter, who was due to arrive on *Clifford,* bearing with her the colony's first hive of bees. The ship came in one rough, dark night and to everyone's consternation ran aground inside the heads. The colonel rushed agitatedly out in an open boat to supervise its refloat. Somehow, the possession of a fifteen-year-old daughter made William Wakefield more human, and certainly more responsible. His popularity rose overnight. Matrons wished to chaperone Emily, to entertain her, to introduce her to eligible young gentlemen. With her impeccable connections as granddaughter of Sir John Sydney of Penshurst Place, great-niece of the earl of Albemarle and Mrs. Coke of Holkham Hall, she was indeed a social catch.

Jerningham came down to meet her wearing stout duck trousers, and a red woolen smock that was belted over a checked cotton shirt without neck-cloth. His hair was long, his beard unkempt, and he was smoking a short black pipe half submerged beneath the brim of a dirty manila hat. She stared at him in amazement, and particularly at a sheath knife, eighteen inches long in the blade, stuck negligently into his belt.

"I use it for cutting up tobacco," he explained.

"I had expected you to be more of a gentleman," she replied with cousinly candor.

"There are only two gentlemen in Wellington now, according to the municipal roll," retorted Jerningham flippantly. "You will find a husband, dear Emily, from among a new class of Englishman, and like him all the better for his diligence."

"That is not what I mean," retorted the colonel's daughter. "Of course I understand that a gentleman may be gainfully employed, but I am sure it is not necessary to look like *that.*"

There was afterward a temporary improvement, but it did not last. People said openly that young Wakefield was going to the dogs. Samuel Revans, writing to a friend in England, expressed a wish that Edward Gibbon should recall his son: "He lives away from us at Wanganui and leads a life he knows his friends would not countenance. It has been suggested that he should go home, but he is obstinate and will not listen." In the event, his going was to be taken out of everyone's hands in the most tragic way.

In the meantime, Jerningham set about organizing the colony's first race meeting. Having received no response from Nicholas to his advertisement in the *Gazette,* and

not having seen him in town, Jerningham rode out to
Rata Hill.

Cressida was standing on the veranda, her eyes narrowed against the glaring late-winter sunshine. She heard
hoofbeats and saw Jerningham coming at a gallop up the
slope. Her first reaction was to instruct the servants to
say she was not at home. She hesitated. Here was a
heaven-sent opportunity to ask him for the truth about
the Putnams' presence.

If she dared to make use of it.

She walked to the end of the vine-shrouded veranda
and back, her fingers clasped tightly together, the soles
of her small boots tapping on the bare boards, her mind
in confusion.

I could say it quite casually, she thought, not feeling
casual at all: By the way, were you responsible . . .

Of course, he would know what she was about and,
she realized with apprehension, could consider her disloyal in the extreme. He might even tell Nicholas. She
decided to take the risk. She was still smarting from the
insult of Nicholas's anger when that girl made an exhibi-
tion of herself with the bullock cart driver. But in spite
of, or perhaps because of, all the upsets, Cressida yearned
for a new beginning.

She would ask, she decided defiantly. Should she discover Nicholas had been telling the truth, her indiscretion would be worthwhile. God willing, such a truth
might help her to look at him with humility and new
eyes. She steeled herself to go down the steps, hesitated
a moment with one hand on the rail, and then glided
across the lawn.

Jerningham had intended to ride straight on to the
stable yard. Seeing Cressida approach, he drew rein,
leaped off his horse, and doffed his crumpled hat. Slipping the reins over his wrist, he opened the garden gate
to allow her through.

"Good-day to you, Lady Cressida. Is Nicholas not at
home?"

"He is indeed, but I wish to speak to you myself." She
saw his quick, wary frown. "Forgive me if I appear blunt,
Mr. Wakefield. It is better that I come straight to the
point. Was it at your instigation that the Putnams trav-

eled out on *Aurora?*" She waited for his knowing, deri-
sory reply.

But if Jerningham Wakefield was sometimes foolish,
he was also kind. He did not like Cressida because she
made no attempt to hide her disapproval of him, but
something in him now recognized her need. He had
never had any compunction about lying when it came to
helping a friend.

"Yes," he said promptly. "Yes, it was."

Forgetting that she had asked her question in the fervent desire that she should receive this very reply,
Cressida's dislike of him overwhelmed all else, and she
snapped, "May I ask why?"

Jerningham leaned back against the horse, stretching
an arm along the mane, taking the warm, friendly smell
of sweat into his nostrils like a protective skin. By God,
but he would have expected Nicholas, who was so devilish shrewd with women, to have softened this frozen
bitch by now. He would not bed her if she was the last
female on earth. The cant phrases that came so easily to
the Wakefields rolled off his tongue. "It is my father's
wish that as many as possible of the underprivileged who
have potential should be aided to a new start."

"You consider the carpenter Putnam to have potential?"

"No," he replied, idly running his fingers through the
horse's mane, "but his wife has, and therefore their children deserve better than they would have had at Rundull.
I do not mean to criticize your father-in-law, m'Lady, for
it is the way of things at home, but you have asked the
question and therefore you saddle yourself with my reply. Please don't take it personally that I should have
caused you such offense. It was not meant so."

"You will find Nicholas at the stockyards behind the
house," she said distantly and turned around and went
back through the gate, across the lawn and the wide,
leaf-shaded veranda.

So, she had her answer, and to her own shame. Nicholas had not lied to her. She stood at the foot of the stairs
leaning on the banister, her face in the circle of her arm.
The unappetizing scent of the new wood touched her
nostrils. "Cannot you give us happiness other than at the
expense of one another?" she whispered angrily.

Jerningham undid his mount's halter and tied him to a

ring in the wall. He was pleased with himself for having done his friend a good turn. He eyed the big, squat homestead so warmly clad with vine. But for him, it would not have been there, settling cozily into the countryside.

Shortly the Land Commissioners would be here sorting things out. With the granting of the title to his estate, Nicholas would be sitting prettier than he could ever be at home. Jerningham did not think of the home country with a capital as others did. Nicholas had conjectured mistakenly when he said Edward's son would grasp his adventure with both hands, knowing the fleshpots of London awaited him when the novelty had worn off. This was his Home. Jerningham never intended to leave.

Now he must persuade Nicholas to take an interest in the running of the country. Everyone said he should be on the legislative council. They all wanted the name le Grys in the annals of such history as was being made. But Nicholas, for all his hard work on the estate, still wore the air of a bird of flight. Today at lunch, when the colonel heard that Jerningham was riding out to Rata Hill, he had said, "Get Nicholas into the town. He comes only to buy and sell, and occasionally to go to the Dickens Society. But it was your father's intention that the boy should take a leading role in the management of the colony's affairs, and he would indeed be disappointed to hear that the fellow is concerned only with the land."

The dogs set up a frenzied barking. Nicholas turned and saw the familiar figure swaggering through the young orchard that separated the sheep yards from the homestead. He had been working with the men, docking the tails of some ewes that had somehow escaped the knife the year before. His first reaction was to tell Jerningham he was too busy to talk to him. Then suddenly, a gate burst open, and escaping sheep were leaping and jerking on their thin white legs across the grass. Leo and Peter, with cries of dismay, mounted and galloped off in their wake, the sheepdogs flying out in front. There was nothing to do but wait for order to be restored. Nicholas climbed onto the slip rails, and sat with his palms resting on his wide-spread knees, watching the visitor approach. He came with a bounce, ruddy-faced and stalwart, his long hair and unruly moustache swept by the wind as he walked, his hat clutched in his hand.

"I've come to tell you we're planning a Derby Day," Jerningham announced cheerfully. "You had better put Cossack into training, so that Francis Molesworth's Calmuck Tartar don't run off with all the prizes." Resting one sturdy shank on the lower rail, he took out his evil-looking black briar and began to fill the bowl.

"Derby Day!" echoed Nicholas derisively, pushing his hat onto the back of his head, squinting into the sun. "And where, may I ask, are you going to find a stretch of level ground?"

"The sands, old boy. The sands, of course. We'll estimate the date of the lowest spring tide. The beach would be uncovered from the mouth of the Hutt River to Petone *pa*. I have already persuaded the establishment to grant a public holiday. *And* I've got nine horses entered at ten guineas each."

Nicholas's dark eyes took on a quizzical look. In his more lighthearted moments he could not withhold a certain reluctant admiration for Jerningham. "You know as well as I do I am too busy to train Cossack." But he already felt a tug of excitement at the thought of racing his steed across the hard sands, with the roar of the surf on one side, the shouts of the crowd on the other.

"All work and no play makes Jack a dull boy," quoted Jerningham tritely, turning away from the wind and putting a lucifer match to his foul pipe. "Your lady wife will wish to attend. I cannot see you wandering up and down with her while men like Watts and Virtue and Bannister, whose neddies don't hold a candle to yours, take the plaudits of the crowd. I might add, my uncle is having a cold collation prepared at his residence, which happens to be close by the finishing line."

Nicholas's mind flew to the Derby Day of 1839. Every detail of it came alive. Rose in her India muslin gown, her beautiful face glowing beneath the brim of the bonnet that had caused all the trouble at Petone; her eyes flashing like emeralds as she bounced up and down cheering the horses in; Rose having her fortune told by one of the gypsies on the hill, hugging to herself the piece of heather they gave her, and the secrets they whispered in her ears. To him, one hag had merely said, "The line will go on." He had been turning away when something stopped him, made him swing back, though he did not for one moment believe these witches and soothsayers of the hedgerows knew any more than anyone else about the future. "You do not say 'my' line. I wish to know. Is it *my* line that will go on?" The ragged creature had replied, her black eyes evil and knowing, without even a surface flicker of goodwill.

"Yours and hers. But first there will be violence and loss, and no way either of you shall avoid it. You will pay for this line, my fine sir. But yes, it will go on."

On the great day the natives' dogs were tied up, the pigs penned safely in the *pa*. Jerningham, galloping along the beach, enjoying himself hugely, rounded up sleepy natives, explaining why they might not today lie basking in the sun; begged whalers to haul their boats in or take them out to sea; persuaded owners of idling craft to closely furl their sails, so that the flapping might not startle racing steeds.

Carts, wagons, and bullock drays were pressed into service for the long procession out from town. Gentlemen wore elegant dove-gray belltoppers and white gloves. Some of the leading hostesses, dressed in lacy gowns with ruffled sleeves, came in a spring cart, sitting on chairs ingeniously covered in flags. Mrs. Watts, whose husband was one of the gentleman jockeys, arrived proudly in a gig recently imported from New South Wales. A separate wagon carried the band. A flotilla of boats of all shapes and sizes brought those who preferred to travel by sea.

Booths, tents, and stalls were put up on the edge of the sand. A man wheeled a barrow selling ginger pop. Five or six hundred citizens assembled to see the races begin, the artisans' wives and children dressed in their best, the ladies twittering beneath parasols. In the event only seven horses started, one having been killed by a bullock rampaging on the beach soon after landing from England. It was one of the hazards of bringing animals on a long voyage: they sometimes went mad on arrival.

It was a wonderful day. Another first for the new colony. Cossack, with Nicholas wearing the Rundull colors of gold and blue, won three races. He looked in vain for Rose and his little son. When he could not see them, some of the triumph went out of the day.

It was Joseph who had kept them away. He chose that date, as though deliberately, to run a fever. Rose attended him with meticulously cloaked resentment, aware that Daniel was silently gloating.

Joseph was a colorless child even when he was well. Now, with his hair lank and his eyes dull, she found him singularly unappealing. She got through the day by removing herself in spirit, dreaming she was galloping over the sand with her arms around Nicholas's warm, hard waist while the plaintive cry of the gulls merged with the pounding of Cossack's great hooves on the hard sand.

Cressida took heart from a new hope that Rose might actually have come to her senses; that she intended in future to stay discreetly out of sight.

At the end of the wonderful day thirty gentlemen on horseback followed in procession behind the ladies as they returned to town for the race dinner at Barratt's Hotel. It was just like Epsom, they declared happily. As Jerningham had said, Epsom on Derby Day.

36

Hobson was dead, he who had defied death and the pirates of the West Indies only to have his heart broken by the indignities heaped upon him by the settlers. They had the pompous Willoughby Shortland now as acting governor. They were, always had been, equally critical of him. Jerningham had called Hobson an imbecile. But at least he had been a man of honor. Shortland was not. Already it was rumored that he was taking advantage of his position to engage in land dealing.

When news came of Captain FitzRoy's appointment as governor, a bonfire was lit on a high point near the Royal Hotel, and coaxed to a great conflagration with barrels of tar. The onlookers, primed with porter, burned an effigy of Shortland. But, as Cressida had said, by the very nature of things any governor was going to be unpopular. The settlers had tasted independence beyond their wildest dreams and would ride roughshod over anyone who dictated to them now.

Outside the harassments of government at Aurora Cottage, Rose kept her ears pricked for events that might require Nicholas's presence in the town. The arrival of a ship bearing horses or cattle or sheep could bring him riding in. She would go to Flash Jack's store pretending she needed a spool of thread or a piece of ribbon. Then, standing idly by the counter, smiling prettily at him, she would extract the information she needed. At the appropriate time she would wander down to the front, and along to the edge of the forest where the road from Rata Hill cut through.

She began to develop a sixth sense of Nicholas's coming. Several times she was actually there, about to turn the pram around, when he emerged into the open. He would leap off Cossack, and they would walk together along the waterfront. Sometimes he brought her a shoulder of mutton, or a leg. Daniel never knew where the extras came from. He gave Rose his earnings and ate what she served, but for every free gift she put a few more shillings into the fund for Florrie and Adam's fare.

"What does Giles call Daniel, Rose?"

"Nothing." Sometimes, when Daniel was trying to persuade Joseph, who was a slow talker, to say "Papa" she would see a puzzled look on Giles's face. She felt he knew instinctively he did not belong to Daniel. "One day," she said, "I shall tell him he is your son." She glanced up, apprehensive that the child could have overheard. And he had. She could tell by the way he stared studiously ahead over Cossack's ears.

Nicholas chuckled. "He'd be hard-pressed to make something of that at two and a half."

"Don't underestimate him," she whispered. Sometimes the child's silences, the dark, deep expressions she surprised on his face as he watched her, made her almost afraid. Giles had come into the world compensated, she was certain, in a way they had yet to understand.

"So that's the latest!" Nicholas said the first time he saw Charlie. "Ah, well, Rose, you were meant to fructify." And he sighed. Sometimes he would lift Giles up and place him in the saddle, leading Cossack, walking at Rose's side. "He's going to make a great horseman. I'll get him a pony when he's four." Rose hugged the delicious promises to herself, never considering where they would keep a pony, or indeed how they would explain it away. Of course people noticed, and gossiped and surmised. A soupçon of scandal from the artisans' ball had eventually filtered through, but Rose's undoubted involvement with that young aristocrat Miss Flora England kept tongues in check. Besides, there was the enigma of Lady Cressida. So far as anyone could tell, the marriage was satisfactory.

People trod warily. The Library Committee, most of all, felt the discomfort of not knowing, but they pushed the matter to the backs of their minds. They were not the kind of people to apologize or retreat. Besides, they were virtuously aware that even though she was burdened with three children, Mrs. Putnam was still desirable in the eyes of men with a roving eye. She seemed to grow more beautiful with each birth, and certainly never looked like losing her figure. Husbands admitted her name was bandied about lecherously in the taverns. And there was that tasteless sobriquet, *Aurora Rose*. Where had it come from? The voyage out was history now.

Early in 1843, the shepherds reported that sheep on the perimeter of the Rata Hill estate were moving restlessly up and down the hills, not pausing long enough to grow fat. Nicholas rode out and saw with apprehension that some of his splendid new pasture had been rooted up. Then one morning sixty little carcasses were found. He had heard from the Maoris that wild pigs traveled down from the back country in winter to search for roots. One of the natives he encountered wandering over his estate said, "You look for sow. Maybe have piglets, maybe stay to eat lambs. Easy meat."

Nicholas returned grimly to the house, slung a rifle across his back, and rode out with one of the shepherds. From the top of a hill they saw a wild sow, patiently trotting behind the flock with perhaps a dozen piglets at her heels.

"There's the villain," he roared, and dug in his heels. The gelding dashed down the slope and took the gate in a flying leap. By the time the shepherd opened the gate and caught up, Nicholas had shot the sow, knocked the little family out, and dumped their carcasses in the saddlebags. "Ben can bring one of the shire horses and drag that brute home," he said, venting both his wrath and his relief in a kick at the great bristled head.

They ate the suckling pigs with a bitter kind of triumph.

That evening Cressida was rereading Mrs. Maxwell's letter that had come the day before:

I try very hard to make up to my husband for having caused him to leave Ayrshire, but he protests he does not need such attention, for busy though he is with his estate and his saw millers, he is content with this new life . . .

I have often wondered, smiling to myself, what

Mrs. Hobson would have thought had she known she was entertaining in Government House the daughter of a humble shoemaker, but she is not to know, for my husband insists I keep my beginnings a dark secret. People, he says, are happier considering me their equal. He adds that there are enough problems without causing embarrassment and discomfort.

I laugh at this new way of looking at things, but I have come to believe he is right.

"And of course he is right," Cressida said to herself. She had always felt vaguely irritated and, as Mr. Maxwell said, discomfited, by his wife's insistent Scottish honesty. After all, it was one of the virtues of the English aristocracy that they so easily took in red blood, of a suitable kind, she added to herself hurriedly, inevitably and uncomfortably reminded of matters she wished to forget. It was said the kind of disaster that had descended on the French kings because of their inflexible class system could never happen at Home.

She glanced back at her letter.

Our children thrive. So rosy-cheeked and robust. I hope I may be able to produce a baby every year for a while. It is time I heard from you, Lady Cressida. I do not know if you have more children, though I have no doubt you have been blessed with at least one other, for your little girl must be nearly three years old now. Is it that you are too busy to write?

"It's clear she is only one of many," Nicholas said, pausing in his pacing up and down the drawing room, worrying out loud. "There must be boars in the forest. While they remain, these brutes will multiply. Something must be done."

Pushing the envy she felt for her friend's happiness deep inside, Cressida looked up. "Why do we not go on a pig hunt?" She laid down her letter. "Several ladies of my acquaintance have engaged in them."

"They're dangerous devils. A very different species now from their tame ancestors, which were liberated by Captain Cook."

She parried his quizzical look. "I followed the hunt on

a leading rein with my very first pony. I am accustomed to danger. Fox hunting is dangerous."

"Very well," he replied. "But we must go immediately. Tomorrow."

They rode out early in the morning with several of the men. As Ben tightened Charmy's surcingle and Cossack pranced excitedly around the yard, Cressida looked across at Nicholas with bright eyes. Jerningham, God be praised, had not repeated the question she had asked him about Mrs. Putnam. She made herself think of the girl as Mrs. Putnam now, for, like it or not, she was a personality in the town. And after all, Cressida thought warmly, once her immediate outrage calmed, the fact that Jerningham had arranged the Putnams' passage had made a difference.

Nicholas checked first one pistol then the other. The hands each carried a fearsome weapon made from one half of a pair of shears bound firmly to a stick with green flax leaves. Ben slapped Charmy on the rump. Cressida's gloved hands gripped the reins firmly as the mare leaped forward. As her eyes met Nicholas's eyes, he smiled. She looked very well, he owned, in her velvet jockey cap with its green veil, and her long skirt, which she had looped up to show the elegance of her ankle boots. He found himself wondering if young Oliver had yet begun to give Rose riding lessons.

They left the green hills of their estate at the furthermost point, and entered the steep valleys leading up into the Rimutakas, the mountain range that ran north, hugging the clouds. The slopes were closely wooded, the air cold. They forded rushing, noisy streams that rattled like broken glass, saw foaming waterfalls hundreds of feet high drifting into crystal pools. The ferns here were delicate as green lace, the wet moss attractively musty with forest decay.

By midday Nicholas was impatient for a kill. He turned in his saddle. "The Maoris told me the best way to bring a wild boar out of his lair is to unseat a boulder and roll it into the ravine. The row it makes thundering down panics him into running for the open ground. Let's climb this hill and see if we can find a rock that is large enough."

The steep, stony hillside, virtually a cliff face where it looked into the valley, proved to be navigable on its eastern flank. They zigzagged up the stony, pathless slope, the horses' feet sliding on exposed tree roots, swishing through the soft ferns. It was hard going. Their withers were white with foam by the time the summit was reached. The men sat back in their saddles, looking around.

"Here we are!" cried Nicholas, indicating a gray rock nearly as high as himself. "It's not embedded deeply. We should be able to shift it."

They set their shoulders and stiffened their knees, their backs rigid. Heaving and grunting, little by little, they loosened the boulder's hold. It rose, rolled back, rose again, sank again. The men drew away, panting. Wordlessly, at a nod from Nicholas, they began again. This time it moved, teetered, then all at once lost its balance and pitched giddily over the rim. Their eyes met in triumph as it thundered down into the ravine with a roar that shattered the bush silence. The sound of crashing stones and splitting wood mounted in crescendo, the uproar echoing and reechoing through the hills.

Nicholas grinned. "If that don't bring 'em out, nothing will." Picking up a largish stone, he handed it up to Cressida. "You had better have your own ammunition. Don't hesitate to use it." His face was bright and eager, his eyes already glittering with the turbulent feelings stirred easily by danger. Stepping gingerly, the men picked their way to the edge of the ravine and peeped cautiously over. The pig dogs, trembling with expectation, already smelling the blood lust of the hunters, stayed behind, poised for the chase.

Nicholas was squinting through the branches into the scrubby, rocky valley below. Suddenly he cried, "There's a boar! He's making for the creek. Quick!" He was into the saddle in a flash. Almost before his feet were in the stirrups, Cossack was careering down the slope with the other horses pounding, staggering, and slipping on the leaf mold and the loose earth behind him. The dogs streaked ahead.

Holding tightly to the stone in her lap, Cressida gave Charmy her head. The little mare, not easily flurried, pitched forward as fast as she dared, slithering, pausing in her sensible way to consider, diving on, maintaining good speed behind the rasher males.

Puffing and panting, they reached the winding creek. The dogs had already bounded across and were off up the hill. They could all see the boar now, a great ugly gray creature of monstrous size, out in the open, running at full speed. The horses plunged into the stream, and splashed across in a shower of freezing water that flew up into the riders' faces, soaking their clothes. Those out in front leaped for the bank, hooves frantically stabbing at the loose earth, then sliding back as the animals grappled with the uneasy mix of soil and stones. One of the cobs came down on his forelegs, then rallied, and with a great heave floundered on up the bank. Charmy splashed close, intelligently gauged the distance, and reared. Cressida threw her weight forward to add power to the mare's strong shoulders, and they landed neatly on hard ground.

"Hang on to your stone!" Nicholas flung the words out on the rushing wind. His reins were in his left hand, a pistol cocked in his right. The men held their colonial boar spears like lances as they pounded up the slope.

They crossed the rim of the ridge and pelted through scrub into a shallow valley, up over the next rise, and into the forest again. They came to a sudden halt. Before them, rearing to the sky, stood a wall of impregnable rock. Below them yawned a canyon. The dogs had driven the boar into a cul-de-sac from which there was no escape. The men were already off their horses and moving forward, spears held at the ready.

Cressida's pupils dilated as she faced their fearsome quarry. She had been told a wild boar was the most dangerous beast in the world. She looked down at his enormous tusks, notched and broken from a lifetime of battle; at his evil eyes glinting with rage; at the massive shoulders plated with thick, horny scales. A cold dread such as she had never known settled on her. It was said that no ball or shot would penetrate the tough hide of a mountain boar, except in a small, vulnerable area over the heart. If Nicholas fired and missed, if the spears broke, if the boar charged straight forward now, he could dispose of the dogs, the horses, all of them with a backward jerk of that vile head, the upthrust of his razor-sharp tusks.

Nicholas leaped off his horse. He pressed his reins into Cressida's hands, saying in a grim voice, "Get back. And have your stone handy."

She looked down at the object that had appeared so

large and useful when Nicholas handed it up to her. Now it seemed absurd. Nicholas was moving forward, his double-barrelled Lancaster supported in both hands, the men with their spears close behind. The dogs, trained and experienced, had already gone in, and were dodging about, distracting the creature.

Cressida tried to turn, but Charmy was nervous and would not obey. The mare reared up on her rear legs, ears back, the whites of her eyes showing, and came down a pace nearer the rock, still facing the boar. She tried to drag Cossack past, but he, too, reared then sidled mindlessly into the bank, inadvertently pushing Charmy forward. Short of dismounting, Cressida saw she was not going to be able to retreat. She looked desperately across at Nicholas but he was taking careful, calculated aim, and she dared not distract him.

He pulled the trigger. The shot rang around the canyon. The dogs dived on their prey. Emitting a pain-crazed scream, the wounded beast bounded into the air. One of the hands sprang forward, his spear driving in beneath the shoulder. The stick snapped off in his hands. Life blood came gushing out in a ruby fountain that sickened and appalled. Another shot rang out, but the maddened beast, harassed as he was by the dogs, was jumping and diving too fast. The ball caught him a glancing blow on the impregnable hide of his shoulder.

Glassily, in horrible slow motion, Cressida saw one of the dogs seize the back leg in his mouth and hang on; saw the boar, mortally wounded, lurch drunkenly forward; saw the great tusks coming nearer, and behind them the evil, glittering red eyes. He was headed straight for Charmy. With a violent, protective movement she kicked the terrified mare into an about-turn. The tragedy was that, in saving her, Cressida inadvertently jerked Cossack's reins, leading him into the boar's path.

Still in slow motion, she saw the great evil head come back, the razor-sharp tusks jerk upward. With a shriek the gelding reared. Frantically, uselessly, Cressida flung the stone. The cobs had panicked and rushed away. Charmy scrambled up the bank. Cressida slipped out of the saddle and let her go.

The boar was down and Cossack was on top of him, kicking, screaming, jerking, his great powerful legs flailing in death agony, his entrails hideously trailing, his stricken, tortured eyes turned toward Nicholas as he slithered across the flat rock. Nicholas dropped the rifle and reached for his pistol. Another shot rang around the echoing valley and the great beast lay still.

A deadly silence fell upon them all. Unable to face Nicholas, Cressida turned in her distress toward the black canyon. A keen-eyed hawk swooped, hovered, then, predatory in its other-worldly knowledge of the forest's affairs, circled, waiting.

Silently, the men crept away, leaving Cressida and Nicholas to their several agonies, their split grief. Now, racked guilt gazed into the eyes of a new and virulent hate, rancorous and implacable as the black rock on which they stood together, their odious nearness burning, cutting, poisoning them. They did not see the men go, or the dogs. Did not notice that one of them rode pillion leaving his mount. They were beyond the world of kindness and care in a vacuum of nauseous death.

Cressida begun to tremble. She moved drunkenly to a ledge and leaned against it for support, looking into a rattling, merry little waterfall, wishing it might have been a fathomless torrent into which she could have fallen. The end was here, anyway. Life had, after all, slipped through her fingers. From the false starts, the failures, the new beginnings, nothing had been built. She heard a click. "I will not move," she thought. She would allow Nicholas to shoot her through the back of the head. She found herself willing it. There was no relief in staying alive. Only emptiness.

The hawk swung around again, its circle tightening. She turned. Nicholas was sitting on the rock, his face resting on his knees, his arms encircling his legs. Another kind of man, she thought illogically, would have been crying. He looked as though he had gone to sleep. She went over to him and stood uncertainly, pulling at her knuckles inside her gloves. At last he moved, lifted his head, stared at her. His face was not ravaged as she had expected. It was very still. There was no emotion. Just a terrible emptiness.

"I am sorry," she said in a queer voice, thinking that at any moment, if he did not move or speak she might laugh or scream or go mad. A voice far back in her brain told her to sit down beside him and put her arms around him, but she had given before, given everything, and still there had been the girl. Whatever she did now, whatever she said, she knew as certainly as she knew the horse was dead, that he did not wish the comfort he so desperately needed to come from her.

She turned away. Charmy had wandered off, her reins dragging. As though nothing untoward had happened, she was snatching at the long, pale grasses and ferns that grew out of the cliff above. She turned her head and nudged familiarly at Cressida's hands, looking for the tidbit that often came her way. Cressida buried her face in the chestnut-colored mane and wept.

It was dusk when at last Nicholas came into town. He tied the cob up outside Barratt's Hotel, removed the saddle, and went in. He took a stool by the bar and ordered brandy. Someone spoke to him, but he did not answer. The publican put the drink in front of him. His fingers twined themselves around the glass, but he made no attempt to lift it to his lips. Two men chatting together at the other end of the bar looked at each other and fell silent. After a time, leaving the drink untasted, Nicholas rose from his stool and flung down the money.

The landlord asked diffidently, "Are you all right, Mr. le Grys?"

He did not hear, for he was already shouldering through the door. He left it swinging behind him and strode down the street, then set off up the grassy slope that led to Aurora Cottage.

Rose was standing on the veranda, looking out over the darkening waters of the harbor. Giles, already dressed in his nightclothes, was holding her hand. A bright spangle of rain had fallen over the town and the air smelled fresh, like linen drying in the sun. She saw the tall figure striding up the hill and caught her breath. Even at this distance she read dejection in the slope of Nicholas's shoulders, and as he came nearer, she saw also the darkness in his face. He came up the path without raising his head.

She waited by the steps in apprehensive silence, her free hand extended to take his. He took it and held it tightly between his own. Recognizing with distress that he could not speak, Rose turned, leading him through the door and into the parlor. The lamp was not yet lit. She let go of the child's hand and put her arms around him. "I am here," she whispered. "I am here."

Daniel, who had watched through the window as Nicholas came, went to the door, his feet silent in his thick socks. He looked in, saw them in each other's arms with the child close by, and turned away. At the back doorway, he stood kicking his heels against the step. Edmund, wandering into the house with tail erect, received a vicious kick. Back arched in indignation, he fled through.

Rose lifted her face. Nicholas's eyes were closed. Her hands smoothed his back beneath the damp coat. There was no impulse of desire, only an instinctive offering of love. Giles picked up a picturebook and sat down on the window seat. Once or twice he glanced up looking vaguely irritated, then, staring intently down at the print, he said loudly, "Once upon a time there was a . . ."

Rose looked around, her face alight like a star. "He can read! He can read!" she cried. "Oh, Nicholas, your little boy is so clever!"

Nicholas's arms dropped to his sides. He crossed the room and lifted the boy. "The first read?" He cleared his throat. "What a dull lad. Three, and only now learning to read!" And then he laughed softly. "A Rundull to the core. I, too, learned to recognize words at this age." He heaved an enormous sigh, and looked across at Rose. "So, life goes on." There was a flicker of a smile as he dropped a kiss on the boy's smooth, round forehead. Edmund sidled in, big-eyed. With Giles in his arms, Nicholas sank into an armchair.

"So, we see another Rundull glorying in his first trick. You will have many triumphs, my boy, and some disasters, too. For every end, perhaps there is a beginning." He looked at Rose and his mouth twisted. "Is that what keeps us going, Rose?"

She had fallen on her knees beside him. Now she smoothed his cheek gently with the palm of one hand, willing the distress away. "I suppose so," she said. "Would you like me to make you a cup of tea?"

He nodded, lifting a hand to his forehead with the pain again showing. "Yes," he said. "A lot of tea. And something to eat."

She rose from her knees and hurried to the kitchen. Daniel had disappeared, but she didn't notice. When she returned, carrying a candle, Nicholas looked up. In the flickering light she saw a thin film of serenity had eased itself across his taut features. Giles, astride his knee, was chuckling at something Nicholas had said. She put the candle down, went back to the kitchen, and cut some thick slices from a loaf she had baked that morning, then buttered them and spread them with the plum jam she had made in the autumn. Because she did not own a tray, she carried the tea in one hand, the plate in the other, and set them on the table with its red chenille cloth. Nicholas began reading aloud from the book. Rose took the plate over to the chair and, perching on the arm, held a piece of bread to his lips. He ate hungrily, in quick snatches, between paragraphs.

"Did you miss your tea?" she asked.

"And lunch."

She put the plate down on the table, handed him the cup and saucer, lifted Giles off his knee, and hurried back to the kitchen. In a little while Nicholas wandered in. He had removed his damp and dirty coat. He stood in shirtsleeves stained with sweat, his arms folded, watching her. Giles came running after him. "I am cooking you some eggs."

Nicholas ran his hands through his roughened hair. "What a splendid idea!" They sat down at the table together. The child stood at Nicholas's knee. Rose made some more tea from Flash Jack's special store. It was dark in the garden now. She drew the pretty flowered curtain across the black glass.

Nicholas pushed his plate aside and took her hands across the table. "I came to tell you Cossack is dead." His fingers tightened over hers, his eyes darkened, but his voice was controlled.

She uttered a little gasp that died in a moan of loss and compassion. "I am so glad you came." Suddenly, superstitiously, she had a frightened feeling that now the thread running through the years was broken, the future might not hold. In a trembling voice, she asked, "What happened?"

"A wild boar."

She let go of his hands, and rose to her feet. With tears in her eyes she stood beside him, pressing his dear head against her breasts. She could feel the emotion rising in him, trembling his shoulders, jerking at his throat. She stayed there, holding him close, until he calmed. Giles said irritably, "Mama!"

"I must put him to bed," she said. "Then we will talk."

But when she returned Nicholas was slumped in an armchair apparently asleep. Tiptoeing into the kitchen, she hung his damp coat over the back of a chair and stood it before the stove, then tiptoed back again. Seating herself on a cushion on the floor, she laid her head gently on his knee.

It was midnight when he awakened. She had long since blown out the candle. Moonlight, shafting through the bow window, lit the room palely. Opening his eyes he reached out with a small nervous movement. She lifted his hand to her lips, and he relaxed, his sleepy face softening. "Ah, Rose."

After a moment or two he stood up, stretched, smiled down at her. "Have we wasted all those hours?" he asked whimsically, looking at the small clock on the mantel. But they both knew it had not been a night for love.

Inside the front door they held each other close, then he opened it quietly and went off down the path. She watched the back of his tall figure moving down the track between the sleeping houses, until it lost shape and merged with the darkness. Turning then, she caught her breath in shock. Further along the veranda, a dark form lay stretched at full length. She moved nearer, apprehensively, and bent down, already recognizing the red flannel shirt. Daniel's mouth was open and he smelled vilely of rum. There was a piece of paper pinned to his chest. By the light of a lucifer match she read the familiar scrawl. *I found this in a ditch.* And there was a large, scrawled *A* as signature.

The match burned down and caught her fingers, but it was not that that caused the intolerable pain.

37

That year, Captain Arthur Wakefield, newly released from his Mediterranean commission, honoring his promise to colonize the Middle Island, sailed in aboard *Whitby*. The town of Nelson was set up across the straits, and an infant government established. Now the Wairau Plains must be surveyed.

Jerningham came to Wellington to warn his uncle of threats made by two great chiefs, Te Rauparaha and his fierce nephew Rangihaeata. "Te Rauparaha came to see me dressed in an old dragoon helmet and black tail coat with his dirty mats flung over the top, excited by drink, declaring the plains have not been paid for."

The colonel said with resignation, "Te Rauparaha also declares the Hutt and Porirua have not been paid for. They still do not understand a sale. Having dissipated their payment, they want the lands back. We must take a firm stand. The natives do not respect one for showing signs of weakness."

"He boasts he will *pung-a-pung* you if you attempt to survey Wairau."

"Kill," translated Nicholas in a clipped voice. He was vaguely irritated by Jerningham speaking Maori in the company of Englishmen. Nicholas had always felt war with the Maoris would come. What were firearms for but fighting? As he had said to Jerningham in the Hans Place house back in 1839 when the latter mentioned bringing guns for hunting, the natives had managed their hunting very satisfactorily before the coming of the white man.

Arthur sailed to Kapiti Island taking Nayti, who had claimed to be a blood brother to the chiefs. "It may be simply that we have had the land for the three years without clearing it. You know the Maori law. The first man to clear a forest owns it by right. We have been dilatory in that."

The visit was not a success. The Maori boy's high birth turned out to be a mere figment of his imagination. Te Rauparaha and his people seized the gifts given by the duke of Sussex and the London hostesses.

In the threatening circumstances, they needed official backing, but the deputy governor, busy feathering his nest with illegal land purchases, would do nothing to help.

"No sea captain worth his salt would shrink from the rantings of a brown bully in a dragoon helmet without trousers," Arthur said goodhumoredly. Reluctantly, they gave in. The colonel's brother was the very soul of tact. Inevitably, during the weeks after *Whitby* sailed, nerves tightened in the town. Rauparaha and his party, it was said, had been transported by Geordie Bolts, the whaler, to Cloudy Bay. A schooner came in with the news that Rauparaha had gone to Wairau by canoe and burned down the surveyors' huts. The tension in the air affected everyone, bringing them closer together.

Miraculously, Nicholas came in time to accept Cossack's death as the whip of fate and, generously, with gratitude, Cressida put behind her the certain knowledge that he had gone to the girl for comfort. With help in the house, and the stalwart loyalty of her old nurse, she found herself growing in strength and tolerance. Their companionship was often lit by moments of genuine affection. Yet there was the ever present knowledge that the girl was only a few miles away. While she remained, the marriage would never achieve the status of a love affair. That was the pity of it.

When Nurse propounded her amazing idea, Cressida's spirits soared. "I could arrange it," Nurse said, in her sensible, managing way. "If I may have the pony trap to go into town and make arrangements . . ."

On the day, wanting to divert her mind, Cressida invited some ladies to take tea at Rata Hill.

They were engrossed in their chatter when Nicholas,

dressed in leather breeches and an old frock coat, wandered casually into the withdrawing room. He pulled up, disconcerted, sweeping off his hat and bowing.

"I am very sorry to intrude, ladies. Forgive me for appearing in my working clothes. We farming gentlemen are not often these days dressed for the drawing room." He looked down wryly at his muddied coat, and the top boots, then apologized to Cressida, "The pony cart being missing, I assumed you had gone visiting. Otherwise I would not have come in, dressed as I am."

Cressida flushed. "Nurse has gone into town. We did not expect you to use the pony cart." Her hands fluttered and her color brightened. "I understood you to be working in one of the far distant fields all day," she said.

He nodded, his eyes appraisingly on his wife, wondering at her nervous manner, surprised that she should feel guilty at having loaned her pony cart to the Dragon. He made his polite adieus, then crossed the yard to the men's quarters to talk to them about the safety and defense of his household. It was increasingly likely, he thought, that Wellington would come under attack.

Meantime, in the withdrawing room, the ladies moved inevitably from fashions to the possibility of war. They were all secretly facing the terrifying prospect of being widowed and thrown on their own resources twelve thousand miles from their loved ones. "The doctor has expressed a wish that a committee of public safety be appointed, but the colonel does not listen," said Mrs. Stokes. "He is overconfident to the point of foolishness. We have no battery, and if we had, there are no soldiers to man it."

"Should the Maoris tomahawk and eat a bishop or two, we might get some intelligent action," asserted Mrs. Sheraton, the red-blooded scion of the Library Committee. "You will, of course, come into Wellington, Lady Cressida, should trouble arise."

"I believe my husband is already making arrangements for our safety," Cressida replied. "There are caves on the property that we intend to stock with provisions. My husband believes they would afford us safety. And should we be forced to flee, in the event of a surprise attack, there are a number of trees nearby that have been killed by the rata vine, and where the vine remains as a curtain across the hollow center. They make wonderful hiding places. My maid Tilly Bird found an excellent hollow trunk only a few hundred yards from the house."

They met each other's eyes then glanced away. Withdrawing room gossip in the town had long since decided the servant girl Tilly Bird was a figment of Lady Cressida's imagination.

At the time of the tea party at Rata Hill, Rose, with the two babies in the pram and Giles walking at her side, was wandering along the waterfront. All at once, to her surprise, she saw Daniel standing by one of the jetties. Daniel. On the waterfront. In the middle of the afternoon! As she lifted Giles into the pram and quickened her steps to a run, it crossed her mind with dismay that Flash Jack might have dismissed him.

"I seen yer goin' along, so I waited," he said, shuffling from one foot to the other, not meeting her eyes. "I got a surprise fer yer, Rose. There's a man 'ere wants ter show us 'is boat."

"Oh Daniel!" In her delight at this unexpected kindness, she quite forgot to ask why he was not working. "How nice of you." Their marriage, too, had gone more smoothly of late. In an exceptional effort to compensate for Nicholas's coming to the cottage, she had been very sweet to him and perhaps out of genuine regret for his own behavior he had seemed to be trying to meet her halfway. Now he indicated a dinghy idling on the water close by the jetty. Rose glanced down at the little craft. A villainous-looking fellow with a black beard was setting the oars in the rowlocks. She looked back at Daniel in bewilderment. "He wants to show us *that* boat? The dinghy?"

"Not the dinghy, silly. The schooner." Daniel pointed to a square-rigged craft rocking on the choppy waters several hundred yards offshore. Rose gazed at him in smiling disbelief. Daniel had never before evinced interest in boats, or, indeed, in anything beyond the day-to-day issues of work and keeping alive. As though embarrassed by her silence, he brushed her fingers from the handles of the baby carriage, and began to push it along the quay.

"But what shall we do with the pram?" she cried, hurrying after him, having to run to keep up. "If we leave it here, anyone might steal it."

"We can take it with us," he replied, as though there was nothing odd or difficult about transporting a large baby carriage in a small dinghy on a choppy sea. They were out on the jetty now, and the wind was snatching at Rose's bonnet, blowing her skirts. She looked down into the dinghy. "In that little thing?" she asked incredulously. "We couldn't get the pram into that, Daniel."

Hearing her voice, the man at the rowlocks looked up. He had shrewd little eyes, and an enormous, liquor-red nose, set slightly askew in a mahogany face. Alarmed no less by his lewd stare than by his overwhelming size, Rose shrank back.

"Get in with the nippers, missus," he growled, as he leaped up the steps.

Astonished that Daniel should have struck up such an unlikely friendship, she whispered, "Who is he, Daniel?"

"I dunno. 'E's not the owner. 'E's a seaman," Daniel replied. " 'E won't bite you. C'mon." With that he lifted Charlie out of the pram, thrust him into her arms, and took Giles himself, balancing the boy on one hip as he picked up Joseph.

Giles said, "Lemme down," and slapped Daniel's wrist disdainfully. Daniel, intent upon what he was doing, seemed not to notice. The seaman was hovering over them, hands on hips.

Alarm bells rang in Rose's head. "I don't want to go," she said, but as she began to swing around, she felt a hand in the center of her back, prodding her down the steps. She was moving off-balance and too fast, teetering dangerously, clutching the child. Daniel, for once light on his feet, not clumsy at all, was coming after her with Joseph in the crook of one arm, and Giles sprawling head down beneath the other. They fell into the dinghy. Before Rose could gather herself together, the big seaman was jolting down the steps half carrying the carriage by the handlebar as though it was a featherweight. She tried to rise, lost her balance, and fell back against the hard wooden seat.

Giles, who had bumped his forehead on Daniel's knee, cried out in indignation, "Let me go."

Rose's incipient alarm erupted in a flood of fear. "Where are you taking us, Daniel?"

At once triumphant and uneasy, Daniel looked back at

her with a foolish grin. She thought dizzily that with Giles in her arms she might have leaped overboard, but Daniel was holding the child as though he held a king's ransom. That was the clue to what was happening—Daniel's capturing Giles. The black villain was pushing the dinghy away from the jetty with his oar. He grinned evilly down at her, showing a half mouthful of dirty peg teeth.

"Where are you going?"

"Kororareka," he grinned malevolently.

Dirty little Kororareka, as Flash Jack called the town. Rose was breathless with disbelief. She rounded on Daniel. "We can't go there. What about our clothes? What about . . . everything, Daniel?"

"It's all right, Rose." He smiled at her, hopefully, his eyes pleading, but still with that strange excitement showing through.

"Nice little cutter," said the man, nodding toward the vessel as they approached. "Ten ton. Plenty of room."

They tied up alongside. Rose's fighting blood burned in her cheeks, and her eyes sparked. "I *will not* go aboard." She sat firmly on the narrow seat, clutching Charlie. The man lifted Joseph and handed him roughly up to another sailor on deck. Daniel—a new, driven Daniel whom Rose had never seen before—climbed up with Giles still held tightly under one arm.

"Want to be left to float out to sea?" asked the man callously, preparing to go aboard. Giles had disappeared. There was nothing else to do but go after him. She allowed herself to be hustled up the ladder.

Immediately, they were directed below to a cabin scarcely six feet square. It was occupied by two women: a bulky, red-faced, rough but kindly woman who introduced herself as Mrs. Badget, and a quiet, stringy, mouselike creature with a cough.

There was scarcely room to stand. Three bunks stretched along the walls. A two-foot-wide table with a bench at either side stood in the middle. A narrow shelf above the bunks held tins of biscuits, vegetables, salt beef. The cabin was separated from the hold by battens two inches apart. All Rose's apprehensions came together in a fierce explosion of energy and, snatching up Giles, she made a blind rush for the door.

"Look out!" shouted Mrs. Badget, and Rose swerved aside as two more seamen, hefty and snarling, staggered in with a huge box.

"Here's your stuff, missus." They bumped clumsily across the room, knocking into the table, sending one of the forms flying. "Git out 'er the way, will yer!" They dropped the box with a crash that set Joseph and Charlie screaming. Giles scrambled up on the bunk and watched in frozen silence.

"I can't think why you couldn't come aboard from the jetty like the rest of us," Mrs. Badget grumbled, as she set the form to rights. "You're causing a lot of bother." She added bossily, "And see you keep all your belongings together. There's no space for untidiness, as you can see."

Rose cowered against the bunk. *"Your* stuff," the man had said. She contemplated the unfamiliar wooden chest. She knew what it meant. A kaleidoscopic picture of swiftly mounting guilt—which began in the curate's garden at Rundull, and exploded over the rum-soaked body Flash Jack had dropped so disdainfully on her veranda— flew through her mind. With an uncertain glance at the other two women, she undid the ropes and tentatively lifted the lid.

On top lay a familiar jumble of baby clothes and toys. Rummaging into a corner, she recognized the firm, flat touch of bed linen. Rummaging further, she came upon one of her house gowns. Who had packed them? she wondered distractedly. She had been gone from the house for no more than an hour and a half, and she had gone of her own volition.

Or had she? Rose's speculations jolted to a halt. Daniel had suggested she go to see some clematis he had discovered growing near the ground on the edge of the forest. Daniel, who had never mentioned or apparently even noticed bush flowers before! Though she had searched for ages, she had not found the starry white flowers. Daniel, who was as simple as the planks of timber with which he worked, had tricked her easily because she had been flattered that, after all these years, he had thought of something that might please her.

She made no attempt to dig deeper among the jumble of belongings in the chest, knowing instinctively, piteously, that the beautiful gowns Nicholas had given her would not be there. She thought of other losses. Her precious silver hoard! Tears filled her eyes.

What of her beloved chickens? Would they starve? Who would look after Edmund? And what would Flash Jack think? Would he be worried, or merely angry that Daniel had walked out of his job? She lowered the lid of the chest and stared bleakly at it, fears and questions stampeding through her mind. Who had helped Daniel? His inadequacy was something Rose had learned to live with, as she had learned to live with her own guilt. She knew he was not capable of organizing this kidnap. Then who had? She crept onto the bunk and curled up with the children, shivering like a cornered rabbit.

It was a dreadful journey. On the second night they had to run for shelter. The next forty-eight hours were spent pitching and tossing at anchor in a southeasterly gale. If the days were rough and uncomfortable, the nights defied endurance. Their tiny communal quarters filled up with the rank stench of vomit, intermingling with fumes from the flaring wick of the fish-oil lamp. Gases from the incessantly churning bilge mingled with odors wafting in from the dog kennels and poultry pens in the hold.

The voyage, which should have taken a week, lasted nearly three. Dirty little Kororareka, tucked in between bush hills and white-capped waves, looked like heaven to the exhausted and desperate passengers. They sailed in on a sunny day, through a bay where half a dozen deep-sea vessels rocked at anchor.

"They's New Bedford whale hunters," announced one of the crew. "There's boats 'ereabouts from Nantucket and Martha's Vineyard and Boston. Whale skippers as rough as you'll find anywhere in the world," he added, looking significantly at Rose. She glanced away, hiding her beautiful face behind the rim of her bonnet.

As they swept in on a rising tide, skirting the pretty little island in their path, they passed many small ships, fore-and-afters, schooner-rigged, cutter-rigged, swinging at anchor. Rose's eyes swept hungrily over them looking for one she might recognize from having seen it in Port Nicholson harbor. Already she was fermenting impossible dreams of tricking Daniel, as he had tricked her, into returning to Wellington.

Behind the town to the north the hills rose steep and abruptly, clothed with coarse fern and dwarf cyprus scrub. There was no jetty. The beach was cluttered. Men-of-war, whalers, trading craft, were hauled up on the gravelly sand. Natives draped in mats and blankets lounged on the beach, dozing in the sun, smoking their foul pipes, gossiping idly.

They staggered ashore, their feet sliding awkwardly in the sand, Rose clutching Giles by the hand, Daniel carrying Joseph and the baby. It was the first time they had had an opportunity to speak together without being overheard.

"And how are we to live in this dreadful place where we know no one?" she asked, fierce with the effort she was making to control her apprehensions.

"I'll get a job," Daniel replied appeasingly.

"Will you? I hope you may, but I read the papers, as you do not, and so you are perhaps unaware that Kororareka is not a thriving town like Wellington."

"I'll get work."

"And how are we to live until you are paid?"

"There's hotels."

She knew then that the person who had arranged their departure had also given him money. Someone wanted very badly to get rid of them. A picture flared up in her mind of her little room at Cavendish Square, of the door opening, and of that hard, strong woman whose name she never knew. Her eviction from Wellington had the same pitiless flavor.

There were only four hundred people in Kororareka now. The owner of the two-storied, weatherboard hotel, who had an unpleasant habit of looking Rose up and down all the time he was speaking to her, told them that not very long ago there had been a population of a thousand in the town. "You have come at a bad time," he said. "There's been trouble with the Maoris. That scoundrel Hone Heke's caused no end of a bother hereabouts. He wants war with the whites."

"War!" exclaimed Daniel, turning pale.

"He used to get anchor duty of five pounds from vessels that come into the bay. Now he don't get nothin' because the government has leveled customs dues, and the captains don't see their ways to pay both. They go other places to refresh their ships. So there ain't much work hereabouts now, Putnam. No ships, no work. And Heke's spoiling for a fight."

Rose said in a small, tart voice, "You may have brought your sons into great danger."

"I'm not afraid o' them heathens," retorted Daniel belligerently, kicking the heel of one heavy boot against the toe of the other. He looked shaken, nonetheless.

The owner of one of the public houses had a small cottage on a promontory overlooking the beach, which he rented to them for four shillings a week, about half what Daniel could expect to earn—if he could find a job at all. Rose pushed the pram up a sandy track between overgrown grass and scrub, to the little sod hut thatched with swamp grass. Standing in the doorway, looking around the dark little interior, she burst into tears.

"C'mon, Rose," said Daniel awkwardly, touching her shoulder. "Like yer said once, we're married. We got each other."

Rose turned on him in a fury, but what she saw in his face arrested her. "I am sorry, Daniel," she said compassionately, apologizing for everything that had happened over the years, remembering how he had saved her from the Rundull mob, seeing in her mind's eye the beatific expression that had crossed his face when she said she would marry him.

There were tears in his eyes, too. He raised an arm and brushed them roughly away. If she needed proof of the fact that Daniel had played only an acquiescent part in her abduction, it was there now in the lost expression he wore.

Just as she had brought him from London to New Zealand, so someone else had sent him here. He had not looked ahead to the time when, the plot having worked itself out, he should be alone in Kororareka, inevitably high and dry.

38

Oliver stood before the desk, legs astride, knuckles on his hips, frowning. "Sit down," barked Flash Jack, pointing to a chair in the corner.

"I'm not staying. I came to ask you—"

"Then sit down while you ask. And don't forget, you young whippersnapper, that boys don't look down on men." As Oliver's overgrown frame collapsed obediently into the rough wooden armchair, Flash Jack's fierce expression relaxed and a touch of pride lit his pale eyes. The boy was shaping into the kind of man he would have liked to call his son, and he knew with great pleasure that he had had more than a passing influence in bringing this about. But Oliver was not a child anymore. By Flash Jack's own reckoning, he had grown a formidable six or eight inches in the past year. He was going to be a fine-looking man. "Well?" he asked.

"Where has Rose gone?"

"What do you mean?" The older man frowned sharply.

"They've left the cottage. I mean, *left!* Taken their things."

There was a quivering silence. Oliver was not afraid of Flash Jack, but there were times when he was glad to be across the room or across the deck from him. Now his face was like thunder, but very still. With a violent backward shove, he rose to his full height, the chair legs grating harshly on the board floor. He reached for a ring of keys hanging on the wall, pocketed them, and without a word strode out of the room, through the store, and into the street. One of the assistants called, "Mr. Wilshire," but if he heard he took no notice, and Oliver knew better than to try to attract his attention. Walking with his purposeful, rolling gait, Flash Jack went swiftly to the end of the street, then up the wide grassy slope between the pretty, white-painted dwellings.

They came to Aurora Cottage and paused outside. The curtains were at the windows, the front door was closed. Edmund was perched on the top step, his little heart-shaped face peaky with apprehension. Flash Jack kicked the gate open and went through. As they came up the path, Edmund stretched his neck and uttered a thin cry. Oliver bent down to pat him. Flash Jack tried the door. It was not locked. They entered in silence. In the parlor were the familiar chairs with the bright cushions Rose had sewn; the table with its red chenille cloth; the little pile of library books, neatly stacked.

They went on to the kitchen. The stove stood cold and bleak. There were no pots and pans in evidence. No kettle. In the bedrooms there were no blankets on the beds; no clothes. The cot had gone, but a box stood in a corner of the children's room. Flash Jack lifted the lid, and they stood side-by-side looking in on a neatly folded garment of emerald green velvet, a glow of oyster silk, a froth of India muslin, and a peep of tarlatan. Gently and gravely, Flash Jack lowered the lid as one might close a coffin. Edmund slid tightly across Oliver's ankles, meowing piteously.

Neither of them had spoken since they left the office. Now, clearing his throat conspicuously, Oliver said, "I had better feed the cat."

Flash Jack went to the back door and stood, hands in pockets, gazing out over the sloping, grassy ridge and the distant, bush-clad hills. Drifts of cloud feathered the windy sky. After a little while, he crossed to the chicken run and stood looking in. The chickens were highstepping up and down. They paused to regard him with beady displeasure. He opened the door and they stalked out, ruffling their feathers, nagging in crotchety little outbursts, "Heck, heck, heck." He lifted the lid of the grain box Daniel had built, took out a handful of golden seeds, and scattered them on the grass. The birds came scampering and pushing and pecking. Oliver was standing on the step now, his face crumpled like an unironed cloth.

"They've not been fed," Flash Jack said gruffly. "Fill their water trough, boy." He stood watching while Oliver fetched a bucket and took it to the tap.

Oliver turned his head. "How shall we find them?"

"You don't find grown-ups," replied Flash Jack curtly. He went back into the house again.

Oliver came after him. "Rose would not have gone without saying good-bye. She wouldn't go without telling me."

Flash Jack pulled at an earlobe.

Oliver looked as if he was going to cry. "I tell you, Mr. Wilshire, she would *not* have gone without telling me."

"Except that she did, boy. She did." He reached out and gripped Oliver's arm, gave it a little shake, then his hand fell to his side. He turned to look again through the opened door into the parlor, lifted his head, and heaved a sigh, sieving the air through his large teeth. "I'll send someone up for that box. Can you take the cat home?"

Oliver nodded.

"And feed the poultry and collect the eggs, until I get another tenant?"

"The chickens are not yours," said Oliver distinctly. "Rose bought them with her own money."

Flash Jack frowned then relaxed with a faint smile. "That's right, boy. That's absolutely right."

"I'll move them over to our place. I could sell the eggs and send Rose the money when we find out . . . Do you suppose Mr. le Grys knows, Mr. Wilshire?"

"Keep away from le Grys," he snarled, suddenly aggressive, larger than life. "D'you hear me? Keep away from le Grys."

"Why?"

"Because there's a damn lot you don't know about this world, and you don't want to learn it too fast." Then, with one of those unexpected changes of mood, he said thoughtfully, "Perhaps it's a good thing they have gone. There's going to be trouble with the natives. It will be one less family to worry about." He turned toward the door. "But you're right, boy. We should know where they are. Give me a couple of hours." Whistling through his teeth, he crossed the veranda and went down the path. Once outside, he headed directly for the waterfront.

Oliver closed the door after him and returned to the kitchen. Rose had never told him where she kept the money tin. He began at the cupboards by the back door, working around the room. It was hidden beneath the wood box under a short plank from which the nails had been discreetly removed. Picking up Edmund, he strode off to look for a suitable corner in the doctor's garden where he might place the chicken coop and hide Rose's precious savings.

Nicholas now had the main part of his thousand acres cleared. Of course it was not all legally his. Only the hundred acres for which he had paid in London could really be called his own, but he lost no sleep over that. When the Land Commissioners came, he would be more than ready for them. All the frustrated energy that came out of his marriage and his banishment had gone into working the land.

Five hundred land claims had already been remorselessly cut down. The virtuous missionaries who were so intent upon "protecting" the natives were found to have in their possession 216,000 acres for which they had not even paid! The Land Commissioners had cut them to 62,000. The settlers were delighted.

One day Nicholas sent his shepherd, Peter, into town to get attention for a festering sore. "Find out the latest news from Wairau," he called, as the man rode out of the stable yard. The medical hall, as well as being a pharmacy, was something of a gathering place.

Later that afternoon, hearing the fast pounding of horse's hooves, he hurried to the stable yard, knowing Peter would not ride so fast except to bring bad news. He came flying past the house and pulled up with a jerk, his horse snorting and stamping, its saddle cloth soaked with sweat, its withers white with foam.

"There's been a bloody massacre!" the shepherd cried, as he leaped out of the saddle. "They say Wakefield and all his party have been slain by Rauparaha and Rangihaeata. The town's in a frenzy."

"My God!" Nicholas pulled up with a jerk, stunned. A Wakefield dead! "You're certain?" he asked.

"I think there's no doubt. They say the chiefs have got

away and are marshaling an army in the north. Wellington is expecting an attack."

"Give Sandy a good rubdown before you stable him. Tell Ben to saddle Duke." Duke was the fastest horse at Rata Hill now. Nicholas strode swiftly back to the house.

Cressida, with her workbasket beside her, was mending a torn shirt. She looked up, smiling a tentative welcome. Beatrix was playing with her doll on the floor, the spaniel lying with his nose in her lap. She, too, looked up as Nicholas swung into the room, but her face remained grave. The Dragon insisted a child speak to its elders only when spoken to. Nicholas, being unacquainted with these rules, found his daughter unforthcoming.

"I am going into town. Peter has returned with news of a Maori uprising. Arthur Wakefield is dead."

Uttering a cry of distress, Cressida jumped to her feet, her sewing materials scattering on the floor.

"I believe we will be safe enough here," Nicholas said. "But make ready to go to the cave, should it be necessary. I will give orders to the hands to be prepared."

Cressida asked in bewilderment, "Why are you leaving us? Surely, you have all the facts from Peter. Why should you go into danger?"

He interrupted her. "I have no reason to believe there is danger. Yet. But should the townspeople not be making what I consider to be adequate arrangements for their protection . . . " He hesitated, then announced, his voice harsh with guilt and pity, "I shall bring the Putnams here."

There was a sudden stillness in her face, a draining away of color.

"I appreciate that you may be dismayed at such a move," he said, "but I must ask you to remember that I am responsible for the boy. Even were you to express a willingness to look after him, I know that Rose would not let him go."

She wanted to scream, "The girl is gone and I am glad, glad, glad!" She opened her mouth, but the intolerable hurt constricted her throat, choking the words. Slowly, she closed her lips, bleeding from the heart, drenched in bitterness and humiliation too great for bearing. She stood in silence while he strode out of the door.

She heard him taking the stairs two or three at a time;

heard him pound down again. The clock on the mantel inexorably ticked away the moments of opportunity. Then there was the beat of a horse's hooves, and it was too late for confession. With trembling fingers, she picked up the shirt she had been mending and sat down again. Mindlessly, she put the needle through the linen. Mindlessly, she drew it out again.

There was a knock at the door and Nurse appeared, hard-bosomed with indignation. "M'Lady, I don't wish to distress you, but I am obliged to inform you that Esau and Manata have gone. I met them fleeing across the yard. They were quite wild-eyed, m'Lady. They shouted to me that the most fierce and bloodthirsty chiefs in the land were about to attack, and that they did not intend to stay and be butchered. It seems that Peter—"

Cressida raised a hand. "My husband has gone into Wellington to ascertain the truth." She added, "He went to bring the girl back, and the ch-ch-child." She pressed the sewing down hard into her lap and closed her eyes, screwing them up, tightening her mouth, choking with grief.

The Dragon crossed the room swiftly, her face drawn with lines of concern. "You did not tell him, m'Lady?"

"How c-could I!"

"Had you consulted me, m'Lady, I would have advised it."

It was some little time before Cressida could speak. "I had to ch-choose, Nan," she managed pathetically, at last. "I was so sh-shocked by his c-callous disregard for my feelings . . ." She wiped her eyes on a lace handkerchief. "I felt the n-n-need to p-protect myself."

She could not go on. Overcome with misery, she reached out both arms as she had done in childhood, encircling her old nurse's ample hips, and burying her face in the padded folds of her skirts.

"There, there, my little dear. Don't take on so. You will disturb the child."

But the violence of Cressida's emotion would not be stemmed. Clinging to the old woman, she cried as though her heart would break.

Reaching the town in record time, Nicholas made straight for Barratt's. In spite of the growth of other hotels, everyone still made for Barratt's.

There were already a dozen horses at the rails, all warmly covered, and with a look of having been ridden hard. Nicholas swiftly rubbed his mount down, covered him, then went around to the front, pushing his way through the crowd of apprehensive citizens.

The coffee room was full. He nodded to acquaintances, paused to speak to friends. Everyone was hungry for news. Few, it seemed, were in possession of concrete facts.

"It seems that twenty-two Europeans, including Captain Wakefield, have lost their lives in the most lamentable and bloodily atrocious circumstances," said Dr. Evans, grimly.

"The bodies were appallingly mutilated. In a burst of mad blood lust, Rangihaeata is said to have cleaved the skulls . . ." The little group around Nicholas lapsed into an appalled silence.

He moved around, gleaning what information he could.

"After the massacre the two culprits fled to Kapiti Island."

"They came back here, to the mainland."

"They traveled up the Manawatu River to hide with Te Rauparaha's tributary tribes."

"They have gone north to Taupo or Rotorua."

"Te Rauparaha intends to incite all the central tribes to march on Wellington."

Mr. Roe, the new editor of the *New Zealand Gazette,* asked, "Is not Jerningham Wakefield up the Manawatu River with his Maori friend?"

"I believe so."

"If Kuru chooses to call on the tribes of his wives and those of his father he could easily raise a thousand men. If young Jerningham hears the news, and undoubtedly he will, for the bush telegraph operates at fantastic speed . . ."

"I doubt he would act rashly," said Nicholas, exuding far more faith in Jerningham than he felt.

"He is devoted to his uncle Arthur."

"And he is foolhardy."

"Hotheaded in the extreme."

Dr. Evans stood up and expressed himself ready to go to Auckland. "I could perhaps rouse the concern of the government sufficiently to send a regiment of soldiers south, as well as get permission and money for the building of a battery. We must be able to defend ourselves."

Someone pointed out that the government brig ws in the harbor.

He nodded. "But I cannot go immediately. In order to present a watertight case to the authorities, I must have precise details of the confrontation at Wairau, for we all know the government to be biased in favor of the Maoris, and the missionaries are bound to say that the New Zealand Company surveyors started the affair. I must wait until eyewitnesses arrive. There is a rumor that one of Rangihaeata's wives, who is also Te Rauparaha's daughter, was murdered, and that was what incited the killings."

"A whaler told me she died by mere chance, a stray bullet hitting her during some fair fighting. They used her death as an excuse for the atrocities."

"They do not use excuses," said another in disgust. "They are at heart barbarians and cannibals."

Nicholas had heard enough. Jamming his tall hat on his head, he stalked out and made his way purposefully up the hill to Aurora Cottage.

It was evening when he returned home. Long needles of rain came with him, darting up the valley. Cressida, standing at the window looking out over the darkening landscape, heard it stabbing at the kauri shingles, pricking, pinging. Then the wind gathered it up and lashed it against the windows.

Nicholas rode around to the stable yard, handed Duke over to Ben, and entered through the back door, the rain coming with him in furious gusts.

The Dragon was waiting for him. "Mr. le Grys, would you be so good as to afford me a moment . . ."

Nicholas cast her a look of such malevolence that she fell silent. He took off his wet coat and flung it over a kitchen chair, brushed his hands through his wet hair, and strode through the room, along the passage, across the hall, and into the withdrawing room. Slamming the door behind him, he leaned against it.

Cressida was still standing at the window. Her hands were trembling, but she was otherwise very still. She turned with lifted head and began her carefully prepared speech.

"I am of the opinion that you admire a woman of spirit," she said. "I am sure you will therefore agree I have shown quite exceptional spirit in what I have done. I have acted in the hope and expectation that our marriage may survive. I have tried to make you love me, and I have not succeeded, if only for the reason that Mrs. Putnam has been following on our heels since the day of our marriage."

She paused, taking a deep, calming breath. "Our marriage could have been successful, had she stayed away. I believe I could have made you forget her. So, with this thought in mind, I have removed her, as it is clear from your manner that you are aware, to Kororareka, where I hope and pray she may remain."

Nicholas heard her out in silence. Not by the flicker of an eyelid did he react to the stilted and carefully rehearsed discourse.

When she finished he walked to the fire, lifted one booted foot to the fender, noted with detachment that the horse sweat was drying rankly on the tail of his coat where it fell across his knee, and said, "Wellington is in turmoil. They anticipate a bloody slaughter. It is as well that Rose and the child are safe. I thank you for that." He paused and lifted his left hand to rest at his waist, his right toying loosely with an unlit cheroot.

"Now, as to our situation. I am indeed gratified that I have been blessed with so brave a spouse. You have reminded me in the past that you are accustomed to danger. First the fox hunt. Then the wild boar. Next comes the cannibal with his tomahawk. But you are a good shot."

He moved away from the fire, walked to the window at the opposite end of the room, turned slowly, and went back to lean an elbow on the mantelpiece, as he had been wont to stand at Rundull beneath the crossed swords and the head of William the Conqueror set in stone. "But I digress," he said. "Tonight you have made a fool of me, m'Lady." He looked down at her with fierce, pulsating strength. "You made a fool of me before Flash Jack Wilshire!"

Cressida caught her breath.

"I believe him to be discreet," Nicholas went on, "but

I may be wrong. If I find myself tomorrow the laughing-stock of the colony . . ." He paused deliberately.

It was Cossack's death all over again. "Nicholas!" He seemed not to hear her cry of bitter despair, of guilt, of loss, of regret for all the mistakes, the opportunities missed through pride and hurt.

"I propose to keep my house in order, as Flash Jack Wilshire advises," Nicholas said, and his voice had a cutting edge. "Let your Dragon know immediately that she has no authority here other than with the child. If she is unwilling to submit to my ruling, she may return on the next sailing. She has interfered once too often in my life."

He raised his head, the black eyes flickering, so that she did not see through to the intolerable pain that had brought him so close to madness he scarcely knew what he said. "Perhaps you would be interested to know, m'Lady, that it is entirely the Dragon's fault that you are here at all. Had Rose not disappeared from Cavendish Square the day after our wedding, I would have released you to bring her with me."

Deeply wounded, Cressida started forward in shock and distress. "How can you say that!"

He reached for a lucifer match, struck it with delibera-tion, using the movement to cover his emotions. "I would have done it."

"You speak of simply disposing of me!" she cried, bleeding from the intolerable outrage of his words. "Toss-ing me back to my family!"

"As I understand it, you were happy there," Nicholas replied, drawing a long breath, blowing the smoke out, watching it spiral; hating himself, hating her: burning with the terrible pain of losing Rose again. There was a long, long silence.

All her longing for happiness, for Nicholas's love, for a new life, burst fiercely through her misery. "Send the girl home!" she cried passionately, advancing toward him with hands outstretched, looking so achingly like Rose that for a moment Nicholas felt a lifting of his distress and that old confusion.

Cressida saw the softening and, encouraged, burst into an unrehearsed chaos of longing. "Send her back to

Rundull where she belongs. She brought herself here. You have no responsibility. She is disposable . . ."

She had already seen his face change, but she could not stop. Her voice rose in panic. "She is only a kitchen maid, Nicholas! Only a kitchen maid. It is one thing to roll a kitchen maid in the hay. It is quite another for a gentleman of your position to become so besotted with her that you would ruin your whole life, and that of your family. Get rid of her, Nicholas! For God's sake, get rid of her. Put her on a boat—cabin class—do that for her—for them all—and send them home so that we may start afresh, and be at peace."

All through the hysterical outburst, he had not moved. Now he said merely, "I have no need, m'Lady. You have got rid of her. You have done it for me." He moved away from the fire, the cheroot between his teeth, flicked his coattails over his forearms, walked the length of the room and back. Then with a violent gesture, he threw the cheroot into the flames.

"Now to us. We may not survive this uprising, or any uprisings that could follow over the years. But there is always the chance of a child being saved. One can hide a child. They are sometimes, in their own peculiar way, immensely indestructible. There is the vexed question of an heir for Rundull."

"You will never inherit, Nicholas. Never," she cried. "Accept it and make the most of what you have here. Take an interest in the running of the country, as the Wakefields wish. Allow yourself to accept the fact that you have taken to the new way of life, for you have. I can see that there has been great satisfaction for you in creating this estate. Of course it was not of your choosing, but it is what has come out of the melting pot for you, and you have shown yourself to have all the . . ." She saw the darkness in his eyes and her voice faltered. "Mr. Gibbon Wakefield was right in seeing you as . . ." The brave, kindly meant words fell away, and she put a hand to her trembling lips.

As though there had been no interruption, Nicholas said calmly, "You will, of course, be willing to cooperate. Your pretty speech touching on the fact that I am a gentleman of position, while devoid of sentiment, convinces me of that."

He flicked a piece of dirt off his knee onto the Aubusson carpet, and watched it fall.

She put a hand to her bosom, weeping inside.

When he spoke it was slowly and quietly, almost as though he was thinking out loud.

"What I am saying, m'Lady, is that you are henceforth, quite cold-bloodedly, out at stud."

Dear Felicity,

I have tried for the past three years not to write this letter, but I can no longer resist. Please, I beg of you, send me the money to return to England with my little daughter and my nurse. You are my dear friend and sister, and I know you love me. You also know your brother, and I am sure will forgive me if I say you know his cruelties. You must be aware, though you have all refrained from mentioning it in your letters, that the kitchen maid Rose is here with Nicholas's son. I pray to the dear Lord that you will receive this cry for help with compassion, and say that you will welcome Beatrix and me home again.

I fain would tell you news of the colony, but my heart is too heavy. I can think of nothing cheerful to say. Only I wish to get away and live among those who care for me, and where my child may be safe.

Your loving sister-in-law.

39

Jerningham, paddling downriver to Wanganui with a party of natives, heard the appalling news shouted from the shore. "Rauparaha has killed Wide-Awake and forty white people." The story rang out from every little hut and settlement. Armed with a rifle, pistols, and cutlass, nervously gratified by offers of *uto* from his Maori friends, Jerningham set off overland.

Wellington had ground to a halt. The repertory company canceled its performances; both musical societies were silent. Owners of precious instruments took them to safe hiding places. News filtered through from the north that Te Rauparaha was gathering the tribes together with the intention of sweeping the white race from the land. The settlers' appeal to Acting Governor Shortland for official sanction to arrest the murderers fell on deaf ears.

The friendly natives, baffled by the Englishmen's inability to move, talked with rising blood lust of fearful vengeance; of trapping the Kapiti chieftains who were now stirring up the northern tribes. In vain the English talked to them of police procedure, of jail sentences, of soldiers and the Queen's protection.

"What good has Queen Wikitoria done for you?" they scoffed. "Captain Wide-Awake has been tomahawked. How could a mere woman stop that? Besides," they pointed out with native logic, "Wikitoria is not here." They grew insolent. Even loyal Te Puni strutted belligerently around the town, stating scornfully that a race under a *wahine* ruler was bound to be weak. Up at the

Hutt a constable attempting to arrest a native for theft was surrounded by flourishing spears and tomahawks. Two more were seriously injured.

Jerningham rode out to Rata Hill so deeply grieved that Cressida could not find it in her heart to hate him. She took him to the withdrawing room, which was as comfortable now as any English home with satinwood cabinets, its family portraits, its great stone fireplace full of logs, the flames reflecting in the gilt mirrors and ornate silver candlesticks. Nicholas poured him a brandy.

"It was so stupid and unnecessary," Jerningham blurted out. "Te Rauparaha did not even wish to kill my uncle. Rangihaeata persuaded him. Such a capital fellow he was. Such a capital fellow. They had killed some surveyors and expected *uto*. Rangihaeata said, since as chiefs they would not take punishment for the killing of slaves, 'Let us therefore have some better blood.' So they killed the white chiefs." Jerningham's voice trembled. "It was their stupid snobbery."

"*Uto*," said Nicholas, for once using the Maori, for *uto* was more than vengeance, incorporating as it did so much of the pride and the dignity of those who dealt it out.

"We will never understand their way of thinking," Cressida said. "We have now seen the true Maori beneath the thin veneer of civilization. One day, unless a strong government takes drastic measures, we will undoubtedly all be slaughtered."

"A strong government!" repeated Jerningham bitterly. "So we are to have this man FitzRoy as her majesty's representative. He is not experienced in colonial administration. He is merely another sea captain, like Hobson. People are already saying, if FitzRoy comes, it will be time to pack up and go. I intend to write to Westminster and the English papers, as well as ours. People at home shall know how the fat government officials up in Auckland ignore us. My uncle should have had official backing when he went about his perfectly legitimate business in Wairau."

Cressida left to arrange for another place at lunch. Cook, who had been trained at Hatfield House, the family seat of the Salisbury family where waste was synonymous with good living and good living with hospital-

ity, never minded how many unexpected guests arrived.
Today a Maori had wandered up to the house, taking the
short route over the hills from the coast, bringing a flax
kit of rock oysters that were now in a pigeon pie.

In one part of her mind Cressida felt Nicholas should
warn his friend no good would come of bursting aggressively into print, slandering the authorities; yet, in another, she felt a small hunger for revenge. He has ruined
my life, she reminded herself fiercely.

In the withdrawing room Nicholas was saying, with an
edge to his voice, "Do you remember that day in Hans
Place when you were trying to persuade me to emigrate?
'They're peace-loving people,' you said."

"My father did not know they were so warlike," said
Jerningham miserably. "And, of course, many of them
are not."

"But the savagery is there underneath, as my wife has
said."

"Tell that to those intolerable missionaries," Jerningham
urged, passionate in his distress. "They are saying the murderers acted in self-defense. They welcome Te Rauparaha
at chapel morning and evening. Yet his wives and his
slave women wear the rings of the murdered men, and
his houses are full of their clothes, their arms, and their
watches. As an act of bravado, he has even pitched a
stolen tent in his *pa!*"

Nicholas kicked at a smoldering log. A mound of coals
collapsed in an unearthly glow of pearl, scarlet, and gray.

"Maoris will easily adopt the form of Christianity but
they do not adopt its spirit," said Jerningham.

"Let me give you another drink." It occurred to Nicholas that Jerningham was perhaps getting some rough
justice for turning his life upside down, but there was no
satisfaction in the thought. It was dreadful to see him
hunched up there in the chair looking so shocked and
miserable, suffering not only his personal loss but bitterly
also the loss of faith in his Maori friends. Why the devil
could not Cressida be more sympathetic? He thought of
Rose, of her quiet, penetrating warmth.

"The government won't accept that Maoris do not
understand the English way of turning the other cheek.
They see only that they can do what they like and will
not be punished. That is why we will eventually, as

m'Lady suggests, have war." Jerningham broke down and cried.

It was a frightening time. Te Rauparaha and Rangihaeata, from their fortified *pa* at Otaki, boasted of murders quietly done in the Wellington area, and of more murders to come. In the absence of word from Dr. Evans in Auckland, the citizens saw no alternative but to take matters into their own hands. They managed to muster four hundred bayonets. Within days they had enrolled themselves as volunteers under the express sanction and superintendence of the mayor, the justices of the peace, and the police magistrate, who swore them in as special constables.

"And now we must have a committee of public safety," said the mayor. They chose carefully and made the appointments. Willfully disobeying the acting governor, they built a battery on Flagstaff Hill, and installed two mounted eighteen-pounders. Major Durie set about drilling a rifle corps of a hundred men. The gentry made up a troop of twenty cavalry. The horses, unaccustomed to drums or the rattling of sabers, went berserk.

It was all to no avail. The government brig returned to Wellington carrying Major Richmond, whom the government had appointed as police magistrate for Port Nicholson. "There will be no war," he said firmly, having demanded the disbandment of the corps. "Te Rauparaha has been persuaded by Mr. Hadfield that Captain Wakefield's death will not be avenged."

"Not avenged!" the citizens cried, "but revenge is all the Maoris understand. They will now consider the *pakeha* not only timid, but powerless. They will lose what little respect still remains for white authority."

Major Richmond was not to be moved.

"The missionaries have established themselves tyrannically as the consultative body on native behavior," said Major Baker bitterly, putting his musket down. Mysteriously, Acting Governor Shortland had somehow managed not only to let the settlers down, but also to lay some kind of blame on Arthur Wakefield for his own death.

"HMS *North Star* is coming from Auckland with a detachment of the 80th Foot acting as supernumerary marines, but they have particular instructions that the troops must not land unless they are needed for an active operation," said Richmond.

At least they cared that much. The settlers continued to live on their nerves. All through the latter part of the year—they did not call it spring anymore for there was so little change in the seasons—everyone kept a loaded gun ready.

The Wanganui citizens were terrorized by a series of earthquakes. Part of Shakespeare Cliff had fallen away, and fissures in the ground were emitting sulfurous vapors.

Also they had struck a deadlock over land. The company offered money; the natives wanted goods. "*Homai no homai.*" they said. "A gift for a gift." The Maoris understood dispossession of land through conquest but not its transference from one party to another. They wondered if that was the real truth behind the Wairau affair. Some settlers gave up all expectation of acquiring land and concentrated on cutting flax for rope fiber.

In Wellington, the citizens waited and seethed. When was FitzRoy coming? They wanted a proper inquiry into Wairau. When he did come, he deprecated in the strongest terms the feelings displayed in their newspapers, and in the newspapers at home, against the native population. He made it clear he was referring to young, indiscreet men.

He sent Jerningham home in disgrace.

Nicholas was surprised at his feelings of sympathy and regret. Cressida felt nothing.

FitzRoy hustled in the Land Commissioners. Nicholas was issued with government scrip for three hundred acres. He felt it as a mere puff of wind like the one that blew the governor's cocked hat into the water after his levée.

"I may fight it in court," he said, as he rode home with Cressida in the buggy, contemplating the mile upon mile of fencing he had erected to keep his longhorn cattle and his sheep from straying. "If I can find the time. Or I may simply cock a snoot at them."

"You will need title deeds for your heirs," said Cressida. "Matters here will not be so free and easy for all time."

He laughed again, contemptuously. "My heirs will not need it, for they shall have Rundull. You know as well as

I do that Adeline hasn't got it in her to produce a son, nor Henry what it takes to put it there."

"I wish you would not express yourself so coarsely." She gazed straight ahead up the lush green valley dotted all over with fat white Lincoln ewes that would be lambing soon, doubling the flock.

"My heirs shall have Rundull," he repeated, without apology. A hundred years ago, he had pointed out to her that she had married a coarse man.

Matters had not gone well between them since Nicholas's discovery that Nurse had arranged Rose's abduction. Only in bed, sometimes, were there moments of forgetting and tenderness. On that level, their marriage worked. Cressida tried hard to forget that particular closeness was due solely to Nicholas's desire for a son. But she could not stop the pain, deep as a well, when she saw by the light of the moon through the windows a particular softening of his features that was new and different. She fought against the knowledge that he was merely using her body as a substitute, and thinking of the girl, but she knew in her heart that this was so.

My dear Cressida,

It is with immense sadness that I am rereading your letter. I have wept over it long and sorrowfully. I was afraid for some time to approach HM knowing full well what her answer would be, but you having implored me so heartrendingly, I have at last plucked up the courage.

Of course, the answer is as I anticipated. In all circumstances you must keep the promises you made at the altar to love, honor, and obey your husband.

HM requires me with great firmness not to write at length upon this matter. Neither did she wish to listen at length. She says merely that life is hard for women.

We have had a visit to Chatsworth since I last wrote. The Duke of Devonshire had a wooden porch put up in a great hurry at the entrance to the house in case HM should get wet stepping from her carriage. Later, of course, it will be replaced in stone. . . .

* * *

Cressida's eyes strayed sightlessly around the room. What did it matter? She could not now in her condition undertake a long voyage.

"Listen to this, m'Lady. It's from Jerningham. He says," Nicholas read out in an amused voice, " 'The colonial office did not consider the charges proved against that bounder Shortland. They have appointed him governor of Nevis in the West Indies.' Upon my soul!" He noticed the expression on her face and asked, "Have you bad news? That is my sister's handwriting, is it not? How are matters at home? The frump Adeline is not, I trust, with child."

"Felicity does not mention it." Cressida crumpled the sheet in her hand and rose to her feet, standing very erect. "But I have news for you. I am myself in that condition."

His head came up, his eyes brilliant. She found herself turning away, as she had not meant to do, lest she should see triumph thinly disguised as pleasure in his eyes. "I must speak to Cook—" She broke off, for he had jumped to his feet. He came toward her. She did not look up at his face, only at the strong brown hands extended in some sort of . . . what? Gratitude? It did not matter. She waited only for his kiss, then repeated, "I must see Cook." His arms fell to his sides. As she crossed the hall, her fingers went involuntarily to her cheek, touching the spot where his lips had been, and she felt a little pang of regret that she had not stayed.

Daniel had been truculent and more silent than usual since coming to Kororareka. He had not counted on the bad turn he was doing for Rose rebounding on himself. With that bustling, efficient woman from Rata Hill behind him everything had seemed so easy. Now, in the ugly little seafront town, where every evening the inhabitants were drunk on rum and arrack; without friends; making do in the discomfort of the rented dwelling that was little more than a shack; seeing the silent condemnation in Rose's eyes, he would have given anything to be able to retrace his steps. Not that Rose made life difficult for him. Except that she would not allow him to touch her.

"You can't do that," he had protested indignantly the

first night, when she wrapped herself in a sheet like a
butterfly moth in its cocoon. "I got me rights."

"And I have my rights," Rose returned coolly, though
she was feeling very far from cool, knowing she had no
rights at all. "I have a right to a decent home for my
children. And library books . . ." her voice broke. "And
friends. And pets and chickens . . ." She watched him
with big, frightened eyes as she spoke, ready to duck,
remembering how Adam hit Florrie when she tried to
stand up to him.

He lunged. Quick as a cat she darted aside. "If you
touch me I shall scream," she threatened, "and then the
boys will be upset and you will get no sleep."

Baffled and angry, Daniel shouted, "Wives can't—"

"This one can, as a matter of f-fact." Rose bit her
lower lip to still the trembling.

"When? 'Ow long?"

"How long will it be before we return to Wellington?"
she countered, knowing despairingly that whoever had
given him money would have made certain there was not
enough for the return journey.

He looked so crestfallen and so shocked that her courage seeped back. "The next time you have your will of
me will be in our own home."

"We're never goin' ter get back there!"

"Then you're never going to touch me again. And
don't shout at me, Daniel. The walls here are thin, and
I'd rather not be the laughingstock of this horrible little
town."

The shack was ill furnished, the cooking arrangements
primitive. There were no comforts.

"You had better tell me how much money you have,"
Rose had said to Daniel, the day they moved out of the
hotel. "It will have to last until you find work."

He fumbled obediently in his pockets, looking crushed.

Hardening her heart against him, Rose picked up the
pathetic little pile of coins from the slab table. "We must
have a spade and seeds. When you're not looking for
work, I'd be glad if you would dig up a patch of ground
for vegetables."

"It's not goin' ter be easy." The shack was surrounded
by fern and scrub.

"No," she agreed. It was strange, this feeling of power

she had acquired. Was it, she wondered, how the ladies of Castle Rundull felt as they ordered their staff around? But as Daniel's shoulders slumped, she remembered what he had done for her, if unwittingly, and she slipped an arm around his shoulders. "You are right," she said, "it is not going to be easy. We will have to help each other." Encouraged, he grabbed her lustfully around the waist, spoiling the tender moment.

"Who gave the money to you?" she asked sharply, pushing him away.

He shuffled his feet, muttering resentfully under his breath.

"Was it Lady Cressida le Grys?"

"No. An old woman."

"From Rata Hill?"

"I don't know." All at once, he surprised her by saying yearningly, "Rose, you was nice ter me. We was gettin' on. I thought, if we was away from 'im . . ."

"Oh, Daniel! Daniel!" Her voice broke, and she wiped her eyes with the back of her hand.

Rose knew she could not stroll idly here with the children as she had done in Wellington. It took all the courage she could muster to walk into the town to look for her spade. There were several houses of ill repute. Maori prostitutes hung out of upstairs windows waving to sailors, enticing them in. The girls flaunted print gowns, brightly colored roundabouts, and glittering earrings brought (according to Mr. Urquart who owned their shack) by traders from the exotic East. In the street and on the beach lusty, swaggering, bare-torsoed men eyed Rose lasciviously, even when she was with Daniel.

One morning, unlike the wild winter mornings of Wellington with their tearing, rocking winds, but sunny with a sharp breeze from the sea, Rose tied her bonnet closely around her face, carefully tucking the pretty ribbons out of sight, and pinned a long shawl around her shoulders, masking her dainty figure, and set out to buy the spade. She hurried along the beach track, pushing the baby carriage with Charlie contentedly enjoying the bumps, nervously aware of the sailors in their blue monkey-jackets and duck trousers standing idly around on the sands, of the raffish-looking crewmen who eyed women like hawks. She was not afraid of the natives who lounged

on the beach in their mats and blankets, though they
were different from those she had known.

Giles said in the imperious way he had, "Don't pull
me, Mama."

"We're in a hurry, darling boy." She tried not to sound
nervous.

He dragged behind, kicking at the tufty grass with his
tiny boots. "I don't like this place. I want to go home."

"We'll go as soon as we can." Rose smiled down at
him, thinking that the children might be her protection.
Joseph was looking at her with Daniel's downcast eyes
and the uncertain expression that filled her with guilt.
She knew, though he was only two years old, that he was
aware of all her spontaneous, overflowing love going to
Giles. Try as she might, she could not love Joseph. His
very acceptance of her uncaring was an irritation.

Maoris squatted in the street smoking their pipes, enjoying the winter sunshine. They glanced at her without
particular interest and she smiled nervously back. A sailor
swaggered past with a native girl on his arm, giggling, her
long earrings shaking.

There were spades, inexplicably, in the doorway to a
butcher's shop. Rolling the pram wheels up against the
weatherboard front and enjoining Joseph to look after
Charlie, she entered, holding Giles by the hand. Too
late, she realized she had come upon a quarrel. "*In a
Heke*," screamed a native woman, her face contorted as
she pointed to a fat hog hanging from the rafters. Fearfully, Rose backed away, pushing Giles behind her.

"This is *tapatapa*!" shouted another Maori.

"I will tell Heke," shouted a third, sticking out his
tongue, waving his arms, and contorting his face. Rose
grasped the handle of the pram, hurried on with the
strident laughter of the Maori woman and the white man
ringing in her ears.

She was trembling when she came to the South Sea
Warehouse, a rough weatherboard building jammed between a public house and a thatched *whare* of slab and
fern. There was a sign outside announcing the proprietor
to be a ship chandler, sea-stock dealer, ironmonger, gun-
smith, grog seller, and gunpowder purveyor. She pushed
open the door.

The big room was filled with anchors and cables, rolled

sails, blankets and casks, iron pots, ball moulds, boat compasses, and, in an unattractive litle heap by the door, a pile of knuckle dusters that made Rose's blood run cold. Over in the far corner, near to a rough sort of counter, lounged an odd assortment of human beings: huge, coal-black Negroes; half-breed Indians; piratical, earringed, foreign-looking men. The air was blue with strong tobacco and sharp with the tang of tarred rope. A big fellow swaggered across the room and placed himself deliberately in Rose's path. He wore an open-necked jersey with a metal cross on a chain. A figure of the Virgin hung by black ribbon from one ear, a shark's tooth from the other. Rose drew back in dismay. Suddenly one of his big hairy arms was around her shoulders, hot and sweaty and with a grip of iron; his stale breath in her face reeked of rum. "Why, if you ain't the prettiest little . . ." With one hand he swept Giles up, gripping her shoulder with his free hand, spinning her around. "C'mon," he said, pausing only to leer at the crowd at the back of the store, "we'll take the nipper with us . . ."

With a shriek of terror, Rose brought the side of her hand down with all her strength on the man's knuckles. She might have been a fly for all the notice he took but as Giles, uttering a roar of fury and indignation, hit him in the eye, the brute recoiled, both hands going to his face.

Rose caught her son as he fell and fled out of the door, followed by a roar of coarse laughter. She thrust Giles into the pram on top of the others, gripped the handles, and ran as fast as her legs would carry her, the pram leaping and bumping, the children screaming.

The next day there was a commotion on the beach. From the front door, the only door—keeping discreetly out of sight—she saw the Maoris gathering, saw their arms waving, heard their shouts. There must have been twenty or thirty of them. A brown giant in a dog-skin cape stood on a rock making an angry speech that was received with roars of approval.

Another Maori took his stand, followed by another and another, each oration raising the level of excitement of the crowd, until they were all brandishing their spears and *meres* in the air, dancing and leaping in the savage posture dance called the *haka*. Rose's blood ran cold as they jumped into the air, knees bent, and yelled their chilling war cries.

Perhaps the breeze changed, or perhaps the half-naked warrior who leaped forward then, brandishing his spear, had a voice louder than the rest, for Rose heard his cry: "War! War! War with the white people. We will drive them from the land."

She heard a small sound and turned. Giles was gazing out across the beach, looking thoughtful. "Bad men," he said.

Rose caught him up and held him against her heart.

40

Rose wept for her sunny kitchen, her carefully nurtured fruit trees and flower beds, her shady veranda, and even for the neighbors, whose familiarity, though they did not quite approve of her, had given a certain comfort.

But she was nothing if not resilient. "It was God's fault," she said to herself, defiantly shifting the blame. "He gave me Nicholas and Giles. And He sent Flash Jack to help. He didn't consider Daniel's feelings." Meantime, she was grateful to be freed of Daniel's nightly violence and his fumblings.

Daniel went out again in search of work and returned with bad news. The town was in a state of unrest. No one wanted to give him a job. The wild chieftain Hone Heke and his men were swaggering through the town, pilfering from shops, bullying residents, insulting women. "The police magistrate 'as gone ter get the missionaries. Don't go out, Rose. Lock the door."

There was no lock. "You must go back into the town and buy a bolt," Rose said, "and while you're there, buy some fishing lines. If you are unable to find work, you will have to fish for our food."

Daniel returned looking frightened. He had gone to Lord's store and found the place in an uproar. A crowd of Maoris led by the notorious Hone Heke had not only plundered the store, they were endeavoring to carry off Mr. Lord's Maori wife. Daniel had bravely gone on to the South Sea Warehouse, though he had no sooner made his purchases than they slammed the doors.

"Maori trouble," they said. "Hone Heke is on the warpath." Rose remembered the woman who had called the great chief a hog. "*Tapatapa*." A gross insult. There was bound to be revenge. But she did not tell Daniel of her own experience in Lord's store. It was enough that she should be afraid.

Daniel put the bolt on the door, then went obediently to the beach to fish.

"Lock up after I've gone," he said.

Rose shut the door and pressed the bolt home, but as soon as the room darkened, she had an intolerable sensation of being back in the tiny cupboard room off the kitchen at Rundull Castle. The heavy gloom clawed down upon her. She sprang to the door and flung it wide, holding her face up to the winter sun, looking across the pretty bay, breathing gratefully of the fresh, free air that still retained the power to fill her with delight and lift her, often, to the heights of ecstasy.

"It has been fun," she said to herself. And it would be fun again. Perhaps the gods were jealous because she had Giles and, in a way, Nicholas.

A small voice at her knees said, "I heard you laughing, Mama." Giles spoke reproachfully, critically, as though she had broken the rules by laughing when there was nothing in their situation to laugh about.

She bent down and picked up the little black-haired boy, covering him with kisses. He was so like Nicholas he turned her heart over. "Only because I am happy and the luckiest person in the world, my darling boy."

"I want to go home," he said fiercely. "It was dark in there."

"It won't be dark again," she reassured him. "And we will go home in a little while." She turned. Joseph was standing in the doorway, clinging to the jamb.

"Charlie's crying," he said in the abject, apologetic manner that was so much a part of him.

Rose heaved a sharp sigh and put Giles down.

Later that afternoon the Maoris began again to assemble on the beach. The lounging sailors were not there anymore, only a few workmen busy on their boats. Some of the craft in the bay pulled up anchor and left. Those lying on the beach were run into the water. When the Maoris began their speech-making, they had the sand virtually to themselves. Today there were many orators, each more powerful, more magnetic, more vociferous than the last. The rhetoric floated with intense clarity across the beach and up the scrubby hill. A brave in a flowing feather cape (so magnificent Rose could see its glossy colors from where she stood) waved his long, feather-tipped *taiaha* and shouted, "Is Te Rauparaha to have all the credit for killing the Europeans?"

Rose's eyes dilated. She knew from Maori folklore that quick, sly skirmishes were the Maoris' natural form of attack. Nicholas would be especially vulnerable on his outlying station. Some people said the Maoris, in the event of war, would attack the farms before coming to grips with the town. Her head buzzed, and her heart nearly failed her.

Then the *haka* began, that travesty of what a dance was meant to be with its battle cries to make one's blood run cold. Rose gathered up the children and rushed around to the back of the shack. Though distressed beyond bearing, she worked at diverting them with the *poi*, the light ball that her friend Epecka had given to them. When at last the noise died down she brought the children back. Now, looking across to the beach she saw three respectable-looking European gentlemen watching the scene.

Taking Joseph and Giles by the hand, she hurried down the path toward them, but before she had gone more than a few yards one of the men broke away, leaping and jumping through the scrub and fern toward the beach where the fierce warriors were now beginning to disperse. The other two held a short consultation, then one of them followed the first. Rose was about to call out when she saw the third fold his arms across his chest, stamp his legs apart, and settle down to wait.

He wore a clergyman's white collar with tweeds and gaiters. He was a sturdy-looking man, with short hair brushed upward, so that he resembled a bright-faced schoolboy. Rose spoke, and he turned in surprise. Then, with singular politeness, he removed his hat and bowed. "I beg your pardon, Mrs. Putnam. I was not expecting . . ."

Amazed and delighted to be recognized, Rose dimpled. "How did you know?"

He broke in with a jolly laugh. "This is a very small place. Allow me to introduce myself. I am Henry Williams. I have come down from the Anglican mission at Paihia with the subprotector of Aborigines, to try to sort out this sorry affair.''

Rose put a hand on his arm and looked up with big-eyed anxiety into his face. "I heard one of the men mention the chief Te Rauparaha in connection with war. Have you heard news of trouble in Wellington?"

The missionary nodded sadly. "It is true. Captain Wakefield and a surveying party were attacked—"

"The settlers?" Rose burst out, oblivious of the Wakefield tragedy. "What about the settlers? Has anything happened?" She could not go on.

"Nothing," he reassured her. "Mr. Hadfield, whom you may know, has taken those troublesome chieftains in hand. They look on him as a saint, and upon my soul, I sometimes think they may be right."

Rose put a hand to her heart and closed her eyes. Nicholas safe! As Williams's eyes traveled curiously over the long, dark lashes on the creamy cheeks, the rounded lips now parted over pretty teeth, his face was a study. Rose's lids fluttered up and she uttered a breathy little gasp of relief, a whisper of thankfulness.

He cleared his throat self-consciously. "I trust you have not been too upset by what is happening down on the beach. It's that mischievous chieftain Hone Heke. Some of his men came to take Mr. Lord the butcher's Maori wife back to the *pa*. She not only refused to go, the foolish creature was reported as having called Heke" —Mr. Williams's weatherbeaten face took on an expression of battered resignation—"who you may know is nephew of the great Hongi Hika, the chief with the greatest *mana* of all time, an *upoko poaka*. Do you know what that is, Mrs. Putnam?"

"It is a pig's head," said Rose gravely.

"Indeed. And it is tantamount to putting a curse on him," Williams said, looking concerned. "I heard you were in the South Sea Warehouse. It would be unwise . . ." He paused, his eyes roving once more with a kind of amazement over her pretty face, her golden hair that lifted in tendrils on the inshore breeze, " . . . er, yes, unwise and perhaps even dangerous for you to move around alone, anyway at the moment. Where is your husband?"

"He has gone fishing."

"Fishing, eh?" he sounded stern.

"He has no work as yet," Rose explained. "He is not fishing to entertain himself."

"I understand." The missionary glanced back at the crowd. The Maoris were beginning to filter away. Some of them ran down to a row of beached canoes and began sliding them into the water.

"I hope this is the end of the foolishness," he said, "but I suspect not. Heke realizes that the British flag is proof the land has passed to the British queen, but unfortunately he believes that its loss automatically makes him a slave, so he threatens to cut down the flagstaff." Williams uttered a sharp little exclamation of irritation. "The American consul has enflamed him with tales of the successful revolt of the American colonies. Now the barbarian has an American flag flying from his canoe."

In spite of everything, Rose gave a gurgle of laughter.

"It is no laughing matter, Mrs. Putnam," said the missionary gravely. "He is a blustering, childish fellow, but nonetheless dangerous for that."

She asked in a suitably solemn voice, "Are you aware that Mrs. Lord is obliged to pay *uto* for the insult? That is the way to calm him."

Williams's eyebrows rose in surprise. He said with exceptional pleasure, "So you have been making an effort to understand the natives? Yes, you are right. Heke has demanded a large keg of tobacco in payment for his hurt feelings, but Lord has refused, and his Maori wife is also defiant. It is now a matter of diplomacy."

Williams glanced across at the beach where the Englishmen were standing with a little group of important-looking natives in feathered cloaks. "My colleagues have at last persuaded them to listen. I hope we may now escort the offending chief to Lord's and with luck arrange for the *uto*." He smiled down at Rose, but his eyes were worried.

"You are not well placed on this headland, Mrs. Putnam."

Her head came up. "We are perfectly all right here," she said firmly. One day, she was certain, one of Flash Jack's schooners would come in, and she intended to be on hand to go aboard. It was the only way—the only possible way—she could ever return to Wellington.

"Then I hope you will keep away from the beach, Mrs. Putnam." The missionary hesitated, not quite knowing how to go on. He wanted to say that the lean, tough hunters of the sea's biggest game were hunters of women as well. He cleared his throat and compromised lamely, "It is not a good place for such as you."

"I do not intend to go down to the beach. I doubt, anyway, if I would understand those men—from the scraps of conversation I have heard."

"They speak a barbarous mix of ship slang, scraps of French from French whalers, and vulgar English pronounced in the native way. When this little bit of nonsense is over, bring your husband and children to the Sunday services in the mission church." He shook her hand, marveling as he so often did on human nature. Who would have guessed that yokel Putnam was married to a lady. His thoughts stilled. A lady . . . ? He turned to look after Rose as she climbed back up the hill with the two little boys. He had been so taken up with her he had not even spoken to the children. He who was, indeed, more fond of children than some of the adults his Christian conscience adjured him to love. Rose's back was straight, her head high. A lady? He had been away from civilization for so long his critical faculties had grown blunt. His brother's wife would know. For a good Christian woman, she was a quite exceptional snob.

"Guts," he said to himself consideringly. "That's what it is." The same quality, somewhat differently packaged, he had seen in that odd puss Miss Tilly Bird, who professed to be a housekeeper by profession, yet who rode Mr. Squire's horses like an English countrywoman at the hunt, and played the piano like an angel. The colonies turned up some rum combinations, and no mistake.

Daniel, who had taken his lines off around the headland, returned laden with mackerel and herring, knowing nothing of the commotion in the bay. The sea, he said, was full of fish, and when the tide went out it left the wet sand pitted with tiny holes denoting the presence of those delectable little cockles and *pipis* that Oliver used to bring to Aurora Cottage. There was going to be plenty to eat. Rose told him of her meeting with the missionary, but not that Mr. Williams had advised them to move inland.

Daniel returned the next day from his fruitless efforts to find work with news that Mr. Lord, guided and encouraged by the missionaries, had given the offended chieftain a bag of rice and some sugar. Contentious custom dues had prevented tobacco coming into the bay. The chief, mollified, had given his promise not to cut the flagstaff down. Rose was unconvinced. Maoris had a way of circumnavigating promises without actually breaking them.

A few days later, Rose awakened before dawn. The shack was full of the roar of the sea breaking on the sands. It was cold and damp in the little bedroom. Drawing a shawl around her shoulders, she tiptoed out to the living room and stirred the ashes in the fireplace, then piled some driftwood on the glowing embers. Crouching down, she blew into the coals until little probing yellow and blue fingers crept around the wood, and the dry, gray, twisted branches began to crackle.

Miraculously, Rose's two books, the Bible given to her by the curate at Rundull as a parting gift, and a dictionary from Flash Jack's store, had been packed in the box that had brought their few possessions. She did not particularly like the Bible and often did not understand it, but fearing the admission constituted some kind of heresy, she soldiered on. The dictionary, though dull in itself, was cumulatively rewarding. With growing pride, she knew she was acquiring a better grasp of her native tongue. Now she settled down in the flaring light of the smelly fish-oil lamp, and opened the Bible. An hour later, glancing up, she saw the first light of dawn at the window. Hugging her shawl closely around her, she went to the window and stood looking out across the bay.

The sun was a mere sliver of red on the skyline, the sky itself a barbarous mixture of orange and gold. As she watched the red disk widening and swelling, Rose stood rapt and uplifted by its unholy splendor. A racing dart of silver light leaped across the black waters toward the land, and she saw in its path a native canoe, moving like a thin stick insect toward the land. As though aware of their exposure, the dark figures in their high-prowed craft bent to their paddles, and the canoe leaped forward out of sight.

Fearfully, Rose slipped the bolt on the door, and,

keeping close against the outside wall, went to the corner of the building. As her eyes grew accustomed to the light, she saw the canoe coming into the beach. A warrior splashed ashore, then another and another. The sun's rays touched something metallic. An axe? A cutlass? The canoe slipped away into the black of the sea, and the Maoris it had left were swallowed up by the land.

The rounded treetops of Maiki Hill curved in an unbroken silhouette against the wintry sky. By noon everyone knew the flagstaff was down. Heke had taken his bribe of rice and sugar and kept his promise. No one had asked him not to sit in his canoe in the bay while Te Haratua and his men climbed the hill and performed the deed for him. Honor was satisfied in the Maori way. Putting the staff back, said the missionaries, would merely provide the mischievous chieftain with a wonderful opportunity to cut it down again. Who was to stop him?

Soldiers would stop him, the governor declared, and grimly dispatched a vessel to New South Wales for help. Meantime, he demanded ten muskets from Heke by way of compensation; then, because he did not understand the Maoris' way of thinking and against advice, he gave a fatal impression of weakness by handing back the fine as a present. Heke continued to patrol the bay with the American flag flying high from the stern of his canoe, emulating those colonists who had driven the English from their land.

During the second week of August, Rose, watching anxiously for one of Flash Jack's vessels, saw the barque *Sydney* come in.

"There's goin' ter be war," said Daniel, looking frightened. "They say there's a hundred an' sixty troops aboard."

Rose swallowed an almost overwhelming desire to tell him it would be his fault if his sons died. But it was too late for recriminations. Besides, being cruel to Daniel meant forgetting what he had done for her, and she had promised herself she would never do that. Standing on the headland next day, anxiously scanning the horizon, Rose saw a sail and her heart quickened, but it was only the sloop *Victoria* with HMS *Hazard* in tow. She sent Daniel down to the beach to try to find out what was going on.

"They say there's a detachment of the Ninety-sixth

from Auckland aboard *Victoria*," he reported. "An' the gov'nor is come on *Hazard*." Bishop Selwyn rowed out to meet the governor, and a little group of dignitaries came ashore. Daniel reported that they were going to Waimate to talk to some of the friendly chiefs. Two days later they returned. It seemed a friendly chief called Waka Nene had said he would guarantee the good behavior of the chiefs if the governor would abolish customs dues, so that shipping would return and Hone Heke could collect his harbor dues.

With fear Rose watched the troops sail away, knowing Heke's absence from the discussions threw a shadow over the validity of his countrymen's promises. "None of them understand the native way of thinking," she said in exasperation. "I wish, how I wish, I could talk to them." With both the beach and the town out of bounds for a woman, she was virtually a prisoner in the shack.

Daniel eventually found a job doing ships' repairs, but the pay was not good: eight shillings a week, of which their landlord took half for rent. Rose remembered hearing from the Maoris that a tea could be made from the prickly weed called bidi-bidi as well as from young manuka shoots. Neither was palatable, but she and Daniel drank it. There was plenty of tea in Mr. Lord's store, but they could no longer afford it.

When the cold winds came sweeping over the hills from the southwest, bringing a deluge of rain so that Daniel was unable to go fishing, potatoes became their basic diet. On fine evenings they ate like kings on mackerel, herring, and flounder. Then the cold winter air turned balmy and Rose began to work zealously with the sterile soil Daniel had dug, planting pumpkin seeds, carrot seeds, and peas from Mr. Lord's store. She never went back to the South Sea Warehouse, even with Daniel. Daniel's *mana*, she sensed, was not enough to protect her from its wickedness.

Goats that ran loose all over the bay were a constant menace. Rose was forever running out with a broom to chase them away. Joseph never ventured outside alone, but the fearless Giles was perpetually at risk. One day a goat butted him into the bushes. Giles emerged enraged from the scrub to go sturdily after the animal, fists clenched. Rose swung him high in her arms. "You may not be as bold as that while you are not yet four," she said. "Not until you are big and strong like your papa."

"Why can't we go home?" demanded Giles crossly, refusing to be mollified.

She cuddled him close. "We will go soon," she promised, but her faith was not as strong as it had been. When the mizzling rain blanketed the hills and everything grew damp, when the firewood would not light and the children grew querulous, Rose toyed with the idea of writing to Flash Jack. But she never did. Always in the back of her mind there was that pinhead of suspicion that he could have been behind her dispatch from Wellington. She did not care to think too deeply about his reasons, only remembering that he and Nicholas had fought over her at the Te Aro ball.

She could not write to Nicholas, for if Lady Cressida had arranged the abduction, she would certainly watch the mail. Rose's love for Nicholas was—had always been—on one level oddly selfless. On that level, she knew she must not upset his marriage.

One Sunday when Daniel was at home, Rose went out on the headland to look for sow thistles and wild turnip. Beating through the cypress scrub and ti tree, finding nothing, she wandered on. It was the clearest of clear days, with a huge pale sky and one slim cloud like a rushing wave tearing whitely across. Soon she found herself on a low cliff looking down on an estuary. She closed her eyes, feeling the warmth of the sun on her lids, smelling the salt and the musky aroma of the ti tree, the dank dark earth, and the perfumed essence of the bush on the hills behind. The sea breathed softly. The sea birds wheeled in silence. She gave herself up to the sweet land breeze, allowing it to catch her and float her down the hill, where she knew she had no right to go, then onto a Maori track between the ti tree bushes. In a few moments she was on the beach.

She looked around swiftly, excited and nervous. All at once, she scarcely knew how, her boots and stockings were off, her skirt was tucked up at the waist, and she was running through the waves, kicking up the spreading foam, laughing for sheer joy. The sea breathed faster, sounding troubled, and she laughed over it, showing she did not care. She danced along the sand, arms flung

wide. How wonderful it was just to be alive and free!
Free of that dreadful little shack. Free of Daniel. Free,
free, free!

She did not see the Maori approach in her fast and
silent way.

"Tenakoe."

Rose stared in fear. The woman was young, with thick
hair sweeping down over her shoulders to touch the
girdle at her waist. The coarse material of her cloak told
Rose she was not of high caste. In her hand she carried a
flax kit.

"Me Merama," she said.

Rose smiled. "I am Rose. What have you there?" she
asked, speaking in Maori and pointing to the kit.

The broad brown face with its thick lips and flat nose
spread into a smile.

"I have . . . I had Maori friends," Rose explained.

The woman opened her kit. At the bottom lay an
assortment of fish and shellfish. Rose reached in and
brought out an oyster. "Where do these grow?"

"Come. I show you."

They walked together, skirting the pretty tidal pools,
making their way out toward the point. The little frilled
shells of the oysters, exposed in their hiding places by a
retreating tide, proliferated on the wet rocks.

Soon the small kit Rose had brought for the greens was
filled to the brim. They sat with their feet in a tidal pool,
eating raw oysters and watching the scuttling crabs, the
waving green sea weed, teasing the limpets into sucking
frantically against the rocks.

Rose returned to the shack singing softly to herself.

"Where 'ave you been?" demanded Daniel, looking
worried. "You've been gone for hours."

Rose showed him the kitful of oysters. "I have been
down to the beach." He opened his mouth to protest, but
she went on swiftly, "I had to get away." She picked up a
pan and moved toward the smoldering fire. For the first
time since the trouble began, she felt happy. As she
passed Daniel she encircled his shoulders with her free
arm, giving him a quick hug. "I am not a bird to be kept
in a horrid cage," she said.

Daniel looked baffled. "Don't go again."

She planted a kiss on his forehead, like conscience

money, because she had every intention of disobeying him.

In the event, Rose did not immediately venture back to the sands, for if the flames that licked around the pot of vengeance had died down, the pot itself still simmered. True, shipping was finding its way back into the newly freed port; and Pomare, as head of the inland waters, again took his toll from boats venturing up the inlets. Nonetheless, several houses were sacked, their English owners badly frightened. Heke lusted for the return of the land he had been happy enough to sell for the novel conveniences of the white man. "Pots and pipes are soon broken," he said now. "The land remains." And that other Maori proverb was heard too often for comfort: "Man is mortal, but the land is a living thing." It was what Te Rauparaha had in mind when he slaughtered the surveyors at Wairau.

The uneasy winter turned to spring, and imperceptibly to summer. In spite of the meanness of the soil and the marauding goats, Rose's seeds sent up their delicate shoots, and in due course the little vegetable garden flourished. Cooking over an open fire was a deprivation after the wonder and convenience of the iron stove at Aurora Cottage, but cooking outside, with the bay spread before her, with the hoarse shriek of the gulls overhead, had a particular charm for Rose. Even a touch of romance. Often, late at night, she would sit alone by the dying embers on a flattened patch of fern, and gaze out across the darkening water, dreaming of Nicholas, yearning for her beloved home, and praying that one of Flash Jack's cutters would come.

One hot night, when the moon had bathed the bush hills in a misty glow of quite ethereal beauty, Rose thought she heard the rattle of gunfire and had a strange feeling that the sea was beating up softly in the darkness to take her. Looking inland, she saw Kororareka in ruins with smoke spiraling up through the empty air. She shuddered awake to find herself damp with dew.

41

———————•———————

The Mission church services which provided Rose with the only contact she had with whites provided her also with a clarification of the muddle of facts Daniel had brought home. Mr. Maunsell explained from the pulpit that the sergeant of police, accompanied by four men all armed with swords, had been to KawaKawa to apprehend a European. Unfortunately, a grandchild of Chief Kawiti happened to be at the house, and in the ensuing scuffle received a cut finger. The next day, the victim's brother came with a small party to demand redress. The resident magistrate advised tying a rag on the finger. On the day following, a larger and more fierce deputation arrived. The day after that they came armed. The missionaries had strongly advised the paying of *uto*, suggesting a calf might be welcome.

"This has now been handed over," said Maunsell, "but regrettably with bad grace. Please, I beg you all to employ the utmost tact in all dealings with the Maoris."

He underlined his own disquiet afterward, as they stood outside the church, saying to Daniel, "I think you should try to find alternative accommodation, Putnam."

Rose stepped forward. She was smiling brightly, but there was a fixity of purpose behind her eyes. "We are perfectly all right where we are, thank you, Mr. Maunsell." The reverend gentleman, looking irritated at her intervention, raised a hand, but she ignored it, adding, "There is a *pa* up the estuary some way. Why should not the natives attack from that side?"

"Mrs. Putnam is right, Reverend," put in a tall man with military bearing whom Rose knew as Captain Wright. "Last night natives broke open my stable, and certainly they did not come in from the bay. They threatened to shoot me if I resisted. They have taken eight of my horses. Mr. Tacy Kemp is even now remonstrating with them."

The Putnams were forgotten in the ensuing buzz of excitement. Collecting up the children, Rose slipped away with Daniel in tow. A few days later he came home with the advice that there were a number of empty cottages at the back of the town. Many people had gone, abandoning their property.

"We could have one of them free."

"We cannot simply walk in and take over someone else's house, Daniel." She did not want to tell him about the wish and the prayer, the hope without foundation, that Flash Jack would come and save them.

Besides, she was afraid to live nearer the town. There was always a motley crowd cooling their heels outside grogshops and native brothels. Even as they walked to church, the runaway apprentice boys and the unkempt, bearded men who were said to be escaped convicts from Botany Bay and Van Dieman's Land eyed her with obscene stares.

Christmas came and went without celebration. There was no money to spare for presents, and they could not afford festive fare. Rose plucked some scarlet pohutakawa flowers, arranging them in jam jars Daniel found on rubbish dumps. It was something.

On January 6, four cottages were plundered and the owners left destitute. Then word came that there had been robbery and personal violence at Matakana, twenty-five miles north of Auckland. The spirit of lawlessness was spreading south. That evening, mending the children's clothes as Daniel sat as usual, staring blankly at the wall before him, Rose felt a coldness drift around her as though she were all alone in a threatened world.

She jumped up and went into the tiny room where the children slept. The moon threw a shaft of yellow light across the bunk where Giles and Joseph lay, touching Giles's face, angelic in sleep. She fell on her knees beside him, her face on his pillow, her forehead brushed by his crisp, dark hair.

Ever since that strange dream Rose had known something dreadful was going to happen. She sent up a prayer that they might come through the blackness that was creeping in as a part of the hills and the bush and the Maori discontent.

The next day the few boats that were left in the bay slipped out to sea. They will go south, Rose thought with fear, perhaps meeting Flash Jack's ships, telling their skippers not to come to Kororareka. Suddenly she could no longer bear the tension. Nothing encountered in the wide open spaces, she told herself fiercely, could be worse than this crushing imprisonment.

She picked Charlie up and put him into the carry-kit. The two older boys glanced up in surprise. "We're going out," she told them, smiling confidently. Everyone had said stay at home. She had tried and she could not do it.

Taking Joseph by the hand, with Giles following closely at her heels, she crept guiltily around the shack, then went out onto the ridge and down the little path leading to the forbidden beach. If Daniel had learned to read, she thought resentfully, she could have left him a note.

It was blissfully quiet there. The hot summer sun beat out of a lapis lazuli sky, the sand stretched smoothly across to the estuary. The sea's white, silky fingers of foam made little forays up the sand, changed their frothy minds, and sank back again. The gulls wheeled and squawked. Behind and beyond, the hills rose steep and green.

Rose removed the children's clothes and her own footwear, tucking up her skirts as she had done on that other day. The two elder boys romped and shrieked with excitement, kicking up the water with their toes until their plump little bodies glistened with the salt spray. Charlie toddled delightedly close to the edge, clutching her hand, squealing, swinging drunkenly away, shouting with delight. At eighteen months he was a strong child though not normally lively. Joseph, who adored him, ran to and fro, jerking his little hand, encouraging him farther in.

She was dressing them when she saw the canoes come around the point from the bay. Swiftly she drew them together in the shadow of a rock while the long, slender craft swept by. There was a stillness about the children as of small animals sensing danger. They did not ask why she was hiding them. Not until the last canoe had disappeared into the estuary did they stir and begin the walk homeward.

"Can we go to the beach tomorrow, Mama?" asked Giles, his eyes bright, though his feet dragged wearily up the narrow track through the cypress scrub and ti tree.

"So long as you don't tell Daniel, darling boy."

"I won't tell." Giles gave his promise with alacrity.

She turned Joseph around to face her. "Do you understand you must not tell Papa?" Joseph, unquestioning and timid, nodded.

The walls of their drab little prison did not matter now. The sea became a friend. At night Rose lay listening to the living tide, feeling at one with the water's breathing and sighing. Sometimes they left for the beach soon after Daniel went to work, taking food and drink with them. After lunch the children would sleep in the lee of a rock while Rose read or dreamed. Giles grew brown-skinned and more beautiful than ever. Charlie and Joseph burned a little and freckled, but gradually their skins, too, toughened. Daniel did not notice.

And then one day, Merama was there, quiet as the land, indistinguishable from the rock under which she waited, predatory as a fox intent on its prey.

"*Tenakoe*, Rose."

Rose started. "*Tenakoe*," she replied uncertainly.

"I come take you for ride in canoe to *pa*."

A prickling apprehension crept up Rose's spine. She looked around nervously to see if any Maori braves lurked near, but the bushes were still beneath the hot sun. Nothing moved except the dancing waves.

"I cannot take the children on the water, thank you all the same. We are going home now," she said. Grasping Giles's hand she swung around, but Merama swiftly, silently blocked her path. "I come to get you," she said.

Rose's apprehension turned to fear. "What do you mean you have come to get me?"

"You speak Maori."

"That is no reason why I should go to the *pa*." She added apologetically, though she was sick with fear, "I am sorry, Merama. I really must take the children home."

"I come to get you," the woman repeated, and now she sounded sly.

The children gathered around, tugging at Rose's skirts.

As if some sixth sense told her where to strike, Merama swept Giles up in her arms. Rose leaped forward, her hands grasping the empty air as Merama ducked, then sped around the rock, fast as a swallow diving. Charlie and Joseph screamed. Giles added his lusty roar.

Rose flew in pursuit. It was the Wellington bush all over again. They rounded a promontory and there in front lay a canoe that had been hidden by another jutting rock. In a flash, Merama was seated and moving out into the stream. Giles, apparently stunned with shock, sat stiffly at her side.

"Stop! I will come. Stop, Merama!" Rose shrieked. "We will all come."

The Maori woman drew the paddle into the canoe. Turning, Rose dashed back to the screaming children and swept them into her arms. Staggering beneath their weight, slipping and slithering across the hot sand, panting with fear, she floundered with them into the shallows. They were going to their deaths. But at least they were going together. The native slid the canoe back inshore and reaching up, took Joseph. Rose lurched into the narrow craft with Charlie in her arms, and settled as best she could, her wet skirts clinging to her ankles.

"Mama!" shouted Giles, his great black eyes looking as though they would jump out of their sockets. "Where are we going?"

With effort, Rose managed a stiff smile. "We are going visiting, darling," she said her voice wobbling and croaking. And then to Merama, holding the panic down, "Why are you . . . where are you . . . ? Aware of three pairs of apprehensive eyes on hers, Rose managed another stiff smile. "Why are we visiting your *pa*, Merama?"

Bending to the paddle, ignoring her passengers, the native began a long, slow, rhythmic chant.

Rose never forgot that dreadful journey upstream, the bush-clad banks creeping closer as the estuary narrowed, the tension mounting, the useless regrets multiplying. If she had stopped for one moment to consider, she would have realized the Maoris with their bush sense were bound to know. It had been willful and stupid of her to bring Giles into danger. Giles who anyway belonged as well to Nicholas, held by her in trust for him.

They could have traveled upriver for no more than an hour—though it seemed a lifetime—before there were signs of habitation. A clearing on the eastern bank signified the approach of the *pa*. Merama turned the canoe and paddled in toward the shore. Several Maori braves who were tilling the soil looked up and called a greeting. The canoe nosed into the landing and Merama, pausing only to pick up Giles, leaped ashore and set him down on the grass. Rose had no recourse but to follow. Giving the boys a tight-lipped smile, meant to be reassuring, she picked up Joseph and handed him out, then jumped with Charlie.

A tattooed woman with heavy breasts and undulating hips was coming toward them, her long, thick hair bouncing on her shoulders. The little boys stared at her in astonishment. There was a blue stained spiral figure on either side of her chin, a semi-circular mark over each eyebrow, lines across her thick lips running down inside her mouth, and a mark resembling a candlestick on each cheek. She was dressed in the feathered mat of a highborn *wahine*.

"I Rangi," she said. "My father who is chief wish to speak." In the friendliest manner, she bent to rub noses. Rose responded stiffly.

"Come," said Rangi, and turned her back on the river.

"Why should he want to speak to me?" Rose asked as they crossed the grass.

"You talk Maori and he dying. Chief's last wish must be granted."

Rose's blood ran cold. She had heard that the whims of a dying man could send his couriers all over the country scouring for delectable tidbits. If he should wish for the sweet flesh of a child . . . Her arms tightened around the placid, smiling Charlie. She looked down at Giles and Joseph trotting innocently beside her. She looked up at the big tattooed woman, her eyes glazed with terror. Rangi smiled back reassuringly. "Is all right," she said.

All right! Rose's heart was drumming against her stays so that she could scarcely breathe. She glanced around surreptitiously, but there was no escape. The three children were her trap.

The *pa* enclosure was about a hundred yards wide, and perhaps five hundred yards long. They passed the sleeping houses, high buildings elaborately carved with round windows to admit light and let out smoke. Some women sitting on a veranda with their *turu turu,* the weaving stick Rose had seen in Te Puni's *pa* in Wellington, watched the little procession with smiling interest.

They turned a corner. Rangi shouted triumphantly, "Here come *pakeha!*"

Rose thought she would faint from fright. She reached for Giles's hand, gripping it tightly. Out in front, on either side of a sleeping house, stood row upon row of braves lined up with spears and *meres* in their hands.

Automatically, she turned to run, but Merama was close behind, blocking her way. Rangi pointed and Rose saw a skeletal old man lying on a mat on the ground, directly outside a flamboyantly carved *whare.* Over and above her fear, somehow on another level, Rose remembered with distaste that food was never wasted on the dying. Neither were they allowed to die inside a building, lest the body from which the spirit had departed should attract evil spirits.

Rangi gestured to Rose to stand before the old man. Her fingers tightened on Giles's hand. Swinging him up in her arms, Merama broke the grip. Rangi took Charlie from her. They all went to the end of the veranda. The children were quiet, as though overwhelmed. Rangi urged her forward. The old man's tomahawk and musket lay at his side. On the wall behind hung a beautiful greenstone *mere.* His eyes were unfocused, but as Rose moved directly in front of him, he fixed her with an obscene glare. "Pick up the parcel and unwrap."

Rose's eyes swiveled. There was a packet wrapped in dressed flax lying at the chief's side. She fell on her knees and began with hasty, trembling fingers to undo the knots. As the wrapping fell away a disgusting stench emerged, and she shrank back, then with a cry of dismay leaped to her feet, looking down with horror at a beautiful greenstone *mere,* the most precious possession of the Maori, smeared with human excrement.

The old man said, speaking slowly, partly in Maori and

partly in pidgin English, "I want the white people to know what you know. Heke has sent me this. It is a question for my people to answer."

Speechless with disgust, Rose looked back at the *mere*. Her mind was already racing ahead. When the Maori spoke of important matters he spoke symbolically. The *mere* symbolized all that was best in the Maori. The filth?

The chieftain said, "We are being deprived of our heritage. Our dignity has been defiled, our prestige and *mana* lowered by the white man's possession of our land. Heke asks me the question, should we clean the *mere* or leave it soiled? And, what is more important to you, he has asked the same question of Kawiti, who is not even his friend and who truly hates the English. Heke is a patriot, but Kawiti is a plunderer and a thief."

Rose answered in Maori, her voice a mere whisper, "What will your answer be?"

"My answer has already gone. His desire will be gratified. The *mere* will be cleaned."

A stout, athletic savage with a fierce and cunning face came creeping forward, and sat down beside the old chief. "The tribe is assembled," he said. "Do you wish to speak?"

This must be the *tohunga*, Rose decided, the Maori priest who held such enormous and sometimes evil sway with the tribe. The old man nodded, the *tohunga* gave a sign, and the army of braves moved forward. Rose felt a touch on her arm. Rangi pointed toward the end of the veranda where Merama now stood with the children. "Come," she said.

Rose followed. The little boys, their eyes riveted on the scene, their expressions rapt, showed no sign of fear. Rangi said in a low voice, "You may not go. Not yet," but she handed Charlie to Rose. The braves lined up before the dying man.

The voice of the chief rang out, extraordinarily strong for one in extremis. "Hide my bones quickly where the white man may not find them. Hide them at once. O, my tribe, be brave," he said. "Be brave that you may live. My two wives will hang themselves." He paused. Two ancient women came out of the building behind to prostrate themselves at his feet, howling their eager assent.

"I am going. Be brave after I am gone."

The fierce old *tohunga,* who had stayed watchfully at his chief's side, sat up with eyes blazing. The dying man rose almost to a sitting position, murmuring, "How sweet is man's flesh!" Then, with a gasp, he fell back.

The priest bent close to his ear, shaking the body roughly as though to bring it back to life. Fascinated and horrified, Rose knew that the priest was shaking the departing spirit out of the body.

"Kia Kotahi Ki Te Ao! Kia Totahi Ki Te Po," he roared. "Now, now, be one with the wide light, the sun! With night and darkness, O, be one, be one!"

Pandemonium broke loose. There was a sound of musket fire, women screamed, the *tohunga* shouted in the dead man's ear. Rose felt a tug at her skirt and looked down. Giles, with a very determined look on his face, pulled her toward him, then sprinted in the direction of the nearest sleeping house. Merama and Rangi had joined the frenzied throng.

With Charlie on one arm, and Joseph's hand in hers, Rose took to her heels. Giles had already slipped behind the building. Waiting only to ensure that she followed, he headed for the river. She bent and caught Joseph up clumsily under her free arm. Holding him on her hip with legs and arms flailing, she raced in the same direction. Once or twice she flung a look behind, but no one was following.

The canoe was where Merama had left it, close against the bank. Giles scrambled in and Joseph after him. Rose stepped aboard, put Charlie down, untied the flax rope and using the paddle against the bank, pushed off. They shot into midstream.

She had not been in a canoe since those blissful days at the Hutt River when she and Oliver and Giles used to go nosing among the flax bushes looking for the nests of the fierce blue kingfishers, picking the bulrush spears to stuff their pillows, but she had not forgotten how to paddle. The tide had turned and the water flowed swiftly downstream. As they sped around the first corner the noise died away. Looking back for the last time, Rose experienced a feeling of unreality and with it a sense of black dread that was more than fear. "Dear God," she prayed. "Send Flash Jack to save us."

"I want to go home," said Giles scowling. "And Jo-

seph and Charlie want to go home, too." Bending to the
paddle, avoiding that all-knowing look on the fierce little
face opposite, Rose remembered saying in the little hospital room on *Aurora,* "Don't mock him. He is your
son." Now she was more than ever aware of a Rundull
strength in Giles.

They reached the neck of the estuary without mishap
and Rose maneuvered toward the shore. Giles and Joseph scrambled out onto the sand. Rose followed with
Charlie in her arms. The afternoon's events had either
passed him by or had already been forgotten, for he wore
his normal amiable expression. They hurried along the
beach and up over the headland, with Giles speeding out
in front, and Rose tempering her steps to Joseph's anxious plodding.

Daniel was standing by the shack, looking lost. "The
fire's out," he said. "Where 'ave yer been? I want me
tea."

"Listen to me, Daniel," Rose said. "Listen well, for I
want you to take this story to the police magistrate. If
you cannot find him, give it to one of the missionaries."

"I'll go after tea," said Daniel truculently, when she
had finished telling him of the chief's warning. "What
sort of wife are yer, Rose, if yer can't even 'ave a man's
tea ready?"

Her nerves gave way then, and she shouted at him.
Like a fishwife, she thought afterward with awe. "I am
the kind who looks after her family. Get down into the
town," she screamed, "and do as I say!"

Kororareka had its warning. To Rose's utter disbelief,
nobody took much notice. The men remarked stiffly and
with embarrassment that it was going a bit far to present
a white woman with a defiled *mere.* Mr. Maunsell said
the natives would have to learn to treat Englishwomen
with respect.

"Heke is nothing if not spectacular," Mr. Williams said
tolerantly. "A showman."

"Keep your wife at home, Putnam," advised Mr.
Maunsell, looking uneasy.

"You would think the bearing of three children would
have given her some sense of responsibility," remarked
one of the missionaries' wives.

Rose looked frantically around the gathering outside the little mission church for someone who would take her seriously. Her eyes fell on Captain Wright, who had championed her before.

He gave her a wry smile. "I know what you are going to say, Mrs. Putnam," he began before she could speak. "They are blockheads and fools who persist in ignoring women because they are women, and in crediting savages with the ability to think as Englishmen. You colonial wives will inevitably on occasion see the cruder side of life, and I am sure will not be unduly scarred." He smiled. "Tell me, though, why are you so—forgive the bluntness—pigheaded about living so near the beach?"

"I do not believe we are in any more danger than those in the town. In fact, less," she asserted. "Besides, I would not wish to be cut off inland should the town be sacked. I could not trek south through the bush with three children. There is only one way out of here for such as me, and that is by sea."

He nodded gravely, giving Daniel a cursory glance, noting that she spoke in the singular, as though she were on her own.

"And there is going to be war," she added.

"Yes. There is going to be war. Those fools are simply precipitating it by re-erecting the flagstaff. I wish I could persuade them to leave the damned thing lying on the ground until there are sufficient troops here to defend it. But Governor FitzRoy does not understand the natives, Mrs. Putnam. And the missionaries treat them as naughty children. If you treat a cannibal as a naughty child, sure as hell he will eat you up."

Rose uttered an hysterical little laugh and wiped her eyes.

His face softened. "You are very isolated here, Mrs. Putnam. Have you, er, anyone to talk to?"

Rose made a face. "Nobody goes out. And besides . . ." She did not want to say she would have little in common with the rough women of the town.

He looked at her acutely. "There are many like you, Mrs. Putnam, if it's any comfort," he said.

Rose went back to their headland feeling warmed by his kindly interest.

On January 9, in broad daylight and without violence,

Hone Heke cut the flagstaff down again. The governor was swiftly informed, and a proclamation issued for the capture of the chief.

"Am I a pig that I am thus to be bought and sold?" Heke asked, highly incensed by the promised reward of £100. Retaliating, he offered the same amount for the capture of the English governor.

HMS *Hazard* and *Victoria* once more returned to the bay. The Reverend Henry Williams protested against the resurrection of the flag, but the colonial secretary insisted on giving it a military guard. The defense might have worked had the soldiers not been relieved by friendly natives from Chief Waaka Nene's tribe.

Heke, knowing no Maori would shed blood in defense of an inanimate object, walked audaciously up the winding track on Maiki Hill and once more slew the pole. Then, spoiling for a fight, he paddled with his braves under the stern of *Victoria*, firing muskets derisively in the air.

Such behavior was not to be borne. They brought in a pole from the forest and once more hoisted the flag. That night, mysteriously, it vanished, spirited away by a chief who had been born under the tree from which it had been cut. Trouble, or even death, could befall him if Heke cut it down. It was the one light moment in a grisly week. Officials purchased the mizzen mast of a foreign vessel that happened to come into the harbor. No Maori could have been born under that. The police magistrate treated further threats with contempt. There were ninety marines and sailors on *Hazard;* one lieutenant, one ensign, two sergeants and fifty rank-and-file soldiers as well as a hundred and ten civilians were under arms.

The Reverend Henry Williams went to Paroa to explain the Treaty of Waitangi once again to the chiefs; the Maori Magna Carta that they had signed for the bribe of a blanket.

On February 28 four war canoes crowded with armed natives swept down the bay. Rose saw them and felt cold to her heart. Charlie and Joseph were sleeping. She and Giles ventured out a little way onto the headland. Apart from *Hazard* and *Victoria* lying at anchor, the bay was deserted. It looked achingly beautiful in the late summer sunshine. She watched with dread as the canoes turned into the estuary and disappeared. She came back inside, knowing that this was the beginning.

Daniel came home looking frightened. "The Maoris 'ave plundered Captain Wright's 'ouse an' burned it down. An' now there's smoke comin' from farther up. They think there's some other 'ouses bein' attacked." He stood in the doorway looking inept with his big hands hanging at his sides.

Rose said fiercely, "You were brave once, Daniel. You saved me from the Rundull mob. You must be brave again." He seemed not to understand. She went to him and put her arms around him, knowing with compassion and guilt that she had taken away his pride and the self-respect that had been his strength.

"We must think of the children," she said, "who cannot look after themselves. At least we have the children," she added, meaning that Daniel had Joseph and Charlie.

And she had Giles.

42

At last it was officially recognized that the Maoris would attack. FitzRoy sent to New South Wales for help, and Sir George Gipps agreed to dispatch two companies of the 58th Regiment, the famous Black Cuffs. Captain Wright moved in with Mr. Polack at the northern end of the beach, where they were busy building a stockade as a refuge for women and children.

Lieutenants Phillpotts and Parrott, two officers from *Hazard*, rode out toward Matauhi Bay to reconnoiter a party of Heke's men. Chief Kawti's scouts unhorsed them, disarmed them, and took them to Kawiti, who sent them back on foot. The Maoris were in the ascendancy, laughing at the whites, trying their strength, growing more cocky by the day.

A three-gun blockhouse was erected on a small hill several hundred feet above the town, close to the track leading to the flagstaff, and the few troops available moved into barracks on the flat below. A gun with a crew of bluejackets and marines from HMS *Hazard* was placed at the other end of the town, where an entrance to the valley made it a likely place of attack. *Victoria* lay at anchor in the bay with forty stand of arms and a thousand rounds of ball cartridge for the militia.

All work ceased while the town waited. Daniel drilled with the civilians and helped to build the stockade. The war was not going to wait for the arrival of the Black Cuffs. Goats came in, eating Rose's spinach and the last of her carrots. Time and again she went out onto the headland to search the horizon for ships. With one palm against the other, fingertips beneath her chin, her face lifted to the empty sky, she prayed like a child. Her prayers winged out uselessly. Nobody came.

It began on March 3. Rose was poking the fire into a blaze under the soup she had made for the boys' lunch, when she heard shouts coming from the beach. She dropped the poker and ran outside. To her amazement, she saw Mr. Phillpotts, the young lieutenant who drilled the civilians, dashing across the sand with some of his men in tow. They leaped into the longboat and rowed out toward *Hazard*.

She scanned the horizon for ships, the black, owl-haunted hills for smoke. When the Maoris planned an attack it was said they sent up gray spirals of smoke as a warning. Nothing moved in the hills or on the sea except the longboat slipping through the calm waters. Then, men began to appear on the frigate's decks, shouting, running up and down, unfurling sails. Rose's eyes once more scanned the hills.

And there it was. Creeping snakelike up through the trees, lifting above the topmost branches of the bush hills, through the misty air until it touched the sky—a gray, thin, sinister cord of smoke. The frigate weighed anchor, swept swiftly around the headland, and disappeared from sight.

Without making a conscious decision, Rose began automatically to gather clothes together, putting them into a little heap beside the door. Inside one of the kerosene boxes they used as chairs she found a discarded sugar sack.

Purposefully, quietly, she filled it with clothes, then gathered up what food they had, packing it in the tin used for boiling their linen. Charlie and Joseph watched her in silence. Giles came out of the boys' bedroom.

"What are you doing, Mama?"

"I am packing, darling boy."

His little face lit up. "Are we going away?"

"Yes," she said, and crossed her fingers superstitiously.

"Are we going home?"

"I hope so, darling boy."

Nothing happened. The intolerable waiting continued all morning. Rose gave the boys their soup, and some of the hard bread left over from the previous day. She made an effort to eat with them, but her apprehension had grown into a great lump in her throat and she could not swallow. Every few minutes she went outside to search the horizon for ships, returning desolate.

It was late afternoon when the first sounds came. A noise like the pounding of a horse's hooves. Rose froze. The hoofbeats came nearer. She went swiftly to the door and looked fearfully out.

Someone was cantering up the track on a tall bay. A woman! Even as Rose collapsed with relief against the doorjamb she recognized something familiar about the way the visitor held her head and the dark curls escaping from beneath the outrageous cabbage tree hat.

"Teresa!" She started forward, joy flooding through her, her feet lifting off the ground.

Teresa flung her hat in the air shrieking, "So it is you! So it is you!" She slid out of the saddle, and flinging the reins over the horse's head, sliding them down her arm, ran forward. With a great, incredulous gasp that dwindled away in a sob, Rose went to meet her, all the loneliness, fear, despair of the long months falling away. They held each other tightly, crying together "like two old Maori women at a *tangi*," they said afterward, laughing.

"Oh, Rose, that I should find you here!"

They wiped the tears away and grew gradually calmer. Teresa said, "I have been riding for simply ages—since before daybreak—hoping to get a ship out. My employer deemed it necessary to come and join the troops."

"Your employer?"

"I have been working as housekeeper for a Captain Squires who lives up the estuary. A long way up. His house, the house where I lived, has been sacked and burned by the Maoris. We had to fly with our lives." Teresa gestured despairingly toward the empty bay. "And now, no ships."

"I have been praying Flash Jack would come in one of his schooners."

"Of course he should," asserted Teresa crisply. "I cannot think why he is not here. But then," her eyes clouded, "there is trouble in Wellington. Did you know?"

Rose nodded.

"They say the English are building redoubts and palisades, and that there are men-of-war in Port Nicholson. I truly believe, Rose, that we are to be driven out of the country. Now I have come to take you to the stockade that Mr. Polack has built. All the women and children are going there."

"First, tell me what is happening."

"Hone Heke and Kawiti's forces are gathered at a joint camp at Te Uruti, and their followers are looting the properties around. *Hazard* went in this morning to disperse the raiders. They sent an armed pinnace ashore. The natives fired on it. By the way, Rose, I am known still as Tilly Bird. You will remember that, will you not? Just until we are certain my husband has given up the search and returned home."

"Of course."

"Come. Let us collect what we can of your things." They turned. The three little boys stood in the doorway, looking shy.

"Why," cried Teresa in amazement, "you have three children now! She looked from one to the other and said in her outrageously candid way, "Daniel's son's, I declare!"

Rose flushed scarlet, but she managed to say demurely, "Daniel is my husband. Of course they are his sons."

Swinging Giles up in her arms, Teresa gave him a hearty kiss on the cheek. "You don't remember me, do you, little man? I am your Aunt Tilly Bird." Still with Giles in her arms, she stepped inside, grimacing as she looked around the mean little interior. "What brought you to this, Rose?" Then swiftly, without waiting for a reply, "We have so much to tell each other. My mount is of even temperament. I could carry one of the boys pillion, and one in front. Perhaps Daniel could collect your belongings."

It seemed oddly fitting that as they set off down the track Daniel should come hurrying along, too late for decisions, but in time to act as packhorse.

Outside the stockade, made of *manuka* stakes lashed together with flax, civilians were on guard, armed with muskets and strung about with cartouche boxes. The women and children from the town were streaming in. One of the soldiers took Teresa's gelding away.

Inside the stockade, there were rough-looking women from the town—some of them half-castes—sailors' whores decked out still, in spite of their distressful situation, in bright earrings and glittering necklaces. Women were huddled in groups comforting one another. Children cried bewilderedly.

Mr. Polack came forward. "Ah, there you are, Mrs. Putnam," he said with evident relief. "This is rough hospitality we're offering, but at least we're all together, and we have ammunition in plenty. Our powder magazine is situated in the cellars."

"Here?" Rose's voice lifted to an incredulous squeak. "*Here*? With all these women and children?"

"Where else?" Then he added uncomfortably, "We believe help is on the way. Young Bishop Selwyn is known to be heading north on his schooner. He professes to be a friend of Hone Heke."

"He will not stop Heke. No one will stop him now." She clutched Giles's hand, her face livid with terror. "You purport to shelter our children! On a powder magazine! This is rough hospitality indeed."

Polack said gruffly, "There is nowhere else, Mrs. Putnam."

"Why not put the powder outside?"

His eyes lifted toward the sky, late-summer blue and flecked with clouds. "Powder must be kept dry," he said. "In the event that it should rain, we would lose the lot. Besides," he added heartily, "the bishop will doubtless talk the rebels out of their aggression."

Rose turned away, sick at heart.

Daniel arrived with their clothes, added their provisions to the store, then went obediently back for more. The children were intrigued by the crowds. There were more than three hundred people in the stockade. An older girl took them off to play, while Rose and Teresa went to the kitchen to see if they could help. There was a mountain of food from the stores as well as the private-house stocks, but no one knew how long the siege would last. Mr. Polack reckoned their food stocks would last a week.

Daniel brought their blankets and they settled in a corner beneath a cover erected by the soldiers. The bedrooms were already full to overflowing.

That first night was the worst. As the dark hills obliterated the sun and the twilight deepened, an awesome silence settled over the little enclave, the only sound the sea as it crept sobbing up the sand. As a heavy blanket of darkness spread itself across the bay, there was the sound of weeping as though, the children being asleep, their mothers had to unloose the pent-up emotions of the day.

Rose and Teresa sat with their backs against the wall of their little partition and talked softly of what had happened since they last met. "I would think Lady Cressida arranged your departure," Teresa commented matter-of-factly. "Flash Jack would not do it for, as you know, he is in love with you."

Rose's cheeks flamed.

"Come, Rose, this is not a moment to be coy. Perhaps you do not wish to know, but nonetheless you must realize it is true. It is a pity," she added in her outrageous way, "because I shall need a husband, and he would suit me very well."

They grew close over the long days of their incarceration, finding much in common in spite of their widely disparate backgrounds. "Cheney will of course divorce me, and then if Flash Jack does not wish to take me on, I shall have to find some suitable sheep farmer," Teresa said, "for I shall never be able to go home. Meanwhile, I shall divide my visiting between you and Lady Cressida."

"I have no home now."

"Flash Jack will doubtless find you another," she replied airily. The planning and embroidery of Teresa's future kept their minds intriguingly occupied while they waited for the saving ships to come.

In the long nights, lying on her fern palliasse on the ground, gazing at the sky beyond the sheltering rooflet, Rose contemplated the boldness, the sheer brash audacity, of Teresa's plan. The runaway had decided to return as Lady Teresa Mountburn, using her maiden name, intending to deny all knowledge of Wellington and the Te Aro ball. "Miss Flora England?" she would say carelessly. "Clearly the lady must have resembled me, but I have no knowledge of her. Did she also have a chipped front tooth?" She laughed softly, showing Rose where one of her pretty white teeth had suffered a misfortune, adding a touch of quaintness to her slant-eyed beauty.

And there was the stark unreality of going from the Putnams' humble home to the dignity of Rata Hill.

"Lady Cressida will know you have come from me. She will not welcome you."

"But of course she will." Teresa was engagingly down to earth. "She has not so many suitable friends of her own age that she can afford to snub one of her kind. She is very lonely, Rose." Their eyes met, gravely. "She is lonely because you have her husband's heart."

So the nightmare of that week was alleviated by audacious plans as well as by the entertainment of the children. Teresa and Rose taught them to be soldiers, drilling them, diverting them, making them feel useful and important. Giles loved the soldiering.

Every morning the mists of late summer obscured the hills, but when the sun rose they could see Maiki with its two blockhouses. Day after day nothing stirred there except that the sailors from *Hazard* and the soldiers who shared guard duty came and went. But they could not see the harbor, for the tall palisade obscured the view.

In the evenings Teresa gathered the children together, thumping an imaginary pianoforte. She taught them rollicking, cheerful songs.

" 'Twere better she learnt them hymns," muttered one of the women.

Rose sang with them. Optimism was strength. Had she not been strong as a lion while waiting for marriage to Daniel and their call to *Aurora* at Gravesend? Sometimes she felt as though she had lived a hundred years. Yet I am but twenty-two, she marveled.

The store of food went down with alarming speed. After three days, half of it had disappeared. Rose and Teresa took turns minding the children and working in the kitchen. They both needed an outlet for their nervous energy.

On the fourth day, Archdeacon Williams came from Paihia to add church property from the mission station to the settlers' valuables in the stockade.

"The *Sir John Franklin,* an American schooner, is coming in," he announced. There was a burst of clapping.

It sailed right up the bay and lay inshore. The crew loaned their only gun to the beleaguered citizens, setting it up behind the stockade. Bishop Pompallier, who had a promise from Hone Heke that the Roman Catholic Church would not be desecrated, sailed in to reassure the civilians that they need not think of an immediate exodus. Then he went back on board.

The next morning Bishop Selwyn arrived in his schooner. "Hone Heke is my friend," he said, genially addressing the refugees. "He has pledged that he and his warriors are intent only upon breaking British dominance and hauling down the colors. They do not wish to massacre the whites. He has given orders that those who keep their shutters fastened will not be attacked. His followers dare not disobey."

Rose leaped up from where she was sitting on the ground. Her skirt was dirty now, for there were no facilities for washing. Her hair was tied neatly at the back of her neck with a piece of cord. She looked no more than a girl, but there was adult purpose in her eyes.

"Do you not understand," she cried in exasperation, "what the chief is saying?"

The Bishop's brows rose in surprise.

Daniel started forward, his face scarlet with embarrassment.

Ignoring him, Rose shouted, "It matters not who I am. Perhaps I understand the Maoris better than some. Heke is saying merely that if we sit quietly here in the stockade, and the soldiers sit idle in the blockhouses, he will be able to cut down the flag and sack the town without firing a shot. But that if we appear to defend . . ."

The Bishop flushed. There was an uproar from the crowd. "Mrs. Putnam is right. She is right. Listen!"

The tall young Anglican advanced. "Could you not let your husband speak for you, madam?" he asked, looking with curiosity and displeasure into Rose's stormy eyes.

"No," retorted Rose, quite amazed at herself. "We women lack physical strength, but often we have more understanding than men. I believe that as many as can be taken aboard what ships there are should go now. If we are so safe here," she added explosively, "why has Bishop Pompallier gone aboard his schooner?"

Daniel was beside himself with embarrassment. "You're a troublemaker, Rose. That's what you are, he muttered. The crowd was gathering around Selwyn, openly hostile now.

Rose absently patted Daniel on the arm, a gesture of condolence without regret. When she spoke it was with lifted head and direct eyes. "I have become a colonial woman, Daniel. Colonial women are going to have to be different from English women. You will just have to get used to it."

The squat old whaler *Matilda* and several schooners arrived in the bay, but Commander Robertson of *Hazard,* who was in charge, did not wish to give the enemy the impression that the whites were running away. No one would be allowed on board until there was enough transport for everyone. Besides, there was the question of food. None of the boats was stocked in preparation for a mass exodus. Word came that the U.S. warship *St. Louis* was lying near Paihia. A rumor, swiftly scotched, said the governor was about to land. Rumors flew, disturbing the volatile, angering the calm.

Bishop Selwyn left on his schooner for the Paihia mission station, which lay across the water, saying he would be able to watch proceedings through his glasses.

"And there you will have the added advantage of not sitting on a powder magazine," remarked Teresa sweetly, her hazel eyes gleaming with very unholy malevolence. She shared the common view that the missionaries were not such great fools that they did not know how to look after themselves.

"Perhaps you would like to take your chance with us?" asked the kindly bishop with a twinkle.

"I will take my chance with my children," she retorted.

On the fourth night of their incarceration, when food was running low and nerves were stretched to the breaking point, Mrs. Lockhart, a slatternly Maori woman who kept a brothel in a high-gabled house in town, slipped out of the enclave with a shawl over her head. One of the townsmen saw her go, silent on her bare feet, and knowing she was said to be Hone Heke's spy, told the soldiers.

It was too late. No British soldier was capable of catching, or indeed of hearing, a Maori who did not wish to be seen or heard. They waited with taut nerves. The next day, and the next, were quiet. Where were the ships? Their bay of islands was not so far by sea from Auckland. They worried that the frantic calls for help had not, after all, arrived; that they had been ignored by the governor. Fear made them unreasonable. It would be

FitzRoy's fault if they were slaughtered. And if they were not, they would run him out of the country.

The storm broke at dawn on Tuesday, March 10. The stockade was barely stirring when the plaintive note of the *ruru* sounded across the hillside. Immediately recognizing the distinctive Maori bush call, Rose jerked upright on her fern palliasse, shivering. A burst of gunfire coming from the direction of Maiki Hill was returned almost immediately from one of the ships in the bay. The stockade sprang to life. Men rushed to man the *Sir John Franklin* gun. Women screamed. The noise was deafening.

"Come!" cried Teresa. "Let us at all costs get the children into the house." Daniel, one of the five score of armed civilians from the hastily drilled militia, sprinted for his musket.

Lifting Charlie in her arms, grasping Giles by the hand, Rose ran for the greater shelter of the house. Teresa, carrying Joseph, sped at her heels. The interior of the house was already crowded with those who slept there in beds, under the stairs, on sofas and floors. Surging forward to see if there was anything to be seen, vigorously guarding their territory, they officiously blocked the front door.

"The window. Push them through." Even as she spoke, Rose was flinging up the sash and sliding Giles over the sill into the comparative safety of the packed room. Picking up her skirts, Teresa stepped after them, wriggling her slim form into the crush.

Rose made no attempt to follow. Teresa could be trusted to look after the boys. She herself had no wish to be incarcerated within four walls. She wanted above all to be where she could see what was happening; where she might do something to help, if indeed there was anything to be done.

Up on Maiki Hill gunsmoke rolled above the trees. Then, as the early-morning mist cleared, they saw the barricaded doors of the upper blockhouse open and the defenders pour out. They waited. Even the children stopped crying. The unexpected silence was more frightening than the gunfire. But it did not last. All at once the air was rent with a series of inhuman yells that froze the blood.

The flagstaff rocked dizzily, drunkenly, against the sky.

Rose put a hand to her throat. What had happened? She thought she knew. Disturbed by some deliberate sound, the soldiers had rushed outside, perhaps unarmed. The Maoris would have been there, silent as the mist and as sinister; invisible against the blockhouse wall, or so close against a tree trunk as to be part of the tree. They would have waited only until the blockhouse was empty, then swift as arrows, they would have moved in, cutting the soldiers off. That was the way the Maoris worked. She had not forgotten Epecka and Matenga's tales of war.

The flagstaff continued to rock, jerking wildly back and forth. Moments later it fell, and what looked like a red shirt was run up in place of the flag.

"It is supposed to be all he desires," said Teresa, speaking through the window in a sharp, nervous voice that was nonetheless tinged with hope. "To fell the flag."

But the missionaries were wrong again. There was another burst of gunfire from the hill. It was known that the slopes hid old Maori trenches tufted with long grass. They would afford perfect shelter for the natives while they fired upon the town. Now, cannon fire and shot flew out into the bay, barely skirting the palisade. Smoke rising from *Hazard*'s guns hovered on the water. Smoke from the blockhouse spread grayly across Maiki Hill.

Women and children screamed. There was a stampede in the house. Teresa, looking desperate, clung to Charlie, and braced her knees to keep Giles and Joseph free of the crush. Men carrying old-fashioned flintlock muskets, which were all they had, pounded through to the magazine, shouting to people to clear the way. Rose, having only the veranda roof for shelter, flattened herself against the wall.

Teresa asked in a strangled voice, "Do you think I might try a hymn?"

"Something jolly." Rose gave vent to an unlovely laugh that caught in her throat and froze her lips.

The gun behind the palisade burst to life in a volley that filled the air with the acrid smell of gunpowder.

"Onward Christian soldiers . . ."

Nobody else joined in. The crying and screaming and wailing drowned all but the highest notes. Rose cleared her throat, but her voice would not come. Anyway, she did not want to sing. She wanted to do something. She wanted to help drive the enemy away. She did not want to stand still and wait to be killed. Every nerve in her, every sinew, was on fire. Even consumed with terror she needed to be involved.

The crowd quieted just a little, as though to draw breath, and Teresa's voice rose at last above a smaller tumult ". . . with the cross of Je-e-sus . . ." A breeze carried the gunsmoke high. Suddenly a horde of Maoris, hundreds of them, were leaping through the *manuka* on the heights, pouring down toward the lower blockhouses, their wild, continual yelling striking terror in every heart.

The gates of the palisade opened and a soldier on guard against the wall fell. Rose sprang mindlessly across the veranda, over the grass. The man's inert body lay huddled on the ground. She fell to her knees, automatically extending aid, and as she did so, a soldier on the other side gave a queer little jerk, then fell with arms outstretched, his musket clattering to the ground. Heedless of her own safety, Rose grasped the jacket of the first victim and dragged him in. Someone rushed past her, picked up the second body and threw it over his shoulder as he swung back into the comparative shelter of the stockade.

43

Somebody shouted, "The sailors are retreating. Keep the gate open!"

Feverishly, Rose cast around her, found some *manuka* stakes, and propped the gate wide. They limped in, dozens of them, some badly wounded. One man, covered in blood, staggered in as though unable to see. She ran forward and supported him to a shelter, settling him upon one of the fern palliasses. He fell back, and she saw there was a musket ball lodged in his chest. Other women had come to help and were tending the wounded, comforting them.

Someone bellowed furiously, "There's a posse of natives exposed on the hill. Fire into them!"

And then a roar of command, "Hold your fire! Heke has kept his promise so far, but Kawiti made no promises. If you fire you could be responsible for a general slaughter."

"We can get away," shouted another voice. "The ships have come!"

But it was too late for relief. Too late to go. "Our gun has fallen!" Consternation gripped them all. Men rushed out to bring in the dead gunners. A musket ball struck the corner of the building. Panic broke out. The air pulsed with terror, the ground with rushing feet. Everyone was shouting.

"We're defenseless!"

"Run! Get to the ships."

"Don't run! You'll be caught in the crossfire."

496

"We'll be blown up if we stay."

"Stop!"

"Run!"

"The ships! The ships!"

The sailor in Rose's arms slumped. Nervelessly, she dropped him. His head fell askew on the palliasse, his eyes stared sightlessly up into her face. Numbly, she put a hand to her forehead, unknowingly spreading the man's blood into her hair.

Someone shouted, "There's a white flag!"

There was indeed something flying from the flagstaff on the hill. Abruptly the guns stopped firing. Rose scrambled to her feet and swung around, looking for Teresa and the children.

A shout went up, reverberating through the house and the stockade. "A white flag! Run! Run for the ships."

A girl came through the gates looking stunned, in her arms the butchered remains of a child. Her face was dripping blood, a silent, terrifying reminder—if they needed it—of the savagery that could come their way.

Someone said, "For God's sake, lady, get me water." Mindlessly Rose gathered strength to stagger back toward the house, pushing her way through the surging mob, not knowing where she was going, saying deliriously, "Water!" Then there was a jug in her hands and she was weaving back again, finding the man somehow, without remembering what he looked like or where he was. There were cautionary shouts, "Don't take the white flag seriously. It could be a trick."

The guns stayed silent. Two more men were carried in on a stretcher. Rose went around to the wounded with her jug, numbly offering it from blood-covered hands. She had stopped thinking about being either scared or saved. When Oliver's white face suddenly appeared before her she thought, "So I have gone mad," and was without surprise.

"Rose." She felt strong hands grip her arms. She was being shaken so roughly her head rocked on her shoulders. "Rose! Rose! Wake up, Rose, it's me. And Mr. le Grys . . ."

She felt herself falling; better dead than mad. The water was cold in her face; the voices loud, curt, unkind. "Put her head between her knees." She tried to sit up but they pushed her head down, down. And suddenly she was laughing hysterically, with her stomach heaving and her head swimming. She could see both Nicholas and Oliver in her mind, clear as sunlight. Someone picked her up.

"Thank God you're all right," said a queerly real, familiar voice. Then, "Rose, *are* you all right? Rose?"

Surely that was Nicholas's voice? "All this blood!"

The crowd surged forward, buffeting her as they drove toward the gates; pushing, shoving, grimly fighting to get out in front. To escape. Then arms closed around her, strong arms holding her tightly. It was Nicholas. Incredibly, impossibly, it *was* Nicholas!

She began to laugh and cry, and the crying was laughter. She could see him now, his dear, dear face smudged with ash or dirt or powder; his black hair awry. "Oh Nicholas!" she said again.

"No one knows how long these demons will hold their fire," Nicholas said. "We have to get everyone aboard. Where is Giles?"

"Nicholas!" It was a great incredulous shout, more of a scream, and Teresa, with Charlie in her arms and Joseph and Giles holding on to her skirts, flung herself at him, incoherent with relief.

"Teresa! Gad!" He gave her a quick hug, enclosing Charlie as well, grinned, surveying her briefly, her tangle of black curls, her excessively grubby clothes. Then he bent down and picked up Giles, looking with concern into his little face. "Are you all right, son?"

Giles's face was buttoned up as though he was about to cry. "Are we going home?" he asked, his voice unsteady and at the same time exasperated.

"Yes," replied Nicholas unequivocally.

Oliver picked up Joseph. They stumbled along with the crowd toward the gate. Already men were furiously fashioning stretchers to carry the wounded.

"Oh, can we not help?" Rose held back.

A soldier shouted, "Get along as fast as you can. Get on board anything. Whatever's available. Don't wait for anyone. The wounded will be brought along."

"Heke has eight hundred men." Nicholas spoke through the anguished cries of families calling to one another, as they jolted along with the crowd. "He has divided them into three. One party holds the hill, another is set to take the town, and the third is ready to attack the stockade."

Information flew in shouts. Commander Robertson of *Hazard*, having led a shore party, was down in the scrub, his thigh shattered by a bullet. Several of his men were making their way out with a stretcher. The lower blockhouse with its three old guns still held.

"Hurry," the soldiers urged the crowd, running alongside with clanking muskets and sabers at the ready. "The Maoris won't wait long."

"Mama! Mama!" The pathetic cries of lost and frightened children rent the air. Strangers hoisted them up out of the confusion of legs, perching them on shoulders where they might be seen. The last families and the wounded were barely clear of the stockade when the roof of Polack's house lifted off in a fountain of flame. The firing began again.

As they struggled onto the sand Teresa shrieked, "There's Flash Jack's *Danny Dolphin*. Oh, but we must go with him. He is perhaps come solely for us."

Oliver said, "We will get you aboard, have no fear. I came with Mr. Wilshire. He has room for all."

"This way. There's plenty of room," shouted the men manning the longboats.

A hoary-looking seaman stood before them, pointing toward the bow of an overloaded dinghy.

"Get in," said Nicholas, and suddenly Rose was splashing through the wavelets and half-helped, half-thrown aboard. "Nicholas . . . Giles! Where's Charlie?"

"I'll see to them," said Nicholas as though the children were none of her affair.

"But G-Giles . . ." She could not leave Giles. She tried to struggle to her feet, then fell back as he was dumped into her lap. She had a giddy view of Teresa, holding Charlie, lifting her free hand in a gesture of farewell. Oliver, looking baffled and concerned, standing beside her holding Joseph. And then the oarsmen dipped their oars, and the little craft headed into the waves.

One of the passengers ventured, "Are you all right, dear?" and Rose realized they were all staring with horror at the blood that was caked on her face, her arms, and spreading with the seawater through her skirt. She began to cry.

Giles said, *"Mama!"* as though he were ashamed that she should give way.

Then the dinghy swung around and Rose caught sight of the stalwart, swarthy figure of Flash Jack Wilshire striding along the sand. Nicholas had already disappeared into the surging, blundering, shouting crowd.

A big, rough woman put a comforting arm around Rose's shoulders. "Don't worry, lovey, we'll all get together later. Your 'usband'll be all right."

Rose started, for the first time since early morning remembering Daniel, and wondering with distress if he had survived.

They clambered aboard the little schooner. The women and children went wearily below. Rose stood tensely at the rails, Giles silent at her side, watching the dinghy bouncing back over the roughening sea.

"Better go below," said one of the sailors kindly. Rose gave him a nervous smile and turned away.

The giant exodus went on all afternoon, the little tenders and dinghies and canoes plying back and forth. The men worked frantically at paddles and oars, not knowing if or when the Maoris might turn their fire on the bay, bringing survivors out to boats already overloaded and insufficiently stocked with food.

There was *Hazard;* the American man-of-war *St. Louis,* which had so generously given its only gun to the town; the English whaler *Matilda;* the government brig *Victoria.* Even Bishop Selwyn's *Flying Fish* was there now. Only later did their critics discover that the archdeacon, along with the Reverend Henry Williams, fearing the Maoris might revert to cannibalism, had bravely collected the bodies of the dead soldiers from the upper blockhouses, carrying out their self-imposed duties under the uncertain protection of Heke's white flag.

As the sun sank toward the darkening hills, one after another, the buildings of the little town went up in flames. A hot wind blew scorching ash over the bay. One or two of the ships moved out of range, others went into the sheltering lee of the island. The passengers grew anxious. Why were they waiting? When the skipper said, "We've one more to come. The man who chartered *Columbine* is still helping," Rose felt her nerves tighten. Nicholas would not want to leave until there was no more excitement to be had, no more work to be done.

Eventually the dinghy went ashore for the last time and she saw the tall, familiar figure come striding through the hazy dusk. Standing at the rail in her filthy, blood-stained rags, unknowingly famished, knowingly destitute, she felt the silk caress of a wave of peace wash over her, and she closed her eyes.

Giles's piping voice broke into her blissful reverie. "Here he is, Mama. Here he is," and Nicholas's son stamped his little boots on the deck, exultantly clapping his hands. Rose smiled tenderly down at him.

It was twilight and Kororareka was a ghost town, overhung by a pall of smoke, sacked by Maoris, and, disgracefully, by the rougher elements of the departing whites. One after another, like great, gray bats, the ships spread sail and departed with their exhausted refugees, leaving their dead, and their homes, with a kind of shattered relief.

Out on the headland the shack where Rose had lived through seven deeply unhappy months stood like a memorial to the death of Daniel's stumbling, groping, hopeless hopes. Rose had been right. Nobody wasted shot and shell on it. It was too humble, too insignificant, even to attract the vandals.

The crew of *Columbine* washed Rose's clothes as best they could, and brought her hot salt water in which to bathe and wash her hair.

"Does this remind you of anything?" she asked Nicholas, gazing blissfully around the cabin as she sat, knees beneath her chin, in a tiny hip bath, her wet hair streaming down her back.

Nicholas, dirty and exhausted, his clothes torn, his dark hair patched with ash and dust, said, "We've come a long way since then," and they both fell silent.

"History repeats itself. I read that in one of the library books. Four years. Would you say history could be made in four years?"

His mouth smiled but his tired eyes were somber. "You are a part of the history of this benighted country," he said. "It has been right for you, has it not?"

She nodded, glowing, cupping the water in her hands and spreading it with a voluptuous movement over her shoulders, her breasts. "Oh, yes. Oh, yes, it has been so right for me. So wonderful. So . . . almost perfect." Her eyes lifted to his, the dark lashes curling back against lids and cheek. "Nothing can be quite perfect for me without you, Nicholas. To be near you . . . to be sharing the same life . . . that is the . . ."

He waited, faintly smiling.

She smiled too, sensuously. "The realization of a dream, when you are there. But when you are not . . ." Her lids flickered down, and she said in a very small voice, "You have never told me why you married . . . her."

He heaved an enormous sigh. "What knowledge I have of it, and that is little enough, only fills me with frustration and bitterness. It is perhaps better not to dwell on it."

She began again to lift the little handfuls of water, dropping them. "It is just that . . . I was so sure you *meant* to marry me. You asked me, and I said yes, and I cannot think—I have never thought—that you did not mean it." Her gaze drifted up, misty and sad.

"I have not told you," he said, "because . . ." He passed a hand across his eyes, battling with an instinctive loyalty to the poor woman whom others had made his wife.

"It was not because I was arrested that night. You proposed to me after . . ."

"Why were you arrested?" For the first time he wanted to know.

"I went for a walk and got lost. I was captured by some rough people and taken to a tavern."

He tried to cast his mind back to London, to the grand pillared mansion in Cavendish Square. The very memory was unreal. Even her explanation seemed not to have the ring of truth. "I found you gone," he said heavily. "I didn't know what to do. I was a little mad with shock. I sat down to think, and the brandy bottle was there . . . I don't remember much, except being with Jerningham Wakefield and seeing you at a window. I remember that much. I must have been hellishly drunk."

"Me? At a window?"

"No. I thought it was you, but it was Cressida. I was heard to propose. At the top of my voice, they said. Her father. Everyone. Oh God, Rose." He put both hands to his face. "We could have married secretly and sailed away. I made a mess of it. A foul, unholy, miserable, sodden mess of it. In my arrogance I told my father what I intended to do. That was the end."

His hands dropped to the bunk, stiffly supporting him. His face was haggard. He spoke quietly, tensely. "You don't know how God-damned bloody powerful, how ruthless, a family like mine can be. How defenseless an unimportant younger son. And yet he has a duty—an inborn knowledge of an unshakeable duty—to provide an heir, to be ready to take over should the fates decree. But I had made my decision to throw all that aside. I wanted you more than I had ever wanted anything in my life. More than Rundull."

With his eyes closed against the unbearable pain, he did not see her rise, but he felt her gentle arms around him, and then she was holding his head against her warm breasts, her wet and naked skin. Suddenly he knew the reason for this lust for Rundull; this madness in him that cried out for Henry's death, for Adeline to prove barren. He had given up his waiting duty for the greater prize of Rose, and then she had been taken from him, irrevocably displaced by a woman whom he could not love. Something fierce and mad, ruthless and unforgiving in him said that since he could not have Rose, then he must have Rundull—over the dead body of his brother and Adeline's son.

With infinite tenderness, Rose began to undo the buttons on his filthy shirt. "Come," she said sweetly. "It is all over for a while." Her whole being was alive with the knowledge that Nicholas had, after all, wanted her. That it was fate and fate alone, in the guise of his family and his position, that had let her down. "We have each other now," she said. "Let us make the most of it for as long as it lasts."

They sailed into the Auckland harbor on a brilliant morning. The quays were packed with goodhearted citizens anxious to provide clothes, food, money even; to take the refugees into their homes. Nicholas and Rose, with Giles trotting between them, were arrested almost immediately by a glad cry.

"Mr. le Grys!"

They looked up. A pretty young woman in a blue pelisse and small hat came running toward them. "I saw *Columbine* come in. Why," she exclaimed with pleasure, "you have found . . . Mrs. Putnam, is it not?" She looked down at Giles, who was looking up at her with interest. "And this is your little boy whom I saw when he was only a few days old. Giles," she said, smiling. "You do not remember me, I am sure, Mrs. Putnam. We met only briefly on the beach."

Rose dimpled. "Oh, but I do, Mrs. Maxwell. I even remember you carried a lovely parasol and wore a yellow gown." How could she forget the one woman who had been kind to her on that frightening morning?

Nicholas said, his eyes twinkling, "In the melee Mrs. Putnam was separated from her family. I found her aboard *Columbine*. I have established, though, that her husband and the other children are safe and on their way. *Danny Dolphin*, the schooner that picked them up," said Nicholas outrageously, "has gone direct to Wellington, and as you already know, I am bound for Sydney to buy blood stock, so there is naught to do but take the stranded pair with me. At least they will get home eventually."

"Oh, how kind." Mrs. Maxwell was already leading them along the quay. All around, other ladies were picking up strangers, inviting them to their homes. There was hustle and bustle, cries of delight and gratitude. "I shall find you some decent clothes, my dear, for we are much of a size," she said, looking with sympathy at Rose's torn gown.

"Go with Mrs. Maxwell," said Nicholas looking vastly amused, pressing a handful of sovereigns into Rose's hand. "When you are decently attired in borrowed garments, run into a store and buy yourself some clothes. I must conduct the business of handing *Columbine* back to her owner, and make inquiries as to when there is a sailing to Sydney."

Mrs. Maxwell grasped Giles by the hand, and taking Rose's arm, said, "Let us hurry, for there are ships going all the time to Sydney and you know what gentlemen are. Mr. le Grys is likely to hustle you aboard, if the sailing fits, not understanding how important it is for ladies to be prettily dressed."

Feeling wicked and smug as a cat, Rose said demurely,

"Yes, let us hurry," for at any moment it was possible that *Danny Dolphin* might come flying in with Daniel and crush the dream like an eggshell.

Dear Lady Cressida,

I am writing to tell you that I have seen your dear husband, first when he came to Auckland with the delegation to try to persuade our unpopular and, one must own, inept and dilatory governor to move against the Maoris. I may tell you, Mr. Maxwell was vociferously behind him, as are the majority of the citizens of Auckland. Then again we saw him after his return from the north with the refugees.

Of course, all right-thinking citizens are up in arms against FitzRoy. However, it is rumored that a warship is coming from Sydney bringing Captain Grey to replace him. He is said to be familiar with the native way of thinking, which Captain FitzRoy certainly is not, or this catastrophe could not have occurred.

You will be pleased to hear, I am sure, that the little family Putnam who hail from your dear husband's village are safe and well, though they became tragically separated, as did a number of families when they fled for their lives. Mr. le Grys most kindly, though mistakenly as it turned out, undertook to escort the mother and child himself, though it meant their being diverted to Sydney.

Cressida put a hand over her eyes to obliterate the dreadful words. But the letter had to be read.

In the event, her family arrived only hours after they sailed. However, the tragedy was quite overshadowed for us, perhaps selfishly, by the arrival also of Lady Teresa Mountburn, whom I believe you know, and who is a dear friend of my husband's younger sister. Lady Teresa was gallantly looking after the two smaller Putnam children. It is a shame that Mrs. Putnam should have gone off worrying, not knowing that they were in such caring hands. . . .

*   *   *

Cressida crumpled the letter in suddenly nerveless fingers. Hoisting herself out of the chair, she went to the long window and stood leaning against the frame. Numbing though the news was, it did not constitute a real shock, for she had known in her heart when Nicholas left that he was going to collect the girl and his bastard. And bring them back. The house he had built on the edge of town was complete; the boy's pony in the field. Not that he had mentioned the matter to her, but the gossips had.

"Nobody likes the idea of absentee landlords," she had found herself saying with a glassy smile, "but nonetheless they are a part of the company's plans and must be tolerated. There are, as you know, insufficient houses for the growing population and many people wish to rent. My Lord Rundull has been persuaded to make some investments."

Submitting to pressure to join the delegation to Auckland, Cressida thought bitterly, was merely a convenient method of leaving her in her present delicate condition with the full approval of their friends. He had gone in spite of the fact that they had troubles of their own; turned his back on Wellington, where, though the gentlemen tried to keep the ladies in ignorance, they all knew matters were very serious indeed. There was now a large earthwork in the town, more than three hundred feet long, with trench and parapet enclosing the bank, some houses, and one or two of the stores. The government commissariat stores building was in a stockade enclosure constructed after the manner of a palisaded Maori *pa*.

War threats in the north and disputes in the Hutt Valley had stimulated a volunteer spirit. Nicholas had himself been drilling with the troops, using the old tower flintlock muskets brought by the company for bartering with the natives. All able-bodied men between eighteen and sixty were soon to be liable for service.

Cressida looked down the green valley patched with afternoon sunshine. Would it make any difference, she asked herself, if the coming baby should be a boy? She turned the thought over in her mind, visualizing the two of them strolling together with their son between them. And then the dream collapsed, replaced by a vivid picture of Nicholas lying beneath the stars on a dreaming

sea, with the girl in his arms. The pain was so intense
that she cried out.

There was a tap at the door and Nurse entered with
Beatrix prettily dressed in frills, tiny white slippers on her
feet, her curls tied with ribbon.

"I thought I heard you call, m'Lady."

Cressida said without looking up, "No, I did not call."
Then to the child, "Come, my dear . . . I will read to
you."

Nurse said, eyeing the little stack of mail on the sofa
table, "You have not finished with the post."

"No." Keeping her telltale eyes hooded, protecting
herself from her nurse's sharp scrutiny, Cressida leaned
down awkwardly, picked up a letter from the top of the
pile and slit it open.

> Dear Sister-in-law,
>   I write hurriedly and with the greatest news. Adeline
> is at last with child. We are all delighted . . .

The old woman asked considerately, "Is there bad news,
m'Lady?"

"No," Cressida replied, looking up, all at once ani-
mated in a manner quite beyond her control. "No, not at
all." She reached out a hand to the child. "Come, my
darling. I will read you a story. The letter can wait."

They went together to the settee, Beatrix chattering,
while Cressida's mind wrestled with the news.

What a devastating blow this would be for Nicholas!
The sweet, wild justice of Adeline's pregnancy slaked in
Cressida an unexpected thirst for revenge, drowning recognition of the fact that if the child should be a boy she
might never return to England. She was glad that Nicholas would come home to this bitter disappointment; a
blow quite satisfyingly equal to her own.

During those wonderful weeks in Sydney Rose felt herself to be in an enchanted world. With Nicholas's money
she bought sensible shifts of linsey-woolsey to replace
those she had had to leave behind, but he it was who
insisted on muslin and brocade.

"You must have buttoned boots. . . . This cape with
the sable collar." Seeing her golden head lifted above the

fur like an elegant flower, her curls spilling like pollen, his mind flew back to that day when he had dressed her in his sister's clothes. The first revelation, he thought. The first time he had realized her potential.

He bought recklessly. "Three bottles of perfume, if you please. And the fur muff. What about a hat? Is it not quite the tippy for ladies nowadays to wear hats?"

Blissfully, Rose fingered lengths of silk. "You are so generous."

"They may not all survive," he whispered in her ear when the shop girl turned her back.

Color flared in Rose's cheeks as she remembered his habit of flinging her on the bed, tearing at her buttons and bows. His lusty lovemaking was hard on clothes.

Drifting back to the hotel on Nicholas's arm as though her pretty boots had wings, Rose could imagine no greater happiness. Giles, too, was in his element, strutting beside them in checked knickerbockers and long, ribbed stockings, carrying his kite and a rubber ball. Giles became loving, creeping in under Rose's heart as he never had before, and she was so touched she cried.

"Now we are a real family," she said to herself.

Inevitably, they had to leave. It was, after all, only an interlude; something to strengthen them so they might hold life's cluttered pieces together for another little while. At the last moment she bought a fluffy toy for Charlie, a picturebook for Joseph, and a shirt for Daniel.

They swept up the harbor on a southwest breeze and there was Wellington, with its white cottages scurrying up the steep hillsides. There were hundreds of them now, all busily puffing their chimney smoke into little gray spirals.

And then she remembered that Flash Jack, whom Nicholas had bested once again, owned Aurora Cottage. She wondered with a start of alarm where the family would live now.

44

They came upon the house in the foothills just outside town. It was all white, with the window frames outlined in strips of green, like long hanging beans. There was a light shingle roof, and a wide veranda along one side as well as at the front. Nicholas prepared to step down from the hired buggy. "What do you think of this? It was built with timber taken from Rata Hill." He added, watching Rose's face covertly, "I haven't had time to find a suitable tenant yet, so you may move in if you would care to."

Rose sat quite still on the narrow leather seat, her hands tightly clasped in her muff, gazing, dazzled, at the beautiful frost-white house. "Oh," she breathed. "You built it for us!"

"You are the easiest person to give to," Nicholas said.

Rose turned her glowing face to Giles.

He nodded.

"It's the least he expected," said Nicholas mockingly. "A little small, if anything." As he lifted the child down, thumping him quite deliberately on the ground, he said, with an edge to his voice, "There are no castles in this benighted land, son." Giles grinned up at him, and with a shock Rose thought she saw a flash of something like malice pass between them, before Giles gave his seraphic smile and Nicholas relaxed.

They went together up the newly made path. "The very devil!" Nicholas swore, looking startled. "Aurora House."

Rose glowed. "You had Flash Jack build it! He knew I would like that."

Nicholas looked annoyed.

The door was flung open and Teresa stood there, arms outstretched in welcome. "You deign to return! Oh, how wicked you are! The town will be agog. We will never keep this from the gossips." She gave Rose a quick hug, then stood back, holding her at arm's length, her eyes roving admiringly over the pretty bonnet, muff, fur collar.

Nicholas, hands in pockets, looked around the hall wearing a frankly irritated expression, like a man whose best story has been topped.

"Flash Jack picked the lock," Teresa said shamelessly. "We had to go somewhere. It seemed sensible. He was very discreet, which may I venture to say, you have not been—driving through the town with Rose all decked out—"

Nicholas snapped, "I happened to come upon Mrs. Putnam in difficulties, so I gave her a lift."

"Well," said Teresa slyly, "you have to hand it to Flash Jack. If he ruined your surprise it was just retribution. He and Oliver went all the way to Kororareka to rescue Rose." Joseph and Charlie came and stood behind Teresa, looking shy. Rose gave them a perfunctory kiss.

Nicholas went back to help the driver with Rose's trunk.

"How kind you were to look after—"

Teresa brushed Rose's thanks aside. "Oh, Rose, where will you wear such finery here?"

"I am braver now. I do not particularly care any longer what people say about me," she said. "What a wonderful house!" There were open doors everywhere. "How many bedrooms?" She darted here and there, peeping into rooms full of sunshine, furnished with beds with pretty covers, flower-patterned jugs and ewers, looking-glasses. There was a parlor that was almost a withdrawing room, it was so large.

Rose came to the kitchen and caught her breath. It was the kitchen at Aurora Cottage, except that it had a bigger, grander stove. With her hands on the bench, she gazed ecstatically out into the sunlit garden. Close to the house there was a clump of *punga* fern, its fronds drooping prettily from furry, chocolate-colored trunks; and beyond, a little copse of pines and birches had been left standing when the land was cleared. Strong, green grass already grew on what would eventually be a lawn. She opened the back door. Teresa, with Joseph and Charlie, stood behind her, enjoying her excitement.

"Why, there's a chicken coop. But it's mine!"

"Oliver brought it over from the doctor's. He looked after your chickens all the time you were away, and sold the eggs. He has a nice tidy sum waiting for you."

Rose was overwhelmed "How kind people are."

Giles came streaking through the trees. "A pony!" he shouted. "There's a pony!" Having shared his delirious delight, he took to his heels again, speeding across the grass, his sturdy legs going like windmills, his arms flailing the air. "A pony!" he yelled as he ran. "A pony!"

Nicholas came around the corner of the house. He said wryly, "I had hoped to have the privilege of introducing him. That boy is a shade too sharp."

They went together across the paddock, and there, munching the long grass, stood a shaggy black Shetland. He raised his head, flicked his ears. Giles went fearlessly up to him. With one of those quirky gestures peculiar to his breed, the tiny pony put his nose in Giles's chest and gave him a playful push that sent him flying. Giles lay on the ground kicking his legs in the air shrieking with glee, while the pony looked down at him with benign interest, blinking his long lashes.

A small voice behind them said, "I don't like that horse."

As Nicholas strode across the garden to Giles's aid, Rose looked down at Joseph with irritation. Then guilt-stricken, she picked him up, gave him a quick hug, then lifted Charlie. "Have you missed your mama?"

They nodded, their little faces flushing with pleasure.

She crossed the garden carrying Charlie, with Joseph at her side, but she had already forgotten them as she watched Nicholas give Giles his first riding lesson.

Taking the pony by the forelock he led him around the field while Giles clung to the mane shouting, "Faster, faster. Make him trot." Obligingly, Nicholas broke into a run. Inevitably losing his balance, Giles slid off. He leaped to his feet. "I meant to do that." He stood, feet apart, endearingly embarrassed, boastful, brave.

Nicholas turned to Rose, his own face lit with a new kind of pleasure. "I remember saying that to my father. In the same circumstances."

Then Edmund came flying across the grass, tail high. He slid silkily across Rose's ankles. Joseph picked the cat up and held him out to Rose, like a gift. "See how he has grown, Mama?"

"He has indeed."

"Oliver looked after him."

Oliver again. She put Charlie down and took the cat. Satiny and boneless, Edmund lay contentedly within the circle of her arm. "Well," she breathed, virtually at a loss for words, "what a homecoming this has been!" She turned to Nicholas. "You were coming for me anyway?"

He nodded. "On my return from Sydney."

"Ah!" She had a warm feeling of being cherished.

Teresa packed her things and left. "I will insist Nicholas drive me right through the town," she said, "and we will bow to everyone we meet. Then the sour crabs will hopefully be confused for some will say he was seen with you and others will swear he was driving with a dark-haired stranger who turned out to be his wife's houseguest."

Before she left Teresa said, "When Daniel comes, Rose, remember attack is the best defense. There are men to be managed, and men to be wooed, and men to be run from. Daniel is easily managed, provided you do not try him too far."

Rose knew immediately when Daniel came up the path that she had indeed tried him too far. Behind the familiar hangdog look there was an inarticulate savagery that caused her to catch her breath.

"It was not my fault we were separated," she burst out. "What did you expect us to do? Hang around in Polack's house and get blown up?"

He said accusingly, "You could've waited in Auckland. . . ."

"I had no money and no clothes, and neither had I any way of knowing whether Flash Jack had taken you direct to Wellington. I knew the ships were overflowing—"

"Mr. Wilshire's weren't," said Daniel, his bitter hurt mixed up with his anger. " 'E'd saved room fer yer an' the brat."

Conscience-stricken, she approached him timidly, extending a hand.

"You smell like a scent factory," he said resentfully. "Where'd yer get that from?"

There was a sound behind her. Joseph and Charlie were standing in the doorway to the parlor, looking distressed. She swept Charlie into her arms, hiding a little behind him.

"When they're in bed," said Daniel, looking pointedly at her pretty gown, "I'll 'ave sumpin' ter say."

She went ahead into the parlor, still holding Charlie in her arms, unnerved by Daniel's aggression. Giles was lying on the floor looking at a picturebook. He glanced up with that knowing, amused look she had seen a hundred times on Nicholas's face, then went back to his pictures.

"It's not a workingman's house," said Daniel indicating the pretty painted table, the carpet, the polished wood desk, the row of bright new books on a shelf.

"You may not always be a workingman." She managed to say the words lightly, though knowing they, too, were a lie.

"I were born an 'umble man an' an 'umble man I'll stay."

"Count your blessings," she said sharply, not wishing to see Giles look at him with contempt.

After tea, she led him to the big overstuffed sofa, and sat down beside him. She was fairly certain that there was a good reason why no time should be lost in winning him over.

She rested her head on his shoulder. "Remember my promise?" she whispered. "I said, when we come back to Wellington . . ." She fluttered her lashes at him. A cunning look came into his eyes and her heart fluttered with fear. She cast around for something to say to cover the awkward moment. "Teresa said you have your old job back. That's nice of Alain."

"I don't want ter work fer Mr. Wilshire," he asserted violently.

"Then I am sure you don't have to." She stroked his rough hand. "There must be plenty of jobs going."

"Not fer me there ain't." Frustrated, he pushed her soothing hand away. I tried but they said Mr. Wilshire's got a job fer me, and it were more than their life's worth. . . . Folks is scared of Mr. Wilshire, Rose."

She leaned over and sweetly brushed Daniel's cheek with her lips. He flushed. "I 'aven't finished. I got more ter say. We can't live 'ere."

"Why not?" She looked smilingly around the room. "It's lovely. We are so lucky."

"It's above our station."

"What's a station, Daniel?" She tickled him in the ribs.

"Now Rose, wipe that innercent look off yer . . ."

"Oh, come, Daniel, laugh a bit." Rose snuggled closer, feeling wicked and worried, like the girl she had been all those years ago, enticing Daniel into marriage in the curate's garden. And for the same reason.

"Now listen ter—" He broke off because she had put her hand where no woman had ever put her hand before. Daniel's choking, gasping emotions played havoc with the carefully laid plans he had made so that he would not be caught again. Shocked, angry, unbearably excited, he gasped, "Rose!"

The taking was rough and clumsy, unloving and greedy, as it had always been. When he had finished with her she lay back feeling depressed and vaguely unclean. Feeling also bewildered and angry because one had to do so many things in life that one would rather not do, simply in order to survive. "Poor Daniel," she thought and a tear trickled down her cheek.

The curate wrote that Grandy was ill. Rose sent the egg money that Oliver brought and her savings, begging him to come and join them.

You will soon get well here, fot he air is fresh and dry, and the climate so healthy nobody remains ill for long. You shall sit all day on the veranda in the sun—for even in winter the sun is hot between the hours of ten and four, though we may have a wood fire at breakfast.

And I will wait on you, as you have waited on others all your life. You will love the children, and you will have all the time in the world to play with them.

* * *

A grandfather for Giles! she thought happily. Every child should have a grandfather. But Grandy was a great-grandfather, she realized in surprise, and perhaps all the better for that. The very old had so much in common with the very young.

In their absence, the town had changed immensely. There was now a theater in Shortland Crescent, a nine-pins alley, a peep show, new taverns on the waterfront, new stores. Carriages swung grandly along a flat, macadamized road. The smell of horse dung and the sun on oiled leather was as pervasive as the cries of the swooping gulls, the scent of the sea, the oranges in their burlap sacks, which came from the Pacific islands, and the blown dust.

All over the country, since the successful sacking of Kororareka, the Maoris were indulging in a great deal of bounce. Toward the end of May warning smoke rose from the hills, giving notice of their intention to attack. Major Richmond ordered fifty men of the 58th Regiment to the Hutt. The brig *Bee* made sail for Petone, landing troops on the beach.

"Sleep easy," Flash Jack reassured Rose. "There's a great fort with flanking bastions been built to command the Hutt Bridge and River. It's got ten-foot-high walls and double-storied blockhouses made of *totara* and *kahikatea* pine. The Maoris will never get through that." But all that winter they lived in a state of alarm. Frightening stories proliferated of fearsome painted and feathered warriors arriving at outlying farms with tomahawks under their mats. They had become reckless and ruthless in their desire for guns.

Teresa having remarked pointedly that Flash Jack was welcomed at Government House on either side of the Tasman, he was placed on the guest list at Rata Hill for cribbage, glees, and dances. One evening, when they were gathered around the supper table, she said, "Mr. Grey is coming to us with a great reputation. You know him, Alain. What is your candid view? Will he put us to rights?"

Flash Jack said cynically, "His reputation grows out of an extraordinary facility for acquiring aid from Providence, as well as his immense skill as a despatch writer. He knows how to impress Westminster."

"Oh, fie!" laughed Teresa. "You are already critical of him and he has not yet begun to displease."

"Also, he was extremely lucky in South Australia—arriving with sole authority, which had been denied to the earlier governors."

"Of course no one will like him," said Cressida dryly, "but surely you must greet him with an open mind."

Taking Teresa's arm, leading her away from the group, Flash Jack asked, "Is the governor to put *us* to rights? you ask. Does this mean, miss, that you intend to stay? I had it in mind to put you on the next sailing to England."

Teresa's head came up. "Indeed, you will put me nowhere, sir. I am not a chattel to be disposed of. Besides which, immediately I set foot in England your most horrible cousin would lay claim to me—like a chattel indeed."

Flash Jack rested his plate on the mantel and took a sip of his wine. "And how do you expect to survive here? Ye gods, you are penniless. Do you wish to sink to the situation of a servant or governess?"

"As you well know, I have been a servant, and I believe, a very good one," Teresa replied with spirit. "And I am not at all penniless. I stitched my jewels into my underwear. Since I am both a good seamstress and a virtuous lady they are intact. I could charge you to build me a house."

" 'Pon my soul!" Flash Jack recovered quickly. "I doubt there are buyers here. People are putting all their money into the land."

"Rose says there is a great deal of money on the other side of the Tasman. Perhaps, on one of your trips to Sydney, you would be good enough to convert a selection of rubies and pearls into cash." She smiled beguilingly at him over her wineglass.

Flash Jack frowned. "Do not think you can twist me around your little finger, miss. Government House will eventually come to Wellington, and then you will be in deuced difficult circumstances without your jewelry. As to the house, a lady may not live alone in such a place as this without respectable companionship."

"Then I shall have to sponge on my friends," Teresa

retorted airily, "until someone is good enough to marry me."

"You are married, miss."

"If you cannot persuade your horrible cousin to divorce me then I shall have to acquire a husband bigamously."

"You are an audacious minx." But Flash Jack spoke with a certain admiration. "Do not trouble yourself too much about the divorce. I will do what I can to ensure the matter is put in hand." He paused. "I will, of course, wish to extract my pound of flesh."

"Yes?"

"Would it be beyond your capacity for inventiveness to lead Rose into Wellington society under the guise of having been a friend of hers at home?"

Teresa's slanting eyes glimmered.

"Then let us say no more. And now, to change the subject. How was the little Isobel received?" He glanced across the room at Cressida, standing with a group of her guests around the piano. "Our hostess has quite regained her figure, I see."

"The child was received on one side with ill-disguised disappointment, and on the other with a certain malicious satisfaction. Despite what you see tonight, Alain, this is not a happy household. I believe I was brought here as a kind of buffer. A friend to both. As I am indeed a friend to Rose and Daniel, who are also far apart."

Somber and thoughtful, Teresa looked back across the room. "Cressida is so extraordinarily like Rose when she is happy, and when she dresses, as she does occasionally, in the flattering colors that Rose chooses. Yet she plays herself down, deliberately I think, out of sheer pride. She would have more of a share of her husband if she swallowed that pride."

Flash Jack fingered his glass. "Do you think they could have made a success of this marriage if Rose had stayed away?"

"Yes. I believe so. That is the great sadness."

"Your grandfather will need a respite from this pesky wind if he is to enjoy the sun," Flash Jack said one day, as he sat with Rose in the garden, cloaked in a pattern of drifting lace from the palm trees. "I'll put up a wall at either end of the side veranda, so that whichever way the breeze blows there will be a sheltered corner for him."

"I haven't heard from Grandy," Rose said. "I hope he still plans to come live with us here."

Their quiet was broken suddenly by a whoop of pleasure from Charlie and Joseph, who were playing in the shallow stream that ran through the bottom of the garden. Oliver was giving Giles a riding lesson in the field. "Hang on with your knees, Giles. Let go of the mane."

"He's a good lad," commented Flash Jack, looking across at Oliver running beside the pony. "Between us we've fashioned a very worthwhile young man." He hesitated, then said carefully, "What a pity the Misses le Grys are not a few years older, Rose. He might marry one of them."

Rose started.

"Did you not know Lady Cressida has another daughter?"

She turned away swiftly, pretending interest in the child who was bouncing on the tiny pony, his face pink with exertion. Anyway, she thought defensively, Nicholas has a son. And around Christmas he would have another. But the news was a shock, all the same. She leaned down and picked some blades of grass, tearing them to pieces in her lap, her eyes downcast. She knew now this was why Flash Jack had come. Not to tell her he would put up a shelter for Grandy. He came to tell her Nicholas and Cressida had been lovers again.

Felicity wrote from England that the old Earl died.

> I was crossing the hall when I noticed the clock had stopped. I sent Snape directly to Papa's room, and there he was, looking so peacefully at rest that we all found ourselves tranquil regarding his death, though it was a pity he could not have lived just a few more days to see the new heir. Adeline's son is handsome and sturdy. . . .

Nicholas said, stony eyed and fierce, "I hope Henry treats Mama with respect and affords her a dignified position in the household." Standing with shoulders squared, looking out on the lush valley below, seeing in his mind's eye the soft green meadows of the Rundull estates, the brooding castle where he would probably never again walk or lay his head, he went on in a voice as hard as his expression, "I am reminded by my father's death that he referred to me as 'an idle and profligate young man.' " He stamped his feet apart, squared his jaw. "If there is a life after death then I should like him to know what I have done here."

He put his hands deeply into his pockets, paced the width of the room and back. "The country is in a bad way, but no doubt it will hobble along quite nicely with the help of FitzRoy's paper money. Flash Jack Wilshire tells me he has sufficient faith to load himself up with these Government Debentures. For my part, I think I shall keep my money in the land. I am told our new governor neither consults nor trusts anyone," he said in a hard, angry voice. "I wonder if he knows how to get the financial support of the British government. I don't trust these damned Maoris, either. He needs to increase our military power. But he must have cash first. I am told the soldiers' pay is five months overdue."

Cressida, sitting, stitching a tear in Nicholas's trousers, listened to the rhetoric in silence, wondering if Nicholas was asking himself, in this queer moment of defeat, if he should take an interest in running the new country after all.

It was a wild spring that year. The hail drove up the valley in freezing sheets, catching the newborn lambs whose mothers were too weakened to protect them, and laying out the little corpses in banked-up hail like shrouds of pearls. Nicholas worked with his shepherds from dawn to dark. They would carry home the orphan lambs on the pommels of their saddles. Ewes that had spent a night on their backs had to be given up for dead.

It was a worrying time, but it was also an exciting one. When lambing was over, Nicholas found himself the proud possessor of seven thousand sheep. A flock could double itself in three years. Arbitrarily ignoring the rules, risking seizure by the Land Court, he bought more land from the Maoris. Shearers moved into the quarters built for them near the woolshed, and shearing began. Distraught, naked-looking sheep leaped out of the yards into spring showers that were sharp and cold.

Cressida had at last grown accustomed to the incessant baaing and bleating, to the farm-activity that inevitably enfolded the homestead, to living close to the land with all that that entailed. Beatrix, who was now four years old, was enthralled with the little lambs who came magically through the back door delivered from the shepherds' hands. She spent many a happy hour feeding them from a bottle, helping Cook protect them as they lurched drunkenly on their frail legs, poking their noses inquisitively too close to the stove, singeing the little rosettes on their foreheads.

Enjoying the child's delight, sometimes Cressida felt she might have become a part of it all if things had been different. But when Nicholas rode into town with a lamb sitting before him on the saddle, its pretty white face gazing inquiringly out of the sugar sack that was gathered around its neck, she knew it was going to Rose. When Mrs. Lewellen asked why Nicholas had bought a nanny goat from Mr. Thomas, she knew it was to provide milk for the children of Aurora House. And it was too bad of Teresa to start that rumor about the girl's having eloped with Putnam from a great house. It is only a matter of time before I shall be meeting her in the withdrawing rooms of my friends, Cressida thought bitterly.

All through that spring and into the Christmas season, Daniel hoped against hope that the child Rose was expecting would bear a strong resemblance to himself. Rose was kind to him, often loving, but she had moved even further out of his reach.

When the child was born, in January 1845, Daniel knew, even before the words were out, what Dr. Stokes was going to say.

"Another boy, Putnam. A lovely, dark-haired son, more like Giles than the others. Go and see him, man."

"I got ter get the boys' tea," he said, shuffling with closed face and heavy brows back into the kitchen.

But something was working its way up through his slow consciousness. Something he had not the wit to take out and examine. In the dark, quiet nights, Daniel would find his thoughts running back to Rundull village; to his sister Gertie, whose husband had died beneath the butt of Nicholas's gun; to that day when vile fate had sent him in to save Rose from the mob rape. Rose, who was not, after all, of his class or his kind or his understanding. He dwelled darkly on the fact that one act of mercy had put him in the hands of the unmerciful. Wormlike, the canker ate into him and spread, taking on a life of its own.

Rose was in seventh heaven. The baby looked exactly as Giles had looked when he was born: thick, black hair; blue eyes already darkening. Yet even in those first days and weeks, he had an air of giving back, of loving in return as Giles never had. She would call him Lance.

Nicholas came when Daniel was away at work. "Another chip off the old block." He smiled indulgently.

"He is a love child," she said, her face suffused with warmth and love.

Nicholas raised an eyebrow quizzically. "Was not Giles?"

"Yes, but in a different way." Giles had been born of youth and passion and naughtiness, his ancestors' castle, knit with the stones of his ancestors' misdeeds, frowning down upon him.

Nicholas leaned over the bed and kissed her—not at all in the way a man should kiss a young woman who was not his wife, only three days after the birth of a child.

Rose whispered, "One day we will be together. I know it in my soul."

45

Upon arriving Governor Grey had taken effective action; his forces took Te Rauparaha and Rangihaeata prisoner. By the winter of 1846, with the two great chieftains out of the way, the country had settled down. There were balls and entertainments. *Victoria* and the barque *Slains Castle* were in port as well as *Driver* whose dashing officers were very much in demand, having engaged en route from war service in China in the suppression of piracy in the East Indies. Of course there were still too few ladies. Anxious men arrived early, hoping to secure good partners. The ladies were obliged to divide their dances.

Nicholas set up a croquet lawn and a cricket pitch. When there was a lull between the seasonal work of lambing, dipping, shearing, and fertilizing, Cressida entertained large parties at lunch. She often had extra help in the house now, for after the arrival of each immigrant ship, Sam Phelps brought out any single girls he came across who were looking for employment. They came willingly enough, crouching on sacks of flour and sugar in his dray, but they did not last long. It was common knowledge that one might find a potential wife at Rata Hill. Useless for Cook to shoo the predatory farm workers out of the kitchen. They took the girls into the bush as soon as it was dark, and after that, everyone was only too pleased to see them married.

Nicholas acquired a kangaroo hound, first cousin to a lurcher. One fine spring day, he brought the dog to show to Giles. "It's time you had a dog of your own," he said. "Would you like a pup from this sharp little creature? He's a genius at hunting the thieving *wekas.*"

Before Giles could reply, the Shetland, Blackboy, who had wandered unnoticed into the garden, stepped up onto the veranda and came toward them. "Good God!"

Giles laughed delightedly. "He's always doing that. He looks in windows, too, to give us a fright."

"He's lonely," said Nicholas. "A cat and a two-toothed ewe must be unsatisfactory companions for a pony." Soon afterward he arrived with a farm hack on a leading rein. "Company for Blackboy," he said, smiling at Rose's surprise. "She's a mild old screw. Oliver might find time to teach you to ride on her."

A great many women who had never set eyes on a horse at home were riding now. Not all the settlers on outlying stations had roads running to their homesteads. They swallowed what apprehensions they might have, pinned their hats firmly on their heads, kilted up their skirts, and took the reins. After the threat of the Maoris, a horse was less than daunting.

When Flash Jack saw Old Screw he said to Rose, "Encourage Daniel to mount her. That creature is tame enough to sit on without learning to ride. I am going to give him some work out in the hills. I don't want him walking. No man can do a good day's work if he has to tramp for miles to get to a job."

"I hope you won't send him to work at the Hutt," she said. She could not have explained why she said it, or even why she used that sharp tone.

Flash Jack looked at her queerly. At the end of February, while clearing the way for legally acquired property, the troops had illegally destroyed a Maori village. There were terrible consequences in systematic raids on white farms. The plunder and destruction had been appalling.

"What makes you think I would send him into danger?" Flash Jack asked, planting his long, strong legs apart, clamping the eternal cheroot between his large teeth.

"Forgive me. I did not mean you might do that." Rose's lashes fluttered down. "Only, I wanted to say that he is not very brave anymore."

"Anymore?" Flash Jack ducked his head forward in astonishment.

"He was brave once," she said loyally, though knowing that she was talking about something else. About Flash Jack's changing attitude to Daniel. About Daniel, who had changed. She had found herself several times lately recalling the mindless violence that had emerged in him to rout the Rundull mob. She did not want his pent-up anger over Lance's birth to erupt on a marauding native. "I know some grants were issued for more houses to be built at the Hutt."

"No houses will be built there until things settle down." Flash Jack spoke casually. Too casually, she thought.

Giles was seven now, and was obsessed with Blackboy, spending hour after hour with him. The little boy and his miniature steed became well known around town.

"You've got no control over that toy," Flash Jack said one day when Blackboy was preparing to enter his store. "You need a horse you can manage. Something a little less shrewd and a lot more intelligent. Something that will obey you." Only the week before he had come upon Giles striding indignantly home, soaked to the skin, while Blackboy ambled docilely behind. Rose said, laughing, that the pony had trotted across to the beach and lain down in the incoming tide.

The next time Nicholas called, Giles, looking up boldly as he sat on his tall cob, said, "Mr. Wilshire says I need a bigger pony now."

Nicholas's irritation showed in his eyes. "The devil he does!"

Nonetheless, Blackboy went to Rata Hill for Beatrix's use and was replaced by Bonnie, a trustworthy little bay mare with an acute sense of responsibility.

Giles rode often with Oliver to Dr. Stokes's farm. Once, he went off by himself, telling no one. Cressida, giving Isobel a lesson on the Shetland, saw the pony with its small rider when they were still some distance away.

"Someone coming to visit," said Isobel, looking pleased. It was lonely for the children as well as the wives. Beatrix and Isobel had companions only when ladies came to tea. She went with heightened curiosity to greet the mite who cantered up the slope.

He was Nicholas's son, there was no doubt about it.

Cressida closed her eyes while the blood pounded at her temples.

"Hello," said Giles with Nicholas's smile, then, pointing with his crop at Blackboy, "That's my horse. It was."

Cressida's eyes clung painfully to the boy's face: The black eyes; the childish mouth, even now showing signs of a familiar chiseled hardness; the high cheekbones. He stood like Nicholas, too. Already, and he could be only seven, the boy had the same air: head held high, one hand at his hip. There was a shift of feeling in her, her shock giving way to an unacceptable acceptance. The child was smiling up at her, like Nicholas at his most beguiling, with the assurance of one who knows he is with friends.

"You have ridden a long way," she found herself saying. "You had better come in and have some tea." She did not ask if his mother knew where he had gone. She had a queer feeling, as though a page had been turned in the annals of fate, that the child had known it was time to come.

That night she reread the letter that had come from Felicity a month ago.

I could not, I really could not tell HM about the new addition to the Putnam family, and your fears, my very dear Cressida. Please do not again ask such a thing of me. She would be so dreadfully shocked. Besides, you cannot be certain of the child's parentage. You really cannot. The woman was living with her husband, except for the voyage from Kororareka to Sydney and back, and I am sure my brother had the very best of reasons for taking her with him.

Besides, I know exactly what HM would say. Again, that women are meant to suffer. And also that you have made your vows and are obliged to keep them, whatever the circumstances. She would never countenance a divorce in either your family or ours. Those who are close to the court, you must know, have certain responsibilities that others have not. Besides, dear Cressida, as HM has said, a woman on her own is nothing . . .

*   *   *

Cressida tore the letter down the center, then crosswise, into tiny pieces, which she dropped into the wastepaper basket. It was the end of the fight. The boy's coming had shown her that. The thread that had tripped Nicholas so lightly as a young and lusty youth had been stronger than any of them guessed. Now it was woven into a web that enmeshed them all. Deep inside she had perhaps known that one day Giles would come, bringing one end of that fine thread to knit its silken strands around Rata Hill.

Later in 1847 they acquired a lieutenant governor to administer the southern part of the country. Mr. Eyre had climbed higher mountains and walked greater distances over wilder terrain than Governor Grey. Grey was jealous of his prowess; Eyre was suspicious of his superior's rhetoric and charm. The ladies of snobbish little Wellington were delighted to have a Residence in their midst. A pivot for the social scene. They could bring out their jewels at last.

Thus, there was a frenzy of entertainment in Wellington. Mrs. Featherston gave a ball for Emily Wakefield, who was about to announce her engagement to Mr. Stafford. Perhaps as a result of the rumors Teresa had sowed—that Rose was related to the le Grys family—she and Daniel were invited.

"If you don't wish to learn to dance," Teresa told Daniel good-humoredly, "you can watch your wife enjoying herself."

That ball marked the beginning of Rose's acceptance on the social scene. Tactfully, people ignored the fact that Lady Cressida kept her distance. They were intrigued by a situation they did not understand.

Teresa waited with impatience for her divorce to come through. At last Flash Jack brought the certificate and she demurely accepted the proposal of a young station owner. Her marriage to Mr. Alexander was set for November 4, when summer would have begun to come to the valley. The reception was to be held at Rata Hill, with Beatrix and tiny Isobel attending her. Giles was to be pageboy.

"You cannot," exclaimed Cressida, outraged, "bring that woman into my home."

"She is thought to be your husband's sister, Cressida,"

replied Teresa innocently. "Or yours. Fallen from grace, indeed, but still a Rundull or a Woolege. Might there not be speculation should you fail to invite your sister to such an event?"

Cressida lost her temper. "You are a wicked girl and a troublemaker."

But Teresa stuck serenely to her guns. "Do you not see, my dear friend, that I have set up a situation that is workable? Nicholas, you must always have known, would not ignore his son. And his son belongs to Rose."

Flash Jack, having generously bought Teresa's jewels, now returned them to her as a wedding present. Resplendent in double-breasted frock coat with side buttons, he gave the bride away at the altar of the Anglican mission church. The guests, twittering happily beneath frilly parasols, whispered about the likeness between Lady Cressida and Mrs. Putnam. Taking Teresa's advice and swallowing her pride, Cressida had ordered from a local milliner a gorgeous hat bedecked with nodding plumes. It was a brave show.

Looking across the scythed lawn, Nicholas, with an aching heart, watched Rose strolling on the arm of Flash Jack Wilshire. If ever he needed proof that she would have fitted in here, bearing him the sons he craved, sweetening his leisure, aiding him in this new and unexpectedly pleasurable life, he had it now.

The Honorable Simon Hazeldene, a "remittance man," banished for the dissipation of his inheritance on drinking and gambling, moved in as tutor to Rata Hill. The family grew to anticipate his drinking bouts, which he slept off in the woolshed or on a beach. Afterward, he could remain sober for months.

"Beatrix has asked her mother if I can share her lessons," Giles said to Rose one day.

Rose turned away to hide her heartache. She knew Giles's going was already a *fait accompli*. Undeterred by a ride of nearly four miles, Nicholas's son began his lessons with Mr. Hazeldene. In wet weather he stayed the night.

Oliver, too, had slipped away, taken up as he was with sailing in Flash Jack's schooners or working on Dr. Stokes's farm. He was looking at girls too. Building his own world.

Lance grew more beautiful every day. He was the riches Rose had built upon earth, as the prayer book adjured her not to do. Charlie was a nice little boy, undemanding and good-natured. He loved the baby and played happily with Joseph. Like Teresa, he was a kind of bridge; a bridge to Joseph as well as to Daniel. Rose did not like the fact that Joseph resembled Daniel. It meant that he also resembled the Rundull Putnams who had tried to kill Nicholas and rape her.

Rose was on the veranda. Flash Jack walked heavily down the path. She saw him coming and waved gaily. "How clever of you to arrive, Alain, when I am thinking about making a cup of your favorite tea."

He stood looking down at her with compassion, a black-edged envelope in his hands. Rose's brows knit together and her eyes sharpened. "The postmaster was looking for Daniel. I decided to bring the letter myself." He pulled up the extra chair and sat opposite, then leaned forward, closing his hands gently over hers. "Rose, dear love, your Grandy is dead."

She could not believe it. She would not. She stared at him with wild, unseeing eyes. "No," she said. "No, Alain." She struggled to her feet, pushing him away. "No!" she shouted, then she ran the length of the side veranda, across the front, and turned in at the door. "I'll make you that tea," she said shrilly. "You just wait there . . ."

"*Rose!*"

She swung around, her face white with shock, her eyes staring. Then, with a strangled scream, she fell against the wall, beating it with her fists and sobbing.

He picked her up and carried her into the pretty sitting room with its flowery curtains, the books he had given her, and the comfortable chairs. He sat her down gently on the sofa and drew up a chair opposite, easing his bulk into it, leaning forward, taking her hands and holding them.

"He can't die. He's all I have," she cried, her voice breaking, the tears streaming down her cheeks.

"No, Rose," Flash Jack said gently. "You've got the children. You've got—"

"I haven't got anyone but Lance," she cried with a passion that startled him and wrenched his heart, "until he goes to Nicholas, like Giles has. Daniel hates me, and Florrie won't come." Her voice broke with pain beyond bearing.

Flash Jack moved to the sofa and drew her head down upon his shoulder, as he had not meant to do. He smoothed her hair and kissed her gently on the head, because he did not trust himself to kiss her on the face.

When at last Rose quieted, he said gently, "I'll make you that cup of tea." He turned her, resting one hand on each shoulder, looking into the wreck of her beautiful face. "Go and wash the tears away, darling, and be brave."

When he returned she was back in the sheltered corner of the veranda that had been fashioned with such love for the old man. She held her son, pink-cheeked and beautiful with sleep, closely in her arms. She looked up, her eyes, though still moist, greedy with possession and a curious hardness that had not been there before.

"Perhaps I am not going to be allowed to have anyone," she said. He thought for a moment she looked slightly mad. Then Lance yawned and gave her a quirky look like a teasing glance from Nicholas. With a great sob, she hugged him close to her heart.

46

Early in 1848, the sobering pronouncement that the 18th earl of Rundull had cut Nicholas's allowance arrived in the same mail as the equally sobering news that an attempt had been made to destroy the statue of William the Conqueror.

The Dowager wrote with the utmost concern,

> The servants believe the culprits were Gertie Taylor's boys, but there is no proof. They bear us great malice for the demise of their father. The legend, as you know, says . . .

"It could have been the end of the Rundulls." Cressida spoke whimsically, but there was a hint of a taunt behind her words. She had been bitter since Rose's appearance at Teresa's wedding.

"Are you worried about the statue's destruction?" she asked Nicholas. "The Taylors have remembered over nine years. No doubt they will try again." She was thinking with a queer sort of satisfaction that the Taylor boys were Putnam's nephews, and therefore nephews also to Rose.

He said cynically, "It is only a superstition. A curse. What is a curse! Mumbo jumbo."

"If the statue should be demolished, the castle, it was said, would be flooded with evil spirits. Your mother told me that. I found it a pleasant, creepy little curse. But in the event that we laugh at the way the *tohungas* lay

curses on those who displease them, had we not better
forget our own?"

He laughed, and then she was laughing too. The
atmosphere in the room was kinder than it had been.
Nicholas said, "It is of no great importance that my
allowance should go. We have the estate. It is all paid
for."

"It is not all legally yours."

"It is mine," he said with unwarranted confidence. His
voice softened, "I am sorry, Cressida, about the allowance, but I will see you do not suffer."

"Thank you."

He put his hands on her shoulders, feeling the warmth
of her flesh through the gown, needing, in spite of his
assertions, some comfort from her.

She looked up into his face. "Have you given up all
thought of inheriting Rundull?"

"Yes. Now that Henry has a son." He heaved a quick
little sigh. "It is time to forget. To make the most of what
we have here."

There was a sound, no more than the scratching of a
mouse, but it stilled them. A confident young voice broke
the silence. "Beatrix says . . ." They both swung around.
Giles was standing in the doorway, ". . . she would like
to ride Bonnie." He was suddenly important and serious.
"The mare doesn't really jump high enough for me. Did
you know I am to be eight next week? I really need a
horse about fifteen hands high."

"Had you not better go home now?" Cressida said,
keeping her voice calm, though her face was white with
anger. "Your mother will be looking for you."

Giles gave her his most beguiling smile. "She doesn't
miss me. She has Lance."

One of Nicholas's names again! When Giles had gone,
she cried, "Have I not endured humiliation—?" Biting
her lips, she turned away.

Later that year, as the winter drew to its close, Colonel
Wakefield suffered an attack of apoplexy and died. A
general sadness spread over the colony. In spite of his
coldness he was greatly respected and would be missed.
There were no Wakefields now, though Jerningham wrote
that he hoped to return.

Emily, the happy bride of Mr. Stafford, had gone to live in the Middle Island. Life was peaceful there now. Sir George Grey, his excellent dispatches to Westminster having paid off, received his long-cherished knighthood. There was a buzz of excitement in the town.

Is it not shocking," asked Mrs. Stokes, "that he should choose Tamati Wake Nene and another Maori as his esquires for the ceremony? What will they say at home? A simple native!"

"Sir George knows what he is doing," said Teresa wisely. "I heard that, one of the chieftains having refused to give up the necessary land for a road, our governor presented his sister with a carriage."

There was a gale of delighted laughter. "It is the kind of diplomacy the Maoris understand," they agreed.

Now there were fenced and cultivated fields all through the colony, thorn and sweetbrier hedges, elegant barouches clattering over the new roads. Dinner wines were imported from France and Germany. There were balls and parties galore. Sir George, mellowed by his honor, came to Wellington and accepted some social invitations as well as extending his own hospitality from Mr. Eyre's official residence.

Nicholas had given the boys a puppy, not after all from the kangaroo hound, but fathered by Cressida's Bertie on one of the working bitches. "When Rover is big enough, I shall take him with me to Rata Hill," said Giles.

"He can't walk so far," retorted Joseph defensively, for Giles took everything.

"I shall put him over my saddle when he gets tired."

Easygoing Charlie smiled. He did not mind Giles taking everything. He still had what was left. He was not burdened with the resentment Joseph had from Daniel.

Now that Old Screw had been added to their stock, Nicholas bought another paddock adjacent to Aurora House. As the disillusioned and discontented took their profit and went home, so Nicholas purchased their land. In the back of his mind lay a plan to barter such legally acquired property for the hundreds of acres he had appropriated adjacent to that for which he held government scrip at Rata Hill.

An extra horse allowed the Putnams to hold their picnics further afield. Charlie, who was six, would sit happily on Old Screw while Lance rode pillion. Joseph, who could never be persuaded to mount, walked with Rose.

That day, that terrible day, was sunny as summer, but without summer's warmth, the winter having been blown out by sharp hail showers and bitter winds. Rose wandered happily along the riverbank, chattering with the children until they came to a clearing. There was a rude bridge over the fast-flowing stream where a tree had come down. It was surprising how slender a hold tall trees had on the ground. When sheltered they managed without taproots, but their network of fibers spread only a short way along the surface of the ground and was insufficient to hold them erect when cleared bush exposed them to the wind.

The boys loved a fallen tree. "On no account go up on the trunk," Rose warned them. Old Screw, relieved of her small load, stood idly flicking her tail, her limbs already locked in a doze. Rose stretched out on the grass, lifting her face blissfully to the sun.

Joseph called in his unauthoritative way, sounding like Daniel, "Mama said no."

There was no warning shout, no scream, only a burst of laughter, yet with it came a smell of danger. Rose opened her eyes, sat up, looked around. Rover was bounding across the tree bridge with Charlie and Lance in his wake. She leaped to her feet.

"No," cried Charlie, already several yards out over the stream, with Lance coming close behind. "Rover! Mama says no! Come back, Rover."

Rose stood transfixed, not daring to shout for fear of startling the boys into losing their balance. And then Joseph shouted again, in a panicky voice that did draw their attention, "Charlie! Come back!"

The child turned obediently, and in that brief, sickening moment Lance ran into him. They overbalanced and went into the water.

Grasping her skirts, Rose raced for the bend in the river. They were both, miraculously, on their backs, being carried forward by the current.

Slipping, plunging, hurtling, grabbing at the plants for support, she plunged down the bank to where a flax bush growing directly at the water's edge spread its sticks and

leaves out into the stream. The two boys swung in where
the water eddied, Charlie in front, Lance a few yards
behind. Charlie came up against the sticks and steadied,
but the impact of his weight bent the sticks back and,
suddenly, to Rose's horror, Lance was sliding around the
tips and was once more caught up in the current.

With an animal scream, she swung back and floundered up the bank. It would take precious moments to
bring Charlie in. Moments in which she would certainly
lose Lance. She did not pause to consider whether Charlie could scramble in with the aid of the flax. In the back
of her mind she knew it was possible. She raced across
the dogleg where the current had slowed. The child was
still on his back. She leaped down the bank, falling headlong, slithering into the water and like a mad woman
forged through it, stretching, plunging, fighting against
its weight, bouncing on the tip of one toe, just keeping
her chin above water.

The child came level. She flung herself forward, right
out of her depth, stretched to her full length. As she sank
she grasped his foot and they went down together, then
gasping, choking, coughing, rose to the surface with Lance
clinging like a limpet around her neck. Half-swimming
though she could not swim, she forged back, kicking,
floating, fighting, until at last she had a grip on the flax
bushes. Thrusting the little boy into the safety of the
green leaves, she scrambled after him, her wet clothes
dragging, catching at her feet, tripping her as she pushed
him roughly up the bank until they were safely on flat
land. "Follow me," she said, and lifting her soaked skirts,
raced back across the grass to where she had left Charlie.

She knew when she saw Joseph weeping.

"He's gone. Charlie's gone."

Then she was screaming to Joseph to go to Lance and
she was running, running. "Charlie! Oh God, Oh God,
where is Charlie!" Or perhaps she was not making a
sound, only running, until suddenly with horror she was
at the end of her running, back where the other stream
came in, blocking her.

She stood staring at the water, the empty, laughing,
spinning water that had swallowed Charlie, knowing with
mindless horror that it was too late. Nonetheless, she
plunged once more into the stream. The greedy, grasp-

ing, sucking water that had taken Charlie rose higher and higher, up to her neck, her mouth, her nose. The floor was still sinking. Flailing her arms, she tried to swim, tried to lift herself and float across but her skirt caught around her legs, dragging her down.

As she sank she could hear the screams of the little boys. "Mama! Mama!" Their terror brought her to a realization of her own danger. She knew deep down that Charlie had gone. That nothing she could do would bring him back.

They returned to Aurora House in a desperate kind of silence. Joseph had stopped crying. Twice, Lance asked innocently, "Where Charlie?" but Rose was unable to answer.

They somehow came home. Daniel and Giles were in the kitchen. Rose saw numbly that there had been some sort of row. Daniel was looking angry, Giles disdainful. They stared at her ravaged face, her wet hair, her clothes clinging to her body; then at Lance, soaked from top to toe; then at Joseph, who was dry.

Lance said in a piping, innocent treble, looking puzzled, "Charlie got dwowned. We felled in water, Charlie and me. Charlie got dwowned."

Rose fell against the doorjamb, sagging, sobbing.

Then Joseph, looking at Lance, his white face crumpled like paper, said with the bitterness of seven years of watching Rose's love enfold others, "She let Charlie drown to save *him*."

A bullish look came over Daniel's face; a black, uncontrollable fury; a compounding of all the insults and disappointments that had begun the day he realized Rose was pregnant with a child that could not possibly be his. He lunged with a closed fist, mindless abuse punching out of him as though expelled by a head of steam. Rose, already toppling with weakness and distress, went down at the first blow.

Giles galloped into town and found Flash Jack. Teresa, miraculously, was in his store. She came and tore the wet clothes off Rose, wrapped her in a warm gown, brought a hot stone bottle, but she could not persuade her to go to bed. Not into Daniel's bed.

The door opened and Lance came in. "Mama!"

She held out her arms and he went into them, looking up at her with puzzled eyes. "Charlie gone?" he said, stating a fact as well as asking for an explanation.

Her arms tightened around him, pressing him against her heart. "My love. My darling love." She gave a hiccuping little sob for the child who had died so that she could keep Nicholas's baby.

She buried her poor bruised face in Lance's petal-soft neck. "It's not fair." She had thought Charlie was safe, his journey downstream halted by the flax. She had not chosen to save one boy and leave the other.

"I didn't," she sobbed, clutching Lance to her. "I didn't, I didn't . . ."

Lance wriggled, laughing, out of her arms. "Mama, where is Charlie?" The black eyes, so huge and familiar, looked into hers; looking like Nicholas in miniature, yet with a sweetness and grace neither Nicholas nor Giles possessed. "Poor Mama," he said fondly and laid himself across her knee, kicking his little legs, humming to himself, innocent, precious, unaware of what he had made her do.

They went to the funeral, divided as they had been since the dreadful day. Flash Jack, disdaining custom, carried the tiny coffin on his shoulder, stalking out in front in his high silk hat, coattails swinging. Rose stood huddled in a black cape he had somehow found for her, her bruised face hidden beneath a little black bonnet Teresa concocted with some ribbons bought in Flash Jack's store. It was a tiny funeral for a tiny boy. Nicholas was absent. In the circumstances, as Teresa told him, it was better that way. Mr. Alexander and Teresa walked on either side of Rose and Daniel, Teresa with her arm through Daniel's arm, Mr. Alexander, kind and concerned, supporting Rose. Dr. and Mrs. Stokes, with Oliver between them, walked behind.

They took him to the little town cemetery with its sparse graves where lay Mr. Betts Hopper, the first of the lively young gentlemen from those first five ships to lose his life, and the Wakefield brothers. They laid him down, little Ned Taylor Putnam, who had been nicknamed Charlie because what he stood for had been insupportable. It had been deemed wise to send Giles to Rata Hill for his lessons as usual, and Joseph had gone to his school, or so they thought. One of Flash Jack's workmen found him wandering on the beach and took him home.

"I suppose they thought he wouldn't know," the man told his wife. "Sometimes kids know more than folks think. Feed the lad up and make a fuss of him, love. He don't look any too good to me."

People were quiet, not knowing which, if any, of the odd rumors they heard was true. Some said Lance was Mrs. Putnam's favorite. But, of course, each baby in his turn was always the favorite. They wondered how Mrs. Putnam came by her bruised face. Putnam, too, had a black eye.

"Giles hit him," Flash Jack told Teresa.

"What nonsense, Alain. The boy is only eight."

"It seems le Grys has been teaching him to box. And he has, let us say, something extra in the way of strength and temper to call on. A chip off the old block," said Flash Jack. "Though I think it was the act of a gentleman, rather than . . ."

She glanced at him inquiringly. "Yes?"

"Giles despises Rose," he said heavily.

Teresa did not answer immediately. Then, "He's only a child," she said.

Flash Jack had never thought of Giles as a child. One of the farmhands at Rata Hill, talking to him in the Ship Inn, said he saw the boy walk away dry eyed and with lifted head from a thrashing Nicholas had given him, saying, "I'll pay you back one day." "And I believe he will," the man said, chuckling.

Flash Jack believed he would, too, but he did not think it was a matter to chuckle over.

Rose dutifully cooked Daniel's meals, but as far as possible she kept out of his way. She knew she had no right to ask his forgiveness, so she learned to live with his hatred.

October's earthquake tossed the little tragedy out of the whispering drawing rooms. Rose, playing with Lance on the veranda, felt the eerie stillness. The noisy, restless *tui* that visited the garden looking for nectar-bearing plants suddenly stopped his antics in the lacebark and was silent. The lazy hum of the bees droned away. Even Lance was aware. He put his bricks down and came toward her, listening to the silence, then, clutching at Rose's knee, looked around fearfully.

All at once the wall behind Rose's chair seemed to leap outward, the floor to rock like the waves on the sea. Snatching the child up in her arms, she leaped down the steps to the lawn, running from danger to danger, not knowing where to go, sensing it everywhere. The chimneys were rocking back and forth like drunken old men. Then with a roar they disintegrated, and the bricks came down over the wooden tiles in a haze of red dust, clattering, banging, and slithering across the eaves and into the garden.

"Chimbley!" exclaimed the child, pointing in astonishment, looking to Rose for an explanation. "Chimbley bwoke?"

There was another tremor, and then another. The debris on the roof slithered. "Chimbley!" shrieked the child again, his excitement rising. Then the ground before them opened silently, and a great crack split the lawn.

"Help!" Rose screamed. She ran and ran, aware only of the stark terror of her aloneness until the sheer weight of the child in her arms forced her to stop.

From the direction of the town columns of smoke rose in the air. On the side of a hill a cottage suddenly burst into flames. Lance was silent now, as though he, too, sensed tragedy.

Time passed. No one came except the birds, rising once more into the sky, rustling in the trees. Tentatively, the crickets began their singing, two seagulls wheeled raucously. The world began slowly to come once more to life.

Still holding Lance tightly in her arms, Rose ventured timorously back into the garden. The great crack in the earth grinned up at her, black and sinister, little soft runnels of earth dribbling in. She went carefully around it and through the broom hedge. The chickens were ruffling their feathers. The cock darted his red and brown head from side to side.

They took her arrival as the signal for protest. "Ree-ch, raw-k. Ree-ch, raw-h-k-k," they shrieked. Old Screw tossed her head, stamped her hooves, and emitted a high, screeching whinny. As if it was my fault, Rose thought. She went to the kitchen door and looked fearfully in. Pans were scattered on the floor, as were a few broken plates. She dared not either take Lance in or leave him behind. She went back into the garden and stood looking mindlessly at the crack.

Daniel's voice came ungraciously from the gateway. "I see you're orl right." She looked up with relief, seeing him with Joseph.

"What's that?" He came and stood beside her. "Pity yer both didn't go down it," he said. "You an' that bastard brat."

"Oh, Daniel! Please." Rose's face twisted. "I don't think I can stand anymore."

Lance, giving Joseph one of his angelic smiles, said, "Chimbley come down," and pointed to the roof, looking greatly awed. Rose clung to him tightly, drawing from him the love she so desperately needed to give her the strength to carry on.

"There's some 'ouses come down near the quay," said Daniel. "An' some gone up in flames. I got Joseph. All the kids was out in the playground." He put a hand on his son's head, as he often did lately, possessive and protective. *My* son, his hard eyes seemed to say.

Rose nodded. She did not see Joseph's look of inept, childish compassion, and he did not come to her. There was too much of Daniel in him for that.

There was amazingly little damage inside the house. Rose's sampler was lying on the floor. She knew when she saw it that Daniel had not resisted the temptation to tread on it with his heavy boot. When they returned to the garden, she leaned over the crack and tossed the sampler in. It was like offering a sacrifice. The broken frame rattled once, then hit the bottom with a dull thud.

Daniel was digging in the paddock for earth to fill the crack, and Joseph was helping carry the sods into the garden, when Nicholas came riding up with Giles. They leaped out of their saddles and Nicholas hurried inside. Rose, who was tidying the kitchen, rushed out at the familiar sound of his footsteps and met him in the hall. His arms came around her, holding her close. It was the first time they had met since before Charlie died. "I'm sorry," he said emotionally, as though he had not come about the earthquake. "It seemed best to stay away."

She clung to him, at last protected, his warmth and his strength seeping into her. "Sometimes I feel I can't go on," she whispered.

He gentled her against his heart. "Ah, Rose. It has been a hard road, but you have to go on."

"Daniel hates me for letting Charlie drown." It was the first time she had been able to face the fact. Saying the words out loud broke something inside her.

Nicholas lifted her face, which was streaming with tears. "You will come through, Rose, as you always have."

She brushed the backs of her hands across her eyes. "Nicholas, can we not go away together?"

"Hush, Rose. Hush, my darling."

"Why can we not?" she demanded. "Your brother has Rundull and an heir. It was for that you could not marry me." A storm of passion broke through. "There is no chance you will ever go back to Rundull. Ever. We can go away somewhere with our baby." She felt his arms stiffen, and he thrust her at arm's length. She looked up into his face with shock. "You still lust after Rundull, which you shall not, cannot have," she cried angrily. "Oh, what a black devil you are! It is an obsession. A madness. You cannot have Rundull, Nicholas. You *cannot.*"

He spoke quietly, "You must try to mend matters with your husband, as I have tried to do with my wife. It is insane to think about anything else."

"We could be together," she shouted at him, "if you did not love possessions more than people."

There was an awestruck silence. "What is Rundull anyway?" she asked when the startled moment had passed. "I told you once, but you did not listen. Old stones. I said, you must not love old stones and earth more than people. All that will be there forever, for other people. We are . . . passing through. I have read the Bible now, Nicholas, as you have not. It is for one another that we live. Not for Rundull Castles and Rata Hills."

"Then I must live for my wife and daughters . . ."

"When it is sons you want? The sons I have. I have them. They are mine," she said, her voice rising again. "You said your mealymouthed sister-in-law would never have a son. Well, she has. But you have not. Now, I say your mealymouthed wife will never . . ."

She stopped as he turned abruptly around, but not before she had seen the fury, the vulnerability, and the pain in his face. She watched him stride across the room and swing out of the door. Then she flung herself face down on the sofa, heartbreak and despair sweeping through her, and a terrible, unbearable sense of loss.

Lieutenant Governor Eyre behaved with courage and kindness. Only three lives were lost, but the damage to the town was estimated at fifty thousand pounds. Some frail citizens panicked and ran into the woods. Others moved into tents. So many wished to bolt that Mr. Eyre put a stop to all ships leaving. Public business in government offices was suspended for eight days. Mr. Eyre, the parson's son, was roundly ridiculed for proclaiming October 20 as a day of solemn prayer, humiliation, and fast.

"The Almighty can scarcely be asked to stop earthquakes if men are foolish enough to settle in a volcanic area," Judge Chapman said with biting sarcasm.

Inevitably, the excitement blew over. The citizens went back to their homes, shrugged their shoulders, and forgot. There was so much to do and scarcely enough hours in the day to do it all. Mr. Eyre sent home for a young lady whom he had met in the West Country. Lady Grey, who had already privately arranged that he should marry the daughter of General Pitt, met the girl at New Plymouth and escorted her to Auckland, with the outrageous intention of sending her home. While the tea parties buzzed with the scandal, Mr. Eyre, the exceptional walker, set out overland, arriving in Auckland in time to meet the brig conveying his bride. The embarrassed governor gave the bride away, and in one of his high-handed acts of integration, arranged also to make it a double wedding with a Maori bride and groom.

Jerningham Wakefield set out from England with an advance party to start up a settlament at Canterbury, leaving debts of three thousand pounds.

47

The summer of 1852 came in with a menacing shriek
of winds and unseasonal hail. The curtains strained at the
windows, and one of the trees in the garden came down.
I should have known, Rose thought later. It was a warning, as the news of the attempted destruction of the
Conqueror's statue seemed also now to have been. When
Nicholas told her, she had merely thought how far she
had left the old ghosts behind, not seeing the shadows in
the glass.

When the holidays came around, the boys once more
clamored for picnics. Rose had said, after Charlie's death,
that she never wanted to go on a picnic again, but they
led her back. She went, because she was trying to rebuild
her broken life. To find a way to live without Nicholas.
She had given up any attempt to mend her marriage.
Daniel had made up his mind not to forgive. There were
only the children now. They saddled the ponies and went
off down a road newly struck through the bush: Giles
riding the cob; Lance on Blackboy, who had returned
from Rata Hill for his use; and Rose riding Old Screw,
with Joseph persuaded onto the pillion seat.

The clearing they found was well away from the river.
As if a river could have made a difference! As if fate
could not do her appalling work in other ways. Afterward, she knew it was Lance who had done it himself.
Lance, as fate's cat's-paw, not knowing why he had to do
it, but doing it nonetheless. "Please look after Rover,"

he said. "He jumps in my way all the time, trying to stop me."

She unbuckled Old Screw's reins and slipped them through the dog's collar. When Rover sat back on his haunches and howled, she patted him on the head. "Go on your way," she said to Lance. "I will look after him." Indulgently smiling, she watched the dog watching the boy go, saw his big, sad, entreating eyes. "You were being a nuisance," she told him, dropping a kiss on his nose.

She relived it all in livid colors a dozen, a hundred times afterward: saw the dog leaping in the air, pulling and jerking at the leather; heard his demented howls as the children ran out of sight. Faintly unnerved, she remembered speaking roughly to him. "Sit still, you awkward creature." He dropped to the ground, chin flat on the fallen leaves, a picture of despair. She stood looking down at him, not thinking, only feeling strange. "They must take you, if it means so much," she said. "We will go together and find them." She loosened her hold on the reins, and was leaning down to release him, when Rover leaped to his feet and was off, streaking across the clearing, the reins dragging and dancing on the ground.

Because of the crackling of the twigs beneath her feet as she ran in his wake, Rose did not immediately recognize the sharp crack that rent the air, until all at once there was a sound of crashing branches and the forest came to life with the shriek of splitting wood. Out in front of her, where the children had gone, where the dog had disappeared, a great tree went over with a thump that shook the earth.

"Lance!" she screamed. "Giles!" She was screaming as she ran, tripping and diving. And then she was at the tree, with dust flying up all around, and Joseph and Giles standing like statues, looking down.

There was no moving the great forest pine. No lifting the branch.

She fell on her knees beside the child. Beside the child's head, because his legs were on the other side of the branch that pinned him. She did not see Giles go. She did not hear the horse's fast plunging footfalls as he raced back up the forest road. She was looking with

agony and despair into her child's gray face, his terrified
eyes.

"Get me out, Mama."

She slid a hand beneath his cheek.

"Get me out, Mama," he whimpered. A tear rolled
down his face, onto her hand.

"Darling," she said. His lids slid down, the dark lashes
lying like little curled combs on his pallid cheek. The
stillness was terrible. More terrible than anything she had
ever experienced. It was she who was dying, from the
heart out. Dying.

The lashes fluttered up. "It's awfully dark," the child
said. His voice was small, frightened.

As best she could, she put her arms around him. She
could not hold him, only shelter him, because of the
branch.

"Mama?"

"Darling."

"Mama, don't let me die."

Then something came up out of the deep past. Something from Rundull village, a world away, and with it a
strange kind of detached strength. "You are going to
Grandy," she said. "To our dear Grandy who loves you."

The dark lids trembled faintly. "I'd rather not," Lance
whispered, but already there was a kind of acceptance, a
thoughtfulness beyond his years.

"Grandy went ahead to wait for you," Rose said. Her
tears fell on the back of his little dark head, like a
blessing. She added in a tortured voice, "My darling, you
will be happy. And greatly loved."

She thought, I am going to die now, too. I am already
dead.

A small wet nose pushed itself under her hand, a
tongue touched her fingers. She felt the dog wriggling
closer, climbing up to her face, licking her frantically in
its excited distress. "No, Rover," she said, as her arm
went around the fluffy body. "You could not have saved
him. He had to go, to pay for Charlie." She knew it with
the utmost certainty, as though she had known it ever
since Charlie died. As though she had read it, like a
curse, in Daniel's vengeful eyes.

She lifted her head and there was Joseph, standing the
way Daniel stood, abject and helpless. She looked at him

and saw that he was all she had now: a child in the pattern of the man who hated her. In her madness she cried, "Go away. I never want to see you again," and as she said it she thought with terrible anguish, Now I have done a little wickedness to match what has been done to me. Oh God, you know I only wanted to love Nicholas. And now I have lost him and both of his sons. Why did you do all this to me? She collapsed on the dry leaves while helpless, hopeless tears of despair poured down her face; with the dog frantically licking them away, and the body of Nicholas's son at her side.

She saw Joseph turn and shuffle off, head hanging. His very acceptance of her cruelty brought a fever of anger. She knew that had he been nearer she would have struck him. She gripped her hands together, holding back the madness within her. Then she lurched to her feet and hurried after him, compassion welling up for his smallness, his dependence, his vulnerability.

"I'm sorry, Joseph," she called, staggering toward him through the tripping vines, arms outstretched. "I am sorry. I didn't mean it. I didn't . . ."

He turned, met the great tragic eyes filled with tears, saw them pouring down her face, and knew sullenly that they were not for him; knew in his little-boy mind that Rose's despair outweighed regret a thousandfold. "It's all right," he muttered, turning away. "I don't mind." He was accustomed to being passed over for brighter, more handsome boys. But what he had seen in his mama's face, heard in her voice a moment ago, had been rejection, for now there was no one better to whom she could go, and still she did not want him. He saw the outstretched arms, but after the barren years he did not know what to do with them.

"Joseph," Rose spoke brokenly, beseechingly. She enfolded his unyielding body, then tried to lead him back with her to the tree trunk. Frightened, uncomprehending, he pulled away and walked, head down, still shuffling his feet, away from her. After all, she had to let him go. She went back to the tree and flung herself upon the ground, one arm around the small, still shoulders, one lifeless little hand beneath her cheek.

When Nicholas and Giles came at last, galloping down the forest path, she was still there. Nicholas leaped off his horse and bent over his son. Rose looked up, her mouth trembling, her eyes swimminng with tears.

"Oh, Rose. My poor Rose." With a stricken expression, he lifted her to her feet and held her against his heart, as he had always held her, for a while, when the world took on a blackness one or other of them was unable to face.

In the distance there was the scatter of a pony's hoofbeats as Giles, quick and resourceful as always, galloped off for help.

"Be brave," Nicholas said. "Be brave, my darling."

But she knew she could not. All the bravery had gone out of her. She could no longer contain her losses. She slipped out of his arms and sank down beside the body of the child who had been her joy and triumph, her bridge to happiness, her last remaining tie with Nicholas. She lifted his hand and held it once more against her cheek, while the tears poured over it. "Don't talk to me. Don't talk to me. Leave me alone," she wept.

Nicholas sat down beside her on the grass, helplessly smoothing her hair. They were still there when the police, Dr. Stokes and Daniel, and the men with hacksaws and a stretcher came.

"Where's Joseph?" asked Daniel. Rose could only look at him piteously. Nicholas tried to lift her to her feet but she would not let go of the child's hand. The helpers turned away, moving awkwardly out of earshot, shuffling their feet in the leaves.

Dr. Stokes said gently, "It is better that you go home, my dear."

She clung to the log, to the child's hand. She heard Daniel ask again, "Where is Joseph?" and then very determined hands lifted her, while more hands broke her grip, and they led her forcibly away.

Nobody knew what had happened to Joseph. The police began the search. Daily the volunteers grew until it seemed the entire population was involved. The friendly chief Te Puni offered to help. He seemed to know something, though he would not talk, merely saying he would go into the bush, but he would need to be accompanied by a white man with the goodwill of an angel and the tact of a diplomat. . . .The Reverend Octavius Hadfield came at speed from Waikanae and the two men disappeared.

"Nothing happened to the boy, said the missionary when they returned with Joseph. Hadfield spoke with his particular brand of serene firmness that had kept the peace between Maoris and whites a dozen times before. Joseph did not speak for nearly two weeks.

"He has lost two brothers," Dr. Stokes explained. Joseph followed Rose everywhere in the cold, cold house though never coming very near. She was beyond deducing that he might be trying to join her, as she, in those first desperate moments after Lance's death, had tried to go to him. When she sat down, he seated himself in a corner and watched her. Too deeply sunk into despair to see, she missed the hope and longing that were growing in his face. The watching drove her mad. Rover watched her, too, but unlike Joseph he cried. The big doggy tears rolled off his jowls, and he would eat nothing. In Rover's doleful eyes she seemed always to read a kind of sorrowful accusation. Once she shouted at him, "You are wrong, Rover. You could not have saved him. No one could have saved him."

Daniel came into the kitchen. "Talkin' to yerself?" he asked. "It's the first sign of madness."

Rose felt she had been going slowly mad for a long time.

"Remember what they said about you in the village?" Daniel asked, and without waiting for a reply went on. "They said yer was a witch. Didn't yer mother meet the ghost by Tanner the Bastard's statue the night yer was born? They say there's a curse on folk what meet that ghost."

Sometimes she thought she might kill Daniel if he did not stop taunting her. Then she would remember what she had done to him, and remain silent.

One morning Rover was too weak to climb out of his basket. Daniel said, "We'd better put 'im down. 'Is ribs is comin' through 'is skin."

Giles, without a word to anyone, employing that familiar, cool decisiveness he had inherited from Nicholas, rode slowly and carefully to Rata Hill with the dog sprawled limply against his knees. Cook's tempting delicacies, and the devoted love of Beatrix and Isobel, brought him back to life, and gradually he forgot.

But Joseph could not be given away. One evening,

unable to bear her loveless isolation any longer, Rose
went to him when he was sitting up in bed, and put her
arms around him. This time, her need to love and be
loved came to him like a charged force, driving out the
cold. He clung to her with a violence that startled her.
Then he spoke for the first time.

"Will you love me now, Mama?"

Rose looked down at the top of his head in shocked
silence.

"I mean, now that Lance has gone as well."

She sat there feeling numb, looking across the empty
years ahead, coming to terms with the fact that now there
was only Joseph, the boy who had grown up in the
shadow of those who had her heart. Instinctively, with
her deep, inner reverence, knowing the laws of the universe, Rose knew also that her obsessional love for Nicholas had led her to flout them. She tightened her arms
around Joseph's thin, bony body. He did not cuddle her
as Lance had, even as did Giles in his most exuberant
moments, but then she realized, with overwhelming shame,
she had never taught him how.

In 1853, the New Zealand Company surrendered its charter, with all its interests reverting to the government. It
seemed scarcely to matter. With the Wakefield brothers
dead, with Edward Gibbon still showing no sign of wishing to visit his dream colony, the old power slipped
silently away.

Oliver, who now gave his age as twenty-one, fell in
love with the daughter of Teresa's nearest neighbor. He
came to see Rose one radiant March day, a tall young
man, muscled and strong from sailing on Flash Jack's
vessels and laboring on the farm. Seated with her in the
shelter of Grandy's shrine, with the warm scents of the
gilly flowers and the lemon trees around them, he said,
"You will love her, Rose, and she will love you. I want
you to know you will always be welcome at our home.
Papa is building a house for us on the farm. He wants to
go on doctoring until he drops. The farm was apparently
always meant for me."

She scarcely heard him. She was thinking that she must
not love this girl, or Oliver, or both of them would be
taken away.

"Do you ever think about your beginnings, Oliver?"

He looked at her queerly. "Do you really mean . . . ?" His sun-browned, open face, which retained virtually nothing of that tragic little creature he had once been, puckered into a question. "Do you really mean I should tell them?"

Silence lay around them while their minds flew back to the horror of the East End of London. To the little boy scrabbling for food in cold streets, stealing lunch baskets from the ghouls gathered around the hangman's gallows. Oliver said uncomfortably, "My life really began in the mews behind Lord Rundull's house in Cavendish Square when I met you. I don't want to remember further back than that. I really don't want to. But I'll never forget meeting you, Rose, though I don't even want to tell Janet about it. It's just between you and me." He gave her a quirky, faintly uncertain smile, all that remained of the child Oliver, lost now in the tall, broad frame of the new man. "I'd just like to call all my daughters Rose, if you wouldn't mind."

They laughed softly together. She thought, without surprise, He doesn't even remember giving that child to the cannibal. She scarcely remembered it herself, so far had she pushed it into the back of her mind.

He said, "I want you to be guest of honor at the wedding. I want this to be a big day for you. I want you to . . ." His voice trailed off and he shifted his feet awkwardly, looking at her black gown.

Rose put a hand to her head, touching the golden hair that was not so bright as before, not so crisp and alive, not so well-dressed. Oliver leaned forward and took her hands the way Flash Jack held them when he was talking seriously to her. "I'd like it if you could look like you used to look before . . . Rose, you were always the best-looking lady."

Her eyes filled with tears. "You know I am in mourning, Oliver."

"You mustn't, Rose. You never did what people thought you should do. I couldn't bear it if you had to wear black to my wedding. And nothing will bring Lance back. Nothing."

A shimmering tear trickled down her cheek.

"You've got to get over it, Rose," said Oliver.

"There is so much to get over," she replied, meaning all the losses—including Giles, and Daniel's respect. Daniel's mindless abuse, though she had learned to live with it, left her weak and despairing.

Oliver said, "Tomorrow I shall bring Janet to see you, and you are to be bright and beautiful and happy for us, and *not* dressed in black, or she will never believe you're my best friend." Then he stood up and went striding down the path. At the gate he turned and waved but she could see the question still in the line of his mouth, the raised brows. She waved back and managed a smile.

It was not so easy, though. Rose felt for the first time as though she had left her youth behind. The eager, restless wind that would set her feet dancing, her curls flying, now only irritated her. The swooping gulls sounded shrill and unfriendly. "Serves you right. Serves you right," they screamed from the high safety of the sky, and the jaunty little garden birds, the fantails and the hedge sparrows, seemed to eye her malevolently.

Other people wanted to say, "You will get over it," but everyone knew a mother never recovered from the loss of a child. As for the loss of two children . . . They shook their heads and told one another how much they sympathized. But they stayed away.

Even going into town to shop was an effort: greeting friends and acquaintances, seeing their faces freeze at sight of her, then settle into embarrassed, kindly smiles. Those who saw her coming would often turn away. "My dear, I simply did not know what to say to the poor thing."

Her feet would grow heavy as though she walked through water—water up to her chin as it had been when she tried to cross the river to search for Charlie—and she would feel her frozen heart slump. She would go home, passing the houses where voices and laughter drifted from windows, where ladies who no longer invited her in, were taking tea in each other's company.

The governor of New Munster, as they were to call him, and his new lady were to give a ball on May 24. The South Island had been officially named New Munster, though no one cared sufficiently for the name to use it.

"You cert'n'ly got ideas above yer station," muttered

Daniel, preparing to throw the beautiful card with its gold lettering into the fire. "How'd yer get 'old of that?"

Rose snatched the card away. "We are obliged to go. It is not possible, whatever you feel about attending, to throw such an invitation away. It is the same as throwing the Queen's invitation in the fire. You may not even decline," she added, clutching to her breasts the passport to a dance with Nicholas. Nicholas, whom she had not seen since Lance's funeral.

"I'll decline orl right," muttered Daniel, clumping his heavy boots on the floor. "Catch me goin' ter Government 'Ouse?"

"I am serious about this," Rose said, facing him calmly. "You are obliged to go."

Daniel looked angry. "You're in mourning."

"I came out for Oliver's wedding. I cannot step in and out of it."

Daniel had not yet recovered from the discomfiture of the wedding: the embarrassment of watching Rose chatting with the gentry, for all the world as though she had been born among them; the terrifying experience of being pushed forward time and again by good-natured guests to stand at her side; the agonizing retreat as the feeling of being the cynosure of all eyes overcame him. He had even overheard some of the unkind remarks.

"What's Putnam doing here, anyway? If he feels so out of place, why did he come?"

And then a merry, mischievous whisper, "Why not ask how she came to marry him? That's what we should all like to know."

Daniel wished he had been brave enough to shout out to all of them why Rose had married him. He did not because he knew instinctively that he would achieve nothing but a swift hustling out of the way.

Flash Jack came to visit, carrying a large box. "Delivery boy," he said saluting, his eyes merry. "I happened to be passing Mrs. Adams's dressmaking establishment."

Rose's brows rose in surprise. "My gown for the ball? She was indeed quick."

Flash Jack wandered across the veranda and settled himself into a chair in Grandy's little shrine. "May I see it?"

"It is not very special," said Rose, thinking of the

lovely clothes Nicholas had bought for her in Sydney, now long out of date. "I am afraid I will cut rather a poor figure. There will be some very beautiful gowns there, I dare say. Teresa's family, who have at last forgiven her, have sent her one from London." She glanced back at the box. "It is nothing, really." So much money had had to go into outfitting Daniel, there had not been much left for her.

Flash Jack took out a cheroot. "Open it," he said.

Reluctantly, Rose undid the string and lifted the lid. "Oh!" she gasped, as she looked down upon fold on fold of magnificent coral silk. "Oh, it is the wrong . . ." And then she saw the warm amusement in Flash Jack's eyes.

"It is for you," he said. "A gift."

Rose blinked, but the gown did not go away. "Oh, Alain."

"I sent for it when I first heard Eyre was coming. I knew there would be some sort of inauguration ball."

There were tears in Rose's eyes. Tears came so easily these days. "Whatever else I lack, Alain, I do not lack wonderful friends."

On the day before the ball, when Daniel's outfit had still not been delivered, Rose went to the tailor.

"Mr. Putnam canceled the order," the man said, looking at her in surprise.

Rose's mouth went dry. "When? When did he cancel it?"

"Only a day or so after it was ordered."

"Thank you," said Rose stiffly, and went out of the shop. She stood in the street feeling stunned, while a cold wind blew her skirts around her ankles. Daniel had told her he had twice been for fittings. She could scarcely believe he would take matters into his own hands like this. Daniel, who since attacking his own brothers in Rundull High Street had never made a decision for himself.

"I have brought it upon myself," she admitted painfully. "It is I who made him like this." Then, with her old, willful illogicality, "But it is not my fault I love Nicholas, and not his fault we could not marry."

That evening, when he came home, she went to the back door to meet him. " 'Ullo Rose," he said, looking cheery, as he had not been for a long time.

She asked as he took off his heavy boots, "Why have you decided not to go to the ball, Daniel?"

His mouth fell open. "Who says so?"

"You have nothing to wear."

His head came down in that now familiar, bull-like, aggressive pose. "We can't say the same fer yer, can we? Yer fancy—"

"Flash Jack gave me that dress," she said. "I should have told you, I suppose. I thought . . ."

"Yer thought I was too stoopid ter see it was more'n yer could afford," said Daniel. "An' what right's Mr. Wilshire got givin' yer clothes, if 'e did, which I don't believe anyways."

"Why don't you ask him?"

Daniel looked taken aback.

"Flash Jack has been very good to me," said Rose. "He has given me a great many presents over the years. And yes, as you say, you have not noticed."

Daniel's face closed in that familiar way. "Anyway, 'owever yer got it," he said, "I'm not goin' an' that's that." His eyes wandered over her pretty face with triumph and malice. "An' yer can't go without me. I arst someone if a married woman can go without 'er 'usband ter Government 'Ouse. That's what I arst, an' 'e said no. So yer can't go," Daniel finished triumphantly.

She knew then it was useless to try to talk him around. "I am sorry for what I have done to you," Rose said, yet knowing if the pages could be turned back she would do the same things again. "I am as I am, Daniel, and I have done what I had to do. I am sorry it has turned out this way for you. You were very kind to me once, and I have always been grateful for that. But I want to say this. I cannot live with hate. You must think again about hating me, because hate destroys people. Tricks are all very well"—she lifted her head and her eyes flashed—"but remember when you play them that I can do the same."

Daniel looked at her with puzzled eyes. "I don't understand yer, Rose."

"No," she replied. "That's the pity of it." She took down her cloak and bonnet from a hook on the wall.

"Where are yer going? I want me tea."

She felt a little of the old impudence returning. A little of the life that had not been in her since the death of the boys. A return of strength that came from the realization that, after all, she could take up the cudgels and fight again. "I am going to play a trick on you," she said, and dimpled. "If you have not already fed yourself when I return, then I will get your tea." She went out of the front door, closing it carefully behind her, and hurried off toward the town.

The next evening Rose dressed herself in the magnificent coral silk, and clasped around her neck the diamond necklace Teresa had insisted on loaning her. "It is obligatory to wear jewels to Government House," she scolded when Rose looked doubtful. She was not walking on air as she had expected. Perhaps it is only that I am now thirty-one, she thought. But it was more than that. The change in Flash Jack's manner bothered her. She had known from the beginning he had no right to order this wonderful dress for her. And as a respectable married woman, she had no right to accept it. She certainly should not have gone to him yesterday and asked him to escort her to the ball. Now she had a nervous feeling he was beginning to tick off on his fingers the good deeds he had done for her.

"Flash Jack takes his pound of flesh," was a common phrase in town.

There was a rattling of harness and the black shadows fled. All at once she was giddy with excitement at the prospect of wearing diamonds and being presented to the lieutenant governor. Flash Jack strode up the path. He swept in, tails swinging, stock high and impeccably tied, wearing a wonderful caped cloak.

"Right! Are we ready?" He eyed Rose up and down with a quite terrifying air of possession. There was a panicky moment when she wanted to turn and run. Then Giles, who had been attending to his horse, came through from the back of the house. He walked past Joseph, who was leaning on the doorpost. "Well," he said thoughtfully, eyeing her exactly as Nicholas used to eye her all those years ago in St. James's. "Well,' said Giles. "I must say, Mama, you cut a pretty figure. A very pretty figure indeed." He added thoughtfully, "I never noticed before that you look like Lady Cressida. But prettier."

Elated beyond bearing by Giles's unexpected attention, Rose twirled her fan nervously.

"Yes," said Giles. Then, "Yes, I see," as though something that had puzzled him was suddenly clear.

"You're right," agreed Flash Jack heartily, rubbing his hands, "but unconscionably slow catching up. Other people have always known she was prettier. Let's be on our way. Dancing is to begin at nine."

"Where's Papa?" asked Joseph, suddenly realizing he and Giles were to be left alone.

"I had to keep him late," replied Flash Jack. "He will be here in a few minutes. And if he ain't, well, big boys like you won't come to harm. How old are you, anyway? Six and seven?"

"You know jolly well I am thirteen, sir," said Giles, flexing his strong young muscles and looking so like Nicholas that Rose's heart wept for what she could not have. "I'll look after the little boy," he said with Nicholas's teasing laugh and punched Joseph lightly in the ribs.

The carriages jostled cheerfully as they rattled along the road to the Residence. And then Flash Jack was handing her down and she made her way inside on his arm. As they approached the reception line, Rose's eyes swept over the tallest men, looking for Nicholas.

"Married ladies may dance, but they may not flirt," said a voice in her ear, and she looked up into Flash Jack's warning eyes.

"Oh, Alain," she whispered, "how wonderful you are to me. How kind."

"Remember that," he said in a low voice. "Try to remember that, will you, darling?"

"As if I could ever forget." Her heart thrilled to the excitement and the danger she had brought upon herself.

It was a magnificent ball, the first vice-regal milestone. Chieftains added a novel ingredient, their thick black hair and brown faces shining above their pristine, carefully folded stocks; their wives beaming, all dressed inexplicably in unrelieved white. Major Baker and other officers who had fought with the Royalists in Spain and Portugal displayed the glittering decorations bestowed upon them by grateful sovereigns. The 65th Regiment and HMS *Leander* had each supplied a band. The *salle de bal*, brilliant with the flickering golden flames from dozens of wax tapers, was a dazzling background for the dress uniforms of the army and naval officers.

There were so many gentlemen that they had to fight for dances, cheating audaciously, writing ladies' names on their programs where no promises had been made, swearing bold lies in order to dance.

"I declare I shall have a ship commandeered and filled with eligible young ladies who do not acquire a husband in the present London season," laughed the governor's lady, looking so happy with her new husband that all hearts warmed toward her, as they hardened against the scheming Lady Grey who had attempted to pack her off home.

With amazing dexterity, Nicholas rid himself of partners in excuse-me waltzes and swooped surreptitiously time and again. "You are to get a prize for being the best-dressed lady here," he whispered, looking black as thunder.

Rose fluttered her eyelashes at him. "You did not offer me the gift of a gown," she said. "And I could not conjure one out of thin air."

"And diamonds! Such a mystery you are," but she knew by the way he spoke that he had already quizzed Teresa in that regard. "This will indeed set the town agog."

She raised her head, the misery of the past months spinning away in a silvery cloud. The gesture went to his heart as no words could have done, and he remembered that night at the palace ball when he had looked at Cressida through narrowed eyes and a haze of champagne, thinking how Rose, given diamonds and silks, would dazzle and amaze. It has come to pass, he thought, his heart aching because it had not come to pass as he would have wished.

Mrs. Stokes, looking matronly and really rather grand in gray silk, caught Rose by the arm. "My dear, your husband has surely not broken his leg or the doctor would—"

"No. Oh, no." Rose flushed. "It is Mr. Wilshire's little joke."

"But it is not a joke, my dear," that good lady said gravely. "It is very wrong to say such things when they are not true." She glanced pointedly across at Flash Jack laughing uproariously at some man's joke. "And also what—"

"You must chastise Mr. Wilshire," said Rose in a rush, "if you do not approve." And then she took refuge in an air of dignified detachment.

Mrs. Stokes looked at her queerly, as though she had been uppish and rude. As perhaps I was, thought Rose, too excited and happy, too warm from Nicholas's arms to feel ashamed.

As they left the ball at sunup, Rose leaned back against the soft leather of the carriage seat, her eyes lifting to the handsome face above her. "How can I thank you, Alain? How can I ever repay you?"

He raised her hand to his lips, his eyes gentle yet at the same time bold. "I usually extract my pound of flesh," he replied.

She said boldly, "You give yourself that reputation. It is the secret of your power, is it not, Alain? I know that is what they say in the town, that you extract your pound of flesh, but I have not heard of you doing it."

His eyes flicked over her, settling on her face with a hungry look that set her heart fluttering. "How you prattle on."

"I should, I suppose, have a conscience about Daniel," she said, speaking quickly, nervously, flicking her fan. "Have you a conscience, Alain?"

He pretended to think for a moment. "No," he said slowly. "Not really. Well, only for everyday use. For special occasions, no, I don't believe I have." And then he leaned down and kissed her, astounding and terrifying her.

"I love you, Rose," he said. "I have loved you for twelve years, give or take a month or two."

She was shocked into silence, knowing suddenly that this was what he had meant when she had asked him— begged him—to take her to the ball. "May it be on your own head," he had said and, foolishly, she had convinced herself he meant she would bring yet another flood of scandal down.

To her surprise he did not kiss her again, only held her hand on his knee, patting it in a thoughtful way. When they arrived at Aurora House he lifted it to his lips. "Sleep well, sweet Rose." Then he sent the carriage on its way and escorted her to the door. Just when she was wondering breathlessly what he was going to demand of her, with a courteous little bow he turned and disappeared into the night.

The rest of 1853 was as gay in Wellington as it was in the capital. Two of Mr. Sheridan's plays were performed in the new playhouse. Sir George and Lady Grey visited. There were dinners and concerts, informal poetry readings, and weekly At Homes at Government House, gracefully presided over by the First Lady of the south. Haydn's symphonies were well played by local talent; there were beautiful quartets for male voices and dancing for the more energetic.

At thirteen, Giles was a tall, strong boy. Rose saw little of him. There were too many reasons why he should not come home. Handsome as a god in Nicholas's image, he spent all his term-time in the classroom at Rata Hill, and all his holidays helping on the property.

"I can always use an extra hand," Nicholas said, and that had to do for both Cressida and Rose. After a day mustering sheep or shooting wild pigs, the boy was too tired, Nicholas said, for the long ride home. He now had a bedroom of his own in the homestead, and most of his wardrobe was there.

Only once had Rose protested, and Giles's answer silenced her with the cruelty of his indifference. "It is where I belong," he said. Yet, she knew he did not love Nicholas. She knew that as surely as she knew Giles was his son. The tie that welded man and boy together was a double-edged one, with pride in the flowing loops. But the love that sustained the knot went one way: from Nicholas.

Teresa came to see Rose often. She brought her little boy, Flash Jack's godchild, and the baby girl for whom Cressida stood godmother. She came in a cloud of happiness, walking on air. "Who would have thought, when I ran from Cheney in New South Wales, that there was so much happiness in store?"

Mrs. Stitchbury came to Rata Hill bringing her five boys. She had not seen another white woman for twelve years. It did not worry either lady that there was lttle—often no—help in the house.

"What a waste of our newfound accomplishments it

would be," Teresa said, "if we were to stand around with our noses in the air giving orders to servants."

One day she told Rose, "Our flash cousin is building two cottages on the estate. Daniel is to work on them. I would like him to stay."

"I doubt he would." The ill feeling engendered in him by her going with Flash Jack to the Residency had fed upon itself. She was afraid of Daniel now. Looking into Teresa's eyes, she saw that her friend knew and was concerned.

She was right in assuming Daniel would not move in with Teresa and her husband. Every morning he rose early and, sitting awkwardly on old Screw, went off to Kauri Creek. In the evenings he was tired and bad-tempered. Several times, when his mount was frightened by a gun or the squawk of a parakeet, he was thrown. The mare, who could always raise energy when she wanted to, would trot home, leaving Daniel to walk.

"Don't you think you should accept Teresa's offer to stay on the estate?" Rose asked with concern on one such evening, when Daniel arrived home dusty and bruised.

"Think I'm goin' ter leave yer ter whore with yer fancy men?"

The long, drowsy days of summer had brought back more of Rose's strength, and with it the spark that lit her old willful spirit. "Why should you begrudge others what you don't want?" she said. But she said the foolish words in jest, without malice, for there had never been any malice in her. Daniel came at her like a charging bull, head down, as he had done the day Charlie died, all the hurt in him bursting out in an uncontrolled and uncontrollable act of fury and much needed revenge. She opened her mouth on a scream of terror that was stopped by his fist.

That night it rained in torrents. The pain raging in her head kept Rose awake for hours. Next morning, the house was silent except for the rain drumming on the roof. Her fingers crept up to her left eye. The skin felt puffy over the painful bruise. Across the room the door was moving faintly. She thought in a rush of panic that another earthquake had arrived. And then, lowering her eyes, she saw Joseph standing just inside the room, with his foot in the door, watching her sorrowfully.

He came timidly over to the bed. "I made you some tea," he said. "And toast. But it's got cold. I'll make some more." A rush of love and gratitude swept through her and she held out her arms. He bent his rough head awkwardly, resting it on her breasts, and then his young arms came around her."

Flesh of my flesh, at last.

"What would I do without you, Joseph," she whispered, kissing him with the light little butterfly kisses he had seen her bestow on Lance. When he drew away, his eyes were moist, his face flushed. If there was a hint of embarrassment in his manner there was also a special joy.

They were there together, Joseph sitting on the bed, sharing the burned toast and the very black tea he had made, when a great thumping sounded at the front door. Joseph scurried out. Rose could hear the murmur of low voices in the hall, then silence. She was drifting into a state of mental torpor akin to sleep when there came a tapping at the door. She opened her one good eye.

Flash Jack came in, treading lightly for so large a man. He stood looking down at her, his face crisscrossed with some turbulent emotion held powerfully in check. "I'll get Dr. Stokes," he said. "Joseph is collecting Daniel's things. I'll take them to Kauri Creek." He hesitated, then added, "That's what I came for, anyway. Daniel hasn't been doing a proper job with all this riding back and forth. With the rain added . . ." His voice trailed off. He turned, as though unable to trust himself to say anymore, and walked out of the room.

Alone again, Rose lay gazing at the ceiling feeling drained. So Flash Jack was taking over. There was help at hand. Wondering where Flash Jack and Joseph had gone she drifted into much needed sleep.

48

That evening, when Cressida went into the big kitchen to congratulate Cook on the dinner, one of the hands was there.

"So late?" she remarked with a smile.

"He's been into town," offered Cook. "On account of the rain, 'e couldn't do no mustering as was arranged. 'E's got bad news, Lady Cressida. We was wondering what ter do about it. Master Giles—"

"What do you mean? Giles is in the drawing room, playing cribbage with my husband." Cressida looked sharply from one concerned face to the other.

"Mr. Putnam's dead, m'Lady. Went orf to work this mornin' on 'orseback, and the 'orse arrived 'ome with 'is saddle swingin' underneath 'im. Mr. Wilshire found 'im lyin' with 'is face in a puddle in the road. Knocked out from 'is fall, they think, and drowned in the . . ."

Cressida bit back hysterical laughter at the sublime suitability of Daniel Putnam's death. Drowned with his nose in a puddle! Then terror came creeping. She turned to the man who had brought this suddenly unacceptable piece of news.

"Are you . . . ?" she managed at last, "are you sure?"

"Quite sure, m'Lady."

"I'll tell my husband," she said in a strange, high voice.

As she went back down the passage she heard the rustle of whispering, then Cook's voice saying loudly, deliberately, as though they realized she would have heard the whispering, " 'Ere you are, Bob. I've kept yer dinner . . ."

She never knew how much people suspected.

She stood in the hall beside the grandfather clock, beneath the heads of the biggest boars Nicholas had killed and the crossed guns that had killed them, and she felt a trembling start deep down in her, spreading until it seemed to be shaking her like a dog with a rat. Outside the dark was racing up the valley. With a sharp jerk the curtains flew inward, flapping, jerking. She went, without realizing that she moved, to close the window.

It was a long time before the shaking stopped. She did not go into the drawing room, though it was time to announce Giles's bedtime. The girls had been hustled off by Nurse an hour ago. Nicholas never interfered with their upbringing but with Giles it was different. "Good heavens, m'Lady," he would say tersely, "the boy is nearly fourteen. Almost a man." He was shortly going to be as tall as Nicholas, and as strong.

Cressida went numbly up the wide staircase and into their room. She looked at the big four-poster where they slept separately, one on either side. Then she went over to the dressing table and stared at herself in the bluish, shadowy glass with its silver frame. Before dinner she had felt an elegant matron, carrying her thirty-four years well. Now she looked old, and afraid.

From a satinwood chest she took the lacy nightgown Felicity had sent her for Christmas. She had not worn it before, deeming its pretty extravagance unsuitable, in the circumstances that Nicholas would not notice. She undressed, brushed her hair into curls around her face, and spread it silkily over her shoulders. Then she went to the vase on the little table in the corner, and picking a pink petal smoothed it over her lips and cheeks.

When Nicholas came yawning to bed she was sitting up against the pillows with the neck of her lacy gown drifting loosely around her breasts. She smiled at him, copying the way that woman had smiled at Teresa's wedding and the governor's ball. She tucked in the corners of her lips, seductively fluttering her lashes, feeling cheap, almost like a woman of the streets.

Nicholas's eyes caressed her white flesh, drifting curls,

and then her unspoken invitation swept him forward with lust, and the small flowering of love that could so easily lift its frosted head when Cressida reminded him of Rose. This time it did not die. Cressida raised an arm with a faintly voluptuous gesture, and he flung his clothes to the floor. She smiled bravely over her distaste at seeing him naked: all of him crudely, offensively, exposed. She tried to keep her eyes at shoulder level as he came toward the bed.

Then he was snuffing out the candle and saying in a hoarse, urgent voice, "Take this thing off."

Later, looking up at the shadowed ceiling with the moonlight filtering through the curtains, Cressida said softly, "It's not too late to hope for a son."

"No, I suppose not."

As he was drifting into sleep, his breath coming evenly, the fear came creeping again. With a feeling of disgust, she slid her hand down his belly. "Love me again," she whispered, and then as he came vibrantly alive, she pulled him to her, shivering at the disagreeableness of what she had to do. Surprised, sleepily excited, Nicholas mounted her again, thinking that perhaps, after all, it was not too late for her to change.

"Please, God," she whispered in her heart, "send us a son."

Again, it was a small funeral. Flash Jack came to support Rose and gave Daniel's workmates the day off, asking them to attend. Rose felt nothing more than relief that at last Daniel, who had made so much possible, had gone where she could not hurt him anymore.

They laid him beside Charlie, who lay beside Lance, among the new graves in the little town cemetery. Nicholas came, but there was no way they could be alone. He sat by himself at the service, but stood between Giles and Joseph at the graveside, while Flash Jack held Rose's arm with a proprietary air. He was thinking helplessly, but with enormous compassion, that Cressida had known of Daniel's death that night she had flattered and warmed him by taking the initiative, and asking, for the first time, that he should love her. Everyone was glad when the discomfort was over and they could go home. Rose was aware that no one mourned Daniel, though Teresa shed a tear or two. Mr. Alexander looked more worried than sad.

The next day Nicholas came riding up to Aurora House. Rose was sitting alone in Grandy's little shrine. She watched him come along the path, her heart fluttering, but she did not move. He stood before her, looking down. "The house is yours," he said. "And I shall open an account for you at the bank. You will always have enough to live on."

"Oh, Nicholas."

He sat down beside her and took one of her hands. "Fourteen years," he said. She smiled sweetly up at him, remembering how she had prayed every night. Now she had prayed away half the hurdle that lay between them.

He said, "The Maoris are saying Flash Jack moved Daniel's face into the puddle when he was unconscious. I think it is possible. In some mysterious way, they do tend to know everything, and get it right."

She felt the shock go right through her, then guilt rose up, flinging everything else away as she recalled asking Flash Jack to take her to the ball. "Remember Proclamation Day? What might come of this?" he had asked quizzically.

She had said, batting her eyelashes, "You went to so much trouble to get me the gown. Would you have it wasted?"

"Ah, you have a dangerous way with you," had been his reply. "Men are but weak creatures. Yet they can be dangerous, too." She had tossed the threat away on a puff of wind because the promise of dancing again with Nicholas, of looking beautiful in the silk gown, was more than she could resist.

"Of course, it isn't true," she cried now, leaping to her feet, her face peaked and white, her lips puffed with indignation. "Flash Jack is not a murderer."

Nicholas did not reply, and she knew he was thinking, as she was thinking, that he could be.

That night, when Cressida put her arms around Nicholas, he turned away. "I am tired," he said. But he did not sleep, nor did she. After a while he knew she was crying. He rose and went downstairs. He poured himself a brandy and sat gazing into the empty fireplace.

Flash Jack waited a full month before proposing. He

came to the door one blustery August evening that was full of winter dark with rain clouds scudding across the sky. He brought a handsome outfit for Joseph, who had at last begun to grow and was streaking out of his clothes.

"Your mother must be tired of looking at those bony wrists and ankles of yours," he said. "Take these things away, boy, and try 'em on."

For Rose, he had one of the new shallow bonnets that fastened with a tiny burst of flowers beneath the chin, a velvet riding habit, a calling costume with an enormous hooped skirt, and a fringed shawl coat of unbelievable beauty.

She sat on the edge of her chair, looking at him with wide, scared eyes, remembering what Nicholas had said, telling herself feverishly that it must be untrue. "Alain, you are so kind. But you know I cannot wear these. Not yet."

He dropped his long frame into one of the bigger chairs. "You have never worried about what people say," he replied, as Oliver had said after Lance died, adding, "Why start bad habits at your age?"

"Even I know I must conform in this. It does not hurt me to show respect for Daniel's memory. I do not pretend to be brokenhearted. But I must show respect."

"You must have come to hate him in the end."

"He never dealt out more than I deserved," she replied in a small voice, looking down at the embroidery on the shawl, fingering it, thinking that quixotic fate, with all its cruelties, had never begrudged her a pride in her appearance. Her smile was wistful as well as fearful when she raised her head. "I have been lucky in so many ways. He could have turned against me earlier."

A great whoosh of rain swept across the darkened windows. They both looked up, startled, and Rose shivered. "What a dreadful night!"

He was examining something he had taken from his pocket, shielding it with his hands. "And what are you to do now, Rose?" he asked, without looking up.

"I have the house. I may stay here as long as I wish." Forever. She knew she would never leave while Nicholas was at Rata Hill.

"And how will you live?"

"I have enough to keep us going. But I should like to

do something." She looked down nervously at the fringe,
tugging it, letting it go.

"Work?" His head came up.

"Why not?"

"What would you do?" He smiled, humoring her.

"I don't know. I don't know what I could do. I would
like to open a school, but I have not the necessary
qualifications. Giles told me that one of the ladies who
came out on *Aurora,* Mrs. Maxwell, whom I knew briefly,
has started a hospital in the north. But I suppose her
husband has the money to build it. It seems she felt as I
do—grateful for what this country has given her. She is in
touch with Mrs. Elizabeth Fry, who is Mr. Wakefield's
cousin, for advice on health problems. Our governor
also, it seems, asks Mrs. Fry for advice on behalf of the
Maoris." She was prattling, she knew, inanities that would
not interest him.

"Aye," growled Flash Jack. "He would do better to
take an interest in the welfare of his own countrymen."

"I do not know about that." Rose again ran her fingers
through the shawl's fringe, lifting the silken threads, feeling them slide away, gripping them again. "I do not
mean I could start a hospital, even had I the money.
Kororareka showed me how poorly I react to the sight of
blood. It is the 'giving back' I am thinking of. I have had
so much from life. So much."

Flash Jack rose and slowly crossed the room. His enormous shadow flattened itself darkly against the wall as he
stood at the rain-lashed window looking out. Then he
turned. With a quick glance down at whatever it was he
held in his hand, he said, "I have work for you."

"Yes?" She looked up sunnily, expectantly. It could
not be true what Nicholas said. Alain was so kind. Had
always been kindness itself, to everyone.

"Would you care to look after me?"

"Housekeeper?" Momentarily, a light flashed in her
green eyes, then she laughed softly, indulgently. "I have
always understood you have a native housekeeper, Alain.
Is that not so?"

They stood smiling at each other, then when he did not
answer, her brow puckered and she glanced away. "It is
only a rumor," she said uncomfortably. "Gossip. It does
not signify."

He came back across the room, and now what he held in his right hand glittered in the lamplight. She had to arch her neck to look into his palm. A ring set with a great ruby, surrounded by enormous diamonds, that winked coldly in the soft glow of the lamp. He lifted her left hand and slid away the thin band that the Rundull curate had supplied all those years ago, then tossed it carelessly onto the table. It tinkled to the floor and came to rest beneath a chair. "Let me put this in its place," he said, already sliding the ruby home.

Rose's eyes were like those of a cat in the dark.

"Did it not occur to you that I would wish to marry you?" he asked. "I told you once I loved you. You must remember that."

"I thought you knew I loved Nicholas." Her voice was barely above a whisper.

"You cannot have him." Flash Jack spoke with soft violence. "You know that."

"But I cannot let him go."

"Are you saying you will go on living here, taking his money, until there is no doubt in anyone's mind what his poor wife suffers?" He put a forefinger beneath her chin, lifting her face so that she had to look at him. "You who are so thoughtful, Rose. So kind. Would you do that to another human being?" He added harshly, "You cannot go on having babies when there is no husband to shield you." He dropped his hand, but he did not move away.

She stared down at the great, glowing ruby.

At last he said persuasively, "As my wife you would have everything."

She nodded, thinking, Everything but Nicholas. If she married Flash Jack, she knew she would never be alone with Nicholas again. And anyway, she would always have in the back of her mind what Nicholas had said. That Flash Jack had moved Daniel's head into the water when he was stunned.

There was no work for Rose. She was too much of a lady, and too comfortably situated, for menial work, but not enough of one for committees.

Christmas came and went. It was a quiet time for Rose. People were kind, but they did not expect her to join in the jollifications. She and Joseph went to Kauri

Creek for a few days. Though the heat was exceptional
Teresa roasted a goose. They had plum pudding with
brandy sauce and lots of cream. Joseph and the little
Alexander boy were sick.

"It is what Cook would have produced at home,"
Teresa said. "We must not lose the old traditions. Yet
these summer festivals give me a feeling of living back-to-
front."

Their visits to Kauri Creek were a delight. Rose, Teresa, and the children would walk beside the water, watching the wild ducks. Occasionally, Mr. Alexander would
accompany them with his water spaniel and his gun. The
young ducks were a delicacy, though the flesh of the
older ones could be tough.

It was a strange time. Rose was made aware of her
desirability by small gestures shrouded in tact. Bachelors
would drop in at Aurora House, alleging they were "just
passing." Women advised her to take her time and choose
carefully. She spent a great many hours on her own,
riding Bonnie, who had come back from Rata Hill as
Beatrix had another pony now, and working in her garden. One of the bachelor settlers brought a spade and
dug her a flower bed. "Now that you have no husband to
do the work for you, it's up to strong men like me to
help," he said. Rose grew panicky, seeing through their
good nature to a building up of the kind of debt she had
incurred with Flash Jack Wilshire.

Nicholas came, though only as often as he had come
before. The great ruby lay on the mantelpiece. "What's
this?" he asked, picking it up.

"Alain gave it to me."

Nicholas stood kicking the toe of his riding boots against
the fender, staring into the big fireplace that was heaped
with ferns. "Cressida is pregnant," he said at last.

"I know."

There was a long silence. "Wilshire is building a great
mansion."

"I cannot . . ."

They moved together, his arms coming around her.
They stood holding each other, their hearts beating as
they always beat, as one. He stayed all that afternoon,
longer than he had ever stayed before. Joseph came in

and joined them. He seemed to be growing less like Daniel every day.

"How are you getting on at school, Joseph?"

Joseph looked at Rose with a deprecating smile. "I am working, now. Working hard."

"He got a prize for having made the greatest progress last term," Rose said proudly.

"And what about riding?"

"I don't like horses."

"Oh, well," said Nicholas good-naturedly, "some people don't." A moment later he added, "But you mustn't think of the horse as killing your father. It's fear of horses that kills. If he had learned to ride properly he would not have been thrown. He didn't want to learn. He sat on the horse. Simply sat. Horses don't respect such people."

The next day, Joseph said diffidently, "If you're going riding, I'd like to come with you."

Rose smiled warmly at him and he smiled back. His eyes were direct now. She realized with surprise that Daniel's look, that of being in this world on sufferance, had not been permanently a part of Joseph's features.

Early in March Dr. Stokes put Cressida to bed. "You're worrying," he said. "What on earth have you got to worry about?"

Cressida looked apologetic. "I'll try not to."

"Do you know what is the matter?" Dr. Stokes asked Nicholas. "She wants the child, doesn't she?"

"Very much."

"My wife says she talks obsessively about going home. What's that about? Are you thinking of tossing all this in?"

"No. Of course not." He frowned. Cressida had said nothing to him about going home.

"Hmn." They were standing in the big hall. The doctor looked around at the boars' heads and the guns. Like a dog sniffing a scent, he sensed a change in the atmosphere. There was a stagnant feeling here. He said, staring at the ceiling, "It's about time little Mrs. Putnam got married, wouldn't you say, and put all those bachelors out of their misery?" He frowned at Nicholas from beneath lowered, bushy brows.

"That's her business." Nicholas spoke curtly.

"Is it? I'm talking about putting people's minds at ease. Oh, well," said the doctor. "Women sometimes turn queer in pregnancy. Try and help her, le Grys. Try and help."

A week later Cressida took a turn for the worse. The doctor brought a change of clothes and night attire. Giles stayed, too, at Nicholas's request. That evening Nicholas was pacing up and down the veranda, deeply disturbed by Dr. Stokes's latest news, when Giles came to join him.

"What's the matter? You look upset."

"The baby could die," said Nicholas.

There was a sudden stillness about Giles that was uncanny. Nicholas waited for him to speak. He went on staring out across the valley, a remote expression in his eyes.

Nicholas's blood sang in his head and his fingers curled in his palms. He had thrashed Giles twice. He remembered both times. Giles had not cried out. He had not even run away. He had looked at Nicholas with that particular stillness. Rose had been right. Giles was every inch a Rundull. Every drop of blood in him was Rundull blood. And the young bastard was standing there now, willing his heir to die. Nicholas swung around and strode into the withdrawing room, slamming the door behind him.

The next day a ship came, bringing the English post. The Dragon put the letters on a table, the great pile of papers in the hall. She said to Nicholas, "Things are bad. Do you think the girls should go to Mrs. Alexander, sir?"

"Perhaps." For once he did not feel like making decisions. "If they want to."

He heard the bustle of small feet, the hushed, childish voices. They came to the door and, standing very erect as they had been taught, said politely, "Good-bye, Papa." Beatrix added, "Giles is taking us to Aunt Teresa."

He nodded, thinking how pretty they looked. He watched the pony cart roll away down the grassy track. They turned to wave, and he waved back.

After a while he went in to look at the mail. There was so much of it he scarcely knew where to start. He slid aside a fat envelope with an official-looking seal, hesitated over letters in the handwriting of Cressida's mother and her sisters. There was one for him in the bold hand of the Dowager. Nothing from Henry. There never had been. Only that cold missive saying his allowance had been canceled. He extracted an envelope addressed in Lady Woolege's handwriting and went slowly upstairs. He tapped at the door. Nurse came to open it. She looked more distressed than ever.

Cressida was lying still, her face as pale as the pillow, her eyes wide and full of pain. He brushed the soft hair back from her forehead with the fingers of his free hand. "I'm sorry," he said. She made no effort to reply. "There are letters for you. Would you like me to read out the one from your mother?"

Her lids flickered, her face contorted, and she cried out. When the pain was over she nodded faintly.

He slit the envelope.

" 'My darling Cressida,' " he read, then broke off, his face stiffening with shock, his eyes flying over the page. "The Taylor boys . . . determined . . . unfortunate . . . pitch dark . . . must have been waiting for Henry and the boy . . . terrible . . ." He looked up, blinked, looking back at the page with disbelief. "Odd that the clock always stops . . . dreadful . . ." The words danced before his eyes, gathering speed until he could not read them at all. He blinked. "Glad . . . home . . . mourning . . . Her Gracious Majesty . . ."

"What's wrong?" Cressida looked alarmed.

Once more, he lifted his eyes from the page, feeling numb, suddenly remembering the big envelope with the official-looking seal that had come with the mail. "They're dead," he said.

"Who is dead?" She began to cry weakly.

Dr. Stokes hurried forward. "Old chap . . ."

"I'm sorry," said Nicholas, wiping a hand across his brow, feeling shaky and strange.

"Mother? Mother is dead?" Cressida was sobbing now.

"No," he cried. "Henry and the boy. Henry and the boy!" His head spun with shock and triumph. With the glittering sight of the goal around which his whole life had webbed. "Rundull," he said, seeing in his mind's eye the soft green meadows, the castle with its sun-washed stone, "is mine."

It was the doctor who said gently, "Lady Cressida, do you realize you can go home now? As soon as this little lot is over, you can go home."

It was not so easy. All that afternoon and evening the pains came, appallingly close together. Nobody had any sleep. Giles returned and sat with Nicholas. He had not opened any more of the letters. Not even the big one that was addressed to The Right Hon. The Earl of Rundull. He did not tell Giles what had happened. As he grew more tired and more worried he began to think he had imagined it. Occasionally they dozed. Sometimes they were awakened by a scream. Many times—he lost count of how many—he walked to the top of the stairs and stood on the landing for a while, not thinking, just staring at the closed door.

All next day they waited, and the next. Cressida was growing weaker.

That evening the doctor told him, "You had better come and sit with her. There's nothing more I can do. The pains have stopped, but only because the baby is dead, I'm afraid."

"That means . . ."

"Go and see her, old chap. Sit with her."

Nicholas went upstairs with leaden feet and crossed the room. Cressida seemed shrunk into the pillow, her face strange. He leaned over her, saying uselessly, "We're going home."

She was looking at him with a world of defeat in her pale eyes. She whispered something. He had to bend right over to catch her words. "I had . . . so much . . . love . . . to . . ."

Oh, God! He passed a hand across his eyes. "I am sorry," he blurted out.

Her fingers closed over his. He felt scalding tears prick at his eyes, then roll heavily down his cheeks. One fell on her hand. She caressed the damp patch with fingers grown weak, then her face smoothed out, and there was a kind of serenity there.

After a while, Dr. Stokes said, "I'm sorry, old chap. I'm sorry." And again, "There was nothing I could do." A little later, he leaned forward and drew the sheet up over Cressida's head.

It was of course not possible for Rose to go to the

funeral. When Flash Jack arrived in a buggy an hour before the service, she stared at him in astonishment.

"Of course you have to go," he said. "You are Lady Cressida's sister, are you not? People will expect you to be there, crying your eyes out."

Unnerved, she cried angrily, "Everyone knows Lady Cressida did not recognize me."

"Ah, but they will appreciate your forgiveness," he drawled. "Get into your widow's weeds, my dear. Black is highly flattering to your complexion. You were quite at your best at Daniel's funeral." A malicious tenderness gleamed in his eyes. She looked at him bleakly without moving, until he gave her a sharp little push. "Go and get dressed. There is little time to spare."

In the bedroom she pulled out a drawer and lifted the ugly black gown that was Charlie's death and, agonizingly, Lance's going; Daniel's; a garment of a thousand miseries. She shook out the folds and proceeded to dress, her fingers fumbling with the buttons, her mind scattering around the confusion of Flash Jack's intentions. Of course he realized she would be able to marry Nicholas now, and that would scarcely please him. But why should he bully her like this? Yet, she understood that his cruelty was a part of his caring. It was true, she should appear at Lady Cressida's funeral, more particularly because she was shortly going to take her place. Rose tossed her head with her old willfulness. There was going to be talk anyway.

When she emerged, Flash Jack was standing in the doorway looking impatient. "Come on," he said and walked ahead of her to the buggy. As they settled into the seat, she looked timorously up at him. She remembered that someone had once said, "He is a good friend but a bad enemy." Well, she thought with relief, she would have Nicholas to look after her soon.

It seemed the entire colony had turned out for the funeral. Mr. Eyre was there with his pretty wife, looking sad in her black gown. Everyone draped in black like a flock of crows, Rose thought, stifling an irreverent giggle that had nothing to do with laughter. Flash Jack led her to a pew embarrassingly near the front of the church, walking tall with his head held high, ignoring or not hearing her whispered protests. "Not up in front, please,

Alain." She sat stiffly with eyes downcast while the crowd found seats. Then a patter of footsteps, faster, younger, lighter than the rest, made her look up to see the daughters who would be hers, and she found herself staring with unbearable terror into the shocked face of a woman, like a battleship in black, with a great stiff prow. What poise Rose still had left her then as she remembered being hauled out of bed and escorted from Cavendish Square to Penbridge, like a prisoner, all those years ago. The woman's shock appeared equal to her own, but her outrage was paramount. Rose looked pitifully up into Flash Jack's face for help. He was staring straight ahead, but she was sure he was aware of her distress.

Then Nicholas came in, his head bent. Rose was stunned to see the deeply etched lines in his face, the aftermath of shock in his eyes. He, too, moving along the pew, met her eyes. Then he seemed to shrink within himself.

The congregation rose to its feet and the service began. Rose's buttoned-down hysteria turned blessedly to a kind of numbness. Flash Jack put a hand over both of hers, clamping them down, and she realized she had been winding her lace handkerchief around the third finger of her left hand; winding it, tugging it, undoing it, winding it again, until her finger was patched white and red.

After the service, after the graveyard, everyone stood around making small talk. A woman said, as no one had dared say in Cressida's lifetime, "You were related to her, were you not, Mrs. Putnam? There is a certain resemblance."

Rose looked up at Flash Jack for help, but he only looked back at her enigmatically, as though he, too, was waiting to hear her reply. Then Teresa grasped her hand, saying, "She is upset, Mrs. Cooper, and I am sure does not wish to talk. Come, Rose." She led Rose through the crowd to her own gig, and Mr. Alexander helped her up. Rose was aware of Flash Jack's having followed them, but slowly, with a long, idle stride, as though he had only to ensure Rose was on her way, and in good hands.

Nobody spoke as they clattered off down the road. Without being invited, Teresa and her husband came inside. "I want you to pick up some things and come home with us," Teresa said.

Rose toyed with the strings of her bonnet, wanting to

get out of the horrid black clothes. "That's very kind of you, but I'd rather not." She added evasively, "There's Joseph . . ." thinking she must be here when Nicholas came.

"Joseph and Giles, too. Just for a few days." Teresa sounded nervous.

Rose smiled and took her hands. "If you are thinking that Nicholas will come here and people will talk, what does it matter?"

"I simply think you should come to Kauri Creek," Teresa replied, sounding sharp.

Rose's mouth tightened obstinately.

Teresa, looking suddenly helpless, nodded to her husband, and he left the room. "Rose, dear," she said, "there is something I must tell you. The town will know directly. I would not like you to hear . . ." She looked upset. "There has been a tragedy at Rundull and Nicholas . . . well, Nicholas is now the earl."

Rose gazed at her blankly.

"Do you understand, dear?"

Rose said through stiff lips, "His brother . . ."

"They were both killed. Henry and his son. Some people from the village, some people whom you may know, called Taylor, who held a grudge . . . Quite deliberate murder, it seems and . . . well, you must understand," Teresa's voice softened, "Nicholas has to go back to Kent."

She was without breath. Without even the ability to stand. She began to laugh, then to choke. She went on staring at Teresa, her eyes seeming to grow too wide, all the horror and shock cruelly exposed.

"But I cannot go to Rundull," she said pitifully.

"I know, dear. I know." With deep compassion Teresa led her to the sofa and sat down beside her. "Let's talk."

There was nothing to talk about. Rose went on staring, naked eyed, empty hearted, trying to come to terms with the fact that in spite of the fighting, the plotting, the praying, the yearning, she had, after all, lost.

Teresa's husband brought her a cup of tea, but she could not drink it. Distressed, Teresa asked, "Do you think, after all, you should go for Nicholas?"

Mr. Alexander shook his head. "Not today. No, not today, my dear." He looked as though he wished fervently they had left well alone. Teresa begged Rose again to go with them to Kauri Creek, but she would not.

"Take Joseph," she said, knowing Giles would want to stay at Rata Hill. Perhaps something would come out of being alone. They left with many protestations. It was easier to think, then. To look at what had happened. A murder for a murder, she thought in anguish. Ned Taylor avenged so that Nicholas could go back home. And he would take Giles. She knew without being told that Giles would go.

On a certain level Rose was ready when at last Nicholas came. She met him at the front door and led him inside. She said in a high but sternly controlled voice, "You don't have to tell me. I know what has happened. I had no right to love you. It is a pity I could not have seen it before. But then"—her mouth twisted in a travesty of a smile—"I suppose one could say I have had a good deal of happiness along the road. Having Lance, for a while. Having Giles, for a while." Her voice trembled. "Sometimes, having you. It just seems rather strange," she said, picking at the lace on her wrist, "that I could not have seen, in the beginning, that what I . . . seemed to . . . have, to h-have . . . was not meant for me. I've done . . . so much damage. So much damage to so many people. I see it quite clearly, now."

Nicholas stepped forward, protesting. "Rose . . ."

She backed away from him, lifting a hand. "No. Don't come near." She meant, Don't break down this wall I have built up to hide behind until I am as strong as I am pretending to be. Aloud she said, "It is all over. You have won, because you come from the kind of family that wins. I have lost, because I come from losing folk. Mr. Wakefield, in his vision of a new land with opportunity for everyone, did not see that. But of course," she became lightly sarcastic, she who had never used sarcasm before in her life, "your mother was right. You may tell her she was right, after all." Looking down at her pretty gown and then around the perimeter of the well-furnished room, she added with a bitter little smile, "Tell her I have 'got on.' "

"Rose!" He spoke violently, stepping forward and holding out his arms, but quick as a cat she stepped aside.

"Oh, yes," she said, "it would be so easy to slip into bed with you. To spend every day and night with you until your ship sails. But still you would go. Perhaps you might even leave me with another little boy. But I would lose him. Oh, yes, I would lose him because—it has taken me fourteen years to see this, Nicholas, but I do see it now—I am not to have you, or anything of you. So go to your Rundull," she said, the despair and the anger at last breaking through, "for that is what you want, and it seems to me that is what you are allowed to have."

He looked down at her with bleak eyes, a stricken expression on his face. She turned away.

"Rose, I need you."

"We have always needed each other," she replied, still managing to stay calm, though it was all she could do to stop herself falling into his arms. "But we have no control. It is not you and I who decide what is to become of us." Suddenly her fury, her disappointment, her unbearable suffering burst out in a hoarse tirade, "So go to your old stones and your old land, if that is what you must have. If you have not enough intelligence to see that you have built up something here for yourself. *Yourself,* Nicholas, by the sweat of your brow and with your own hands. Something that is yours, yours, as Rundull never will be, never can be. Rundull," she said scathingly, "you really ought to be able to see, is merely stepping into dead men's shoes."

"Rose!"

She went swiftly out of the room, down the passage to the door, and held it open.

She thought he would never move. She stood like a statue, gazing sightlessly out into the garden and across to the steep green slope of the new town that had given her so much, yet could not prevent the past from taking it away. There was a small sound, as though Nicholas had begun to speak, but changed his mind. Then slow footsteps. She looked down at her slippers as he went past, leaving, after all, without a word.

Unable to stop herself, she looked up at his broad back as he reached the path, but he did not turn, and a moment later he disappeared behind the trees.

49

The days were cold and empty, each one as long as a week or a month of happiness. The seagulls swooped over the garden with sharp and lonely cries. "Yah-awk. Yah-awk." When Joseph had gone to sleep and the dark came thundering up to the windows, Rose was reminded that Charlie had lain in the bottom of the river, in darkness. Darkness had overwhelmed Lance, too, at the end.

She went to bed late because there was so much loneliness in the bedroom. It was hard to imagine that Daniel's baleful presence had been company, but it must have been. Even then she would read, loath to snuff the candle because of the memories that came in the black silence. She thought often about Giles's going, which was a part of the great emptiness in her heart. So much love had gone into Giles's upbringing. So much love filtered away into nothing.

When she took flowers to the cemetery she put some also on Lady Cressida's grave, though she could not have said why; except perhaps, because she had looked after Nicholas. Surprisingly, he had not sold Rata Hill. Perhaps it meant so little to him, Rose thought angrily, that he could simply walk away. They had left on the next ship that sailed.

Flash Jack, still cruelly bullying, had made her go to the quay to see the ship off. She was obliged to do it, he said, because of Giles. Yet Giles had given her a mere perfunctory kiss and then he was away, striding along the jetty in the wake of that woman, with Beatrix clinging to one arm and little Isobel to the other; all laughing and chattering with excitement. His sisters, as he said. He had fashioned them into sisters over the last few years.

Back at the house Flash Jack had stood by the mantel-piece looking down at her. "Do you not have any feeling for me?" he asked. "None at all? I always thought you loved me. You were so trusting of me, and so warm and affectionate. So apparently happy with me. I thought, if Daniel . . ." In his distress he floundered. "I mean, I was sure it was only because you were married. I felt you knew you could never have le Grys. I thought, I really thought, I had only to bide my time . . ." When Rose did not answer, because she could not, he shambled clumsily on, "Nobody expected Lady Cressida to die . . . But anyway, he's gone. Fifteen years," said Flash Jack with awe, "and you were beaten by a bloody earldom!"

"I never wanted to be an earl's wife." Rose added in a very small, very defeated little voice, "I only wanted Nicholas."

"Only Nicholas," he repeated heavily, and with venom kicked the fender.

"I have always loved you, Alain."

"Not that way," he said. "Not that bloody way. Not the way you love the horses and that damned bloody cat."

The freezing winter wind raged up across the Southern Alps, flinging fistfuls of hail at the little town, drenching it with rain. Rata Hill, Rose knew, had lost a great many spring lambs. That winter, the passion vine that grew over Grandy's little shrine died, and Rose wept. Every day it seemed to rain. The *punga* fronds hung drenched and sulky in the garden. The drip, drip, drip of the water from the roof said, "Gone. Gone. Gone."

She was embarrassed by the way men eyed her in the town. Several of them, with a singular lack of ceremony, proposed outright.

"You shouldn't be living on your own, Mrs. Putnam. And I need a housekeeper. I'd be good to the boy."

There were so many men desperate for wives. Nice men. Kind men. Men who had difficulty managing on their own. Men who wanted a family to replace the one they had left behind.

When, in the school holidays, Joseph went to sea with

Flash Jack, Teresa insisted Rose stay at Kauri Creek. She took the horses with her, and Edmund. One of Flash Jack's men came in to feed the chickens. She enjoyed the glees and the dancing. She received several proposals of marriage, but she did not mind. It was easier, in that lively atmosphere, to refuse gently and without causing offence.

"But you will have to marry someone," Teresa said kindly one day. "Even an independent lady like you needs a man to look after her."

"It's what everyone says."

"They say it because it's true, Rose. Life is a compromise, darling. And besides, my lovely flash cousin has built the most wonderful house for you. Every thinking person in the colony knows it is for you, and they are beginning to say you are ungrateful and hardhearted not to take it.

"Besides which, Joseph needs a father. You should think of the boy. They all say that. 'Every boy needs a father,' they say. And, oh, Rose, think of all the excursions you would have in his ships! To Sydney for clothes . . ." She flew at her guest, flinging both arms around her, contrite and concerned. "I am so sorry, darling. I did not mean to remind you. I wouldn't hurt you for the world, you must know." Teresa took a lace handkerchief from her pocket and wiped away a tear that was trembling on Rose's lashes.

They were silent for a while after that. Then Teresa said, "Nobody has everything. Cressida never had Nicholas. She was obliged to live with that right to the end."

There had been so many endings.

Mr. Eyre, succumbing to the pressures of his uneasy relationship with Governor Grey, had departed to govern Jamaica. Mr. Petre, who had brought the first steam engine to the colony, had been recalled to take over from his father as lord lieutenant of Essex. And now Governor Grey himself had gone after a farewell dinner for which tickets had to be hawked at half price. Government officials dared not stay away, but Judge Martin sent apologies, and many leading citizens were pointedly absent.

Although Grey was liberal in theory, he had proved far too autocratic in practice for the independent settlers over whom he ruled. His policy of protection for the

Maoris from his own countrymen, who only wanted an Englishman's idea of fair play, had made them hate him, too, in the end. They accepted Lieutenant Colonel Wynyard, his replacement, in polite silence, reserving their judgment. The pattern of governor-settler antagonism had gone on too long. Wynyard approached the challenge warily but with goodwill, fanning a wind of change.

One day, when Mrs. Stokes came to call on Rose, she said, "I have heard that Mr. Tompkins, who manages Rata Hill, has bought a farm of his own, and is having a house built on it. Have you heard from Lord Rundull if, after all, he proposes to sell?"

"I suppose he may as well," Rose replied dully. "Folk say it is not sensible to leave such a large estate. That an owner should be there."

"Oliver expressed surprise," Mrs. Stokes went on. "He said a man who knows enough to run such an estate in this country is going to want to own his own land. It is not as it was at home, where a manager is forced to remain a manager for want of opportunity. It did surprise him, too, that Mr. Tompkins has already saved enough money to put down on his own place, and Lord Rundull gone only a few months."

It was with a feeling almost of relief that Rose rode out to Rata Hill the next day. "When it becomes the property of another man," she thought, "all the ties, all the memories, will perhaps go. Then it may be possible for me to forget." As she approached the bottom of the garden she thought the house had an abandoned air. She dismounted and tied her horse to the fence.

The shrubs were overgrown. All the flowers had gone. She made her way through the rank grass that had been a lawn, and climbed the steps to the veranda. The curtains were drawn. She tried the door, and to her surprise found it unlocked. She went inside, wandering from room to room, drawing the curtains back, letting in the light. There was some furniture, but all the valuable carpets and pictures had gone. The air smelled musty and stale. She went through to the kitchen and out of the back door. A man was crossing the yard with a bridle in his hand. She spoke to him.

"Are you Mr. Tompkins?"

"No," the man replied. "He's away at his new property."

"Does he not manage Rata Hill anymore?"

"Not as you'd notice." The man laughed, but without humor. "He and his wife are camping at the new place. He rushes back here when he has to, just to keep things ticking over."

"Ticking over," Rose echoed incredulously. "By the way, I found the doors of the house unlocked."

He shrugged.

"Where are the rest of the staff?"

"Some have walked off. Some are helping Mr. Tompkins."

"Working for him and being paid by Lord Rundull?" asked Rose, outraged.

He nodded.

She said bleakly. "Perhaps you can tell me what has happened."

"My guess is Tompkins has borrowed money from the bank against his wages." The man came a step nearer and looked into her face. "Are you Mrs. Putnam?"

She nodded.

"You're a friend of the family, aren't you?"

"Yes," she said. "Yes, I am." Already she knew what she could do. "Please tell me your name."

"Redman, ma'am."

"Mr. Redman, would you be so kind as to find Mr. Tompkins and ask him to return, bringing the rest of the staff with him."

The man looked immeasurably relieved. "I'll be pleased to do as you say."

When he had ridden off down the road, Rose returned to the house. She went upstairs and down, opening all the windows and doors. The wind blowing up the valley swept through, bringing in sunlight. The house seemed to come alive. She stood in the hall looking up at Nicholas's trophies; great boars' heads that he had hunted and killed. There were faded patches on the walls where pictures had hung.

She thought of Teresa's wedding when she had walked through the house as a guest, trying to pretend that her presence was acceptable, feeling sorry for her hostess, knowing there was nothing to be done.

She thought of the years Giles had spent here, growing

up, from the time he was seven until they went away together when he was fourteen. So many memories. With a sigh she went back to the veranda and prepared herself to face Tompkins. I, she thought, with a little quiver of alarm, who have never given orders to anyone in my life, have suddenly come to this. She sat down on the wooden seat, pensive with the weight of the unexpected responsibility. I have learned so much over the years. I am sure it is not beyond me, she told herself.

"Us?" asked Joseph incredulously. "You and me moving to Rata Hill?"

"You will like it there," said Rose warmly. "I know it's a long way to ride to school, but you're a good rider now. And you could help on the farm at weekends. I am sure the hands would be pleased to have you."

Joseph glowed. "Do you think they would?"

"Of course." She clapped her hands, suddenly gay, almost excited about what she had to do. "Now you know where Sam Phelps lives. Go and find him. Ask him how soon he can move us up to the estate."

"Why are you doing this, Mama?"

She smiled at him and ruffled his hair. Joseph looked ready to purr like a cat. "I have some debts to pay," she said. She skipped across the room. "I think you might make a very good farmer, Joseph." He had grown tall in the past year. He was also much better looking, now that he held his head high and walked with pride.

"I think I might," agreed Joseph, grinning from ear to ear.

"Oliver will tell us what to do. I once did him a good turn. He is deeply in my debt. Everyone must pay their debts, Joseph. Never forget that. It is one of the rules. I am sure Mr. Alexander will be glad to offer advice as well."

Not for a long time had Rose felt such strength of purpose. Everything seemed to fall into place. The town, as word flew around, was indignantly behind her. Even Tompkins accepted her tyranny.

"Fair cop," he said gruffly and moved back into the cottage. The furniture from Aurora House was laughably inadequate in the big house, but they were able to furnish the rooms they needed. Rose worked all day every day, and gradually brought the garden back to order. Oliver found two single hands to replace those who had walked out in disgust at Tompkins's cheating. Rose enjoyed cooking for them on the big modern stove. They took Joseph out mustering when he was not at school. Joseph also took over the wood heap and the stables. He became a partner and a friend, as well as a son.

"Have you had an answer from Lord Rundull?" he asked one day.

"I did not write."

"What!"

She turned with an assumed casual air from Joseph's startled scrutiny. "I have really been too busy. Besides, I am certain all his friends will have done so." Nicholas had been gone nine months. It took four months to sail to England, and four months for mail to travel back. During the past three or four weeks a letter could have come. On a calendar on the kitchen wall, every day of every month since his sailing had been marked with a cross.

"Odd," Dr. Stokes had said last week, "that you have not heard from Rundull." He looked closely into Rose's face. "I cannot believe he does not write to you. You are teasing, are you not, Mrs. Putnam?"

She shook her head.

"Perhaps his letters have gone astray."

Rose did not mind the silence. Silence was kindly, safe, a form of hope. She lived in a kind of waiting calm. She had not prayed since God had so terribly, grievously, answered her last prayer, removing Lady Cressida with one hand and taking Nicholas, vengefully, with the other. Life has taught me many things, she thought now, but above all, that one may not tell Him what to do. And now I know about the land. I have done so little here, and yet I feel the tug of it. If he does not come back, at least now I will understand. And if he does, then I will have paid back, in the only way I can, for what he did for me.

One evening, Joseph, urged on by Rose, had ridden into town for a concert. She encouraged him to have interests outside the farm. She was sitting on the veranda dreaming, gazing down the long valley, feeling herself a part of the farm's growth. So much had been achieved with the help of her friends and her staff. My staff, she thought, and a little trill of self-deprecating laughter escaped her lips. It had been surprisingly easy to take over as mistress of Rata Hill. Tompkins, terrified of losing his job, which would mean also the loss of his bank loan and his newly acquired acres, treated her with immense respect. Rose felt a new kind of strength as she learned to shoulder the bigger responsibilities and handle the men. Oliver came over every week to advise her and talk to her manager, but he never diminished her by seeing Tompkins alone.

She had seen the estate right through its seasonal cycle now: from the lambing, to the shearing, the dipping, and the haymaking. All around her, climbing up the veranda posts, over the trellises, were late-flowering roses. It was autumn again and the garden was a riot of yellow chrysanthemums. The lawn, freshly scythed, was emerald-green from recent rains.

She closed her eyes and dreamed, as she dreamed every night, that Nicholas had come. The strength of her longing was so great that she started awake, imagining the sound of carriage wheels on the newly surfaced drive, and it was as though the spirit of Nicholas was there. Nicholas, dressed in a gray topper and braided frock coat. She sat quiet and still while the ghost came through the gate and strode across the lawn. Even when she heard footsteps on the veranda, she did not move, afraid to break the spell.

He walked right up to her, bent over, and took her hands, holding them warmly, firmly, and with infinite tenderness. "Rose, my darling," he said, "I have come back to you."

"Oh, Nicholas, is it really you?" But she knew it was. Knew by the pulsating life in his hands, the tenderness of his lips on hers.

Later, when the moon was high in the sky, bathing the valley in a pearly glow, Nicholas said, "Giles loves Rundull. Took to it like a duck to water." They meditated together on that, on the strangeness of a colonial boy not being a colonial boy at all. Not, anyway, under the skin.

Nicholas looked down at Rose with a whimsical, faintly wry expression. "It was odd, but I was the one who felt out of place. I missed the wind," he lifted his free hand, sensuously feeling it as it drifted up the valley, "and I missed Rata Hill. How I missed it," he said, his voice rough with emotion. "You were right, dear Rose. When I left Rundull I had never known what it was like to build something for myself. Going from here, I still had no real conception of what it had meant to me.

"Standing on the castle terrace looking down over those meadows that I had done nothing at all to earn, I suddenly realized that out here I had followed in the footsteps of the first Henry le Grys. I had built my own kingdom. Inheriting Rundull *was* like stepping into dead men's shoes. Your words kept flying through my mind. 'Dead men's shoes!' I found myself thinking. Giles can wear them, if that's what he wants."

"But he can't inherit."

"He can change his name to le Grys, and in fact has already done so, with my blessing. The servants know who he is. And yet . . ." Nicholas hesitated, then went on, laughing a little, "the moment we drove in through the gates Giles took on the mantle of the young master. The village, mysteriously, accepted him at his own valuation. It's odd," said Nicholas. "It does make you wonder about the workings of the universe when a genuine bastard is able to convince the world he belongs. Even my mother, especially the Dowager," he corrected himself, his voice faintly awed as though he had still not taken the matter in, "accepted him. William the Conqueror was a bastard, she reminded me. So I took the opportunity to remind her the Conqueror was the son of a tanner's daughter." He looked down into her face with a proud and loving smile.

"What did she say?"

"My proposal to marry you was, of course," said Nicholas tactfully, "a little closer to home. Do you realize, my dear Rose, that you are to be Lady Rundull? Had you thought of that? How the town will be around you like bees around a honey pot."

Rose started, flushing. Then she lifted her head with the new dignity that had come to her the day she sent Nicholas off to find out what his true values were. It had been the hardest thing she had ever done in her life. "I daresay I shall manage," she said. Then, reverting to the old Rose, she added wickedly, "Perhaps I shall be invited to go onto the Library Committee."

Nicholas grinned, "I, too, shall now take an interest in public affairs."

"Tell me what has happened to the girls." Beatrix and Isobel, who needed a mother, now.

"They went to Saxon Mote, but they'd like to come back, and I would like it, too. We grew close on the voyage. I found I liked having daughters. Would you mind?"

"Of course not. I'd love it." There was plenty of love for Nicholas's daughters: that which was lying dormant because Giles did not want it, and Lance did not need it anymore. "It will be good for Joseph to have sisters. He and I are friends, Nicholas. We have supported each other. That was something else I had to do. To learn to be a loving mother to Daniel's son. And working on the farm has been so good for him. It has made him feel important in his own right. All his life he has played second fiddle to Giles. Now it has come to him to be important in his turn."

"I am glad. Shall I tell you about Giles now, or would you rather not know?"

She caught her breath. "Do you want to tell me?"

"Yes. I believe I do," he said gravely. "This might be what you need to know. It may make you feel it was for the best that Giles should go."

She waited, faintly afraid.

"He knew about the hawthorn tree and the blacksmith. I don't know who told him. I didn't ask. One evening when we walked together by the river, he gestured toward the tree and laughed in my face."

Rose gripped her hands together.

"I told him what I had decided to do. That I would leave him there and get cousin Humphrey and his wife to take over. I said I'd thought it all out, and that you were only thirty-three, and there was plenty of time to produce a dozen heirs. I suggested that as Ned Taylor's death had been avenged, I might bring you back sometime, if we wished to come. If I wanted to leave Rata Hill. If not, perhaps our eldest son . . ." Nicholas fell silent. She waited, breath held, until he was ready to go on again.

"That evening, I went alone for a stroll by the river. I

was walking by that cursed tree when something whizzed
past my ear. I dived for cover and got away. I knew
immediately who it was had tried to kill me, and I knew
why."

Rose put a hand to her heart.

"I went back to the castle at a fast rate. It was dark but
I still knew the path like the back of my hand, as the boy
did not. I went into the hall and sat down in the big
chair. Remember the one, Rose, where I used to sit and
wait for you?"

She nodded. "Under the clock that stops when an earl
of Rundull dies."

"That's it. That is exactly it. Half an hour later Giles
came in, looking tousled, as though he had been searching through underbrush in the darkness, and still carrying
his gun. He didn't see me right away. He was looking
directly upward, at the clock."

It was a long time before either of them spoke. Nicholas was thinking of the statue the Taylor boys had demolished, and the curse that went with its destruction. Rose
was remembering that day on *Aurora* when Nicholas had
come to see his newborn son; recalling he had inferred
that the wild new land he did not want would be good
enough for his bastard. She had known then that Giles
would never forgive. And she had known throughout the
years, that he harbored that memory, waiting. To her
own surprise, she felt very little dismay. It was such a
long time since Giles had moved out of her orbit of
loving and caring. Since he—she could face it now—had
discarded her as being of no more use to him.

"I stayed only to thrash him," said Nicholas. His voice
was grim but he was laughing a little. "I am familiar
enough with the ruthless emotions that come with wanting to have Rundull by fair means or foul. He's a big lad.
Nearly as big now as I am, but I could still thrash him.
He didn't utter a sound." Nicholas fell silent. "Do you
think it possible that all the time he lived with us at Rata
Hill he hated me?"

She did not want to say it, but she knew, had always
known, that was so.

"I've put him in Eton College," said Nicholas. "The
aristocracy are sending their sons there now. I remembered something Jerningham Wakefield said to me when

I reminded him his father had run away from Westminster. He said, if I remember correctly, 'What do you know about the barbarism of a public school?' Something like that," said Nicholas. "So we will see what a little barbarism can do for a barbaric youth. Who knows but it may make a better Rundull of him."

He let go of Rose's hands and, leaning on the veranda rail, looked out across the moonlit hills. "It's not all mine yet. That's another thing I kept thinking about." He laughed, squaring his shoulders in that familiar way he had when a challenge presented itself. "I am going to have to fight the Land Courts."

She pressed his hand. "You will win. You have paid for your land, and you will win."

He felt the warmth, the encouragement inherent in her touch, and put his free hand over hers. "I've always felt the time would come, too, when we would have to fight the Maoris. They're quiet now, but they're not always going to remain so. I thought—I had a lot of time to think—why should they have the land I cleared simply to hunt over? Even by their rules it is mine for the mere fact of having cleared it. Anyway, when they come the land will merely be their excuse. They will come because war is bred into them. What is a warrior without a war to fight? Until we beat the savagery out of them—" He broke off. "My God, Rose, after the 1745 rebellion we hung the heads of traitors at Temple Bar and the people—English people—hired spyglasses at a halfpenny a stare!"

"That was a hundred years ago." Then she remembered Oliver had watched his parents hanged.

"Life's a rum go," said Nicholas thoughtfully.

The wind came drifting up the valley, whispering in the grasses and the silent ghosts came with it. It had been a long road. But now, after all, it seemed that was the route they had to take. She hoped those who had fallen by the wayside, those who slept in the sweet, warm earth, slept quietly, with forgiveness. She leaned her head against Nicholas's shoulder. "We are together at last."

There was a kind of divinity in that.

THE PRICE
OF WELLINGTON

100 red blankets. 120 muskets. 2 tierces of tobacco. 48 iron pots. 2 cases soap. 15 fowling pieces. 21 kegs gunpowder. 1 case ball cartridges. 1 keg lead slabs. 100 cartouche boxes. 100 tomahawks. 40 pipe tomahawks. 1 case pipes. 2 doz. spades. 10 doz. prs scissors. 1 doz. prs shoes. 1 doz. umbrellas. 1 doz. hats. 1 doz. razors. 6 doz. hoes. 1 doz. shaving boxes & brushes. 1 doz. sticks sealing wax. 50 steel axes. 1200 fish hooks. 12 bullet moulds. 12 doz. shirts. 20 jackets. 20 prs trousers. 60 red night caps. 300 yds cotton duck. 200 yds calico. 100 yds check. 2 doz. handkerchiefs. 2 doz. slates. 200 pencils. 10 doz. looking glasses. 10 doz. pocket knives. 2 pounds of beads. 100 yds ribbon. 1 gross Jews harps. 10 doz. dressing combs. 2 suits superfine clothes. 1 doz. adzes.

Adventure in New Zealand
Jerningham Wakefield

ABOUT THE AUTHOR

Anne Worboys was born and raised in New Zealand. She now lives with her husband in a period house in Kent, England. *Aurora Rose* is her American debut.